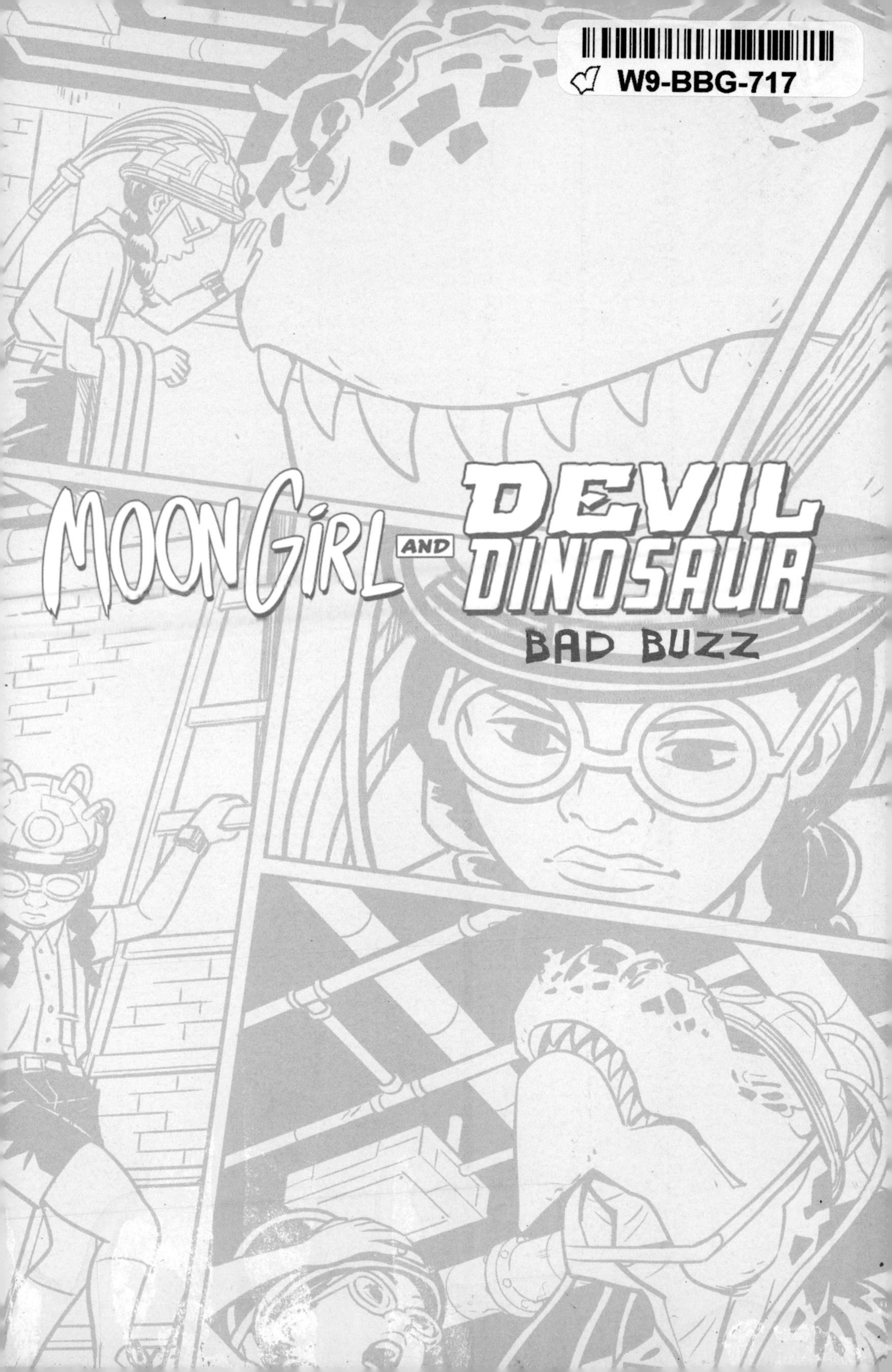
MOON GIRL AND DEVIL DINOSAUR
BAD BUZZ

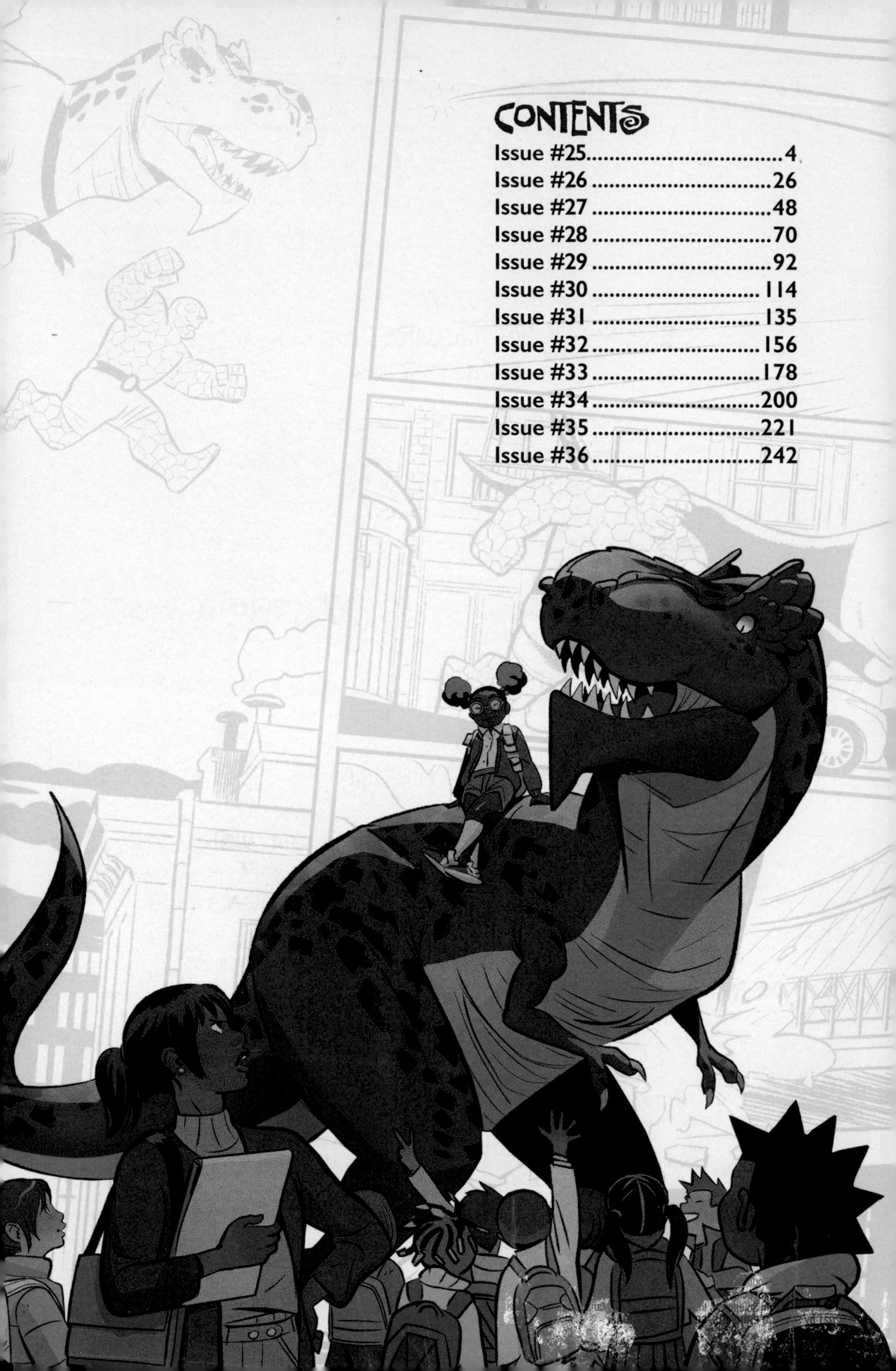

CONTENTS

MOON GIRL AND DEVIL DINOSAUR

BAD BUZZ

writers
BRANDON MONTCLARE (#25, #27–30)
WITH AMY REEDER (#31)

ISSUES #25, #27–30 & #32–26
artist
NATACHA BUSTOS

ISSUE #26
penciller
ALITHA E. MARTINEZ
inkers
ROBERTO POGGI WITH ALITHA E. MARTINEZ

ISSUE #21
artist
RAY-ANTHONY HEIGHT

color artist
TAMRA BONVILLAIN

letterer
VC's TRAVIS LANHAM

cover art
NATACHA BUSTOS
WITH RACHEL ORLOW (#32, #34–36)
& JUDY STEPHENS (#33)

editors
MARK PANICCIA & CHRIS ROBINSON

supervising editor
JORDAN D. WHITE

DEVIL DINOSAUR CREATED BY JACK KIRBY

collection editor JENNIFER GRÜNWALD • assistant editor DANIEL KIRCHHOFFER
assistant managing editor MAIA LOY • assistant managing editor LISA MONTALBANO
vp production & special projects JEFF YOUNGQUIST
svp print, sales & marketing DAVID GABRIEL • vp licensed publishing SVEN LARSEN
editor in chief C.B. CEBULSKI

MOON GIRL AND DEVIL DINOSAUR: BAD BUZZ. Contains material originally published in magazine form as MOON GIRL AND DEVIL DINOSAUR (2016) #25-36. First printing 2021. ISBN 978-1-302-92984-8. Published by MARVEL WORLDWIDE, INC., a subsidiary of MARVEL ENTERTAINMENT, LLC. OFFICE OF PUBLICATION: 1290 Avenue of the Americas, New York, NY 10104. © 2021 MARVEL No similarity between any of the names, characters, persons, and/or institutions in this magazine with those of any living or dead person or institution is intended, and any such similarity which may exist is purely coincidental. **Printed in Canada.** KEVIN FEIGE, Chief Creative Officer; DAN BUCKLEY, President, Marvel Entertainment; JOE QUESADA, EVP & Creative Director; DAVID BOGART, Associate Publisher & SVP of Talent Affairs; TOM BREVOORT, VP, Executive Editor; NICK LOWE, Executive Editor, VP of Content, Digital Publishing; DAVID GABRIEL, VP of Print & Digital Publishing; JEFF YOUNGQUIST, VP of Production & Special Projects; ALEX MORALES, Director of Publishing Operations; DAN EDINGTON, Managing Editor; RICKEY PURDIN, Director of Talent Relations; JENNIFER GRÜNWALD, Senior Editor, Special Projects; SUSAN CRESPI, Production Manager; STAN LEE, Chairman Emeritus. For information regarding advertising in Marvel Comics or on Marvel.com, please contact Vit DeBellis, Custom Solutions & Integrated Advertising Manager, at vdebellis@marvel.com. For Marvel subscription inquiries, please call 888-511-5480. **Manufactured between 3/26/2021 and 5/4/2021 by SOLISCO PRINTERS, SCOTT, QC, CANADA.**

10 9 8 7 6 5 4 3 2 1

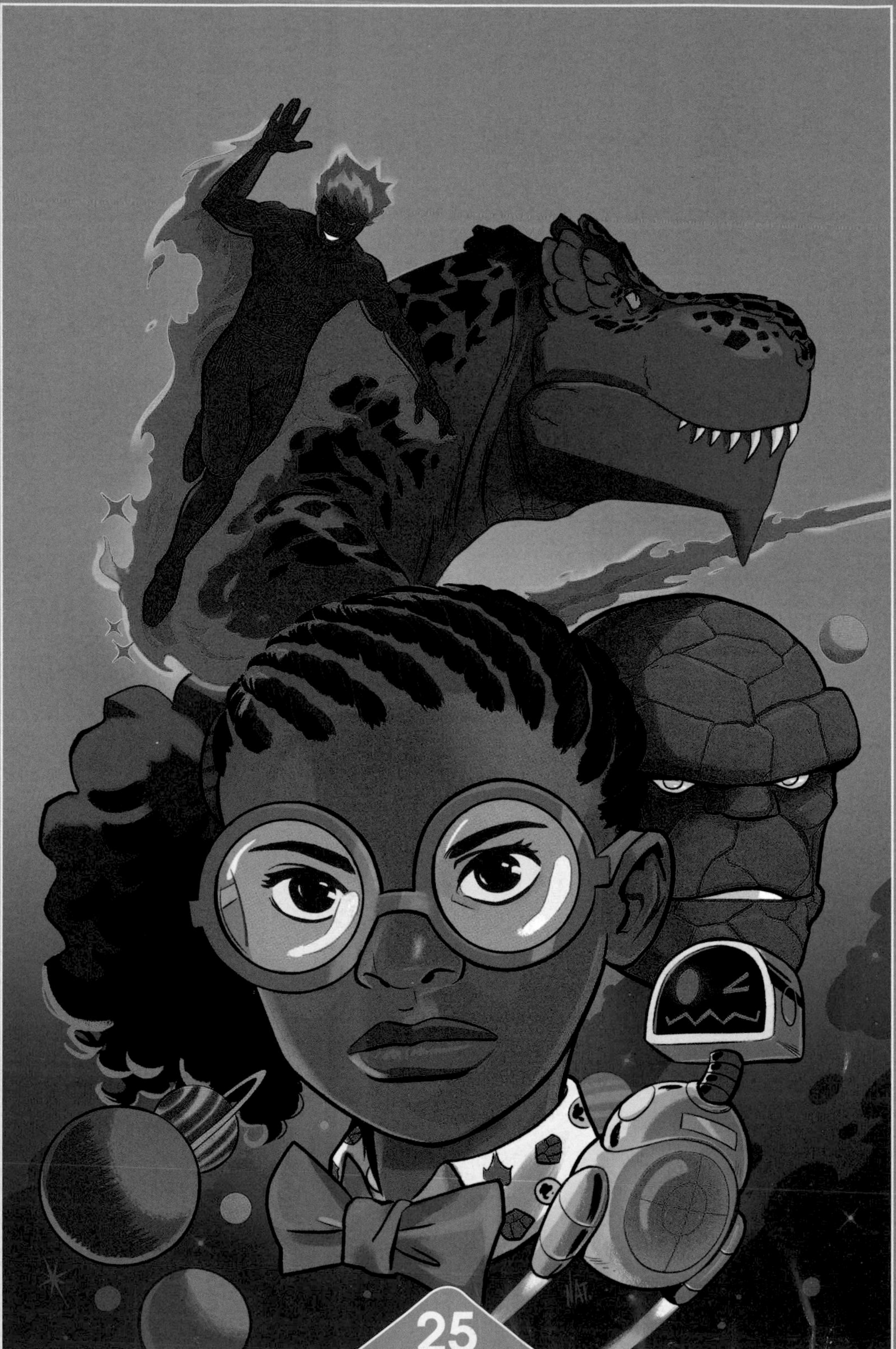
25

"1+2=FANTASTIC THREE"

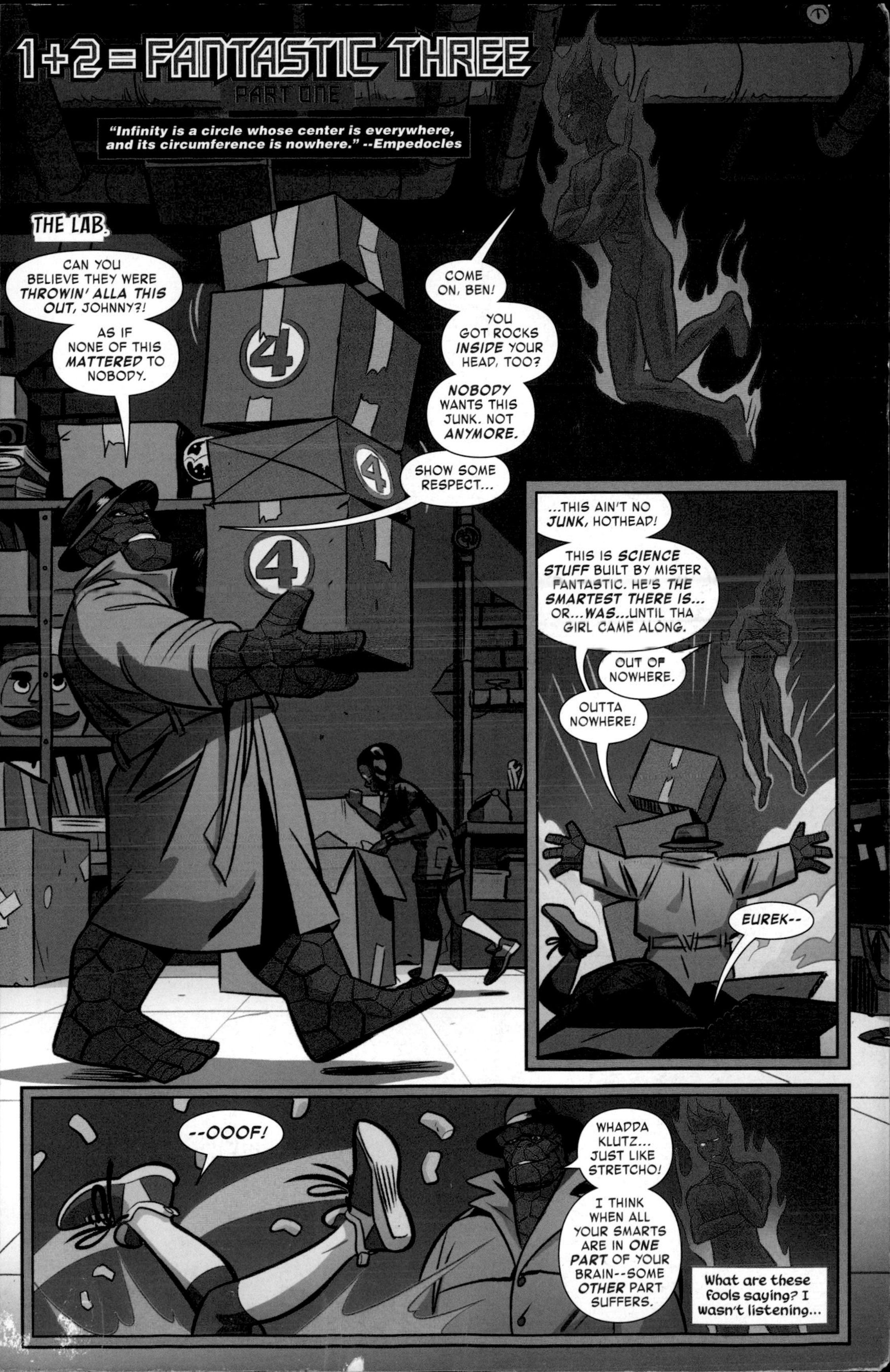
1+2 = FANTASTIC THREE
PART ONE
"Infinity is a circle whose center is everywhere, and its circumference is nowhere." --Empedocles
THE LAB.
CAN YOU BELIEVE THEY WERE THROWIN' ALLA THIS OUT, JOHNNY?!
AS IF NONE OF THIS MATTERED TO NOBODY.
COME ON, BEN!
YOU GOT ROCKS INSIDE YOUR HEAD, TOO?
NOBODY WANTS THIS JUNK. NOT ANYMORE.
SHOW SOME RESPECT...
...THIS AIN'T NO JUNK, HOTHEAD!
THIS IS SCIENCE STUFF BUILT BY MISTER FANTASTIC. HE'S THE SMARTEST THERE IS... OR...WAS...UNTIL THA GIRL CAME ALONG.
OUT OF NOWHERE.
OUTTA NOWHERE!
EUREK--
--OOOF!
WHADDA KLUTZ... JUST LIKE STRETCHO!
I THINK WHEN ALL YOUR SMARTS ARE IN ONE PART OF YOUR BRAIN--SOME OTHER PART SUFFERS.
What are these fools saying? I wasn't listening...

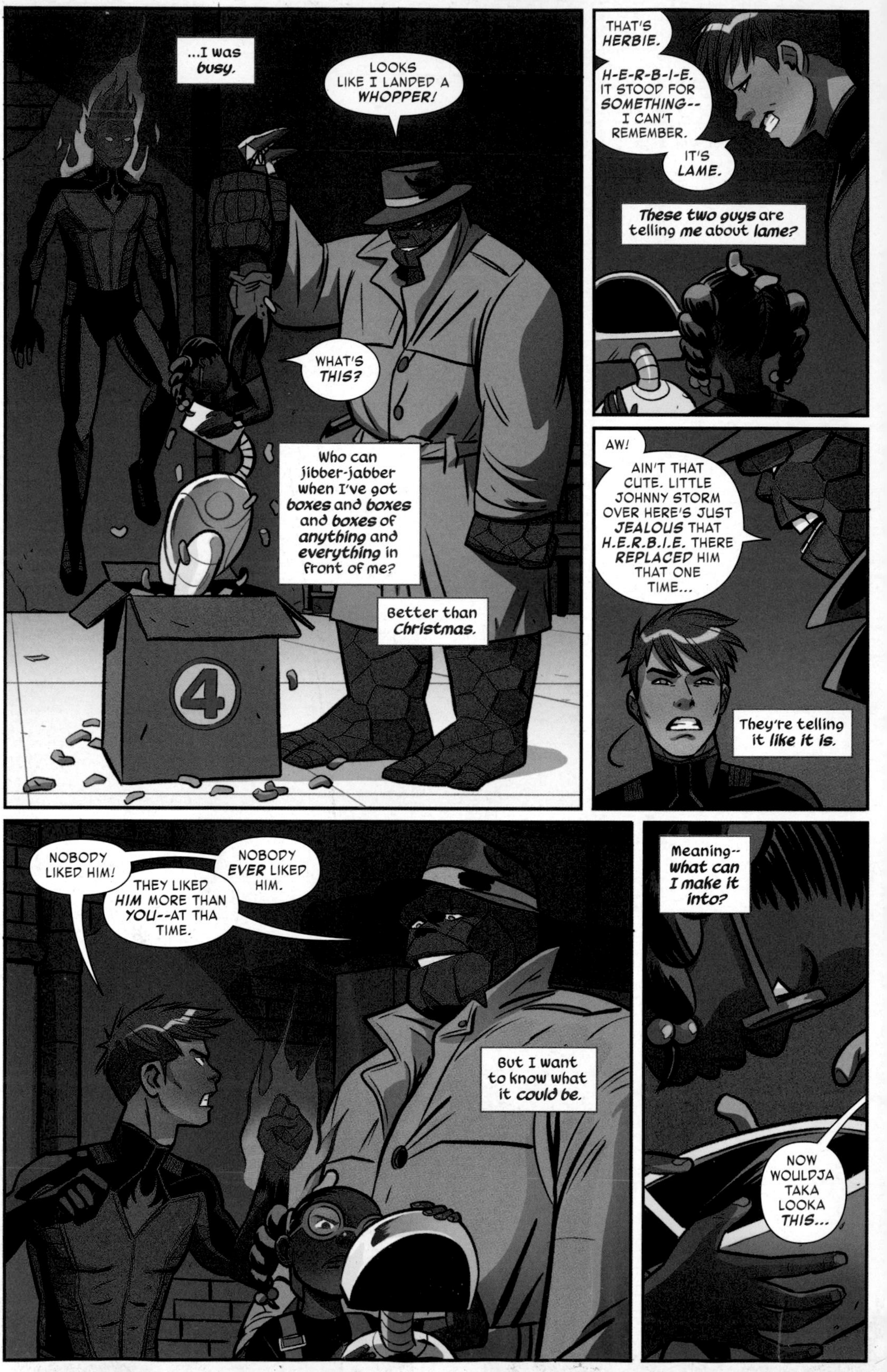
...I was busy.
LOOKS LIKE I LANDED A WHOPPER!
WHAT'S THIS?
Who can jibber-jabber when I've got boxes and boxes and boxes of anything and everything in front of me?
Better than Christmas.
THAT'S HERBIE.
H-E-R-B-I-E. IT STOOD FOR SOMETHING-- I CAN'T REMEMBER.
IT'S LAME.
These two guys are telling me about lame?
AW!
AIN'T THAT CUTE. LITTLE JOHNNY STORM OVER HERE'S JUST JEALOUS THAT H.E.R.B.I.E. THERE REPLACED HIM THAT ONE TIME...
They're telling it like it is.
NOBODY LIKED HIM!
NOBODY EVER LIKED HIM.
THEY LIKED HIM MORE THAN YOU--AT THA TIME.
But I want to know what it could be.
Meaning-- what can I make it into?
NOW WOULDJA TAKA LOOKA THIS...

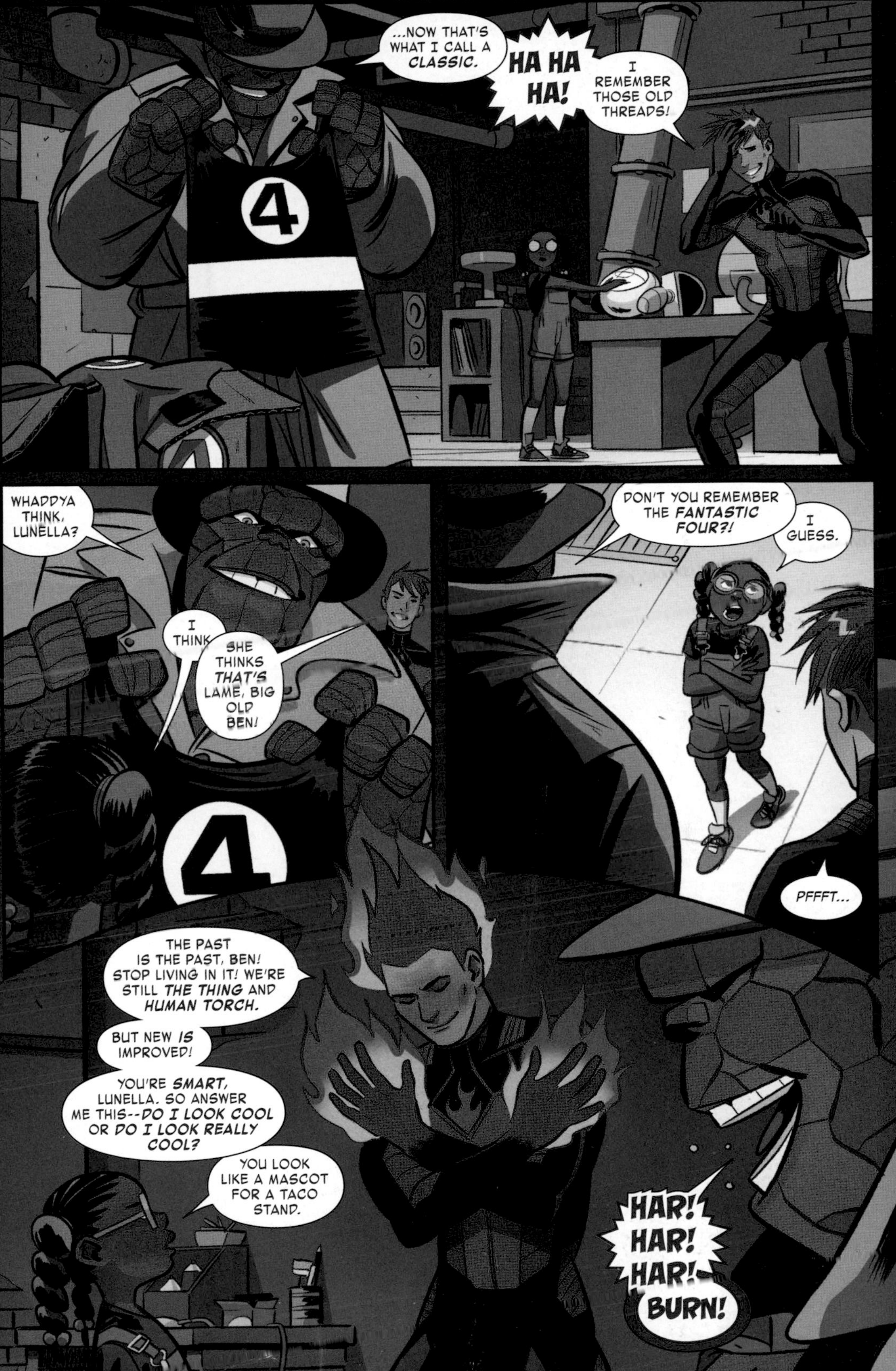
...NOW THAT'S WHAT I CALL A CLASSIC.
HA HA HA!
I REMEMBER THOSE OLD THREADS!
WHADDYA THINK, LUNELLA?
I THINK...
SHE THINKS THAT'S LAME, BIG OLD BEN!
DON'T YOU REMEMBER THE FANTASTIC FOUR?!
I GUESS.
PFFFT...
THE PAST IS THE PAST, BEN! STOP LIVING IN IT! WE'RE STILL THE THING AND HUMAN TORCH.
BUT NEW IS IMPROVED!
YOU'RE SMART, LUNELLA. SO ANSWER ME THIS--DO I LOOK COOL OR DO I LOOK REALLY COOL?
YOU LOOK LIKE A MASCOT FOR A TACO STAND.
HAR! HAR! HAR!
BURN!

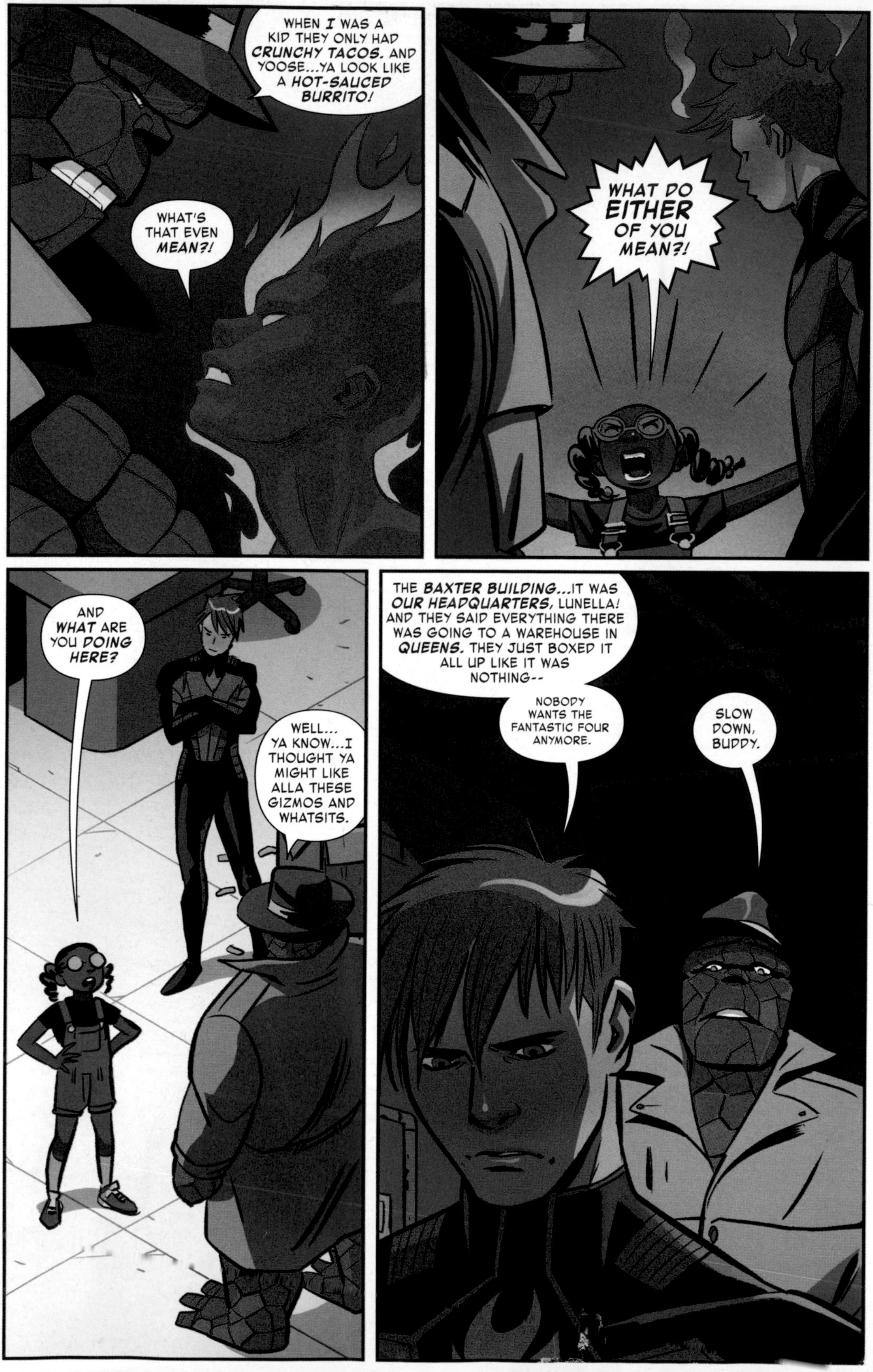
WHEN I WAS A KID THEY ONLY HAD CRUNCHY TACOS. AND YOOSE...YA LOOK LIKE A HOT-SAUCED BURRITO!
WHAT'S THAT EVEN MEAN?!
WHAT DO EITHER OF YOU MEAN?!
AND WHAT ARE YOU DOING HERE?
WELL... YA KNOW...I THOUGHT YA MIGHT LIKE ALLA THESE GIZMOS AND WHATSITS.
THE BAXTER BUILDING...IT WAS OUR HEADQUARTERS, LUNELLA! AND THEY SAID EVERYTHING THERE WAS GOING TO A WAREHOUSE IN QUEENS. THEY JUST BOXED IT ALL UP LIKE IT WAS NOTHING--
NOBODY WANTS THE FANTASTIC FOUR ANYMORE.
SLOW DOWN, BUDDY.

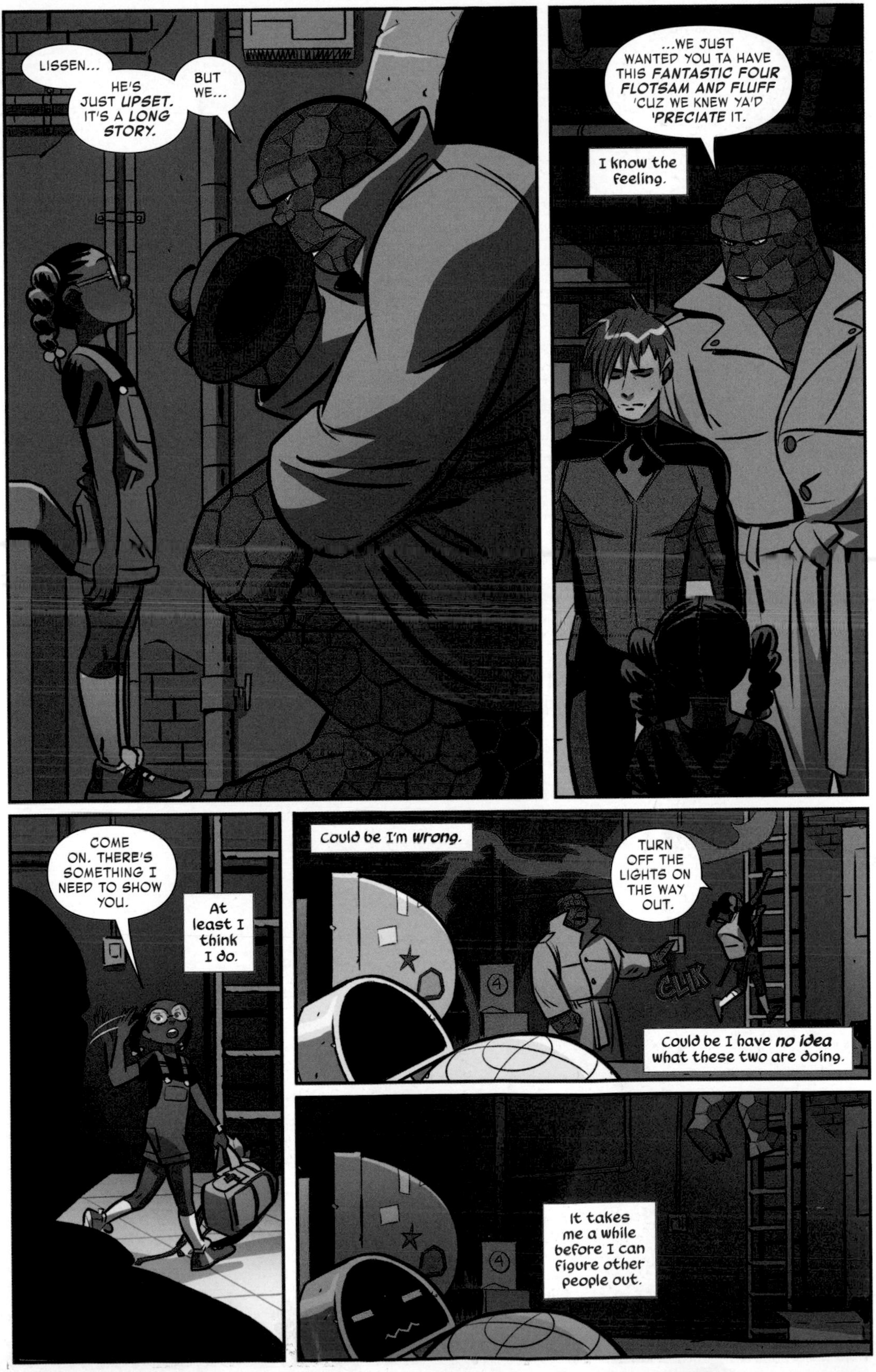
LISSEN...
HE'S JUST UPSET. IT'S A LONG STORY.
BUT WE...
...WE JUST WANTED YOU TA HAVE THIS FANTASTIC FOUR FLOTSAM AND FLUFF 'CUZ WE KNEW YA'D 'PRECIATE IT.
I know the feeling.
COME ON. THERE'S SOMETHING I NEED TO SHOW YOU.
At least I think I do.
Could be I'm wrong.
TURN OFF THE LIGHTS ON THE WAY OUT.
CLIK
Could be I have no idea what these two are doing.
It takes me a while before I can figure other people out.

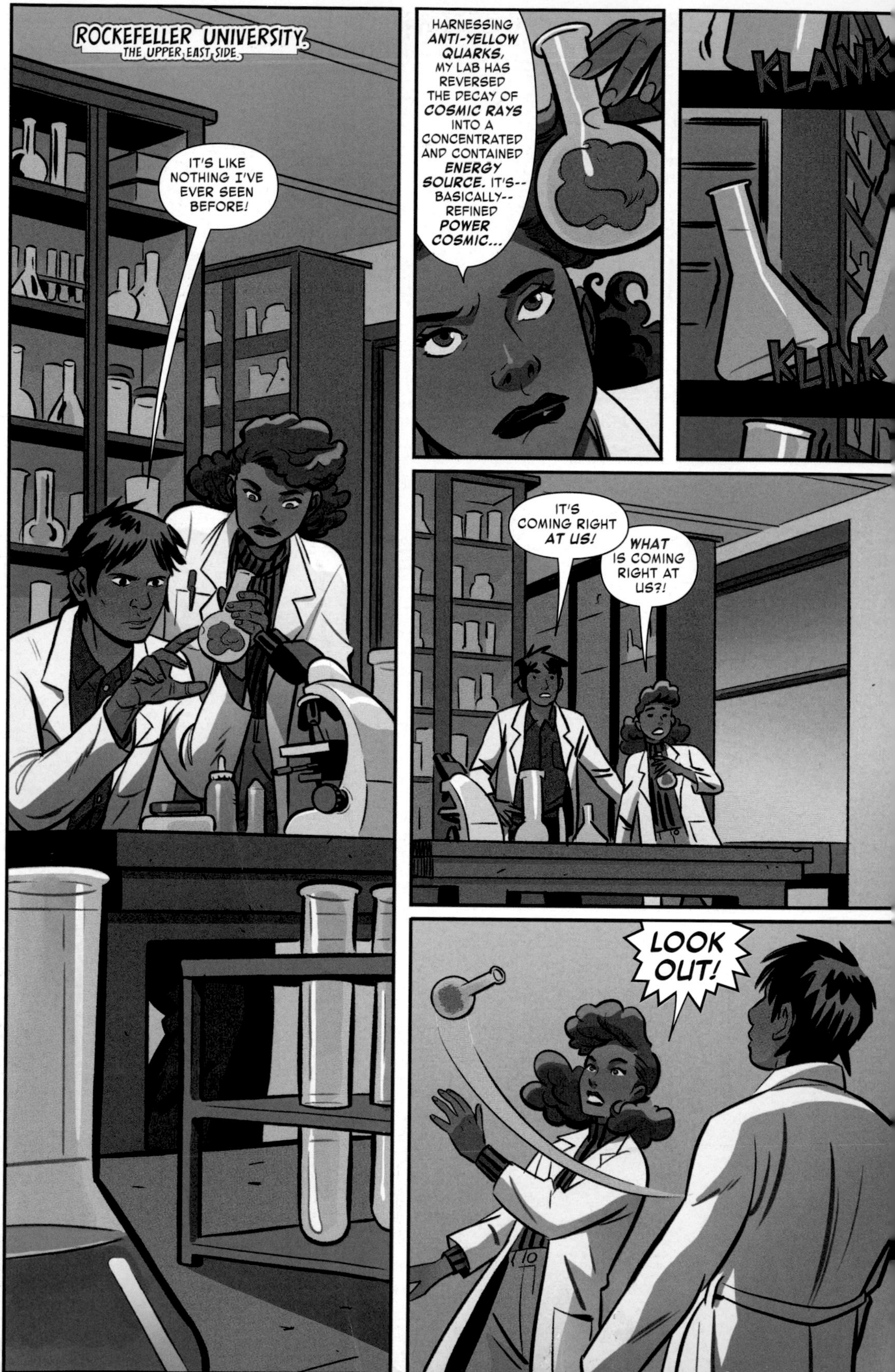
ROCKEFELLER UNIVERSITY.
THE UPPER EAST SIDE.
IT'S LIKE NOTHING I'VE EVER SEEN BEFORE!
HARNESSING ANTI-YELLOW QUARKS, MY LAB HAS REVERSED THE DECAY OF COSMIC RAYS INTO A CONCENTRATED AND CONTAINED ENERGY SOURCE. IT'S-- BASICALLY-- REFINED POWER COSMIC...
KLANK
KLINK
IT'S COMING RIGHT AT US!
WHAT IS COMING RIGHT AT US?!
LOOK OUT!

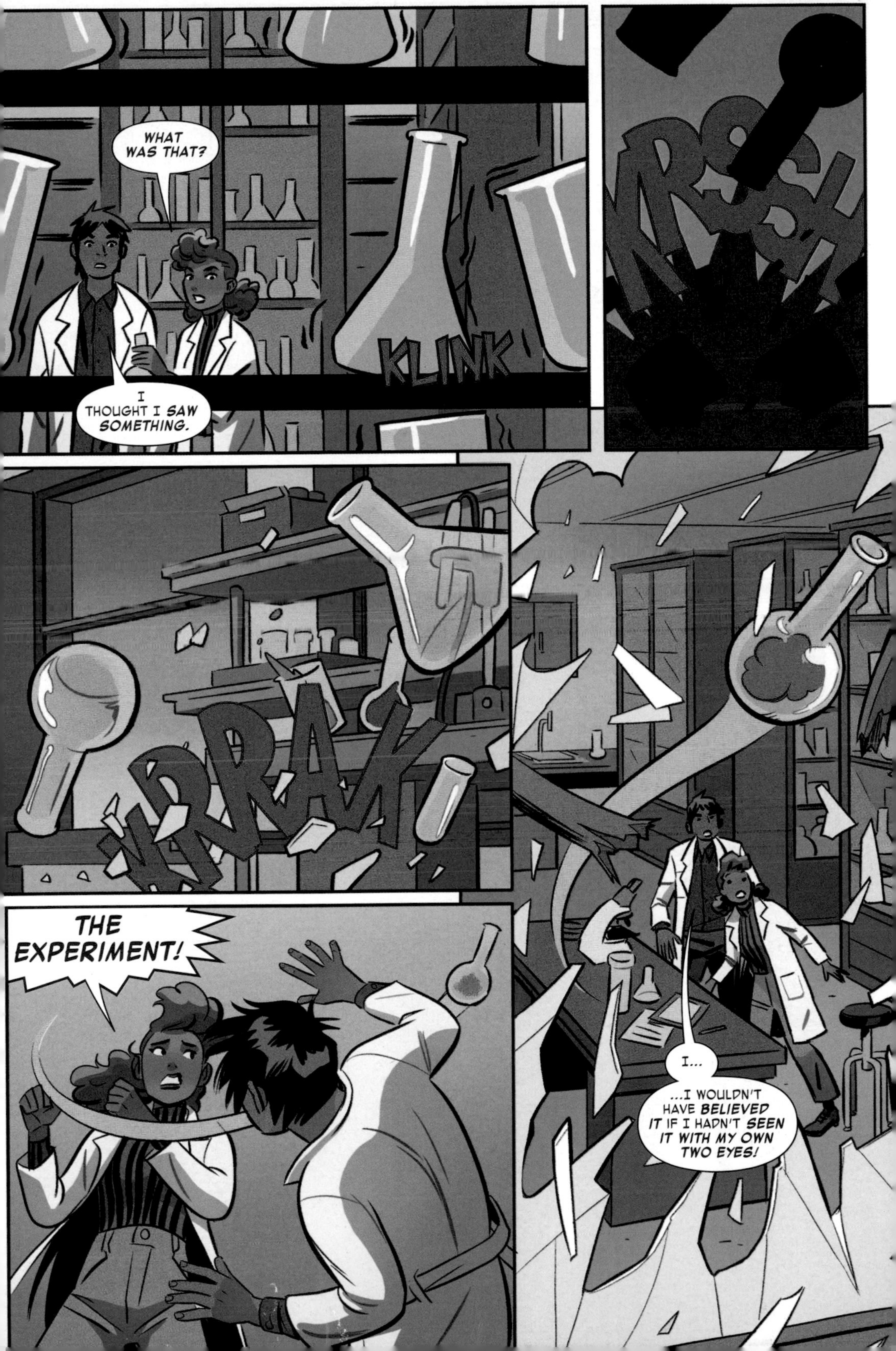

WHAT WAS THAT?
I THOUGHT I SAW SOMETHING.
KLINK
KRRSSH
KRRAK
THE EXPERIMENT!
I...
...I WOULDN'T HAVE BELIEVED IT IF I HADN'T SEEN IT WITH MY OWN TWO EYES!

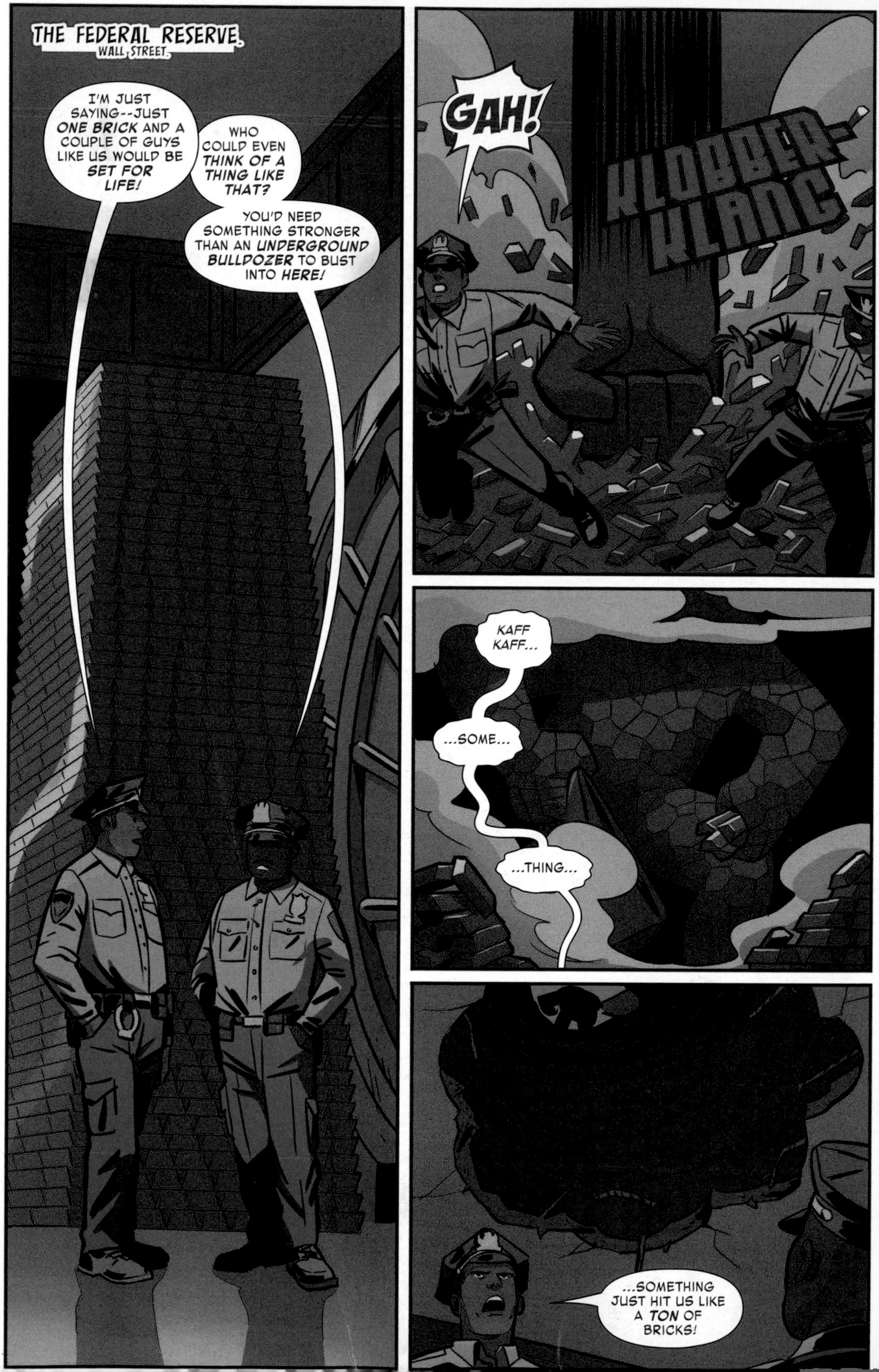
THE FEDERAL RESERVE.
WALL STREET.
I'M JUST SAYING--JUST ONE BRICK AND A COUPLE OF GUYS LIKE US WOULD BE SET FOR LIFE!
WHO COULD EVEN THINK OF A THING LIKE THAT?
YOU'D NEED SOMETHING STRONGER THAN AN UNDERGROUND BULLDOZER TO BUST INTO HERE!
GAH!
KLOBBER-KLANG
KAFF KAFF...
...SOME...
...THING...
...SOMETHING JUST HIT US LIKE A TON OF BRICKS!

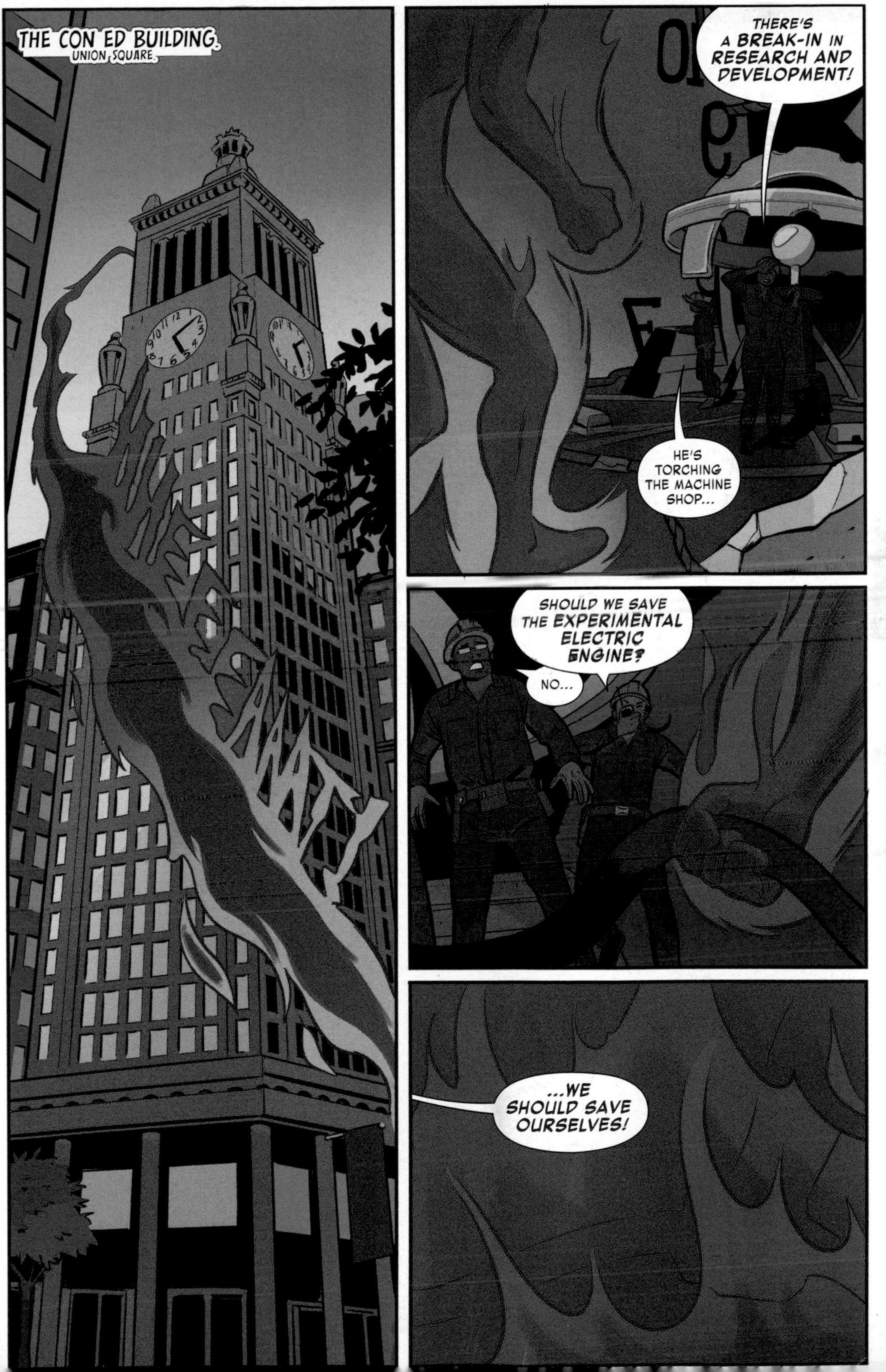
THE CON ED BUILDING.
UNION SQUARE.
THERE'S A BREAK-IN IN RESEARCH AND DEVELOPMENT!
HE'S TORCHING THE MACHINE SHOP...
SHOULD WE SAVE THE EXPERIMENTAL ELECTRIC ENGINE?
NO...
...WE SHOULD SAVE OURSELVES!

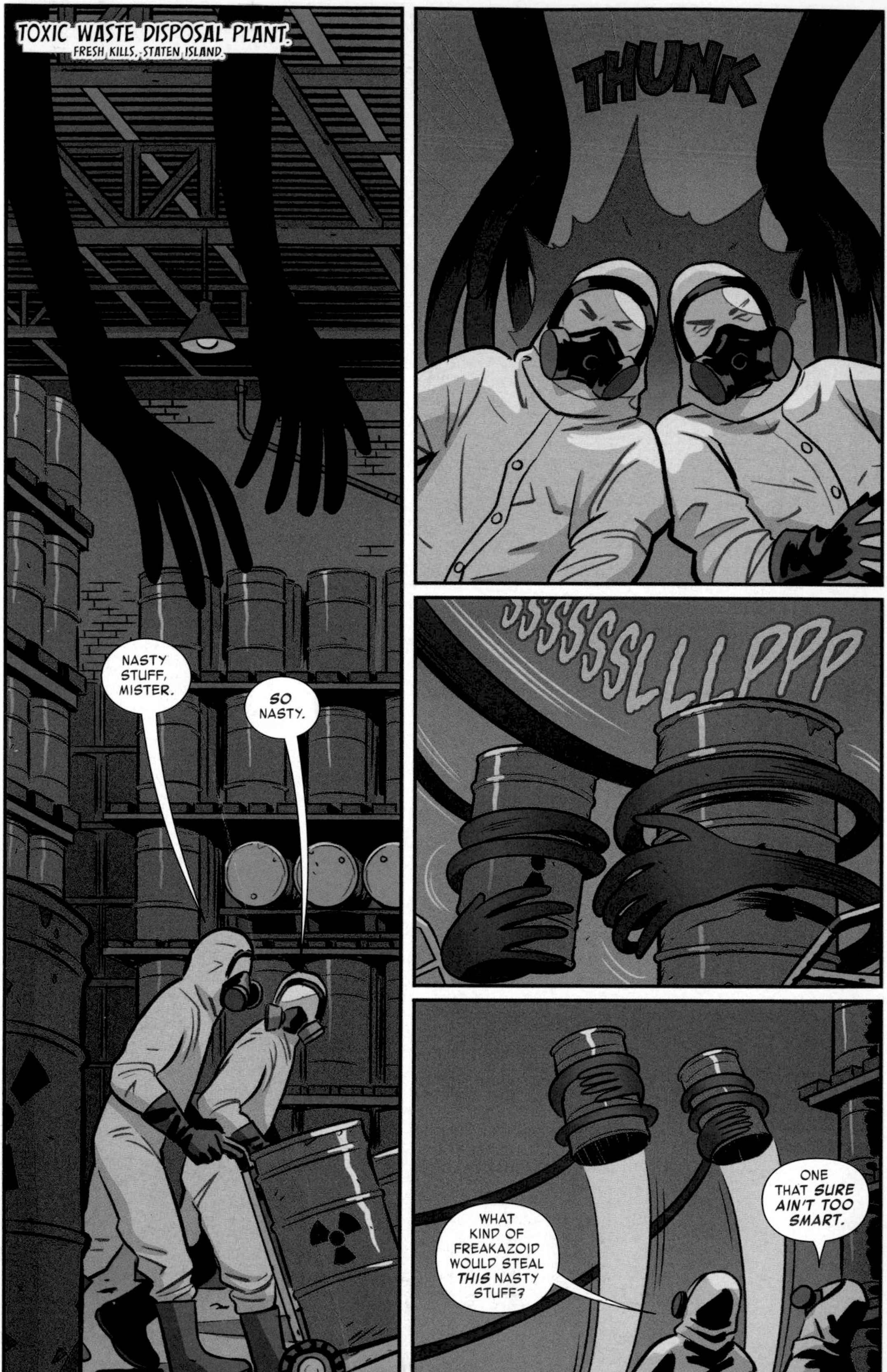
TOXIC WASTE DISPOSAL PLANT.
FRESH KILLS, STATEN ISLAND.
NASTY STUFF, MISTER.
SO NASTY.
THUNK
SSSSSSLLLPPP
WHAT KIND OF FREAKAZOID WOULD STEAL THIS NASTY STUFF?
ONE THAT SURE AIN'T TOO SMART.

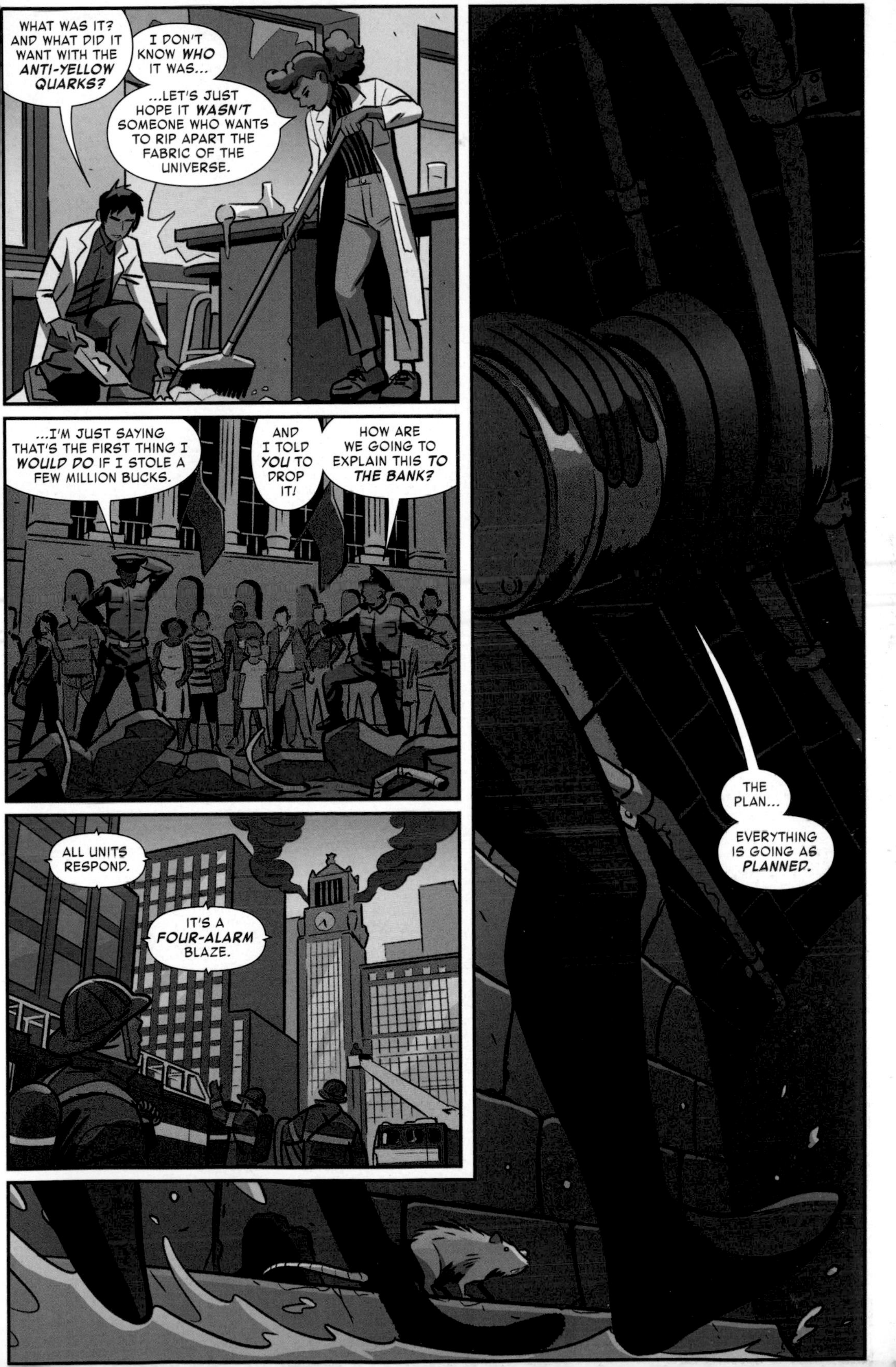
WHAT WAS IT? AND WHAT DID IT WANT WITH THE ANTI-YELLOW QUARKS?
I DON'T KNOW WHO IT WAS...
...LET'S JUST HOPE IT WASN'T SOMEONE WHO WANTS TO RIP APART THE FABRIC OF THE UNIVERSE.
...I'M JUST SAYING THAT'S THE FIRST THING I WOULD DO IF I STOLE A FEW MILLION BUCKS.
AND I TOLD YOU TO DROP IT!
HOW ARE WE GOING TO EXPLAIN THIS TO THE BANK?
ALL UNITS RESPOND.
IT'S A FOUR-ALARM BLAZE.
THE PLAN...
EVERYTHING IS GOING AS PLANNED.

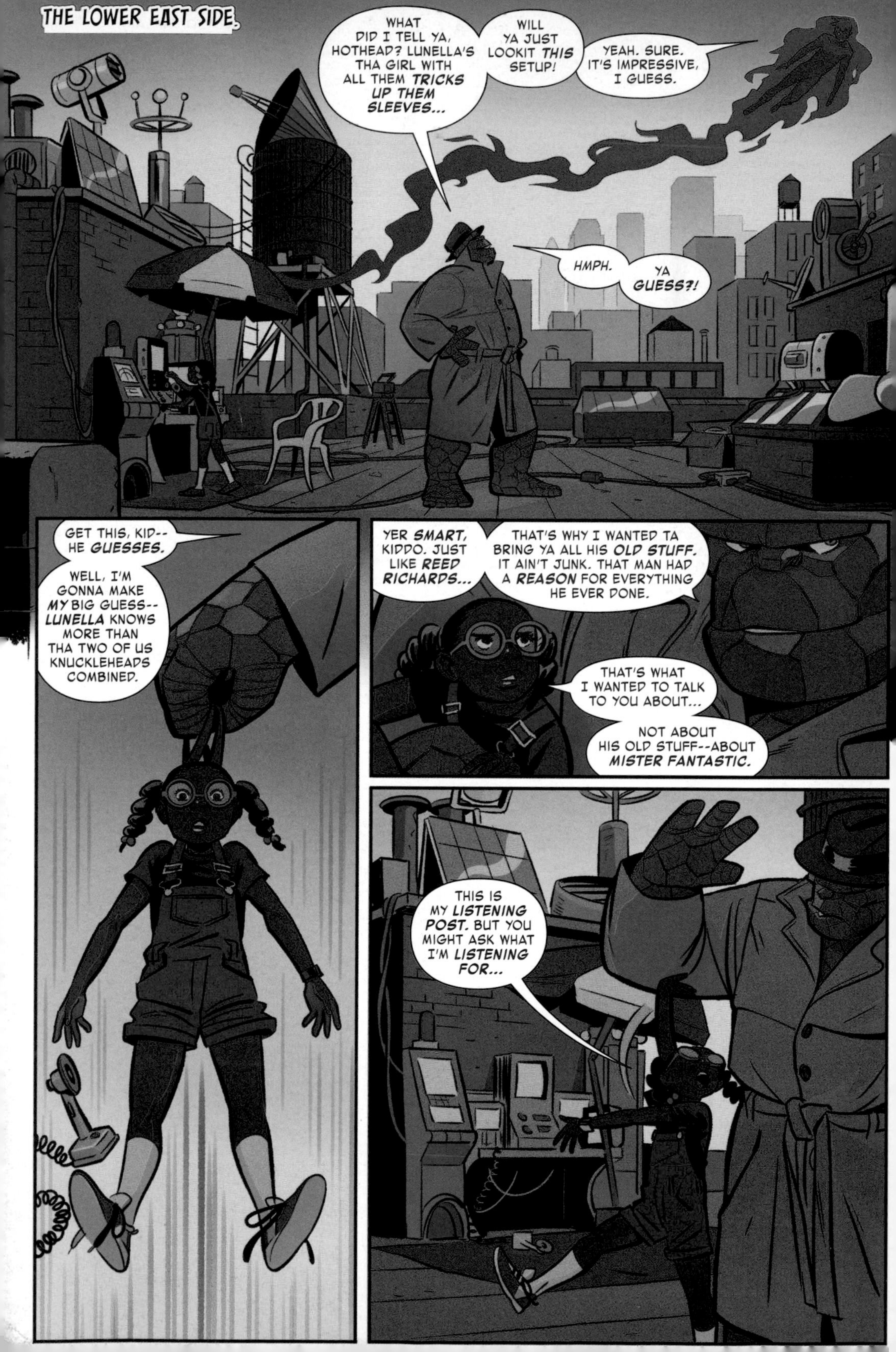
THE LOWER EAST SIDE.
WHAT DID I TELL YA, HOTHEAD? LUNELLA'S THA GIRL WITH ALL THEM TRICKS UP THEM SLEEVES...
WILL YA JUST LOOKIT THIS SETUP!
YEAH. SURE. IT'S IMPRESSIVE, I GUESS.
HMPH.
YA GUESS?!
GET THIS, KID-- HE GUESSES.
WELL, I'M GONNA MAKE MY BIG GUESS-- LUNELLA KNOWS MORE THAN THA TWO OF US KNUCKLEHEADS COMBINED.
YER SMART, KIDDO. JUST LIKE REED RICHARDS...
THAT'S WHY I WANTED TA BRING YA ALL HIS OLD STUFF. IT AIN'T JUNK. THAT MAN HAD A REASON FOR EVERYTHING HE EVER DONE.
THAT'S WHAT I WANTED TO TALK TO YOU ABOUT...
NOT ABOUT HIS OLD STUFF--ABOUT MISTER FANTASTIC.
THIS IS MY LISTENING POST. BUT YOU MIGHT ASK WHAT I'M LISTENING FOR...

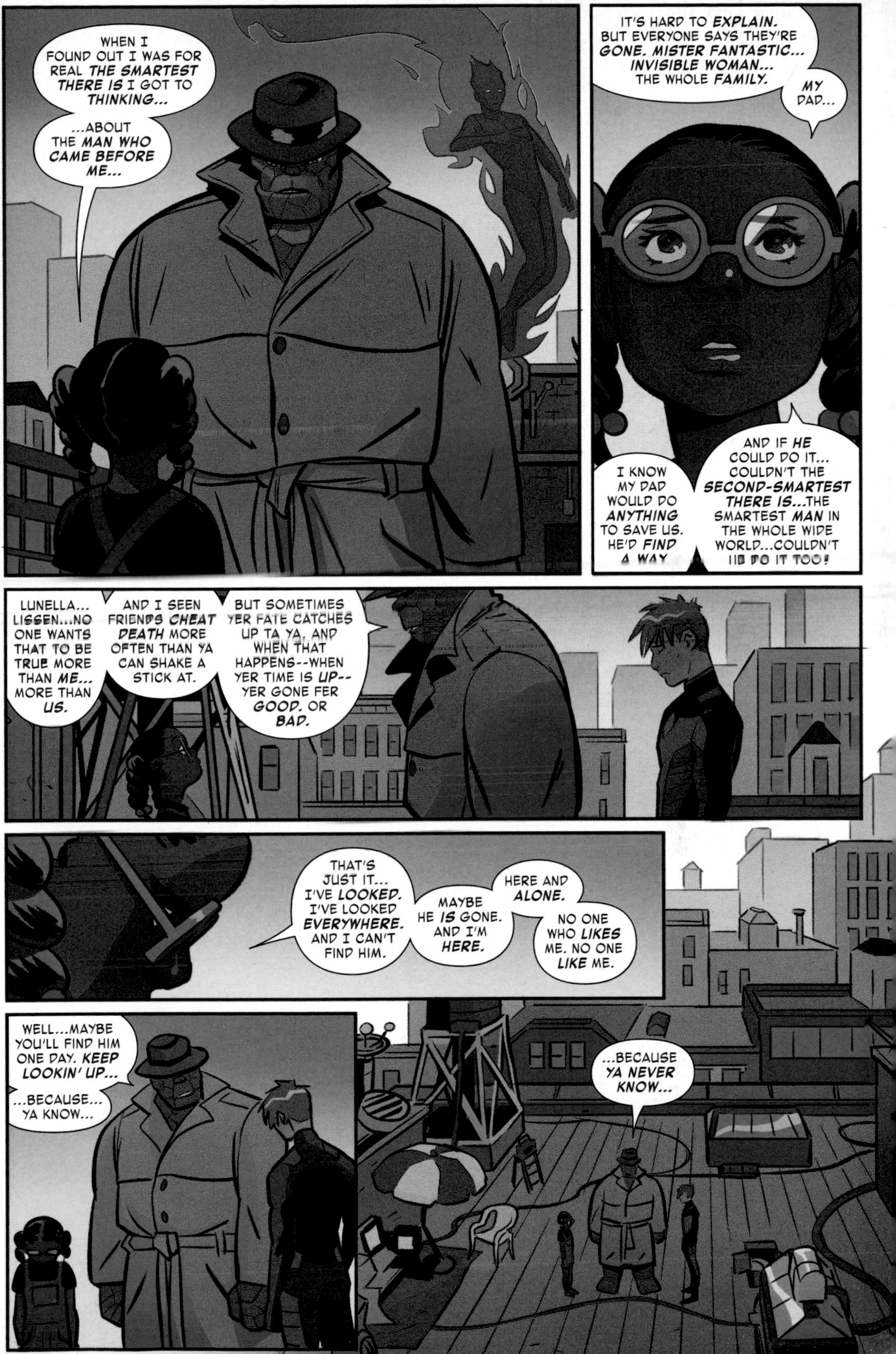
WHEN I FOUND OUT I WAS FOR REAL THE SMARTEST THERE IS I GOT TO THINKING...
...ABOUT THE MAN WHO CAME BEFORE ME...
IT'S HARD TO EXPLAIN. BUT EVERYONE SAYS THEY'RE GONE. MISTER FANTASTIC... INVISIBLE WOMAN... THE WHOLE FAMILY.
MY DAD...
I KNOW MY DAD WOULD DO ANYTHING TO SAVE US. HE'D FIND A WAY.
AND IF HE COULD DO IT... COULDN'T THE SECOND-SMARTEST THERE IS...THE SMARTEST MAN IN THE WHOLE WIDE WORLD...COULDN'T HE DO IT TOO?
LUNELLA... LISSEN...NO ONE WANTS THAT TO BE TRUE MORE THAN ME... MORE THAN US.
AND I SEEN FRIENDS CHEAT DEATH MORE OFTEN THAN YA CAN SHAKE A STICK AT.
BUT SOMETIMES YER FATE CATCHES UP TA YA. AND WHEN THAT HAPPENS--WHEN YER TIME IS UP--YER GONE FER GOOD. OR BAD.
THAT'S JUST IT... I'VE LOOKED. I'VE LOOKED EVERYWHERE. AND I CAN'T FIND HIM.
MAYBE HE IS GONE. AND I'M HERE.
HERE AND ALONE.
NO ONE WHO LIKES ME. NO ONE LIKE ME.
WELL...MAYBE YOU'LL FIND HIM ONE DAY. KEEP LOOKIN' UP...
...BECAUSE... YA KNOW...
...BECAUSE YA NEVER KNOW...

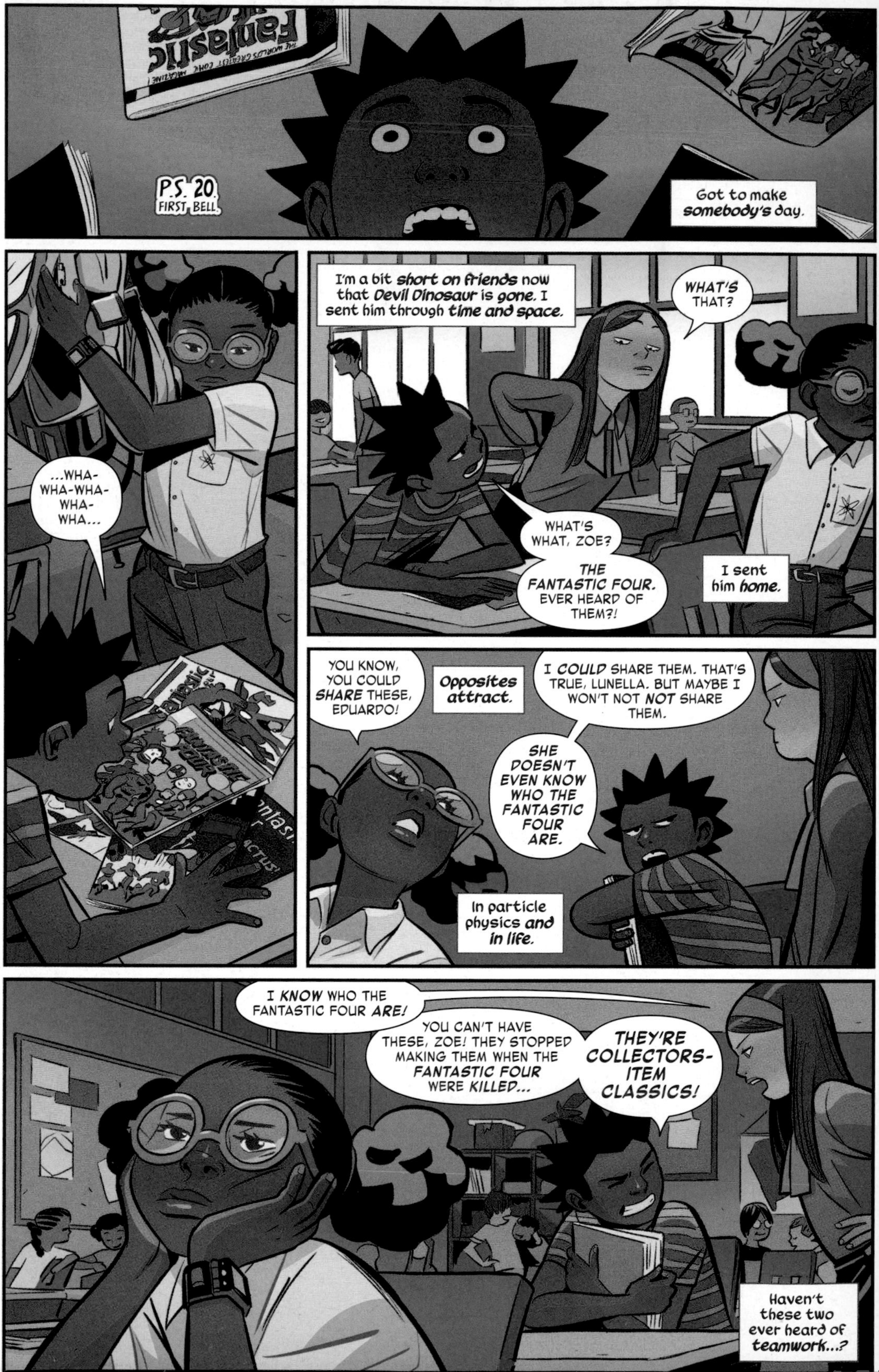

P.S. 20. FIRST BELL.
Got to make somebody's day.
...WHA-WHA-WHA-WHA-WHA...
I'm a bit short on friends now that Devil Dinosaur is gone. I sent him through time and space.
WHAT'S THAT?
WHAT'S WHAT, ZOE?
THE FANTASTIC FOUR. EVER HEARD OF THEM?!
I sent him home.
YOU KNOW, YOU COULD SHARE THESE, EDUARDO!
Opposites attract.
I COULD SHARE THEM. THAT'S TRUE, LUNELLA. BUT MAYBE I WON'T NOT NOT SHARE THEM.
SHE DOESN'T EVEN KNOW WHO THE FANTASTIC FOUR ARE.
In particle physics and in life.
I KNOW WHO THE FANTASTIC FOUR ARE!
YOU CAN'T HAVE THESE, ZOE! THEY STOPPED MAKING THEM WHEN THE FANTASTIC FOUR WERE KILLED...
THEY'RE COLLECTORS-ITEM CLASSICS!
Haven't these two ever heard of teamwork...?

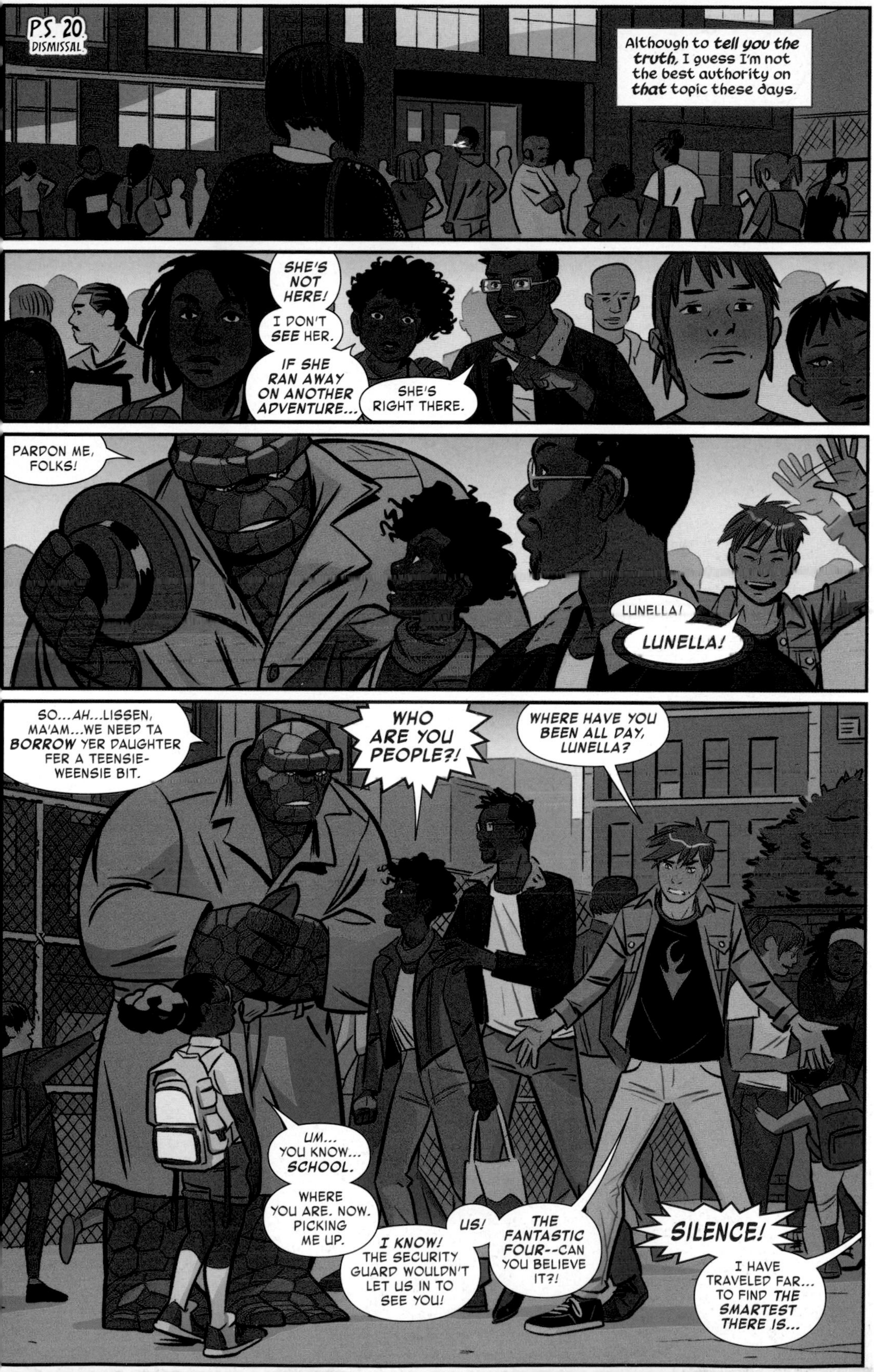
P.S. 20 DISMISSAL
Although to tell you the truth, I guess I'm not the best authority on that topic these days.
SHE'S NOT HERE!
I DON'T SEE HER.
IF SHE RAN AWAY ON ANOTHER ADVENTURE...
SHE'S RIGHT THERE.
PARDON ME, FOLKS!
LUNELLA!
LUNELLA!
SO...AH...LISSEN, MA'AM...WE NEED TA BORROW YER DAUGHTER FER A TEENSIE-WEENSIE BIT.
WHO ARE YOU PEOPLE?!
WHERE HAVE YOU BEEN ALL DAY, LUNELLA?
UM... YOU KNOW... SCHOOL.
WHERE YOU ARE. NOW. PICKING ME UP.
US!
I KNOW! THE SECURITY GUARD WOULDN'T LET US IN TO SEE YOU!
THE FANTASTIC FOUR--CAN YOU BELIEVE IT?!
SILENCE!
I HAVE TRAVELED FAR... TO FIND THE SMARTEST THERE IS...

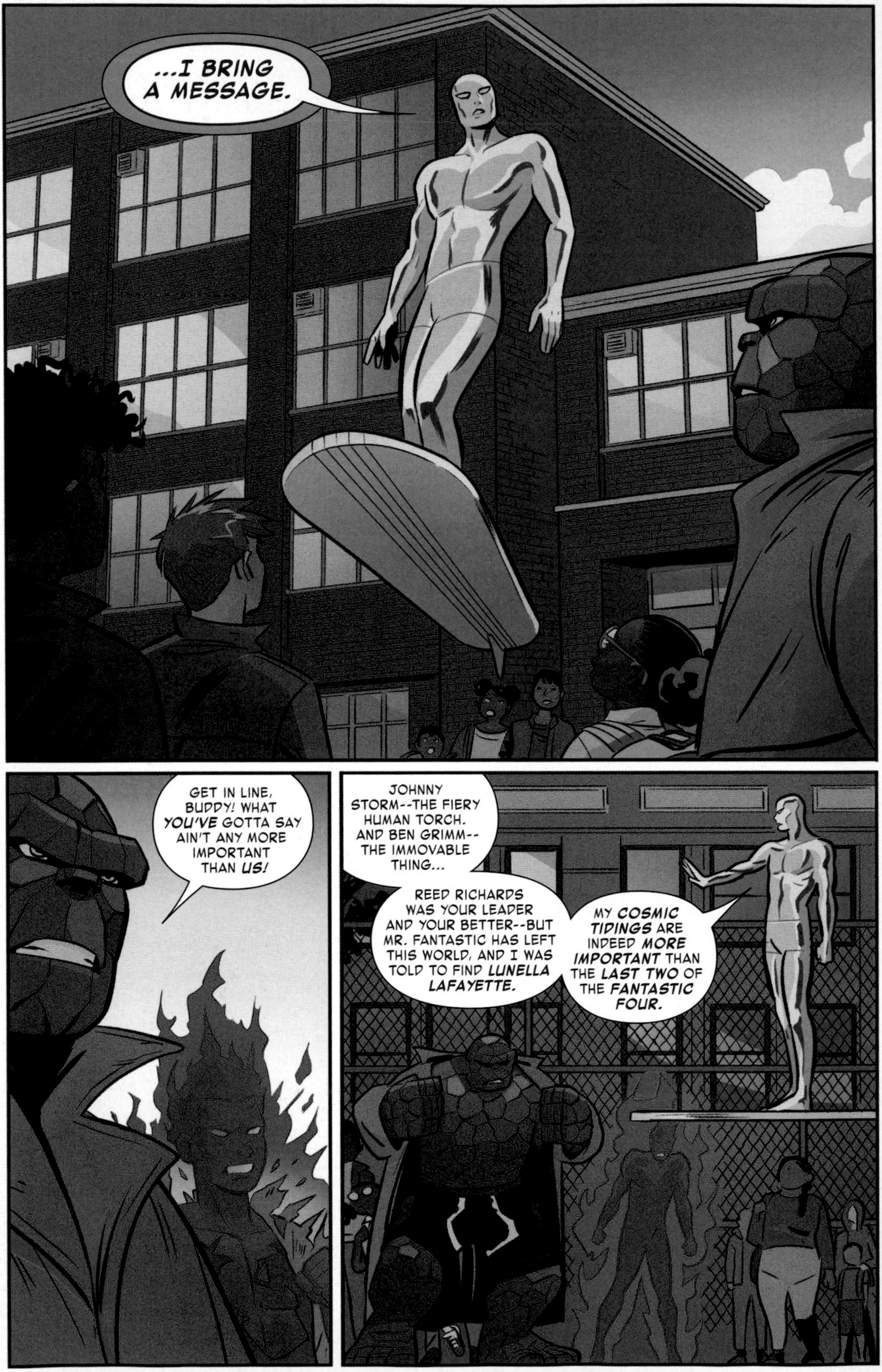
...I BRING A MESSAGE.
GET IN LINE, BUDDY! WHAT YOU'VE GOTTA SAY AIN'T ANY MORE IMPORTANT THAN US!
JOHNNY STORM--THE FIERY HUMAN TORCH. AND BEN GRIMM--THE IMMOVABLE THING...
REED RICHARDS WAS YOUR LEADER AND YOUR BETTER--BUT MR. FANTASTIC HAS LEFT THIS WORLD, AND I WAS TOLD TO FIND LUNELLA LAFAYETTE.
MY COSMIC TIDINGS ARE INDEED MORE IMPORTANT THAN THE LAST TWO OF THE FANTASTIC FOUR.

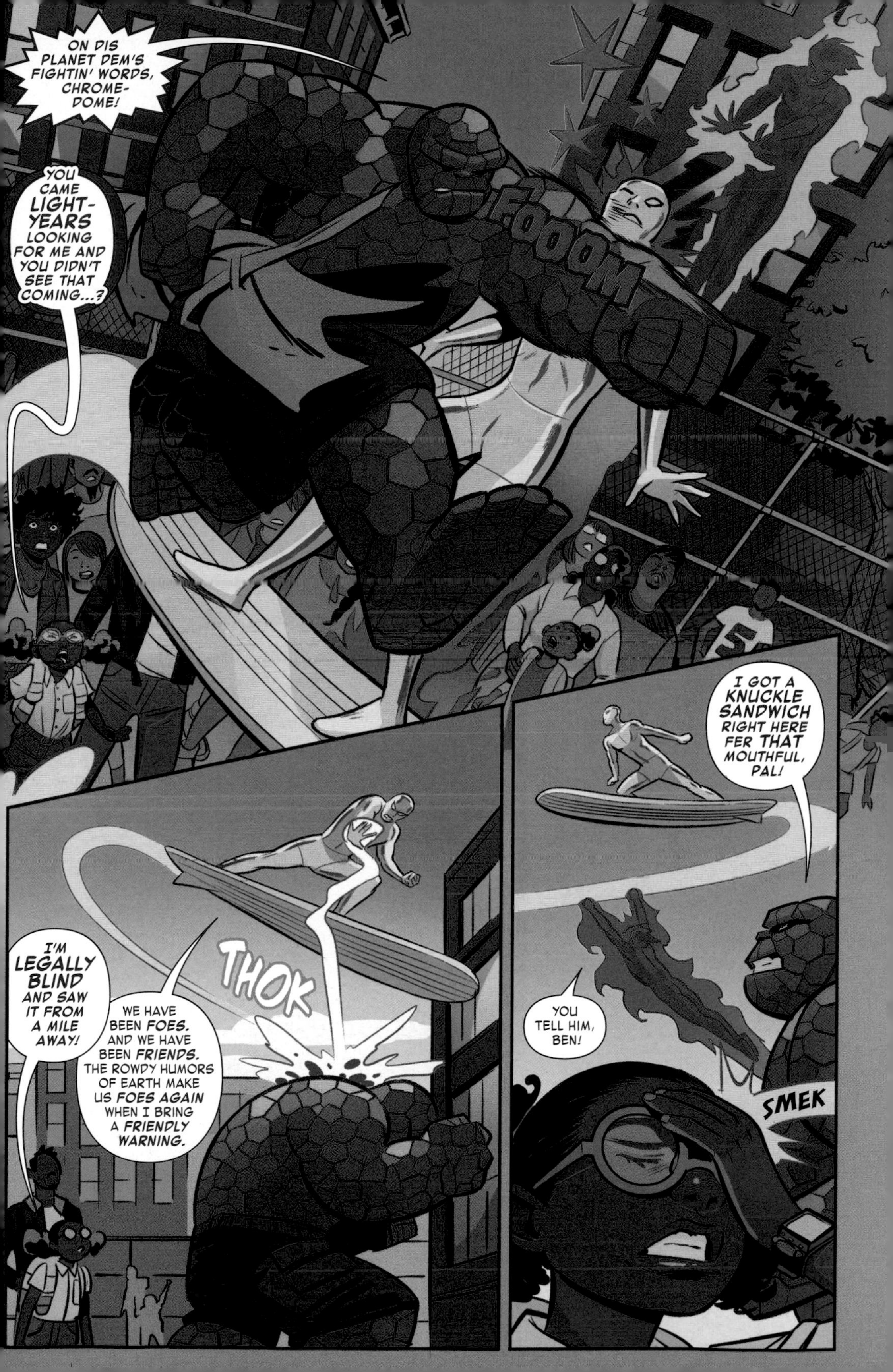

ON DIS PLANET DEM'S FIGHTIN' WORDS, CHROME-DOME!
YOU CAME LIGHT-YEARS LOOKING FOR ME AND YOU DIDN'T SEE THAT COMING...?
FOOOM
I'M LEGALLY BLIND AND SAW IT FROM A MILE AWAY!
WE HAVE BEEN FOES. AND WE HAVE BEEN FRIENDS. THE ROWDY HUMORS OF EARTH MAKE US FOES AGAIN WHEN I BRING A FRIENDLY WARNING.
THOK
I GOT A KNUCKLE SANDWICH RIGHT HERE FER THAT MOUTHFUL, PAL!
YOU TELL HIM, BEN!
SMEK

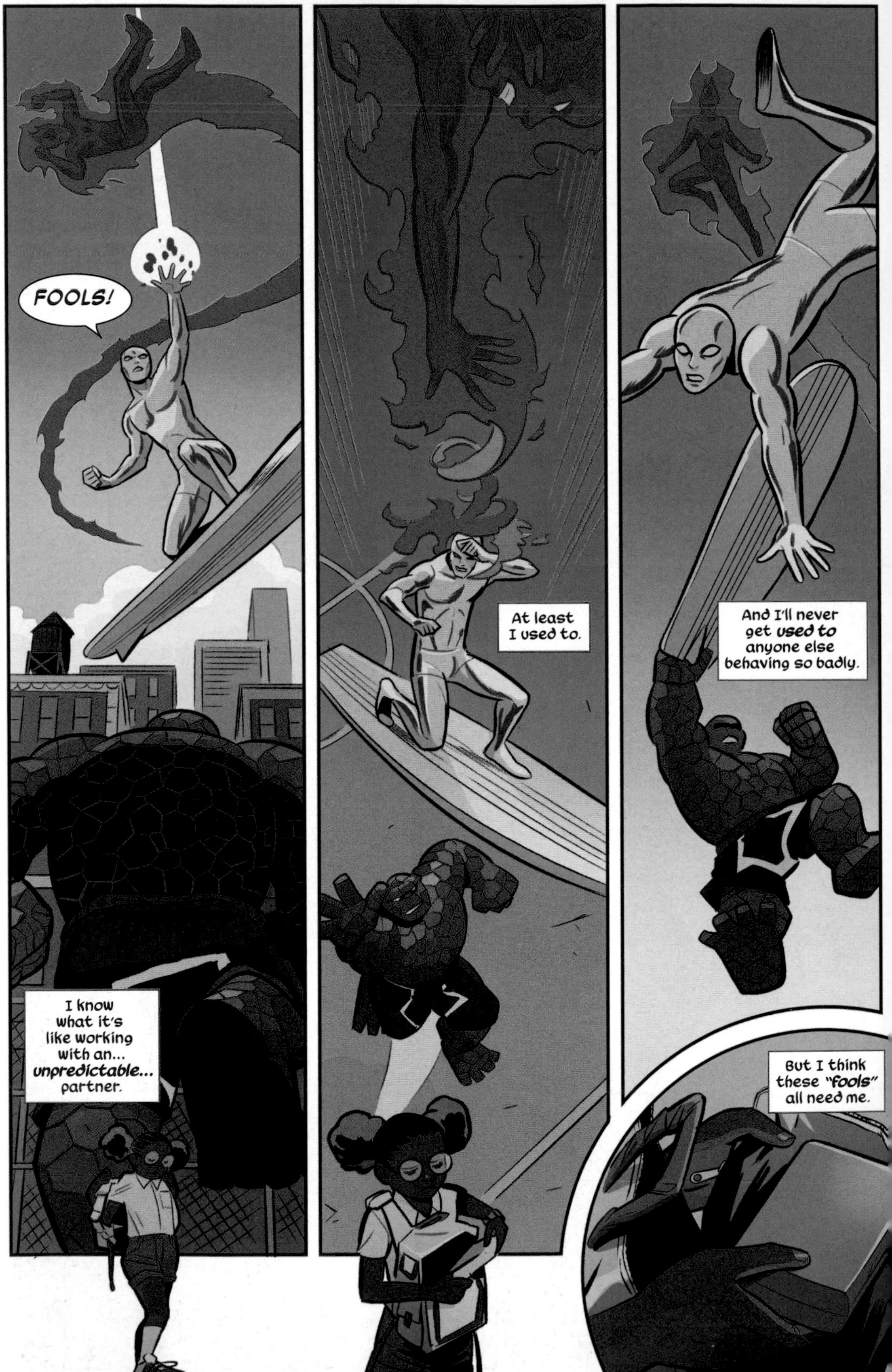
FOOLS!
I know what it's like working with an... unpredictable... partner.
At least I used to.
And I'll never get used to anyone else behaving so badly.
But I think these "fools" all need me.

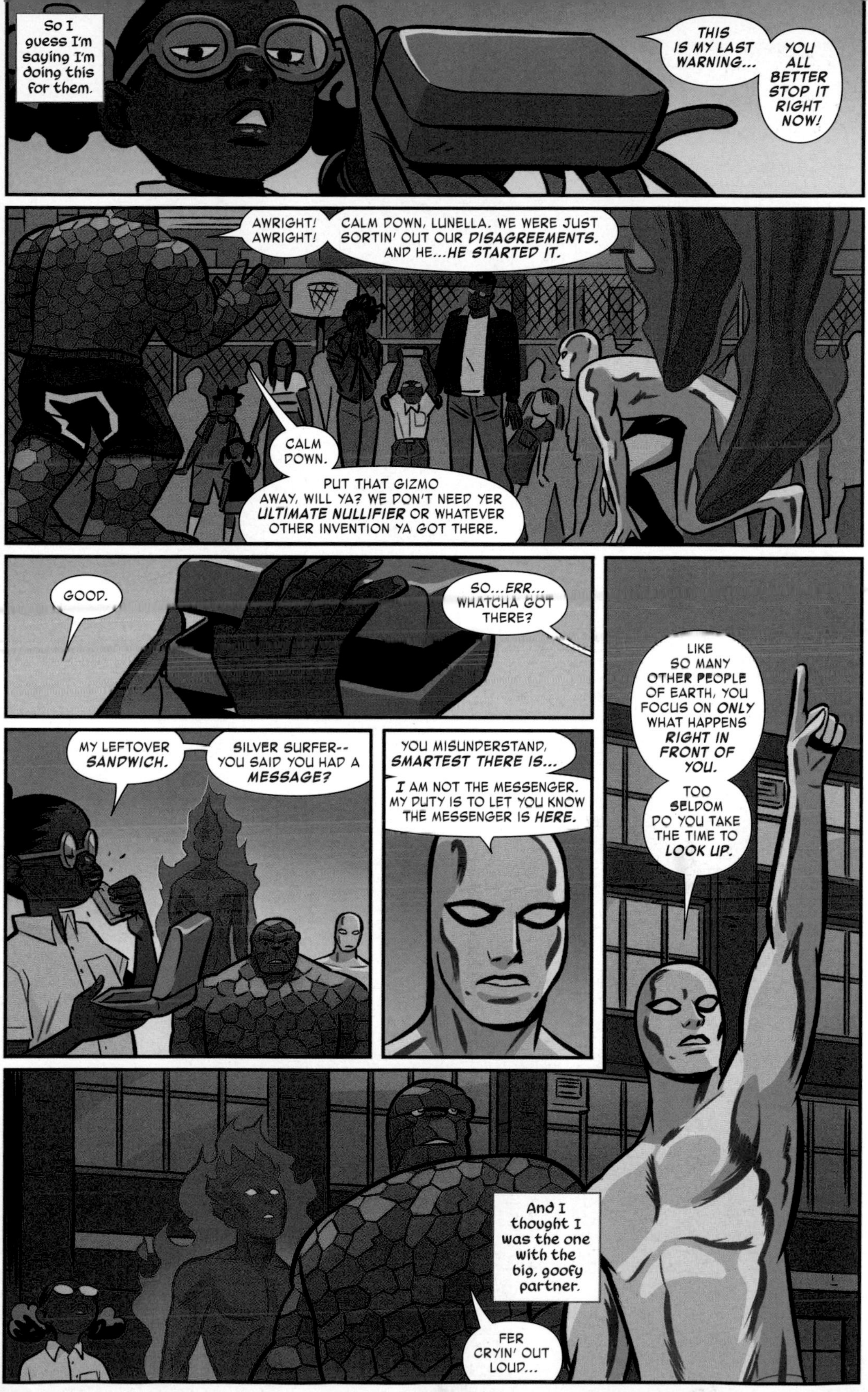

So I guess I'm saying I'm doing this for them.
THIS IS MY LAST WARNING...
YOU ALL BETTER STOP IT RIGHT NOW!
AWRIGHT! AWRIGHT!
CALM DOWN, LUNELLA. WE WERE JUST SORTIN' OUT OUR DISAGREEMENTS. AND HE...HE STARTED IT.
CALM DOWN.
PUT THAT GIZMO AWAY, WILL YA? WE DON'T NEED YER ULTIMATE NULLIFIER OR WHATEVER OTHER INVENTION YA GOT THERE.
GOOD.
SO...ERR... WHATCHA GOT THERE?
MY LEFTOVER SANDWICH.
SILVER SURFER-- YOU SAID YOU HAD A MESSAGE?
YOU MISUNDERSTAND, SMARTEST THERE IS...
I AM NOT THE MESSENGER. MY DUTY IS TO LET YOU KNOW THE MESSENGER IS HERE.
LIKE SO MANY OTHER PEOPLE OF EARTH, YOU FOCUS ON ONLY WHAT HAPPENS RIGHT IN FRONT OF YOU.
TOO SELDOM DO YOU TAKE THE TIME TO LOOK UP.
And I thought I was the one with the big, goofy partner.
FER CRYIN' OUT LOUD...

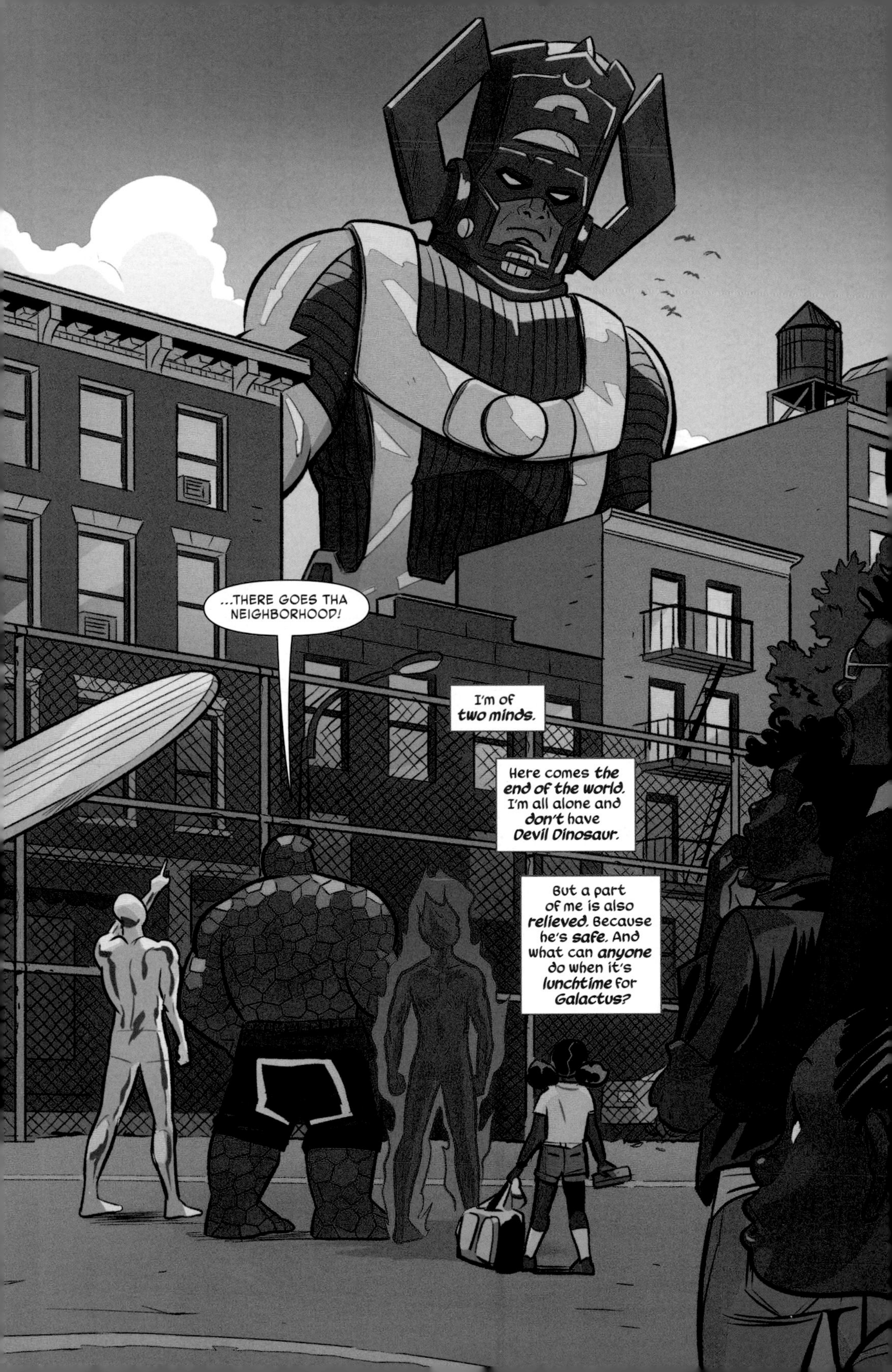
...THERE GOES THA NEIGHBORHOOD!
I'm of *two minds*.
Here comes *the end of the world*. I'm all alone and *don't* have *Devil Dinosaur*.
But a part of me is also *relieved*. Because he's *safe*. And what can *anyone* do when it's *lunchtime* for *Galactus*?

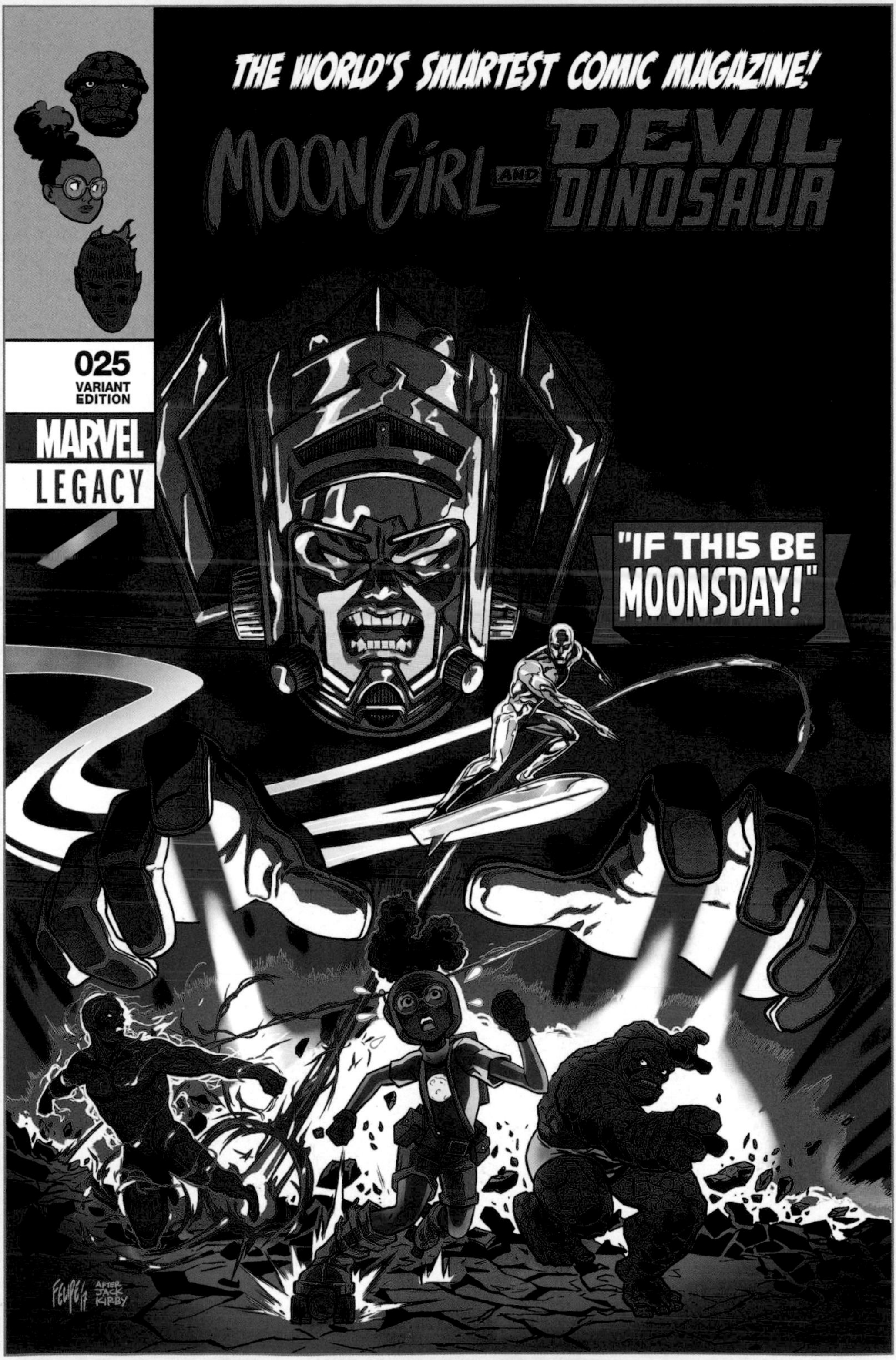
THE WORLD'S SMARTEST COMIC MAGAZINE!
MOON GIRL AND DEVIL DINOSAUR
025
VARIANT EDITION
MARVEL
LEGACY
"IF THIS BE MOONSDAY!"
FELIPE 17 AFTER JACK KIRBY

#25 HOMAGE VARIANT
BY FELIPE SMITH

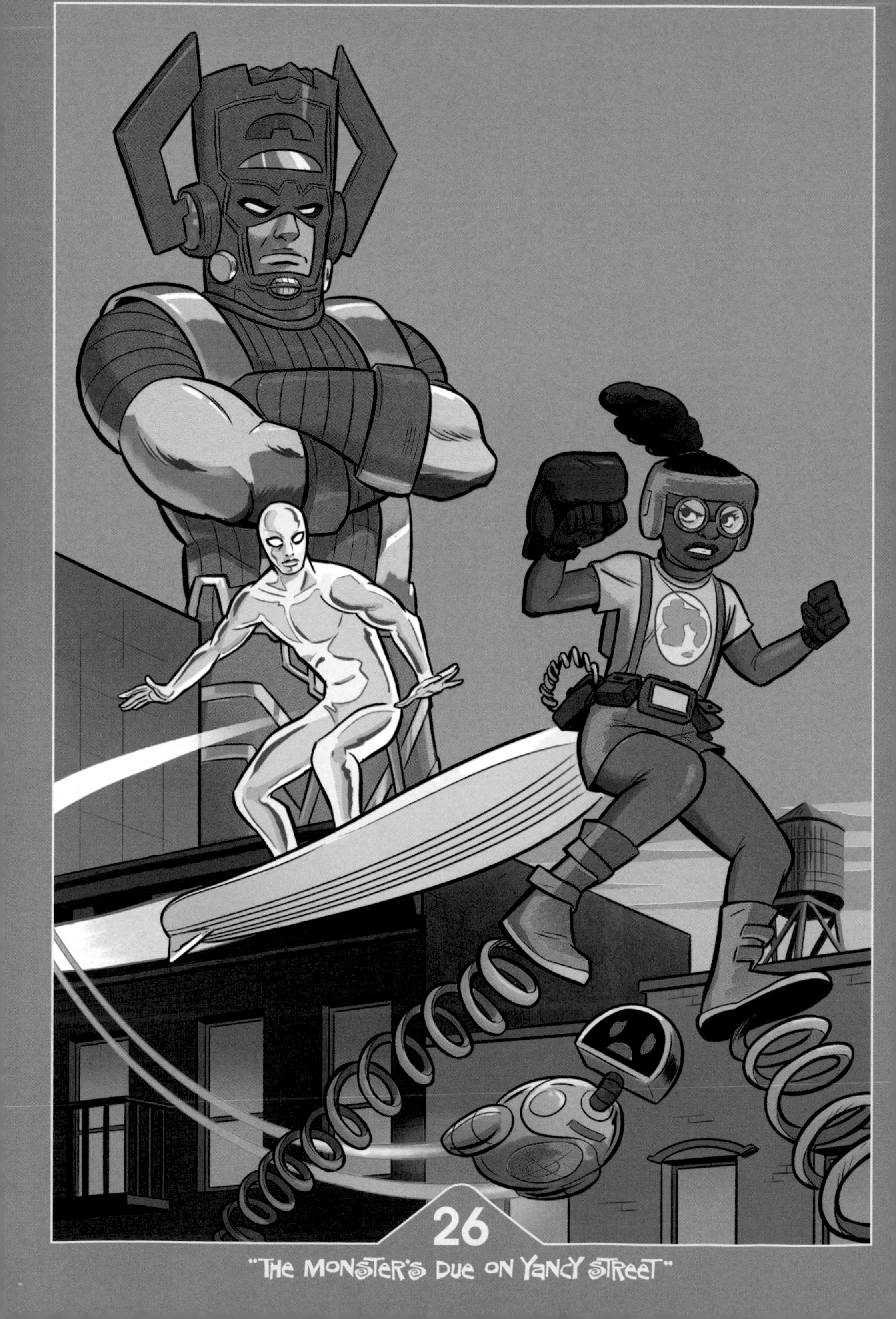

26

"THE MONSTER'S DUE ON YANCY STREET"

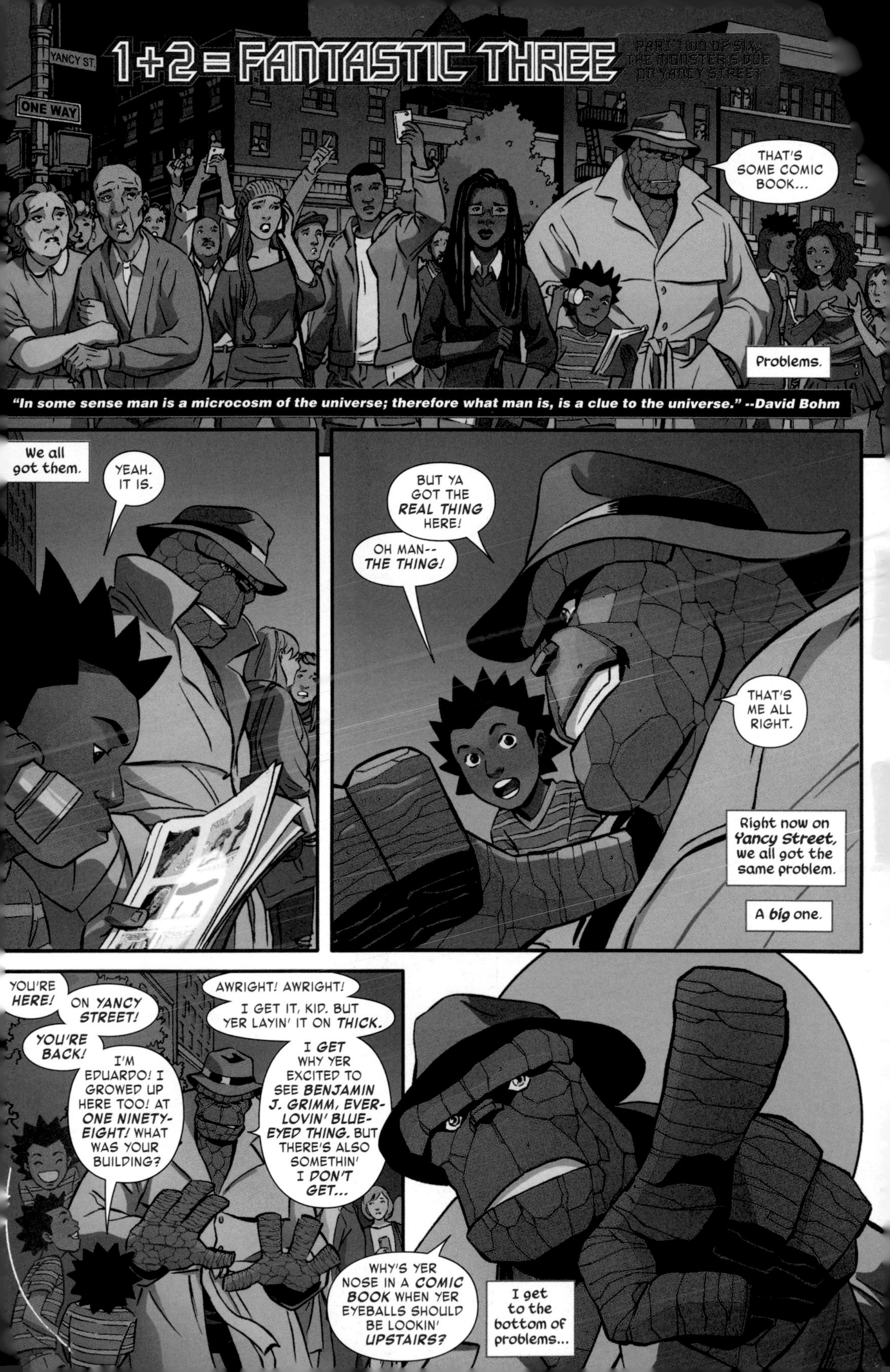

YANCY ST.
1+2 = FANTASTIC THREE
PART TWO OF SIX: THE MONSTER'S DUE ON YANCY STREET
ONE WAY
THAT'S SOME COMIC BOOK...
Problems.
"In some sense man is a microcosm of the universe; therefore what man is, is a clue to the universe." --David Bohm
We all got them.
YEAH. IT IS.
BUT YA GOT THE *REAL THING* HERE!
OH MAN-- *THE THING!*
THAT'S ME ALL RIGHT.
Right now on *Yancy Street,* we all got the same problem.
A *big* one.
YOU'RE *HERE!*
ON *YANCY STREET!*
YOU'RE BACK!
I'M EDUARDO! I GROWED UP HERE TOO! AT *ONE NINETY-EIGHT!* WHAT WAS YOUR BUILDING?
AWRIGHT! AWRIGHT!
I GET IT, KID. BUT YER LAYIN' IT ON *THICK.*
I *GET* WHY YER EXCITED TO SEE *BENJAMIN J. GRIMM, EVER-LOVIN' BLUE-EYED THING.* BUT THERE'S ALSO SOMETHIN' I *DON'T GET...*
WHY'S YER NOSE IN A *COMIC BOOK* WHEN YER EYEBALLS SHOULD BE LOOKIN' *UPSTAIRS?*
I get to the bottom of problems...

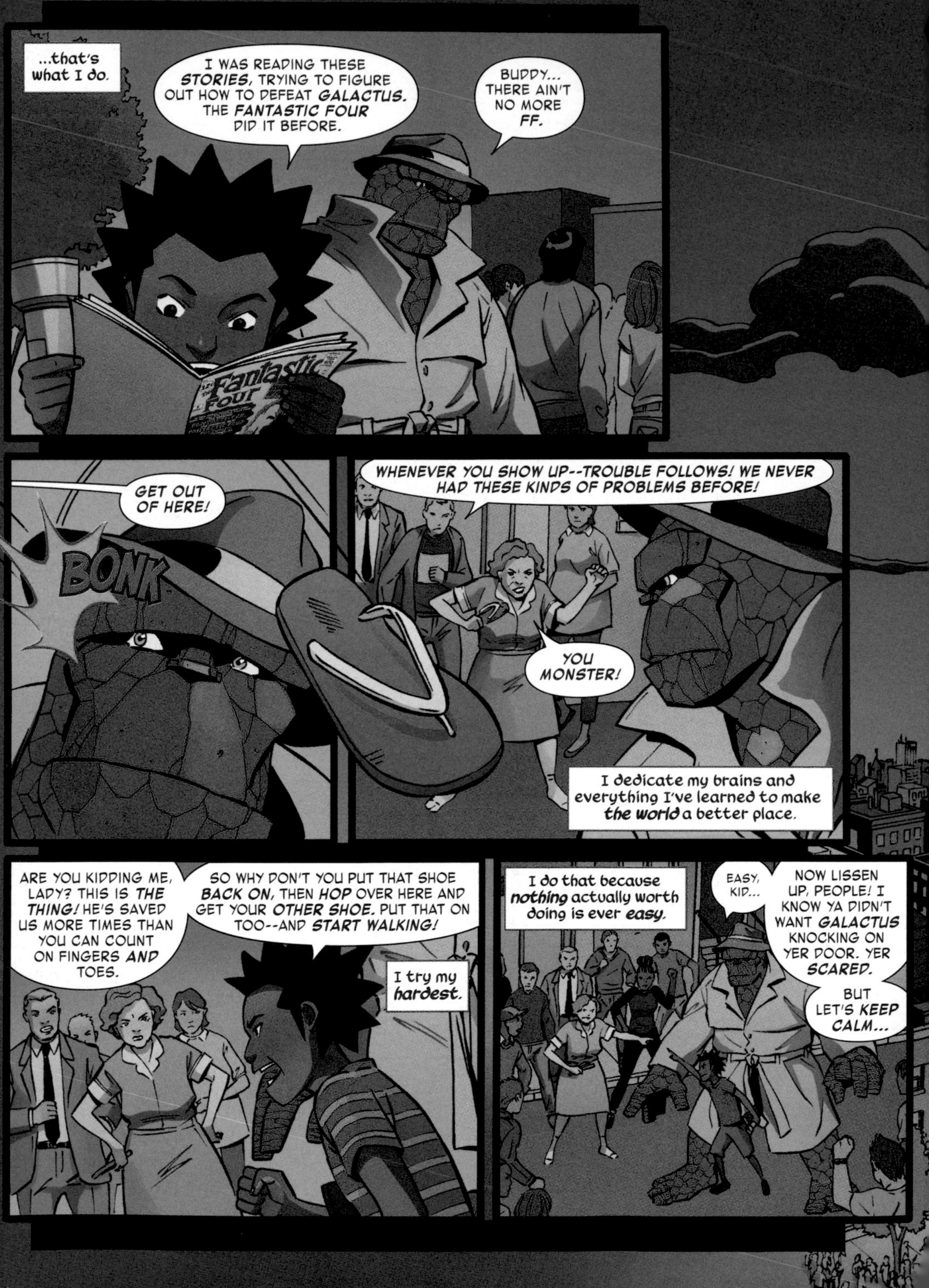

...that's what I do.
I WAS READING THESE STORIES, TRYING TO FIGURE OUT HOW TO DEFEAT GALACTUS. THE FANTASTIC FOUR DID IT BEFORE.
BUDDY... THERE AIN'T NO MORE FF.
Fantastic Four
GET OUT OF HERE!
BONK
WHENEVER YOU SHOW UP--TROUBLE FOLLOWS! WE NEVER HAD THESE KINDS OF PROBLEMS BEFORE!
YOU MONSTER!
I dedicate my brains and everything I've learned to make the world a better place.
ARE YOU KIDDING ME, LADY? THIS IS THE THING! HE'S SAVED US MORE TIMES THAN YOU CAN COUNT ON FINGERS AND TOES.
SO WHY DON'T YOU PUT THAT SHOE BACK ON, THEN HOP OVER HERE AND GET YOUR OTHER SHOE. PUT THAT ON TOO--AND START WALKING!
I try my hardest.
I do that because nothing actually worth doing is ever easy.
EASY, KID...
NOW LISSEN UP, PEOPLE! I KNOW YA DIDN'T WANT GALACTUS KNOCKING ON YER DOOR. YER SCARED.
BUT LET'S KEEP CALM...

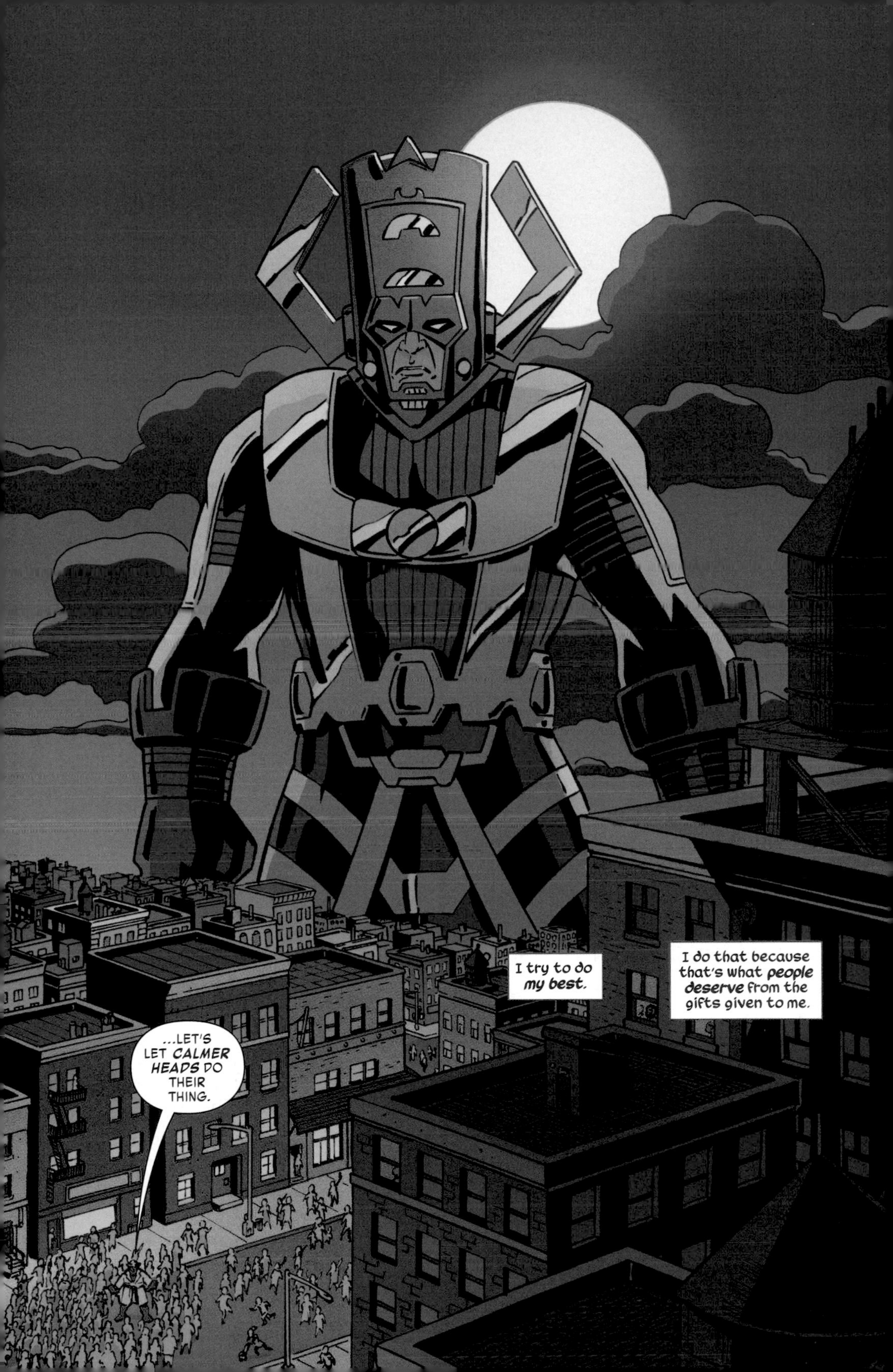
...LET'S LET CALMER HEADS DO THEIR THING.
I try to do my best.
I do that because that's what people deserve from the gifts given to me.

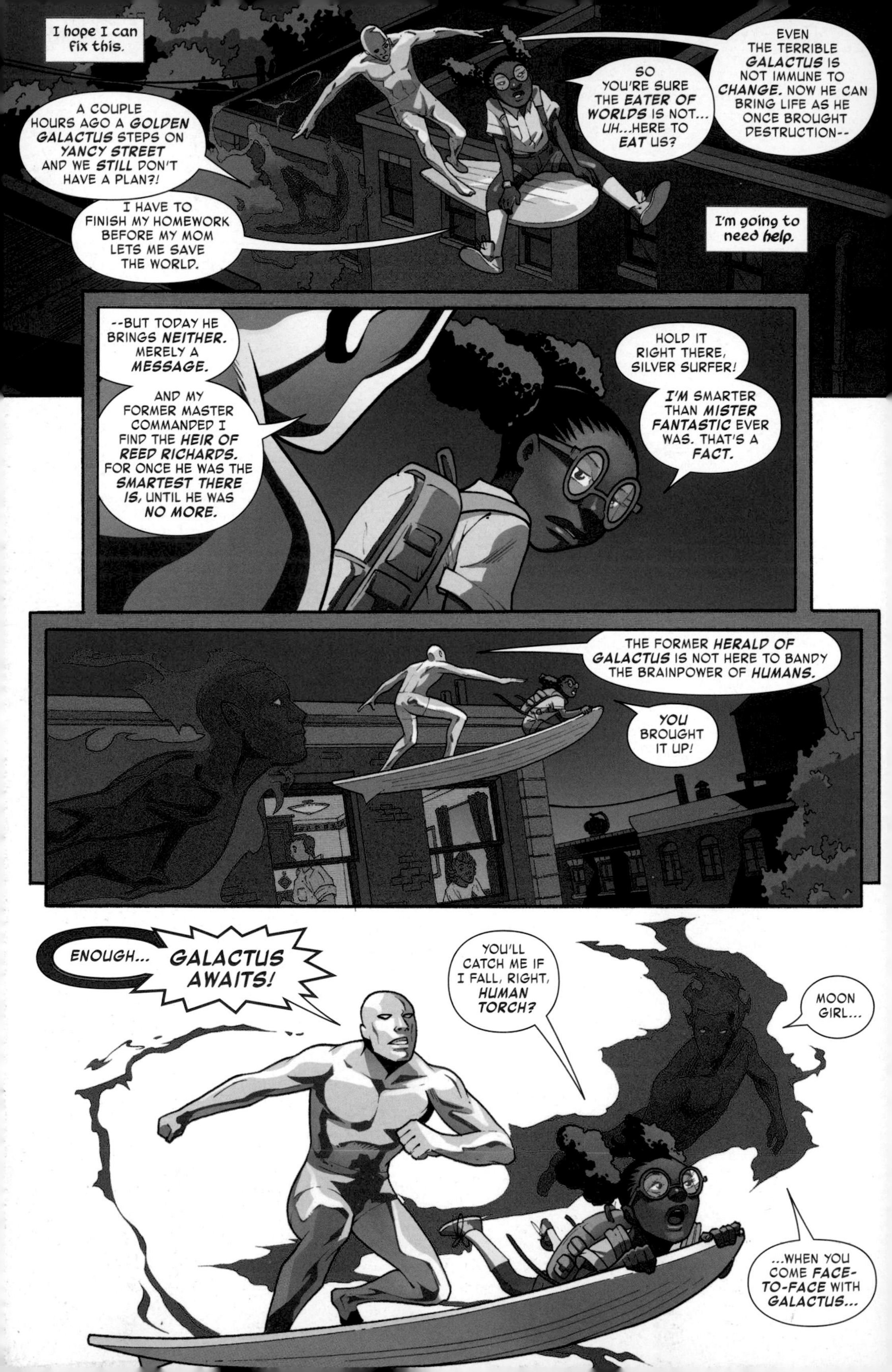
I hope I can fix this.
A COUPLE HOURS AGO A GOLDEN GALACTUS STEPS ON YANCY STREET AND WE STILL DON'T HAVE A PLAN?!
I HAVE TO FINISH MY HOMEWORK BEFORE MY MOM LETS ME SAVE THE WORLD.
SO YOU'RE SURE THE EATER OF WORLDS IS NOT... UH...HERE TO EAT US?
EVEN THE TERRIBLE GALACTUS IS NOT IMMUNE TO CHANGE. NOW HE CAN BRING LIFE AS HE ONCE BROUGHT DESTRUCTION--
I'm going to need help.
--BUT TODAY HE BRINGS NEITHER. MERELY A MESSAGE.
AND MY FORMER MASTER COMMANDED I FIND THE HEIR OF REED RICHARDS. FOR ONCE HE WAS THE SMARTEST THERE IS, UNTIL HE WAS NO MORE.
HOLD IT RIGHT THERE, SILVER SURFER!
I'M SMARTER THAN MISTER FANTASTIC EVER WAS. THAT'S A FACT.
THE FORMER HERALD OF GALACTUS IS NOT HERE TO BANDY THE BRAINPOWER OF HUMANS.
YOU BROUGHT IT UP!
ENOUGH...
GALACTUS AWAITS!
YOU'LL CATCH ME IF I FALL, RIGHT, HUMAN TORCH?
MOON GIRL...
...WHEN YOU COME FACE-TO-FACE WITH GALACTUS...

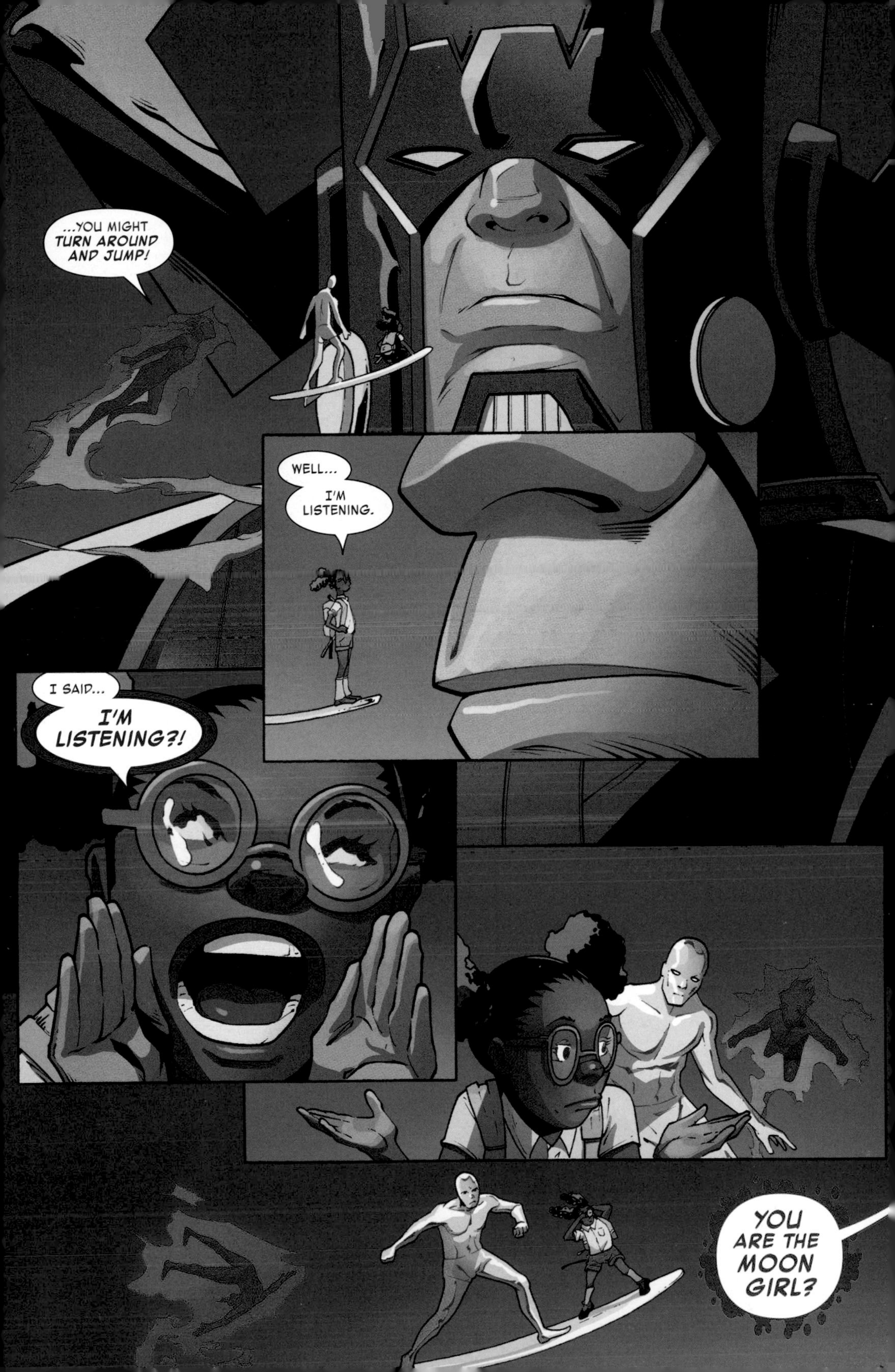
...YOU MIGHT TURN AROUND AND JUMP!
WELL...
I'M LISTENING.
I SAID...
I'M LISTENING?!
YOU ARE THE MOON GIRL?

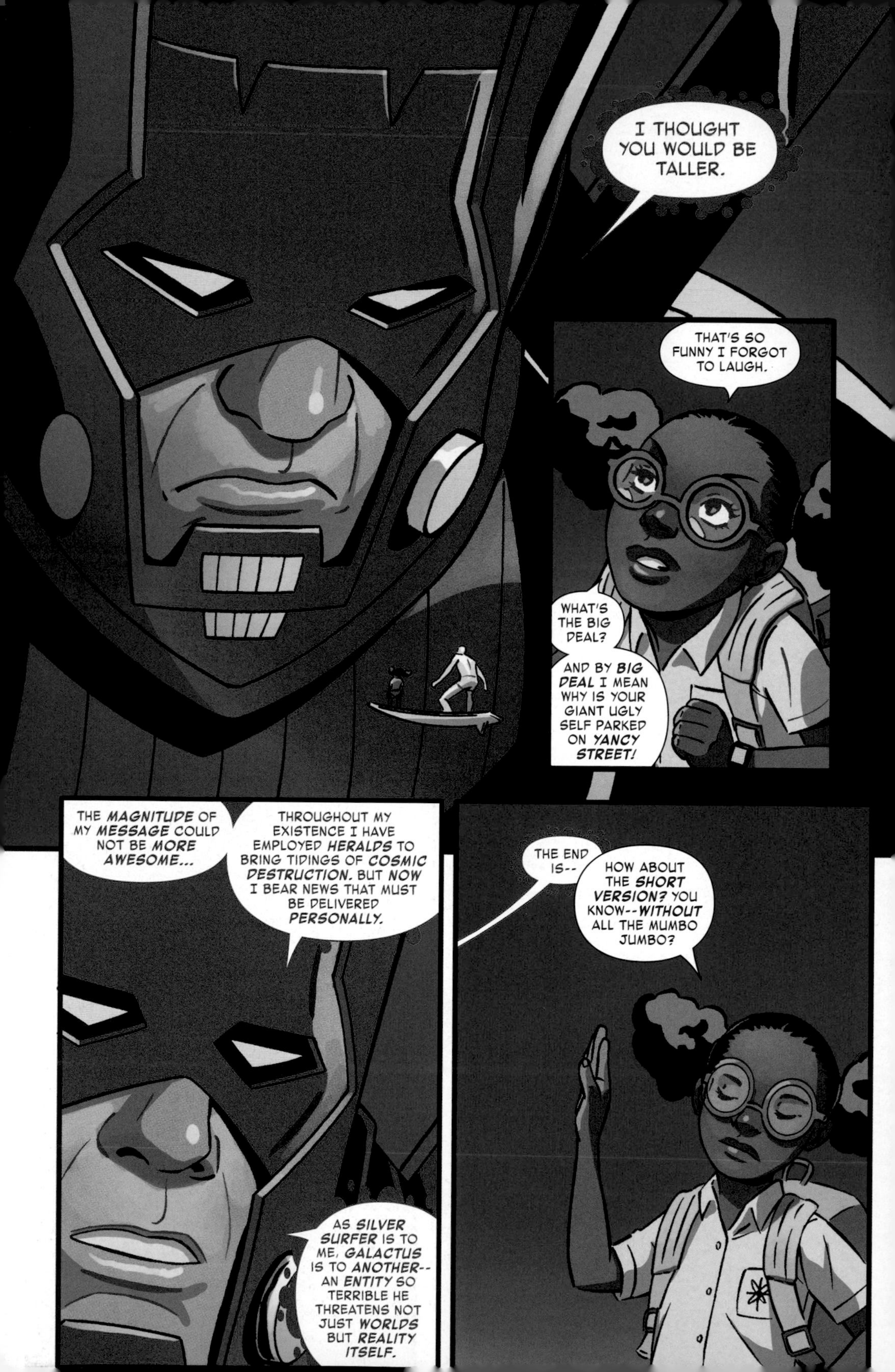
I THOUGHT YOU WOULD BE TALLER.
THAT'S SO FUNNY I FORGOT TO LAUGH.
WHAT'S THE BIG DEAL?
AND BY BIG DEAL I MEAN WHY IS YOUR GIANT UGLY SELF PARKED ON YANCY STREET!
THE MAGNITUDE OF MY MESSAGE COULD NOT BE MORE AWESOME...
THROUGHOUT MY EXISTENCE I HAVE EMPLOYED HERALDS TO BRING TIDINGS OF COSMIC DESTRUCTION. BUT NOW I BEAR NEWS THAT MUST BE DELIVERED PERSONALLY.
AS SILVER SURFER IS TO ME, GALACTUS IS TO ANOTHER--AN ENTITY SO TERRIBLE HE THREATENS NOT JUST WORLDS BUT REALITY ITSELF.
THE END IS--
HOW ABOUT THE SHORT VERSION? YOU KNOW--WITHOUT ALL THE MUMBO JUMBO?

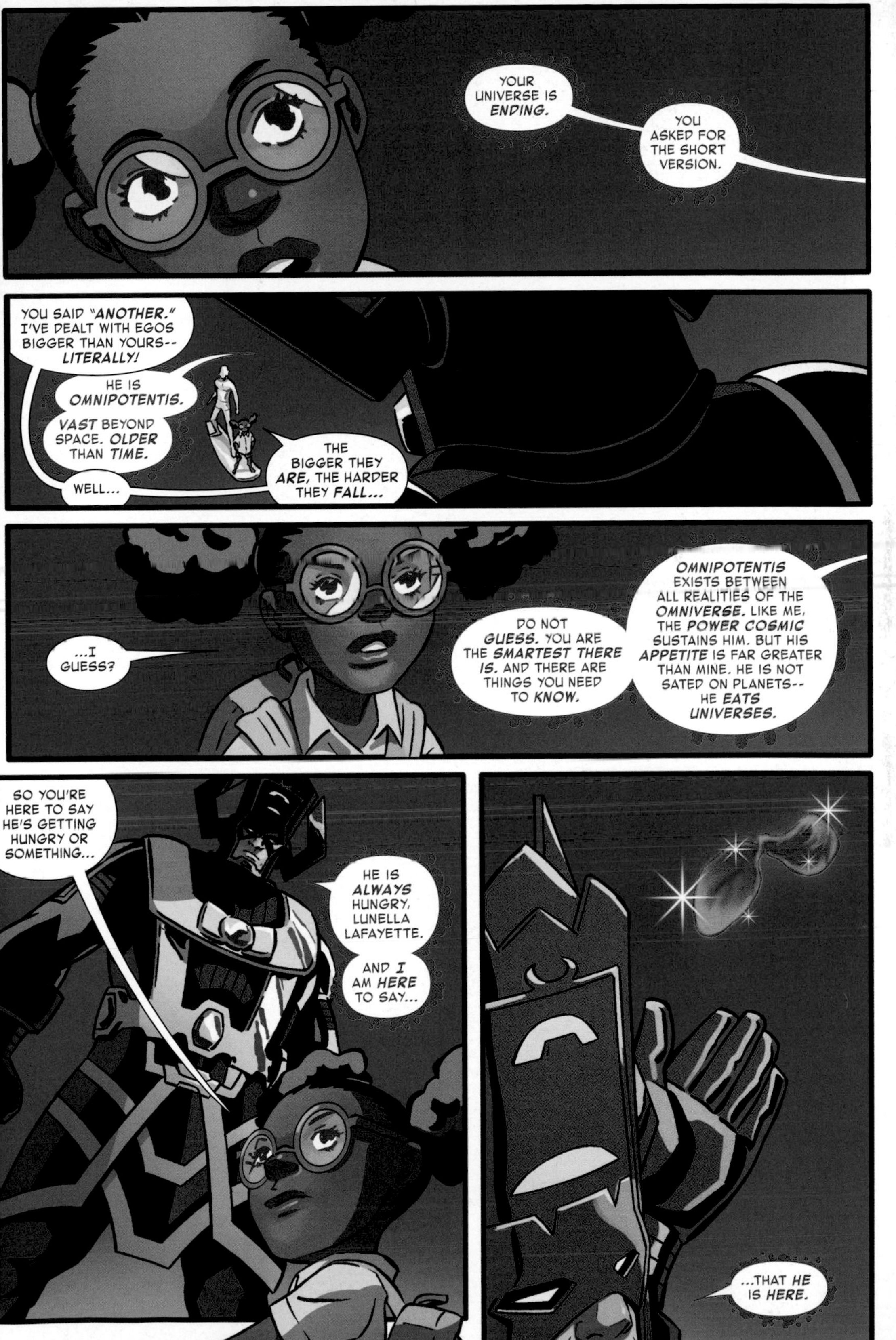
YOUR UNIVERSE IS ENDING.
YOU ASKED FOR THE SHORT VERSION.
YOU SAID "ANOTHER." I'VE DEALT WITH EGOS BIGGER THAN YOURS-- LITERALLY!
HE IS OMNIPOTENTIS.
VAST BEYOND SPACE. OLDER THAN TIME.
WELL...
THE BIGGER THEY ARE, THE HARDER THEY FALL...
...I GUESS?
DO NOT GUESS. YOU ARE THE SMARTEST THERE IS. AND THERE ARE THINGS YOU NEED TO KNOW.
OMNIPOTENTIS EXISTS BETWEEN ALL REALITIES OF THE OMNIVERSE. LIKE ME, THE POWER COSMIC SUSTAINS HIM. BUT HIS APPETITE IS FAR GREATER THAN MINE. HE IS NOT SATED ON PLANETS-- HE EATS UNIVERSES.
SO YOU'RE HERE TO SAY HE'S GETTING HUNGRY OR SOMETHING...
HE IS ALWAYS HUNGRY, LUNELLA LAFAYETTE.
AND I AM HERE TO SAY...
...THAT HE IS HERE.

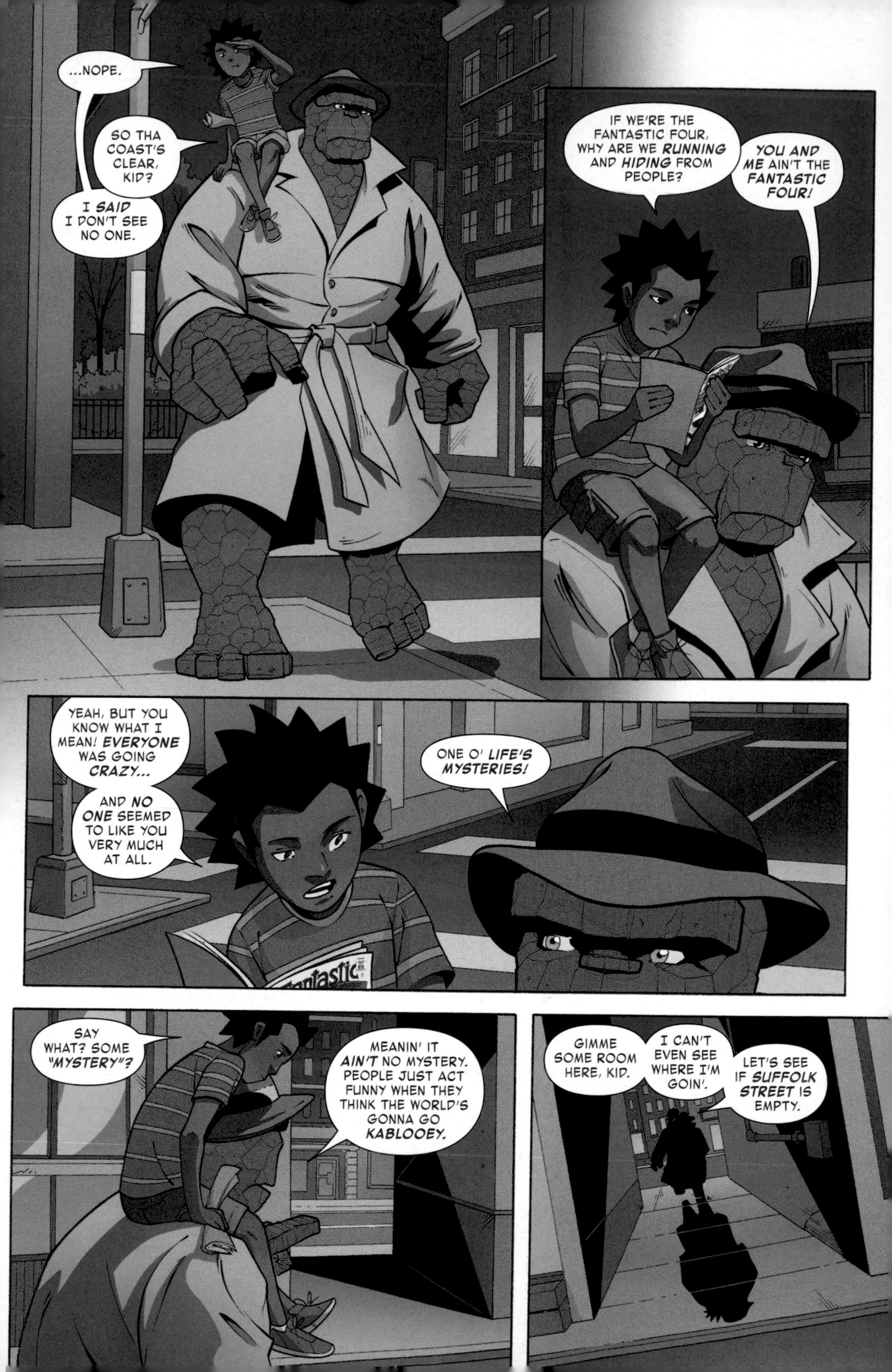
...NOPE.
SO THA COAST'S CLEAR, KID?
I *SAID* I DON'T SEE NO ONE.
IF WE'RE THE FANTASTIC FOUR, WHY ARE WE *RUNNING* AND *HIDING* FROM PEOPLE?
YOU AND ME AIN'T THE *FANTASTIC FOUR!*
YEAH, BUT YOU KNOW WHAT I MEAN! *EVERYONE* WAS GOING *CRAZY...*
AND *NO ONE* SEEMED TO LIKE YOU VERY MUCH AT ALL.
ONE O' *LIFE'S MYSTERIES!*
SAY WHAT? SOME *"MYSTERY"?*
MEANIN' IT *AIN'T* NO MYSTERY. PEOPLE JUST ACT FUNNY WHEN THEY THINK THE WORLD'S GONNA GO *KABLOOEY.*
GIMME SOME ROOM HERE, KID.
I CAN'T EVEN SEE WHERE I'M GOIN'.
LET'S SEE IF *SUFFOLK STREET* IS EMPTY.

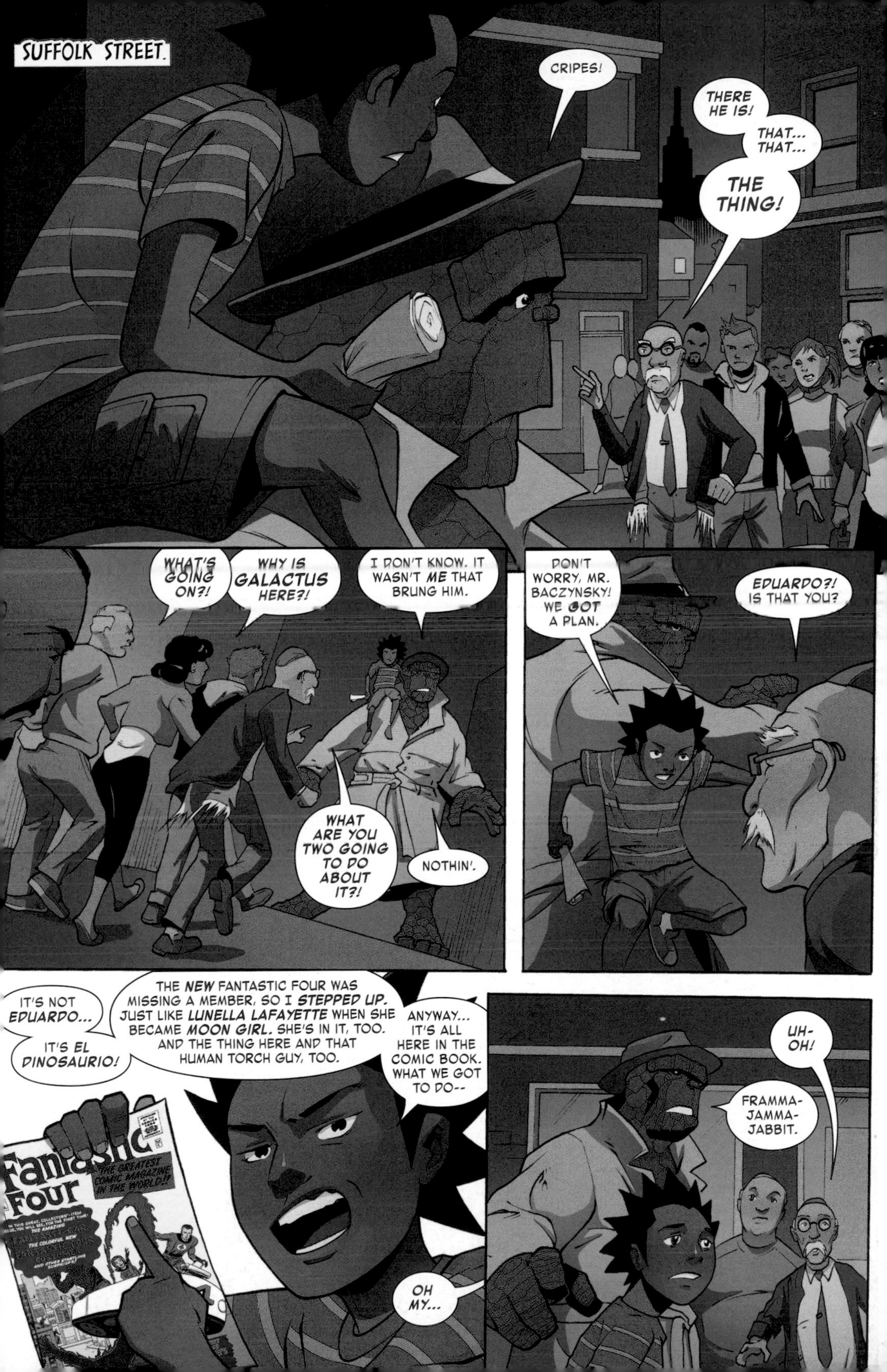
SUFFOLK STREET.
CRIPES!
THERE HE IS!
THAT... THAT...
THE THING!
WHAT'S GOING ON?!
WHY IS GALACTUS HERE?!
I DON'T KNOW. IT WASN'T ME THAT BRUNG HIM.
WHAT ARE YOU TWO GOING TO DO ABOUT IT?!
NOTHIN'.
DON'T WORRY, MR. BACZYNSKY! WE GOT A PLAN.
EDUARDO?! IS THAT YOU?
IT'S NOT EDUARDO...
IT'S EL DINOSAURIO!
THE NEW FANTASTIC FOUR WAS MISSING A MEMBER, SO I STEPPED UP. JUST LIKE LUNELLA LAFAYETTE WHEN SHE BECAME MOON GIRL. SHE'S IN IT, TOO. AND THE THING HERE AND THAT HUMAN TORCH GUY, TOO.
ANYWAY... IT'S ALL HERE IN THE COMIC BOOK. WHAT WE GOT TO DO--
Fantastic Four
THE GREATEST COMIC MAGAZINE IN THE WORLD!!
OH MY...
UH-OH!
FRAMMA-JAMMA-JABBIT.

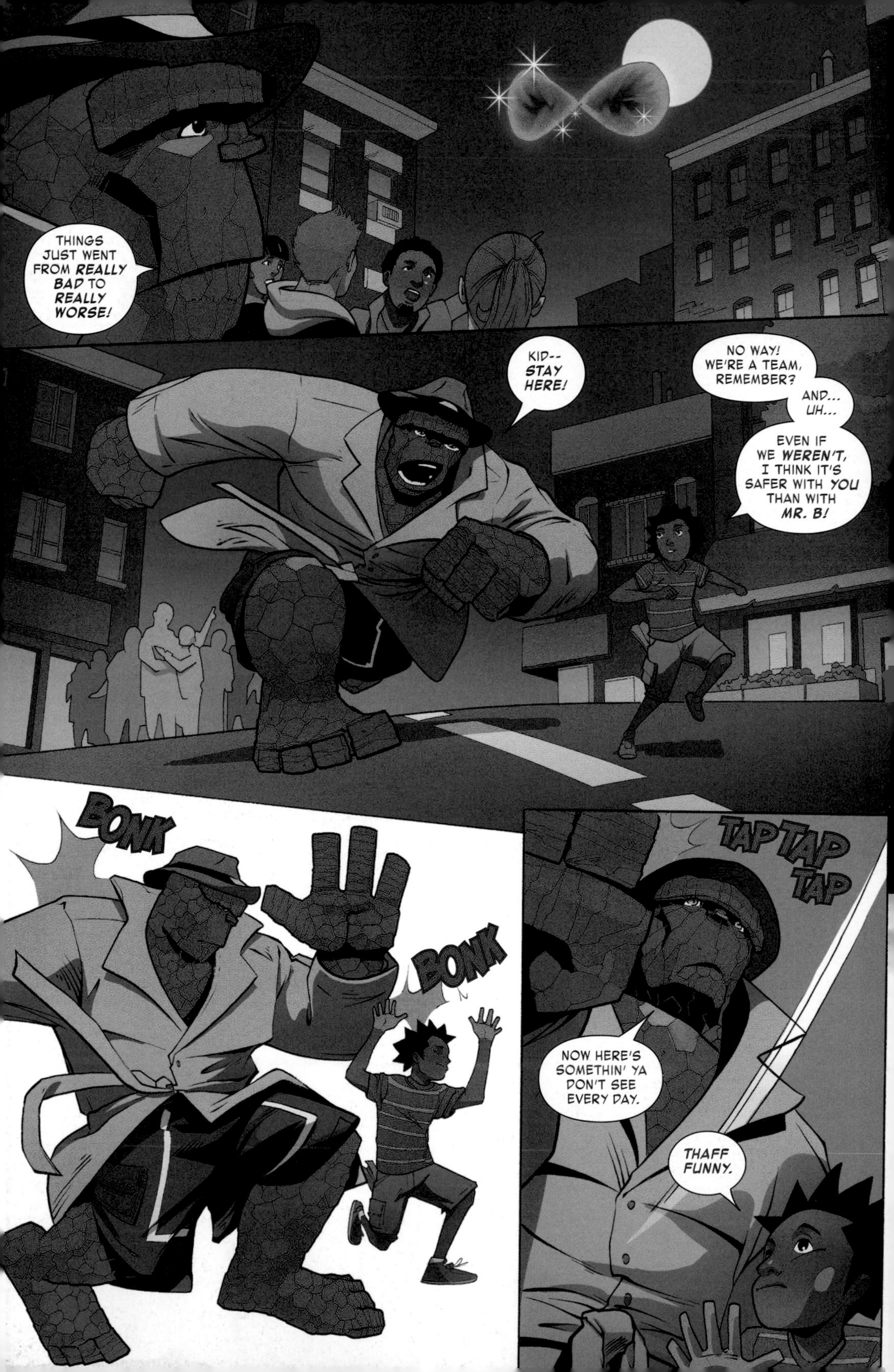
THINGS JUST WENT FROM REALLY BAD TO REALLY WORSE!
KID-- STAY HERE!
NO WAY! WE'RE A TEAM, REMEMBER?
AND... UH...
EVEN IF WE WEREN'T, I THINK IT'S SAFER WITH YOU THAN WITH MR. B!
BONK
BONK
TAP TAP TAP
NOW HERE'S SOMETHIN' YA DON'T SEE EVERY DAY.
THAFF FUNNY.

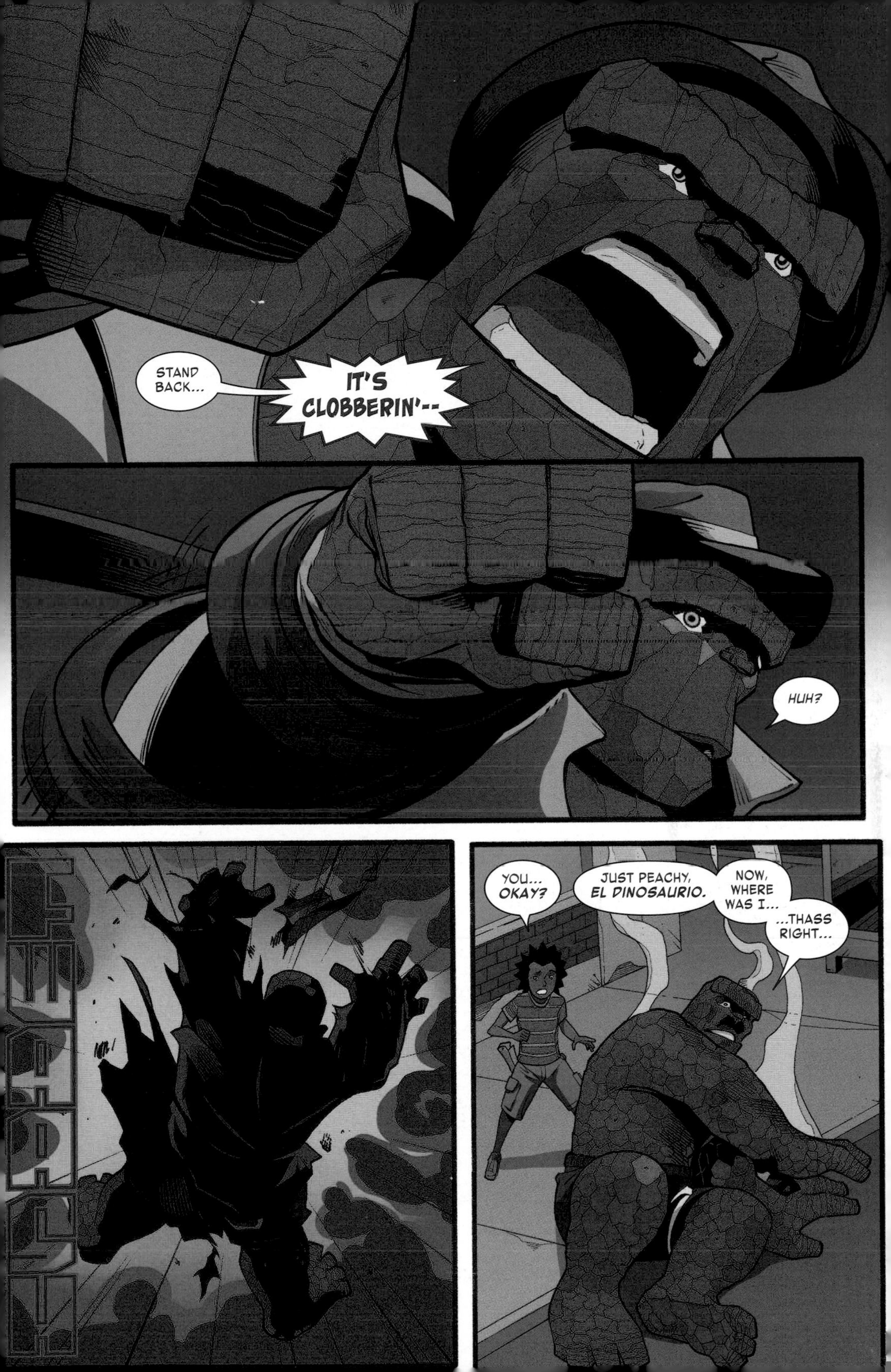
STAND BACK...
IT'S CLOBBERIN'--
HUH?
YOU... OKAY?
JUST PEACHY, EL DINOSAURIO.
NOW, WHERE WAS I...
...THASS RIGHT...

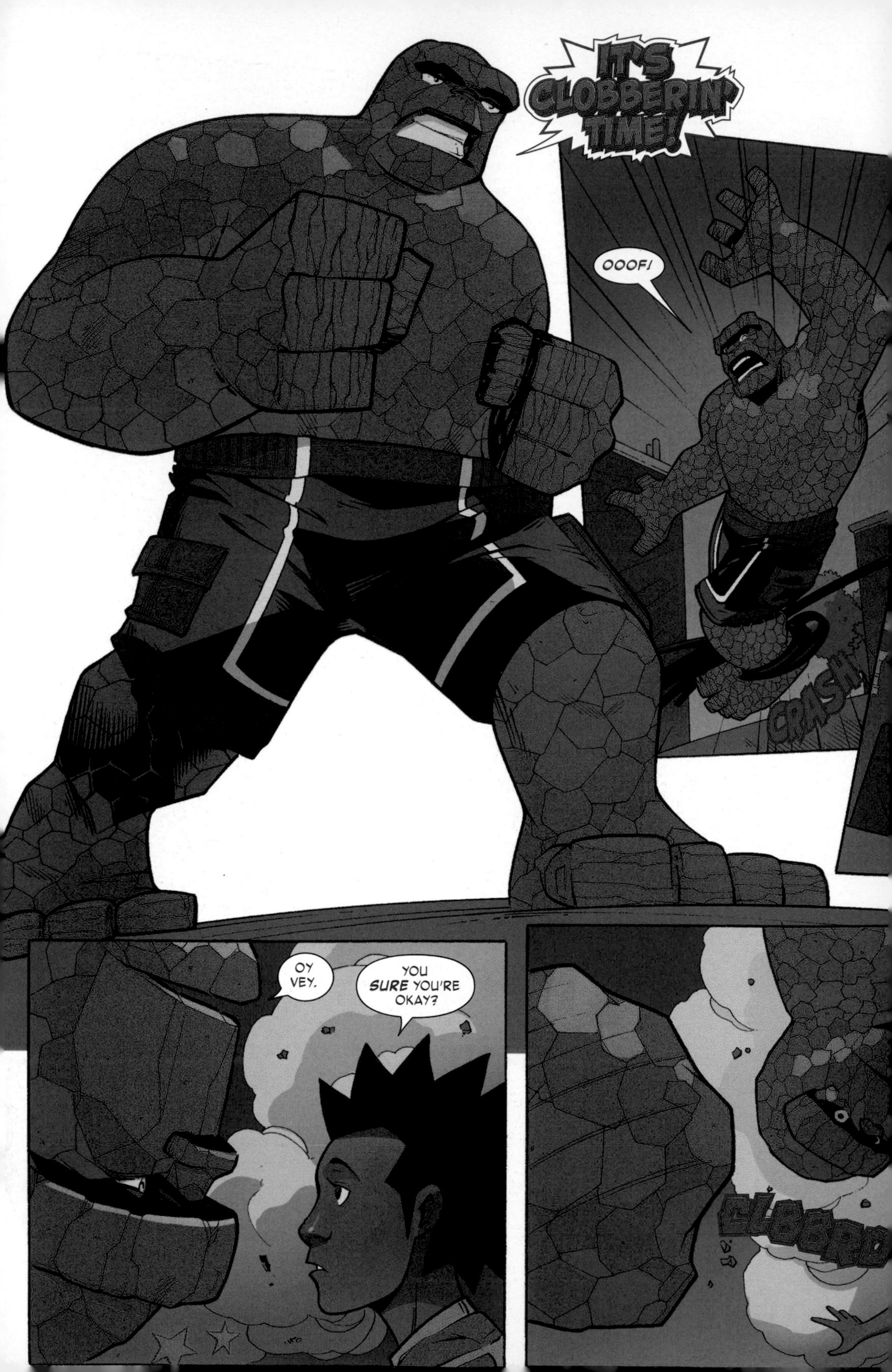
IT'S CLOBBERIN' TIME!
OOOF!
CRASH!
OY VEY.
YOU SURE YOU'RE OKAY?
CLBBRD

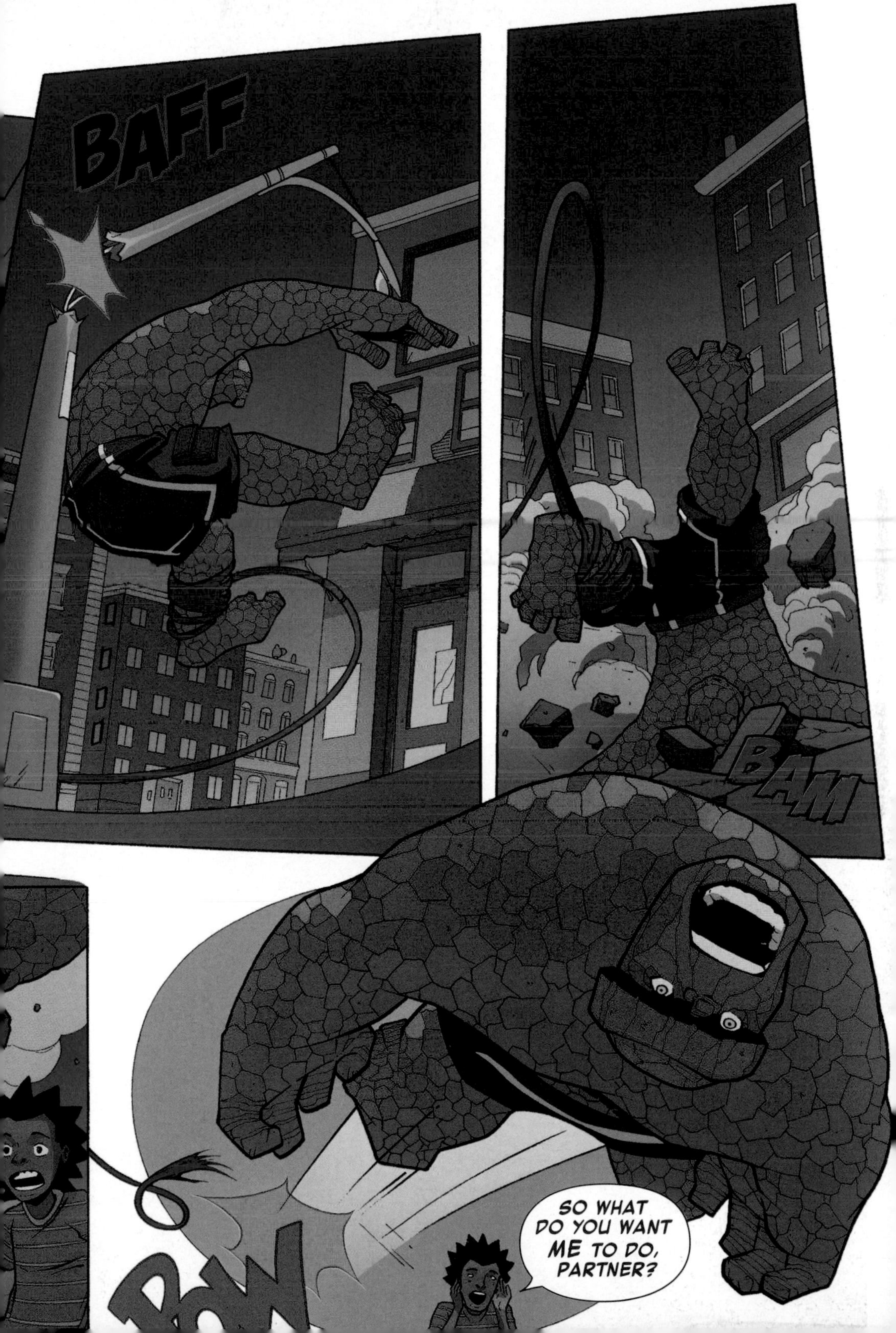
BAFF
BAM
SO WHAT DO YOU WANT ME TO DO, PARTNER?

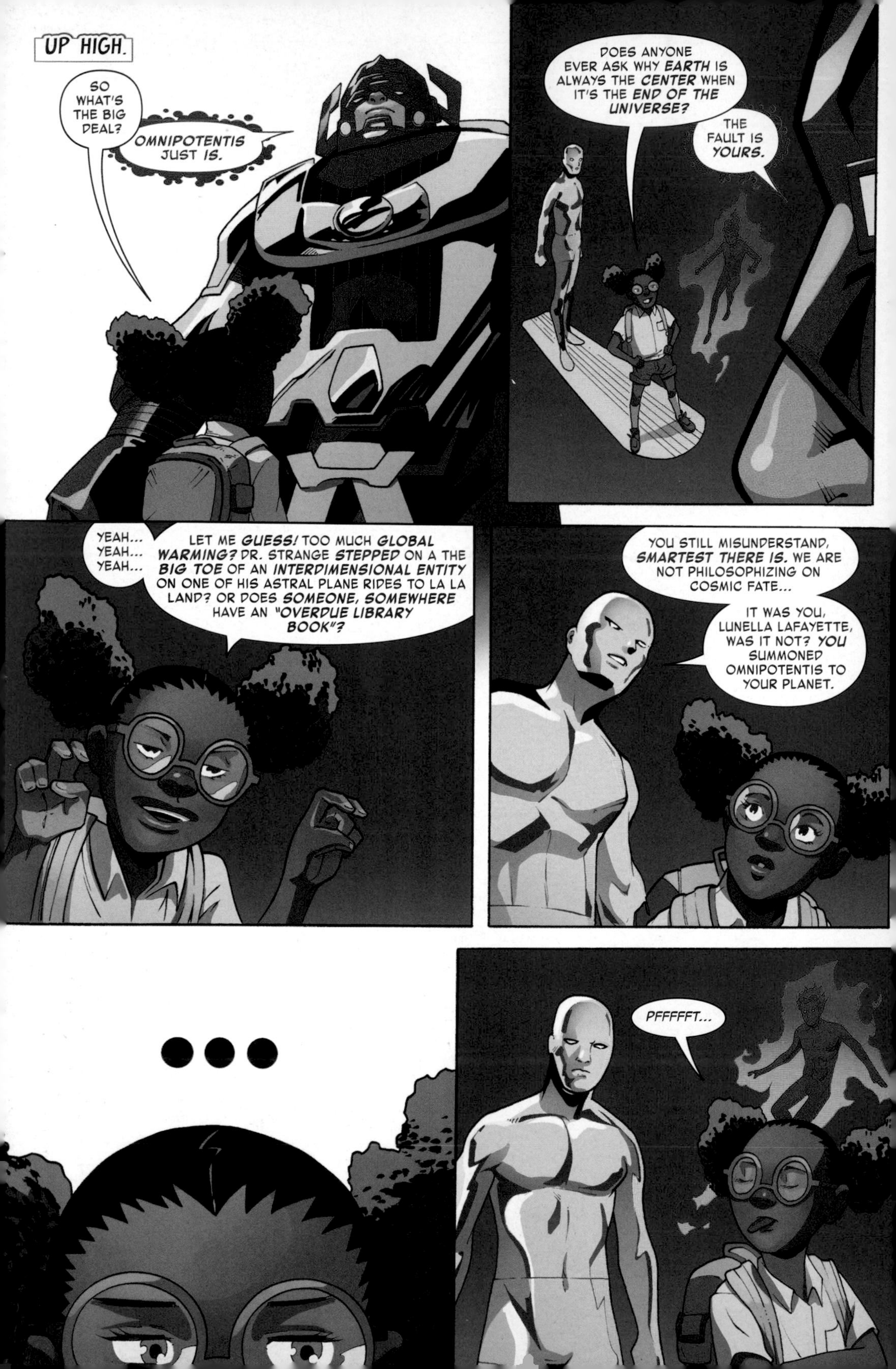
UP HIGH.
SO WHAT'S THE BIG DEAL?
OMNIPOTENTIS JUST IS.
DOES ANYONE EVER ASK WHY EARTH IS ALWAYS THE CENTER WHEN IT'S THE END OF THE UNIVERSE?
THE FAULT IS YOURS.
YEAH... YEAH... YEAH...
LET ME GUESS! TOO MUCH GLOBAL WARMING? DR. STRANGE STEPPED ON A THE BIG TOE OF AN INTERDIMENSIONAL ENTITY ON ONE OF HIS ASTRAL PLANE RIDES TO LA LA LAND? OR DOES SOMEONE, SOMEWHERE HAVE AN "OVERDUE LIBRARY BOOK"?
YOU STILL MISUNDERSTAND, SMARTEST THERE IS. WE ARE NOT PHILOSOPHIZING ON COSMIC FATE...
IT WAS YOU, LUNELLA LAFAYETTE, WAS IT NOT? YOU SUMMONED OMNIPOTENTIS TO YOUR PLANET.
PFFFFFT...

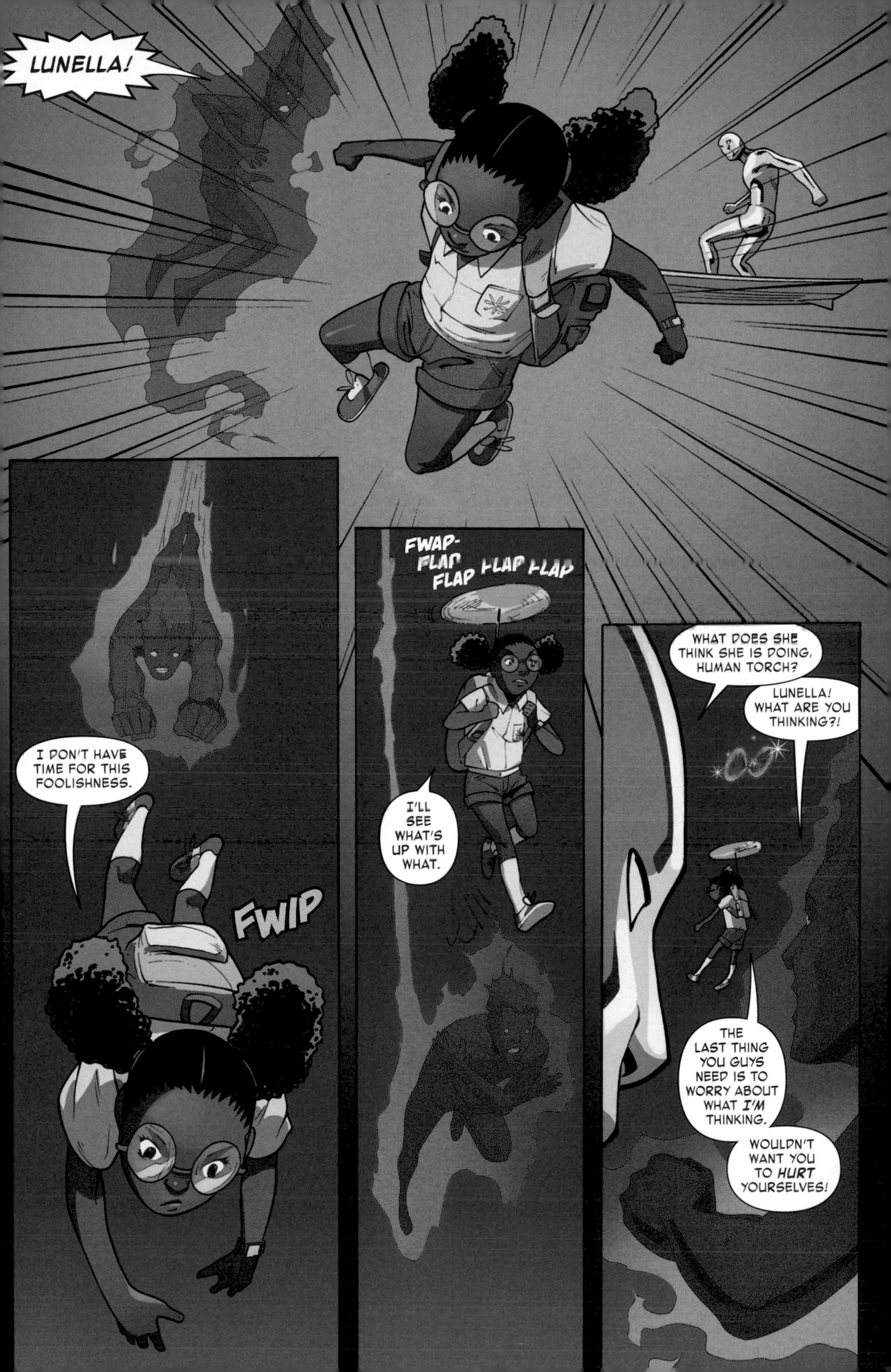
LUNELLA!
I DON'T HAVE TIME FOR THIS FOOLISHNESS.
FWIP
FWAP-FLAP FLAP FLAP FLAP
I'LL SEE WHAT'S UP WITH WHAT.
WHAT DOES SHE THINK SHE IS DOING, HUMAN TORCH?
LUNELLA! WHAT ARE YOU THINKING?!
THE LAST THING YOU GUYS NEED IS TO WORRY ABOUT WHAT *I'M* THINKING.
WOULDN'T WANT YOU TO *HURT* YOURSELVES!

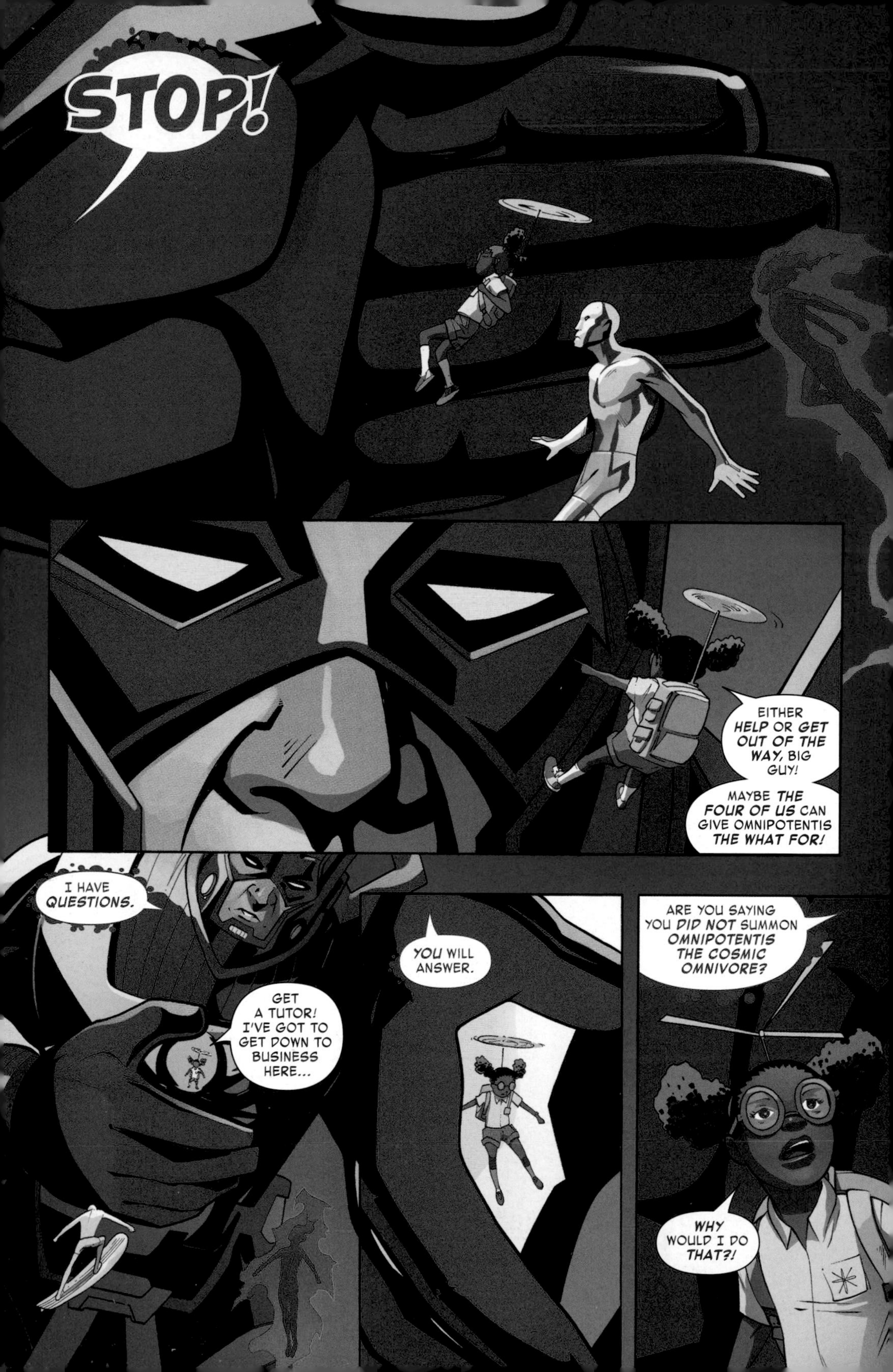
STOP!
EITHER HELP OR GET OUT OF THE WAY, BIG GUY!
MAYBE THE FOUR OF US CAN GIVE OMNIPOTENTIS THE WHAT FOR!
I HAVE QUESTIONS.
GET A TUTOR! I'VE GOT TO GET DOWN TO BUSINESS HERE...
YOU WILL ANSWER.
ARE YOU SAYING YOU DID NOT SUMMON OMNIPOTENTIS THE COSMIC OMNIVORE?
WHY WOULD I DO THAT?!

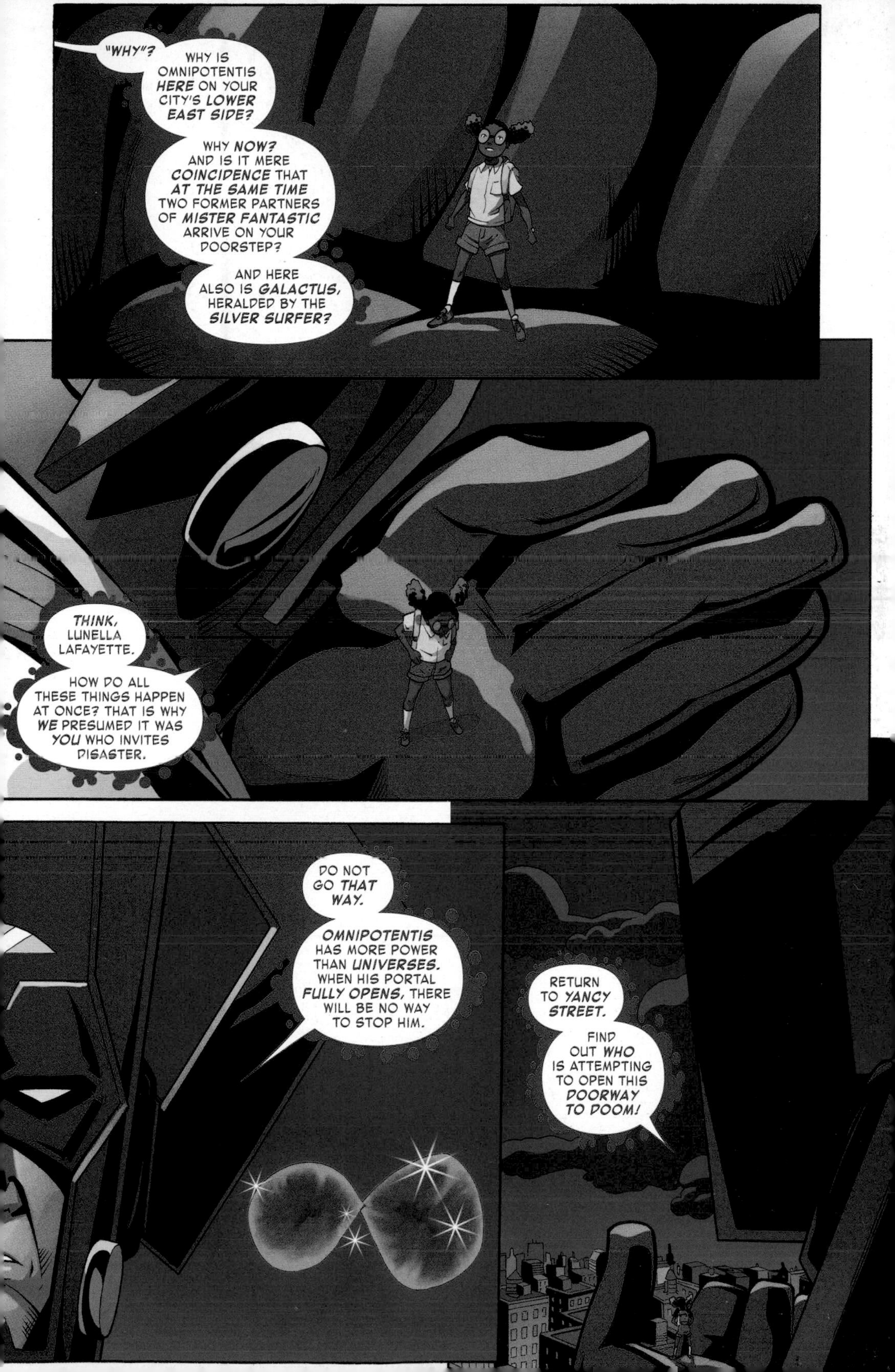
"WHY"? WHY IS OMNIPOTENTIS HERE ON YOUR CITY'S LOWER EAST SIDE?
WHY NOW? AND IS IT MERE COINCIDENCE THAT AT THE SAME TIME TWO FORMER PARTNERS OF MISTER FANTASTIC ARRIVE ON YOUR DOORSTEP?
AND HERE ALSO IS GALACTUS, HERALDED BY THE SILVER SURFER?
THINK, LUNELLA LAFAYETTE.
HOW DO ALL THESE THINGS HAPPEN AT ONCE? THAT IS WHY WE PRESUMED IT WAS YOU WHO INVITES DISASTER.
DO NOT GO THAT WAY.
OMNIPOTENTIS HAS MORE POWER THAN UNIVERSES. WHEN HIS PORTAL FULLY OPENS, THERE WILL BE NO WAY TO STOP HIM.
RETURN TO YANCY STREET.
FIND OUT WHO IS ATTEMPTING TO OPEN THIS DOORWAY TO DOOM!

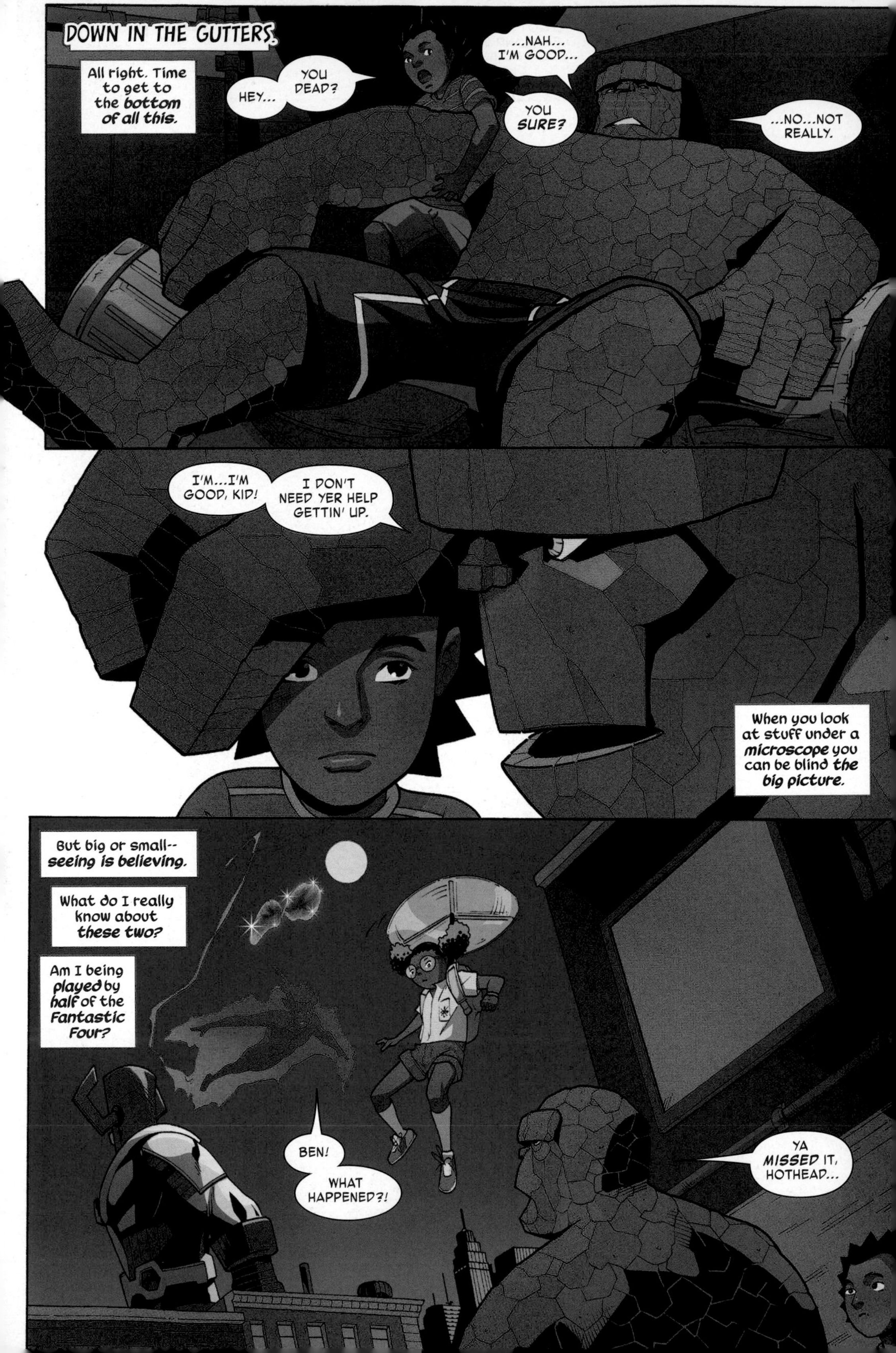
DOWN IN THE GUTTERS.
All right. Time to get to the bottom of all this.
HEY...
YOU DEAD?
...NAH... I'M GOOD...
YOU SURE?
...NO...NOT REALLY.
I'M...I'M GOOD, KID!
I DON'T NEED YER HELP GETTIN' UP.
When you look at stuff under a microscope you can be blind the big picture.
But big or small-- seeing is believing.
What do I really know about these two?
Am I being played by half of the Fantastic Four?
BEN!
WHAT HAPPENED?!
YA MISSED IT, HOTHEAD...

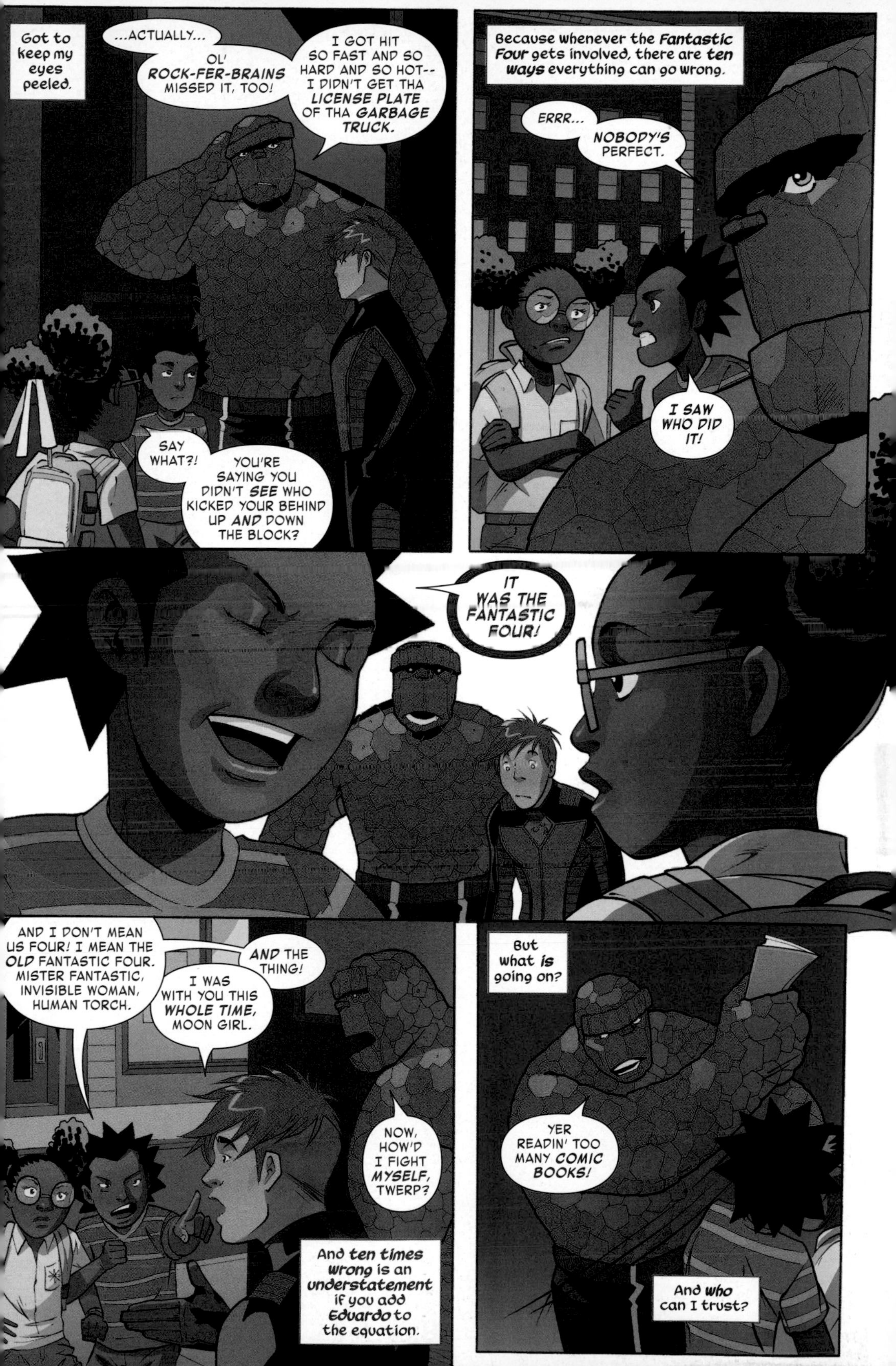
Got to keep my eyes peeled.
...ACTUALLY...
OL' ROCK-FER-BRAINS MISSED IT, TOO!
I GOT HIT SO FAST AND SO HARD AND SO HOT-- I DIDN'T GET THA LICENSE PLATE OF THA GARBAGE TRUCK.
SAY WHAT?!
YOU'RE SAYING YOU DIDN'T SEE WHO KICKED YOUR BEHIND UP AND DOWN THE BLOCK?
Because whenever the Fantastic Four gets involved, there are ten ways everything can go wrong.
ERRR...
NOBODY'S PERFECT.
I SAW WHO DID IT!
IT WAS THE FANTASTIC FOUR!
AND I DON'T MEAN US FOUR! I MEAN THE OLD FANTASTIC FOUR. MISTER FANTASTIC, INVISIBLE WOMAN, HUMAN TORCH.
AND THE THING!
I WAS WITH YOU THIS WHOLE TIME, MOON GIRL.
NOW, HOW'D I FIGHT MYSELF, TWERP?
And ten times wrong is an understatement if you add Eduardo to the equation.
But what is going on?
YER READIN' TOO MANY COMIC BOOKS!
And who can I trust?

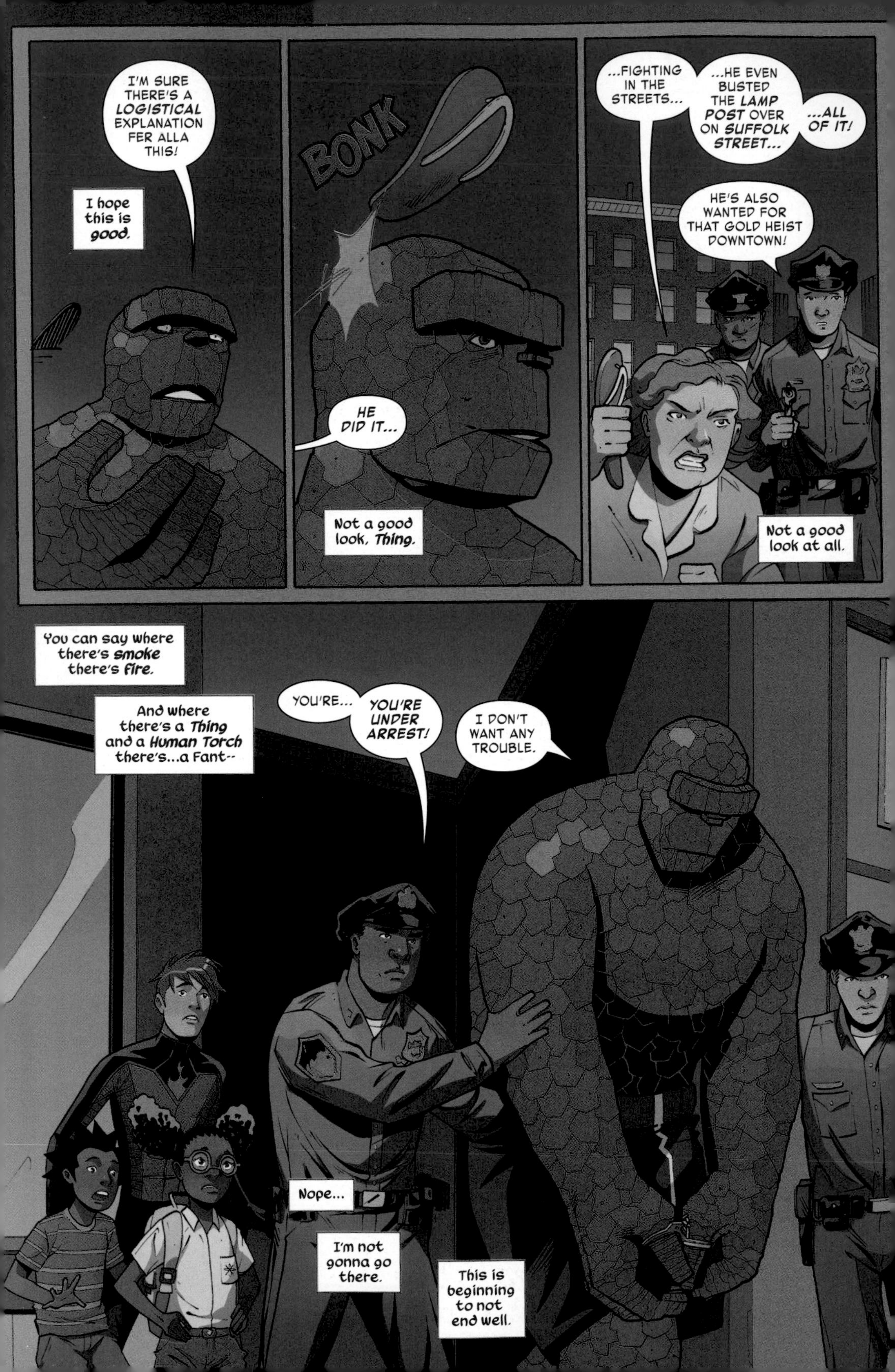
I'M SURE THERE'S A LOGISTICAL EXPLANATION FER ALLA THIS!
I hope this is good.
BONK
HE DID IT...
Not a good look, Thing.
...FIGHTING IN THE STREETS...
...HE EVEN BUSTED THE LAMP POST OVER ON SUFFOLK STREET...
...ALL OF IT!
HE'S ALSO WANTED FOR THAT GOLD HEIST DOWNTOWN!
Not a good look at all.
You can say where there's smoke there's fire.
And where there's a Thing and a Human Torch there's...a Fant--
YOU'RE... YOU'RE UNDER ARREST!
I DON'T WANT ANY TROUBLE.
Nope...
I'm not gonna go there.
This is beginning to not end well.

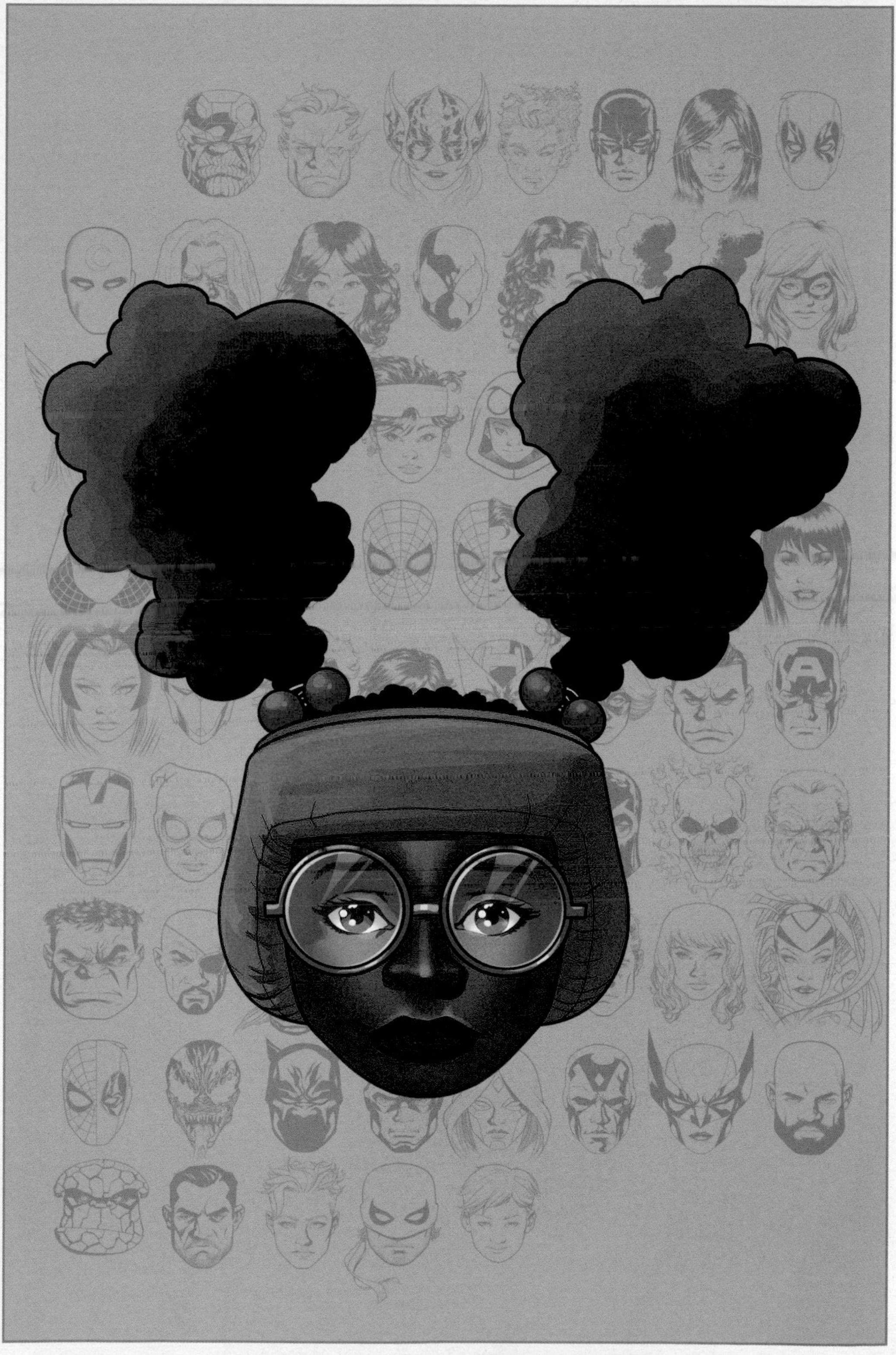

#25 Legacy Headshot Variant
BY MIKE McKONE & ANDY TROY

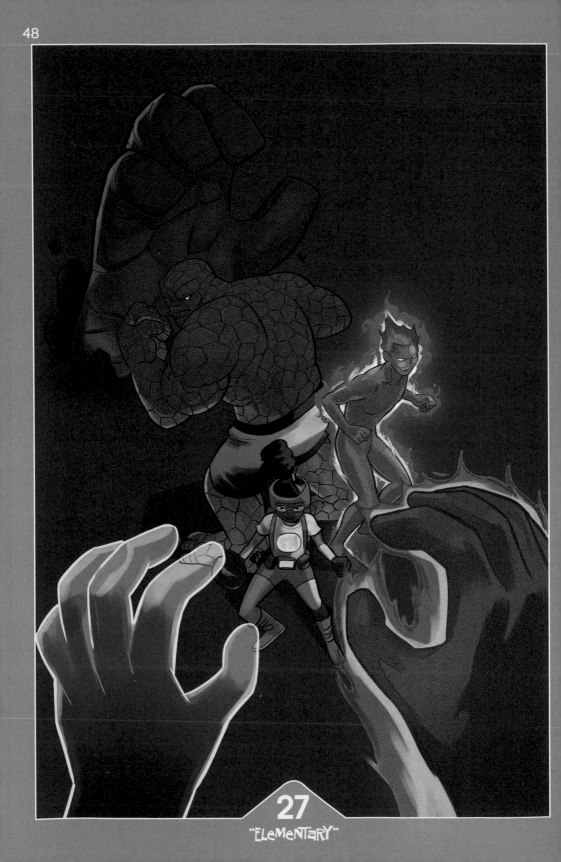

27

"ELEMENTARY"

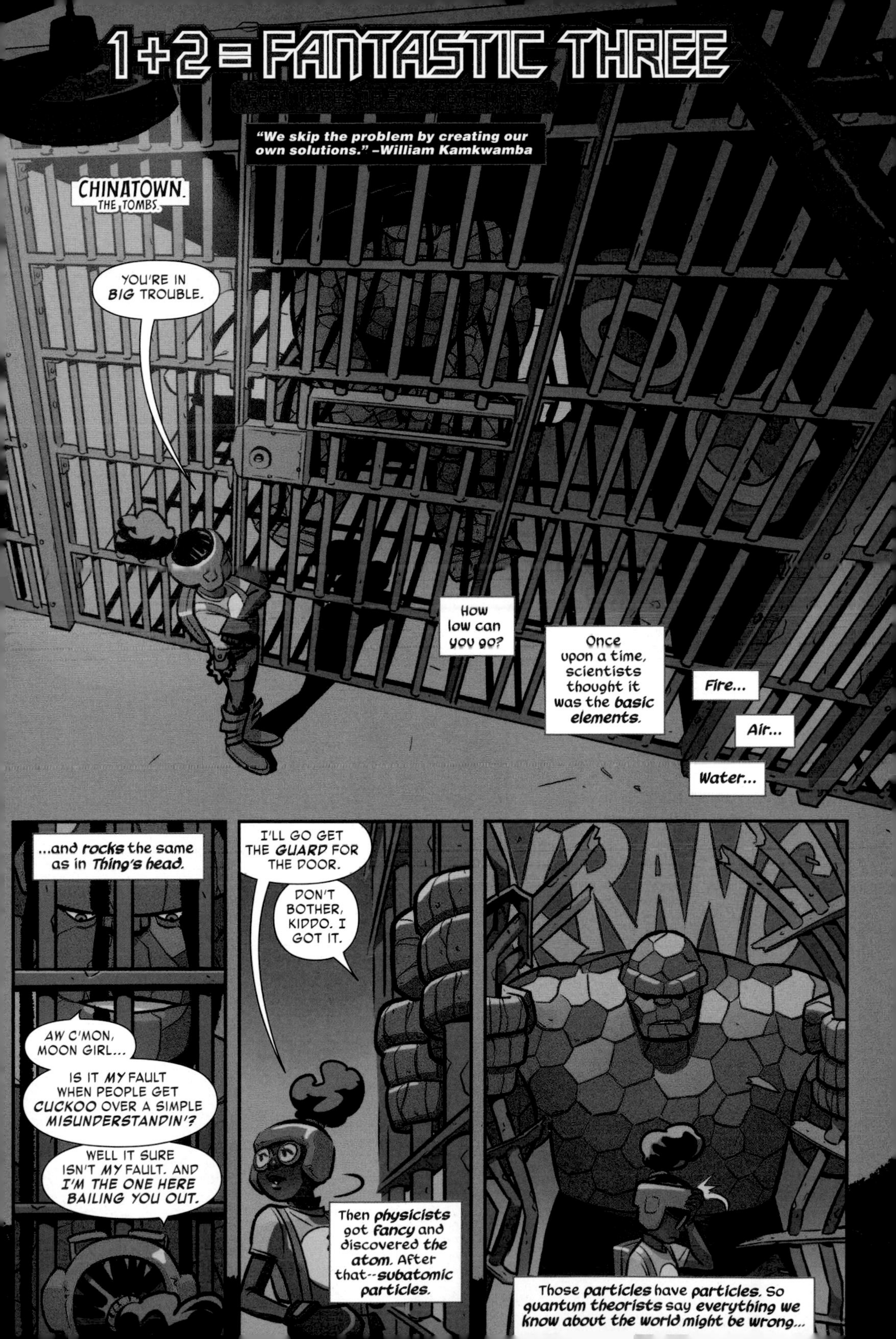
1+2 = FANTASTIC THREE
"We skip the problem by creating our own solutions." –William Kamkwamba
CHINATOWN. THE TOMBS.
YOU'RE IN BIG TROUBLE.
How low can you go?
Once upon a time, scientists thought it was the basic elements.
Fire...
Air...
Water...
...and rocks the same as in Thing's head.
AW C'MON, MOON GIRL...
IS IT MY FAULT WHEN PEOPLE GET CUCKOO OVER A SIMPLE MISUNDERSTANDIN'?
WELL IT SURE ISN'T MY FAULT. AND I'M THE ONE HERE BAILING YOU OUT.
I'LL GO GET THE GUARD FOR THE DOOR.
DON'T BOTHER, KIDDO. I GOT IT.
Then physicists got fancy and discovered the atom. After that--subatomic particles.
Those particles have particles. So quantum theorists say everything we know about the world might be wrong...

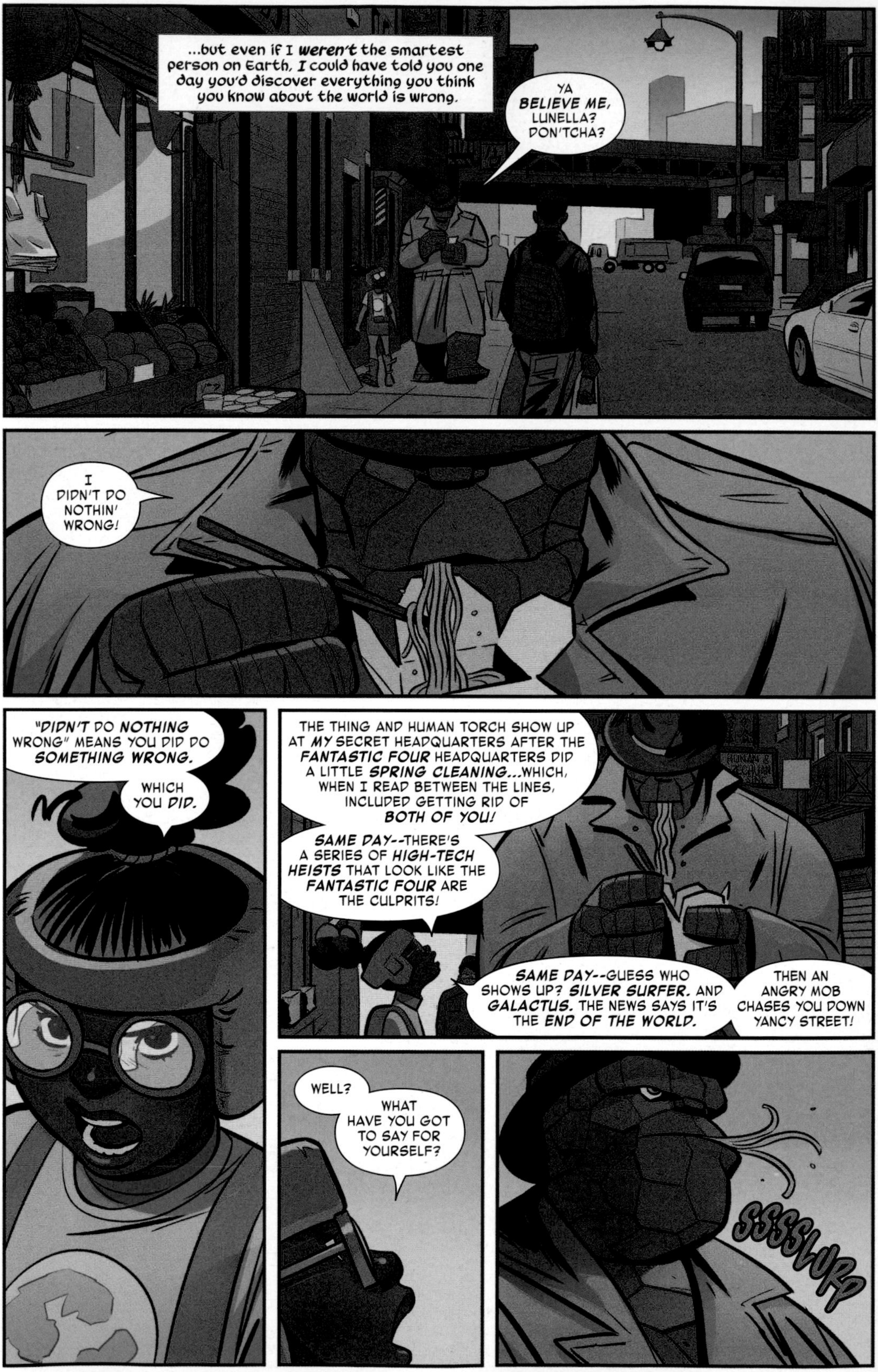
...but even if I weren't the smartest person on Earth, I could have told you one day you'd discover everything you think you know about the world is wrong.
YA BELIEVE ME, LUNELLA? DON'TCHA?
I DIDN'T DO NOTHIN' WRONG!
"DIDN'T DO NOTHING WRONG" MEANS YOU DID DO SOMETHING WRONG.
WHICH YOU DID.
THE THING AND HUMAN TORCH SHOW UP AT MY SECRET HEADQUARTERS AFTER THE FANTASTIC FOUR HEADQUARTERS DID A LITTLE SPRING CLEANING...WHICH, WHEN I READ BETWEEN THE LINES, INCLUDED GETTING RID OF BOTH OF YOU!
SAME DAY--THERE'S A SERIES OF HIGH-TECH HEISTS THAT LOOK LIKE THE FANTASTIC FOUR ARE THE CULPRITS!
SAME DAY--GUESS WHO SHOWS UP? SILVER SURFER. AND GALACTUS. THE NEWS SAYS IT'S THE END OF THE WORLD.
THEN AN ANGRY MOB CHASES YOU DOWN YANCY STREET!
WELL?
WHAT HAVE YOU GOT TO SAY FOR YOURSELF?
SSSSLURP

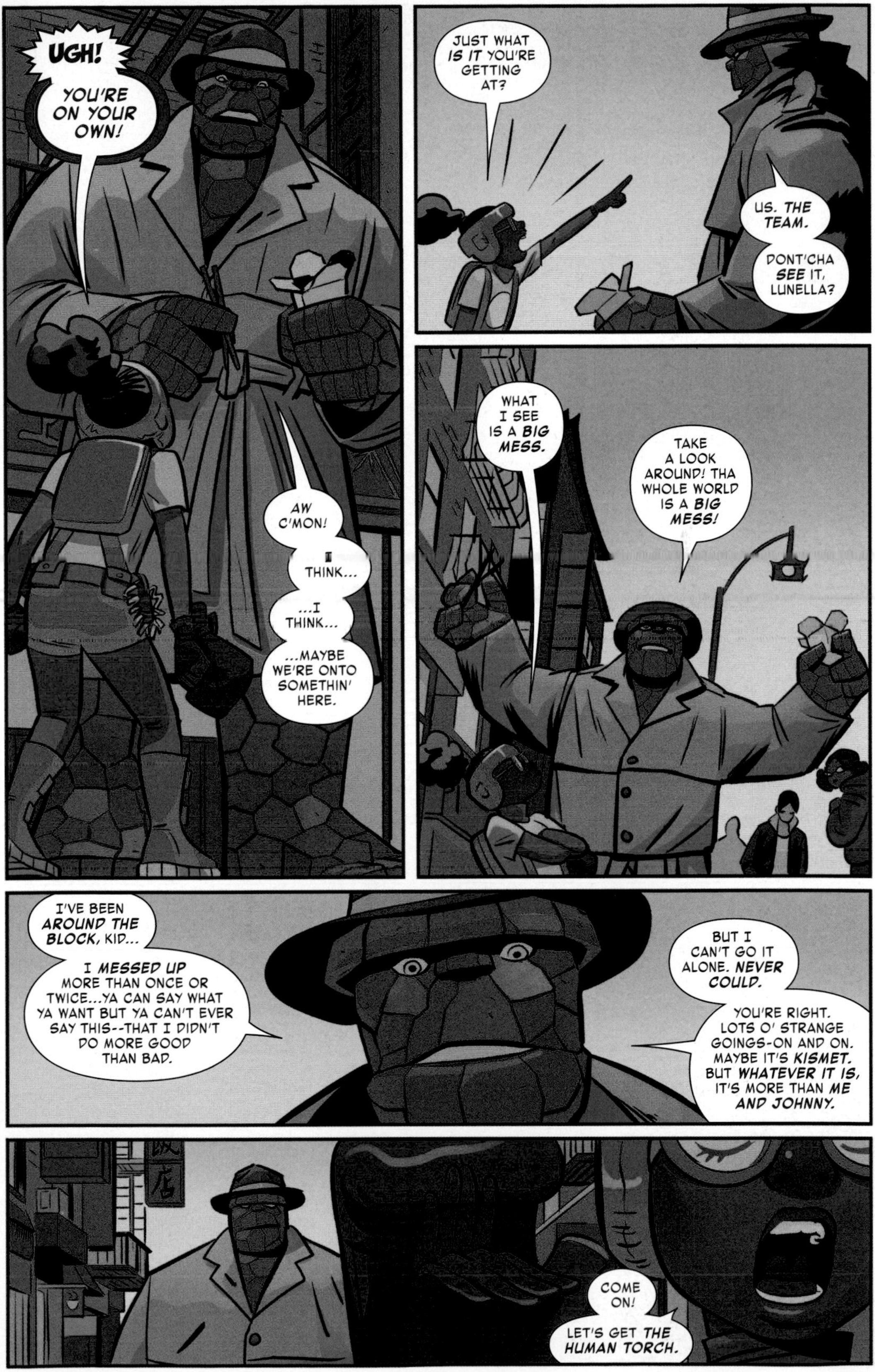

UGH!
YOU'RE ON YOUR OWN!
AW C'MON!
I THINK...
...I THINK...
...MAYBE WE'RE ONTO SOMETHIN' HERE.
JUST WHAT IS IT YOU'RE GETTING AT?
US. THE TEAM.
DONT'CHA SEE IT, LUNELLA?
WHAT I SEE IS A BIG MESS.
TAKE A LOOK AROUND! THA WHOLE WORLD IS A BIG MESS!
I'VE BEEN AROUND THE BLOCK, KID...
I MESSED UP MORE THAN ONCE OR TWICE...YA CAN SAY WHAT YA WANT BUT YA CAN'T EVER SAY THIS--THAT I DIDN'T DO MORE GOOD THAN BAD.
BUT I CAN'T GO IT ALONE. NEVER COULD.
YOU'RE RIGHT. LOTS O' STRANGE GOINGS-ON AND ON. MAYBE IT'S KISMET. BUT WHATEVER IT IS, IT'S MORE THAN ME AND JOHNNY.
COME ON!
LET'S GET THE HUMAN TORCH.

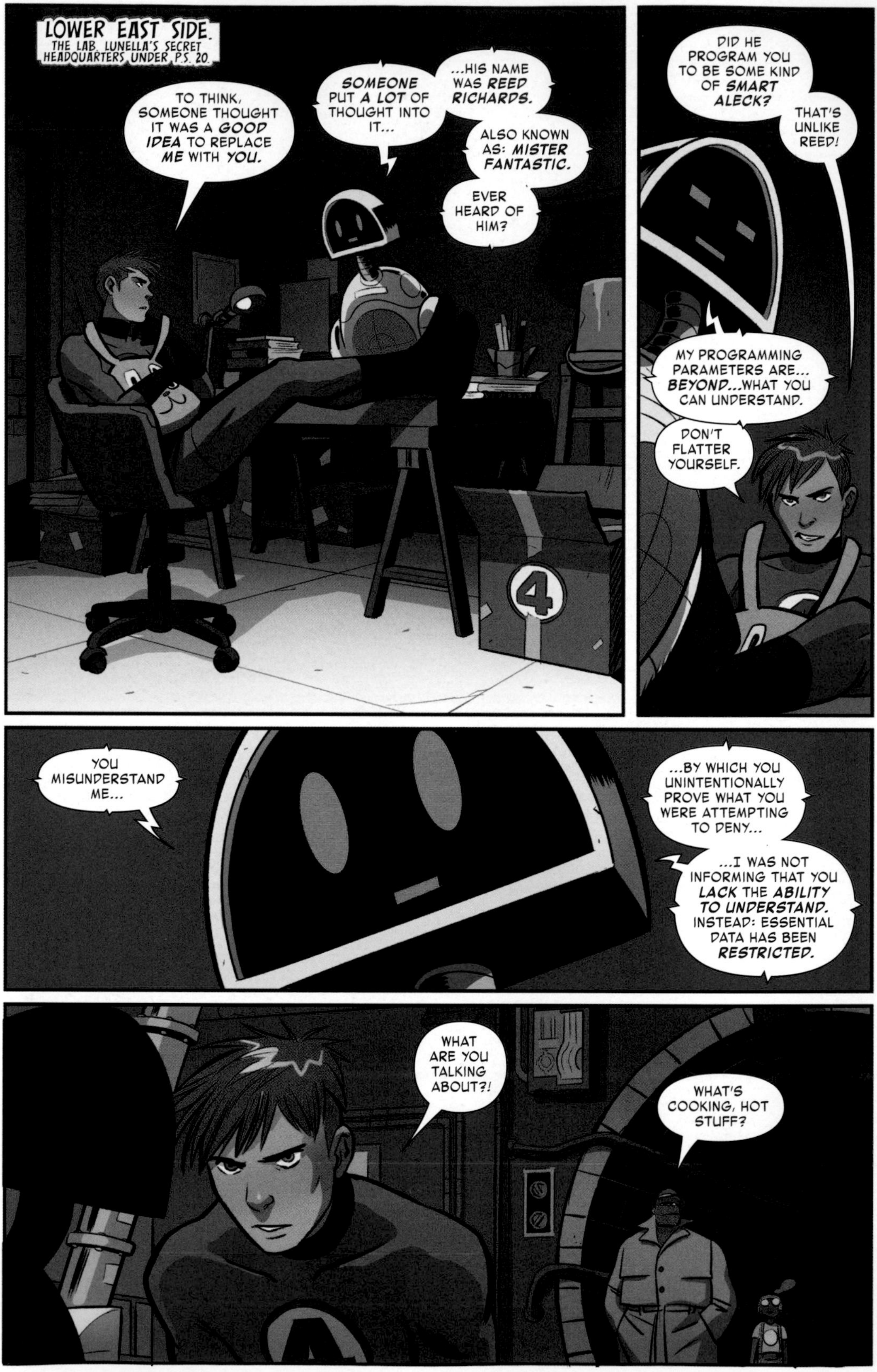
LOWER EAST SIDE. THE LAB. LUNELLA'S SECRET HEADQUARTERS UNDER P.S. 20.
TO THINK, SOMEONE THOUGHT IT WAS A GOOD IDEA TO REPLACE ME WITH YOU.
SOMEONE PUT A LOT OF THOUGHT INTO IT...
...HIS NAME WAS REED RICHARDS.
ALSO KNOWN AS: MISTER FANTASTIC.
EVER HEARD OF HIM?
DID HE PROGRAM YOU TO BE SOME KIND OF SMART ALECK?
THAT'S UNLIKE REED!
MY PROGRAMMING PARAMETERS ARE... BEYOND...WHAT YOU CAN UNDERSTAND.
DON'T FLATTER YOURSELF.
YOU MISUNDERSTAND ME...
...BY WHICH YOU UNINTENTIONALLY PROVE WHAT YOU WERE ATTEMPTING TO DENY...
...I WAS NOT INFORMING THAT YOU LACK THE ABILITY TO UNDERSTAND. INSTEAD: ESSENTIAL DATA HAS BEEN RESTRICTED.
WHAT ARE YOU TALKING ABOUT?!
WHAT'S COOKING, HOT STUFF?

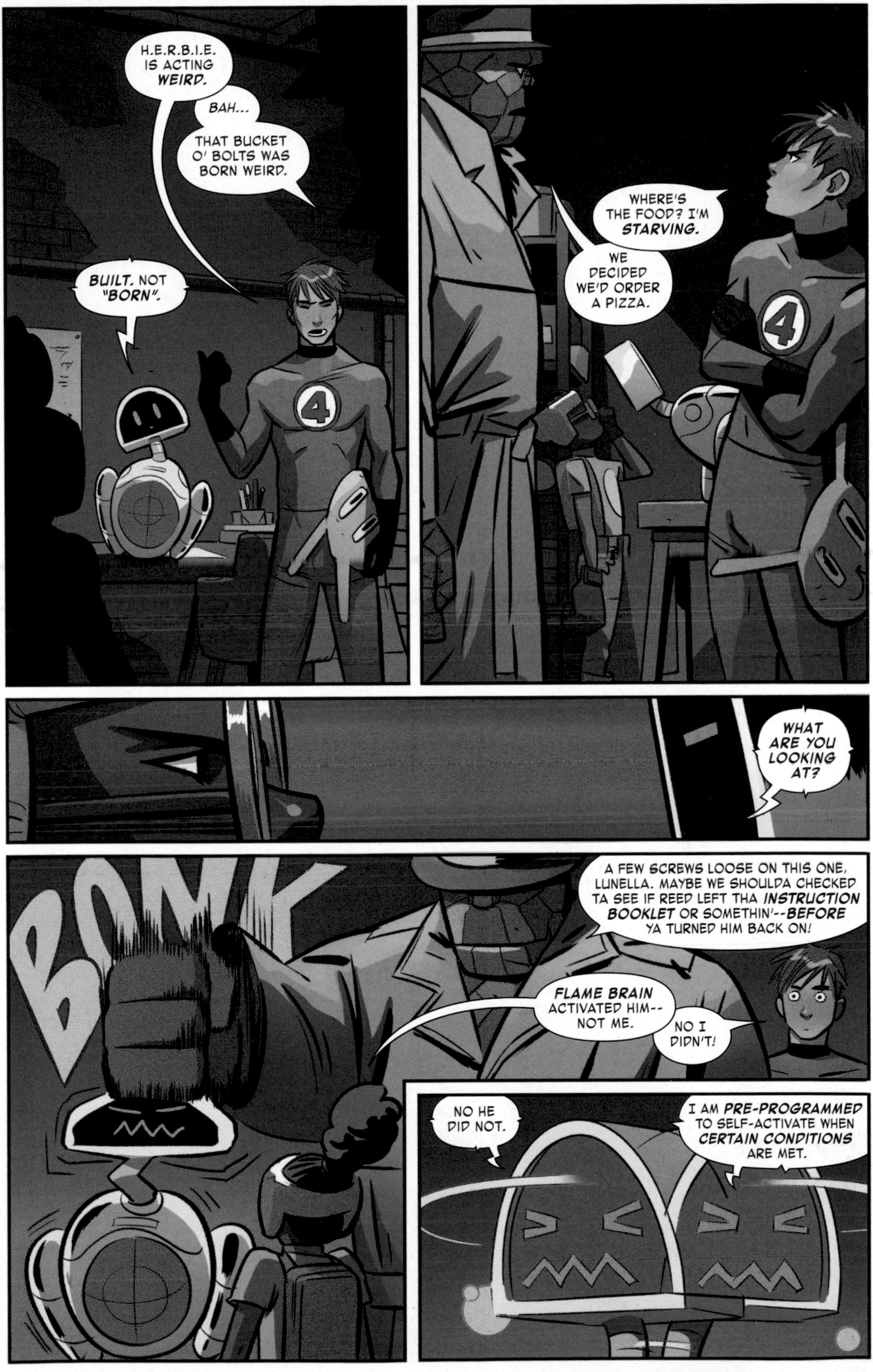
H.E.R.B.I.E. IS ACTING *WEIRD.*
BAH...
THAT BUCKET O' BOLTS WAS BORN WEIRD.
BUILT. NOT *"BORN".*
WHERE'S THE FOOD? I'M *STARVING.*
WE DECIDED WE'D ORDER A PIZZA.
WHAT ARE YOU LOOKING AT?
BONK
A FEW SCREWS LOOSE ON THIS ONE, LUNELLA. MAYBE WE SHOULDA CHECKED TA SEE IF REED LEFT THA *INSTRUCTION BOOKLET* OR SOMETHIN'--*BEFORE* YA TURNED HIM BACK ON!
FLAME BRAIN ACTIVATED HIM--NOT ME.
NO I DIDN'T!
NO HE DID NOT.
I AM *PRE-PROGRAMMED* TO SELF-ACTIVATE WHEN *CERTAIN CONDITIONS* ARE MET.

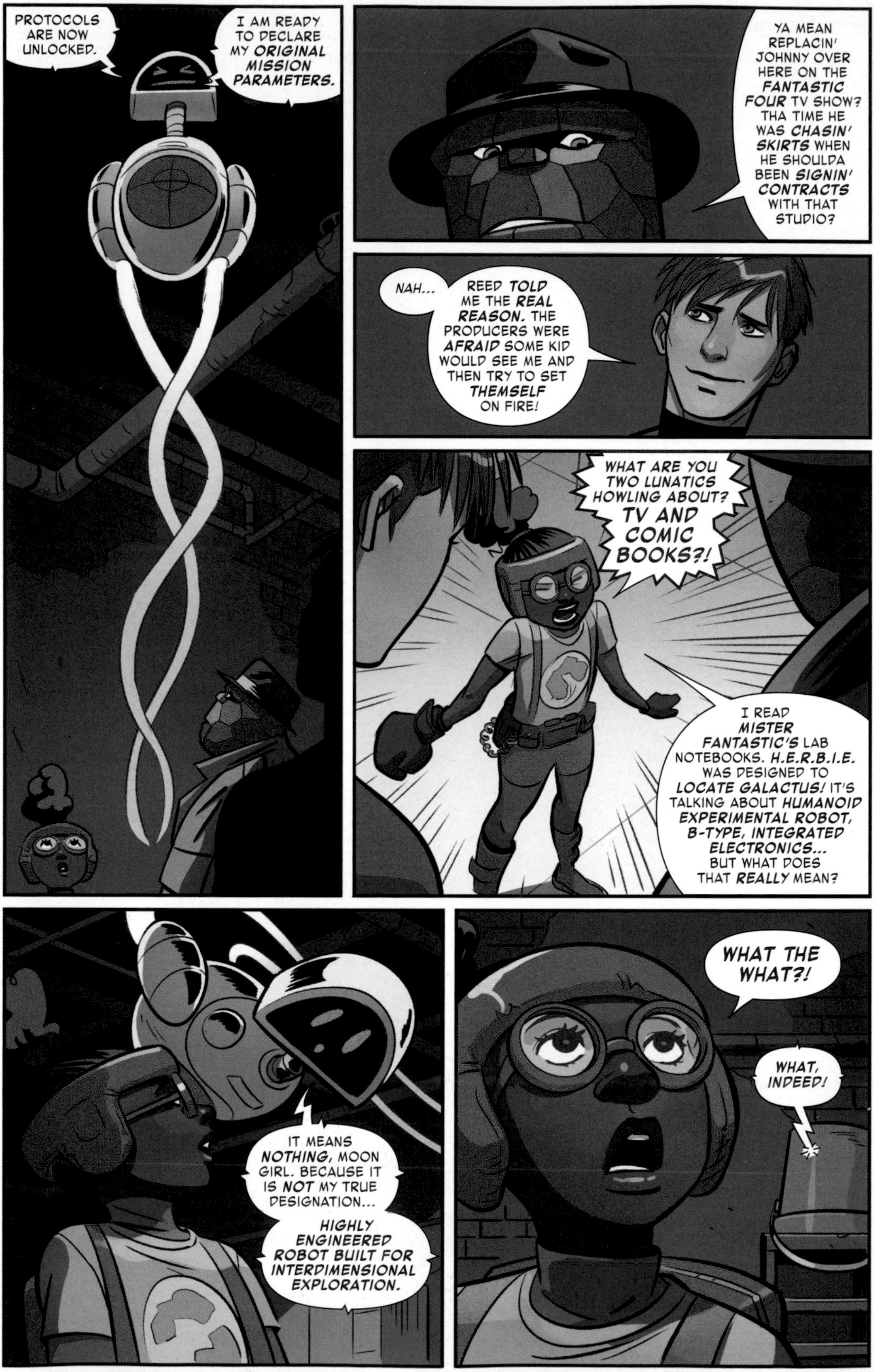
PROTOCOLS ARE NOW UNLOCKED.
I AM READY TO DECLARE MY ORIGINAL MISSION PARAMETERS.
YA MEAN REPLACIN' JOHNNY OVER HERE ON THE FANTASTIC FOUR TV SHOW? THA TIME HE WAS CHASIN' SKIRTS WHEN HE SHOULDA BEEN SIGNIN' CONTRACTS WITH THAT STUDIO?
NAH...
REED TOLD ME THE REAL REASON. THE PRODUCERS WERE AFRAID SOME KID WOULD SEE ME AND THEN TRY TO SET THEMSELF ON FIRE!
WHAT ARE YOU TWO LUNATICS HOWLING ABOUT? TV AND COMIC BOOKS?!
I READ MISTER FANTASTIC'S LAB NOTEBOOKS. H.E.R.B.I.E. WAS DESIGNED TO LOCATE GALACTUS! IT'S TALKING ABOUT HUMANOID EXPERIMENTAL ROBOT, B-TYPE, INTEGRATED ELECTRONICS... BUT WHAT DOES THAT REALLY MEAN?
IT MEANS NOTHING, MOON GIRL. BECAUSE IT IS NOT MY TRUE DESIGNATION...
HIGHLY ENGINEERED ROBOT BUILT FOR INTERDIMENSIONAL EXPLORATION.
WHAT THE WHAT?!
WHAT, INDEED!

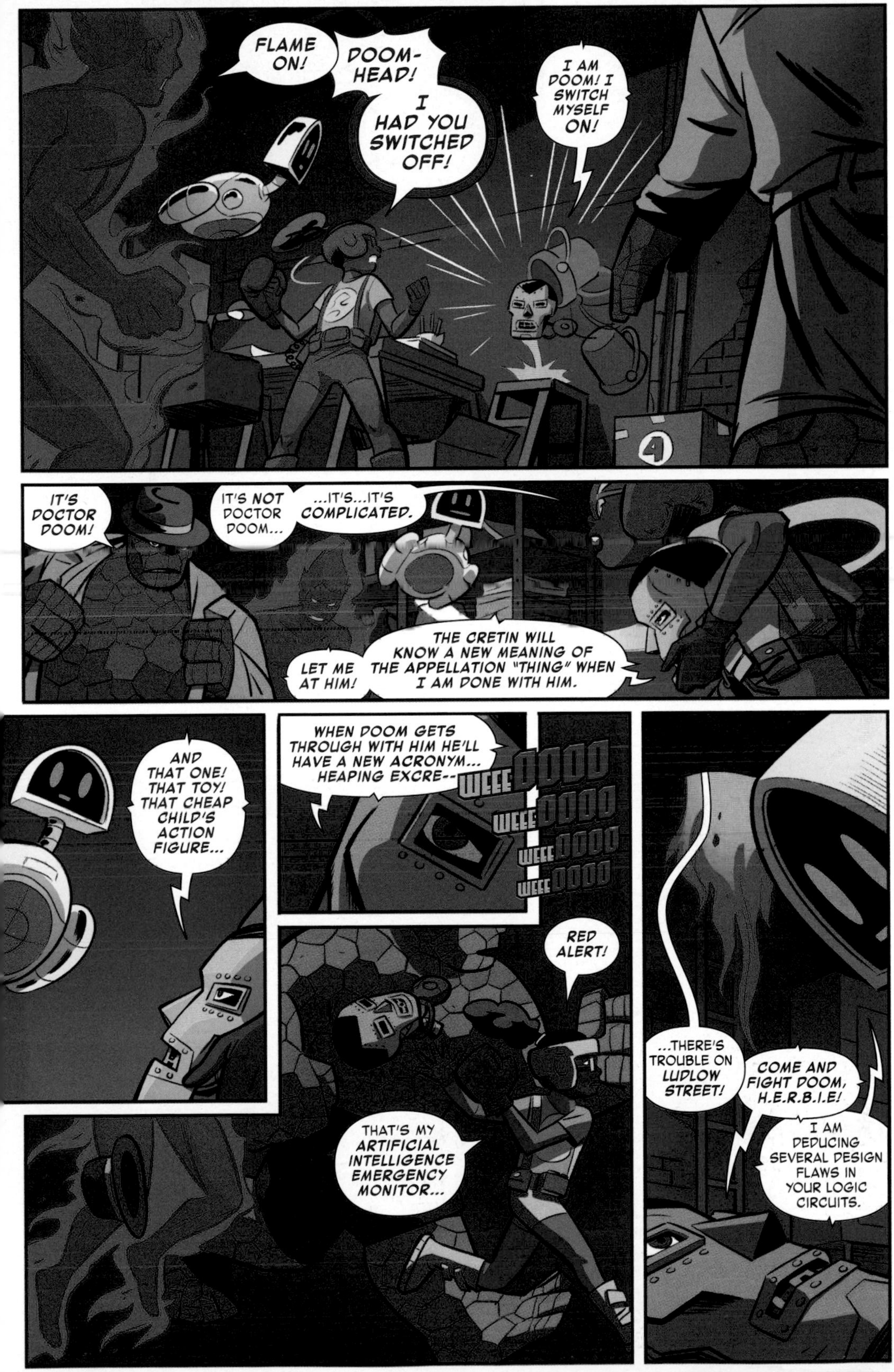
FLAME ON!
DOOM-HEAD!
I HAD YOU SWITCHED OFF!
I AM DOOM! I SWITCH MYSELF ON!
IT'S DOCTOR DOOM!
IT'S NOT DOCTOR DOOM...
...IT'S...IT'S COMPLICATED.
LET ME AT HIM!
THE CRETIN WILL KNOW A NEW MEANING OF THE APPELLATION "THING" WHEN I AM DONE WITH HIM.
AND THAT ONE! THAT TOY! THAT CHEAP CHILD'S ACTION FIGURE...
WHEN DOOM GETS THROUGH WITH HIM HE'LL HAVE A NEW ACRONYM... HEAPING EXCRE--
WEEEOOOO
WEEEOOOO
WEEEOOOO
WEEEOOOO
RED ALERT!
...THERE'S TROUBLE ON LUDLOW STREET!
THAT'S MY ARTIFICIAL INTELLIGENCE EMERGENCY MONITOR...
COME AND FIGHT DOOM, H.E.R.B.I.E!
I AM DEDUCING SEVERAL DESIGN FLAWS IN YOUR LOGIC CIRCUITS.

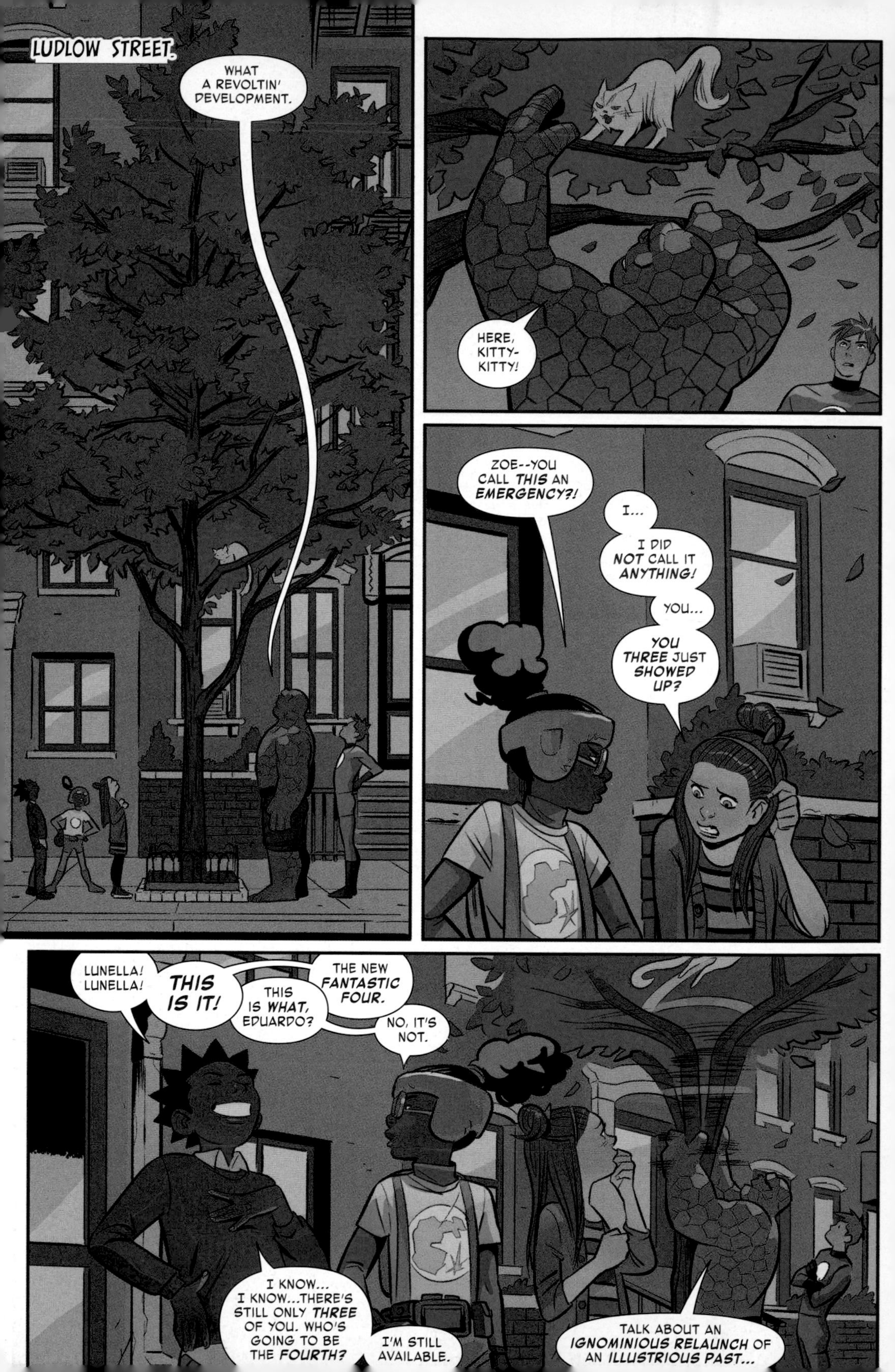
LUDLOW STREET.
WHAT A REVOLTIN' DEVELOPMENT.
HERE, KITTY-KITTY!
ZOE--YOU CALL THIS AN EMERGENCY?!
I...
I DID NOT CALL IT ANYTHING!
YOU...
YOU THREE JUST SHOWED UP?
LUNELLA! LUNELLA!
THIS IS IT!
THIS IS WHAT, EDUARDO?
THE NEW FANTASTIC FOUR.
NO, IT'S NOT.
I KNOW... I KNOW...THERE'S STILL ONLY THREE OF YOU. WHO'S GOING TO BE THE FOURTH?
I'M STILL AVAILABLE.
TALK ABOUT AN IGNOMINIOUS RELAUNCH OF AN ILLUSTRIOUS PAST...

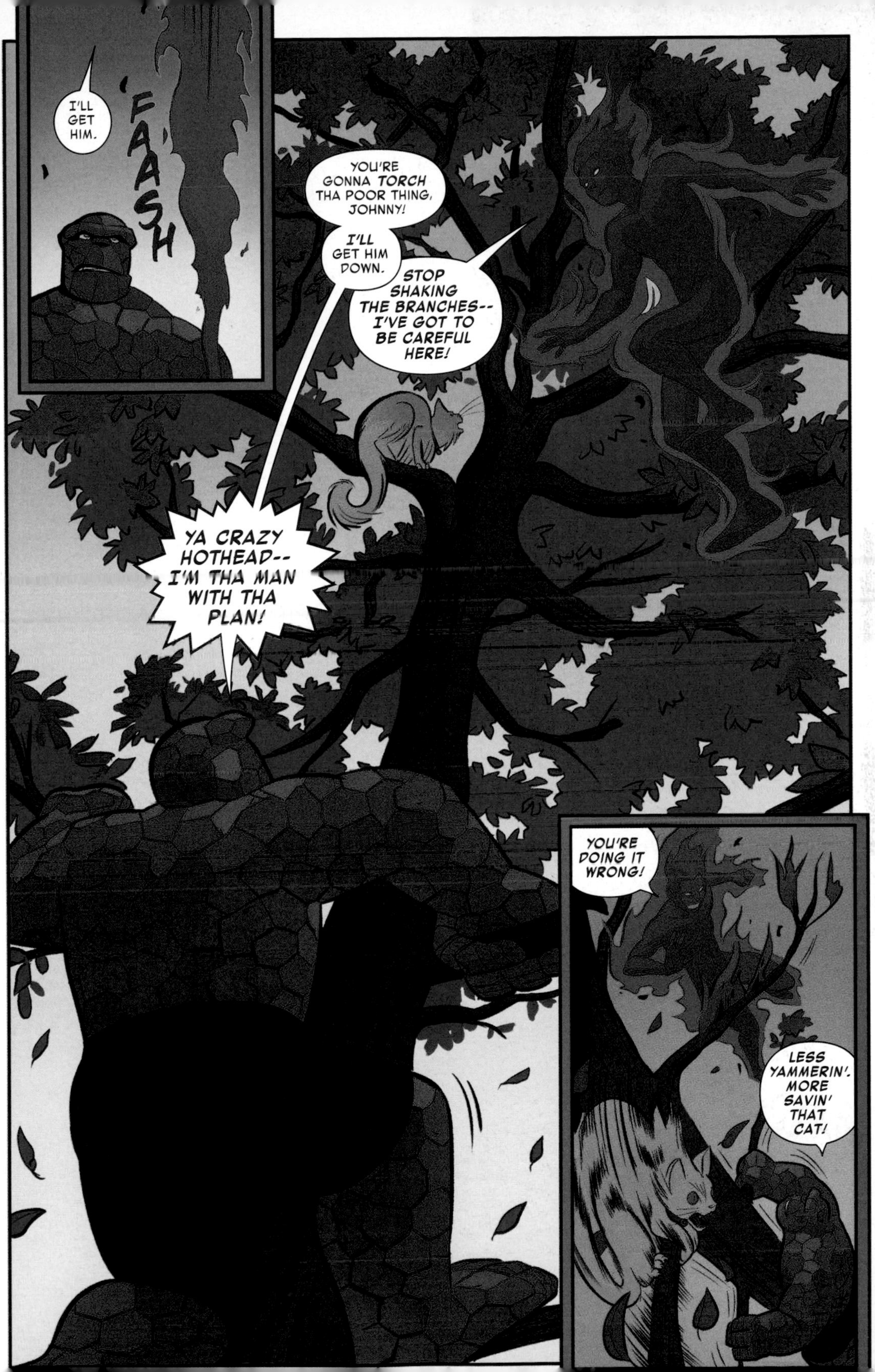
I'LL GET HIM.
FAASH
YOU'RE GONNA TORCH THA POOR THING, JOHNNY!
I'LL GET HIM DOWN.
STOP SHAKING THE BRANCHES-- I'VE GOT TO BE CAREFUL HERE!
YA CRAZY HOTHEAD-- I'M THA MAN WITH THA PLAN!
YOU'RE DOING IT WRONG!
LESS YAMMERIN'. MORE SAVIN' THAT CAT!

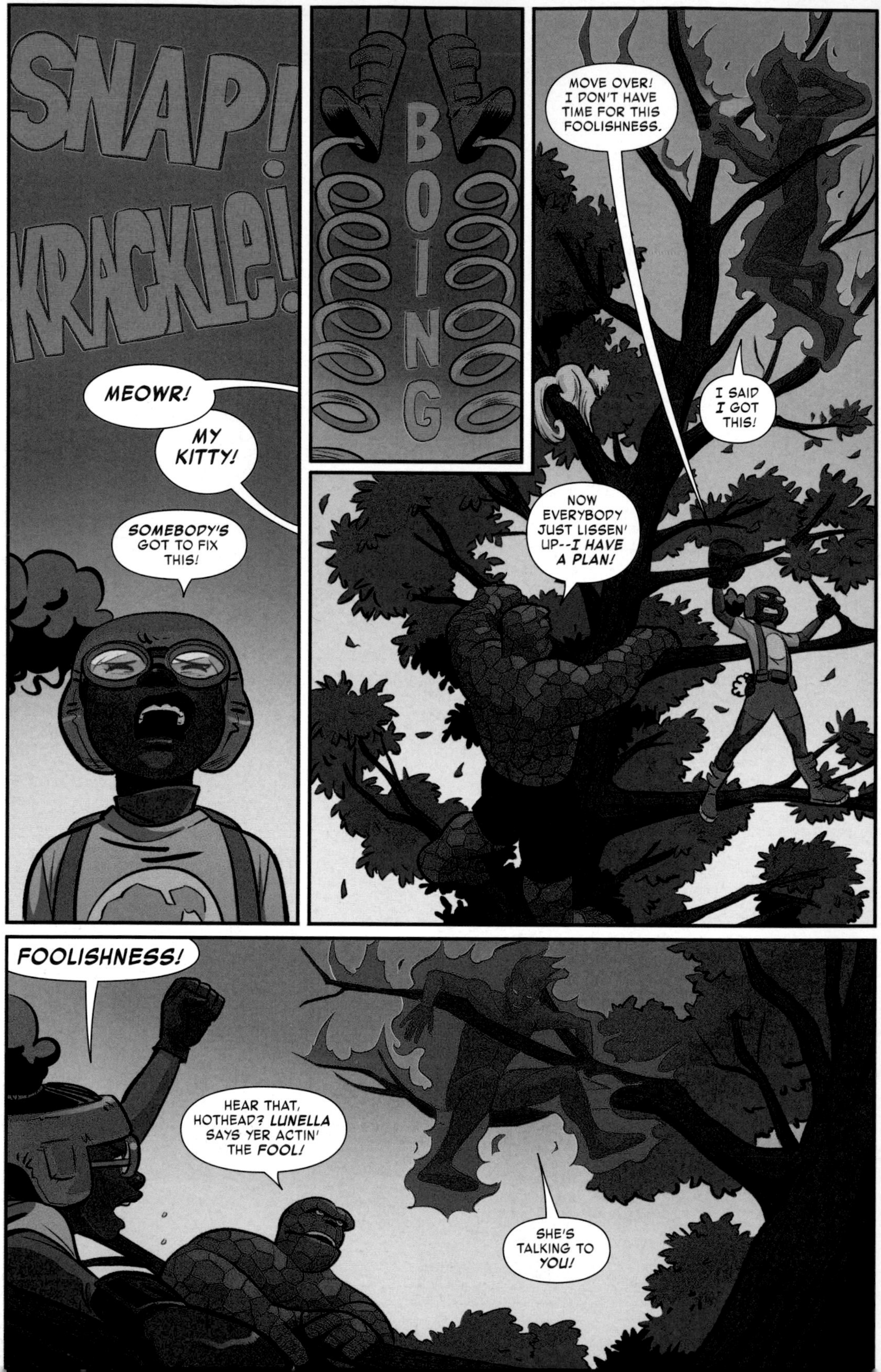

SNAP!
KRACKLE!
MEOWR!
MY KITTY!
SOMEBODY'S GOT TO FIX THIS!
BOING
MOVE OVER! I DON'T HAVE TIME FOR THIS FOOLISHNESS.
I SAID I GOT THIS!
NOW EVERYBODY JUST LISSEN' UP--I HAVE A PLAN!
FOOLISHNESS!
HEAR THAT, HOTHEAD? LUNELLA SAYS YER ACTIN' THE FOOL!
SHE'S TALKING TO YOU!

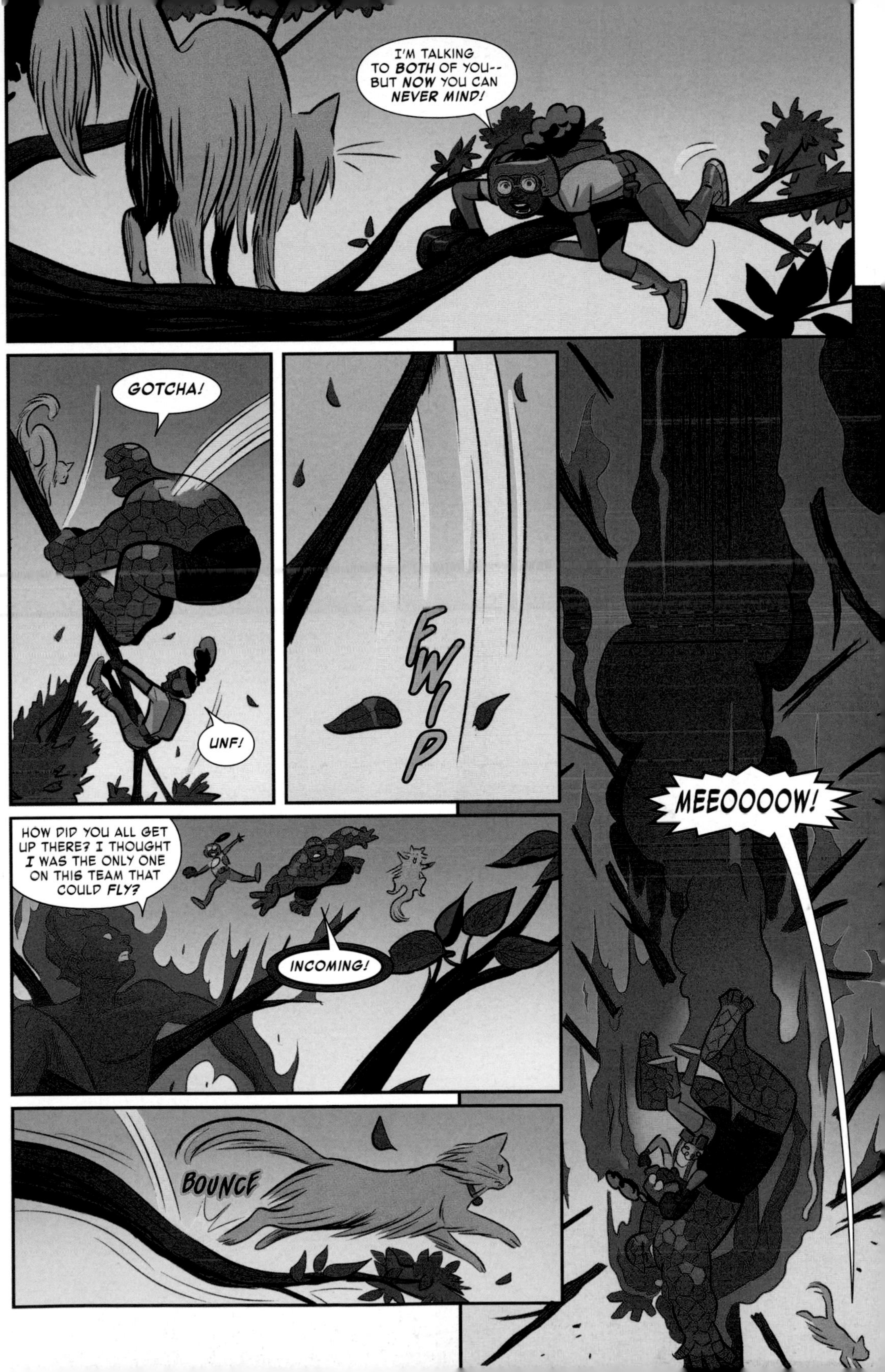
I'M TALKING TO BOTH OF YOU-- BUT NOW YOU CAN NEVER MIND!
GOTCHA!
UNF!
FWIP
MEEOOOOW!
HOW DID YOU ALL GET UP THERE? I THOUGHT I WAS THE ONLY ONE ON THIS TEAM THAT COULD FLY?
INCOMING!
BOUNCE

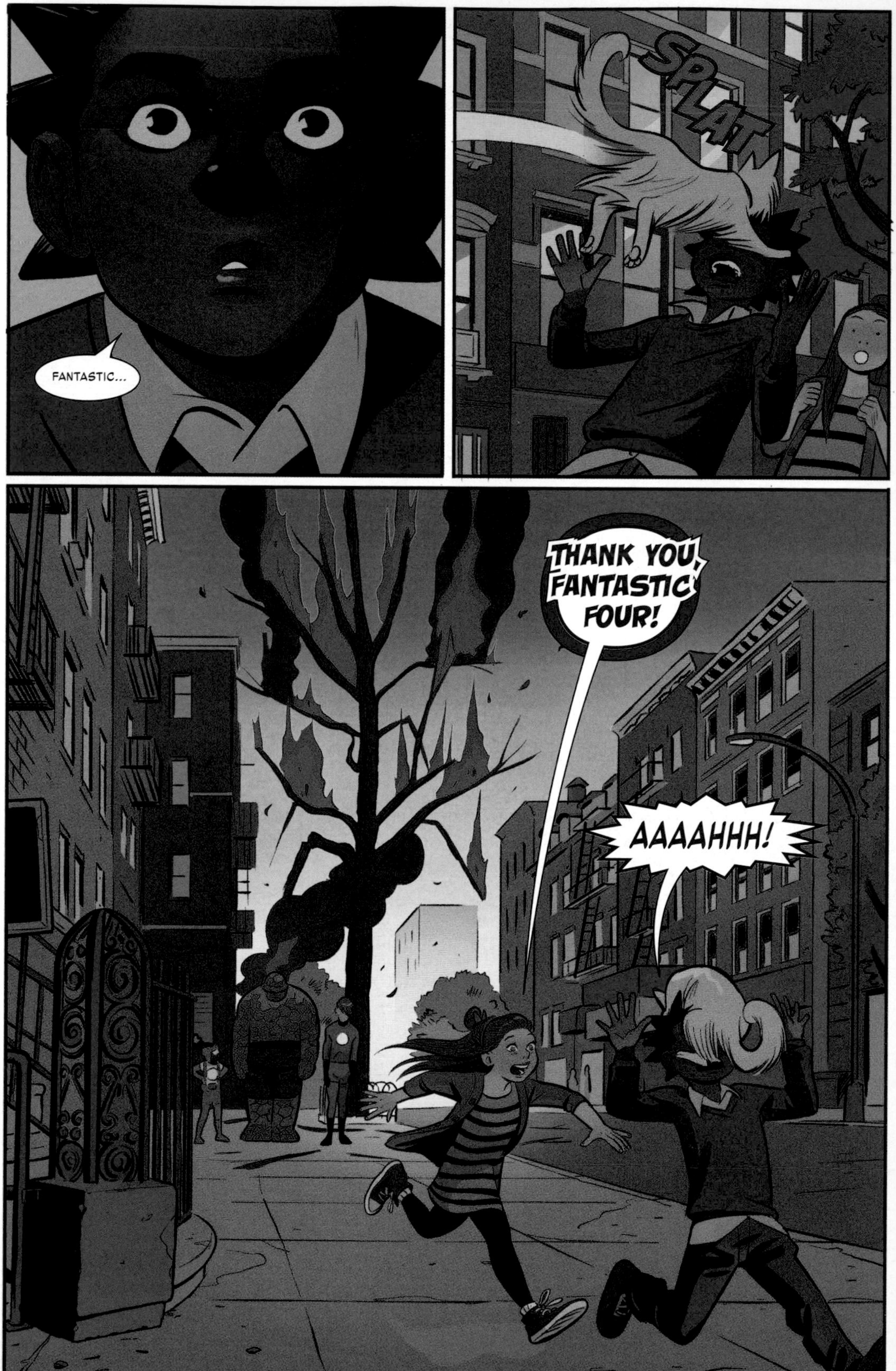
FANTASTIC...
SPLAT
THANK YOU, FANTASTIC FOUR!
AAAAHHH!

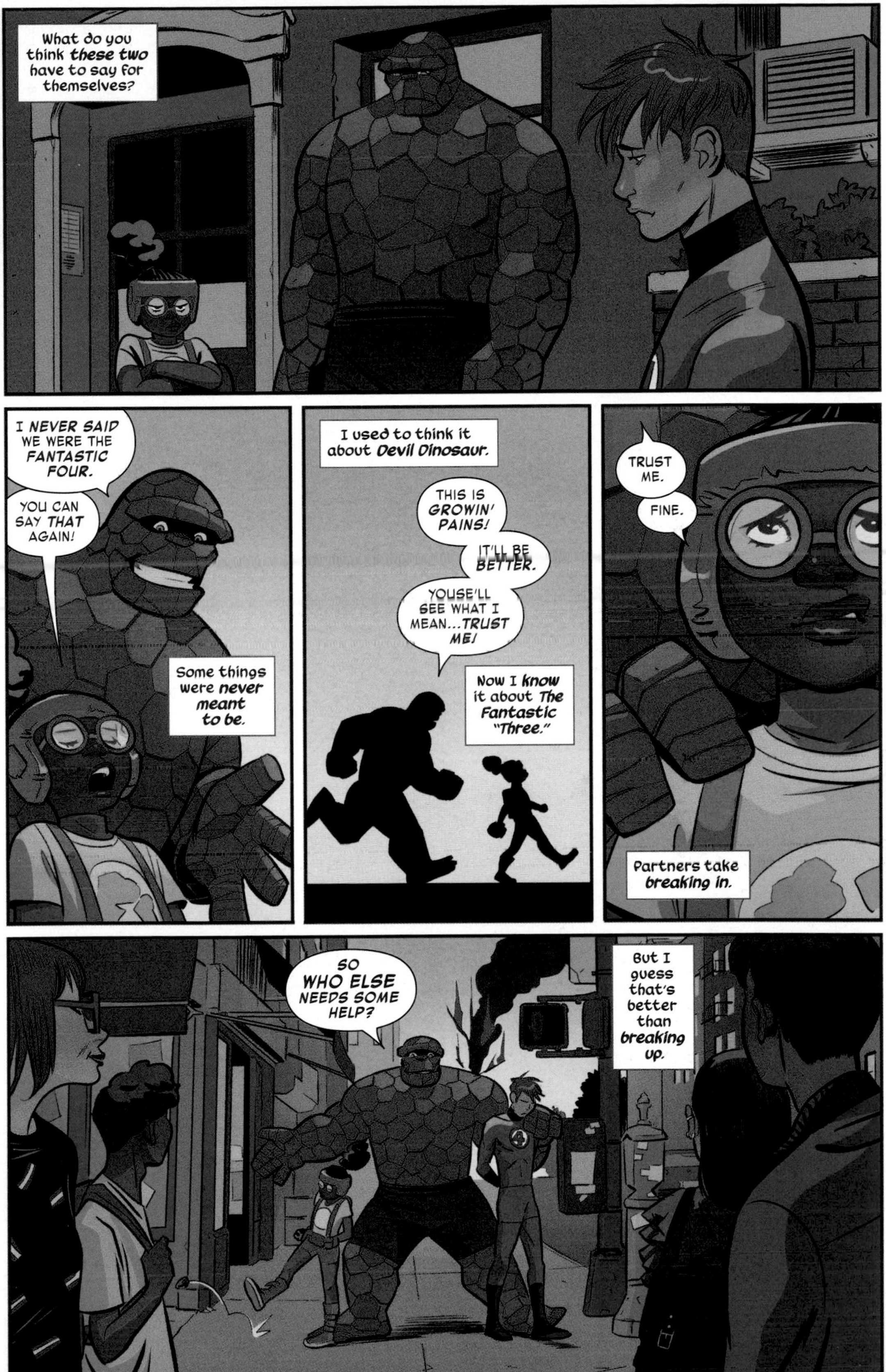
What do you think these two have to say for themselves?
I NEVER SAID WE WERE THE FANTASTIC FOUR.
YOU CAN SAY THAT AGAIN!
Some things were never meant to be.
I used to think it about Devil Dinosaur.
THIS IS GROWIN' PAINS!
IT'LL BE BETTER.
YOUSE'LL SEE WHAT I MEAN...TRUST ME!
Now I know it about The Fantastic "Three."
TRUST ME.
FINE.
Partners take breaking in.
SO WHO ELSE NEEDS SOME HELP?
But I guess that's better than breaking up.

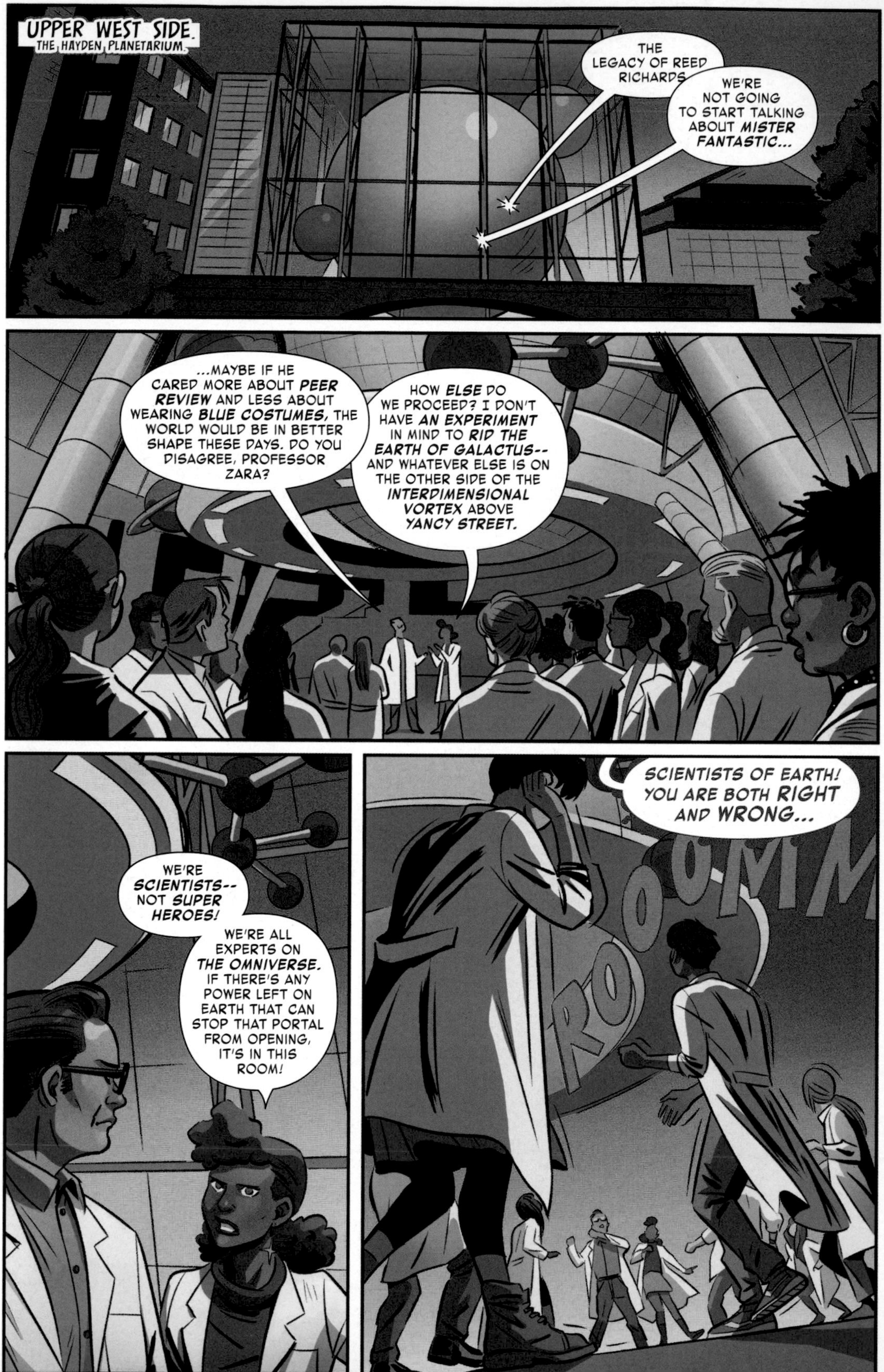
UPPER WEST SIDE.
THE HAYDEN PLANETARIUM.
THE LEGACY OF REED RICHARDS
WE'RE NOT GOING TO START TALKING ABOUT MISTER FANTASTIC...
...MAYBE IF HE CARED MORE ABOUT PEER REVIEW AND LESS ABOUT WEARING BLUE COSTUMES, THE WORLD WOULD BE IN BETTER SHAPE THESE DAYS. DO YOU DISAGREE, PROFESSOR ZARA?
HOW ELSE DO WE PROCEED? I DON'T HAVE AN EXPERIMENT IN MIND TO RID THE EARTH OF GALACTUS-- AND WHATEVER ELSE IS ON THE OTHER SIDE OF THE INTERDIMENSIONAL VORTEX ABOVE YANCY STREET.
WE'RE SCIENTISTS-- NOT SUPER HEROES!
WE'RE ALL EXPERTS ON THE OMNIVERSE. IF THERE'S ANY POWER LEFT ON EARTH THAT CAN STOP THAT PORTAL FROM OPENING, IT'S IN THIS ROOM!
SCIENTISTS OF EARTH! YOU ARE BOTH RIGHT AND WRONG...
ROOOMM

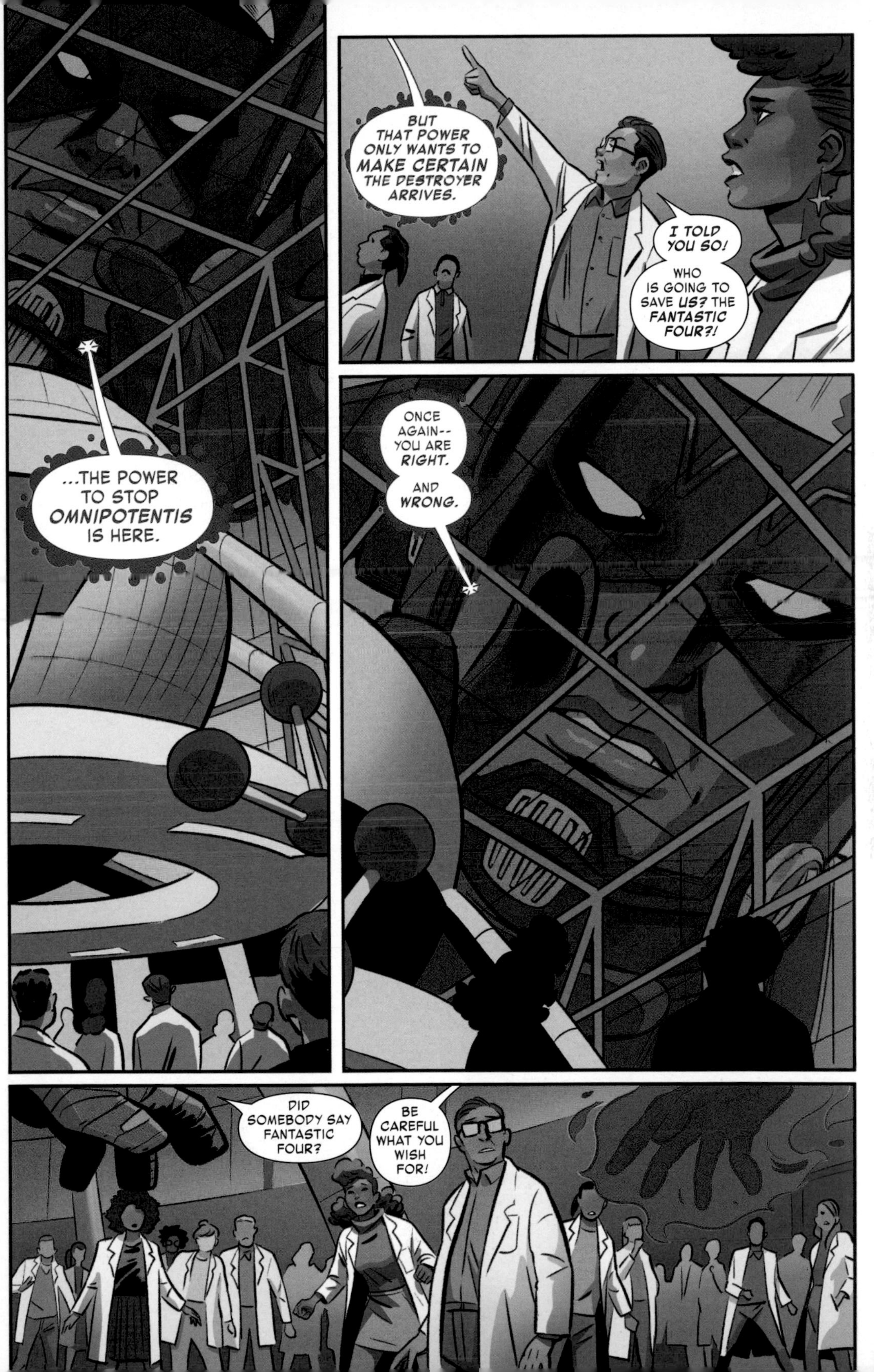
...THE POWER TO STOP OMNIPOTENTIS IS HERE.
BUT THAT POWER ONLY WANTS TO MAKE CERTAIN THE DESTROYER ARRIVES.
I TOLD YOU SO!
WHO IS GOING TO SAVE US? THE FANTASTIC FOUR?!
ONCE AGAIN-- YOU ARE RIGHT.
AND WRONG.
DID SOMEBODY SAY FANTASTIC FOUR?
BE CAREFUL WHAT YOU WISH FOR!

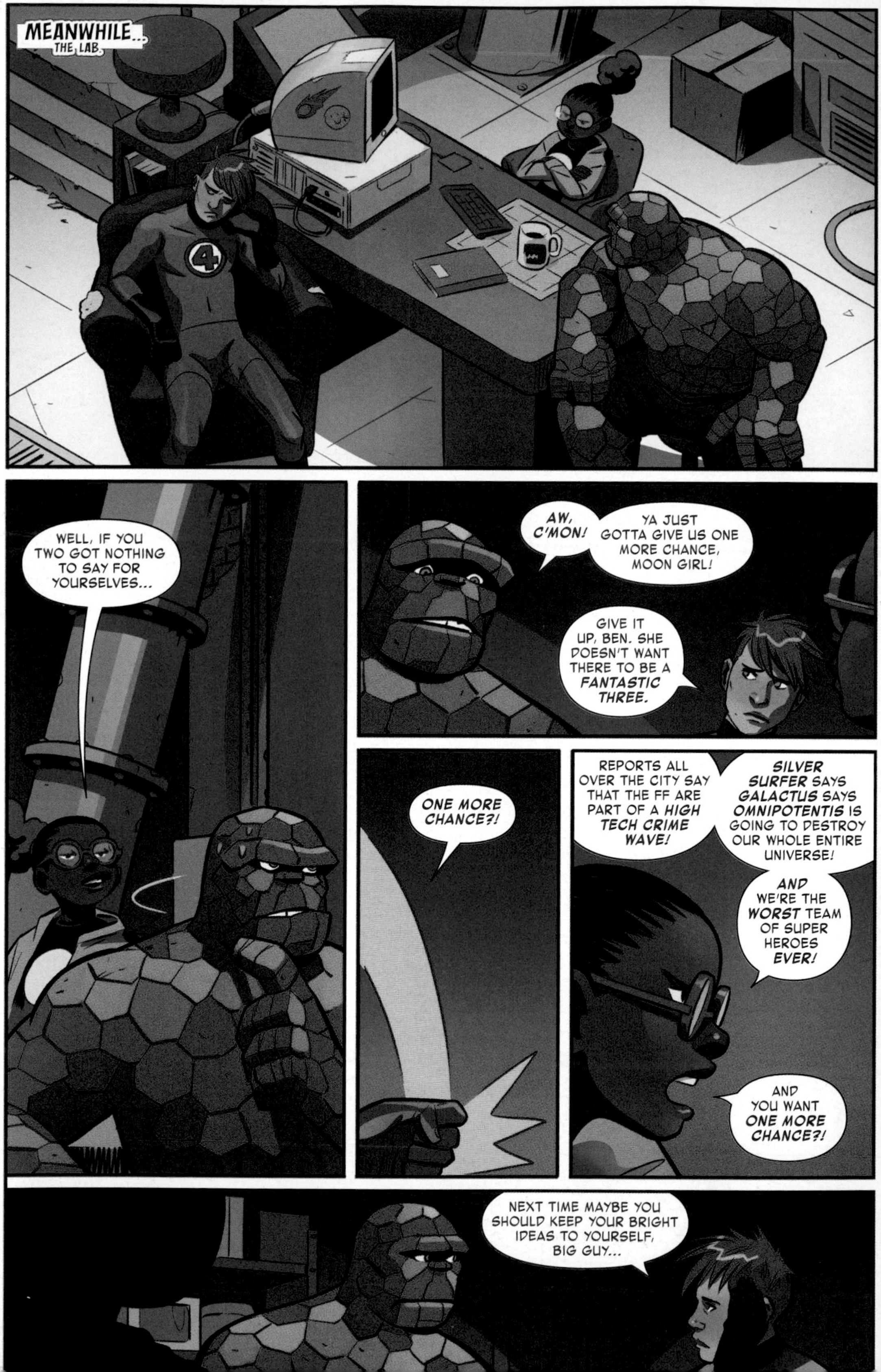
MEANWHILE... THE LAB.
WELL, IF YOU TWO GOT NOTHING TO SAY FOR YOURSELVES...
AW, C'MON!
YA JUST GOTTA GIVE US ONE MORE CHANCE, MOON GIRL!
GIVE IT UP, BEN. SHE DOESN'T WANT THERE TO BE A FANTASTIC THREE.
ONE MORE CHANCE?!
REPORTS ALL OVER THE CITY SAY THAT THE FF ARE PART OF A HIGH TECH CRIME WAVE!
SILVER SURFER SAYS GALACTUS SAYS OMNIPOTENTIS IS GOING TO DESTROY OUR WHOLE ENTIRE UNIVERSE!
AND WE'RE THE WORST TEAM OF SUPER HEROES EVER!
AND YOU WANT ONE MORE CHANCE?!
NEXT TIME MAYBE YOU SHOULD KEEP YOUR BRIGHT IDEAS TO YOURSELF, BIG GUY...

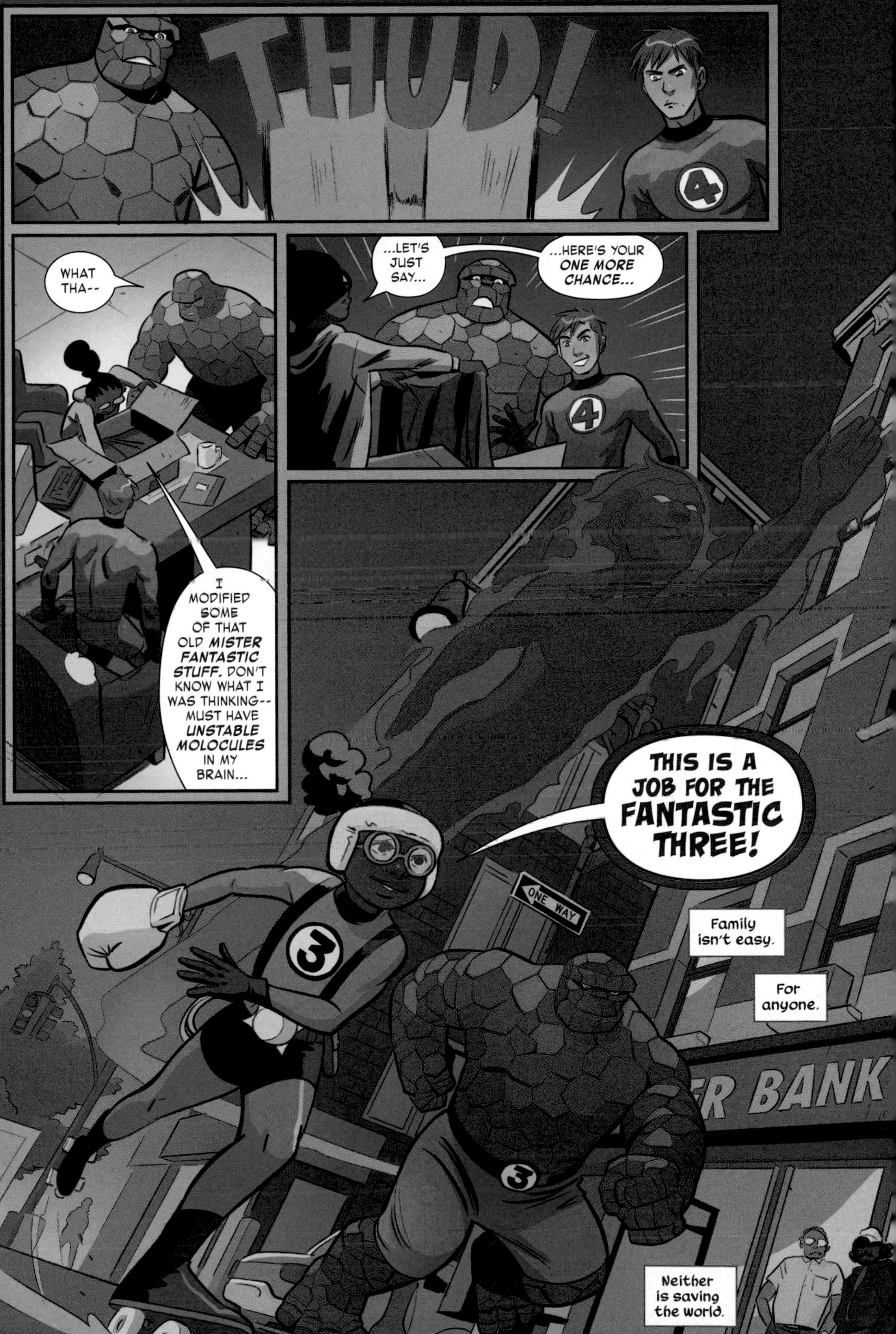
THUD!
WHAT THA--
I MODIFIED SOME OF THAT OLD MISTER FANTASTIC STUFF. DON'T KNOW WHAT I WAS THINKING-- MUST HAVE UNSTABLE MOLOCULES IN MY BRAIN...
...LET'S JUST SAY...
...HERE'S YOUR ONE MORE CHANCE...
THIS IS A JOB FOR THE FANTASTIC THREE!
ONE WAY
Family isn't easy.
For anyone.
ER BANK
Neither is saving the world.

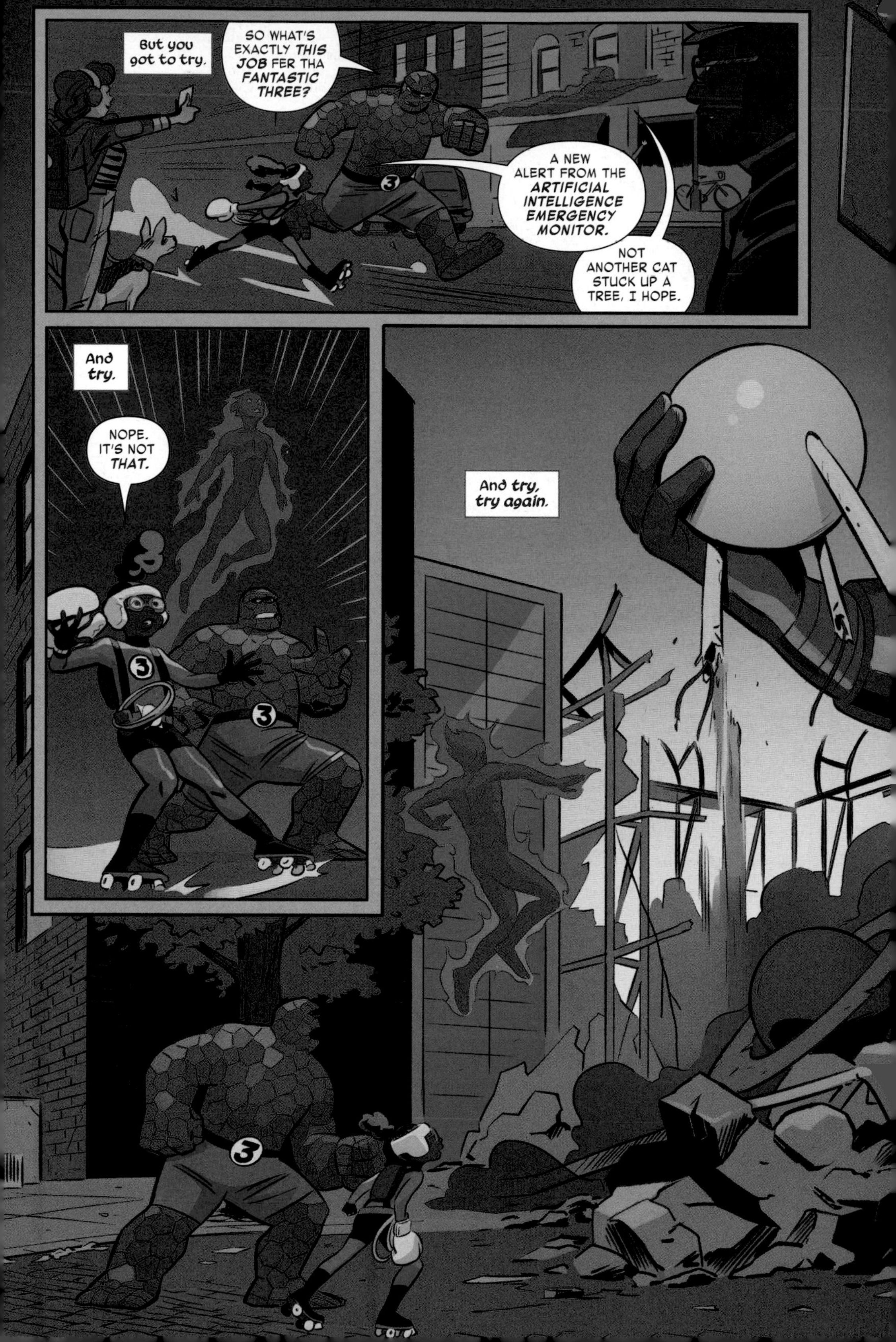
But you got to try.
SO WHAT'S EXACTLY THIS JOB FER THA FANTASTIC THREE?
A NEW ALERT FROM THE ARTIFICIAL INTELLIGENCE EMERGENCY MONITOR.
NOT ANOTHER CAT STUCK UP A TREE, I HOPE.
And try.
NOPE. IT'S NOT THAT.
And try, try again.

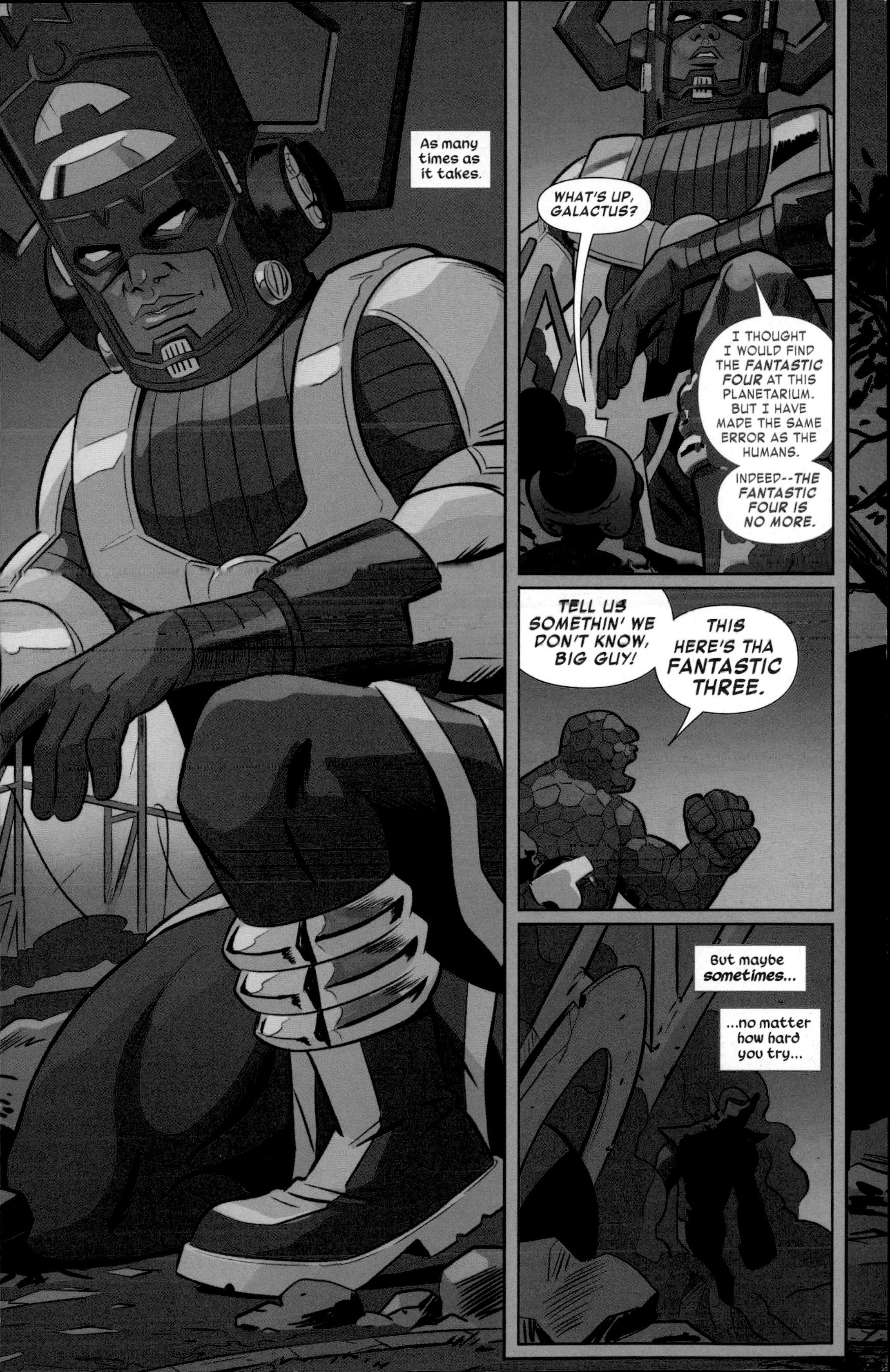
As many times as it takes.
WHAT'S UP, GALACTUS?
I THOUGHT I WOULD FIND THE FANTASTIC FOUR AT THIS PLANETARIUM. BUT I HAVE MADE THE SAME ERROR AS THE HUMANS.
INDEED--THE FANTASTIC FOUR IS NO MORE.
TELL US SOMETHIN' WE DON'T KNOW, BIG GUY!
THIS HERE'S THA FANTASTIC THREE.
But maybe sometimes...
...no matter how hard you try...

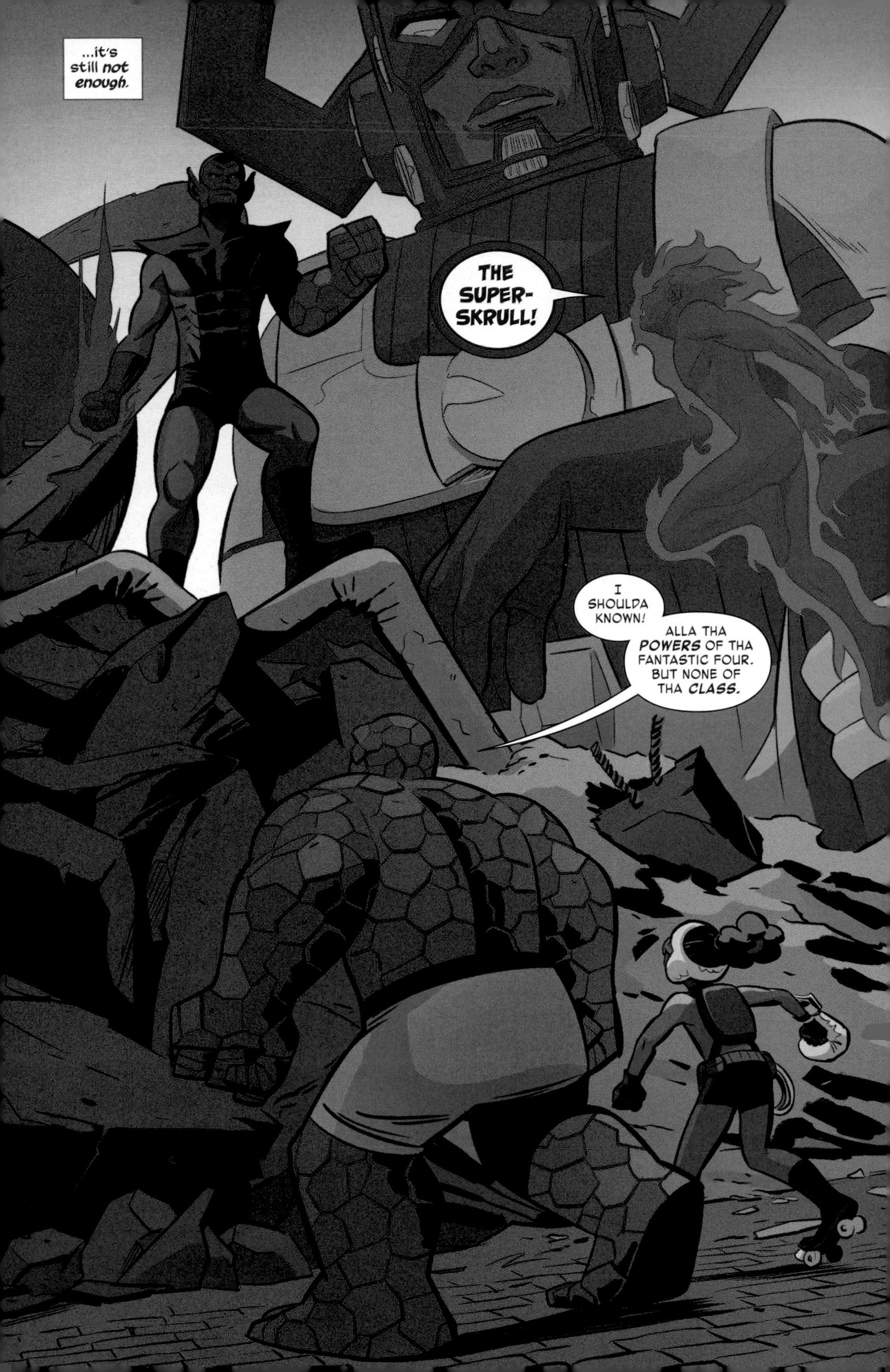
...it's still not enough.
THE SUPER-SKRULL!
I SHOULDA KNOWN!
ALLA THA POWERS OF THA FANTASTIC FOUR. BUT NONE OF THA CLASS.

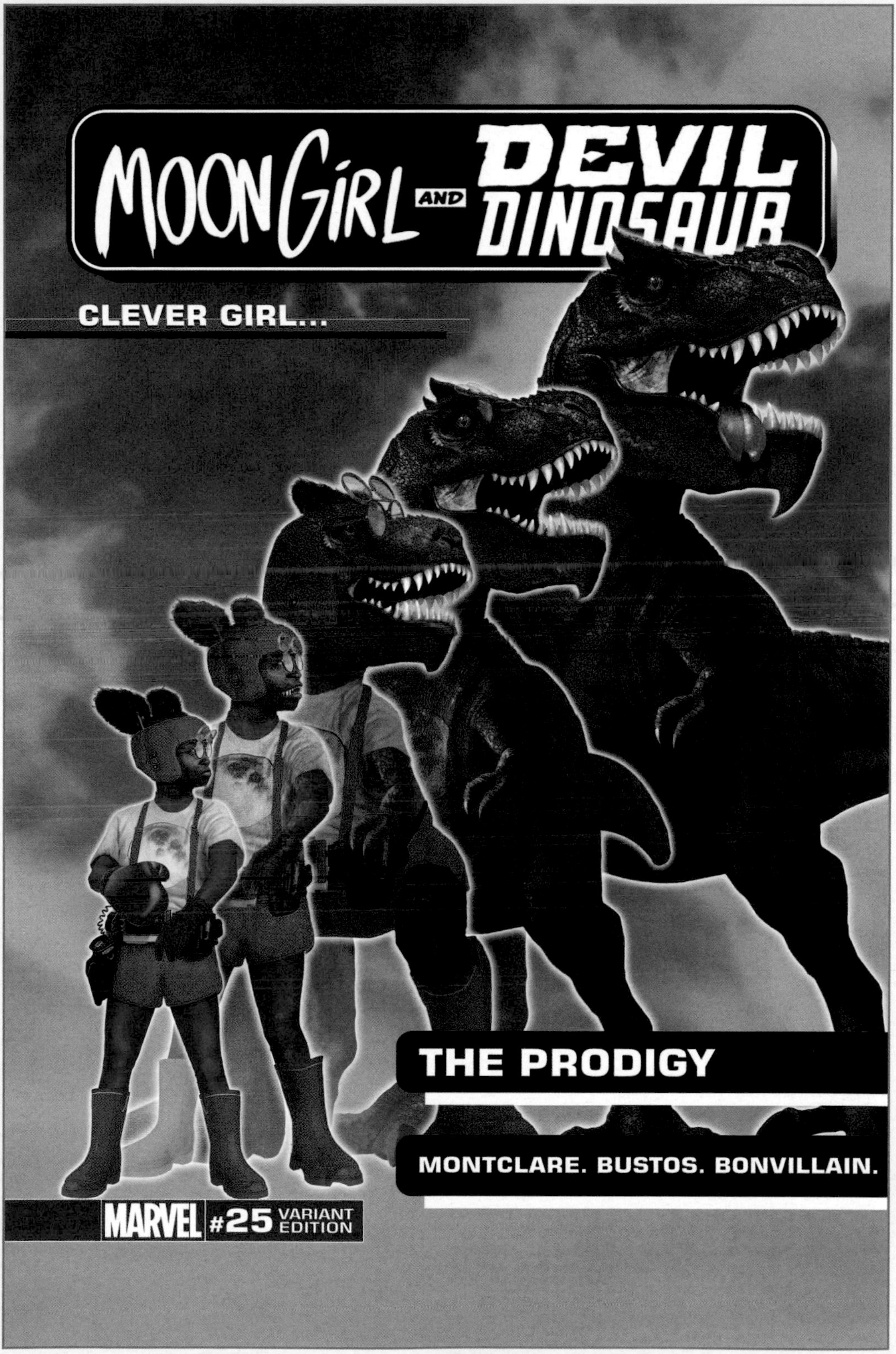
MOON GIRL AND DEVIL DINOSAUR
CLEVER GIRL...
THE PRODIGY
MONTCLARE. BUSTOS. BONVILLAIN.
MARVEL #25 VARIANT EDITION

#25 VARIANT
BY RAHZZAH

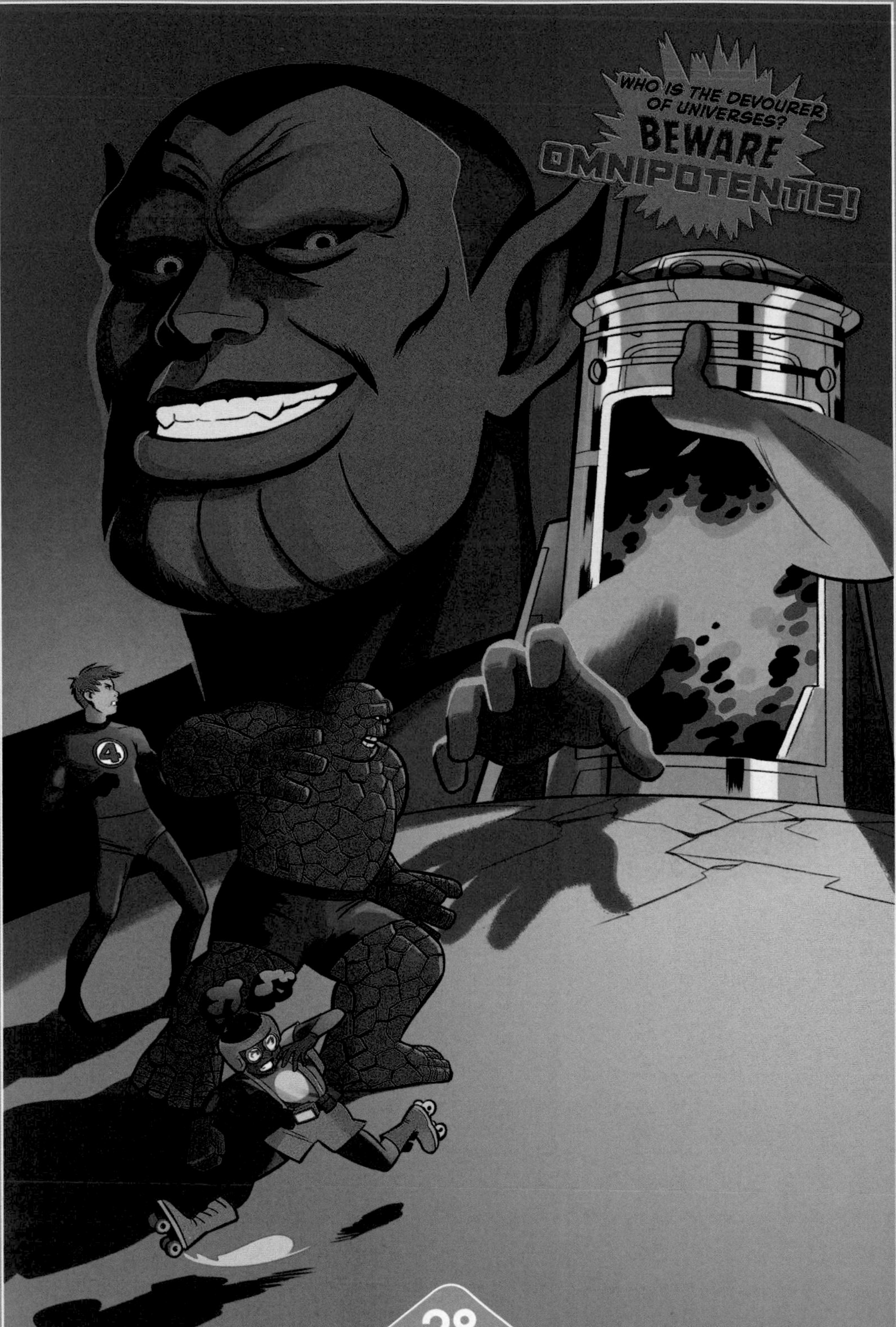
WHO IS THE DEVOURER OF UNIVERSES?
BEWARE OMNIPOTENTIS!
28

"THREE IS NOT ENOUGH"

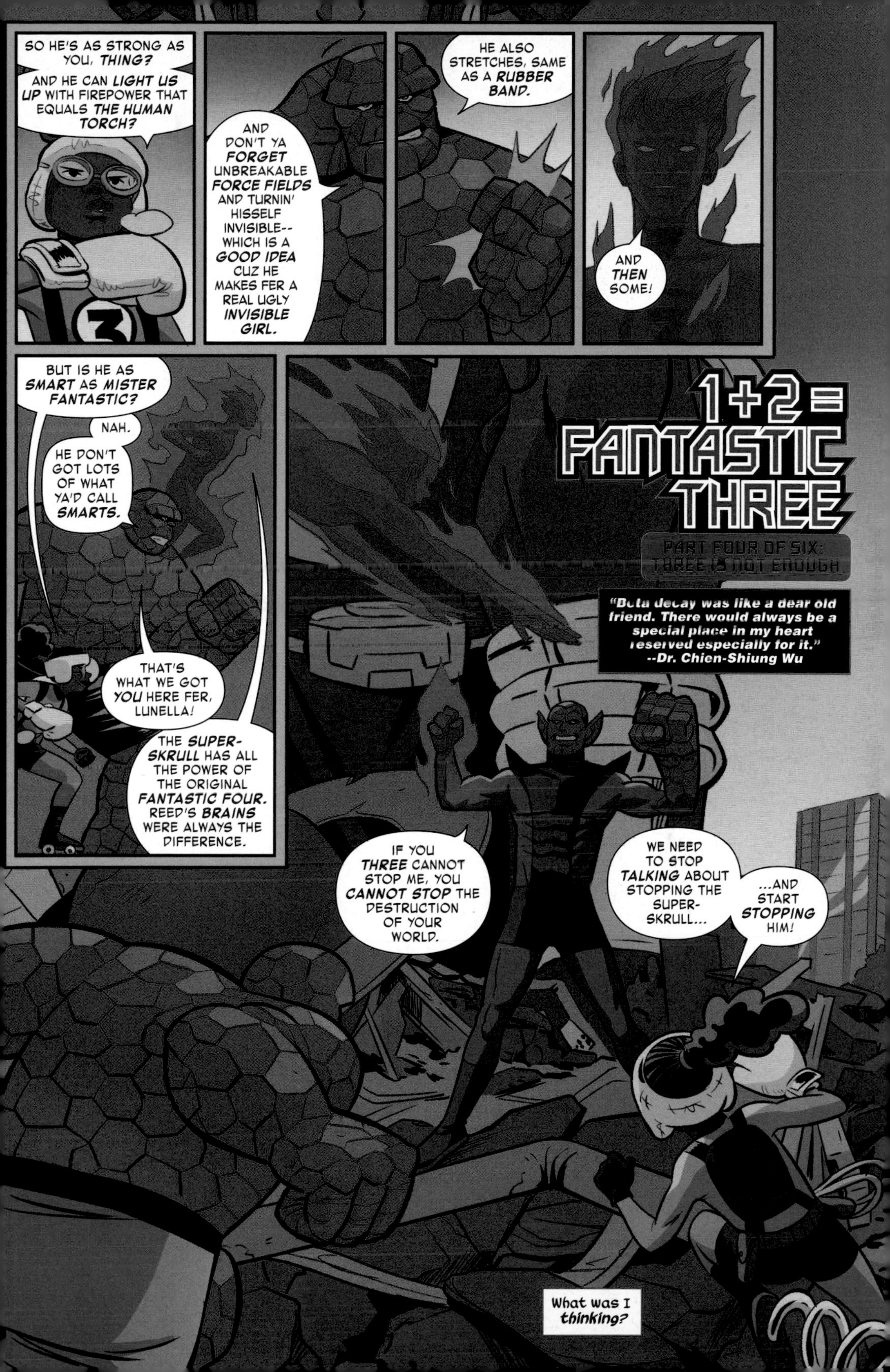

SO HE'S AS STRONG AS YOU, THING?
AND HE CAN LIGHT US UP WITH FIREPOWER THAT EQUALS THE HUMAN TORCH?
AND DON'T YA FORGET UNBREAKABLE FORCE FIELDS AND TURNIN' HISSELF INVISIBLE-- WHICH IS A GOOD IDEA CUZ HE MAKES FER A REAL UGLY INVISIBLE GIRL.
HE ALSO STRETCHES, SAME AS A RUBBER BAND.
AND THEN SOME!
BUT IS HE AS SMART AS MISTER FANTASTIC?
NAH.
HE DON'T GOT LOTS OF WHAT YA'D CALL SMARTS.
THAT'S WHAT WE GOT YOU HERE FER, LUNELLA!
THE SUPER-SKRULL HAS ALL THE POWER OF THE ORIGINAL FANTASTIC FOUR. REED'S BRAINS WERE ALWAYS THE DIFFERENCE.
1+2 = FANTASTIC THREE
PART FOUR OF SIX: THREE IS NOT ENOUGH
"Beta decay was like a dear old friend. There would always be a special place in my heart reserved especially for it." --Dr. Chien-Shiung Wu
IF YOU THREE CANNOT STOP ME, YOU CANNOT STOP THE DESTRUCTION OF YOUR WORLD.
WE NEED TO STOP TALKING ABOUT STOPPING THE SUPER-SKRULL...
...AND START STOPPING HIM!
What was I thinking?

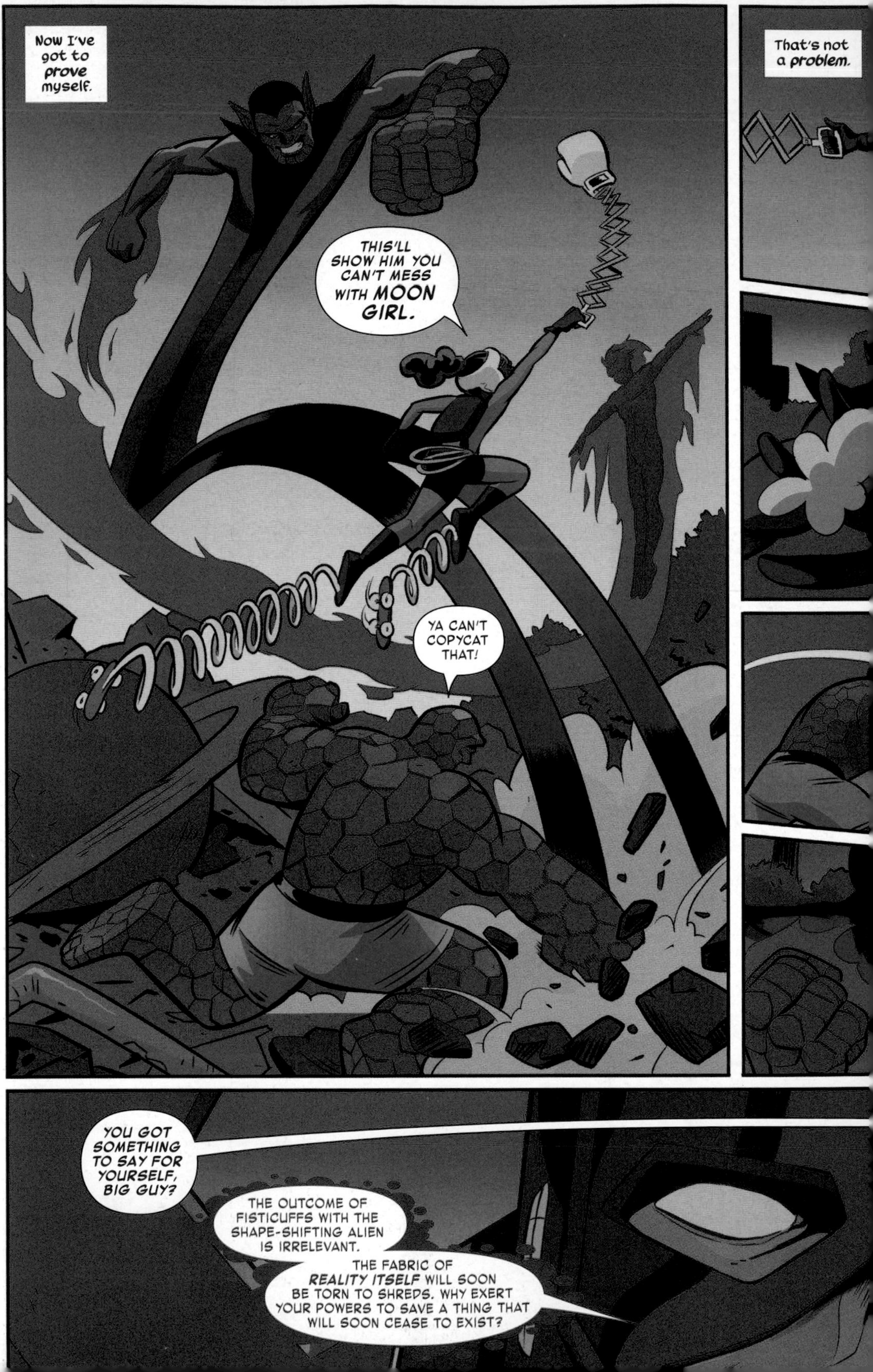
Now I've got to *prove* myself.
That's not a *problem.*
THIS'LL SHOW HIM YOU CAN'T MESS WITH MOON GIRL.
YA CAN'T COPYCAT THAT!
YOU GOT SOMETHING TO SAY FOR YOURSELF, BIG GUY?
THE OUTCOME OF FISTICUFFS WITH THE SHAPE-SHIFTING ALIEN IS IRRELEVANT.
THE FABRIC OF *REALITY ITSELF* WILL SOON BE TORN TO SHREDS. WHY EXERT YOUR POWERS TO SAVE A THING THAT WILL SOON CEASE TO EXIST?

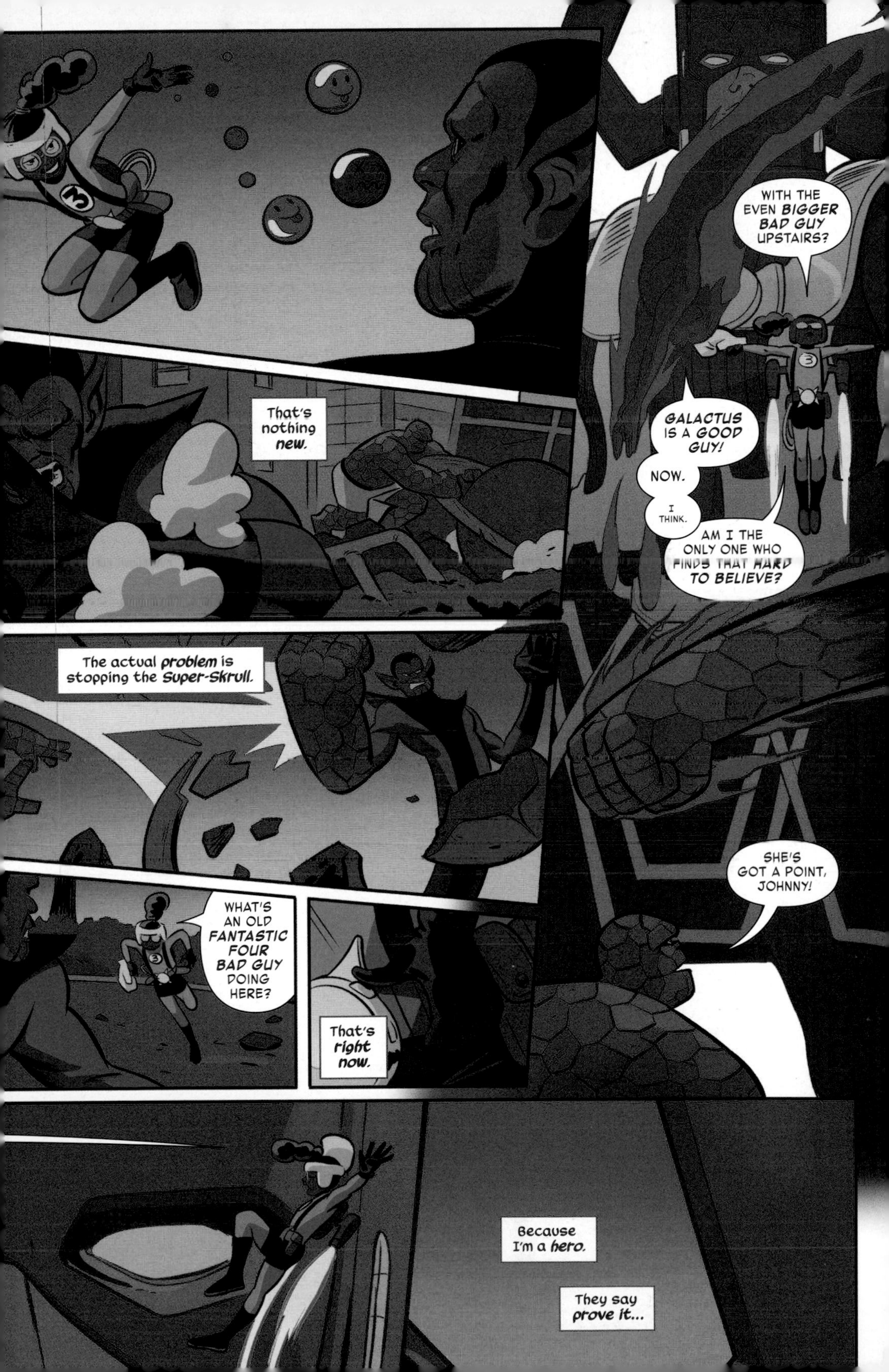

WITH THE EVEN BIGGER BAD GUY UPSTAIRS?
That's nothing new.
GALACTUS IS A GOOD GUY!
NOW.
I THINK.
AM I THE ONLY ONE WHO FINDS THAT HARD TO BELIEVE?
The actual problem is stopping the Super-Skrull.
SHE'S GOT A POINT, JOHNNY!
WHAT'S AN OLD FANTASTIC FOUR BAD GUY DOING HERE?
That's right now.
Because I'm a hero.
They say prove it...

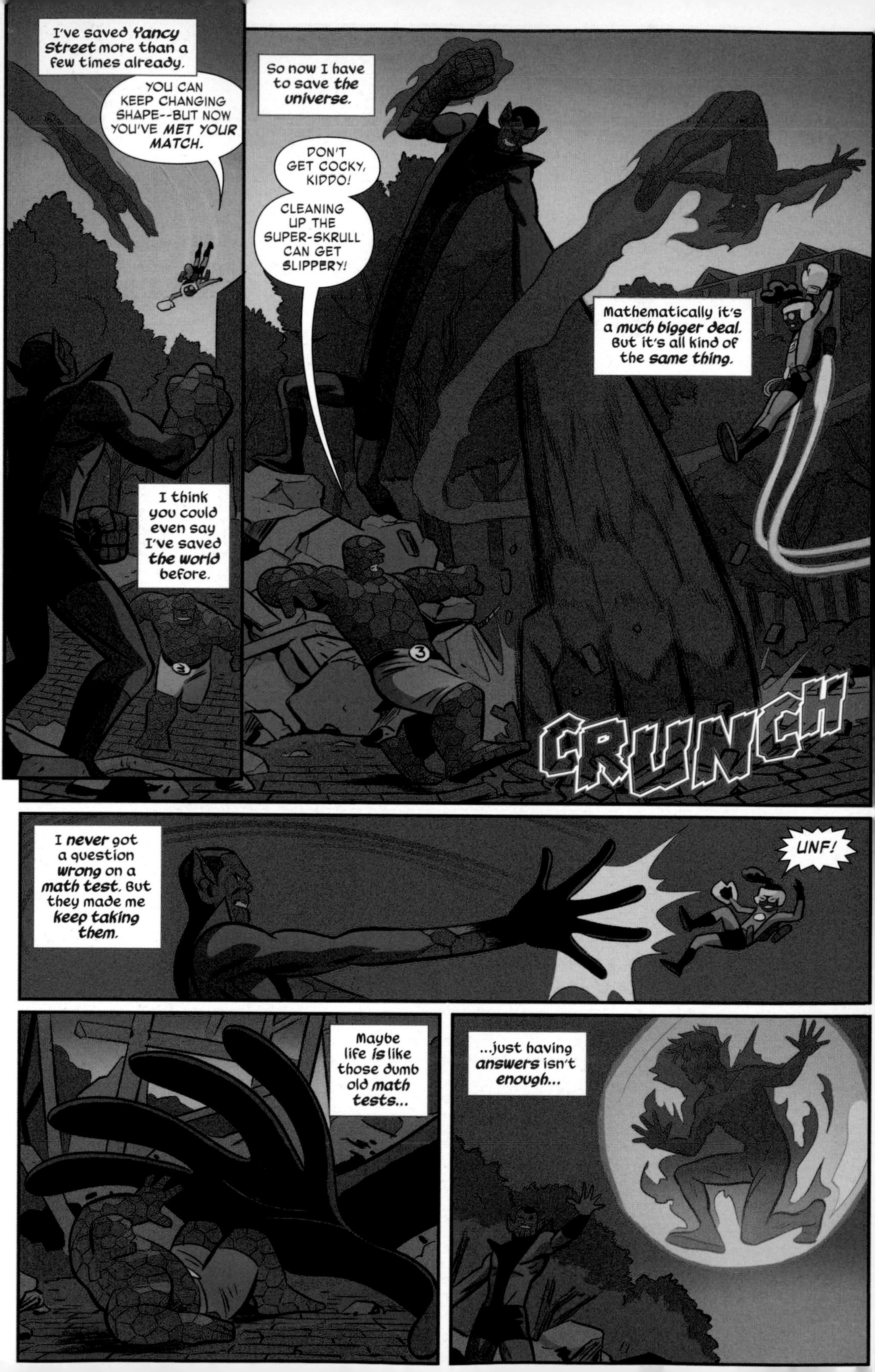
I've saved Yancy Street more than a few times already.
YOU CAN KEEP CHANGING SHAPE--BUT NOW YOU'VE MET YOUR MATCH.
So now I have to save the universe.
DON'T GET COCKY, KIDDO!
CLEANING UP THE SUPER-SKRULL CAN GET SLIPPERY!
Mathematically it's a much bigger deal. But it's all kind of the same thing.
I think you could even say I've saved the world before.
CRUNCH
I never got a question wrong on a math test. But they made me keep taking them.
UNF!
Maybe life is like those dumb old math tests...
...just having answers isn't enough...

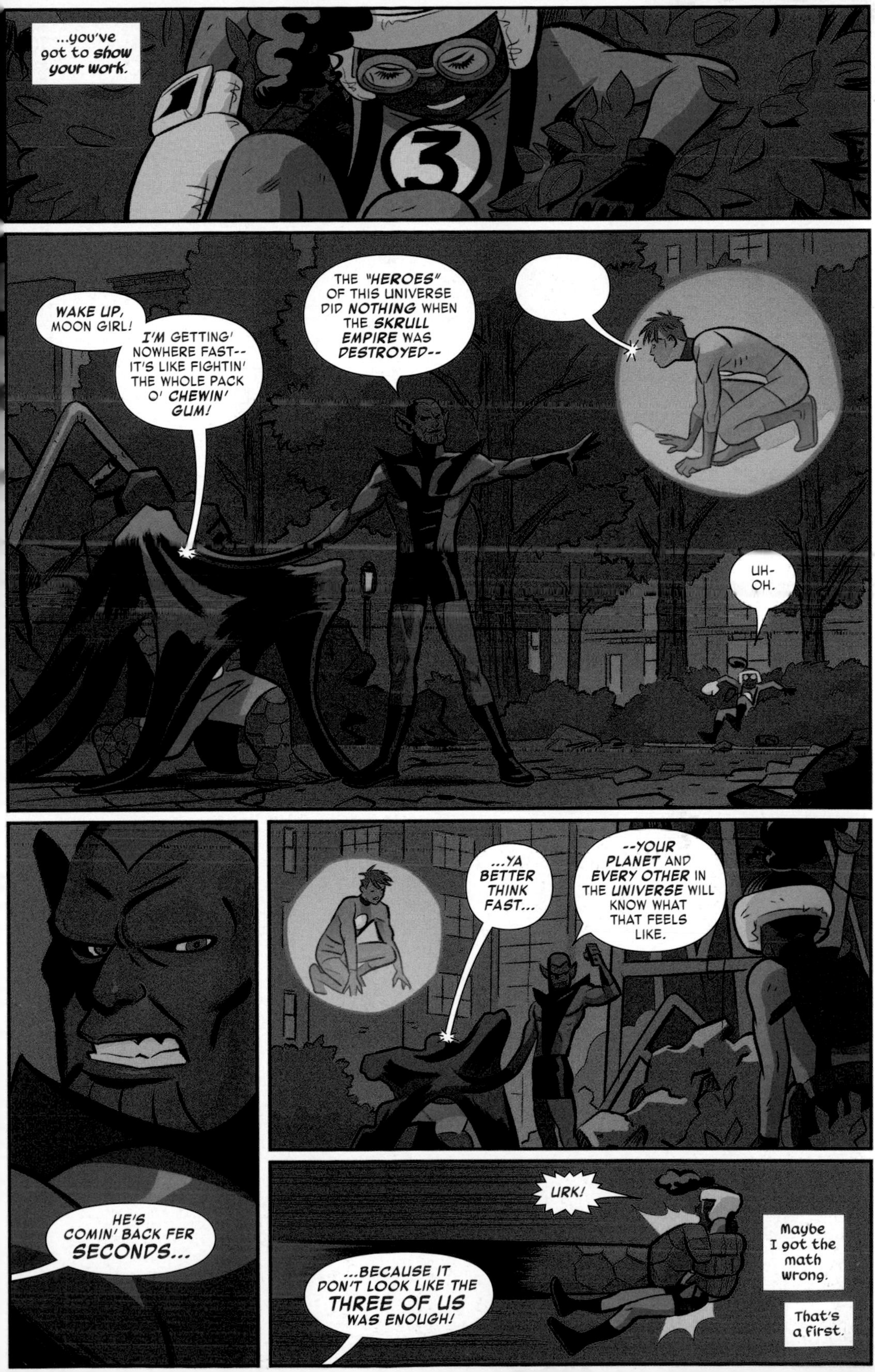
...you've got to show your work.
WAKE UP, MOON GIRL!
I'M GETTING' NOWHERE FAST-- IT'S LIKE FIGHTIN' THE WHOLE PACK O' CHEWIN' GUM!
THE "HEROES" OF THIS UNIVERSE DID NOTHING WHEN THE SKRULL EMPIRE WAS DESTROYED--
UH-OH.
...YA BETTER THINK FAST...
--YOUR PLANET AND EVERY OTHER IN THE UNIVERSE WILL KNOW WHAT THAT FEELS LIKE.
HE'S COMIN' BACK FER SECONDS...
URK!
...BECAUSE IT DON'T LOOK LIKE THE THREE OF US WAS ENOUGH!
Maybe I got the math wrong.
That's a first.

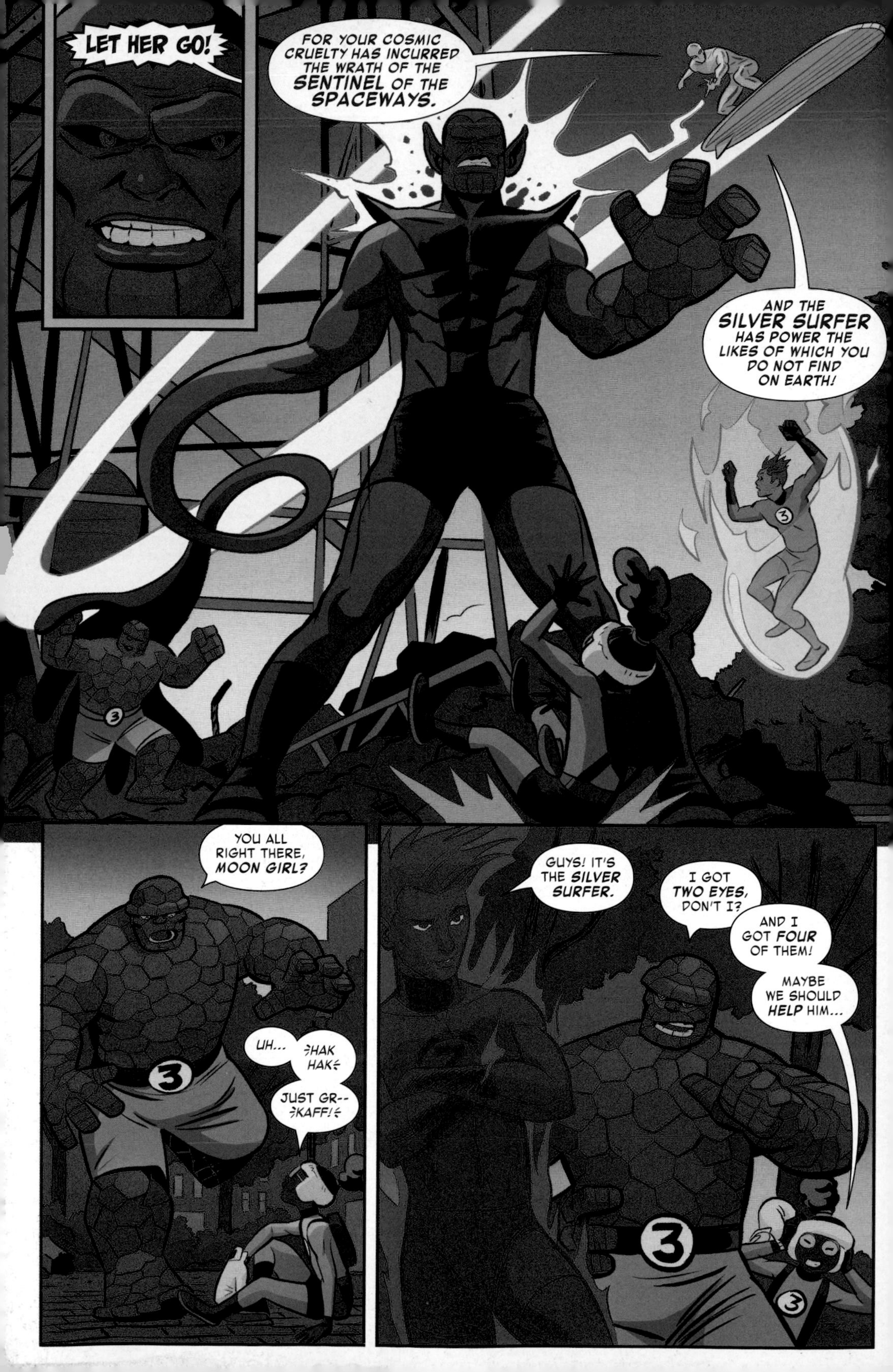
LET HER GO!
FOR YOUR COSMIC CRUELTY HAS INCURRED THE WRATH OF THE SENTINEL OF THE SPACEWAYS.
AND THE SILVER SURFER HAS POWER THE LIKES OF WHICH YOU DO NOT FIND ON EARTH!
YOU ALL RIGHT THERE, MOON GIRL?
UH...
HAK HAK
JUST GR--
KAFF!
GUYS! IT'S THE SILVER SURFER.
I GOT TWO EYES, DON'T I?
AND I GOT FOUR OF THEM!
MAYBE WE SHOULD HELP HIM...

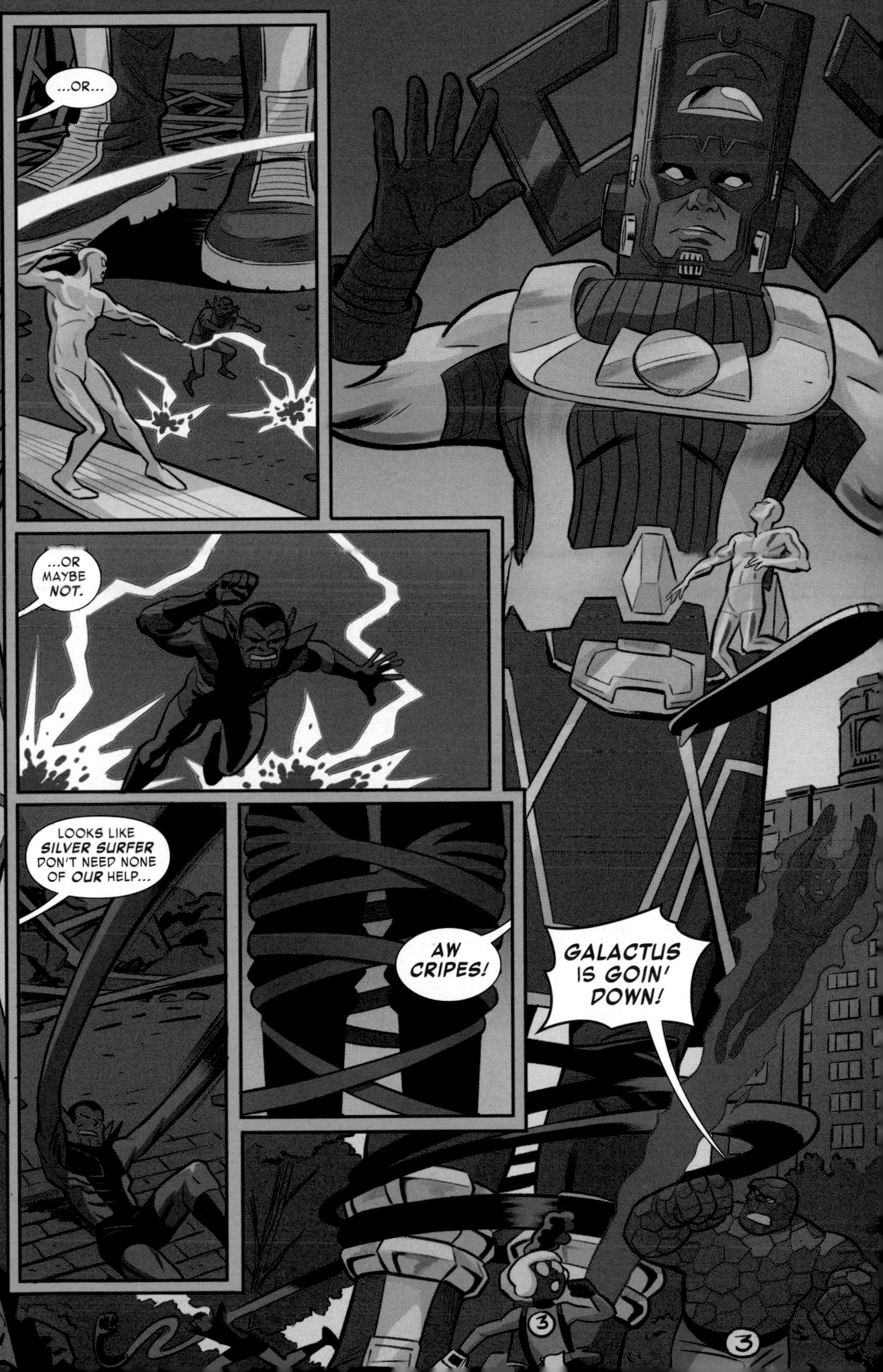
...OR...
...OR MAYBE NOT.
LOOKS LIKE SILVER SURFER DON'T NEED NONE OF OUR HELP...
AW CRIPES!
GALACTUS IS GOIN' DOWN!

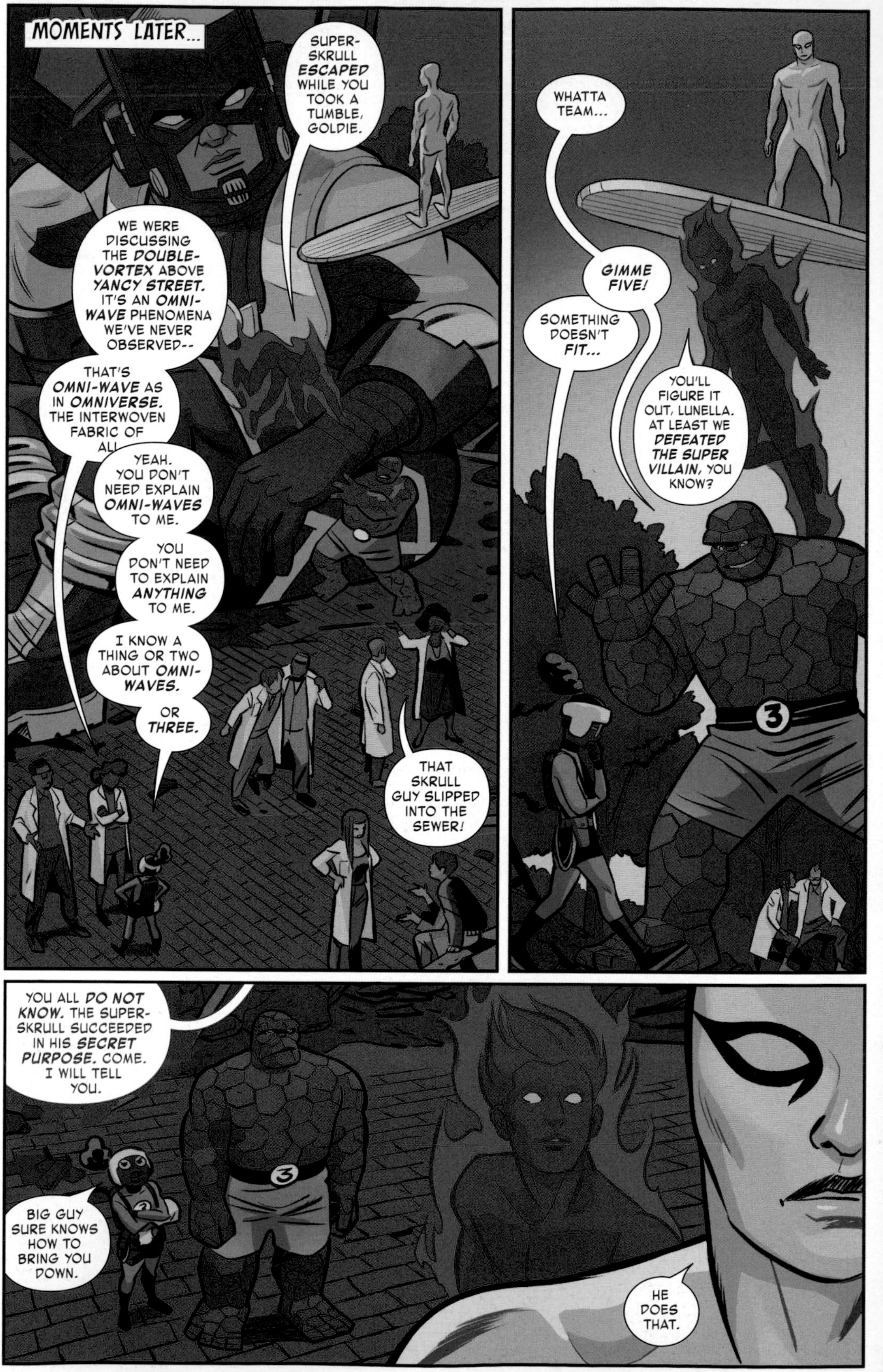
MOMENTS LATER...
SUPER-SKRULL ESCAPED WHILE YOU TOOK A TUMBLE, GOLDIE.
WE WERE DISCUSSING THE DOUBLE-VORTEX ABOVE YANCY STREET. IT'S AN OMNI-WAVE PHENOMENA WE'VE NEVER OBSERVED--
THAT'S OMNI-WAVE AS IN OMNIVERSE. THE INTERWOVEN FABRIC OF ALL
YEAH. YOU DON'T NEED EXPLAIN OMNI-WAVES TO ME.
YOU DON'T NEED TO EXPLAIN ANYTHING TO ME.
I KNOW A THING OR TWO ABOUT OMNI-WAVES.
OR THREE.
THAT SKRULL GUY SLIPPED INTO THE SEWER!
WHATTA TEAM...
GIMME FIVE!
SOMETHING DOESN'T FIT...
YOU'LL FIGURE IT OUT, LUNELLA. AT LEAST WE DEFEATED THE SUPER VILLAIN, YOU KNOW?
YOU ALL DO NOT KNOW. THE SUPER-SKRULL SUCCEEDED IN HIS SECRET PURPOSE. COME. I WILL TELL YOU.
BIG GUY SURE KNOWS HOW TO BRING YOU DOWN.
HE DOES THAT.

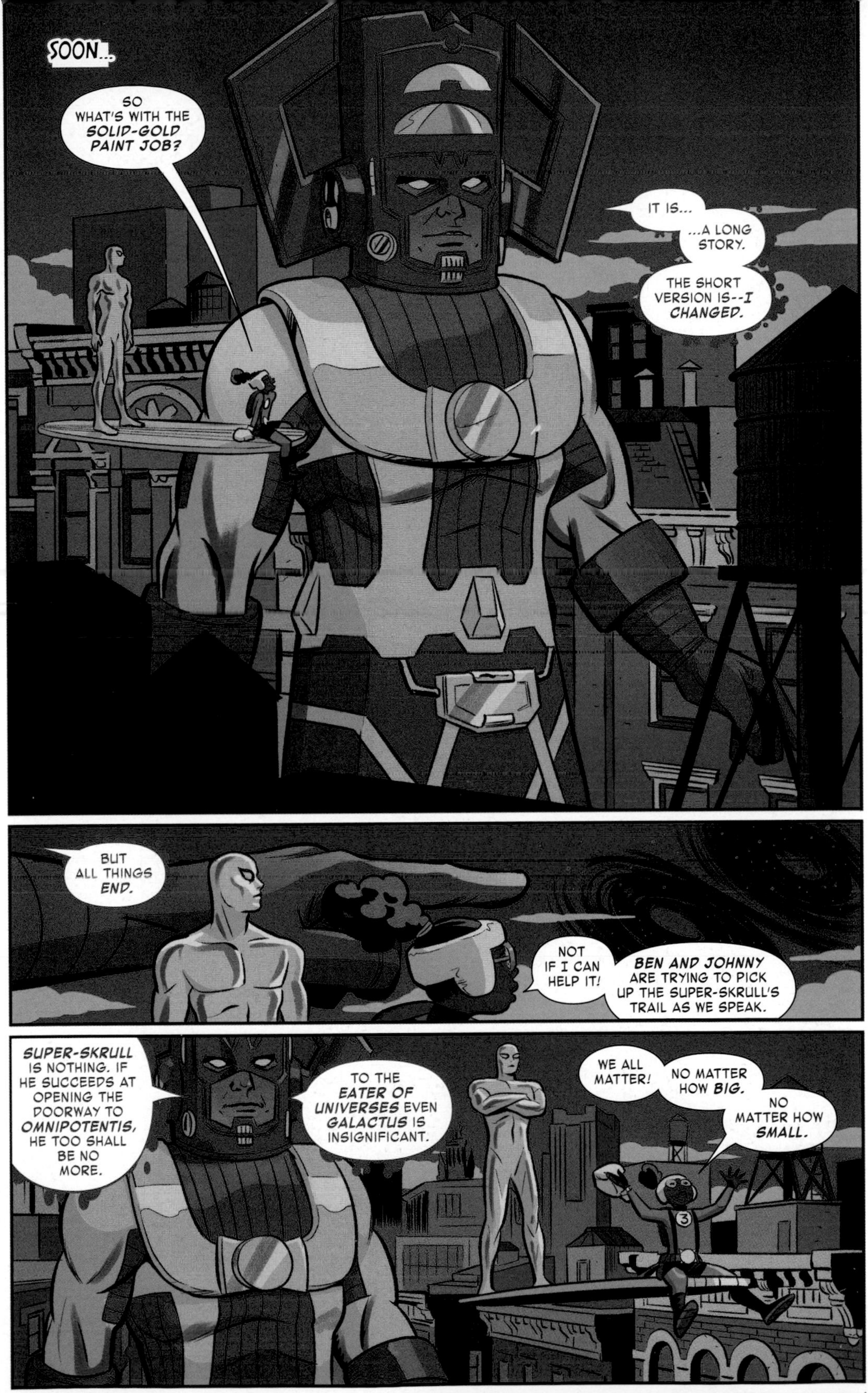
SOON...
SO WHAT'S WITH THE SOLID-GOLD PAINT JOB?
IT IS...
...A LONG STORY.
THE SHORT VERSION IS--I CHANGED.
BUT ALL THINGS END.
NOT IF I CAN HELP IT!
BEN AND JOHNNY ARE TRYING TO PICK UP THE SUPER-SKRULL'S TRAIL AS WE SPEAK.
SUPER-SKRULL IS NOTHING. IF HE SUCCEEDS AT OPENING THE DOORWAY TO OMNIPOTENTIS, HE TOO SHALL BE NO MORE.
TO THE EATER OF UNIVERSES EVEN GALACTUS IS INSIGNIFICANT.
WE ALL MATTER!
NO MATTER HOW BIG.
NO MATTER HOW SMALL.

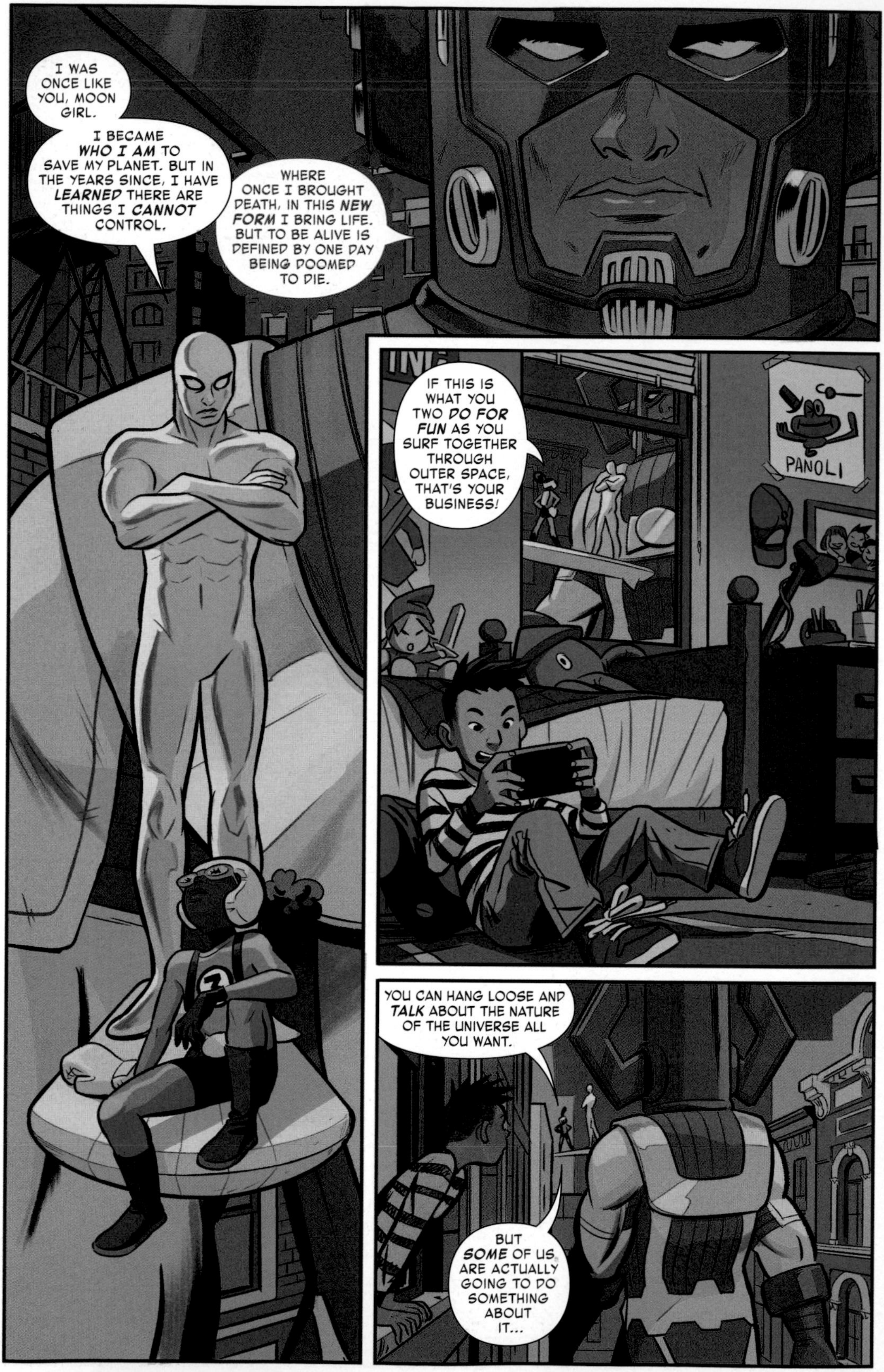
I WAS ONCE LIKE YOU, MOON GIRL.
I BECAME *WHO I AM* TO SAVE MY PLANET. BUT IN THE YEARS SINCE, I HAVE *LEARNED* THERE ARE THINGS I *CANNOT* CONTROL.
WHERE ONCE I BROUGHT DEATH, IN THIS *NEW FORM* I BRING LIFE. BUT TO BE ALIVE IS DEFINED BY ONE DAY BEING DOOMED TO DIE.
IF THIS IS WHAT YOU TWO *DO FOR FUN* AS YOU SURF TOGETHER THROUGH OUTER SPACE, THAT'S YOUR BUSINESS!
PANOLI
YOU CAN HANG LOOSE AND *TALK* ABOUT THE NATURE OF THE UNIVERSE ALL YOU WANT.
BUT *SOME* OF US ARE ACTUALLY GOING TO DO SOMETHING ABOUT IT...

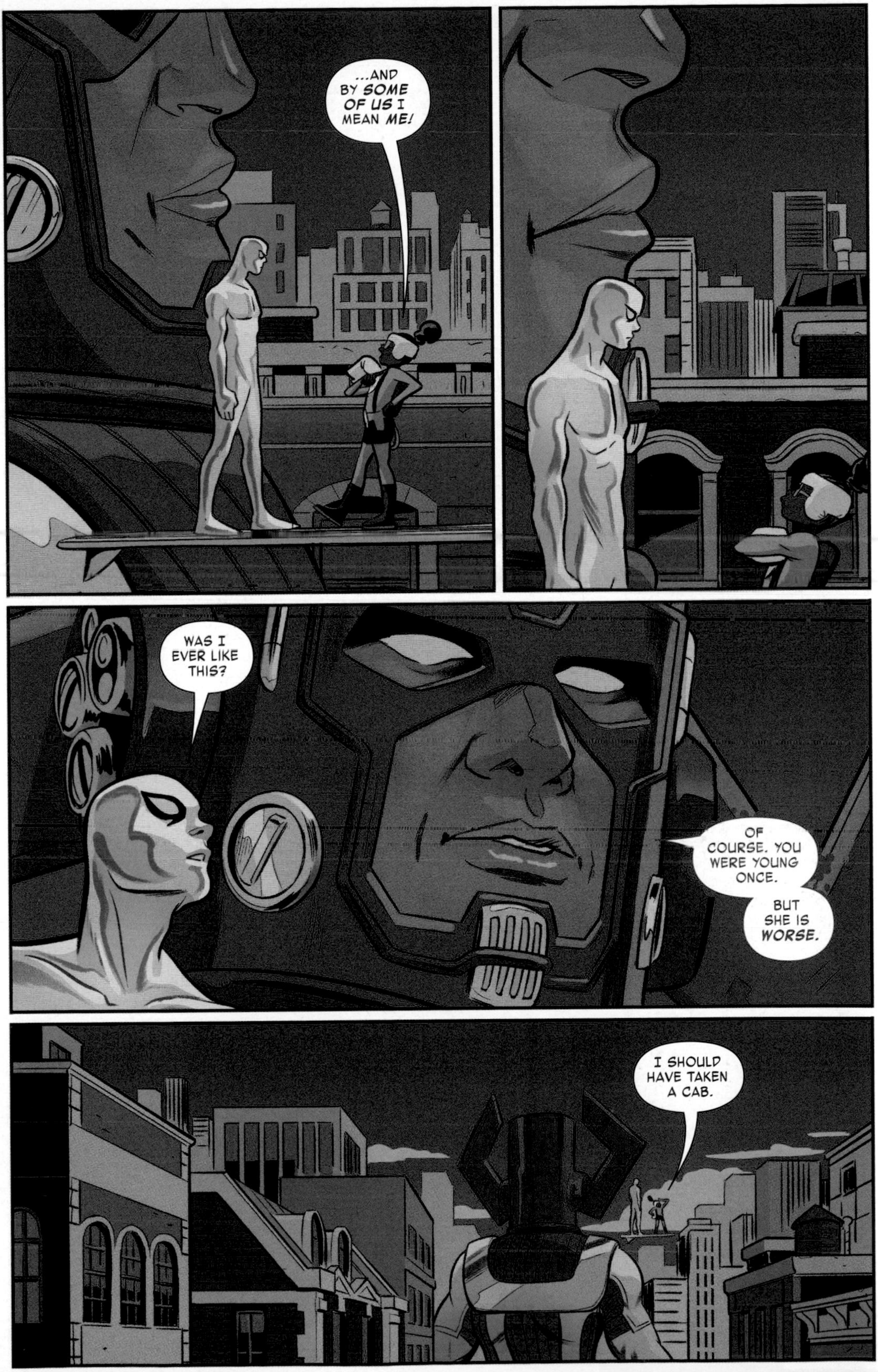
...AND BY *SOME OF US* I MEAN *ME!*
WAS I EVER LIKE THIS?
OF COURSE. YOU WERE YOUNG ONCE.
BUT SHE IS *WORSE.*
I SHOULD HAVE TAKEN A CAB.

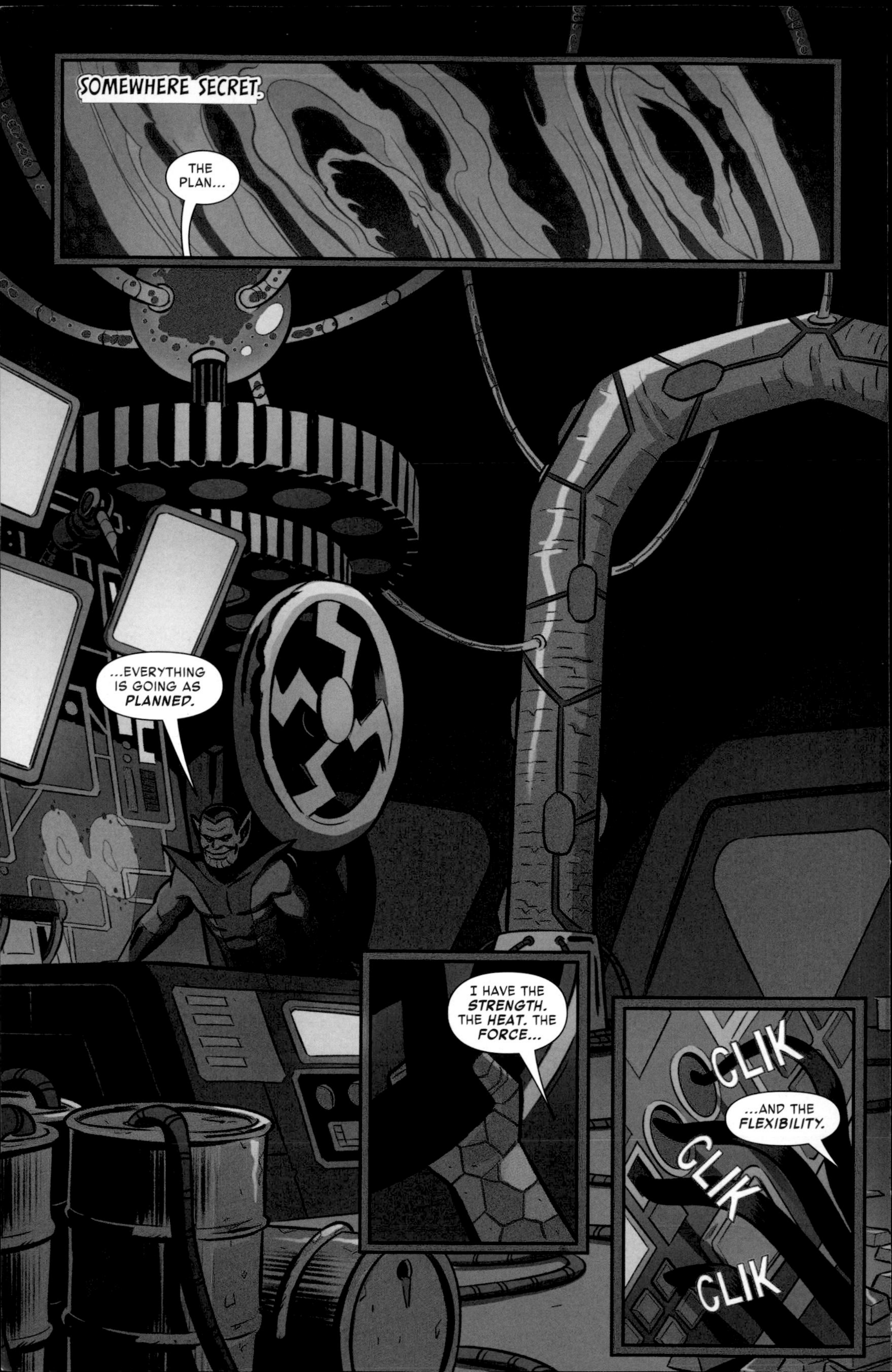
SOMEWHERE SECRET.
THE PLAN...
...EVERYTHING IS GOING AS PLANNED.
I HAVE THE STRENGTH. THE HEAT. THE FORCE...
CLIK
...AND THE FLEXIBILITY.
CLIK
CLIK

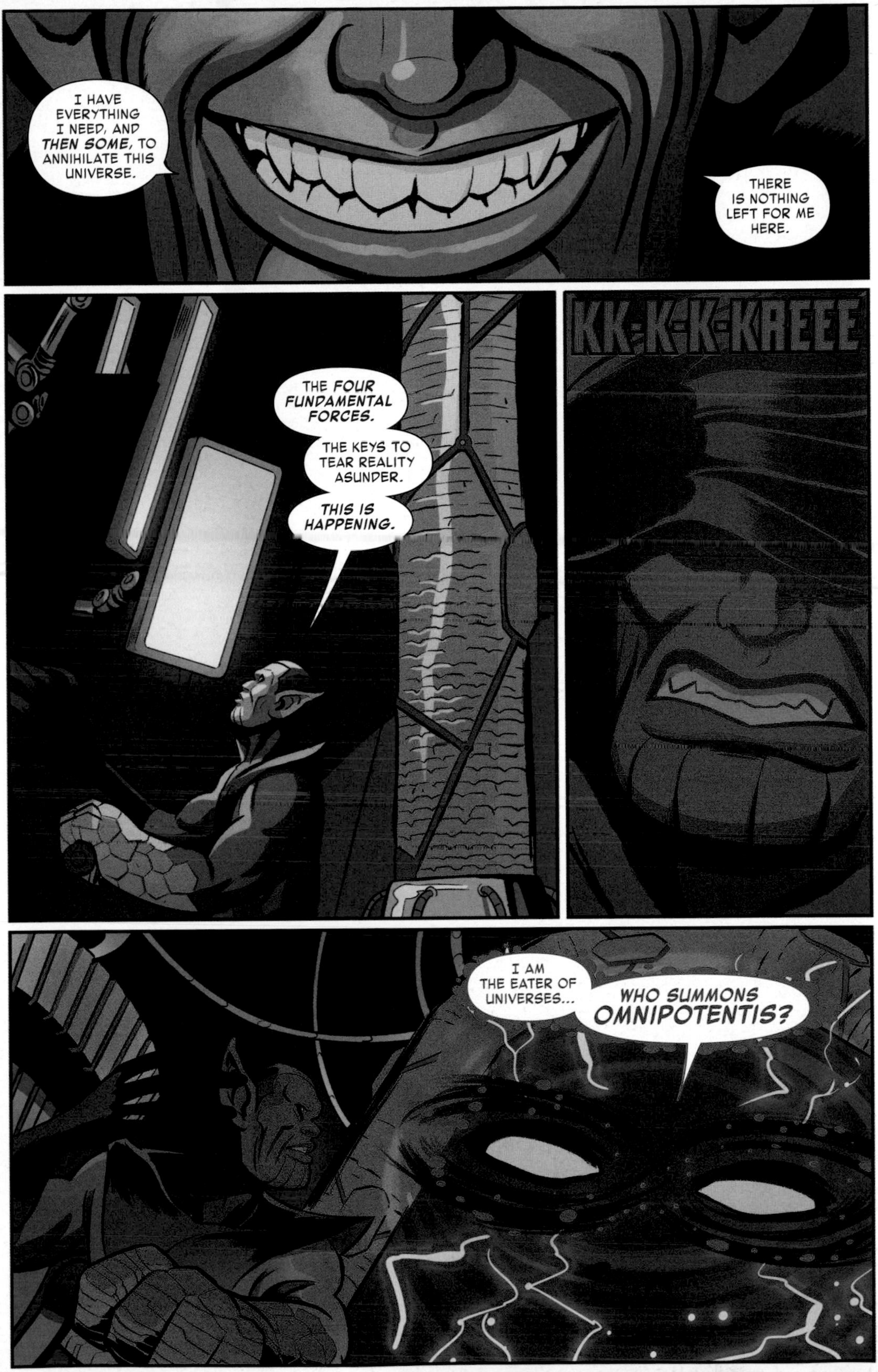
I HAVE EVERYTHING I NEED, AND *THEN SOME,* TO ANNIHILATE THIS UNIVERSE.
THERE IS NOTHING LEFT FOR ME HERE.
THE *FOUR FUNDAMENTAL FORCES.*
THE KEYS TO TEAR REALITY ASUNDER.
THIS IS HAPPENING.
KK-K-K-KREEE
I AM THE EATER OF UNIVERSES...
WHO SUMMONS OMNIPOTENTIS?

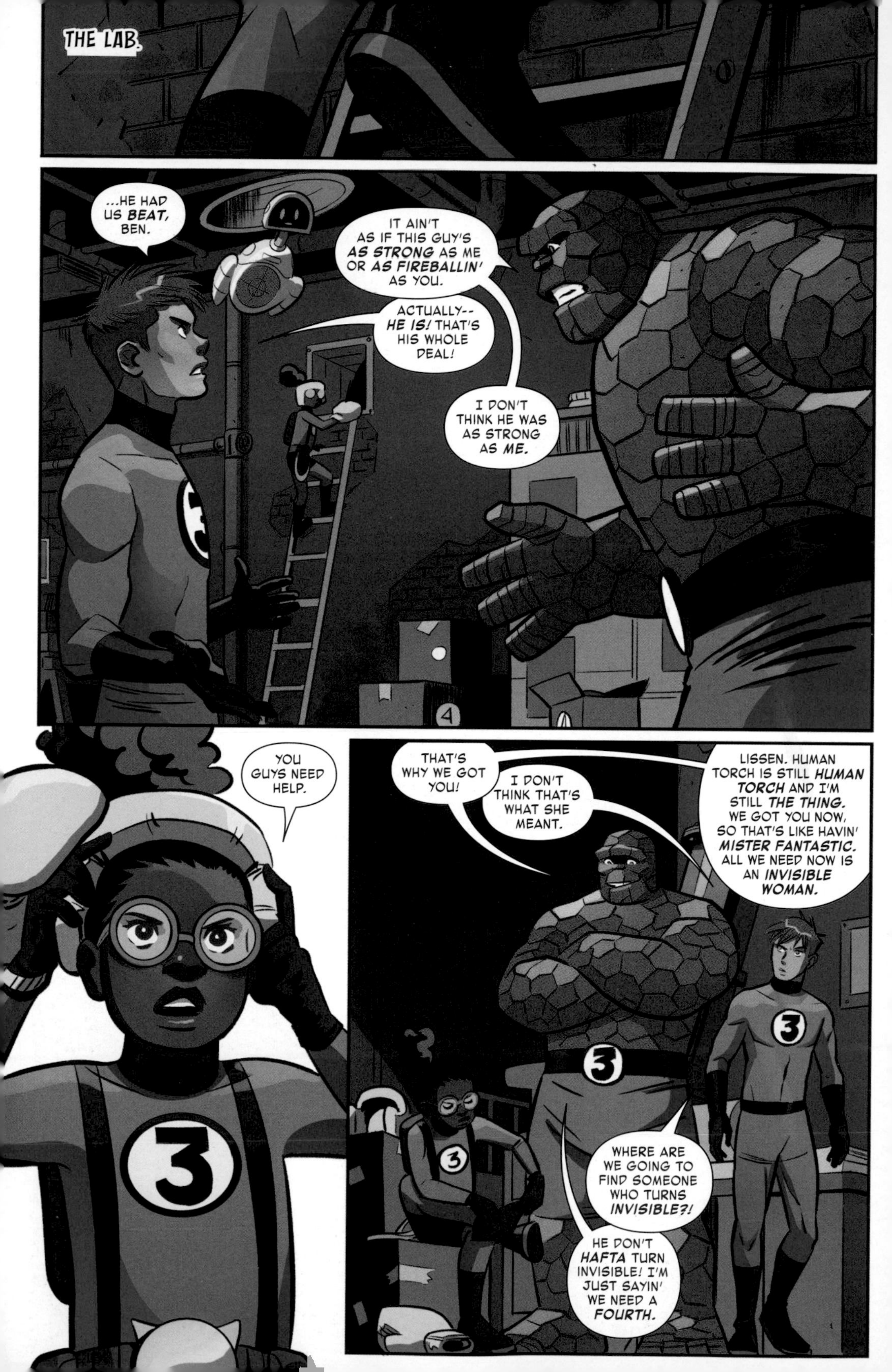
THE LAB.
...HE HAD US BEAT, BEN.
IT AIN'T AS IF THIS GUY'S AS STRONG AS ME OR AS FIREBALLIN' AS YOU.
ACTUALLY-- HE IS! THAT'S HIS WHOLE DEAL!
I DON'T THINK HE WAS AS STRONG AS ME.
YOU GUYS NEED HELP.
THAT'S WHY WE GOT YOU!
I DON'T THINK THAT'S WHAT SHE MEANT.
LISSEN. HUMAN TORCH IS STILL HUMAN TORCH AND I'M STILL THE THING. WE GOT YOU NOW, SO THAT'S LIKE HAVIN' MISTER FANTASTIC. ALL WE NEED NOW IS AN INVISIBLE WOMAN.
WHERE ARE WE GOING TO FIND SOMEONE WHO TURNS INVISIBLE?!
HE DON'T HAFTA TURN INVISIBLE! I'M JUST SAYIN' WE NEED A FOURTH.

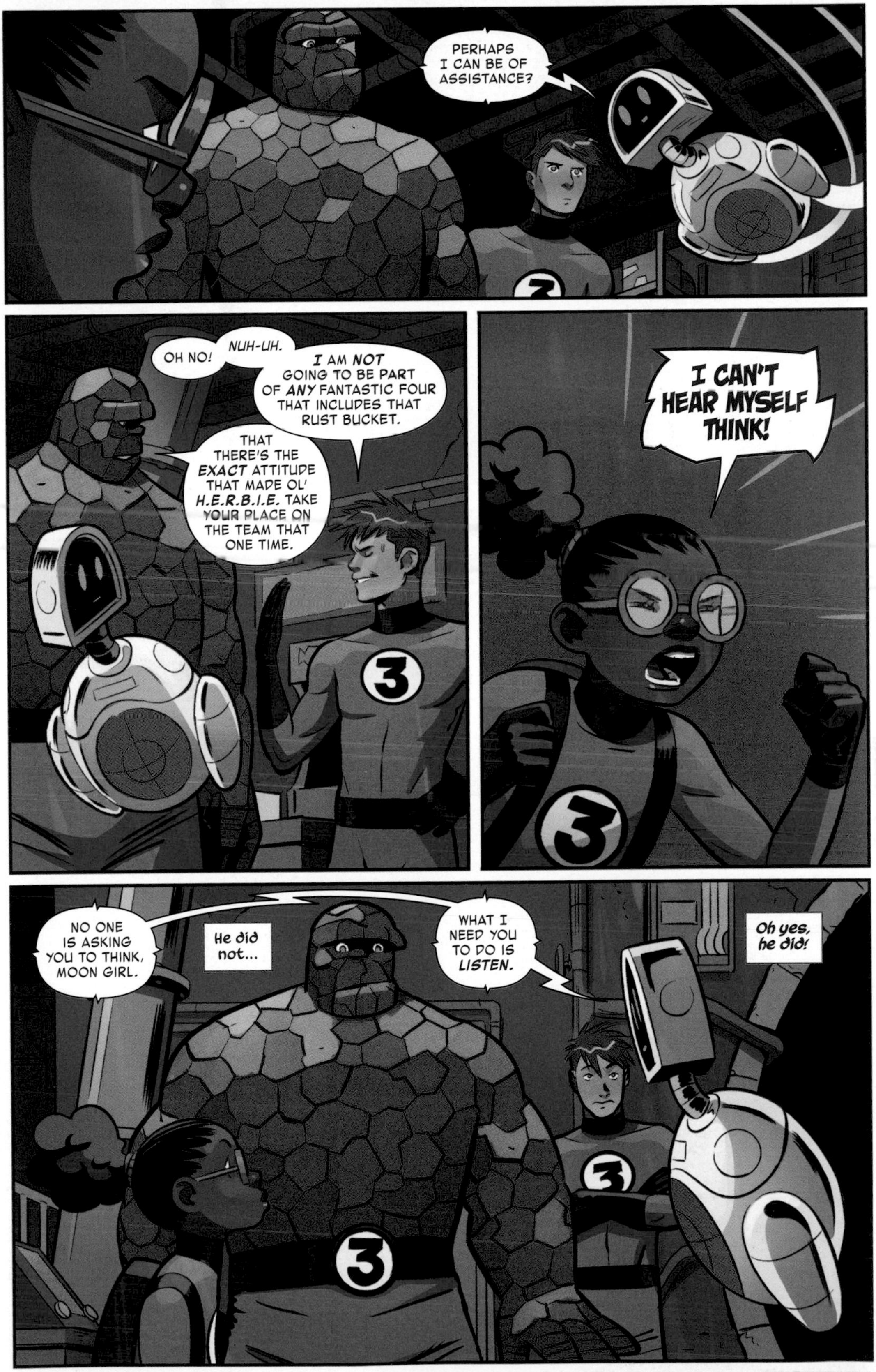
PERHAPS I CAN BE OF ASSISTANCE?
OH NO!
NUH-UH.
I AM NOT GOING TO BE PART OF ANY FANTASTIC FOUR THAT INCLUDES THAT RUST BUCKET.
THAT THERE'S THE EXACT ATTITUDE THAT MADE OL' H.E.R.B.I.E. TAKE YOUR PLACE ON THE TEAM THAT ONE TIME.
I CAN'T HEAR MYSELF THINK!
NO ONE IS ASKING YOU TO THINK, MOON GIRL.
He did not...
WHAT I NEED YOU TO DO IS LISTEN.
Oh yes, he did!

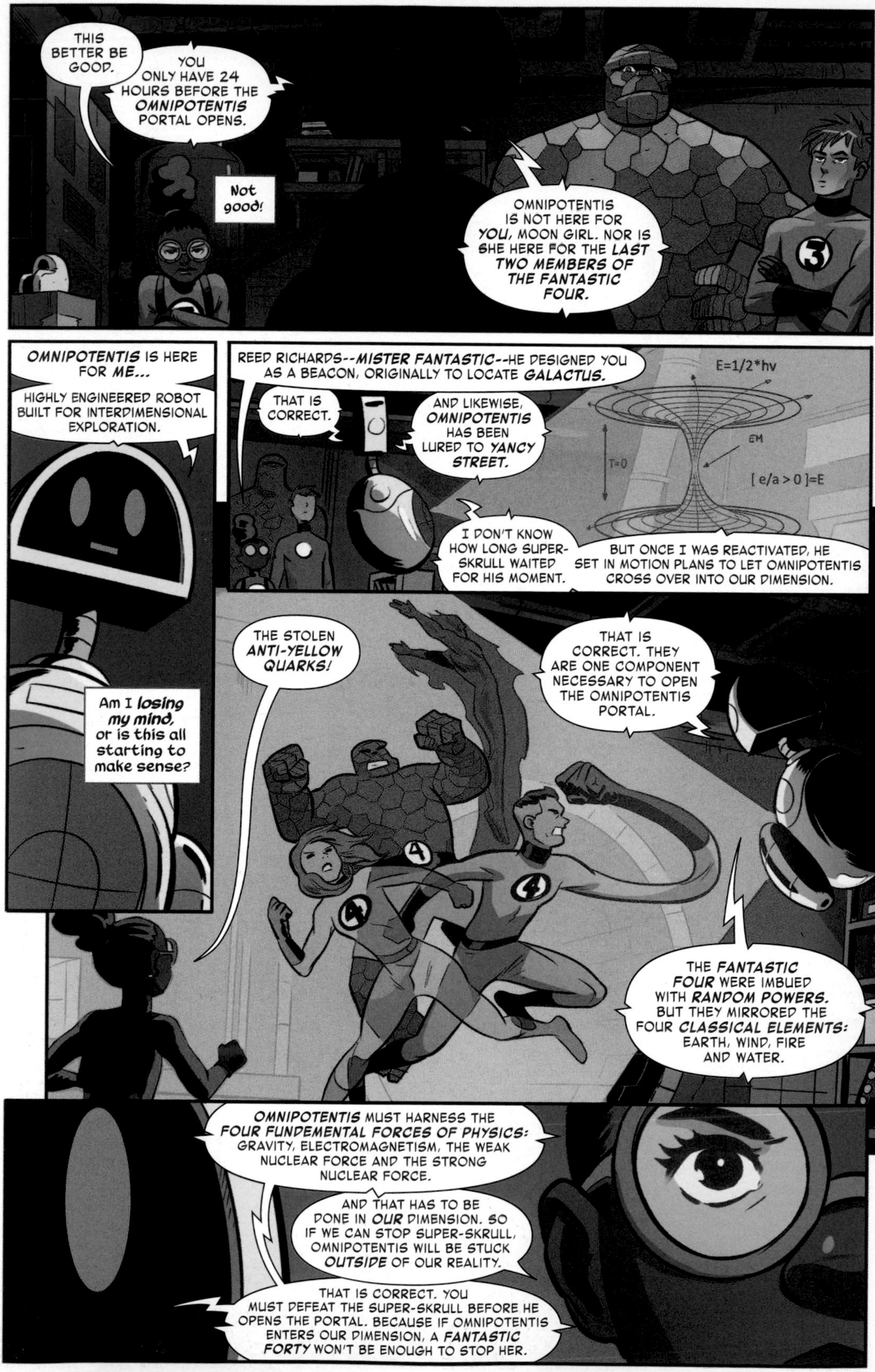
THIS BETTER BE GOOD.
YOU ONLY HAVE 24 HOURS BEFORE THE OMNIPOTENTIS PORTAL OPENS.
Not good!
OMNIPOTENTIS IS NOT HERE FOR YOU, MOON GIRL. NOR IS SHE HERE FOR THE LAST TWO MEMBERS OF THE FANTASTIC FOUR.
OMNIPOTENTIS IS HERE FOR ME...
HIGHLY ENGINEERED ROBOT BUILT FOR INTERDIMENSIONAL EXPLORATION.
REED RICHARDS--MISTER FANTASTIC--HE DESIGNED YOU AS A BEACON, ORIGINALLY TO LOCATE GALACTUS.
THAT IS CORRECT.
AND LIKEWISE, OMNIPOTENTIS HAS BEEN LURED TO YANCY STREET.
E=1/2*hv
EM
T=0
[e/a > 0]=E
I DON'T KNOW HOW LONG SUPER-SKRULL WAITED FOR HIS MOMENT.
BUT ONCE I WAS REACTIVATED, HE SET IN MOTION PLANS TO LET OMNIPOTENTIS CROSS OVER INTO OUR DIMENSION.
Am I losing my mind, or is this all starting to make sense?
THE STOLEN ANTI-YELLOW QUARKS!
THAT IS CORRECT. THEY ARE ONE COMPONENT NECESSARY TO OPEN THE OMNIPOTENTIS PORTAL.
THE FANTASTIC FOUR WERE IMBUED WITH RANDOM POWERS. BUT THEY MIRRORED THE FOUR CLASSICAL ELEMENTS: EARTH, WIND, FIRE AND WATER.
OMNIPOTENTIS MUST HARNESS THE FOUR FUNDEMENTAL FORCES OF PHYSICS: GRAVITY, ELECTROMAGNETISM, THE WEAK NUCLEAR FORCE AND THE STRONG NUCLEAR FORCE.
AND THAT HAS TO BE DONE IN OUR DIMENSION. SO IF WE CAN STOP SUPER-SKRULL, OMNIPOTENTIS WILL BE STUCK OUTSIDE OF OUR REALITY.
THAT IS CORRECT. YOU MUST DEFEAT THE SUPER-SKRULL BEFORE HE OPENS THE PORTAL. BECAUSE IF OMNIPOTENTIS ENTERS OUR DIMENSION, A FANTASTIC FORTY WON'T BE ENOUGH TO STOP HER.

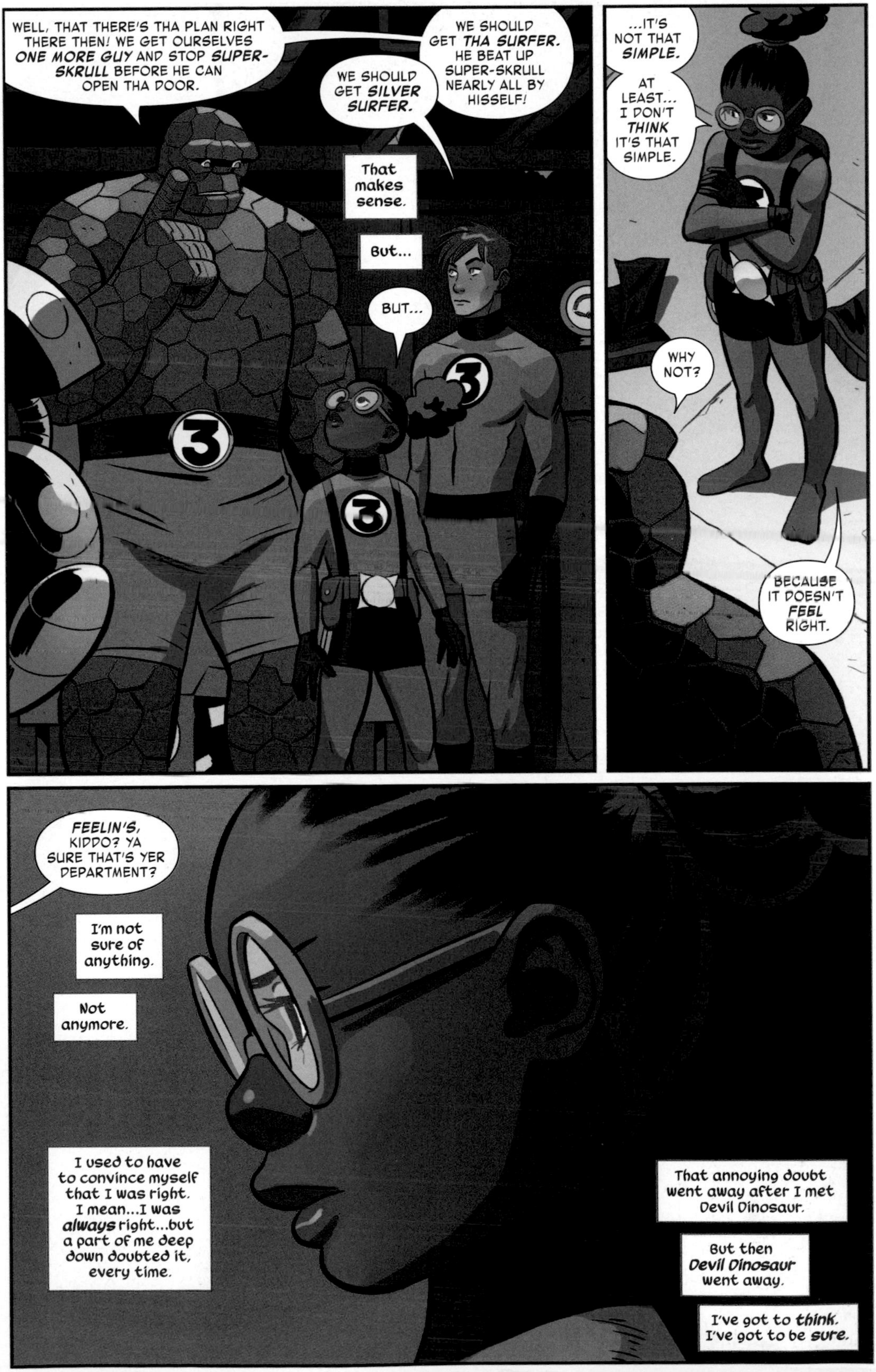
WELL, THAT THERE'S THA PLAN RIGHT THERE THEN! WE GET OURSELVES ONE MORE GUY AND STOP SUPER-SKRULL BEFORE HE CAN OPEN THA DOOR.
WE SHOULD GET THA SURFER. HE BEAT UP SUPER-SKRULL NEARLY ALL BY HISSELF!
WE SHOULD GET SILVER SURFER.
That makes sense.
But...
BUT...
...IT'S NOT THAT SIMPLE.
AT LEAST... I DON'T THINK IT'S THAT SIMPLE.
WHY NOT?
BECAUSE IT DOESN'T FEEL RIGHT.
FEELIN'S, KIDDO? YA SURE THAT'S YER DEPARTMENT?
I'm not sure of anything.
Not anymore.
I used to have to convince myself that I was right. I mean...I was always right...but a part of me deep down doubted it, every time.
That annoying doubt went away after I met Devil Dinosaur.
But then Devil Dinosaur went away.
I've got to think. I've got to be sure.

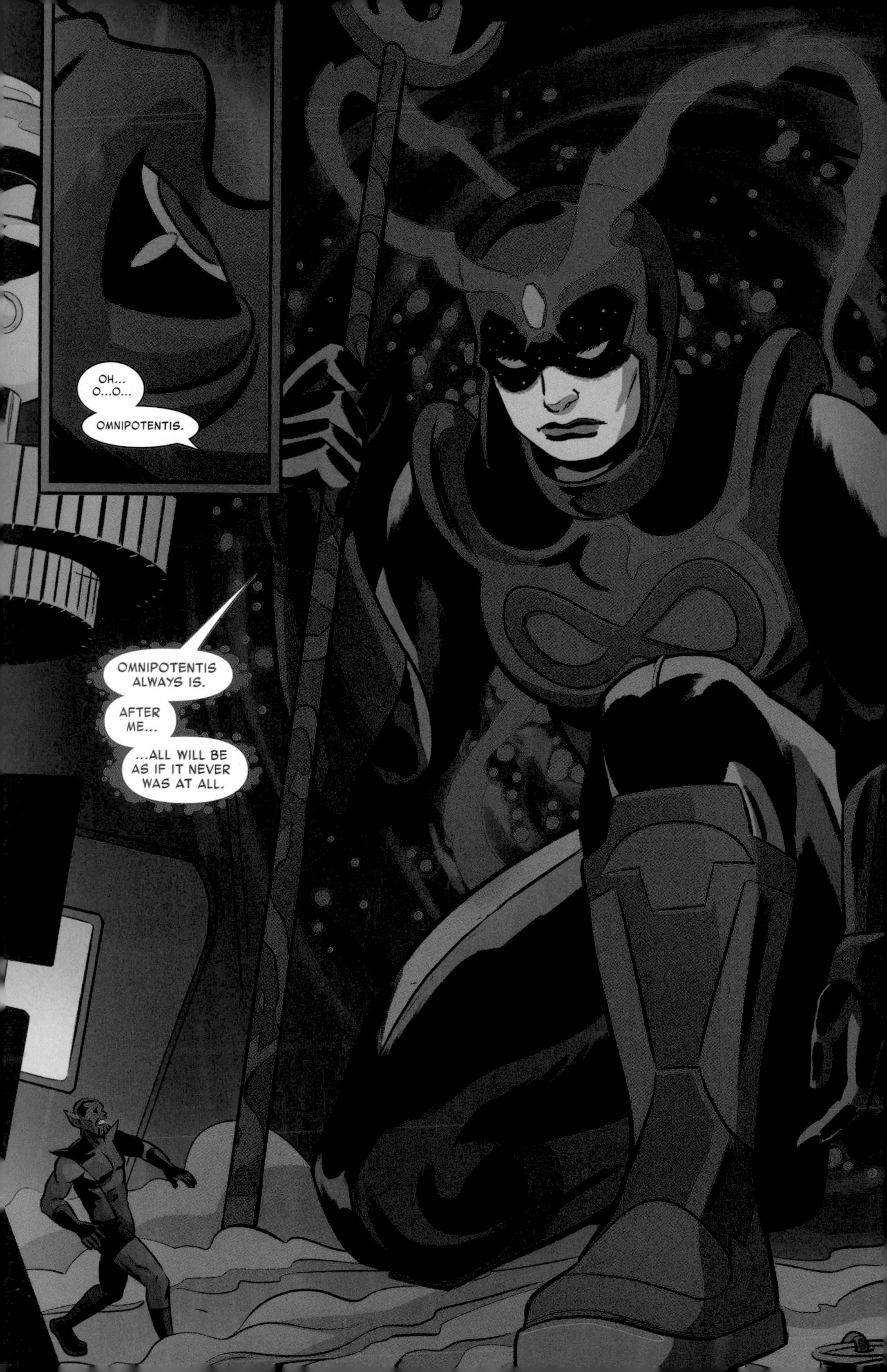
OH... O...O...
OMNIPOTENTIS.
OMNIPOTENTIS ALWAYS IS.
AFTER ME...
...ALL WILL BE AS IF IT NEVER WAS AT ALL.

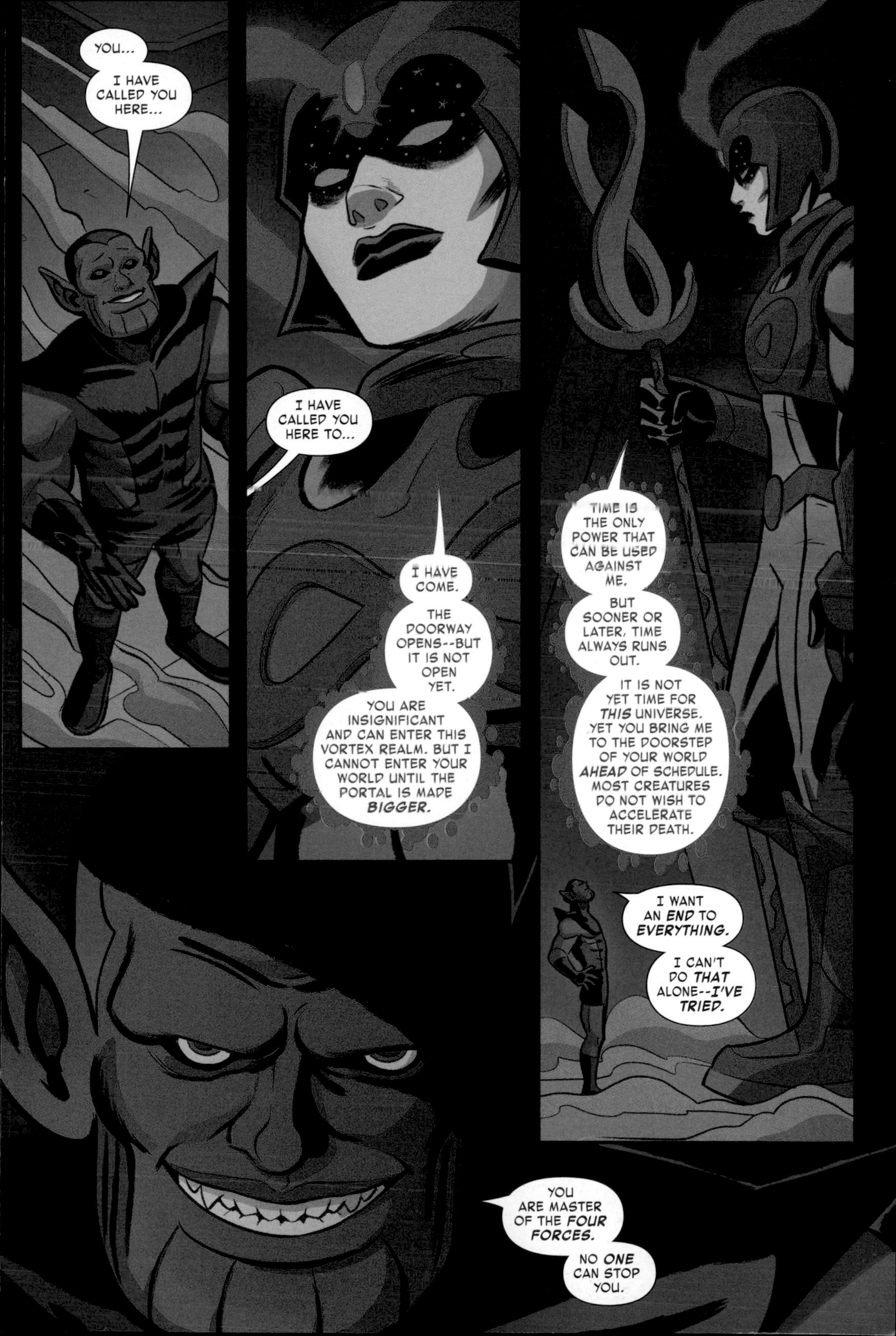
YOU...
I HAVE CALLED YOU HERE...
I HAVE CALLED YOU HERE TO...
I HAVE COME.
THE DOORWAY OPENS--BUT IT IS NOT OPEN YET.
YOU ARE INSIGNIFICANT AND CAN ENTER THIS VORTEX REALM. BUT I CANNOT ENTER YOUR WORLD UNTIL THE PORTAL IS MADE BIGGER.
TIME IS THE ONLY POWER THAT CAN BE USED AGAINST ME.
BUT SOONER OR LATER, TIME ALWAYS RUNS OUT.
IT IS NOT YET TIME FOR THIS UNIVERSE. YET YOU BRING ME TO THE DOORSTEP OF YOUR WORLD AHEAD OF SCHEDULE. MOST CREATURES DO NOT WISH TO ACCELERATE THEIR DEATH.
I WANT AN END TO EVERYTHING.
I CAN'T DO THAT ALONE--I'VE TRIED.
YOU ARE MASTER OF THE FOUR FORCES.
NO ONE CAN STOP YOU.

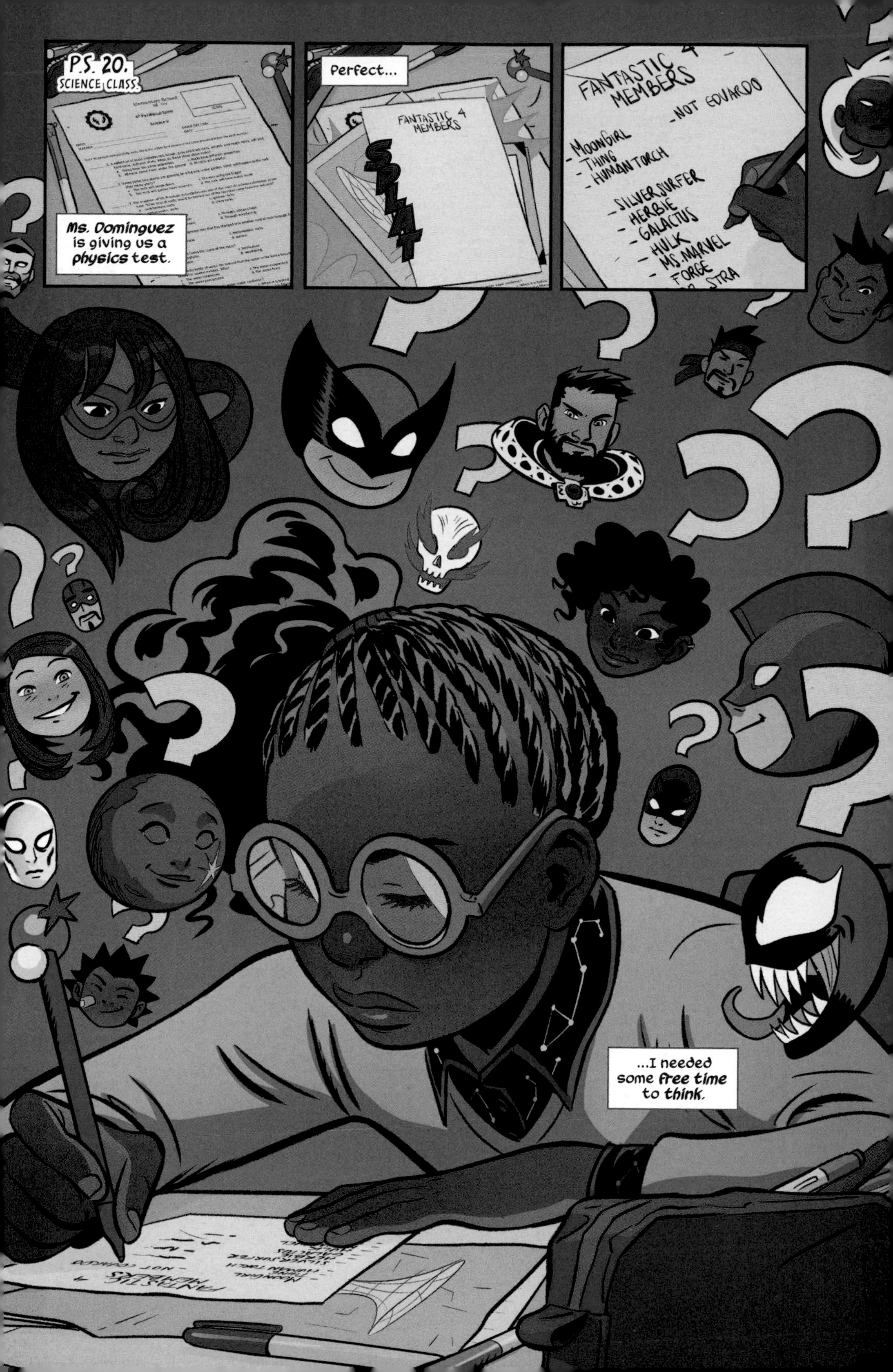
P.S. 20.
SCIENCE CLASS.
Ms. Dominguez is giving us a physics test.
Perfect...
FANTASTIC 4 MEMBERS
SPLAT
FANTASTIC 4 MEMBERS
- NOT EDUARDO
- MOONGIRL
- THING
- HUMAN TORCH
- SILVER SURFER
- HERBIE
- GALACTUS
- HULK
- MS. MARVEL
- FORGE
...I needed some free time to think.

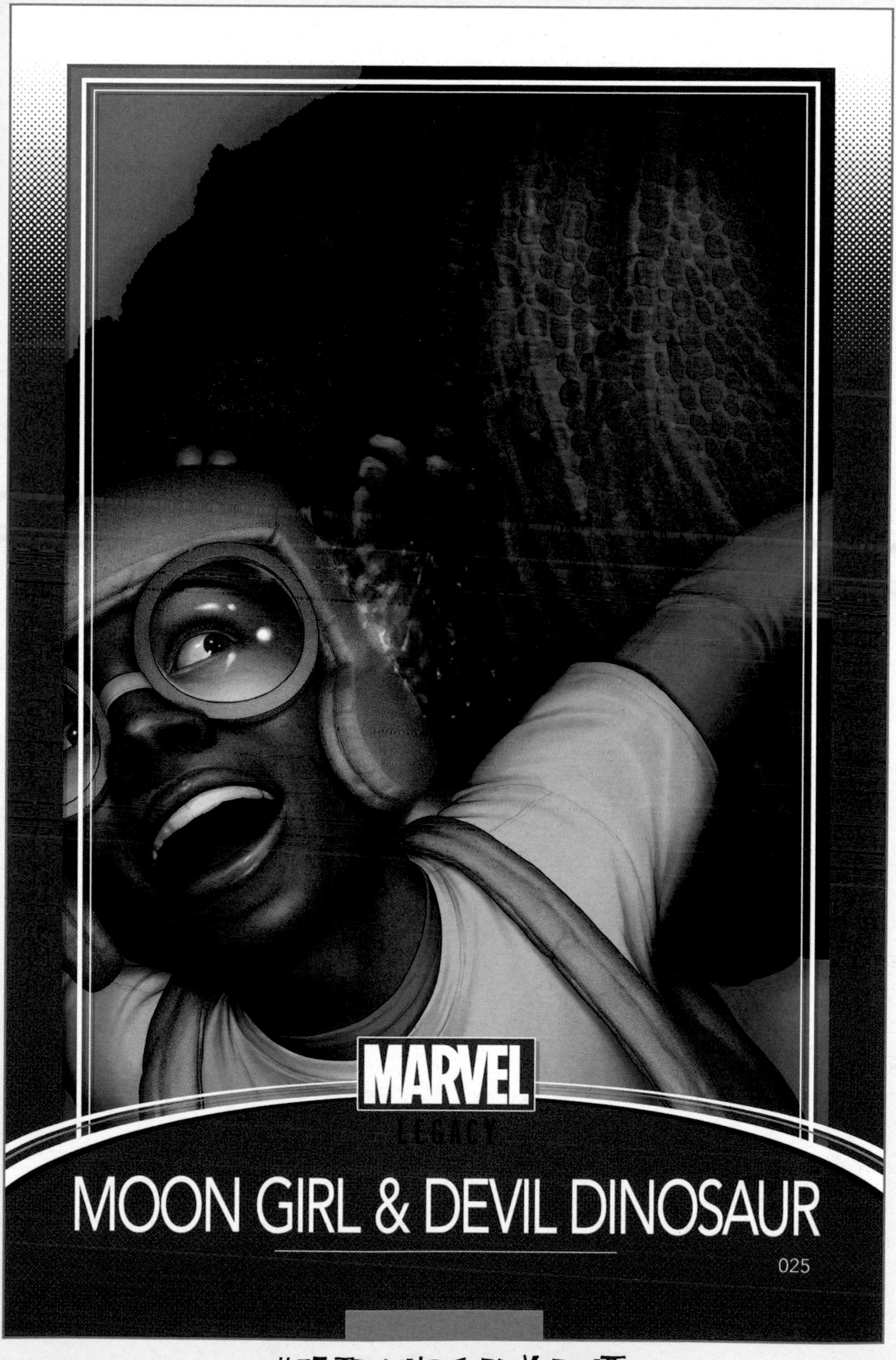
MARVEL
LEGACY
MOON GIRL & DEVIL DINOSAUR
025

#25 TRADING CARD VARIANT
BY JOHN TYLER CHRISTOPHER

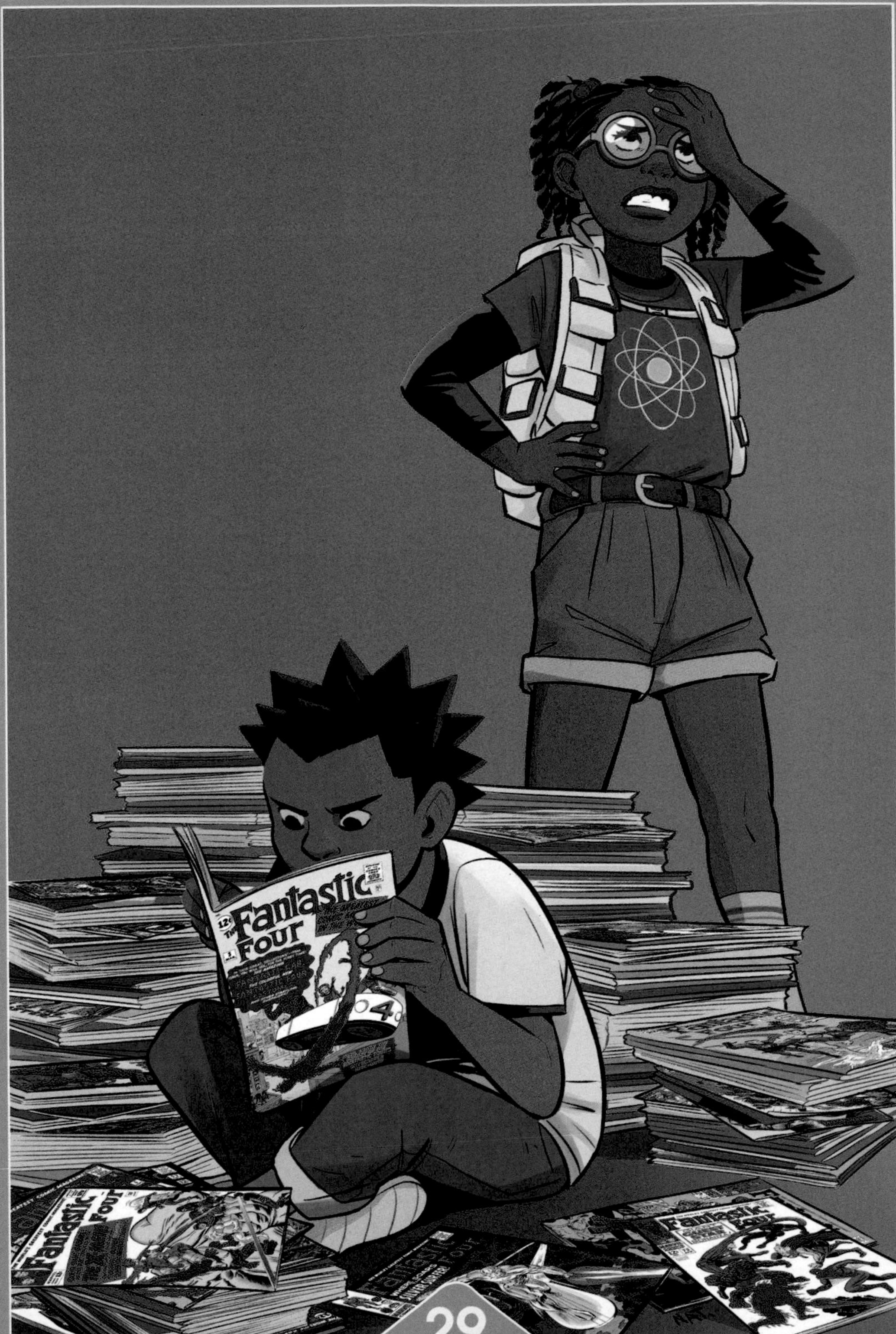
Fantastic Four

29

"The Four Corners of the Omniverse"

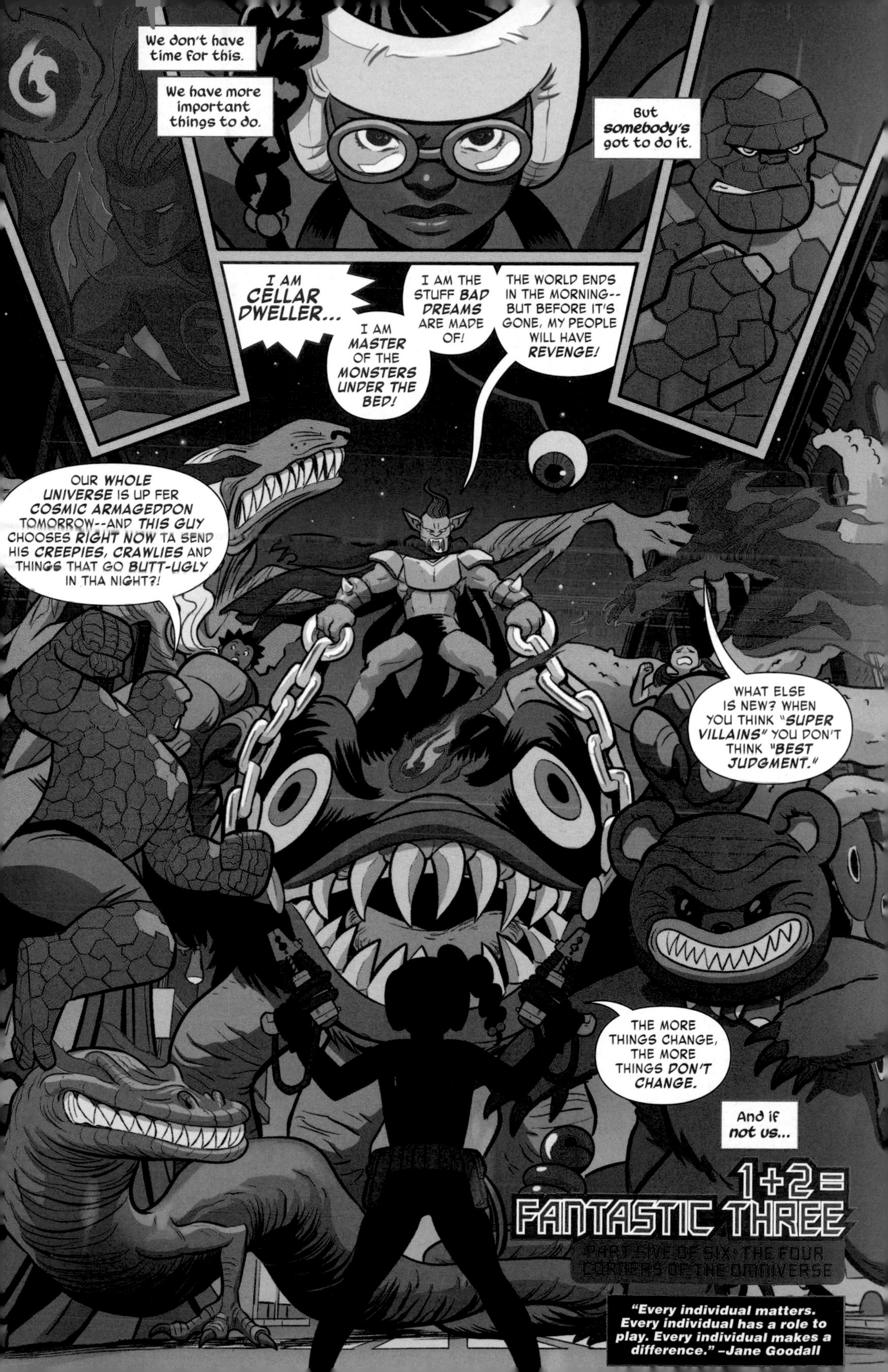

We don't have time for this.
We have more important things to do.
But somebody's got to do it.
I AM CELLAR DWELLER...
I AM MASTER OF THE MONSTERS UNDER THE BED!
I AM THE STUFF BAD DREAMS ARE MADE OF!
THE WORLD ENDS IN THE MORNING--BUT BEFORE IT'S GONE, MY PEOPLE WILL HAVE REVENGE!
OUR WHOLE UNIVERSE IS UP FER COSMIC ARMAGEDDON TOMORROW--AND THIS GUY CHOOSES RIGHT NOW TA SEND HIS CREEPIES, CRAWLIES AND THINGS THAT GO BUTT-UGLY IN THA NIGHT?!
WHAT ELSE IS NEW? WHEN YOU THINK "SUPER VILLAINS" YOU DON'T THINK "BEST JUDGMENT."
THE MORE THINGS CHANGE, THE MORE THINGS DON'T CHANGE.
And if not us...
1+2= FANTASTIC THREE
PART FIVE OF SIX: THE FOUR CORNERS OF THE OMNIVERSE
"Every individual matters. Every individual has a role to play. Every individual makes a difference." –Jane Goodall

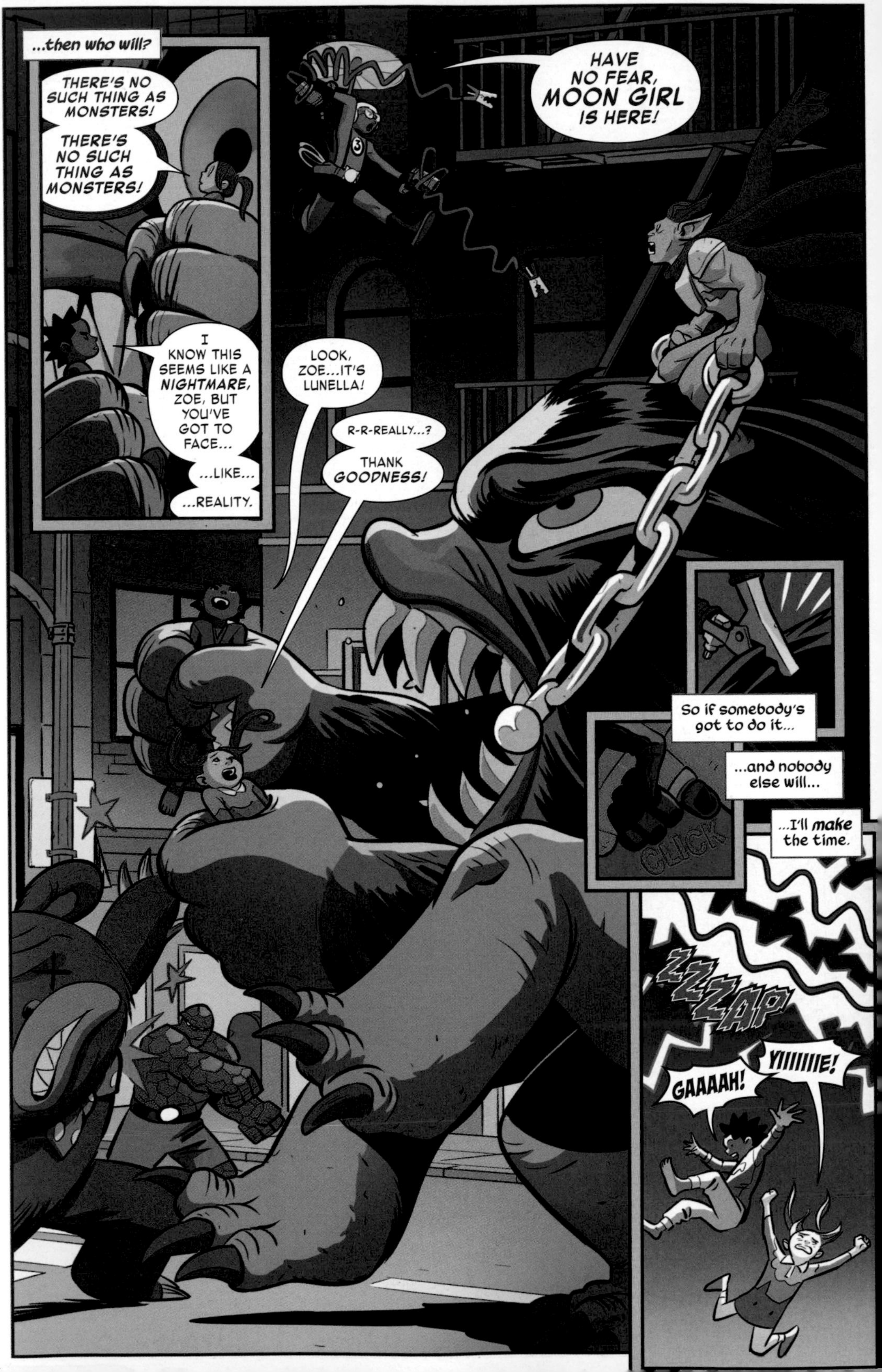
...then who will?
THERE'S NO SUCH THING AS MONSTERS!
THERE'S NO SUCH THING AS MONSTERS!
I KNOW THIS SEEMS LIKE A NIGHTMARE, ZOE, BUT YOU'VE GOT TO FACE...
...LIKE...
...REALITY.
HAVE NO FEAR, MOON GIRL IS HERE!
LOOK, ZOE...IT'S LUNELLA!
R-R-REALLY...?
THANK GOODNESS!
So if somebody's got to do it...
...and nobody else will...
CLICK
...I'll make the time.
ZZZAP
GAAAAH!
YIIIIIIIE!

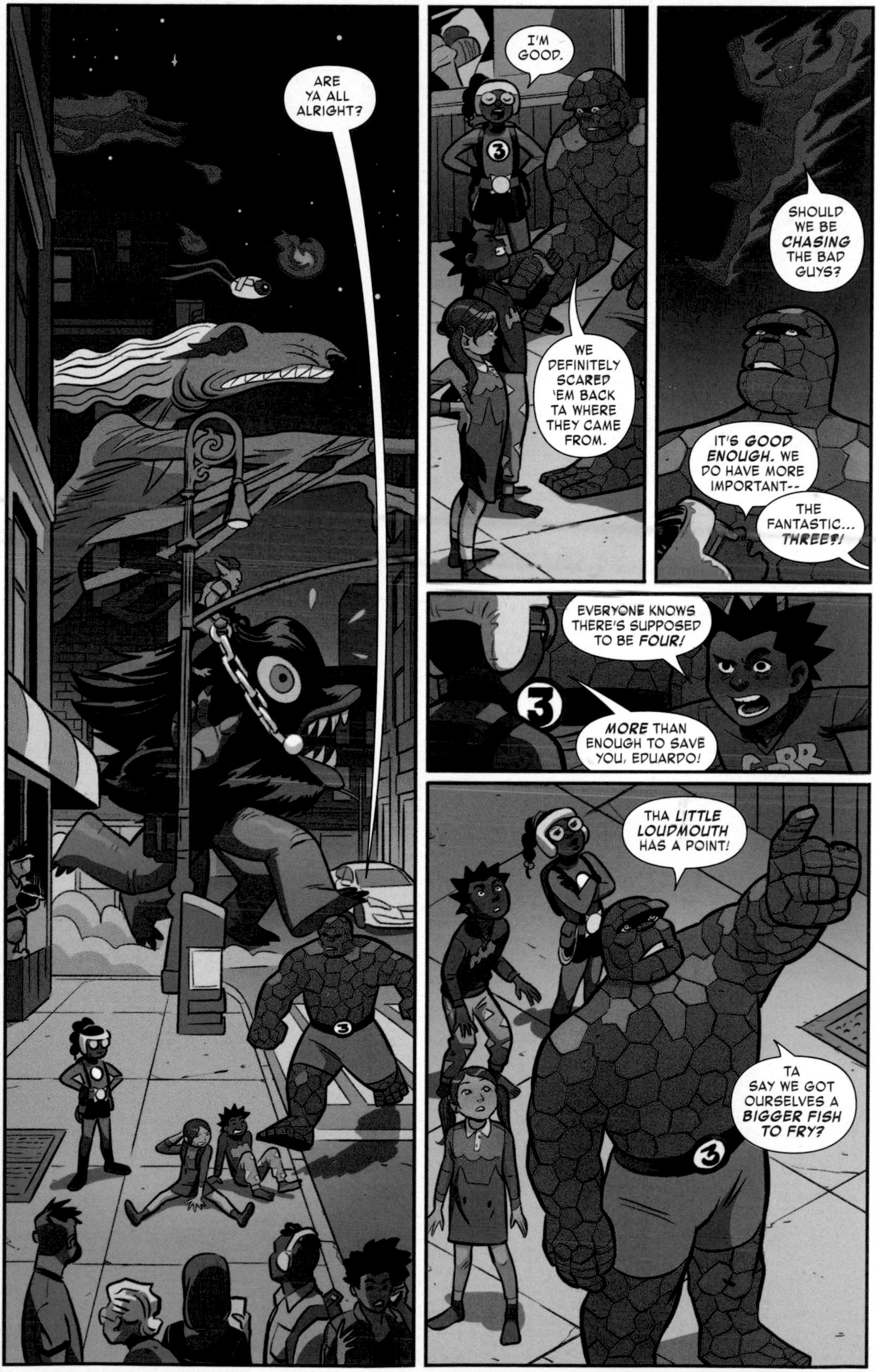
ARE YA ALL ALRIGHT?
I'M GOOD.
WE DEFINITELY SCARED 'EM BACK TA WHERE THEY CAME FROM.
SHOULD WE BE *CHASING* THE BAD GUYS?
IT'S *GOOD ENOUGH.* WE DO HAVE MORE IMPORTANT--
THE FANTASTIC... *THREE?!*
EVERYONE KNOWS THERE'S SUPPOSED TO BE *FOUR!*
MORE THAN ENOUGH TO SAVE YOU, EDUARDO!
THA *LITTLE LOUDMOUTH* HAS A POINT!
TA SAY WE GOT OURSELVES A *BIGGER FISH TO FRY?*

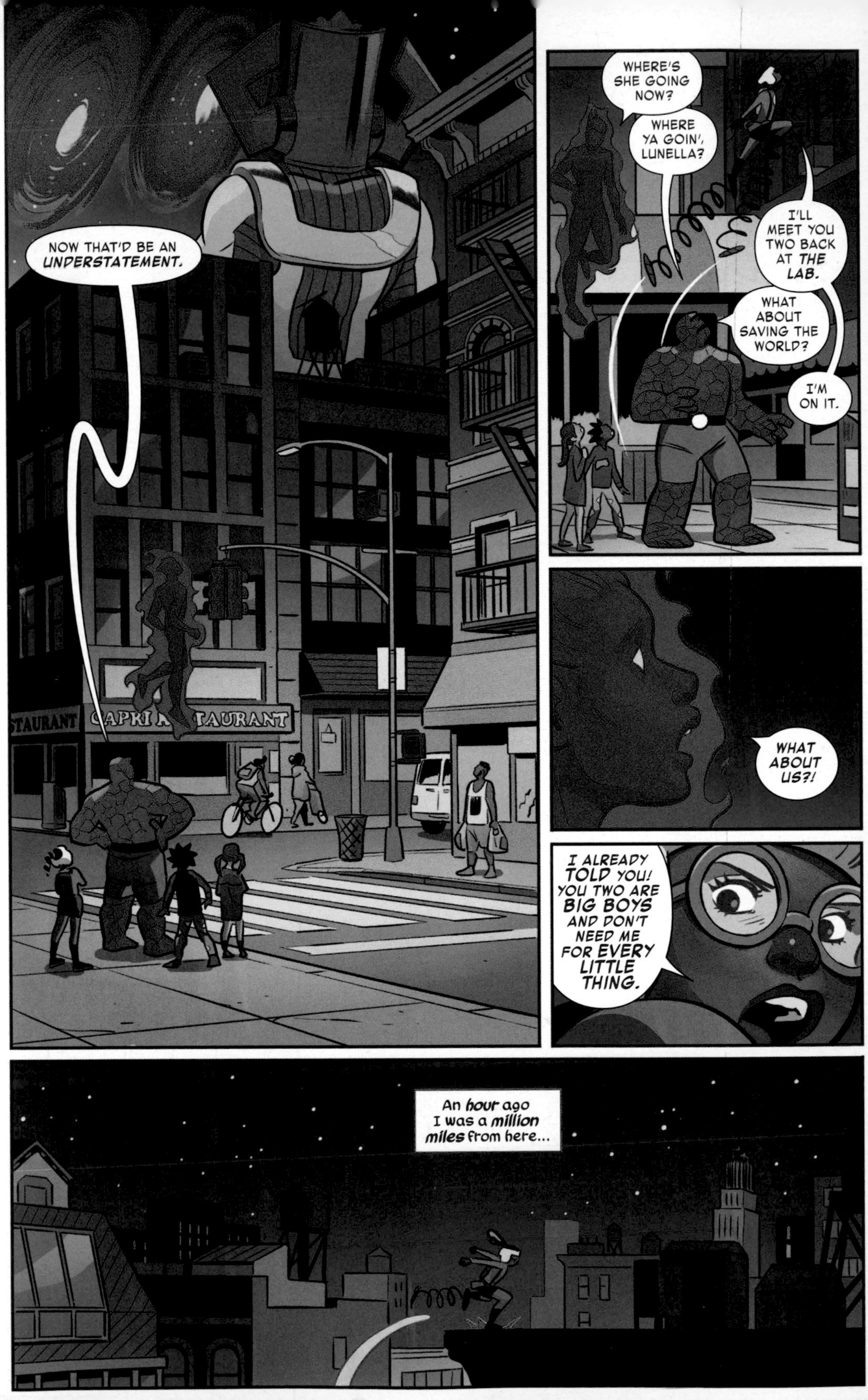
NOW THAT'D BE AN UNDERSTATEMENT.
STAURANT
CAPRI R TAURANT
WHERE'S SHE GOING NOW?
WHERE YA GOIN', LUNELLA?
I'LL MEET YOU TWO BACK AT THE LAB.
WHAT ABOUT SAVING THE WORLD?
I'M ON IT.
WHAT ABOUT US?!
I ALREADY TOLD YOU! YOU TWO ARE BIG BOYS AND DON'T NEED ME FOR EVERY LITTLE THING.
An hour ago I was a million miles from here...

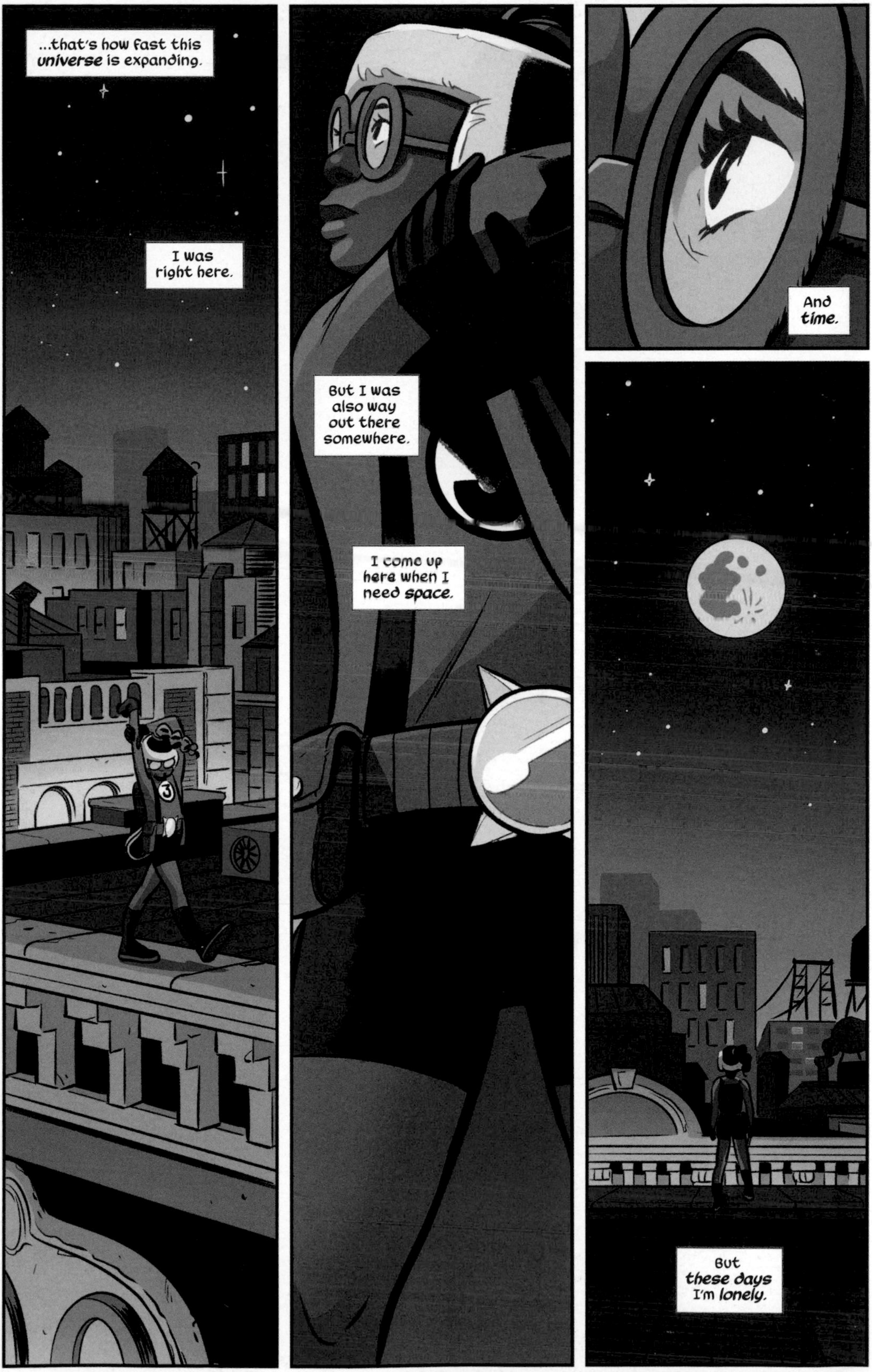
...that's how fast this universe is expanding.
I was right here.
But I was also way out there somewhere.
I come up here when I need space.
And time.
But these days I'm lonely.

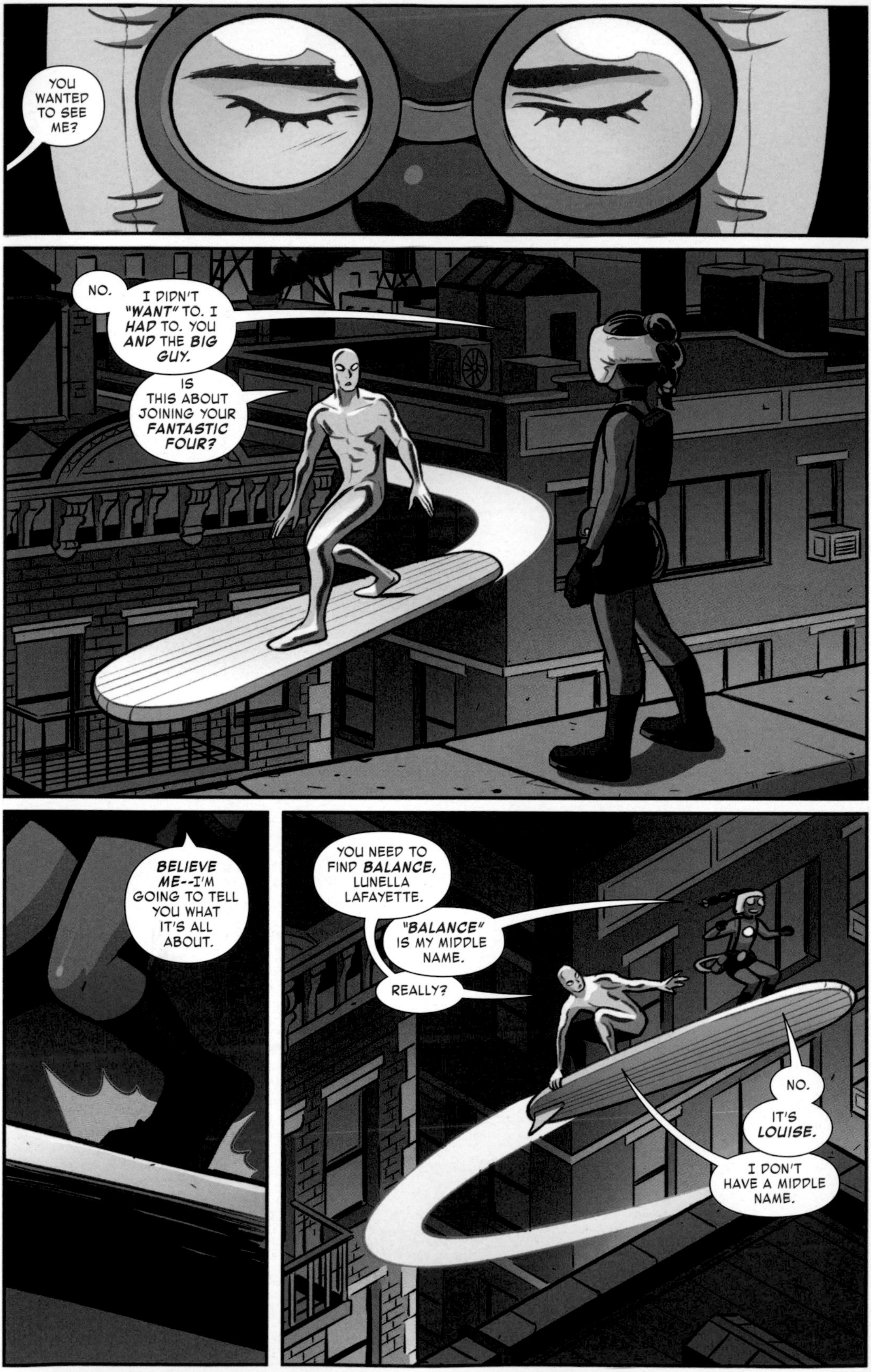
YOU WANTED TO SEE ME?
NO.
I DIDN'T "WANT" TO. I HAD TO. YOU AND THE BIG GUY.
IS THIS ABOUT JOINING YOUR FANTASTIC FOUR?
BELIEVE ME--I'M GOING TO TELL YOU WHAT IT'S ALL ABOUT.
YOU NEED TO FIND BALANCE, LUNELLA LAFAYETTE.
"BALANCE" IS MY MIDDLE NAME.
REALLY?
NO.
IT'S LOUISE.
I DON'T HAVE A MIDDLE NAME.

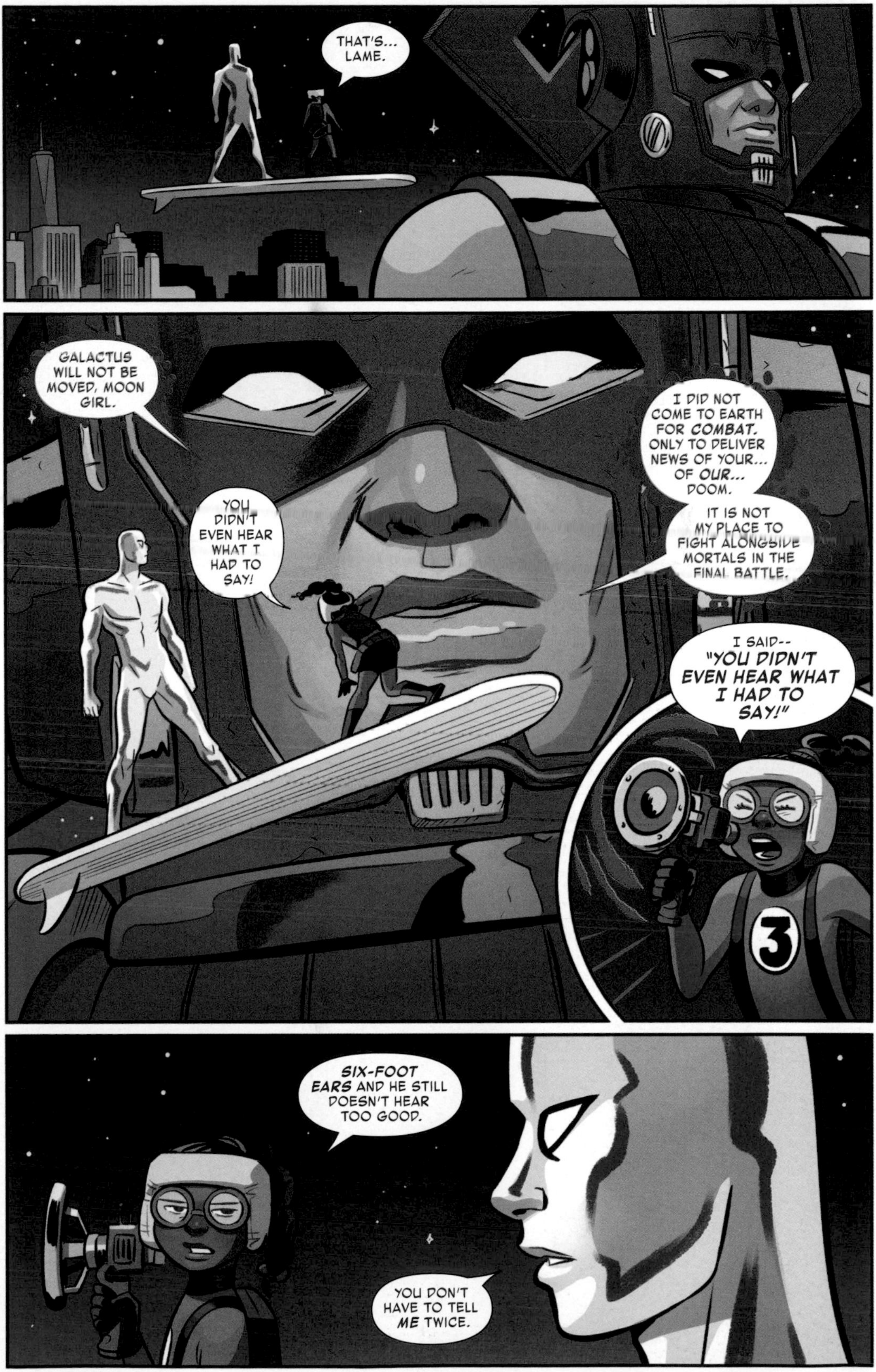
THAT'S... LAME.
GALACTUS WILL NOT BE MOVED, MOON GIRL.
I DID NOT COME TO EARTH FOR COMBAT. ONLY TO DELIVER NEWS OF YOUR... OF OUR... DOOM.
YOU DIDN'T EVEN HEAR WHAT I HAD TO SAY!
IT IS NOT MY PLACE TO FIGHT ALONGSIDE MORTALS IN THE FINAL BATTLE.
I SAID-- "YOU DIDN'T EVEN HEAR WHAT I HAD TO SAY!"
SIX-FOOT EARS AND HE STILL DOESN'T HEAR TOO GOOD.
YOU DON'T HAVE TO TELL ME TWICE.

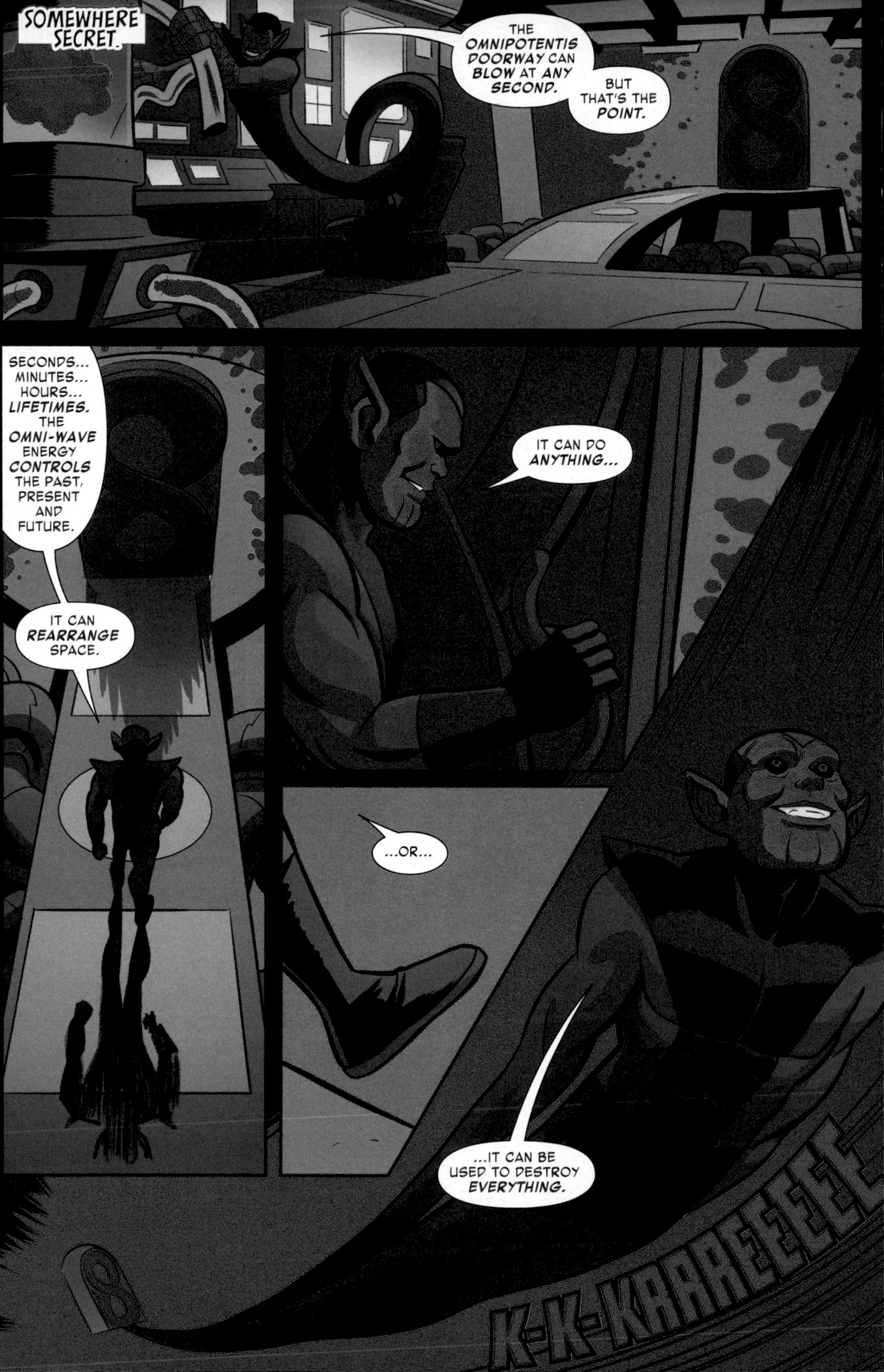
SOMEWHERE SECRET.
THE OMNIPOTENTIS DOORWAY CAN BLOW AT ANY SECOND.
BUT THAT'S THE POINT.
SECONDS... MINUTES... HOURS... LIFETIMES. THE OMNI-WAVE ENERGY CONTROLS THE PAST, PRESENT AND FUTURE.
IT CAN REARRANGE SPACE.
IT CAN DO ANYTHING...
...OR...
...IT CAN BE USED TO DESTROY EVERYTHING.
K-K-KARREEEEE

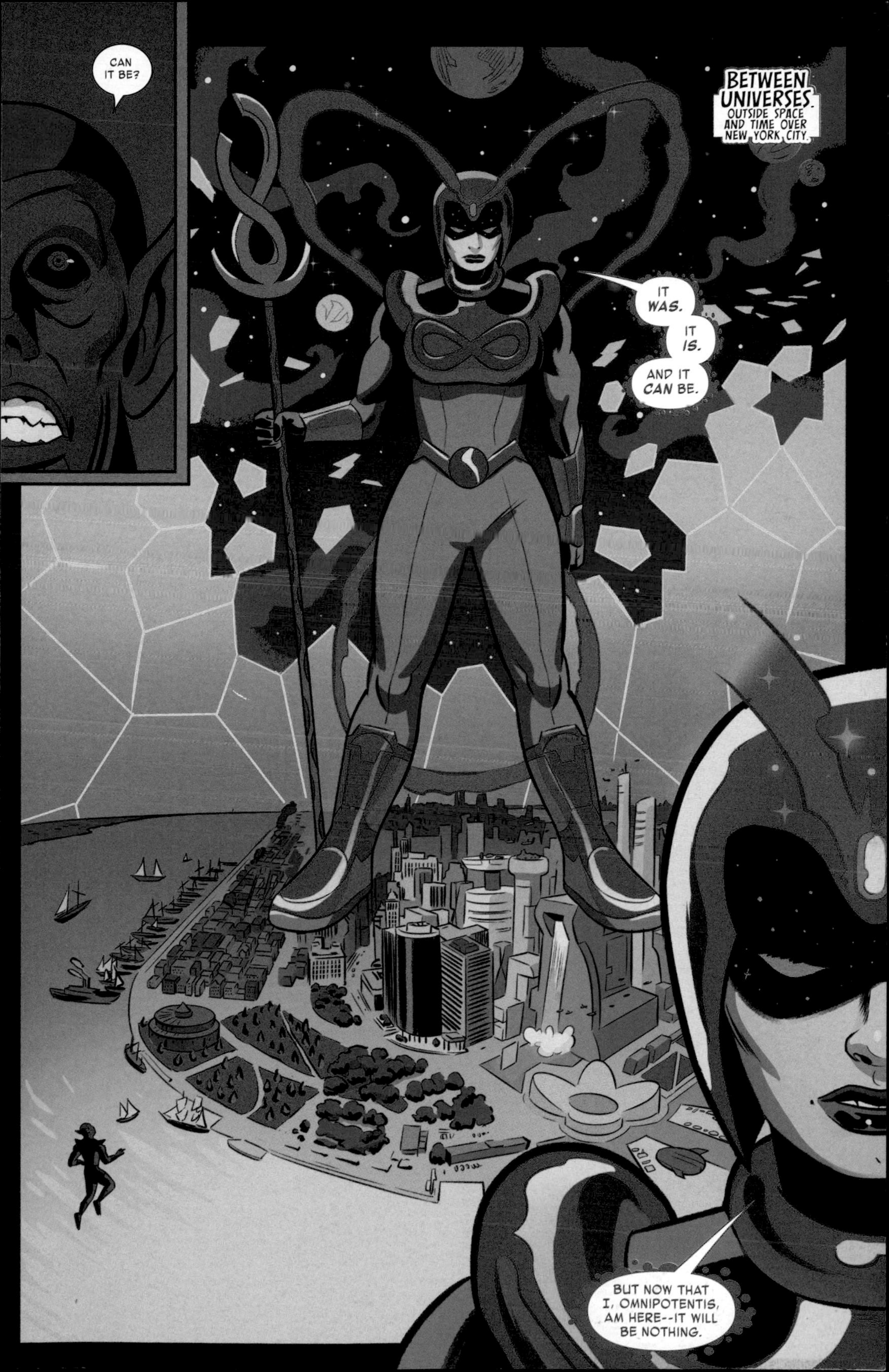
CAN IT BE?
BETWEEN UNIVERSES.
OUTSIDE SPACE AND TIME OVER NEW YORK CITY.
IT WAS.
IT IS.
AND IT CAN BE.
BUT NOW THAT I, OMNIPOTENTIS, AM HERE--IT WILL BE NOTHING.

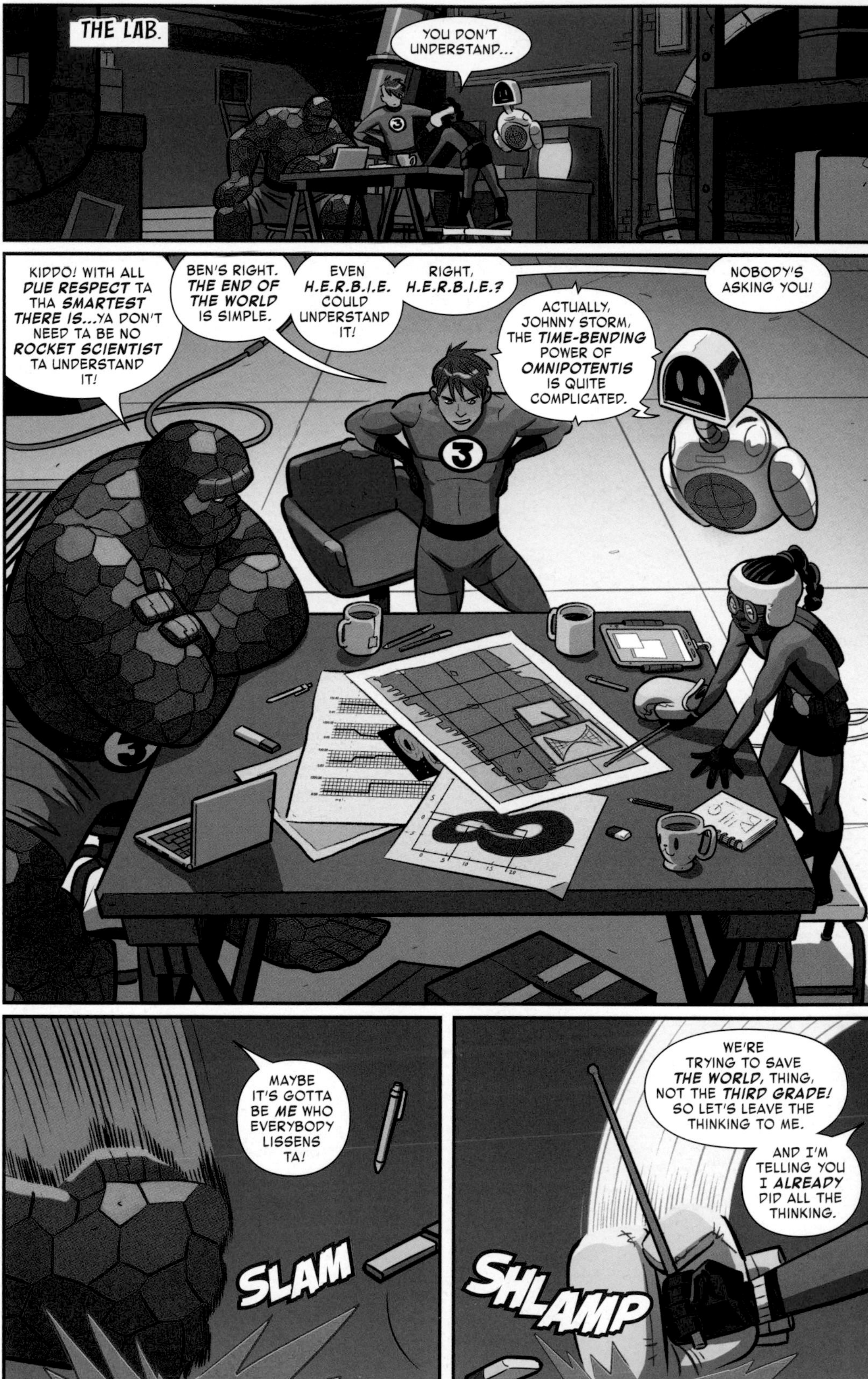
THE LAB.
YOU DON'T UNDERSTAND...
KIDDO! WITH ALL DUE RESPECT TA THA SMARTEST THERE IS...YA DON'T NEED TA BE NO ROCKET SCIENTIST TA UNDERSTAND IT!
BEN'S RIGHT. THE END OF THE WORLD IS SIMPLE.
EVEN H.E.R.B.I.E. COULD UNDERSTAND IT!
RIGHT, H.E.R.B.I.E.?
ACTUALLY, JOHNNY STORM, THE TIME-BENDING POWER OF OMNIPOTENTIS IS QUITE COMPLICATED.
NOBODY'S ASKING YOU!
MAYBE IT'S GOTTA BE ME WHO EVERYBODY LISSENS TA!
SLAM
WE'RE TRYING TO SAVE THE WORLD, THING, NOT THE THIRD GRADE! SO LET'S LEAVE THE THINKING TO ME.
AND I'M TELLING YOU I ALREADY DID ALL THE THINKING.
SHLAMP

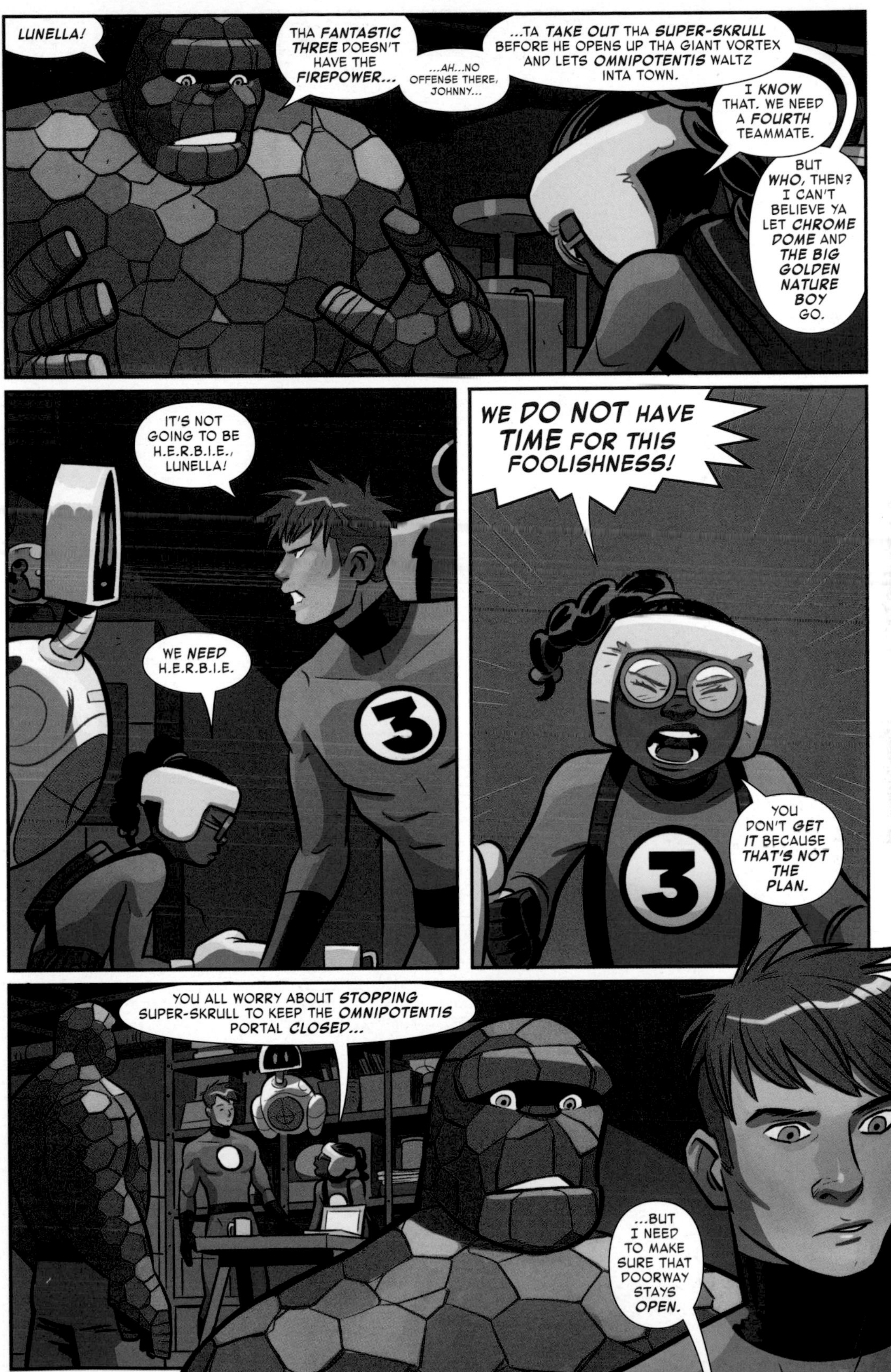
LUNELLA!
THA FANTASTIC THREE DOESN'T HAVE THE FIREPOWER...
...AH...NO OFFENSE THERE, JOHNNY...
...TA TAKE OUT THA SUPER-SKRULL BEFORE HE OPENS UP THA GIANT VORTEX AND LETS OMNIPOTENTIS WALTZ INTA TOWN.
I KNOW THAT. WE NEED A FOURTH TEAMMATE.
BUT WHO, THEN? I CAN'T BELIEVE YA LET CHROME DOME AND THE BIG GOLDEN NATURE BOY GO.
IT'S NOT GOING TO BE H.E.R.B.I.E., LUNELLA!
WE NEED H.E.R.B.I.E.
WE DO NOT HAVE TIME FOR THIS FOOLISHNESS!
YOU DON'T GET IT BECAUSE THAT'S NOT THE PLAN.
YOU ALL WORRY ABOUT STOPPING SUPER-SKRULL TO KEEP THE OMNIPOTENTIS PORTAL CLOSED...
...BUT I NEED TO MAKE SURE THAT DOORWAY STAYS OPEN.

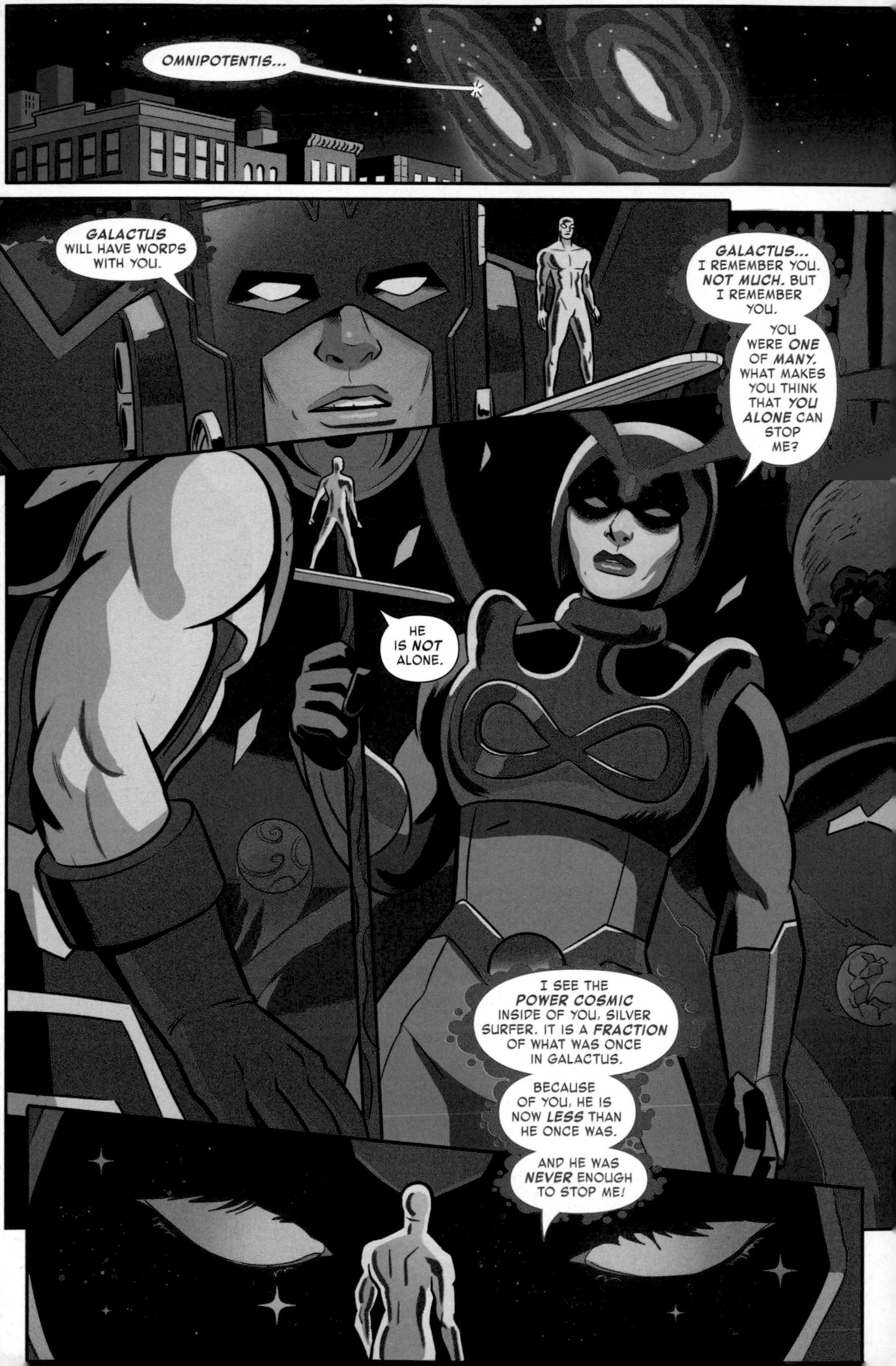
OMNIPOTENTIS...
GALACTUS WILL HAVE WORDS WITH YOU.
GALACTUS... I REMEMBER YOU. NOT MUCH. BUT I REMEMBER YOU.
YOU WERE ONE OF MANY. WHAT MAKES YOU THINK THAT YOU ALONE CAN STOP ME?
HE IS NOT ALONE.
I SEE THE POWER COSMIC INSIDE OF YOU, SILVER SURFER. IT IS A FRACTION OF WHAT WAS ONCE IN GALACTUS.
BECAUSE OF YOU, HE IS NOW LESS THAN HE ONCE WAS.
AND HE WAS NEVER ENOUGH TO STOP ME!

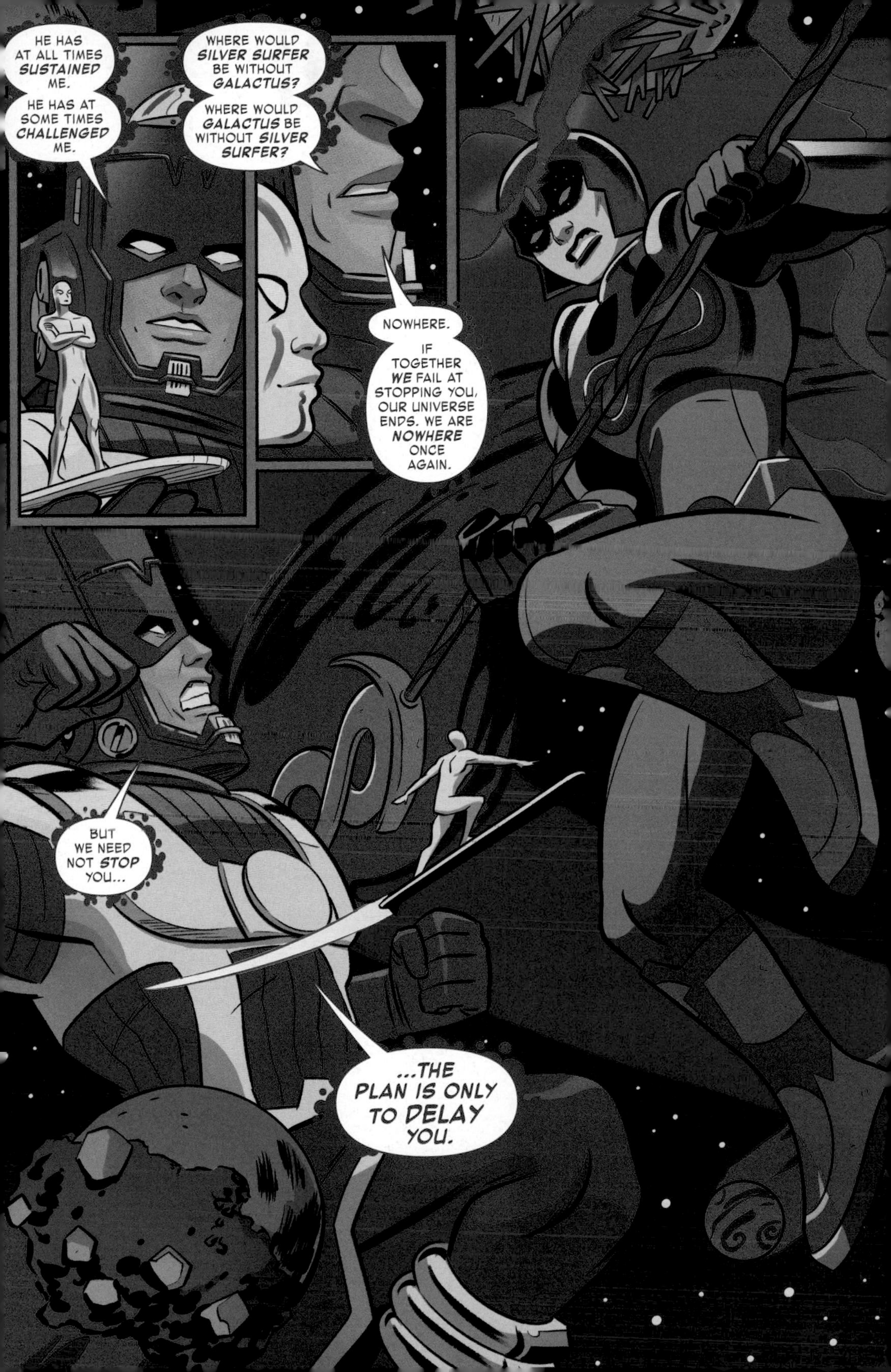
HE HAS AT ALL TIMES SUSTAINED ME.
HE HAS AT SOME TIMES CHALLENGED ME.
WHERE WOULD SILVER SURFER BE WITHOUT GALACTUS?
WHERE WOULD GALACTUS BE WITHOUT SILVER SURFER?
NOWHERE.
IF TOGETHER WE FAIL AT STOPPING YOU, OUR UNIVERSE ENDS. WE ARE NOWHERE ONCE AGAIN.
BUT WE NEED NOT STOP YOU...
...THE PLAN IS ONLY TO DELAY YOU.

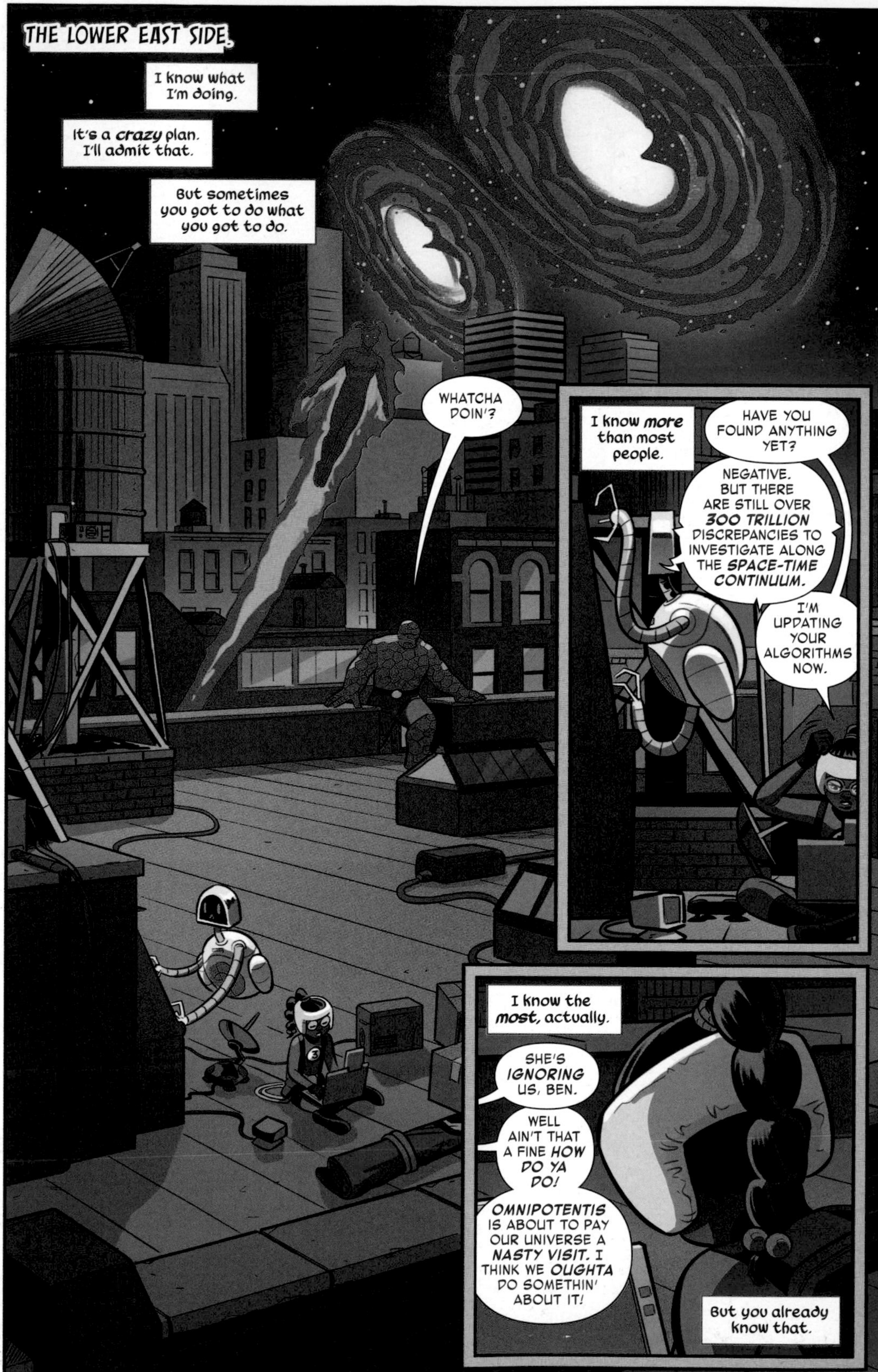
THE LOWER EAST SIDE.
I know what I'm doing.
It's a crazy plan. I'll admit that.
But sometimes you got to do what you got to do.
WHATCHA DOIN'?
I know more than most people.
HAVE YOU FOUND ANYTHING YET?
NEGATIVE. BUT THERE ARE STILL OVER 300 TRILLION DISCREPANCIES TO INVESTIGATE ALONG THE SPACE-TIME CONTINUUM.
I'M UPDATING YOUR ALGORITHMS NOW.
I know the most, actually.
SHE'S IGNORING US, BEN.
WELL AIN'T THAT A FINE HOW DO YA DO!
OMNIPOTENTIS IS ABOUT TO PAY OUR UNIVERSE A NASTY VISIT. I THINK WE OUGHTA DO SOMETHIN' ABOUT IT!
But you already know that.

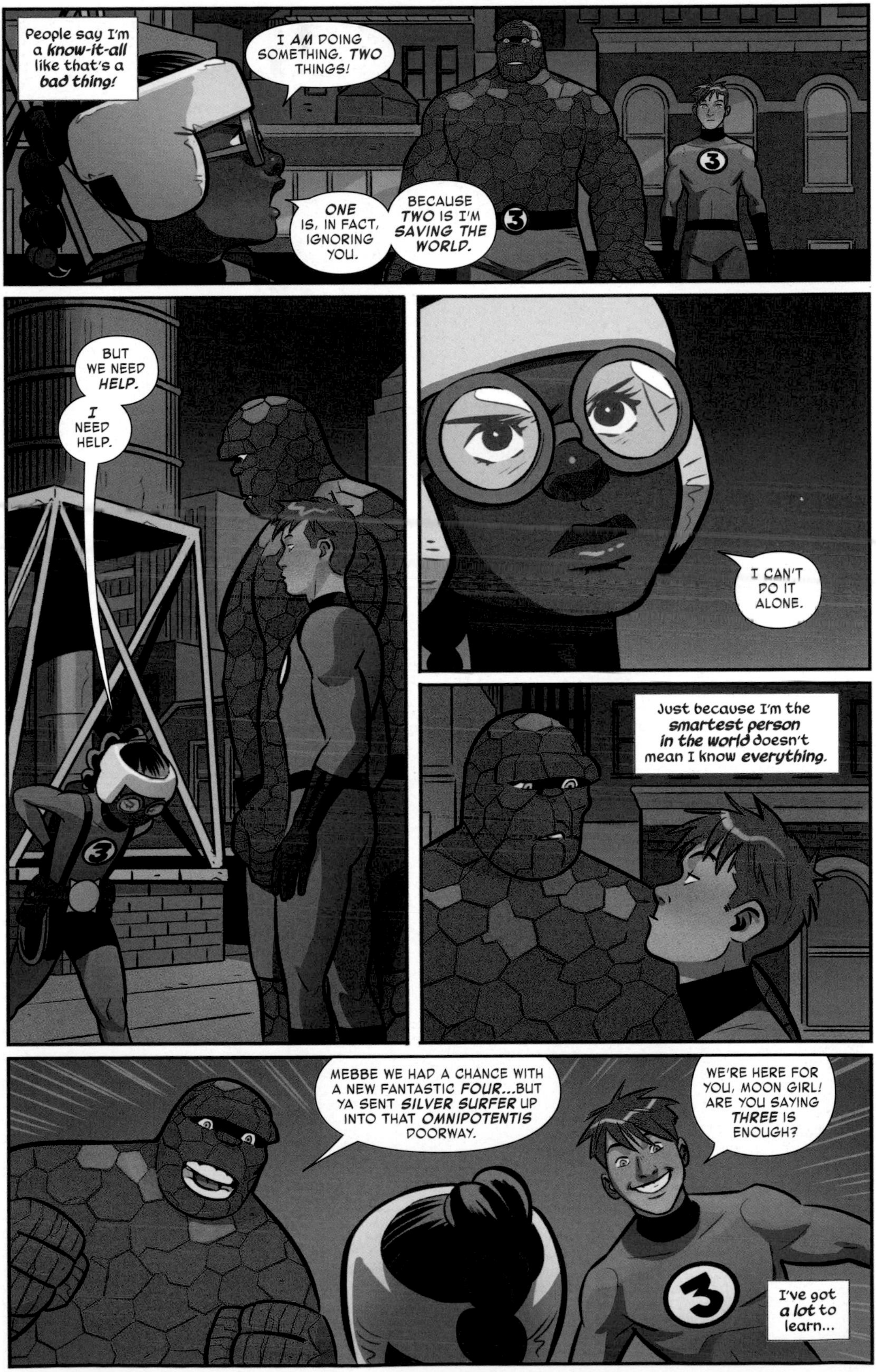

People say I'm a *know-it-all* like that's a *bad thing!*
I *AM* DOING SOMETHING. *TWO* THINGS!
ONE IS, IN FACT, IGNORING YOU.
BECAUSE *TWO* IS I'M *SAVING THE WORLD.*
BUT WE NEED *HELP.*
I NEED HELP.
I CAN'T DO IT ALONE.
Just because I'm the *smartest person in the world* doesn't mean I know *everything.*
MEBBE WE HAD A CHANCE WITH A NEW FANTASTIC *FOUR*...BUT YA SENT *SILVER SURFER* UP INTO THAT *OMNIPOTENTIS* DOORWAY.
WE'RE HERE FOR YOU, MOON GIRL! ARE YOU SAYING *THREE* IS ENOUGH?
I've got *a lot* to learn...

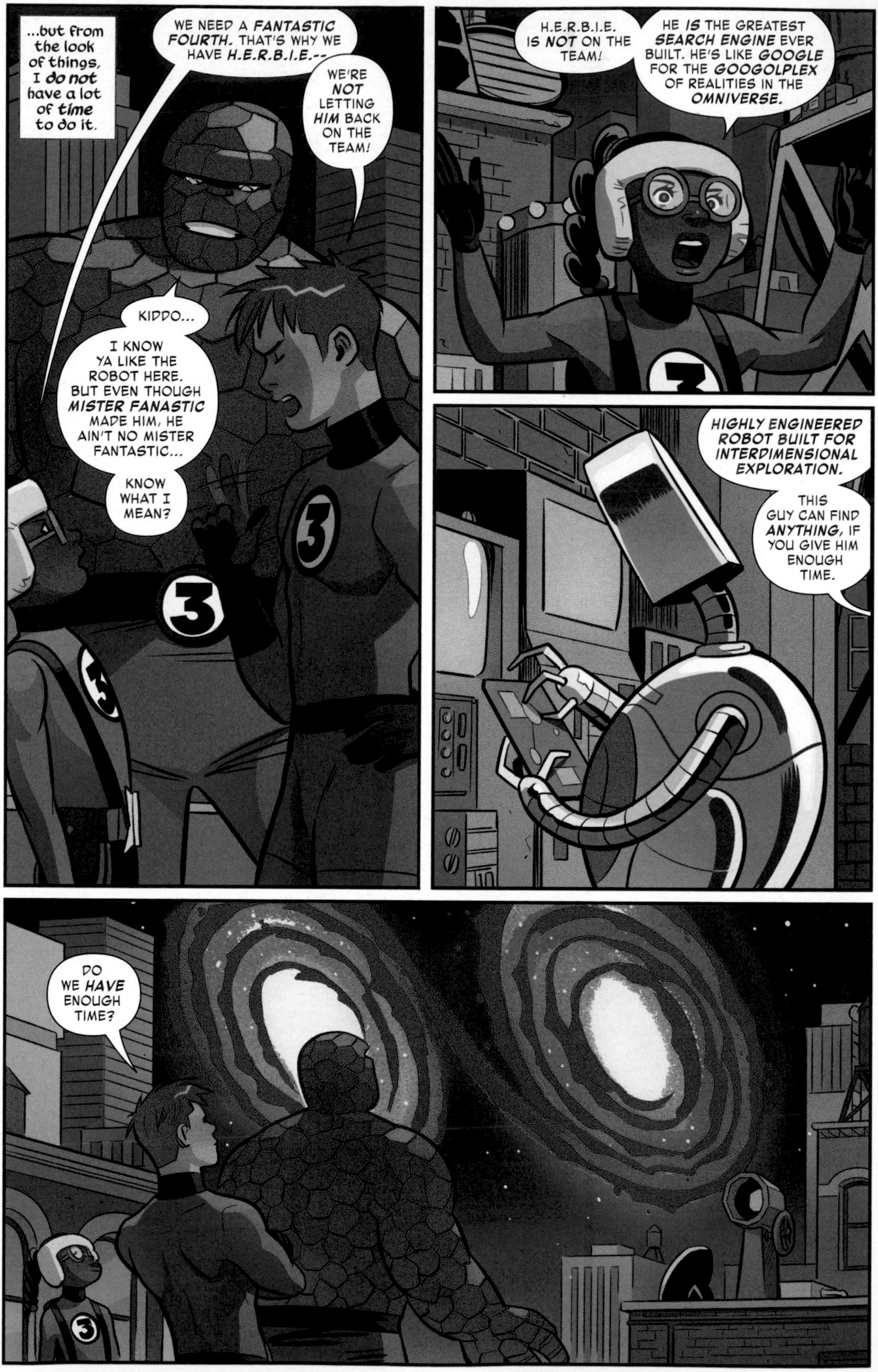

...but from the look of things, I *do not* have a lot of *time* to do it.
WE NEED A *FANTASTIC FOURTH.* THAT'S WHY WE HAVE *H.E.R.B.I.E.*--
WE'RE *NOT* LETTING *HIM* BACK ON THE TEAM!
KIDDO...
I KNOW YA LIKE THE ROBOT HERE. BUT EVEN THOUGH *MISTER FANASTIC* MADE HIM, HE AIN'T NO MISTER FANTASTIC...
KNOW WHAT I MEAN?
H.E.R.B.I.E. IS *NOT* ON THE TEAM!
HE *IS* THE GREATEST *SEARCH ENGINE* EVER BUILT. HE'S LIKE *GOOGLE* FOR THE *GOOGOLPLEX* OF REALITIES IN THE *OMNIVERSE.*
HIGHLY ENGINEERED ROBOT BUILT FOR INTERDIMENSIONAL EXPLORATION.
THIS GUY CAN FIND *ANYTHING,* IF YOU GIVE HIM ENOUGH TIME.
DO WE *HAVE* ENOUGH TIME?

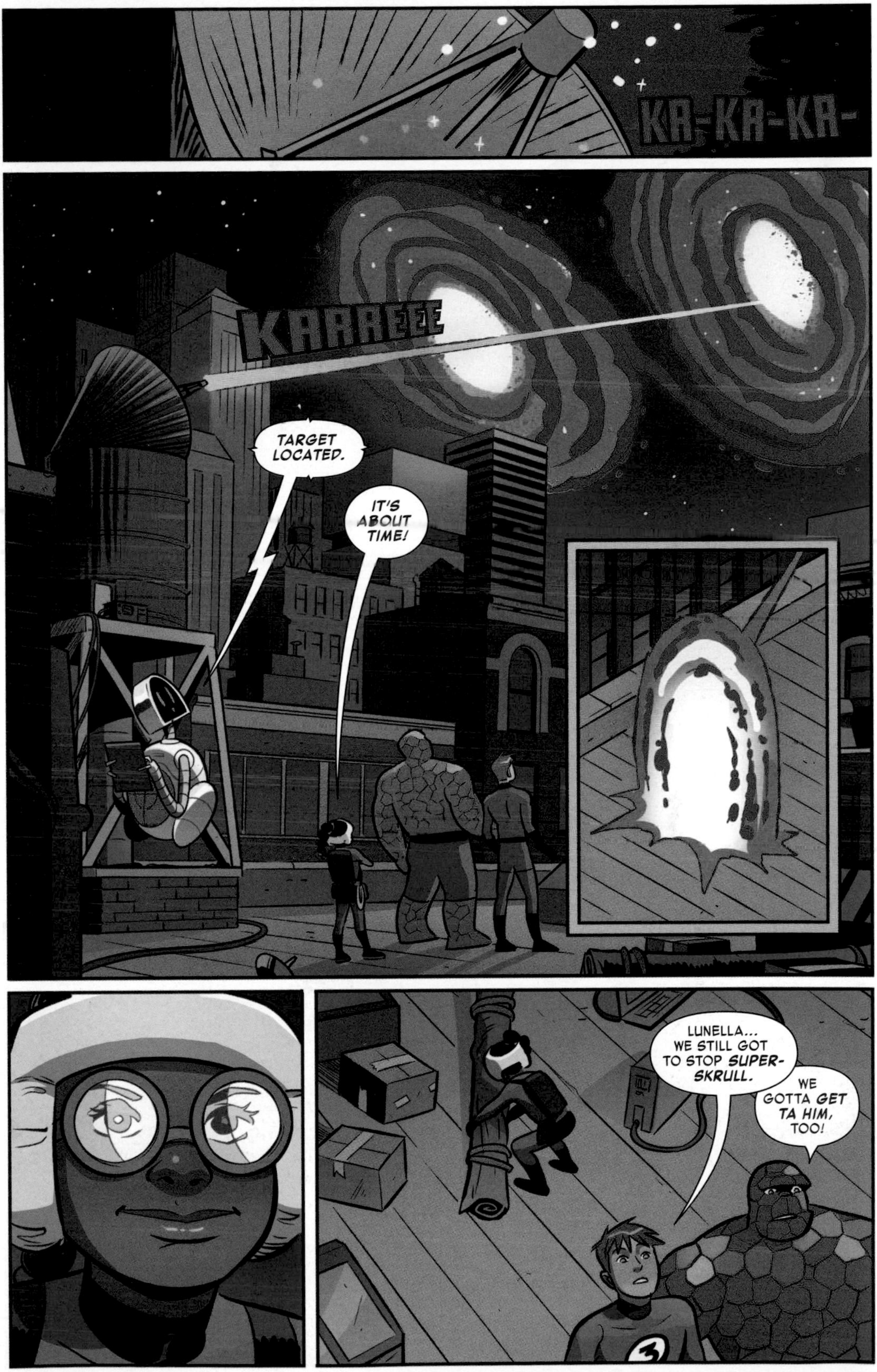
KA-KA-KA-
KARREEE
TARGET LOCATED.
IT'S ABOUT TIME!
LUNELLA... WE STILL GOT TO STOP SUPER-SKRULL.
WE GOTTA GET TA HIM, TOO!

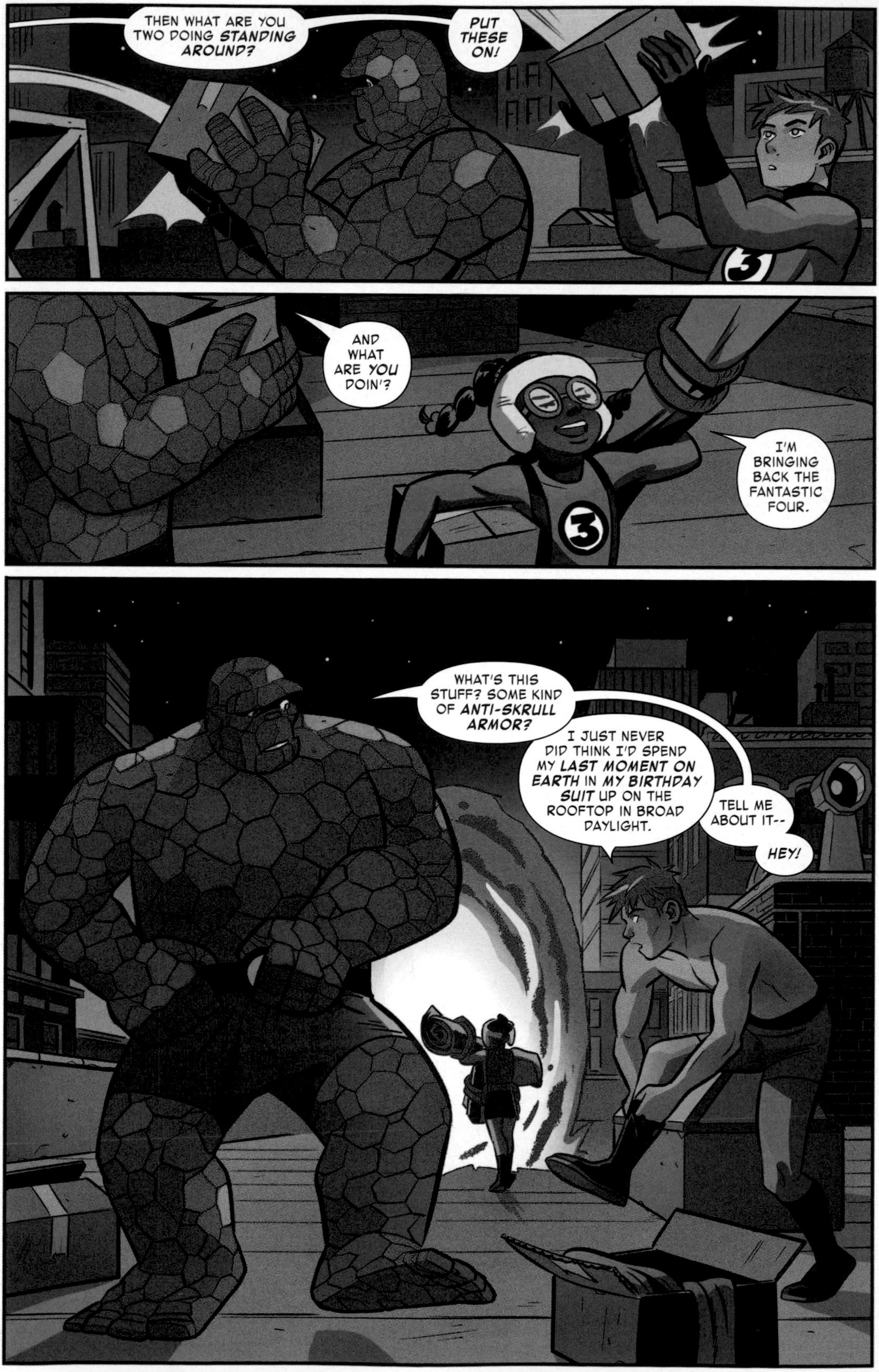
THEN WHAT ARE YOU TWO DOING STANDING AROUND?
PUT THESE ON!
AND WHAT ARE YOU DOIN'?
I'M BRINGING BACK THE FANTASTIC FOUR.
WHAT'S THIS STUFF? SOME KIND OF ANTI-SKRULL ARMOR?
I JUST NEVER DID THINK I'D SPEND MY LAST MOMENT ON EARTH IN MY BIRTHDAY SUIT UP ON THE ROOFTOP IN BROAD DAYLIGHT.
TELL ME ABOUT IT--
HEY!

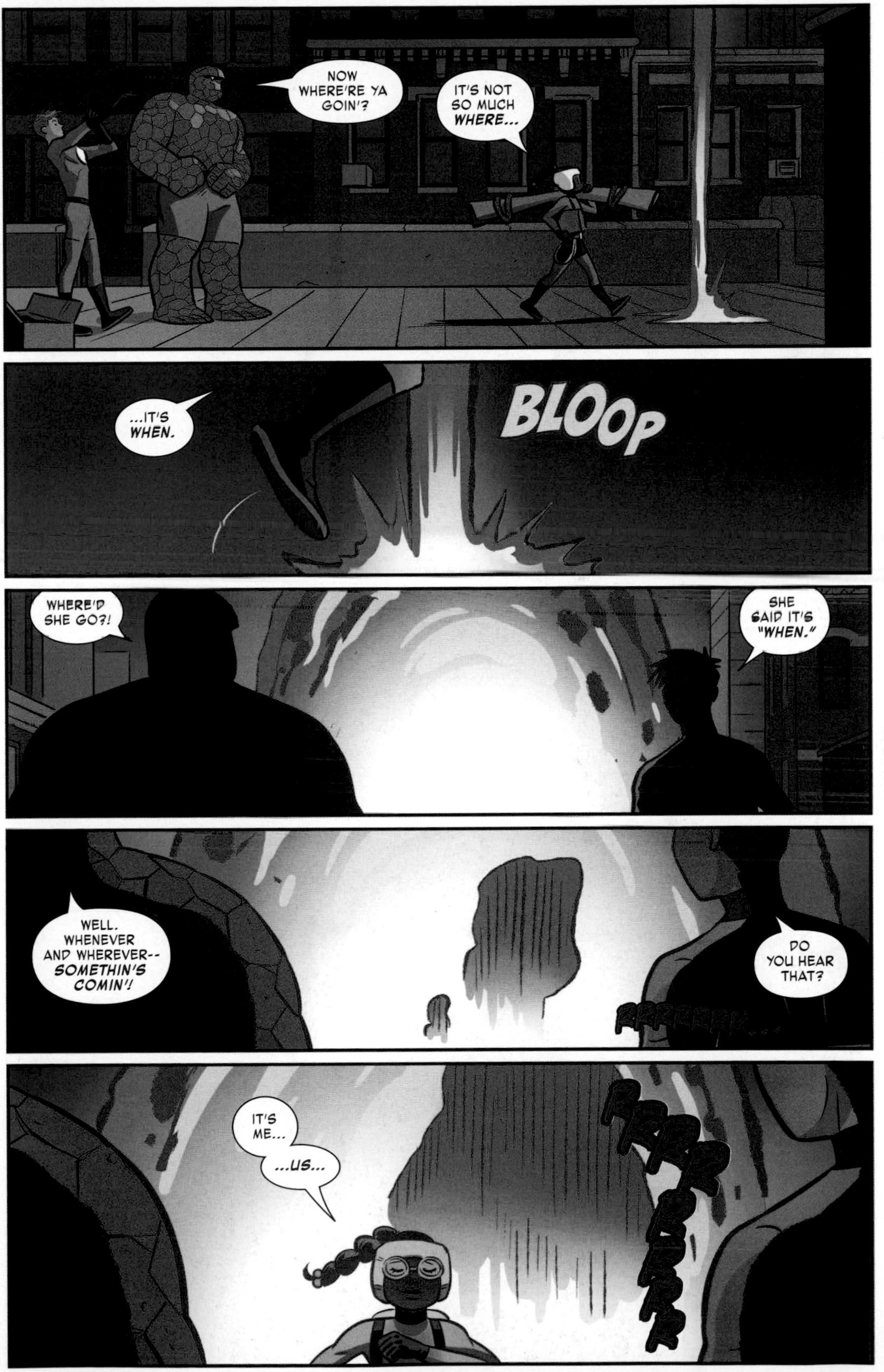
NOW WHERE'RE YA GOIN'?
IT'S NOT SO MUCH *WHERE...*
...IT'S *WHEN.*
BLOOP
WHERE'D SHE GO?!
SHE SAID IT'S *"WHEN."*
WELL. WHENEVER AND WHEREVER-- *SOMETHIN'S COMIN'!*
DO YOU HEAR THAT?
IT'S ME...
...US...

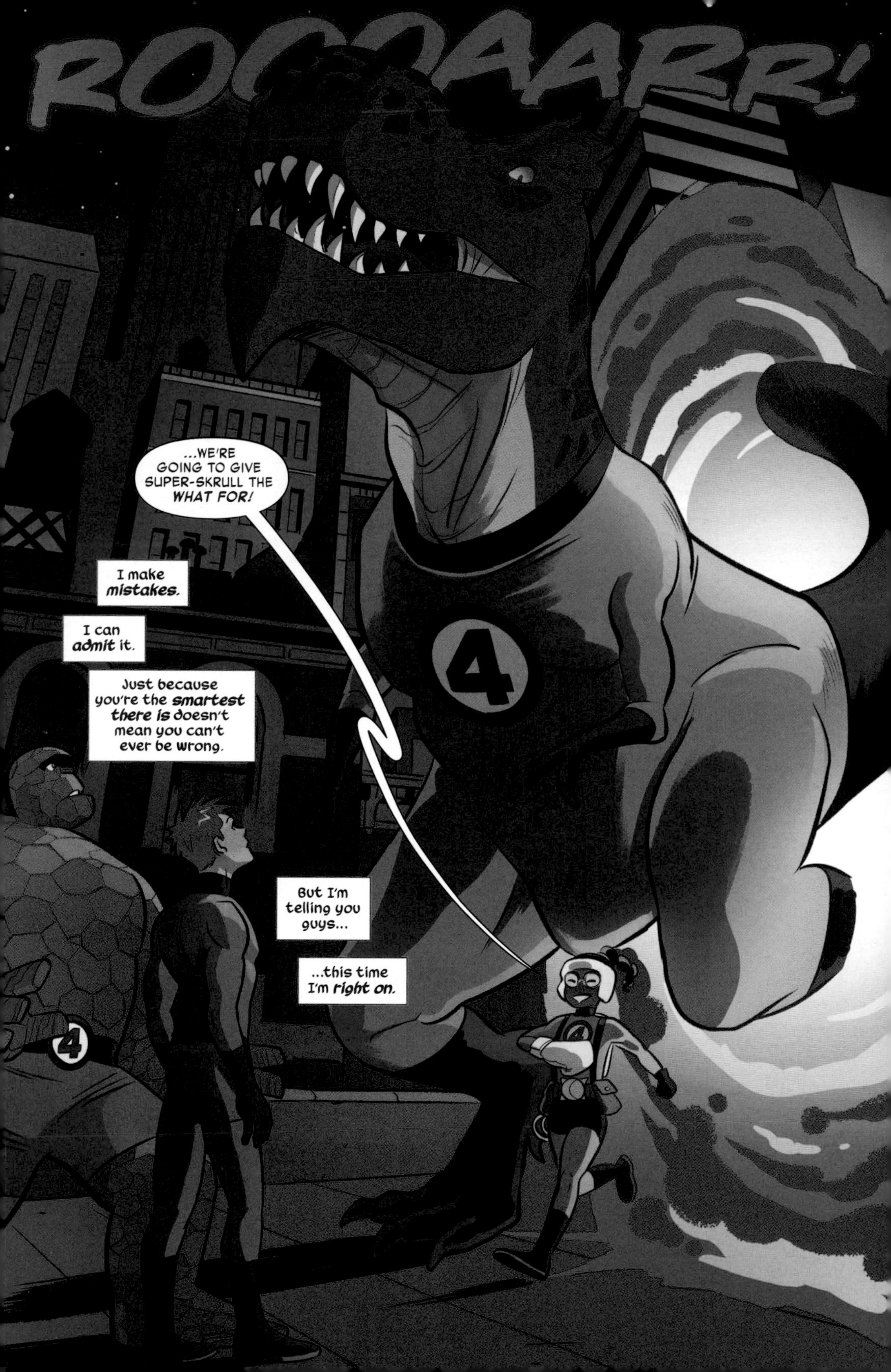
ROOOAARR!
I make **mistakes.**
I can **admit** it.
Just because you're the **smartest there is** doesn't mean you can't ever be wrong.
But I'm telling you guys...
...this time I'm **right on.**
...WE'RE GOING TO GIVE SUPER-SKRULL THE *WHAT FOR!*

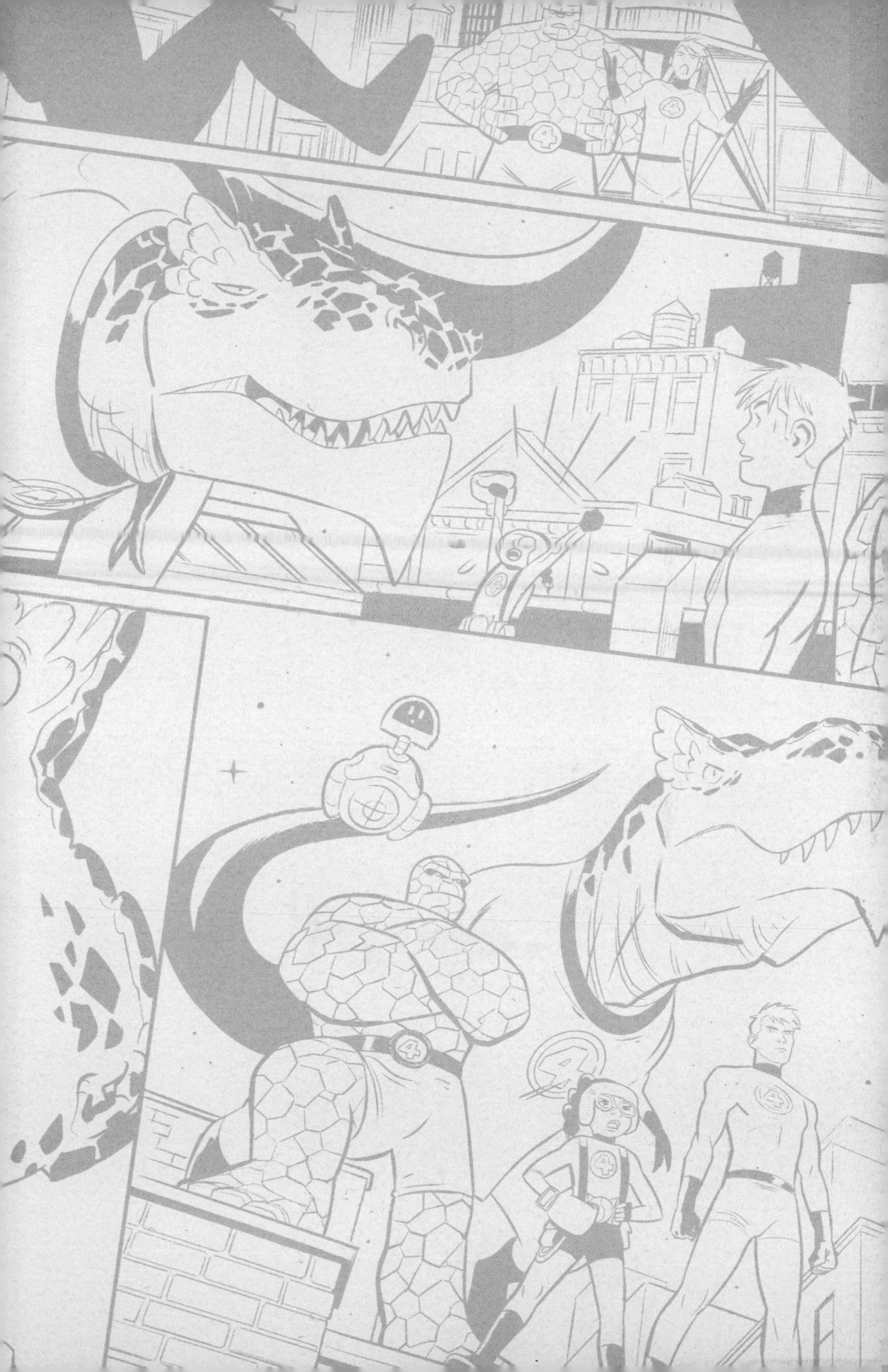

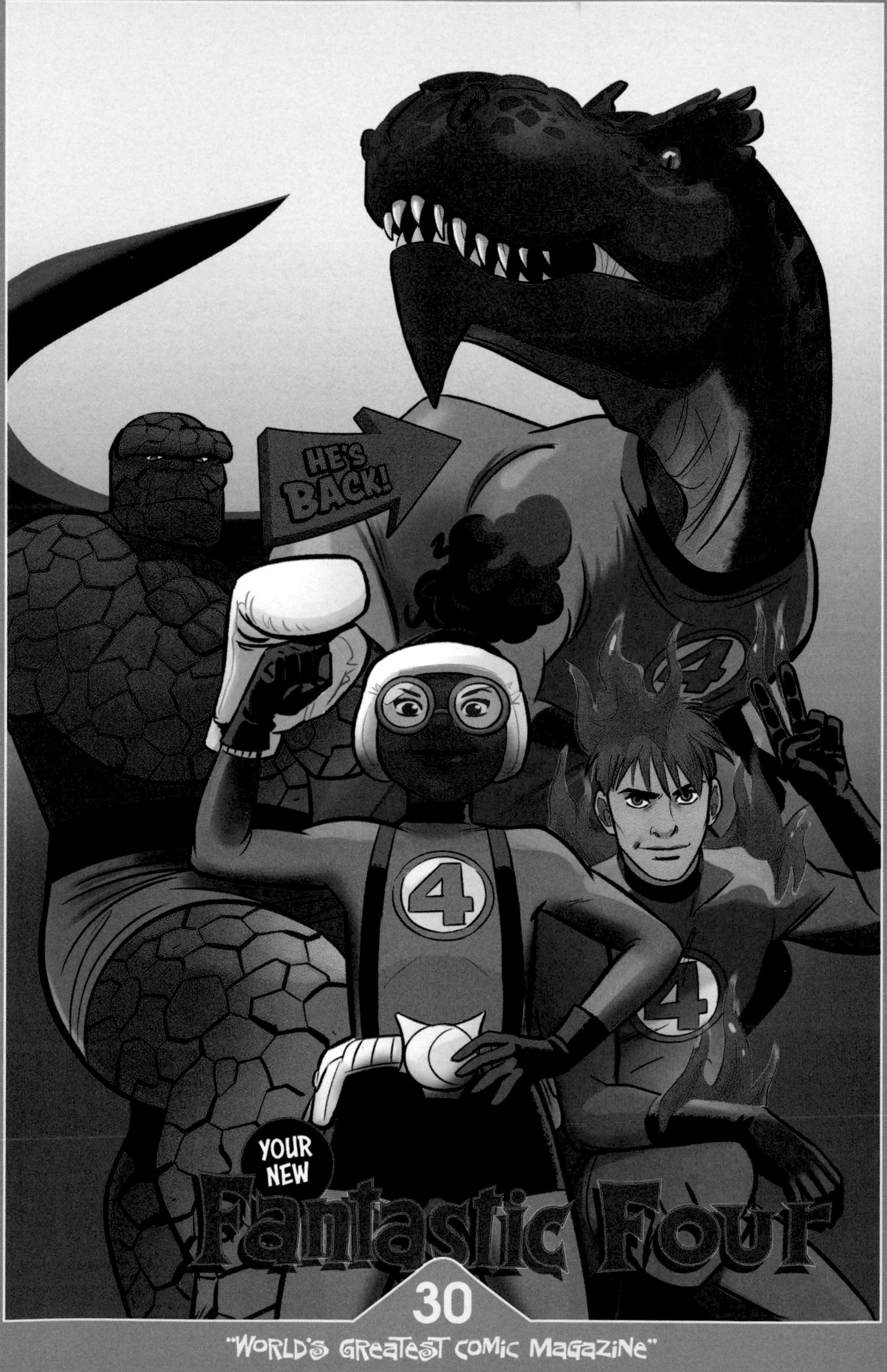
HE'S BACK!
YOUR NEW
Fantastic Four
30
"WORLD'S GREATEST COMIC MAGAZINE"

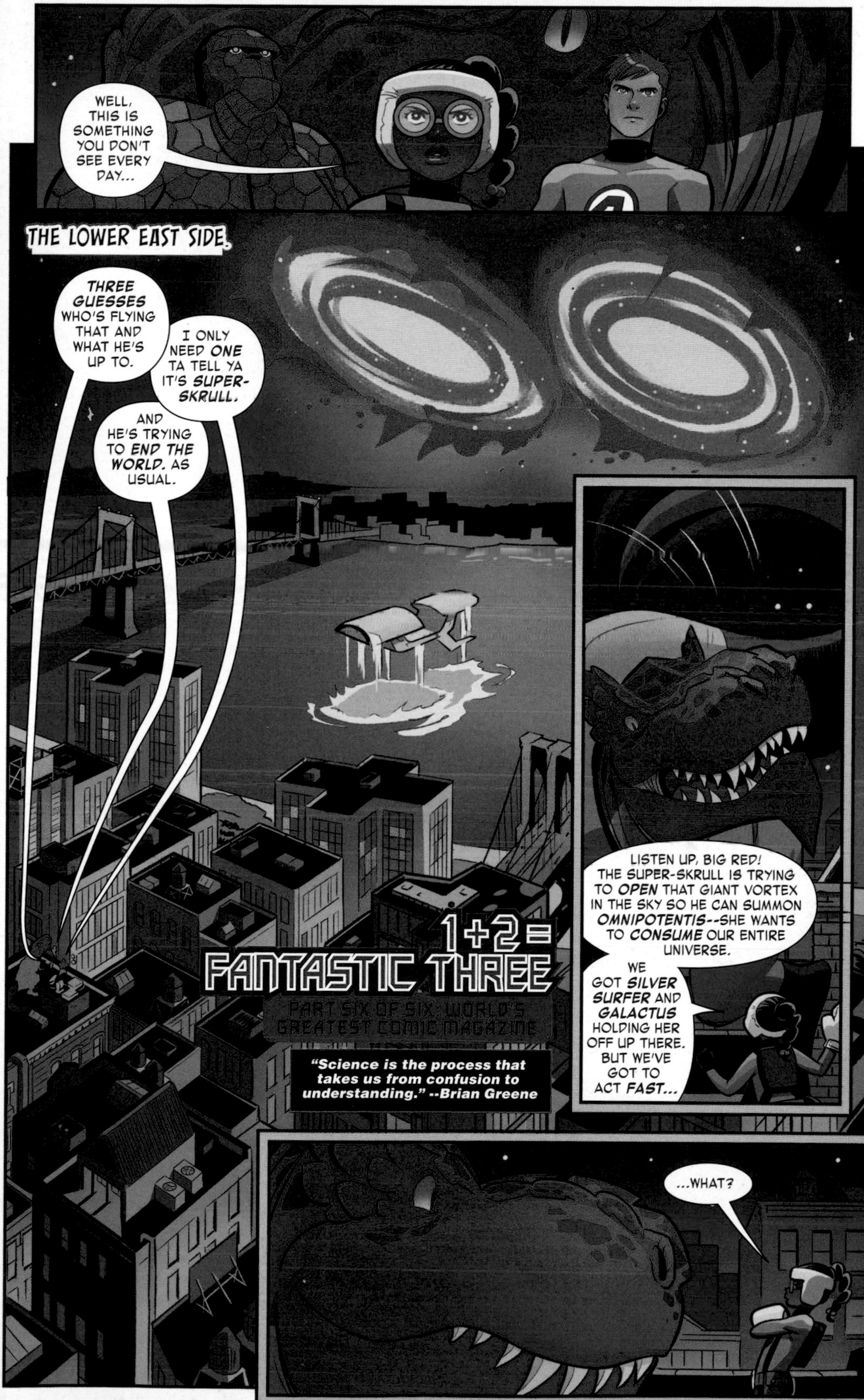
WELL, THIS IS SOMETHING YOU DON'T SEE EVERY DAY...
THE LOWER EAST SIDE.
THREE GUESSES WHO'S FLYING THAT AND WHAT HE'S UP TO.
I ONLY NEED ONE TA TELL YA IT'S SUPER-SKRULL.
AND HE'S TRYING TO END THE WORLD. AS USUAL.
1+2= FANTASTIC THREE
PART SIX OF SIX: WORLD'S GREATEST COMIC MAGAZINE
"Science is the process that takes us from confusion to understanding." --Brian Greene
LISTEN UP, BIG RED! THE SUPER-SKRULL IS TRYING TO OPEN THAT GIANT VORTEX IN THE SKY SO HE CAN SUMMON OMNIPOTENTIS--SHE WANTS TO CONSUME OUR ENTIRE UNIVERSE.
WE GOT SILVER SURFER AND GALACTUS HOLDING HER OFF UP THERE. BUT WE'VE GOT TO ACT FAST...
...WHAT?

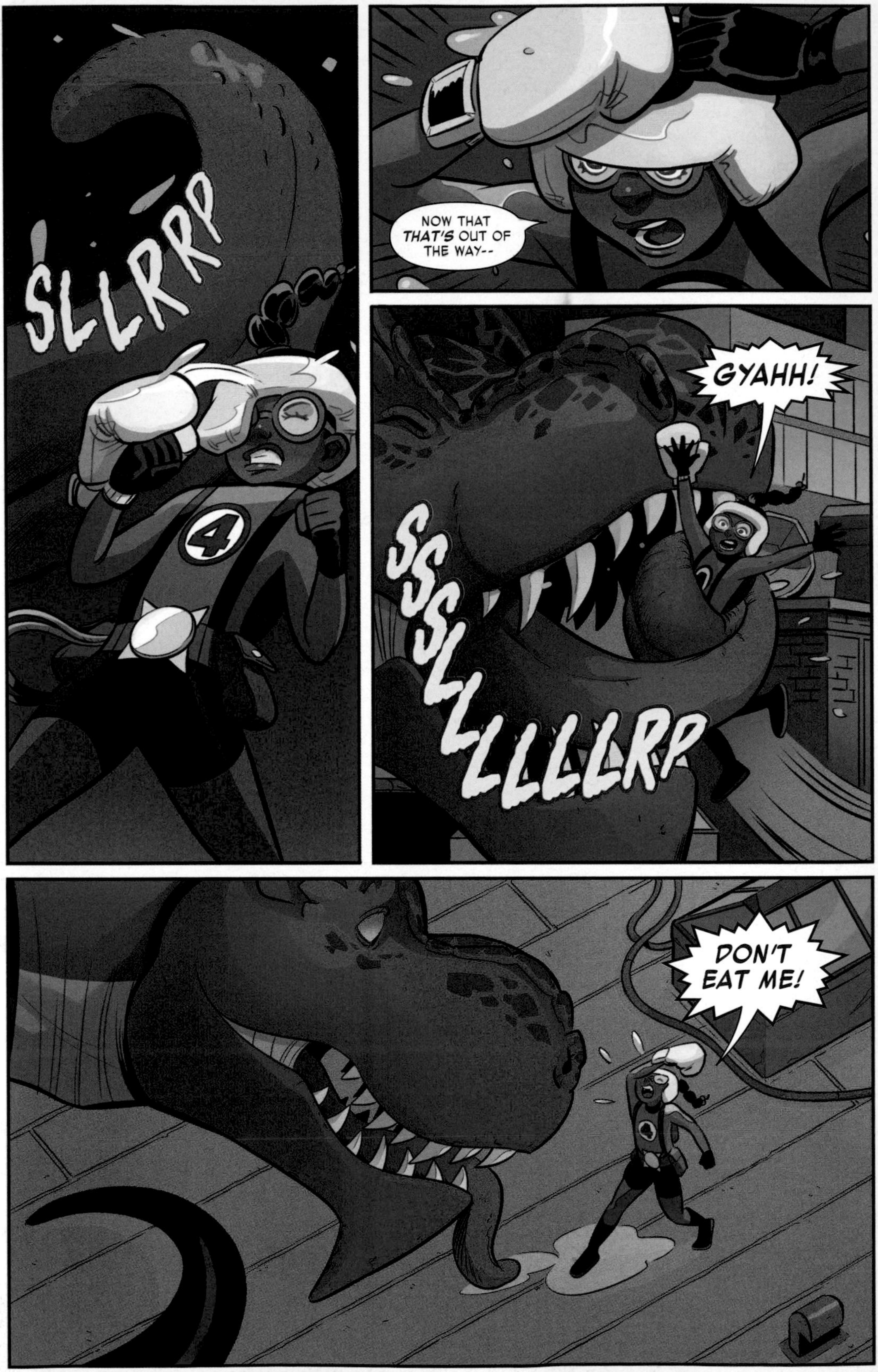
SLLRRP
NOW THAT THAT'S OUT OF THE WAY--
GYAHH!
SSSLLLLLRP
DON'T EAT ME!

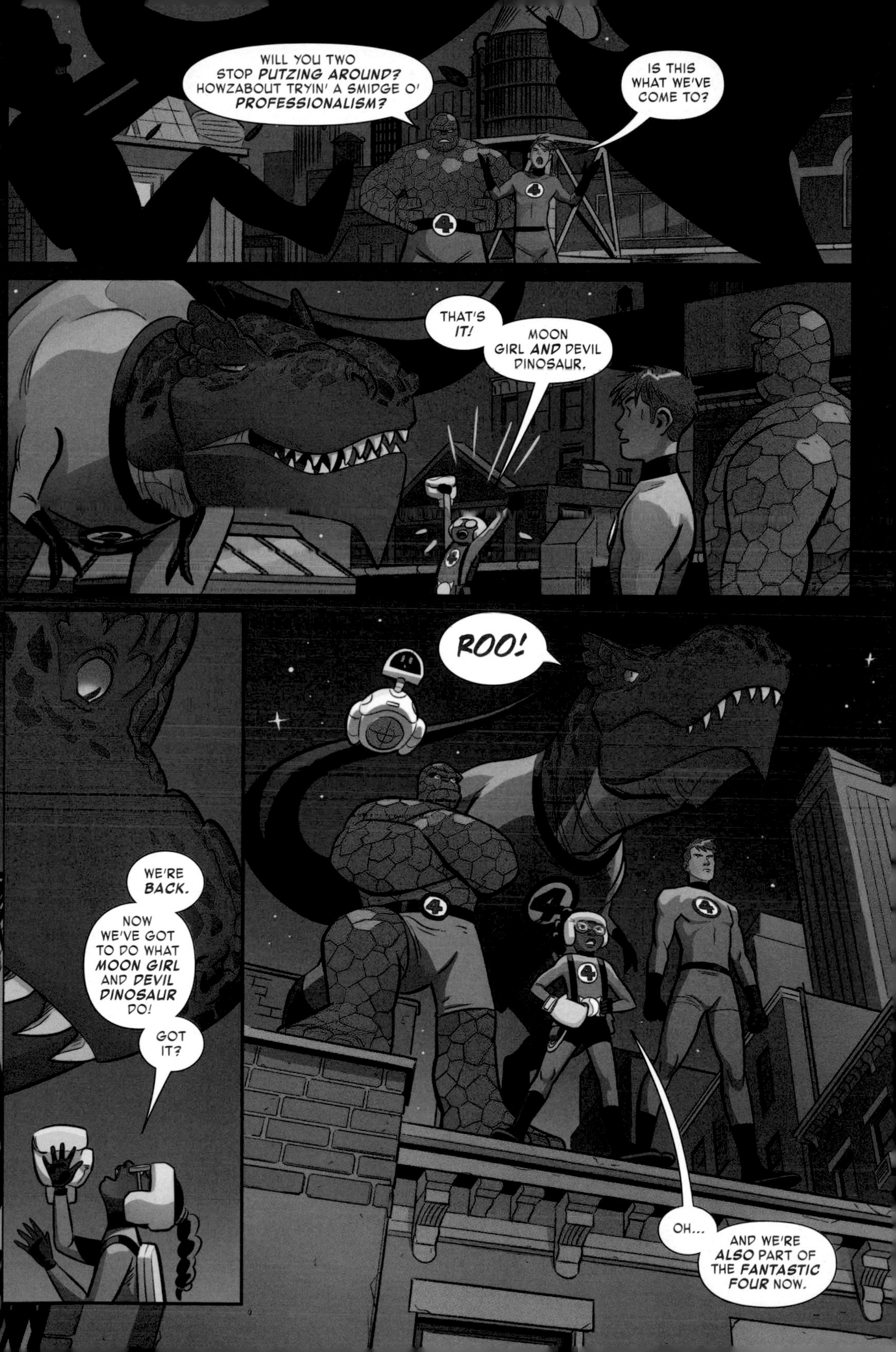
WILL YOU TWO STOP PUTZING AROUND? HOWZABOUT TRYIN' A SMIDGE O' PROFESSIONALISM?
IS THIS WHAT WE'VE COME TO?
THAT'S IT!
MOON GIRL AND DEVIL DINOSAUR.
ROO!
WE'RE BACK.
NOW WE'VE GOT TO DO WHAT MOON GIRL AND DEVIL DINOSAUR DO!
GOT IT?
OH...
AND WE'RE ALSO PART OF THE FANTASTIC FOUR NOW.

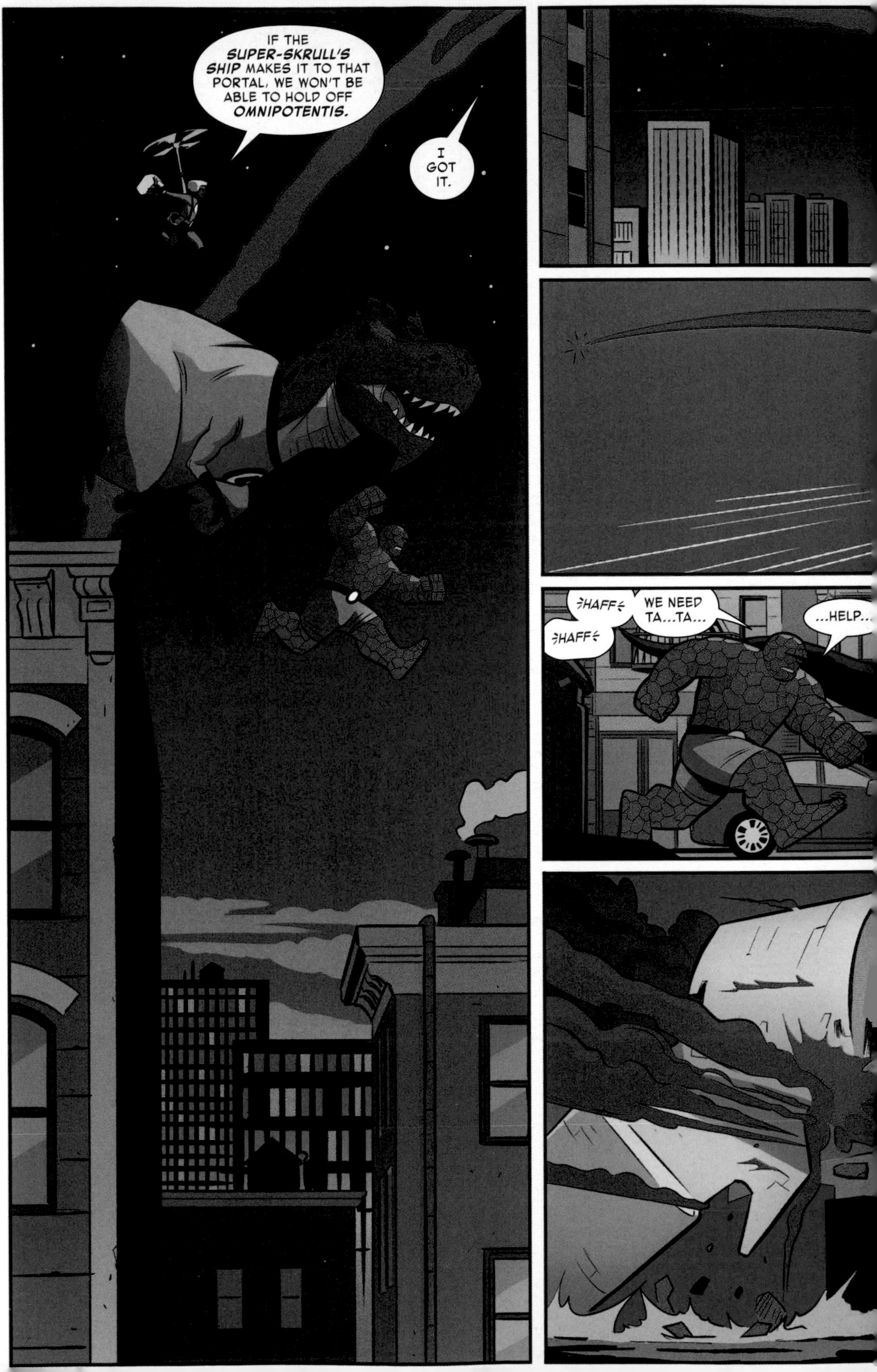
IF THE SUPER-SKRULL'S SHIP MAKES IT TO THAT PORTAL, WE WON'T BE ABLE TO HOLD OFF OMNIPOTENTIS.
I GOT IT.
HAFF
HAFF
WE NEED TA...TA...
...HELP...

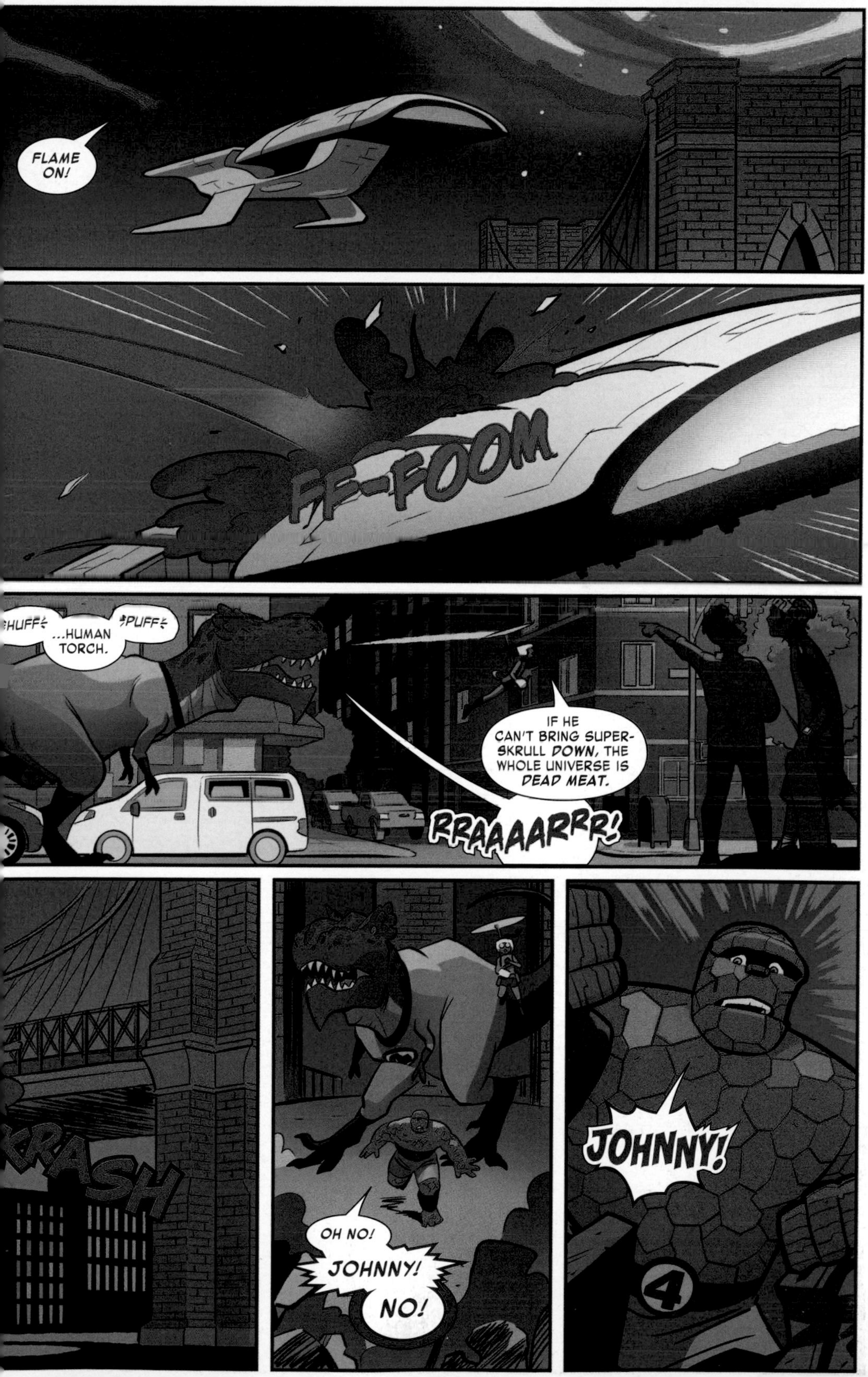
FLAME ON!
FF-FOOM
HUFF
...HUMAN TORCH.
PUFF
IF HE CAN'T BRING SUPER-SKRULL DOWN, THE WHOLE UNIVERSE IS DEAD MEAT.
RRAAAARRRR!
KRASH
OH NO!
JOHNNY!
NO!
JOHNNY!

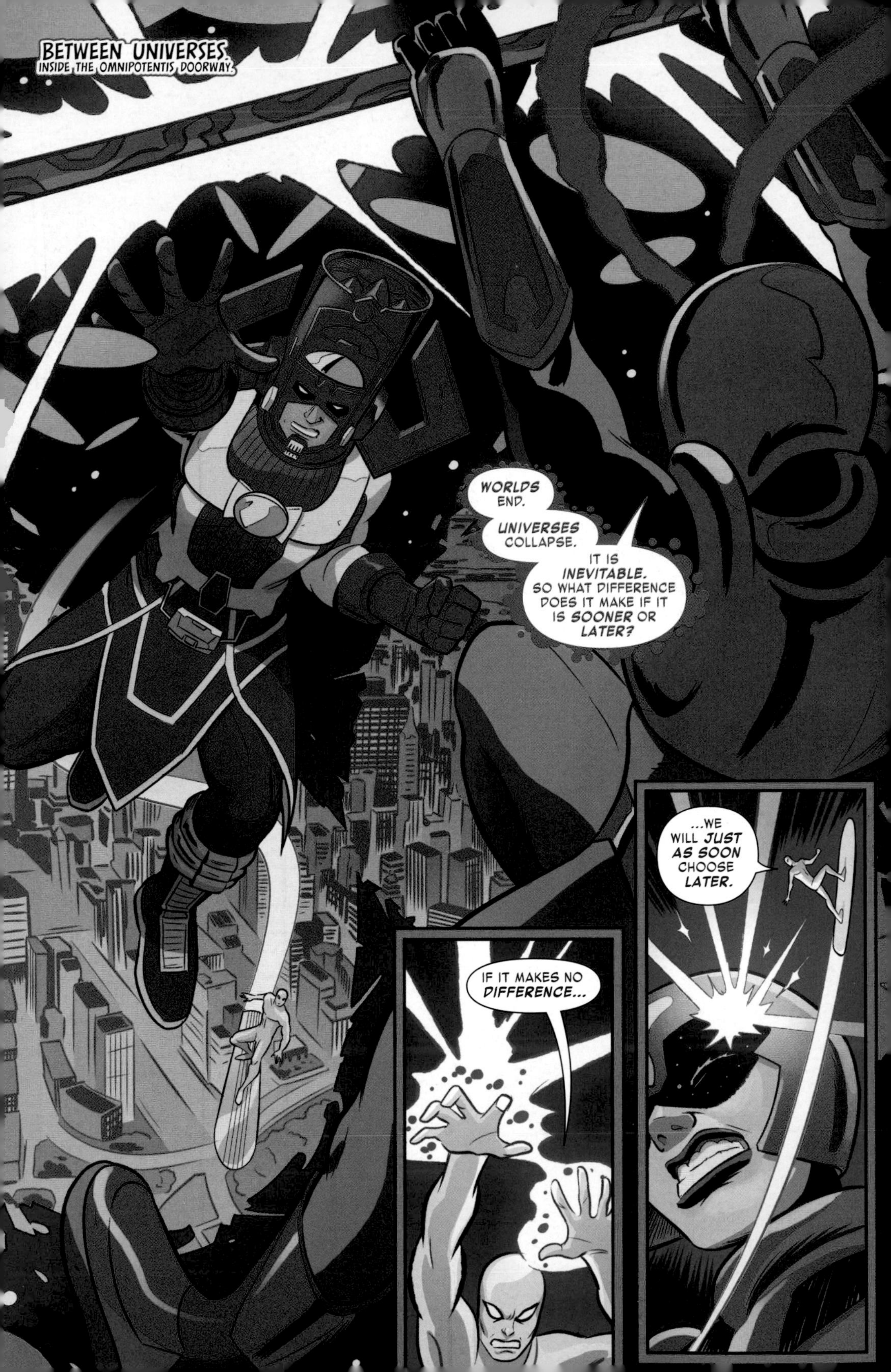

BETWEEN UNIVERSES.
INSIDE THE OMNIPOTENTIS DOORWAY.
WORLDS END. UNIVERSES COLLAPSE.
IT IS INEVITABLE. SO WHAT DIFFERENCE DOES IT MAKE IF IT IS SOONER OR LATER?
IF IT MAKES NO DIFFERENCE...
...WE WILL JUST AS SOON CHOOSE LATER.

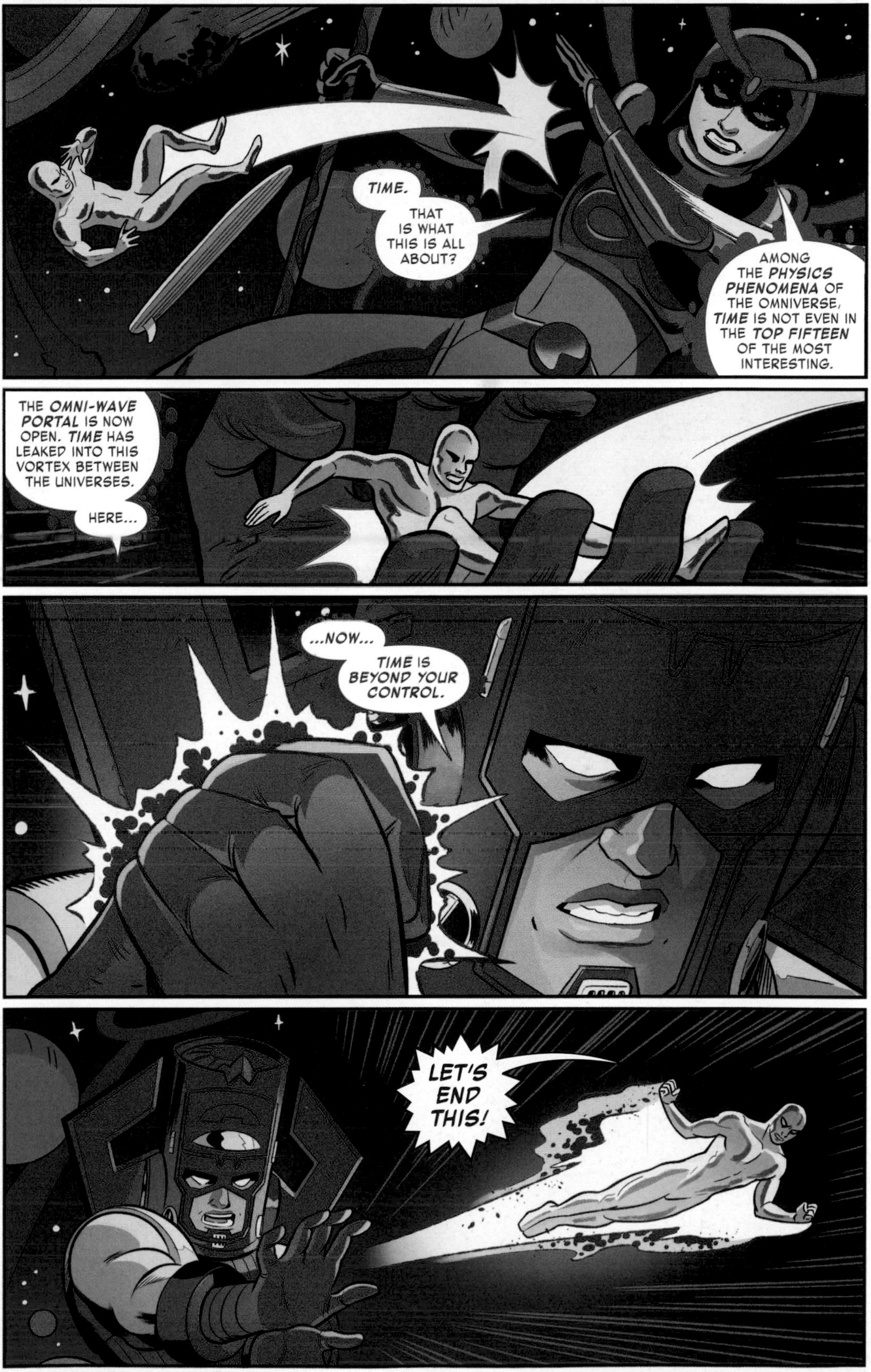
TIME.
THAT IS WHAT THIS IS ALL ABOUT?
AMONG THE PHYSICS PHENOMENA OF THE OMNIVERSE, TIME IS NOT EVEN IN THE TOP FIFTEEN OF THE MOST INTERESTING.
THE OMNI-WAVE PORTAL IS NOW OPEN. TIME HAS LEAKED INTO THIS VORTEX BETWEEN THE UNIVERSES.
HERE...
...NOW...
TIME IS BEYOND YOUR CONTROL.
LET'S END THIS!

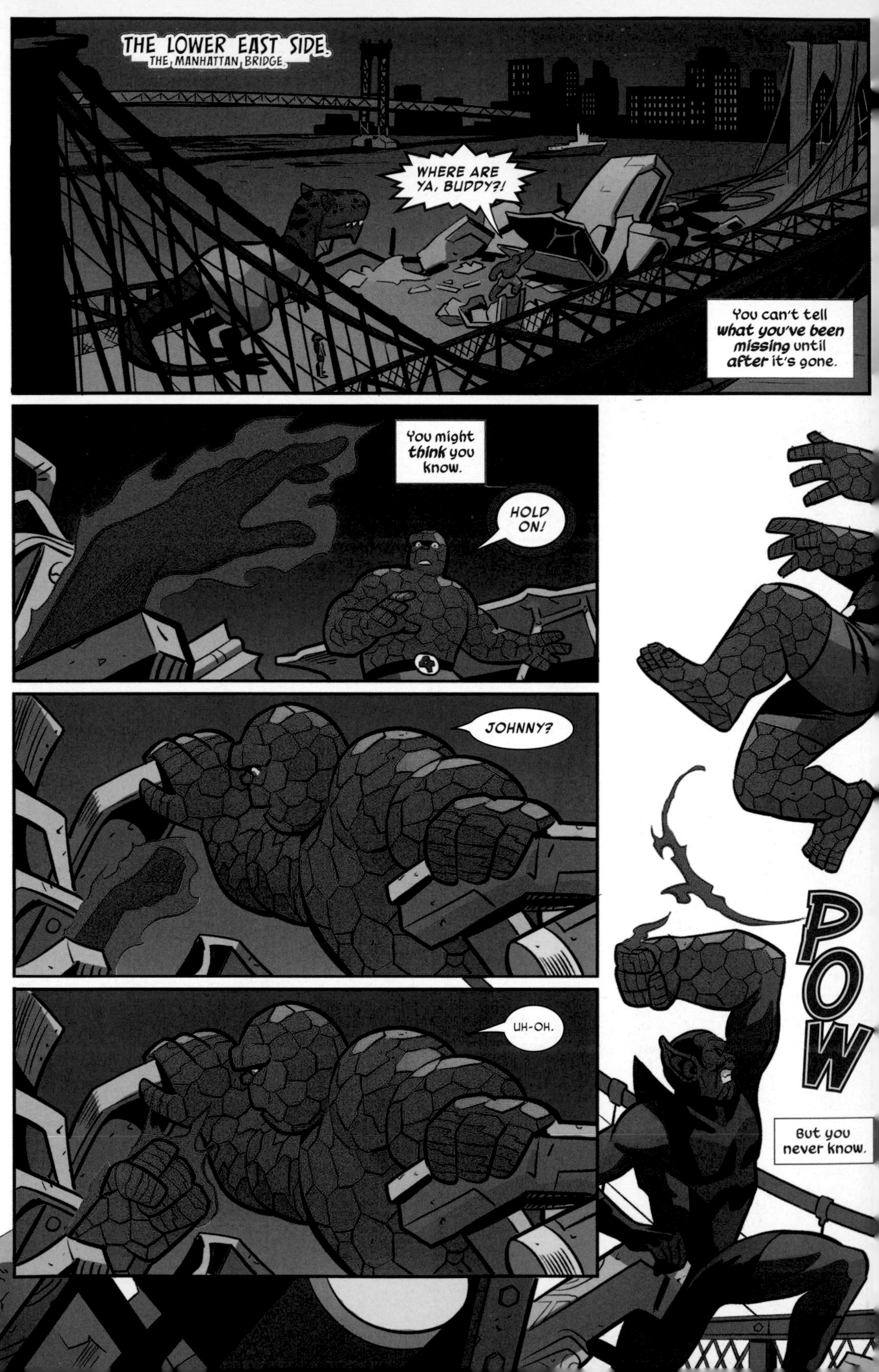

THE LOWER EAST SIDE.
THE MANHATTAN BRIDGE.
WHERE ARE YA, BUDDY?!
You can't tell what you've been missing until after it's gone.
You might think you know.
HOLD ON!
JOHNNY?
UH-OH.
POW
But you never know.

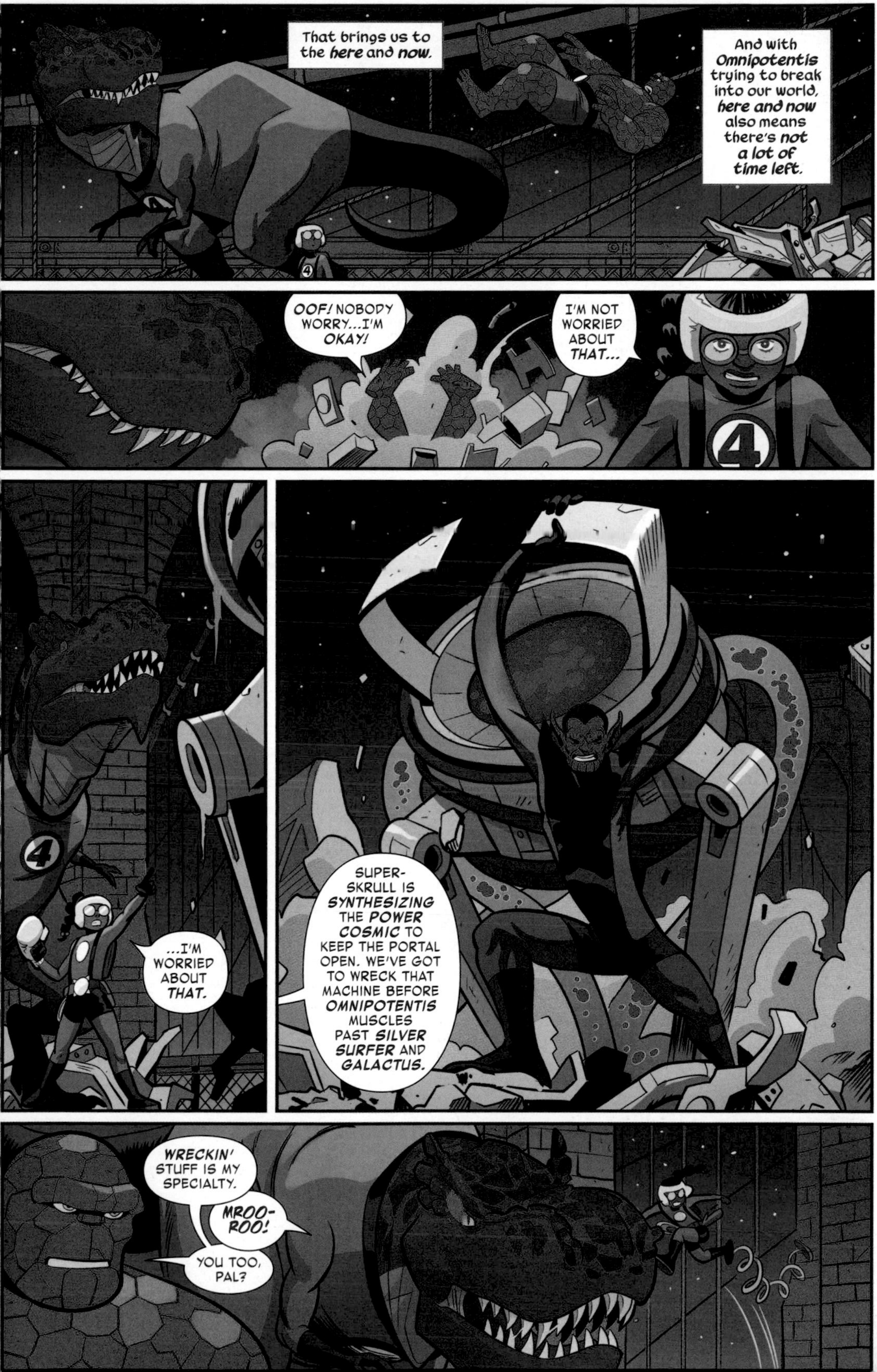
That brings us to the here and now.
And with Omnipotentis trying to break into our world, here and now also means there's not a lot of time left.
OOF! NOBODY WORRY...I'M OKAY!
I'M NOT WORRIED ABOUT THAT...
...I'M WORRIED ABOUT THAT.
SUPER-SKRULL IS SYNTHESIZING THE POWER COSMIC TO KEEP THE PORTAL OPEN. WE'VE GOT TO WRECK THAT MACHINE BEFORE OMNIPOTENTIS MUSCLES PAST SILVER SURFER AND GALACTUS.
WRECKIN' STUFF IS MY SPECIALTY.
MROO-ROO!
YOU TOO, PAL?

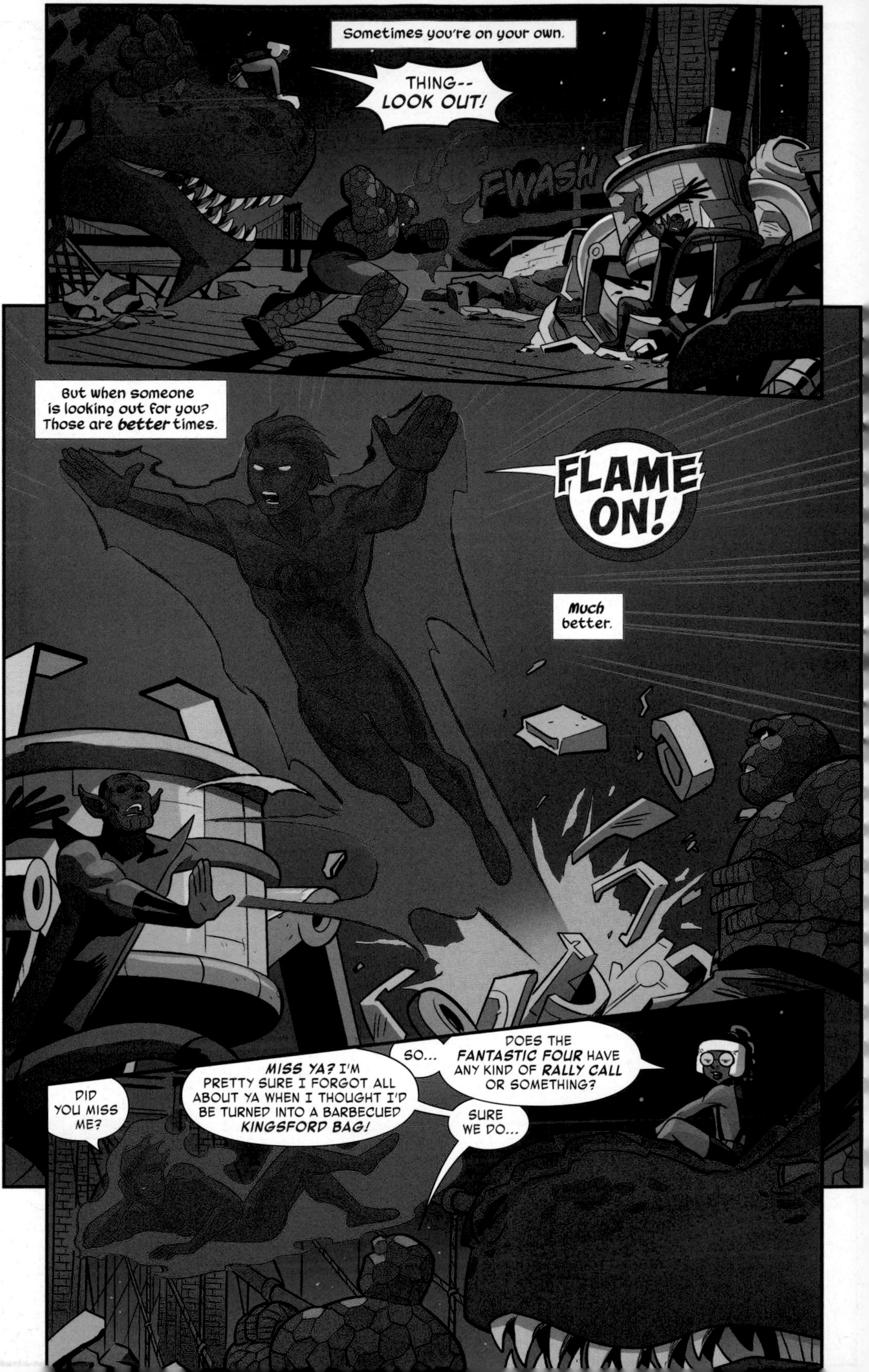

Sometimes you're on your own.
THING-- LOOK OUT!
FWASH
But when someone is looking out for you? Those are better times.
FLAME ON!
Much better.
DID YOU MISS ME?
MISS YA? I'M PRETTY SURE I FORGOT ALL ABOUT YA WHEN I THOUGHT I'D BE TURNED INTO A BARBECUED KINGSFORD BAG!
SO...
DOES THE FANTASTIC FOUR HAVE ANY KIND OF RALLY CALL OR SOMETHING?
SURE WE DO...

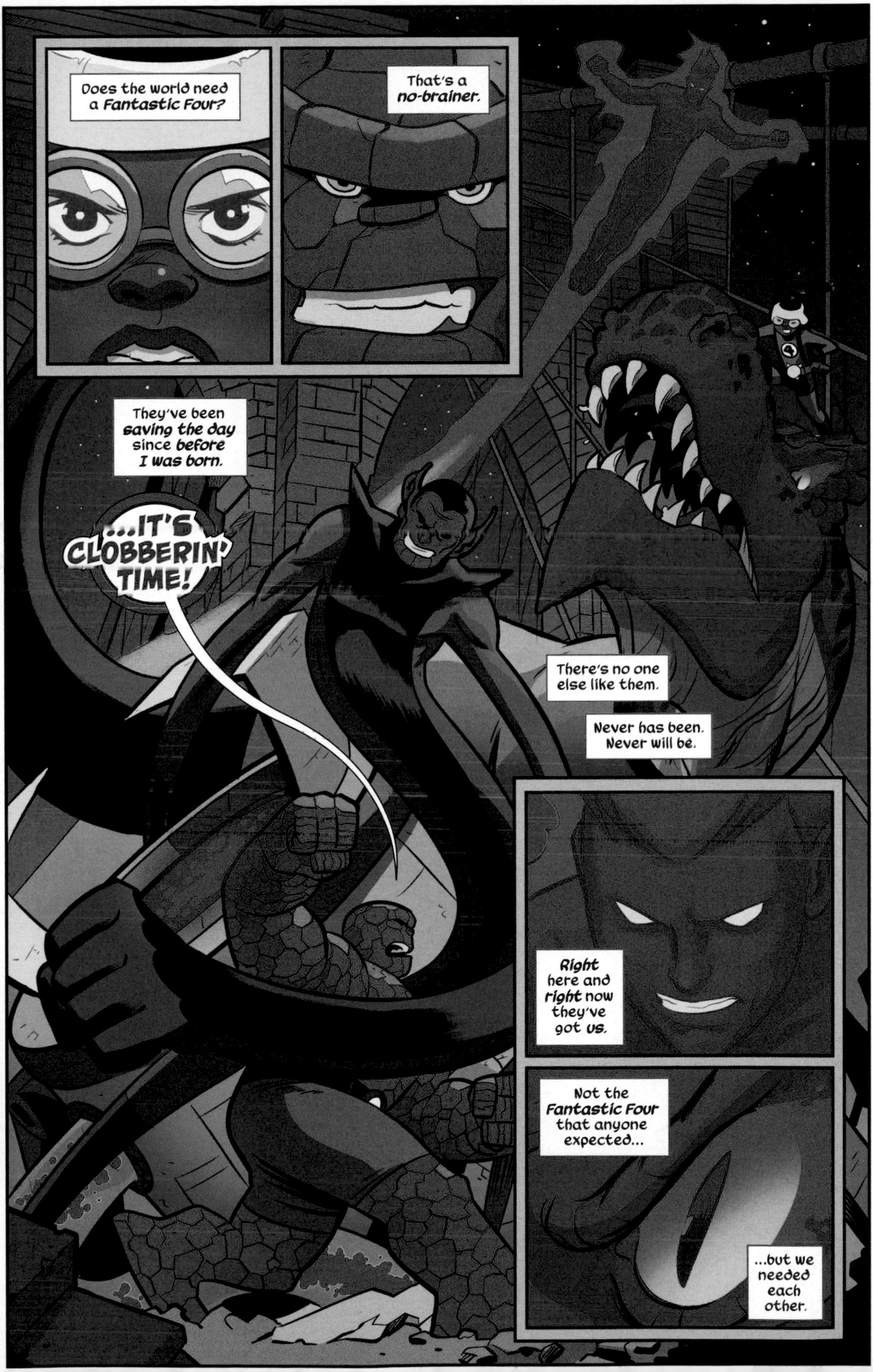

Does the world need a *Fantastic Four?*
That's a *no-brainer.*
They've been *saving the day* since *before I was born.*
...IT'S CLOBBERIN' TIME!
There's no one else like them.
Never has been. Never will be.
Right here and *right* now they've got *us.*
Not the *Fantastic Four* that anyone expected...
...but we needed each other.

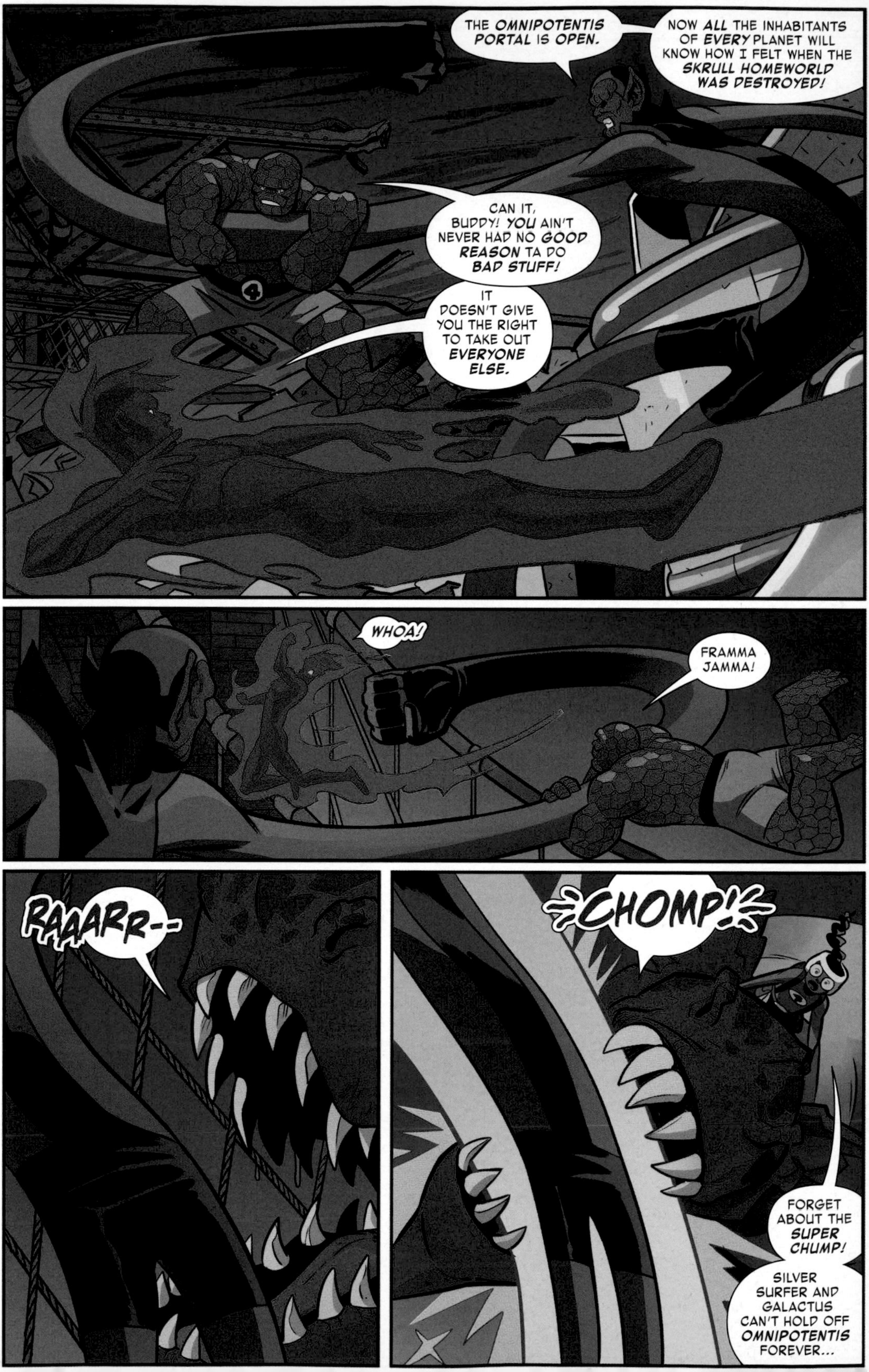
THE OMNIPOTENTIS PORTAL IS OPEN.
NOW ALL THE INHABITANTS OF EVERY PLANET WILL KNOW HOW I FELT WHEN THE SKRULL HOMEWORLD WAS DESTROYED!
CAN IT, BUDDY! YOU AIN'T NEVER HAD NO GOOD REASON TA DO BAD STUFF!
IT DOESN'T GIVE YOU THE RIGHT TO TAKE OUT EVERYONE ELSE.
WHOA!
FRAMMA JAMMA!
RAAARR--
CHOMP!
FORGET ABOUT THE SUPER CHUMP!
SILVER SURFER AND GALACTUS CAN'T HOLD OFF OMNIPOTENTIS FOREVER...

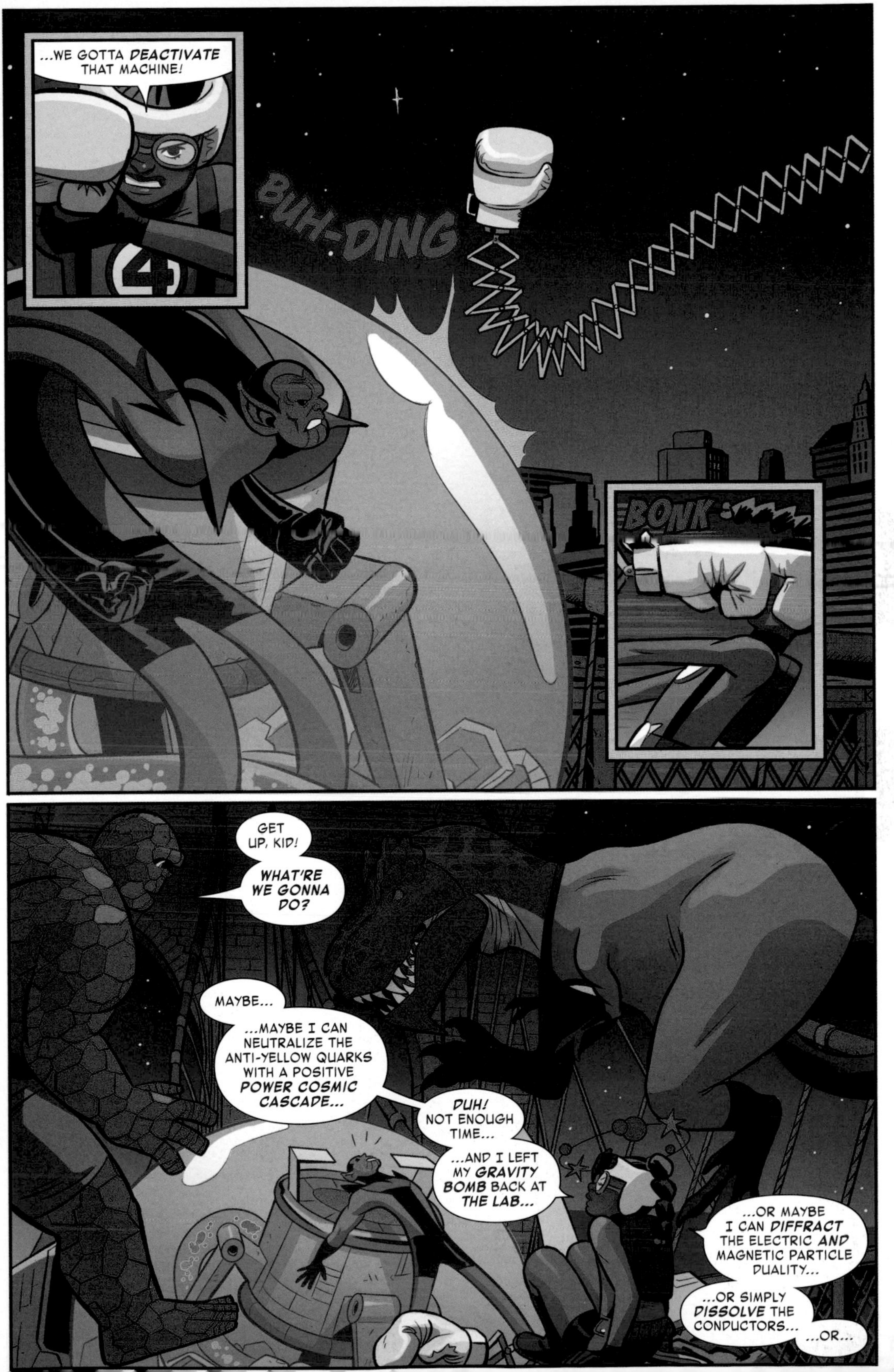
...WE GOTTA DEACTIVATE THAT MACHINE!
BUH-DING
BONK
GET UP, KID!
WHAT'RE WE GONNA DO?
MAYBE...
...MAYBE I CAN NEUTRALIZE THE ANTI-YELLOW QUARKS WITH A POSITIVE POWER COSMIC CASCADE...
DUH! NOT ENOUGH TIME...
...AND I LEFT MY GRAVITY BOMB BACK AT THE LAB...
...OR MAYBE I CAN DIFFRACT THE ELECTRIC AND MAGNETIC PARTICLE DUALITY...
...OR SIMPLY DISSOLVE THE CONDUCTORS...
...OR...

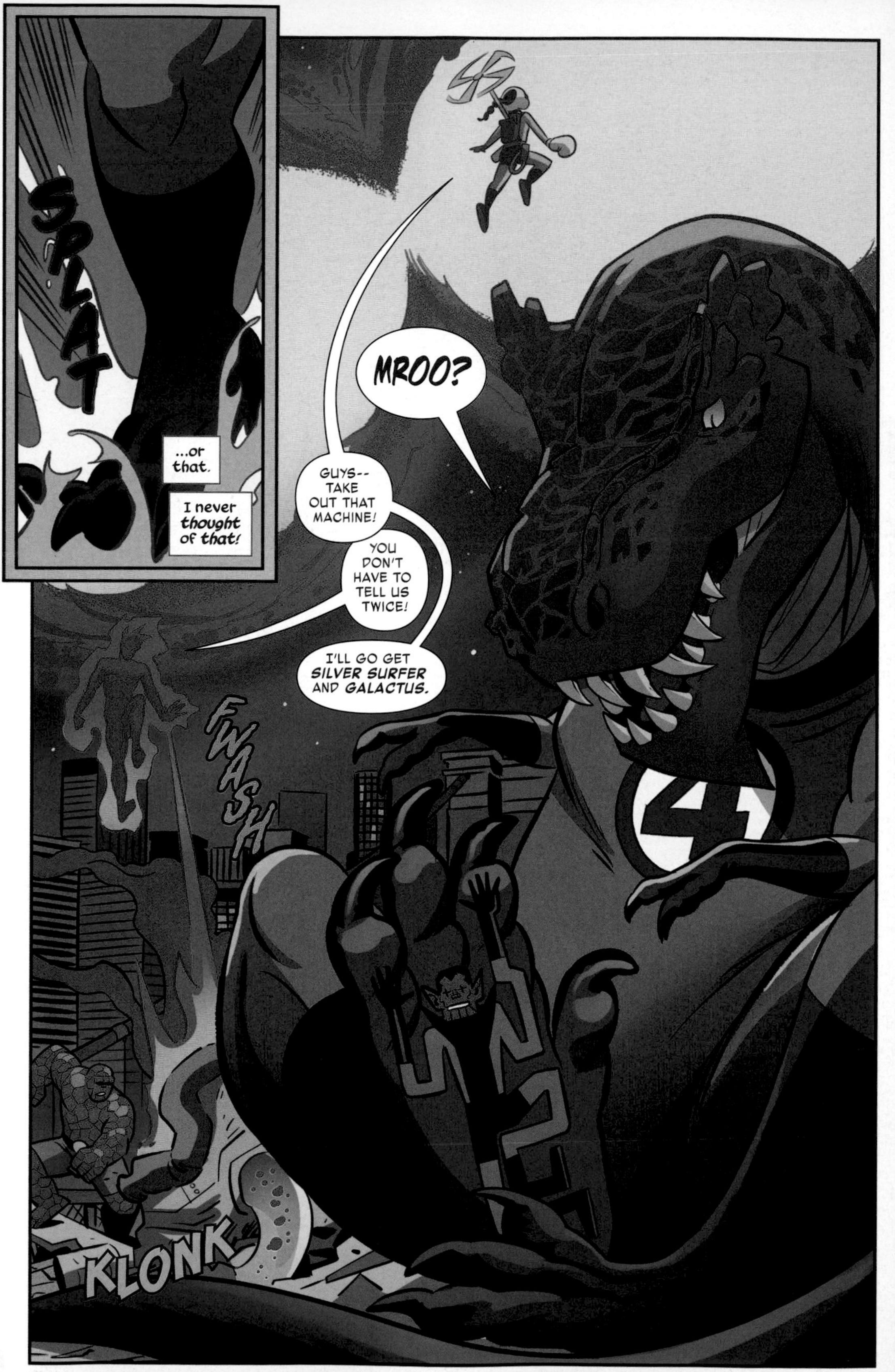
SPLAT
...or that.
I never thought of that!
MROO?
GUYS-- TAKE OUT THAT MACHINE!
YOU DON'T HAVE TO TELL US TWICE!
I'LL GO GET SILVER SURFER AND GALACTUS.
FWASH
KLONK

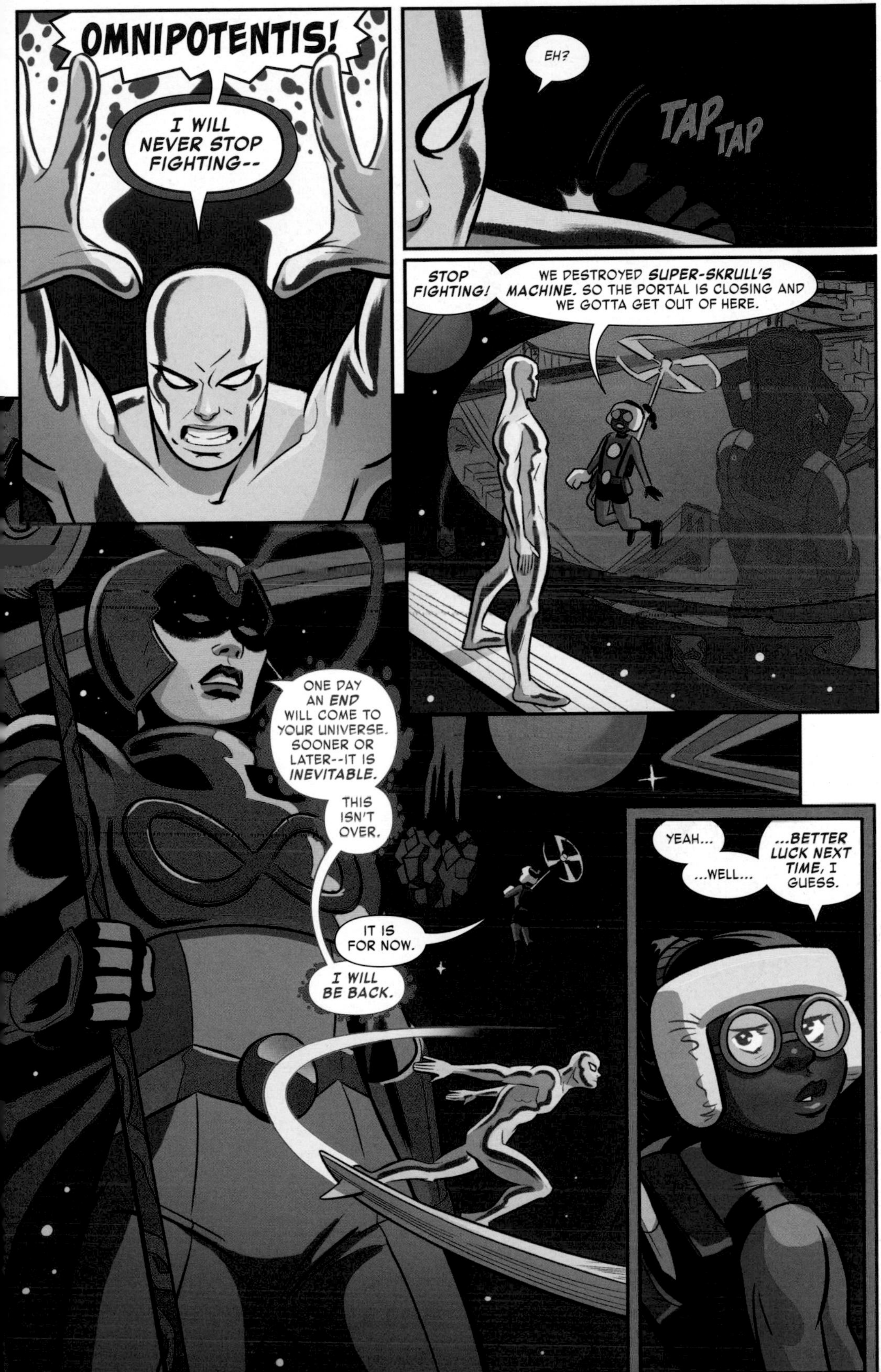
OMNIPOTENTIS!
I WILL NEVER STOP FIGHTING--
EH?
TAP TAP
STOP FIGHTING!
WE DESTROYED SUPER-SKRULL'S MACHINE. SO THE PORTAL IS CLOSING AND WE GOTTA GET OUT OF HERE.
ONE DAY AN END WILL COME TO YOUR UNIVERSE. SOONER OR LATER--IT IS INEVITABLE.
THIS ISN'T OVER.
IT IS FOR NOW.
I WILL BE BACK.
YEAH...
...WELL...
...BETTER LUCK NEXT TIME, I GUESS.

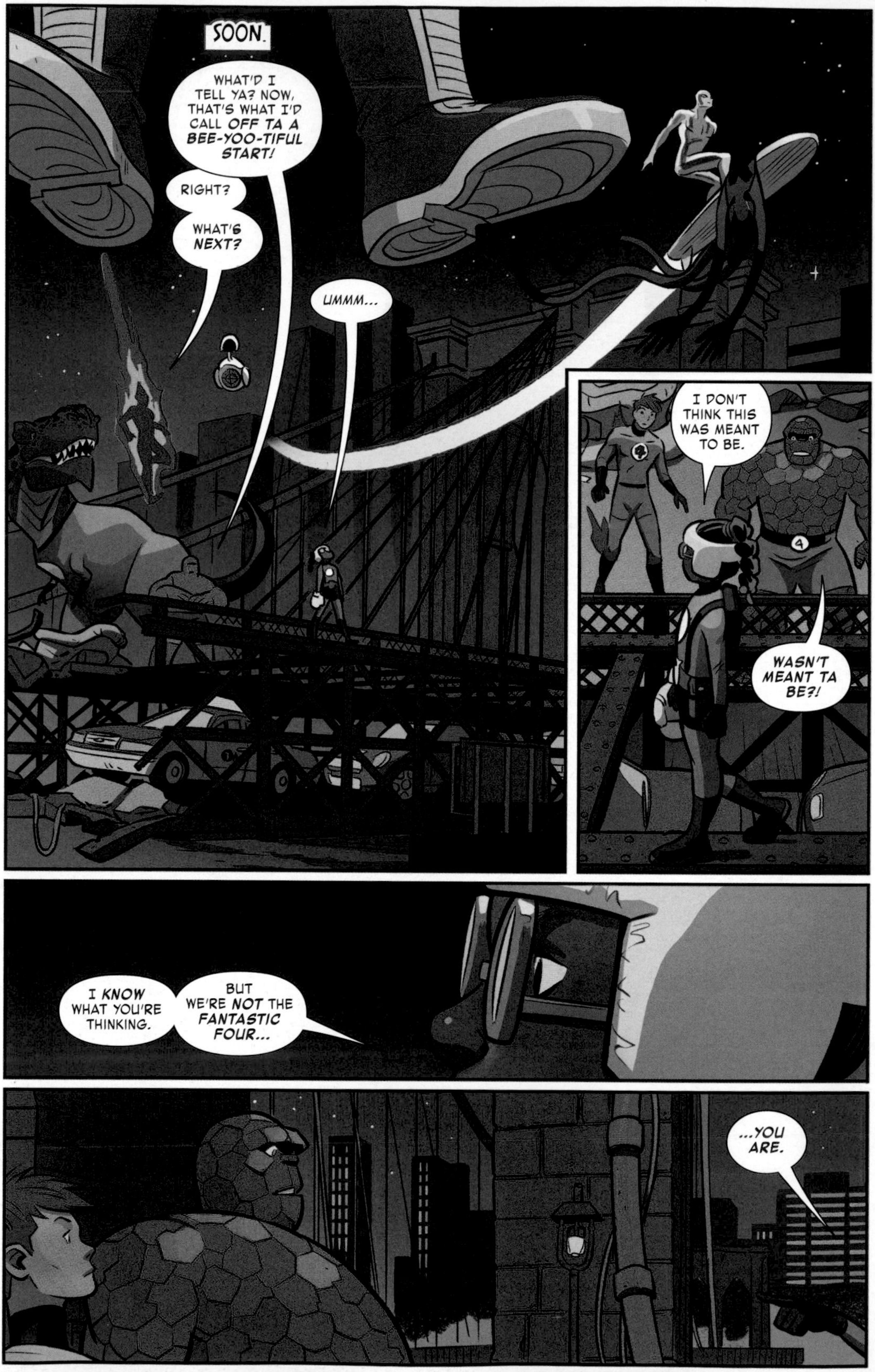
SOON.
WHAT'D I TELL YA? NOW, THAT'S WHAT I'D CALL OFF TA A BEE-YOO-TIFUL START!
RIGHT?
WHAT'S NEXT?
UMMM...
I DON'T THINK THIS WAS MEANT TO BE.
WASN'T MEANT TA BE?!
I KNOW WHAT YOU'RE THINKING.
BUT WE'RE NOT THE FANTASTIC FOUR...
...YOU ARE.

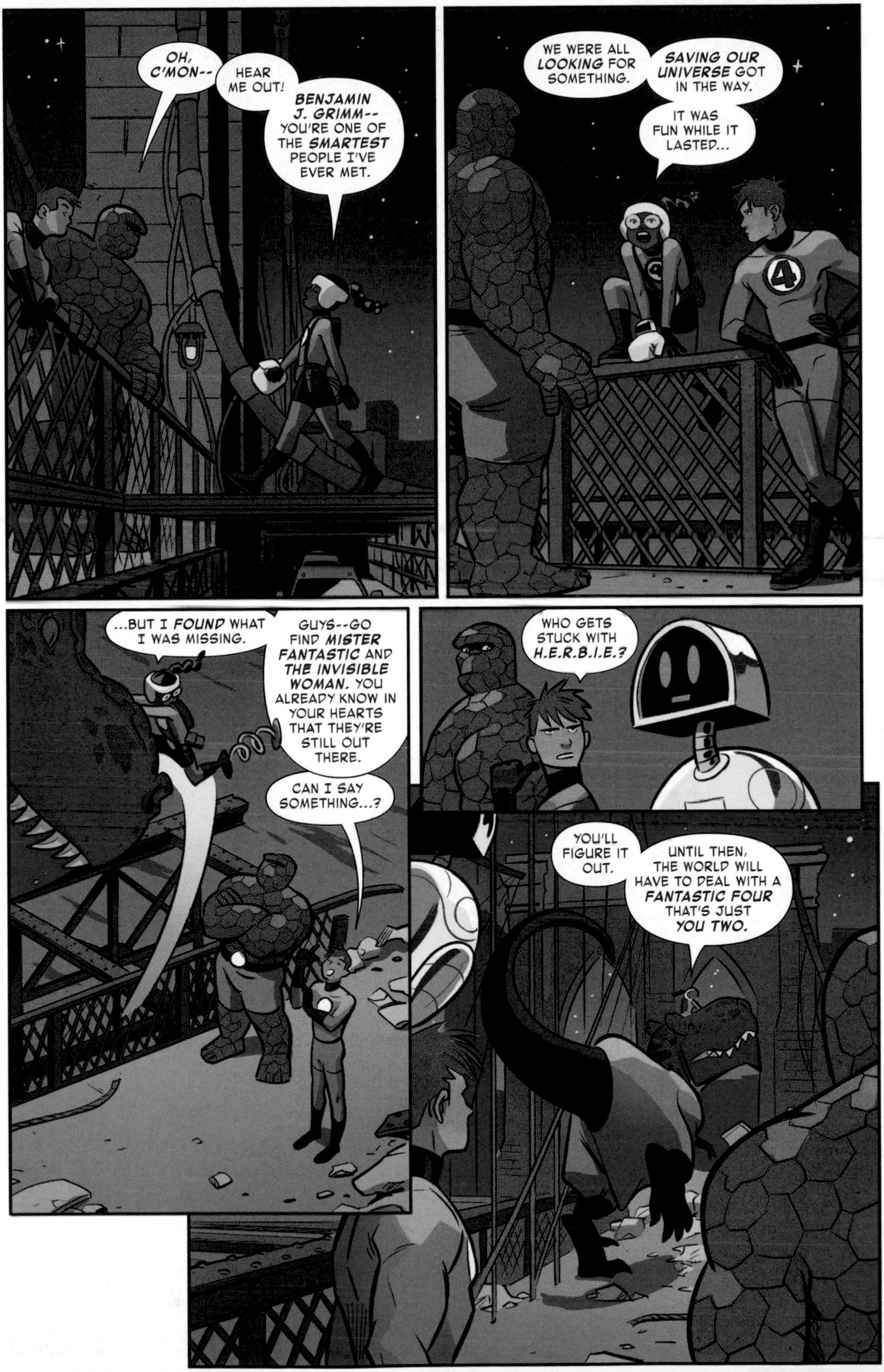

OH, C'MON--
HEAR ME OUT!
BENJAMIN J. GRIMM-- YOU'RE ONE OF THE SMARTEST PEOPLE I'VE EVER MET.
WE WERE ALL LOOKING FOR SOMETHING.
SAVING OUR UNIVERSE GOT IN THE WAY.
IT WAS FUN WHILE IT LASTED...
...BUT I FOUND WHAT I WAS MISSING.
GUYS--GO FIND MISTER FANTASTIC AND THE INVISIBLE WOMAN. YOU ALREADY KNOW IN YOUR HEARTS THAT THEY'RE STILL OUT THERE.
CAN I SAY SOMETHING...?
WHO GETS STUCK WITH H.E.R.B.I.E.?
YOU'LL FIGURE IT OUT.
UNTIL THEN, THE WORLD WILL HAVE TO DEAL WITH A FANTASTIC FOUR THAT'S JUST YOU TWO.

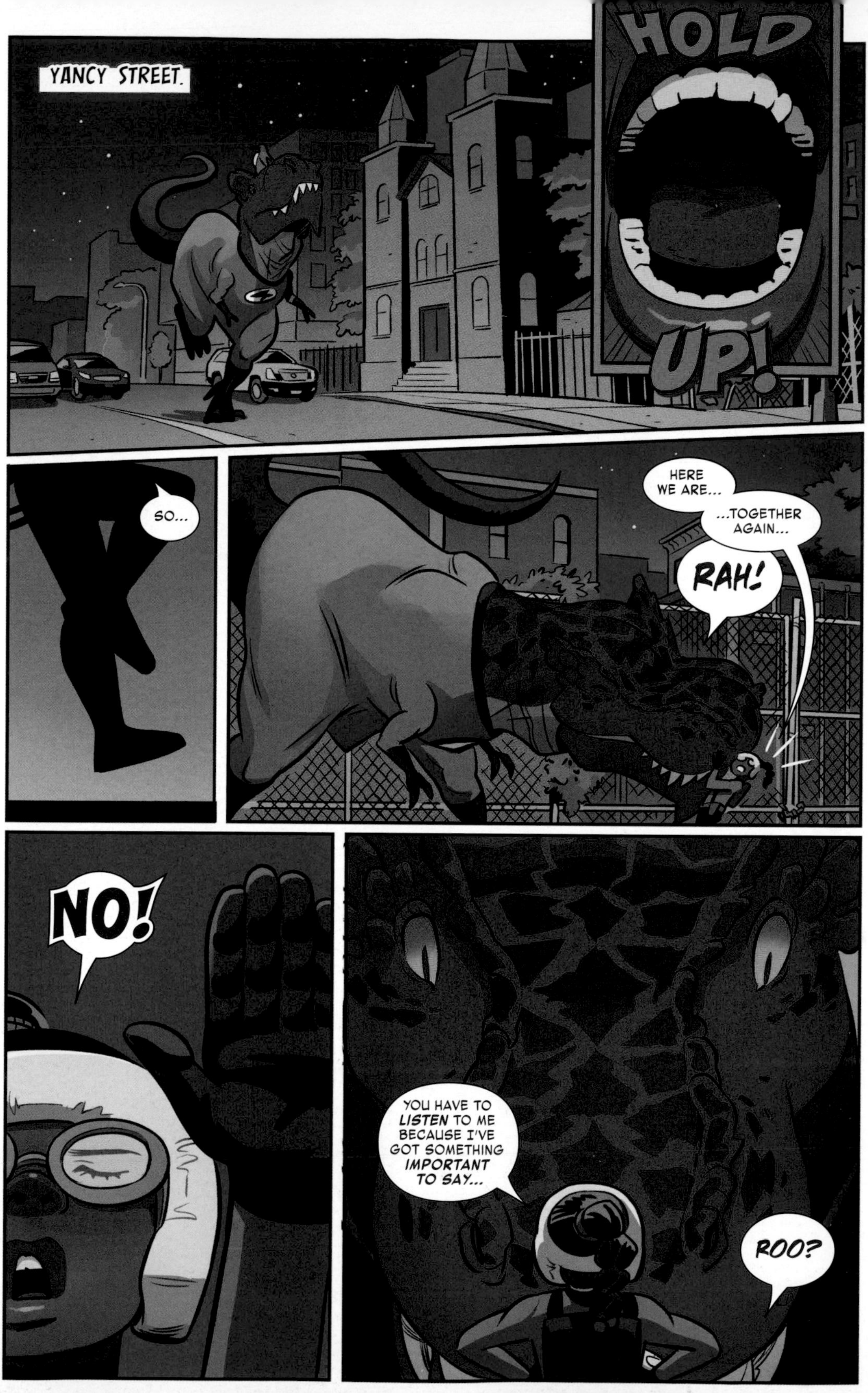
YANCY STREET.
HOLD UP!
SO...
HERE WE ARE...
...TOGETHER AGAIN...
RAH!
NO!
YOU HAVE TO LISTEN TO ME BECAUSE I'VE GOT SOMETHING IMPORTANT TO SAY...
ROO?

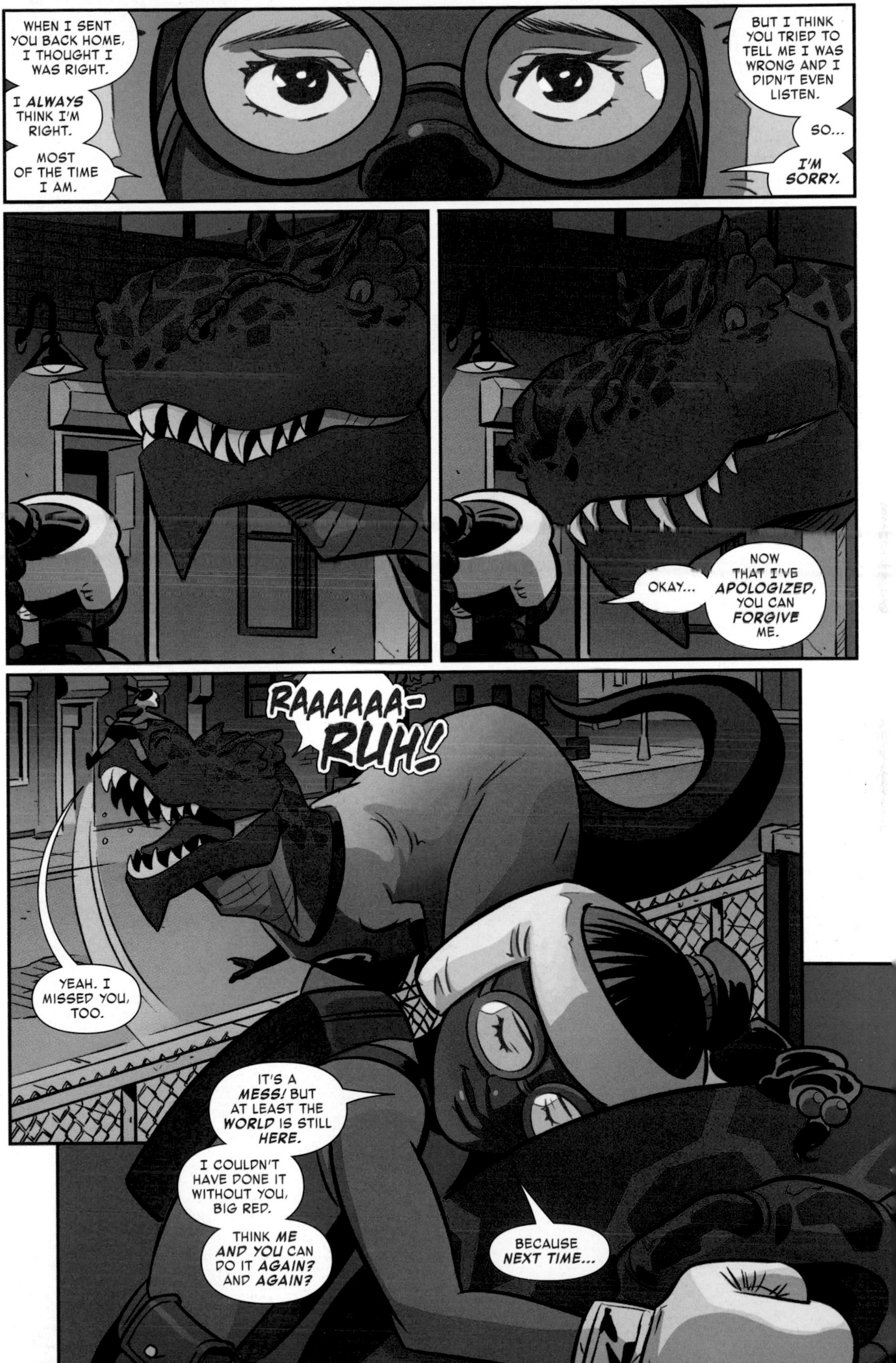

WHEN I SENT YOU BACK HOME, I THOUGHT I WAS RIGHT.
I *ALWAYS* THINK I'M RIGHT.
MOST OF THE TIME I AM.
BUT I THINK YOU TRIED TO TELL ME I WAS WRONG AND I DIDN'T EVEN LISTEN.
SO...
I'M SORRY.
OKAY...
NOW THAT I'VE *APOLOGIZED*, YOU CAN *FORGIVE* ME.
RAAAAAA-RUH!
YEAH. I MISSED YOU, TOO.
IT'S A *MESS!* BUT AT LEAST THE *WORLD* IS STILL *HERE.*
I COULDN'T HAVE DONE IT WITHOUT YOU, BIG RED.
THINK *ME AND YOU* CAN DO IT *AGAIN?* AND *AGAIN?*
BECAUSE *NEXT TIME...*

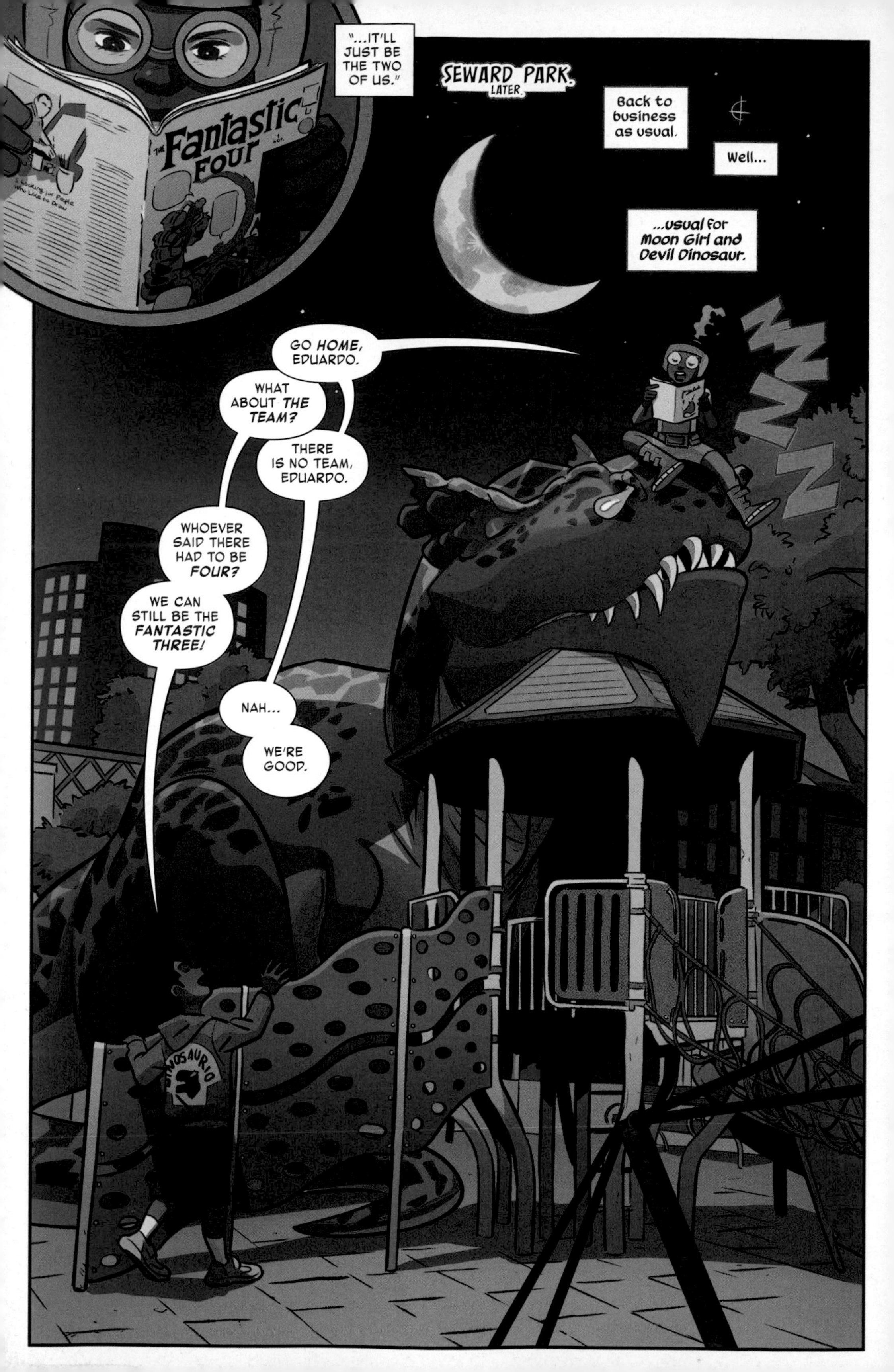
"...IT'LL JUST BE THE TWO OF US."
SEWARD PARK. LATER.
Back to business as usual.
Well...
...usual for Moon Girl and Devil Dinosaur.
GO HOME, EDUARDO.
WHAT ABOUT THE TEAM?
THERE IS NO TEAM, EDUARDO.
WHOEVER SAID THERE HAD TO BE FOUR?
WE CAN STILL BE THE FANTASTIC THREE!
NAH...
WE'RE GOOD.
MMMM
DINOSAURIO

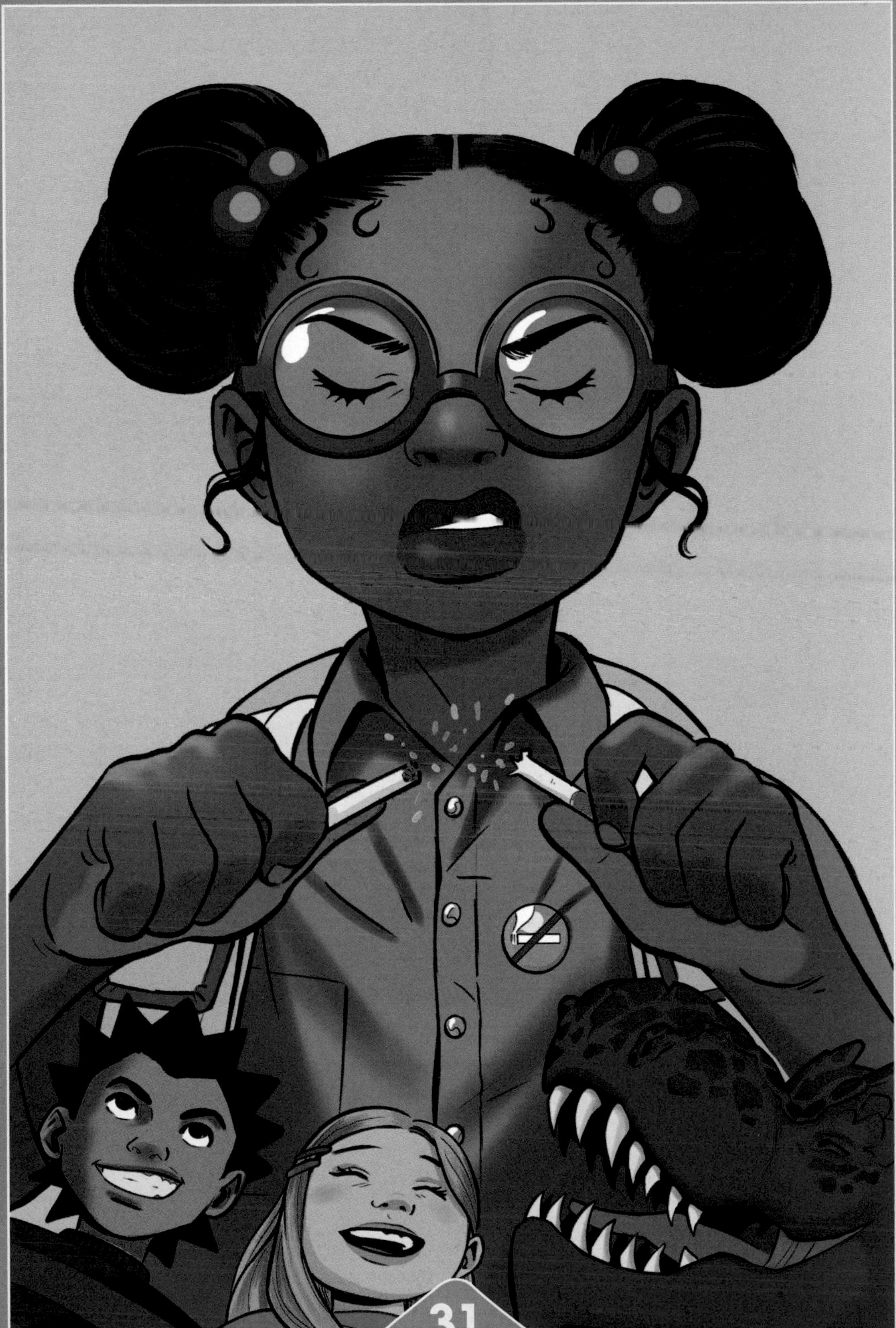

31

"BAD BUZZ"

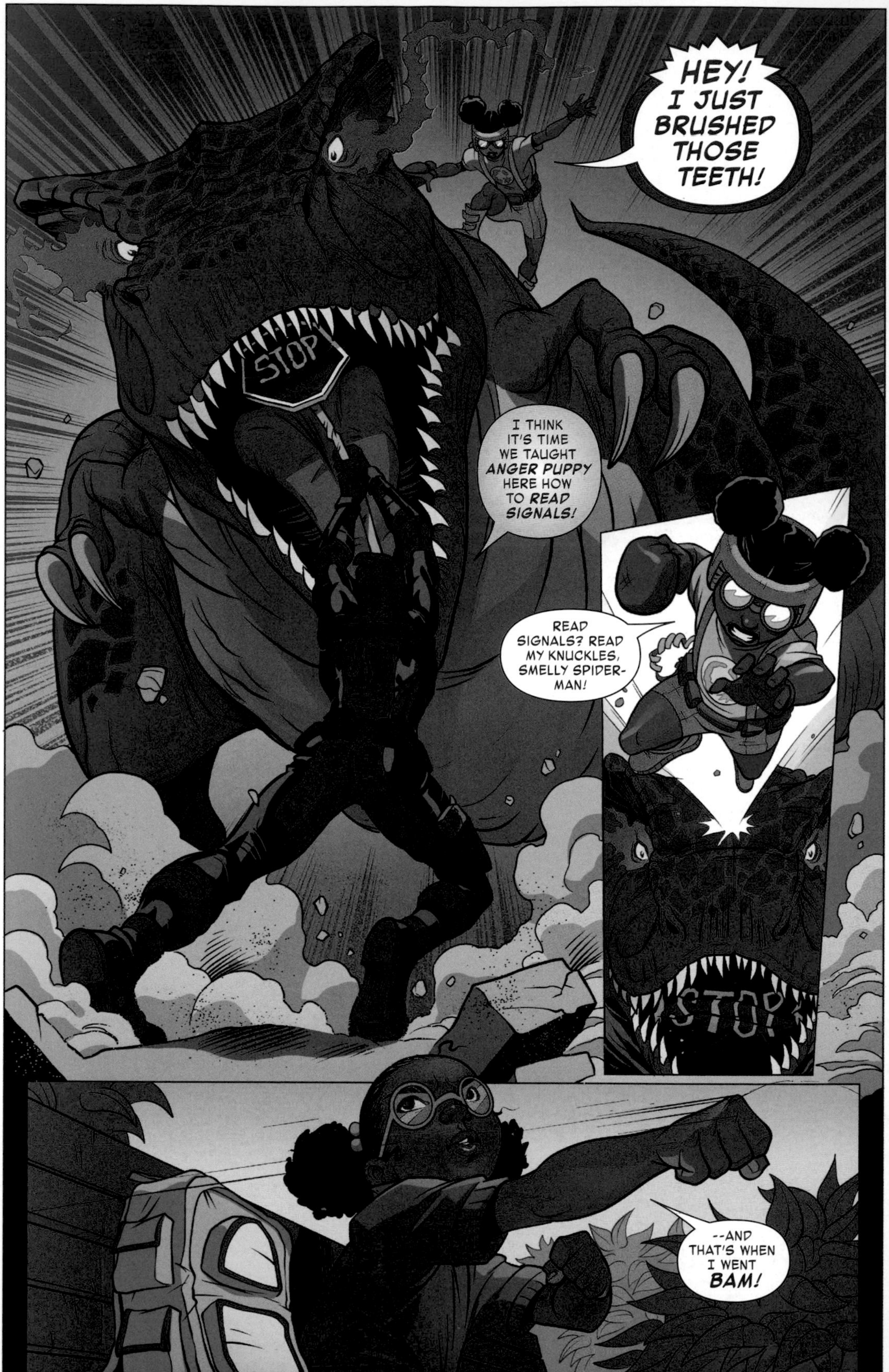
HEY! I JUST BRUSHED THOSE TEETH!
STOP
I THINK IT'S TIME WE TAUGHT ANGER PUPPY HERE HOW TO READ SIGNALS!
READ SIGNALS? READ MY KNUCKLES, SMELLY SPIDER-MAN!
STOP
--AND THAT'S WHEN I WENT BAM!

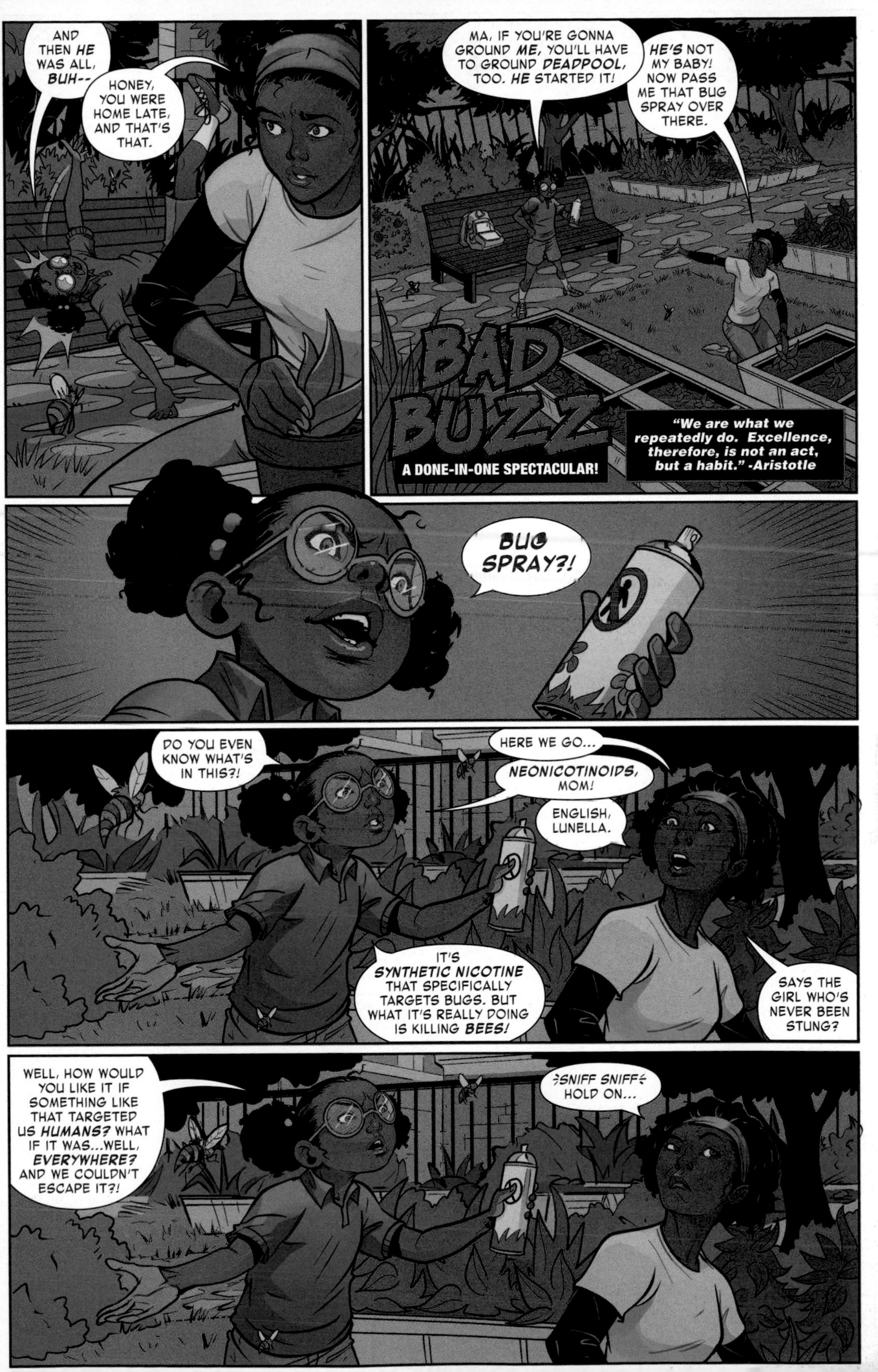
AND THEN HE WAS ALL, BUH--
HONEY, YOU WERE HOME LATE, AND THAT'S THAT.
MA, IF YOU'RE GONNA GROUND ME, YOU'LL HAVE TO GROUND DEADPOOL, TOO. HE STARTED IT!
HE'S NOT MY BABY! NOW PASS ME THAT BUG SPRAY OVER THERE.
BAD BUZZ
A DONE-IN-ONE SPECTACULAR!
"We are what we repeatedly do. Excellence, therefore, is not an act, but a habit." -Aristotle
BUG SPRAY?!
DO YOU EVEN KNOW WHAT'S IN THIS?!
HERE WE GO...
NEONICOTINOIDS, MOM!
ENGLISH, LUNELLA.
IT'S SYNTHETIC NICOTINE THAT SPECIFICALLY TARGETS BUGS. BUT WHAT IT'S REALLY DOING IS KILLING BEES!
SAYS THE GIRL WHO'S NEVER BEEN STUNG?
WELL, HOW WOULD YOU LIKE IT IF SOMETHING LIKE THAT TARGETED US HUMANS? WHAT IF IT WAS...WELL, EVERYWHERE? AND WE COULDN'T ESCAPE IT?!
⸗SNIFF SNIFF⸗ HOLD ON...

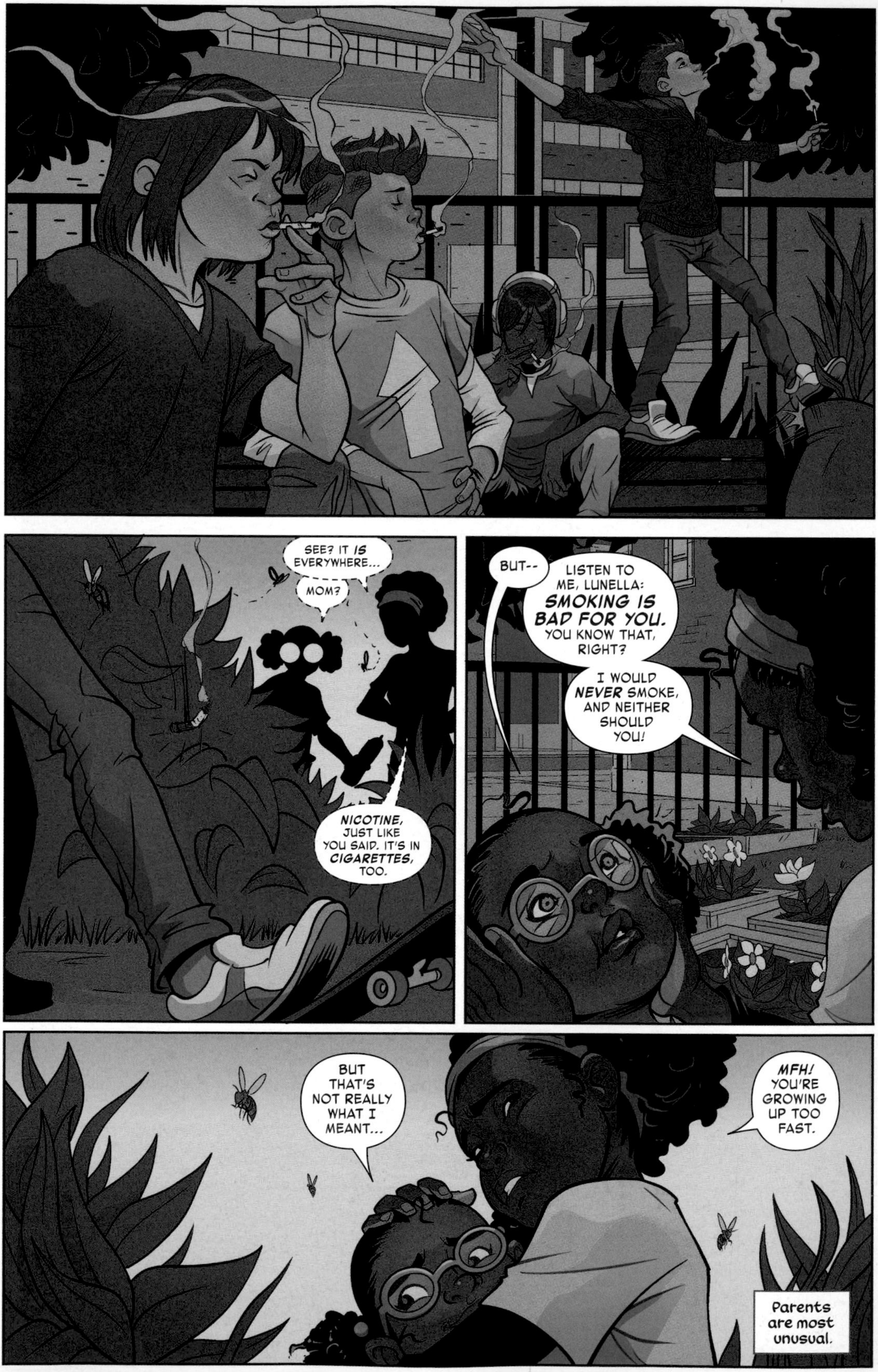

SEE? IT *IS* EVERYWHERE...
MOM?
NICOTINE, JUST LIKE YOU SAID. IT'S IN *CIGARETTES*, TOO.
BUT--
LISTEN TO ME, LUNELLA: ***SMOKING IS BAD FOR YOU.*** YOU KNOW THAT, RIGHT?
I WOULD ***NEVER*** SMOKE, AND NEITHER SHOULD YOU!
BUT THAT'S NOT REALLY WHAT I MEANT...
MFH! YOU'RE GROWING UP TOO FAST.
Parents are most unusual.

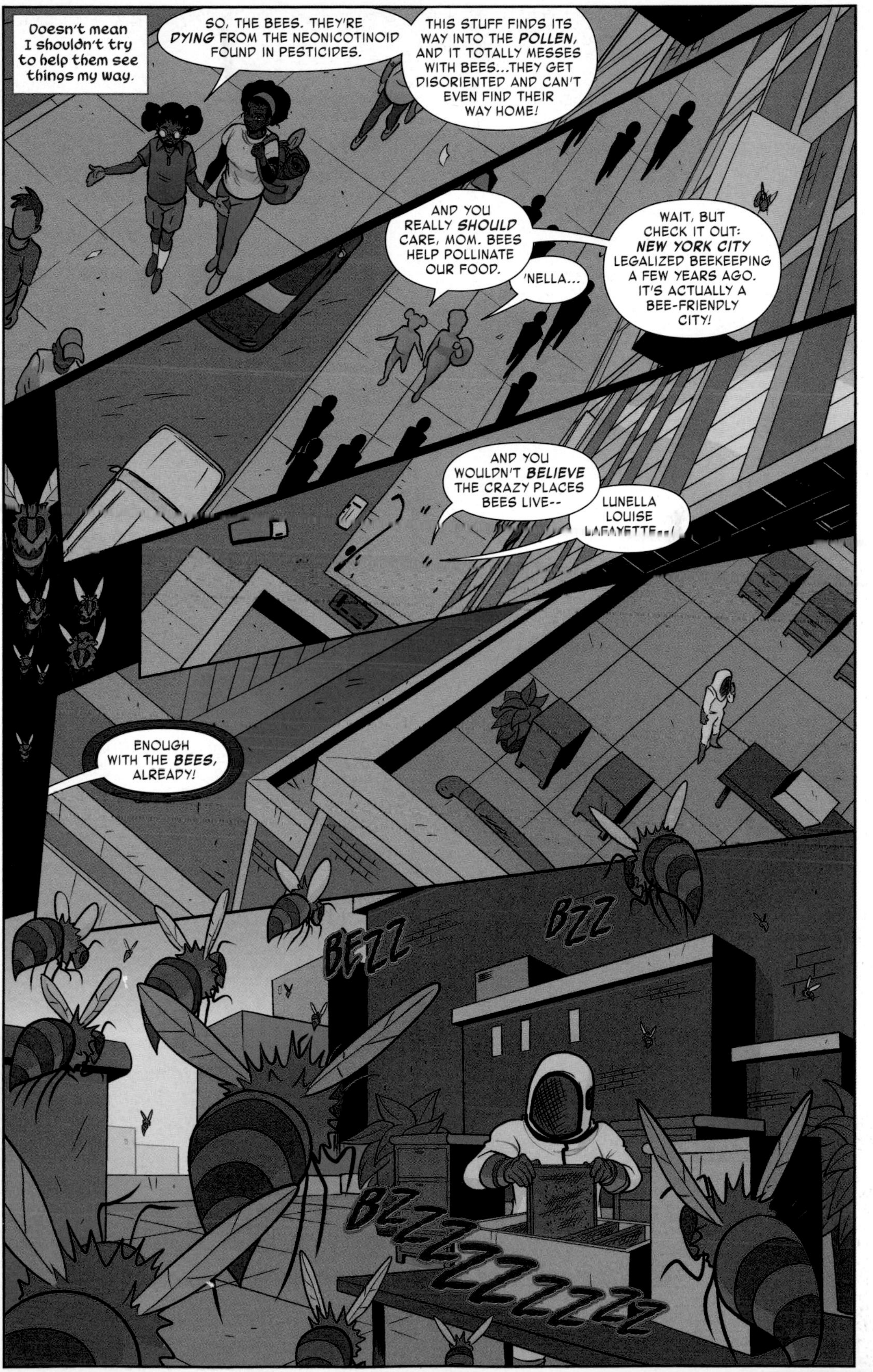
Doesn't mean I shouldn't try to help them see things my way.
SO, THE BEES. THEY'RE DYING FROM THE NEONICOTINOID FOUND IN PESTICIDES.
THIS STUFF FINDS ITS WAY INTO THE POLLEN, AND IT TOTALLY MESSES WITH BEES...THEY GET DISORIENTED AND CAN'T EVEN FIND THEIR WAY HOME!
AND YOU REALLY SHOULD CARE, MOM. BEES HELP POLLINATE OUR FOOD.
'NELLA...
WAIT, BUT CHECK IT OUT: NEW YORK CITY LEGALIZED BEEKEEPING A FEW YEARS AGO. IT'S ACTUALLY A BEE-FRIENDLY CITY!
AND YOU WOULDN'T BELIEVE THE CRAZY PLACES BEES LIVE--
LUNELLA LOUISE LAFAYETTE...!
ENOUGH WITH THE BEES, ALREADY!
BZZ
BEZZ
BZZZZZZZZZZZZZ

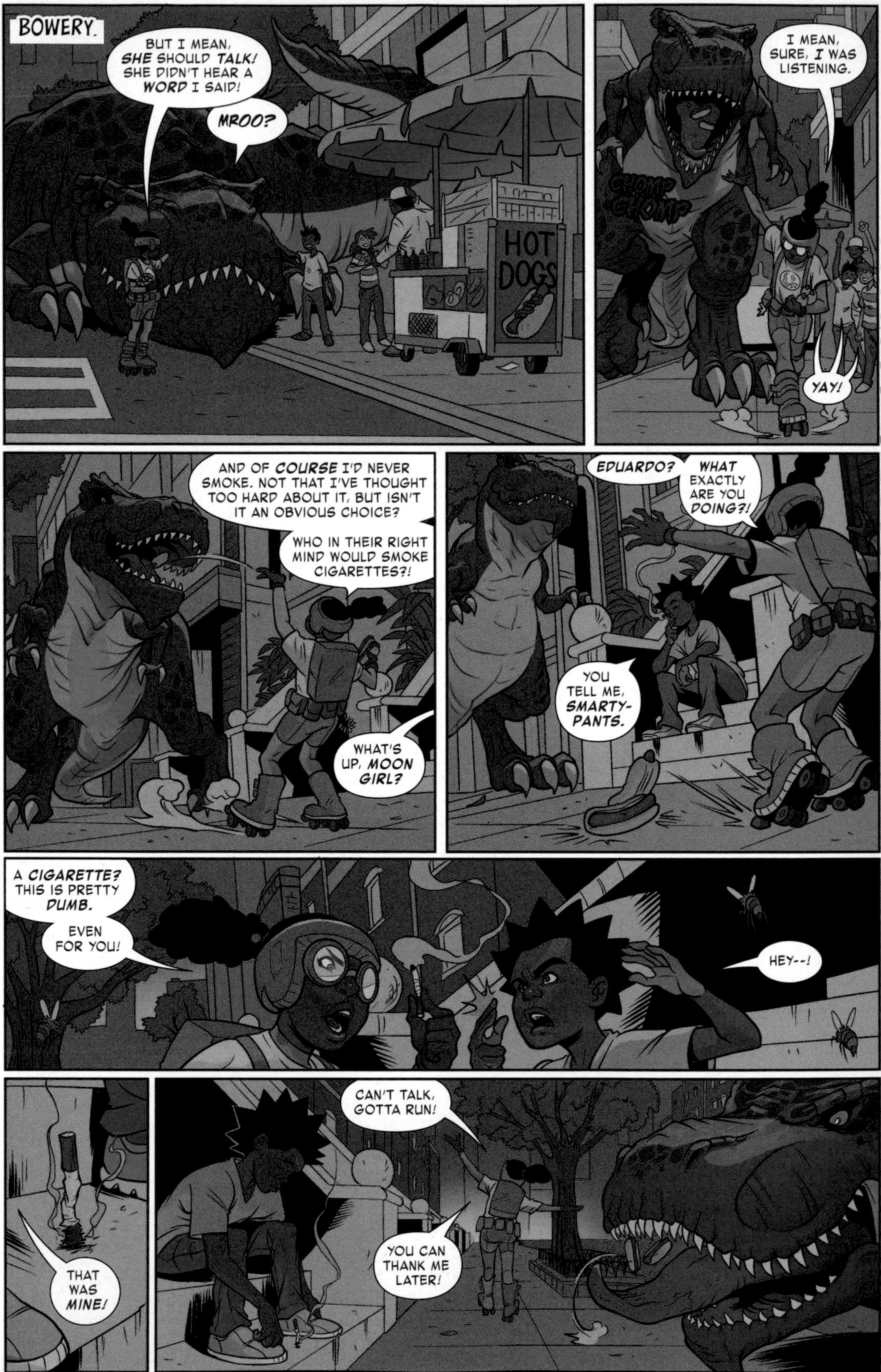

BOWERY.
BUT I MEAN, SHE SHOULD TALK! SHE DIDN'T HEAR A WORD I SAID!
MROO?
I MEAN, SURE, I WAS LISTENING.
YAY!
AND OF COURSE I'D NEVER SMOKE. NOT THAT I'VE THOUGHT TOO HARD ABOUT IT, BUT ISN'T IT AN OBVIOUS CHOICE?
WHO IN THEIR RIGHT MIND WOULD SMOKE CIGARETTES?!
WHAT'S UP, MOON GIRL?
EDUARDO?
WHAT EXACTLY ARE YOU DOING?!
YOU TELL ME, SMARTY-PANTS.
A CIGARETTE? THIS IS PRETTY DUMB.
EVEN FOR YOU!
HEY--!
THAT WAS MINE!
CAN'T TALK, GOTTA RUN!
YOU CAN THANK ME LATER!

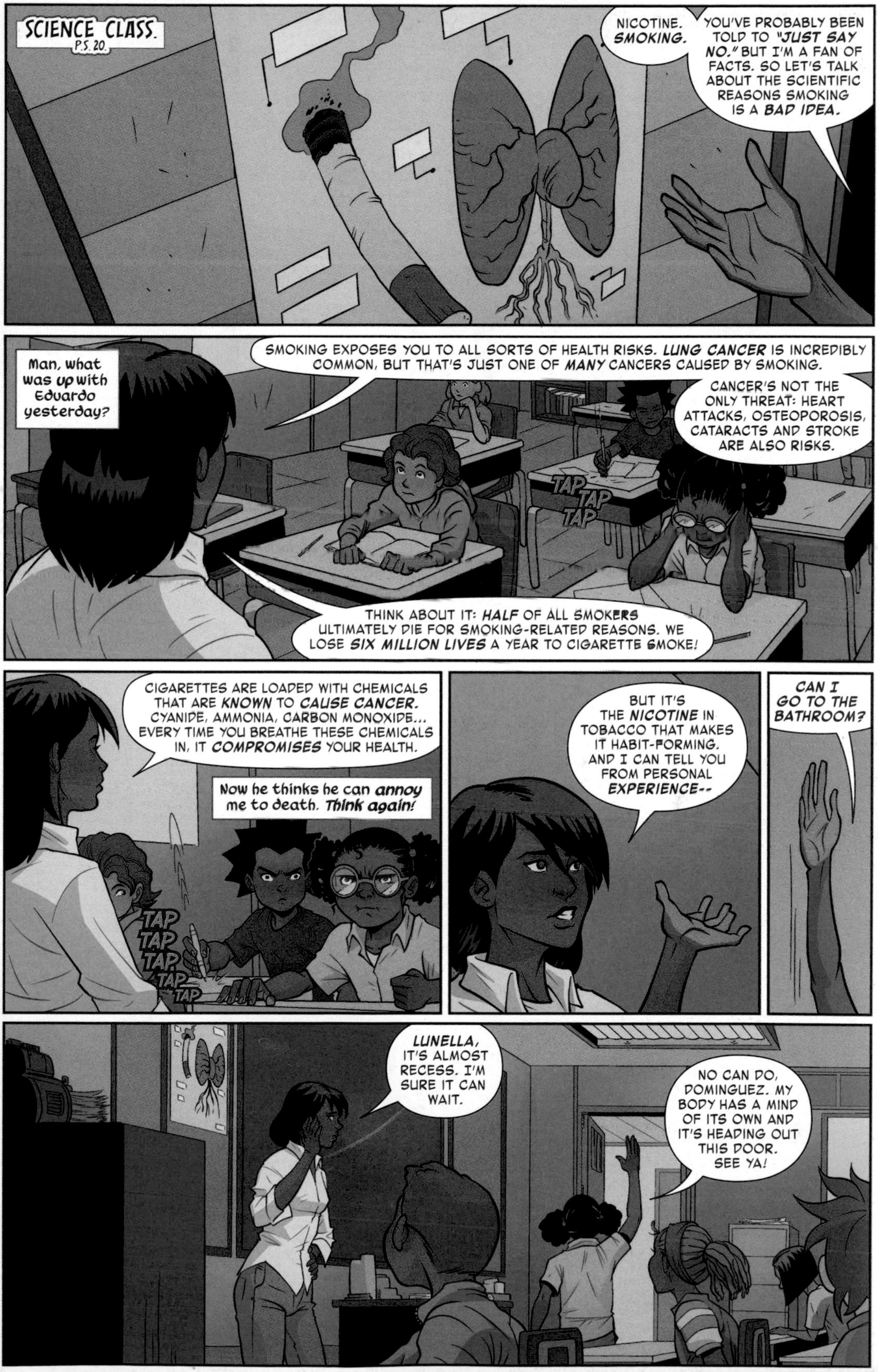
SCIENCE CLASS. P.S. 20.
NICOTINE. SMOKING.
YOU'VE PROBABLY BEEN TOLD TO "JUST SAY NO." BUT I'M A FAN OF FACTS. SO LET'S TALK ABOUT THE SCIENTIFIC REASONS SMOKING IS A BAD IDEA.
Man, what was up with Eduardo yesterday?
SMOKING EXPOSES YOU TO ALL SORTS OF HEALTH RISKS. LUNG CANCER IS INCREDIBLY COMMON, BUT THAT'S JUST ONE OF MANY CANCERS CAUSED BY SMOKING.
CANCER'S NOT THE ONLY THREAT: HEART ATTACKS, OSTEOPOROSIS, CATARACTS AND STROKE ARE ALSO RISKS.
TAP TAP TAP
THINK ABOUT IT: HALF OF ALL SMOKERS ULTIMATELY DIE FOR SMOKING-RELATED REASONS. WE LOSE SIX MILLION LIVES A YEAR TO CIGARETTE SMOKE!
CIGARETTES ARE LOADED WITH CHEMICALS THAT ARE KNOWN TO CAUSE CANCER. CYANIDE, AMMONIA, CARBON MONOXIDE... EVERY TIME YOU BREATHE THESE CHEMICALS IN, IT COMPROMISES YOUR HEALTH.
Now he thinks he can annoy me to death. Think again!
TAP TAP TAP TAP TAP
BUT IT'S THE NICOTINE IN TOBACCO THAT MAKES IT HABIT-FORMING. AND I CAN TELL YOU FROM PERSONAL EXPERIENCE--
CAN I GO TO THE BATHROOM?
LUNELLA, IT'S ALMOST RECESS. I'M SURE IT CAN WAIT.
NO CAN DO, DOMINGUEZ. MY BODY HAS A MIND OF ITS OWN AND IT'S HEADING OUT THIS DOOR. SEE YA!

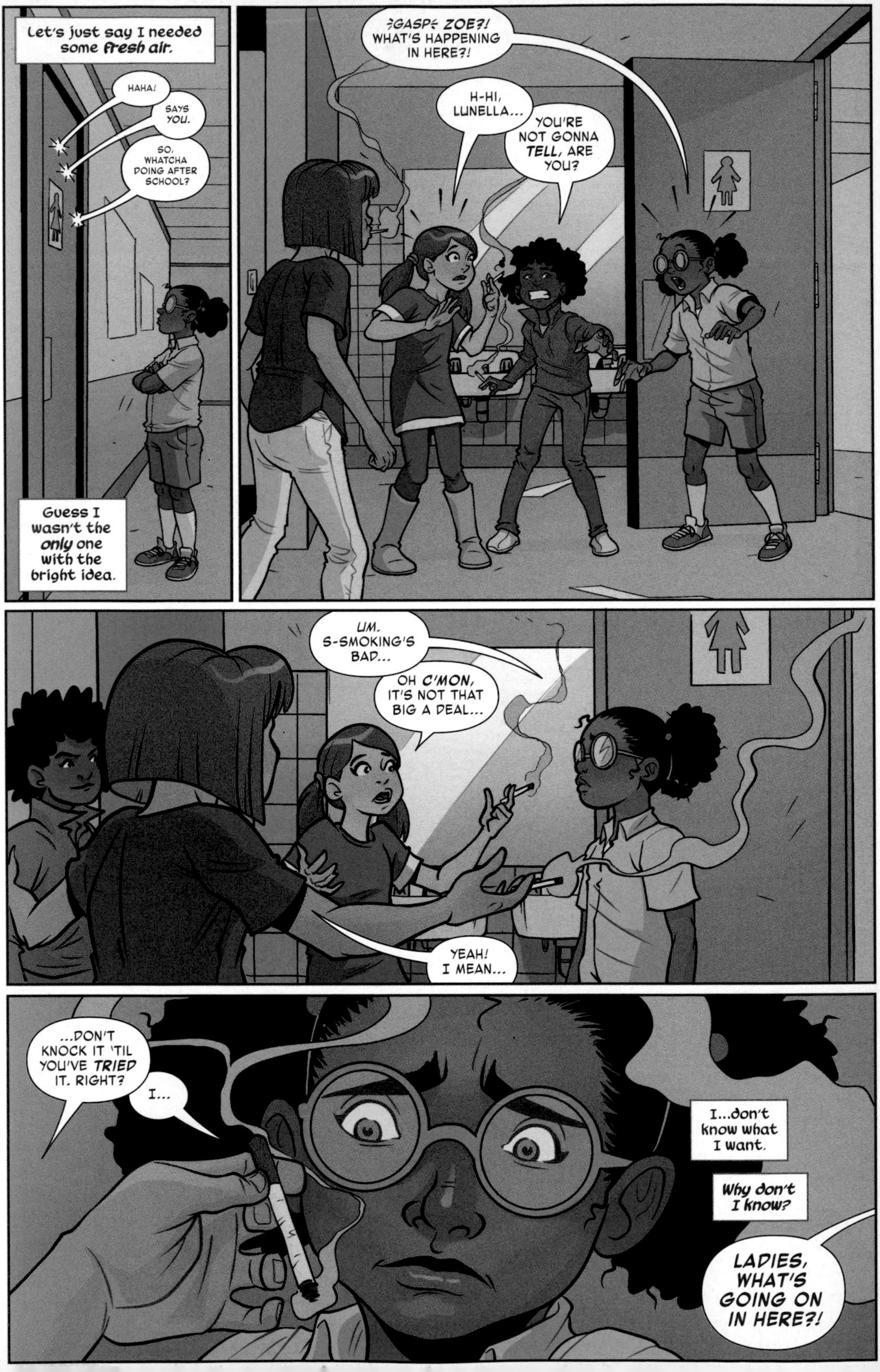
Let's just say I needed some fresh air.
HAHA!
SAYS YOU.
SO, WHATCHA DOING AFTER SCHOOL?
Guess I wasn't the only one with the bright idea.
GASP ZOE?! WHAT'S HAPPENING IN HERE?!
H-HI, LUNELLA...
YOU'RE NOT GONNA TELL, ARE YOU?
UM. S-SMOKING'S BAD...
OH C'MON, IT'S NOT THAT BIG A DEAL...
YEAH! I MEAN...
...DON'T KNOCK IT 'TIL YOU'VE TRIED IT. RIGHT?
I...
I...don't know what I want.
Why don't I know?
LADIES, WHAT'S GOING ON IN HERE?!

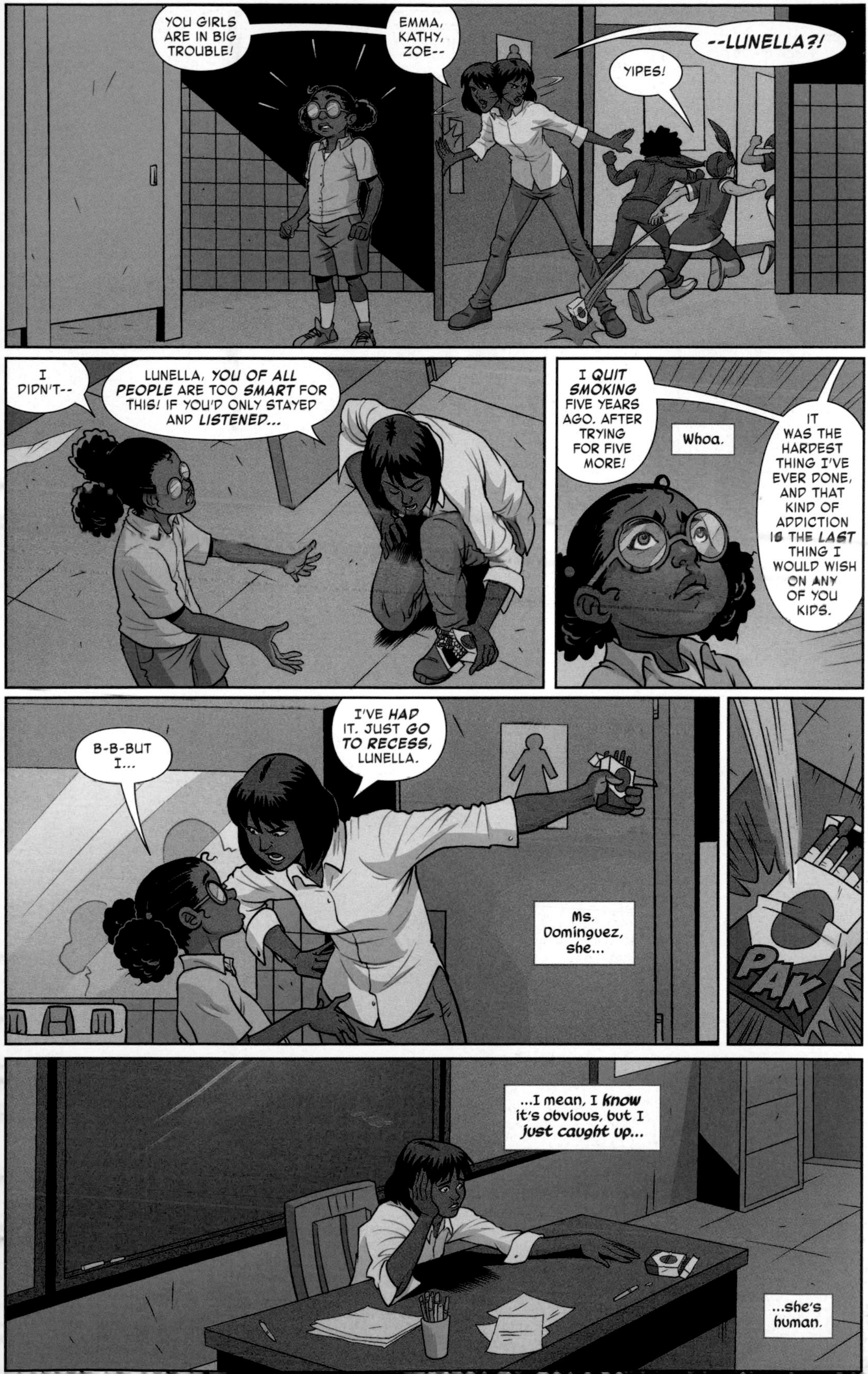
YOU GIRLS ARE IN BIG TROUBLE!
EMMA, KATHY, ZOE--
--LUNELLA?!
YIPES!
I DIDN'T--
LUNELLA, YOU OF ALL PEOPLE ARE TOO SMART FOR THIS! IF YOU'D ONLY STAYED AND LISTENED...
I QUIT SMOKING FIVE YEARS AGO. AFTER TRYING FOR FIVE MORE!
Whoa.
IT WAS THE HARDEST THING I'VE EVER DONE, AND THAT KIND OF ADDICTION IS THE LAST THING I WOULD WISH ON ANY OF YOU KIDS.
B-B-BUT I...
I'VE HAD IT. JUST GO TO RECESS, LUNELLA.
Ms. Dominguez, she...
PAK
...I mean, I know it's obvious, but I just caught up...
...she's human.

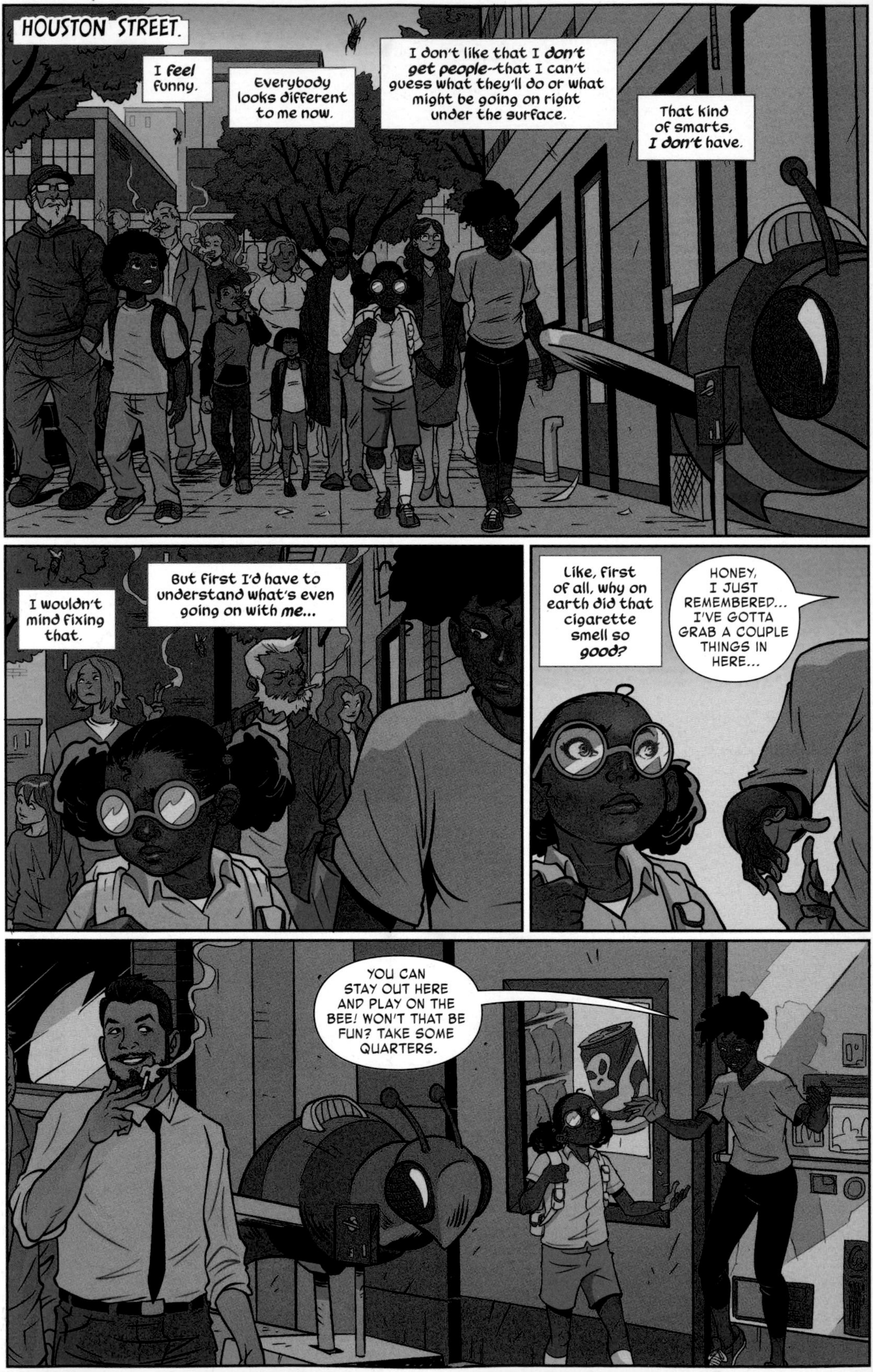
HOUSTON STREET.
I *feel* funny.
Everybody looks different to me now.
I don't like that I *don't get people*--that I can't guess what they'll do or what might be going on right under the surface.
That kind of smarts, *I don't* have.
I wouldn't mind fixing that.
But first I'd have to understand what's even going on with *me*...
Like, first of all, why on earth did that cigarette smell so *good*?
HONEY, I JUST REMEMBERED... I'VE GOTTA GRAB A COUPLE THINGS IN HERE...
YOU CAN STAY OUT HERE AND PLAY ON THE BEE! WON'T THAT BE FUN? TAKE SOME QUARTERS.

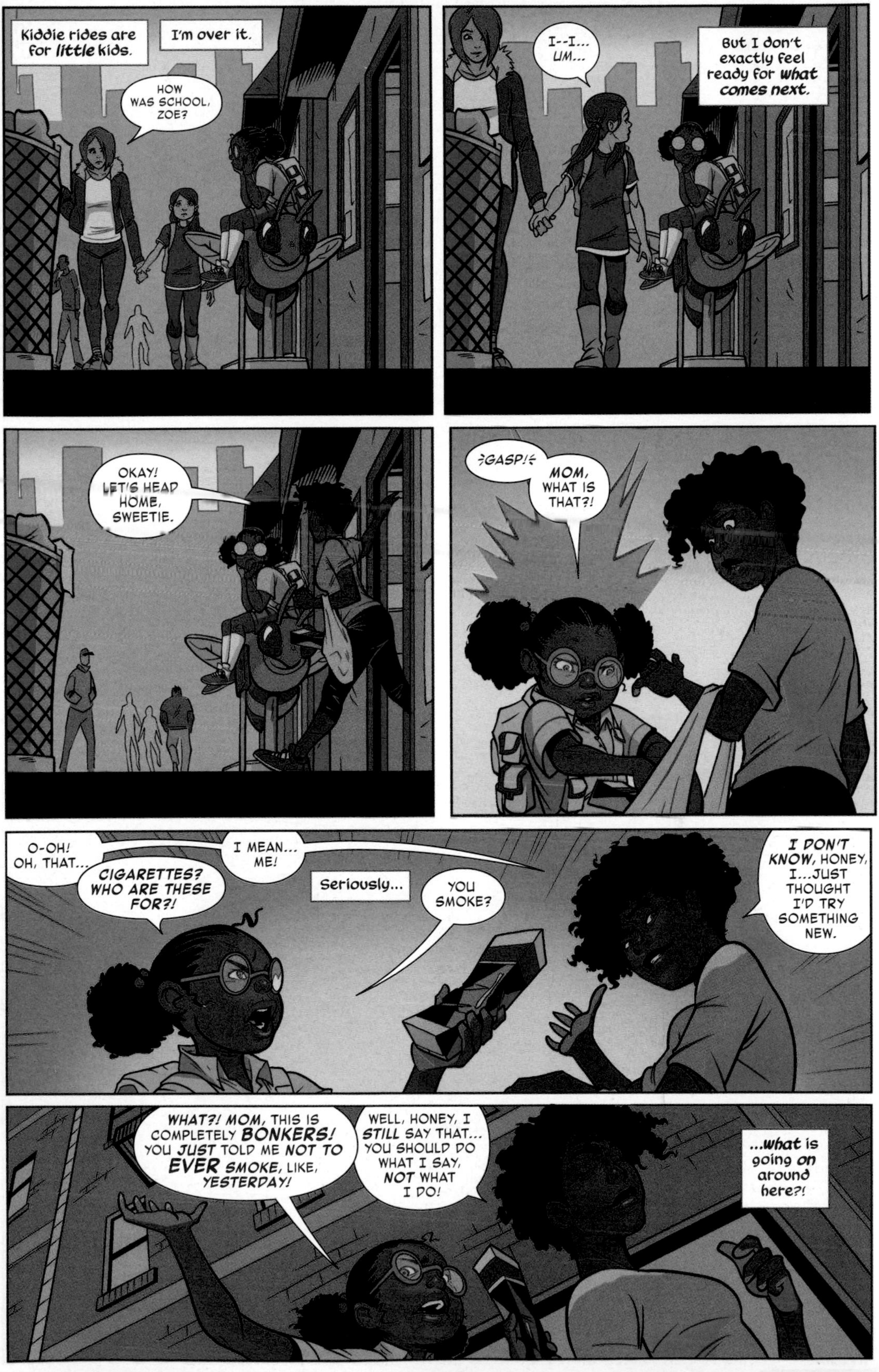
Kiddie rides are for *little* kids.
I'm over it.
HOW WAS SCHOOL, ZOE?
I--I... UM...
But I don't exactly feel ready for *what comes next.*
OKAY! LET'S HEAD HOME, SWEETIE.
GASP!
MOM, WHAT IS THAT?!
O-OH! OH, THAT...
I MEAN... ME!
CIGARETTES? WHO ARE THESE FOR?!
Seriously...
YOU SMOKE?
I DON'T KNOW, HONEY, I...JUST THOUGHT I'D TRY SOMETHING NEW.
WHAT?! MOM, THIS IS COMPLETELY BONKERS! YOU JUST TOLD ME NOT TO EVER SMOKE, LIKE, YESTERDAY!
WELL, HONEY, I STILL SAY THAT... YOU SHOULD DO WHAT I SAY, NOT WHAT I DO!
...what is going on around here?!

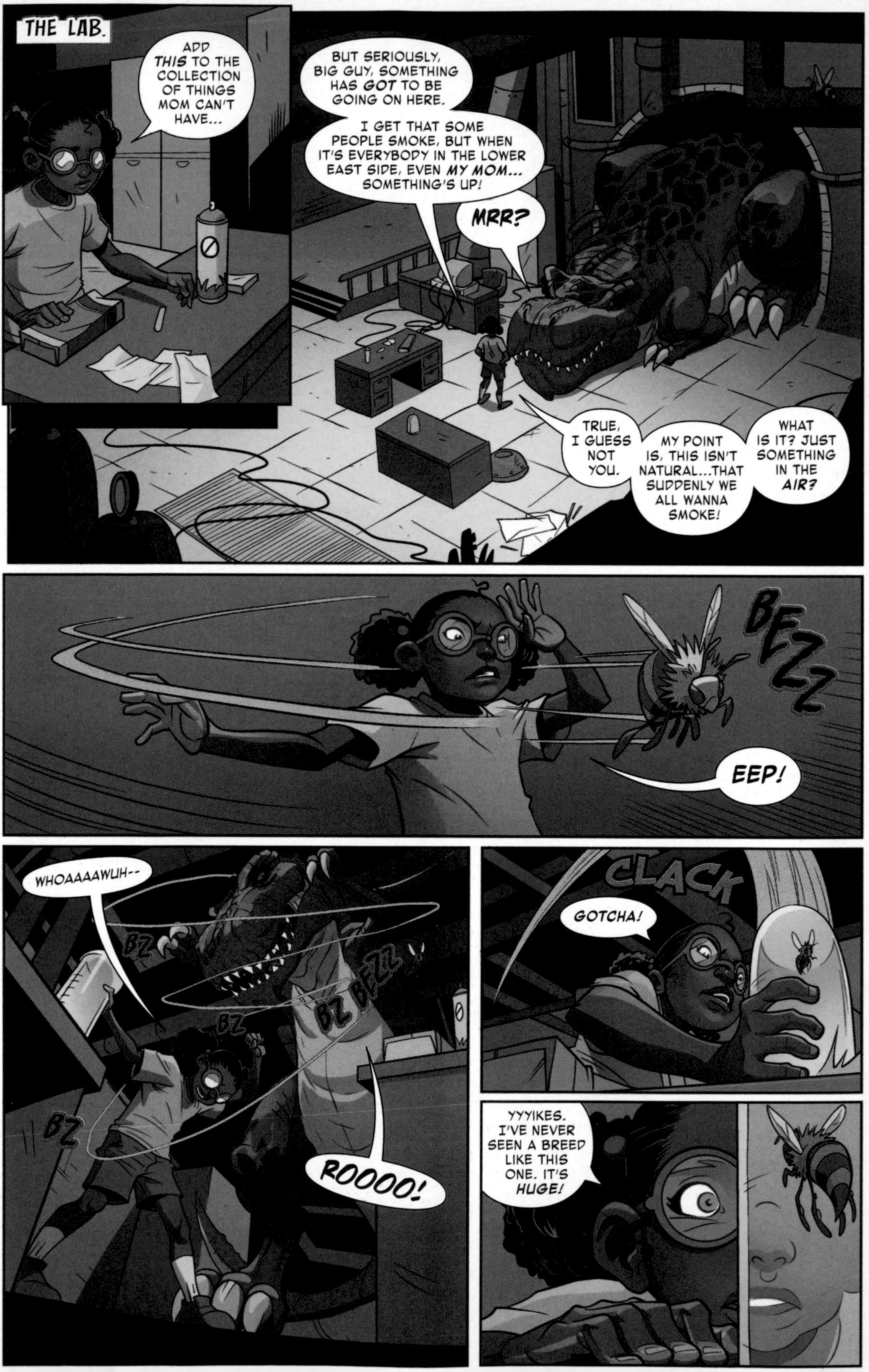
THE LAB.
ADD THIS TO THE COLLECTION OF THINGS MOM CAN'T HAVE...
BUT SERIOUSLY, BIG GUY, SOMETHING HAS GOT TO BE GOING ON HERE.
I GET THAT SOME PEOPLE SMOKE, BUT WHEN IT'S EVERYBODY IN THE LOWER EAST SIDE, EVEN MY MOM... SOMETHING'S UP!
MRR?
TRUE, I GUESS NOT YOU.
MY POINT IS, THIS ISN'T NATURAL...THAT SUDDENLY WE ALL WANNA SMOKE!
WHAT IS IT? JUST SOMETHING IN THE AIR?
BEZZ
EEP!
WHOAAAAWUH--
BZ
BZ BEZZ
BZ
BZ
ROOOO!
CLACK
GOTCHA!
YYYIKES. I'VE NEVER SEEN A BREED LIKE THIS ONE. IT'S HUGE!

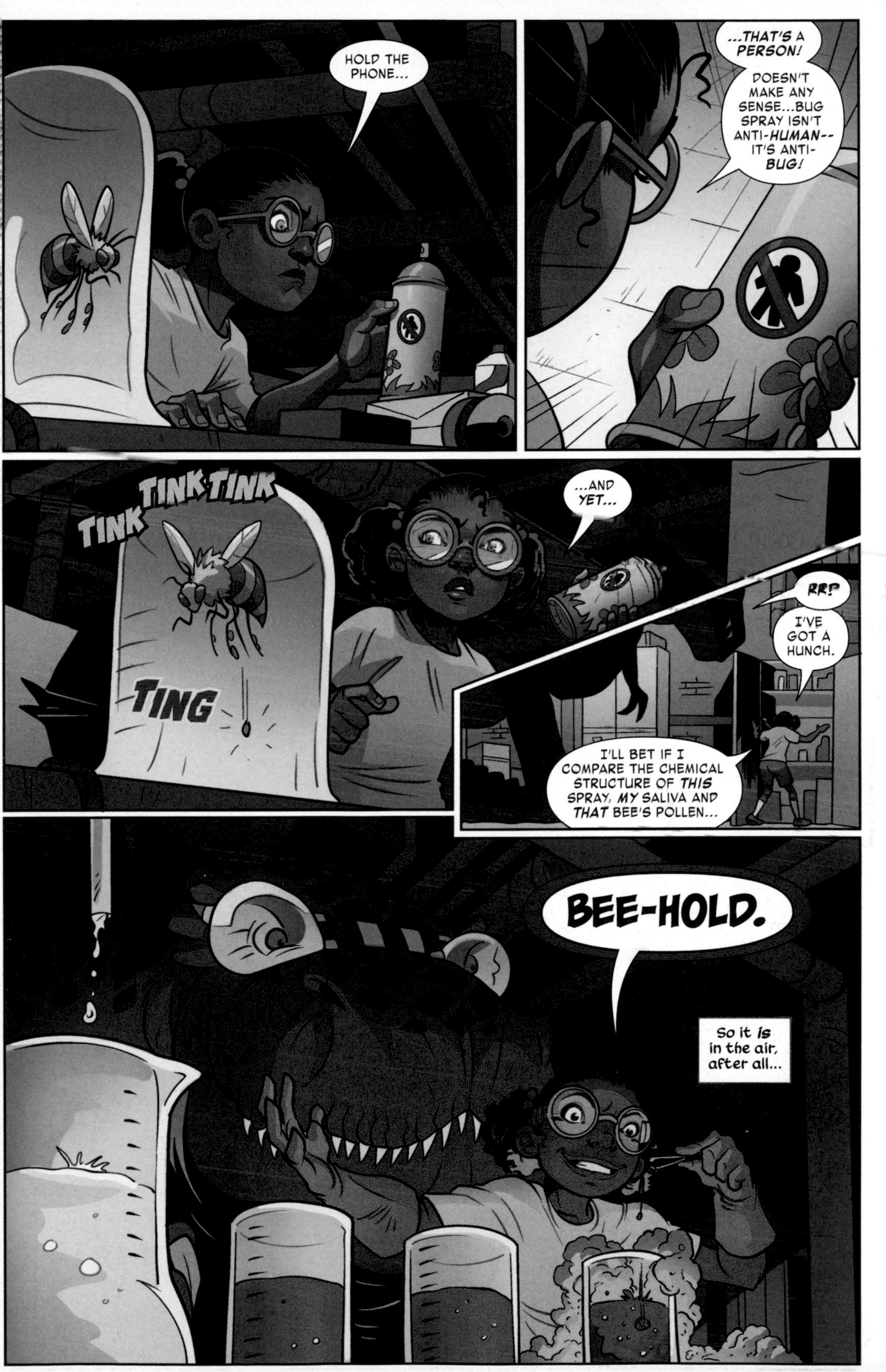
HOLD THE PHONE...
...THAT'S A PERSON!
DOESN'T MAKE ANY SENSE...BUG SPRAY ISN'T ANTI-HUMAN--IT'S ANTI-BUG!
TINK TINK TINK
TING
...AND YET...
RR?
I'VE GOT A HUNCH.
I'LL BET IF I COMPARE THE CHEMICAL STRUCTURE OF THIS SPRAY, MY SALIVA AND THAT BEE'S POLLEN...
BEE-HOLD.
So it is in the air, after all...

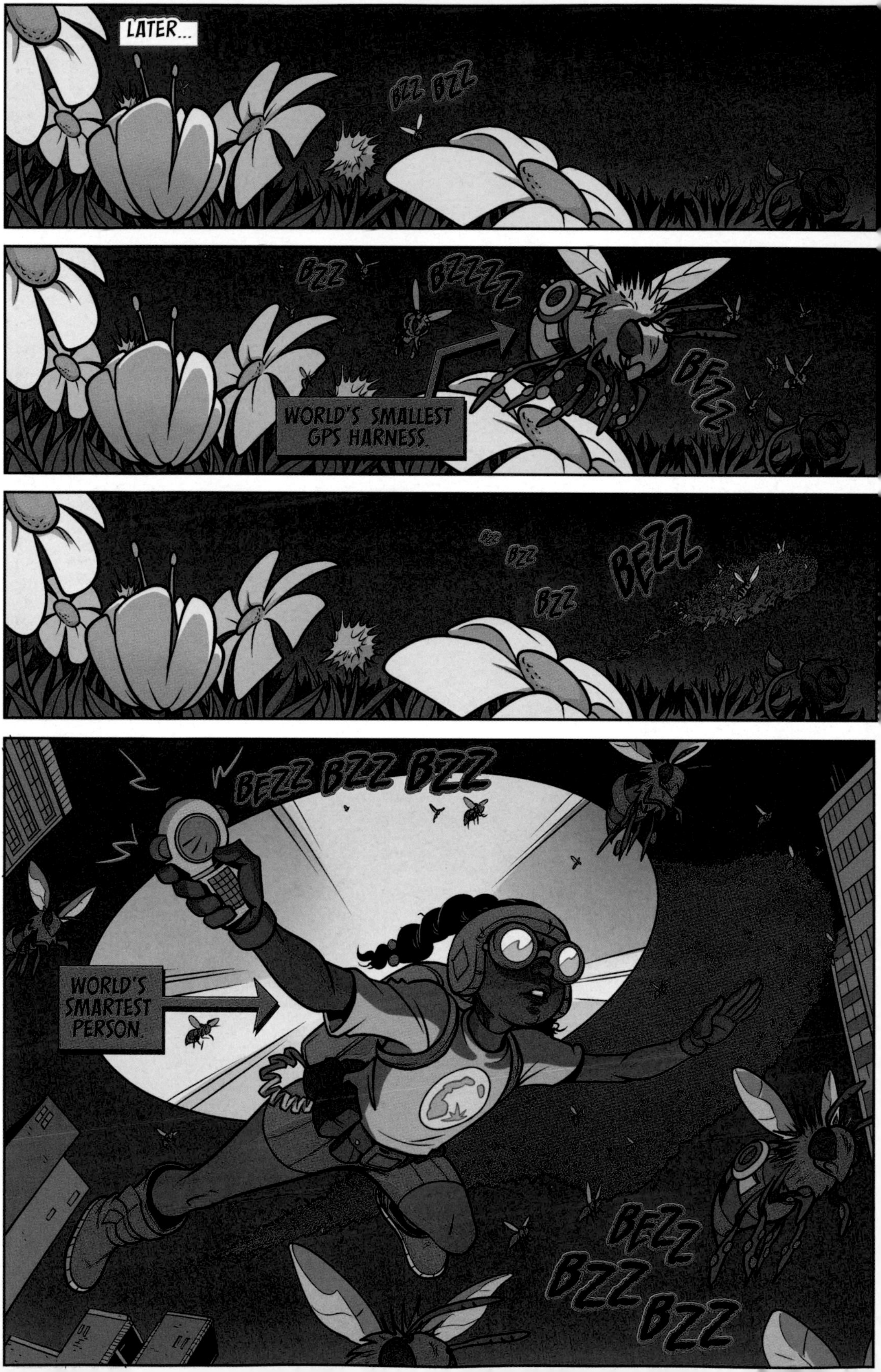
LATER...
BZZ BZZ
BZZ
BZZZZZ
BEZZ
WORLD'S SMALLEST GPS HARNESS.
BZZ
BZZ
BEZZ
BZZ
BEZZ BZZ BZZ
WORLD'S SMARTEST PERSON.
BEZZ
BZZ
BZZ

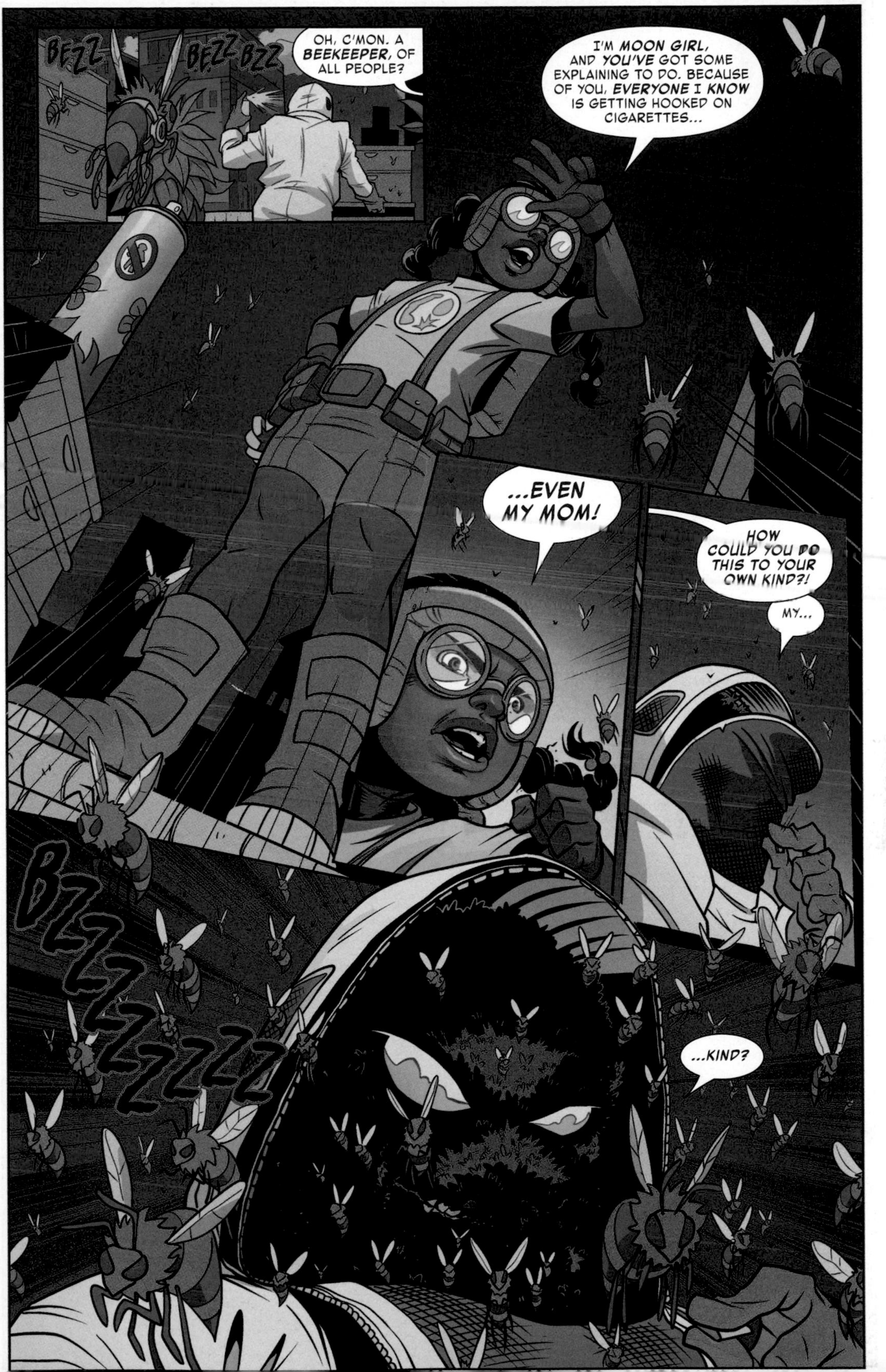
BEZZ
BEZZ BZZ
OH, C'MON. A BEEKEEPER, OF ALL PEOPLE?
I'M MOON GIRL, AND YOU'VE GOT SOME EXPLAINING TO DO. BECAUSE OF YOU, EVERYONE I KNOW IS GETTING HOOKED ON CIGARETTES...
...EVEN MY MOM!
HOW COULD YOU DO THIS TO YOUR OWN KIND?!
MY...
BZZZZZZZZZ
...KIND?

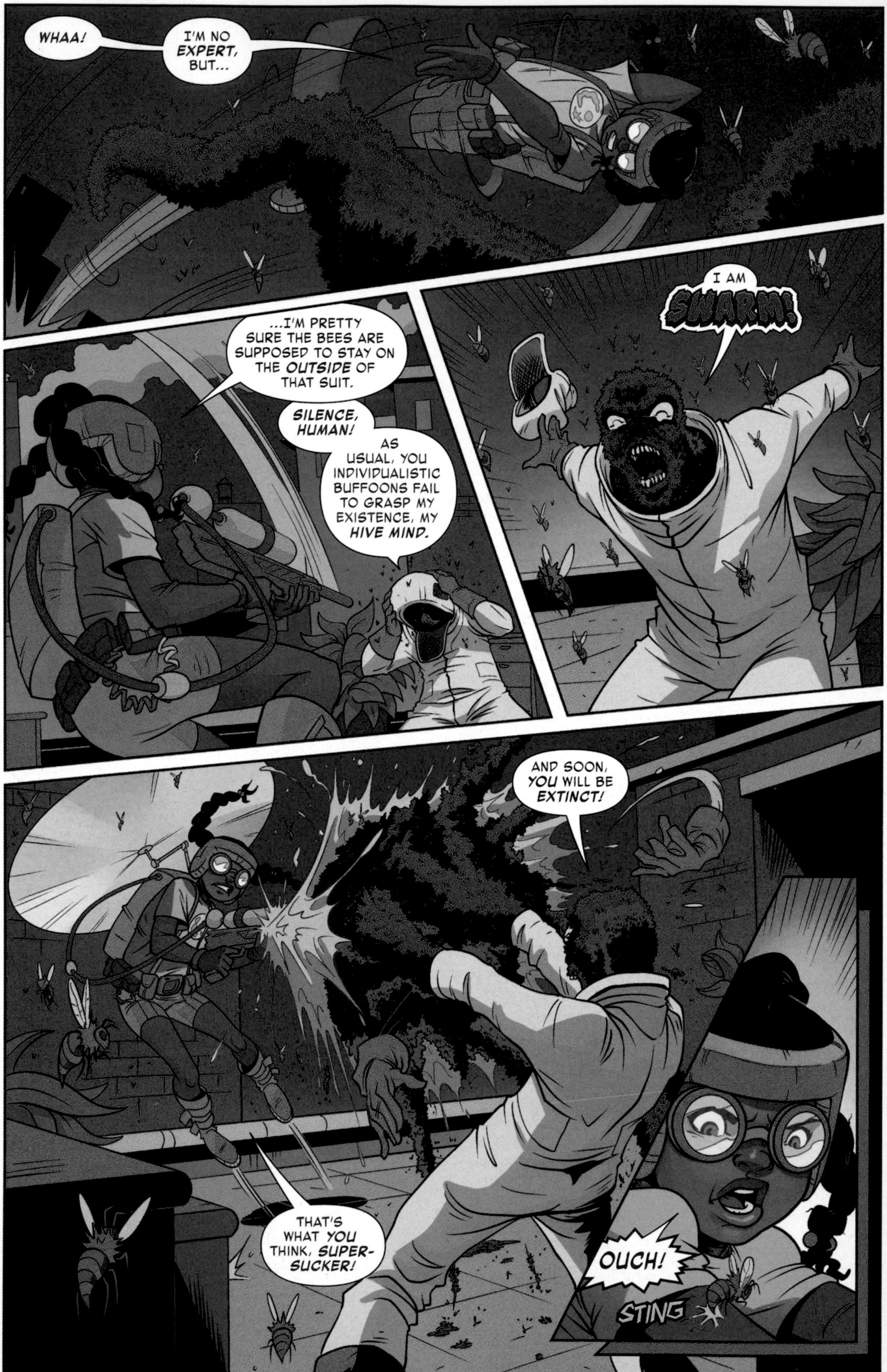
WHAA!
I'M NO EXPERT, BUT...
...I'M PRETTY SURE THE BEES ARE SUPPOSED TO STAY ON THE OUTSIDE OF THAT SUIT.
SILENCE, HUMAN!
AS USUAL, YOU INDIVIDUALISTIC BUFFOONS FAIL TO GRASP MY EXISTENCE, MY HIVE MIND.
I AM SWARM!
AND SOON, YOU WILL BE EXTINCT!
THAT'S WHAT YOU THINK, SUPER-SUCKER!
OUCH!
STING

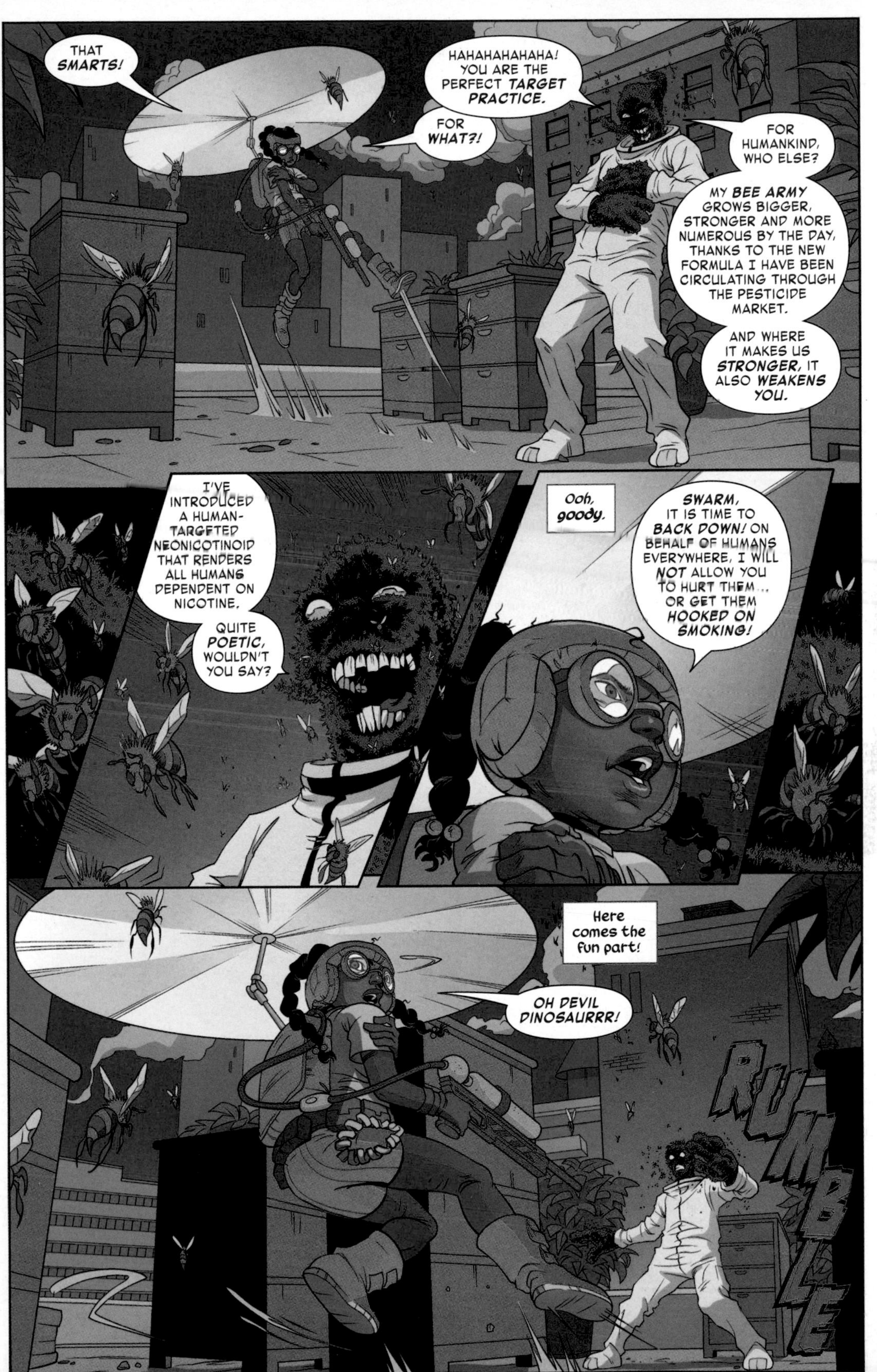
THAT SMARTS!
HAHAHAHAHAHA! YOU ARE THE PERFECT TARGET PRACTICE.
FOR WHAT?!
FOR HUMANKIND, WHO ELSE?
MY BEE ARMY GROWS BIGGER, STRONGER AND MORE NUMEROUS BY THE DAY, THANKS TO THE NEW FORMULA I HAVE BEEN CIRCULATING THROUGH THE PESTICIDE MARKET.
AND WHERE IT MAKES US STRONGER, IT ALSO WEAKENS YOU.
I'VE INTRODUCED A HUMAN-TARGETED NEONICOTINOID THAT RENDERS ALL HUMANS DEPENDENT ON NICOTINE.
QUITE POETIC, WOULDN'T YOU SAY?
Ooh, goody.
SWARM, IT IS TIME TO BACK DOWN! ON BEHALF OF HUMANS EVERYWHERE, I WILL NOT ALLOW YOU TO HURT THEM... OR GET THEM HOOKED ON SMOKING!
Here comes the fun part!
OH DEVIL DINOSAURRR!
RUMBLE

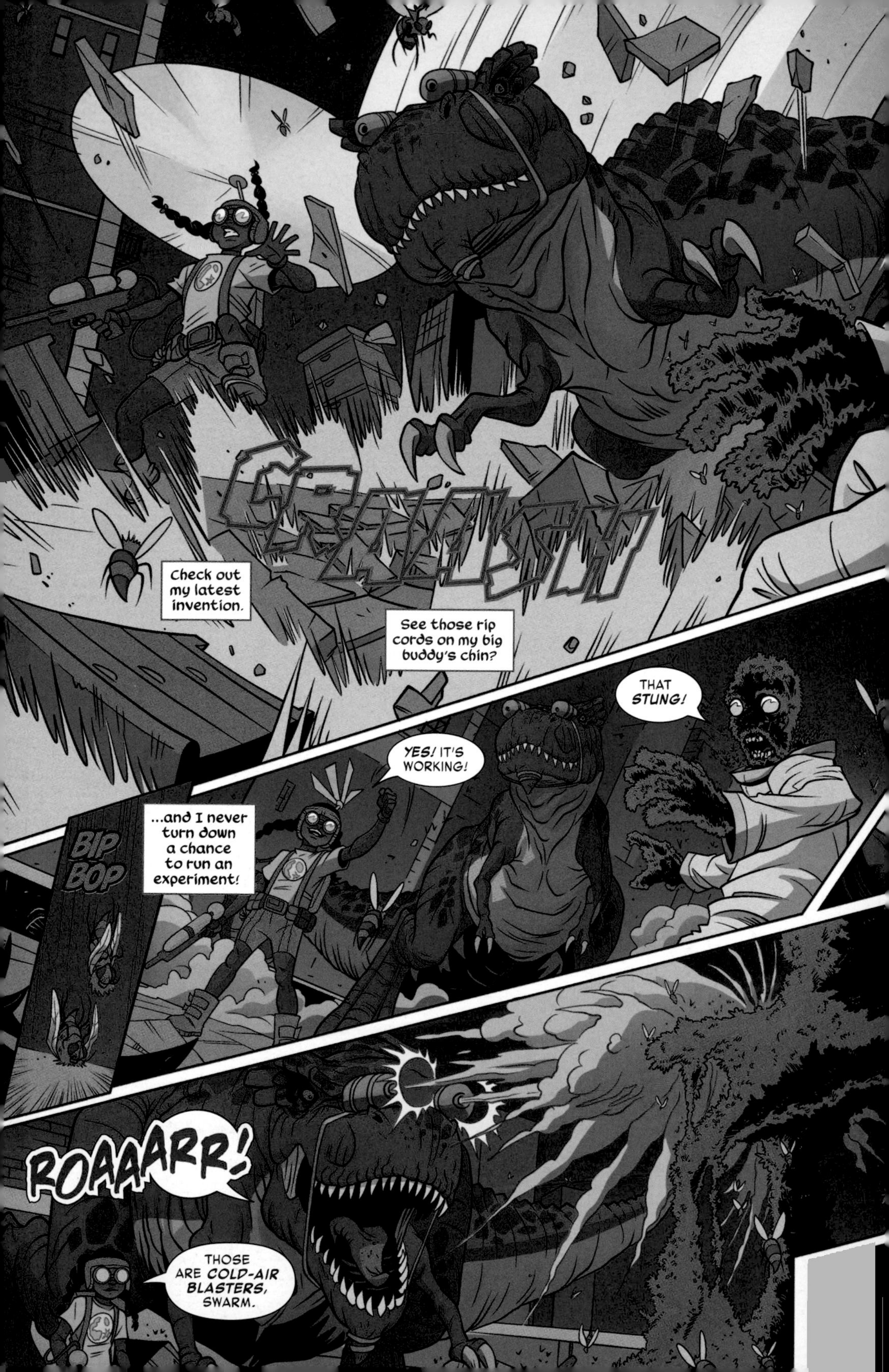

CRAAASH
Check out my latest invention.
See those rip cords on my big buddy's chin?
THAT STUNG!
YES! IT'S WORKING!
...and I never turn down a chance to run an experiment!
BIP BOP
ROAAARR!
THOSE ARE COLD-AIR BLASTERS, SWARM.

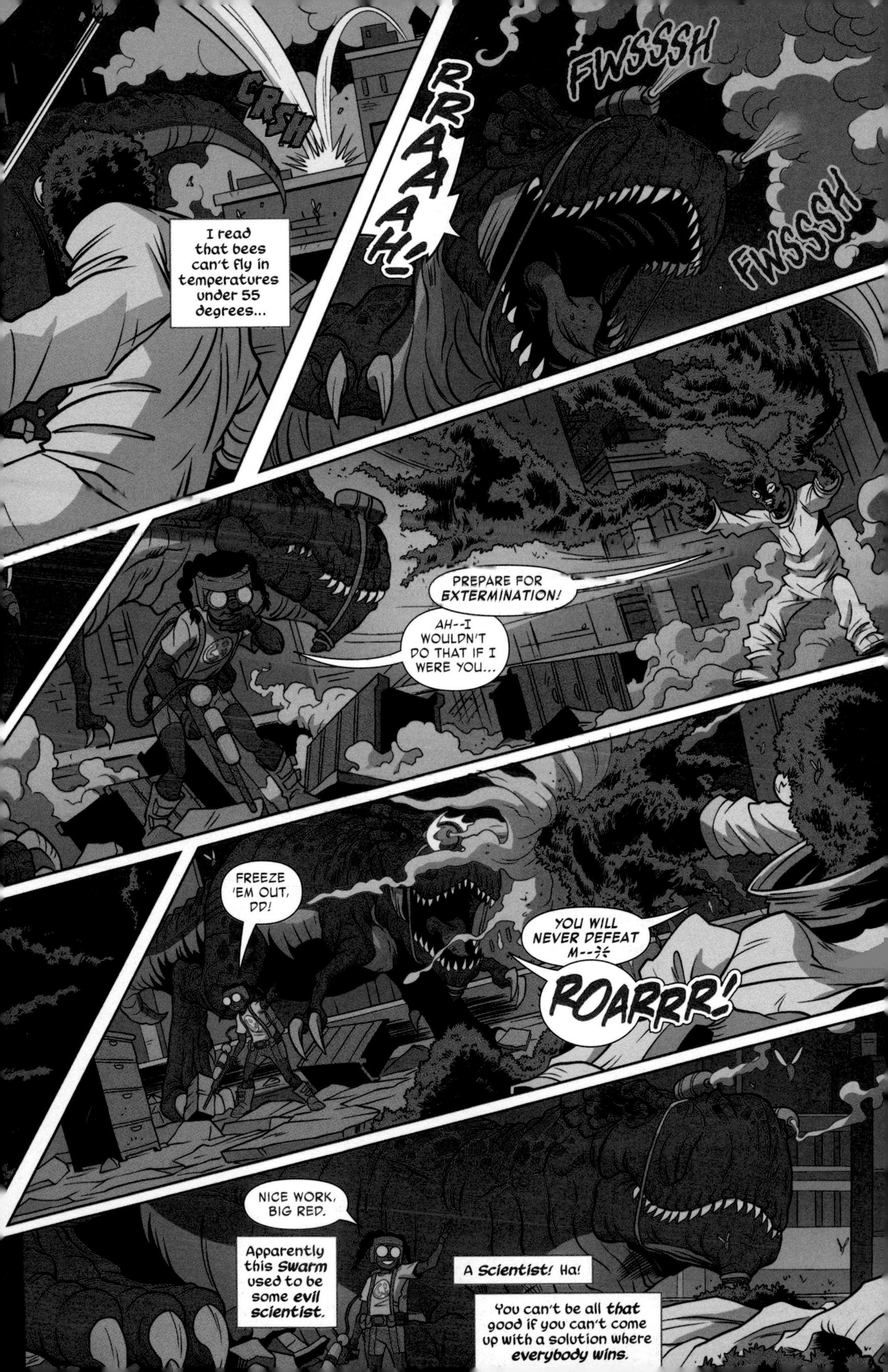
CRSH
I read that bees can't fly in temperatures under 55 degrees...
RRAAAAH!
FWSSSH
FWSSSH
PREPARE FOR EXTERMINATION!
AH--I WOULDN'T DO THAT IF I WERE YOU...
FREEZE 'EM OUT, DD!
YOU WILL NEVER DEFEAT M--
ROARRR!
NICE WORK, BIG RED.
Apparently this *Swarm* used to be some *evil scientist*.
A *Scientist*! Ha!
You can't be all *that* good if you can't come up with a solution where *everybody wins*.

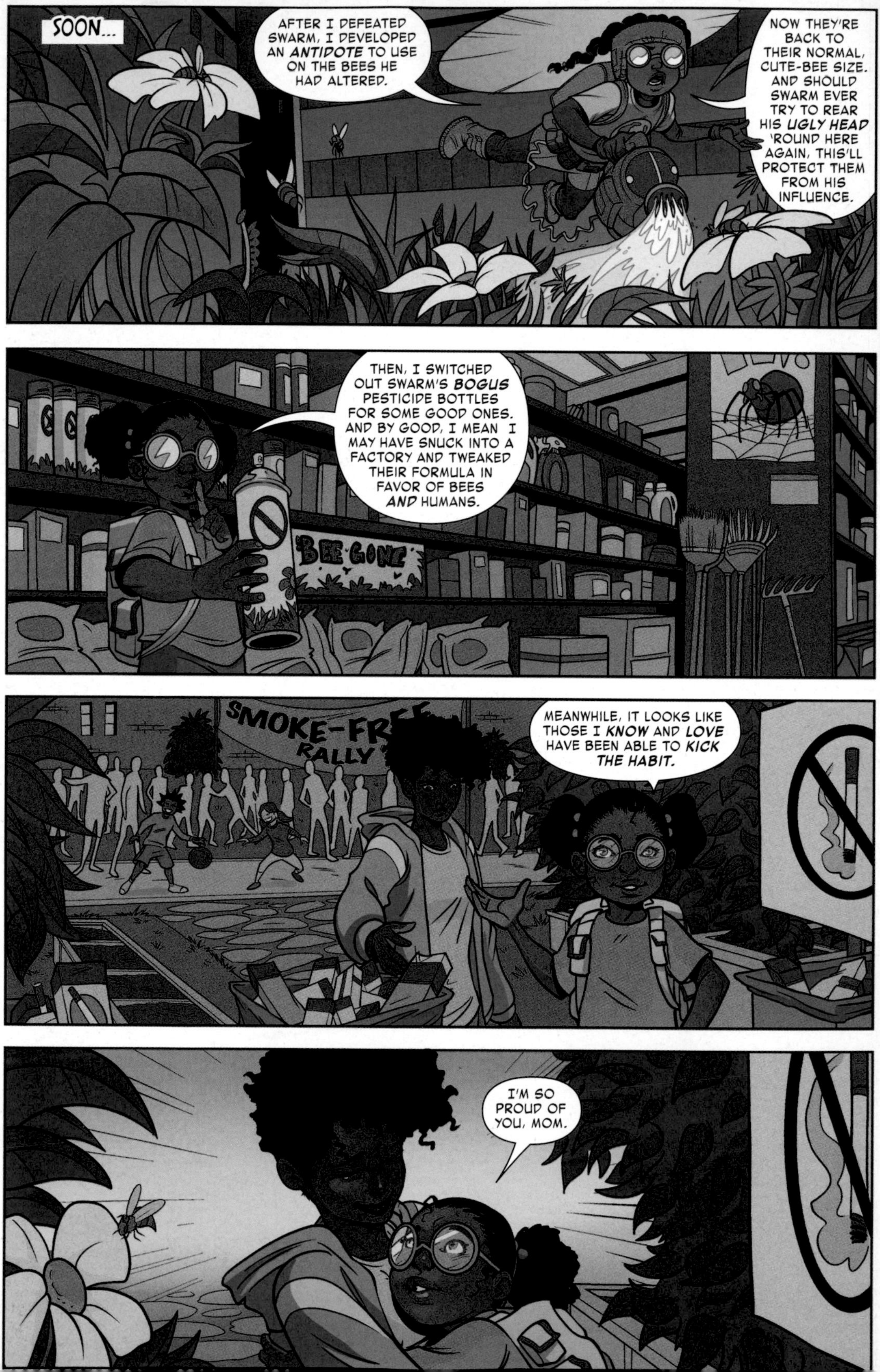
SOON...
AFTER I DEFEATED SWARM, I DEVELOPED AN ANTIDOTE TO USE ON THE BEES HE HAD ALTERED.
NOW THEY'RE BACK TO THEIR NORMAL, CUTE-BEE SIZE. AND SHOULD SWARM EVER TRY TO REAR HIS UGLY HEAD 'ROUND HERE AGAIN, THIS'LL PROTECT THEM FROM HIS INFLUENCE.
THEN, I SWITCHED OUT SWARM'S BOGUS PESTICIDE BOTTLES FOR SOME GOOD ONES. AND BY GOOD, I MEAN I MAY HAVE SNUCK INTO A FACTORY AND TWEAKED THEIR FORMULA IN FAVOR OF BEES AND HUMANS.
BEE GONE
SMOKE-FREE RALLY
MEANWHILE, IT LOOKS LIKE THOSE I KNOW AND LOVE HAVE BEEN ABLE TO KICK THE HABIT.
I'M SO PROUD OF YOU, MOM.

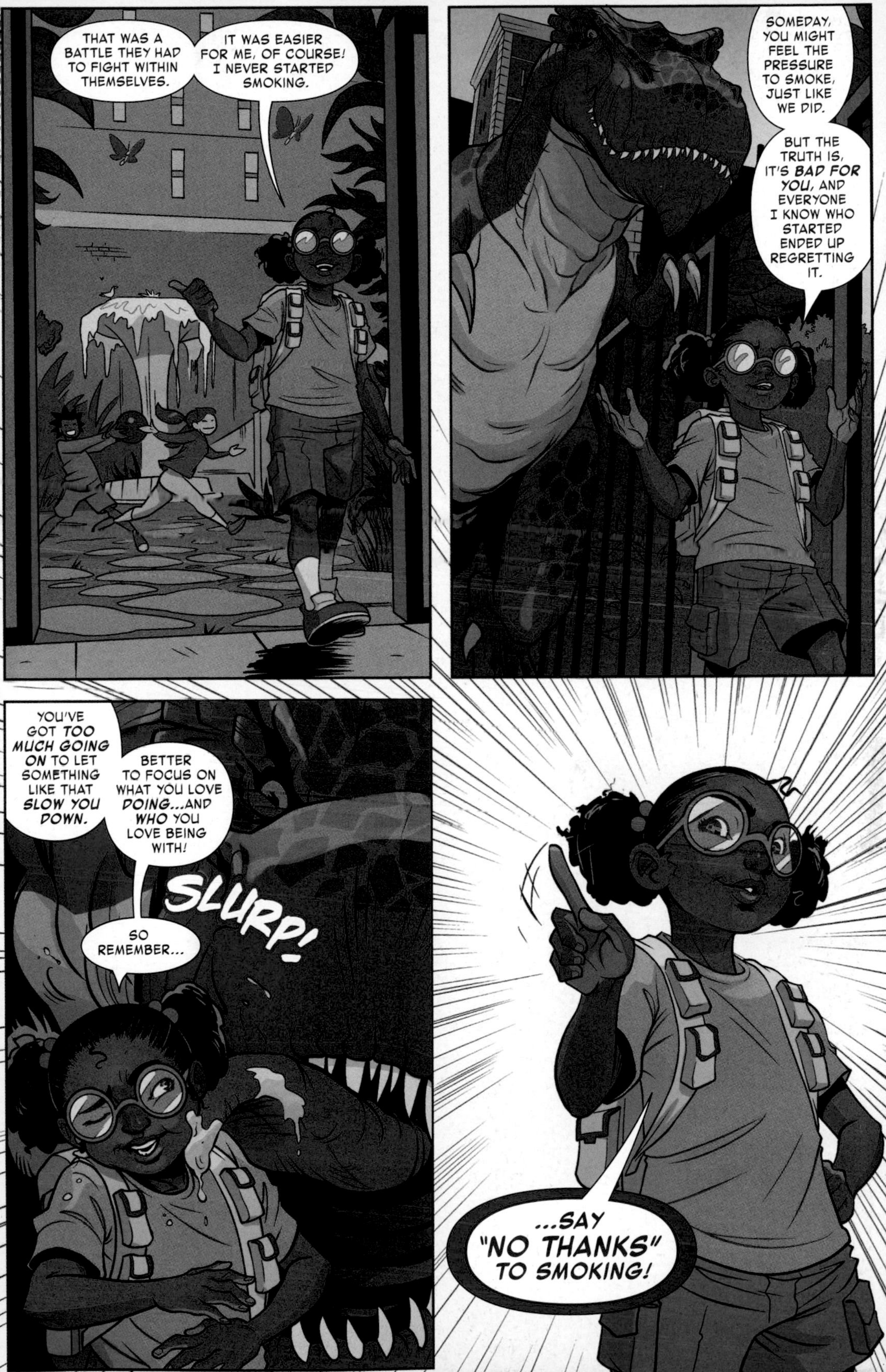
THAT WAS A BATTLE THEY HAD TO FIGHT WITHIN THEMSELVES.
IT WAS EASIER FOR ME, OF COURSE! I NEVER STARTED SMOKING.
SOMEDAY, YOU MIGHT FEEL THE PRESSURE TO SMOKE, JUST LIKE WE DID.
BUT THE TRUTH IS, IT'S *BAD FOR YOU,* AND EVERYONE I KNOW WHO STARTED ENDED UP REGRETTING IT.
YOU'VE GOT *TOO MUCH GOING ON* TO LET SOMETHING LIKE THAT *SLOW YOU DOWN.*
BETTER TO FOCUS ON WHAT YOU LOVE *DOING*...AND *WHO* YOU LOVE BEING WITH!
SLURP!
SO REMEMBER...
...SAY "NO THANKS" TO SMOKING!

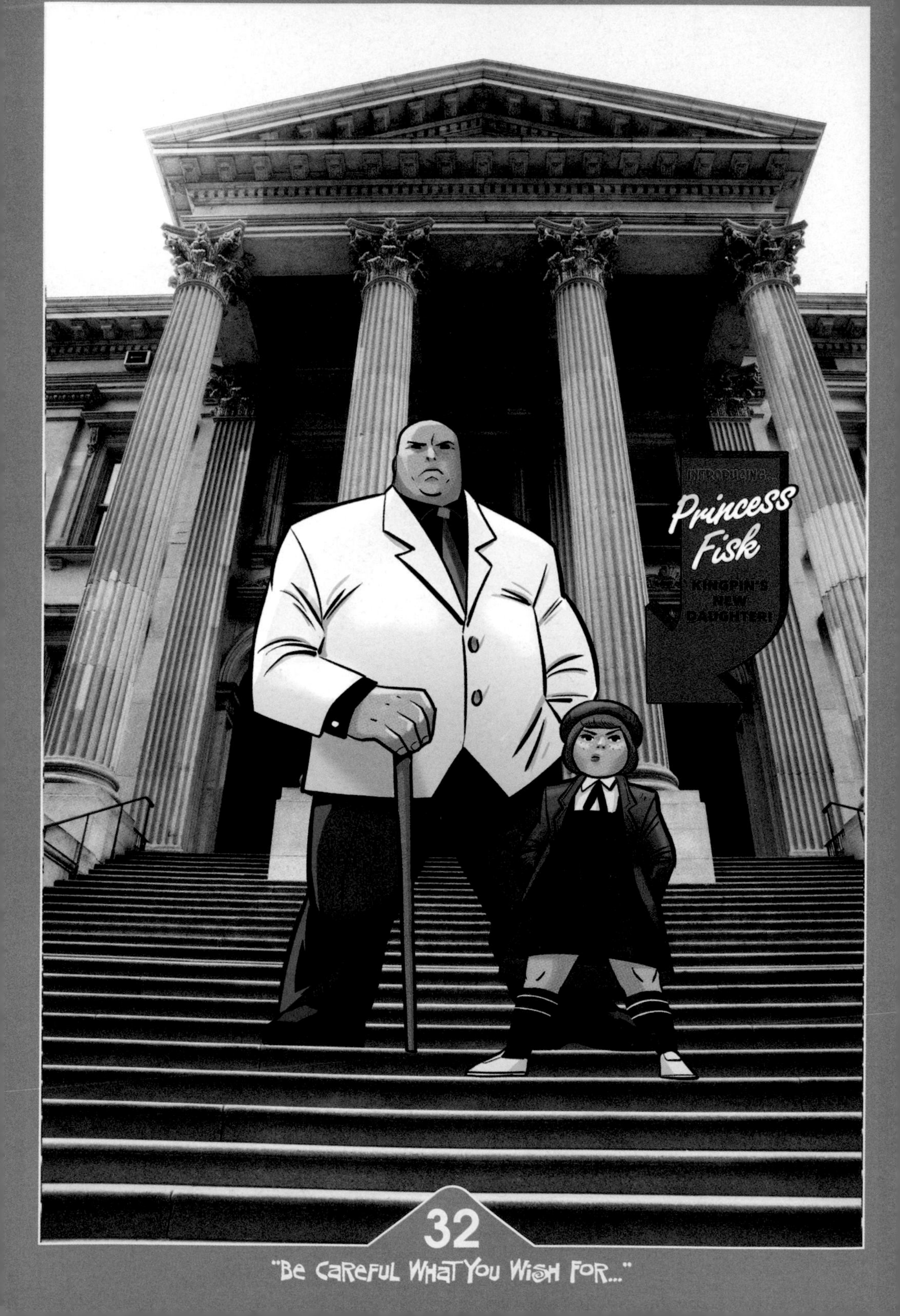
INTRODUCING...
Princess Fisk
KINGPIN'S NEW DAUGHTER!

32

"Be Careful What You Wish For..."

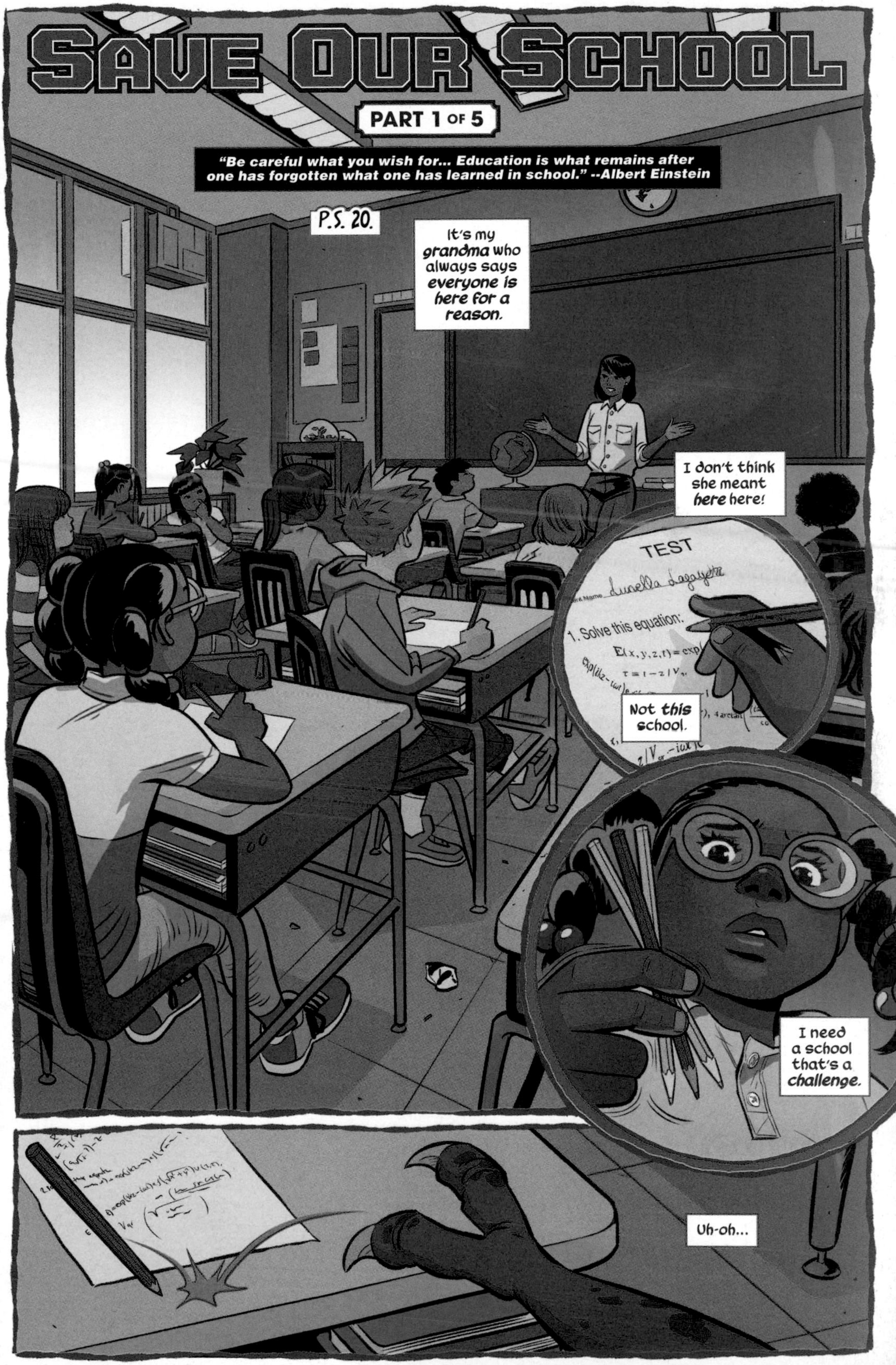
SAVE OUR SCHOOL
PART 1 OF 5
"Be careful what you wish for... Education is what remains after one has forgotten what one has learned in school." --Albert Einstein
P.S. 20.
It's my grandma who always says everyone is here for a reason.
I don't think she meant here here!
TEST
1. Solve this equation:
Not this school.
I need a school that's a challenge.
Uh-oh...

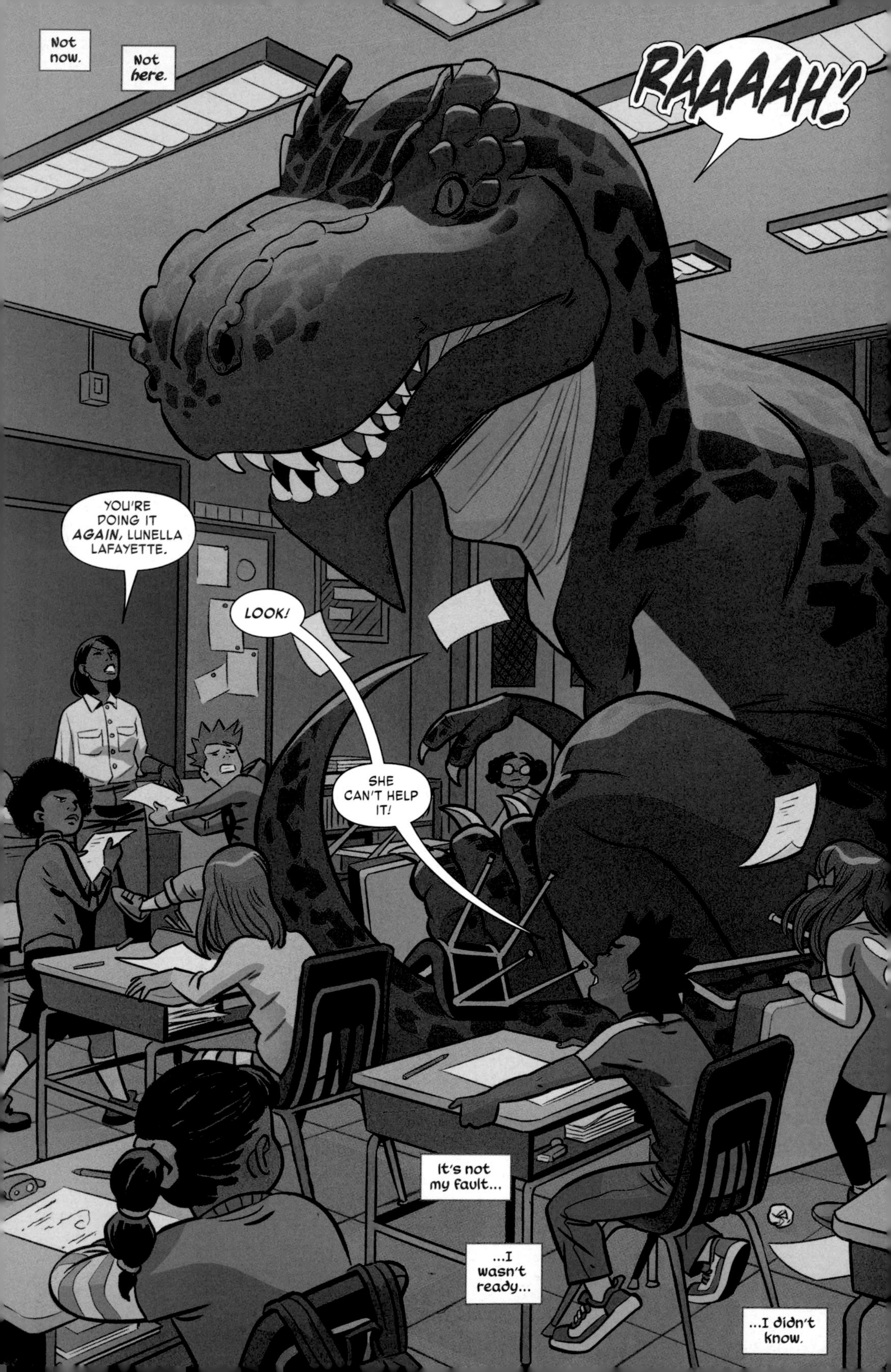
Not now.
Not here.
RAAAAH!
YOU'RE DOING IT *AGAIN*, LUNELLA LAFAYETTE.
LOOK!
SHE CAN'T HELP IT!
It's not my fault...
...I wasn't ready...
...I didn't know.

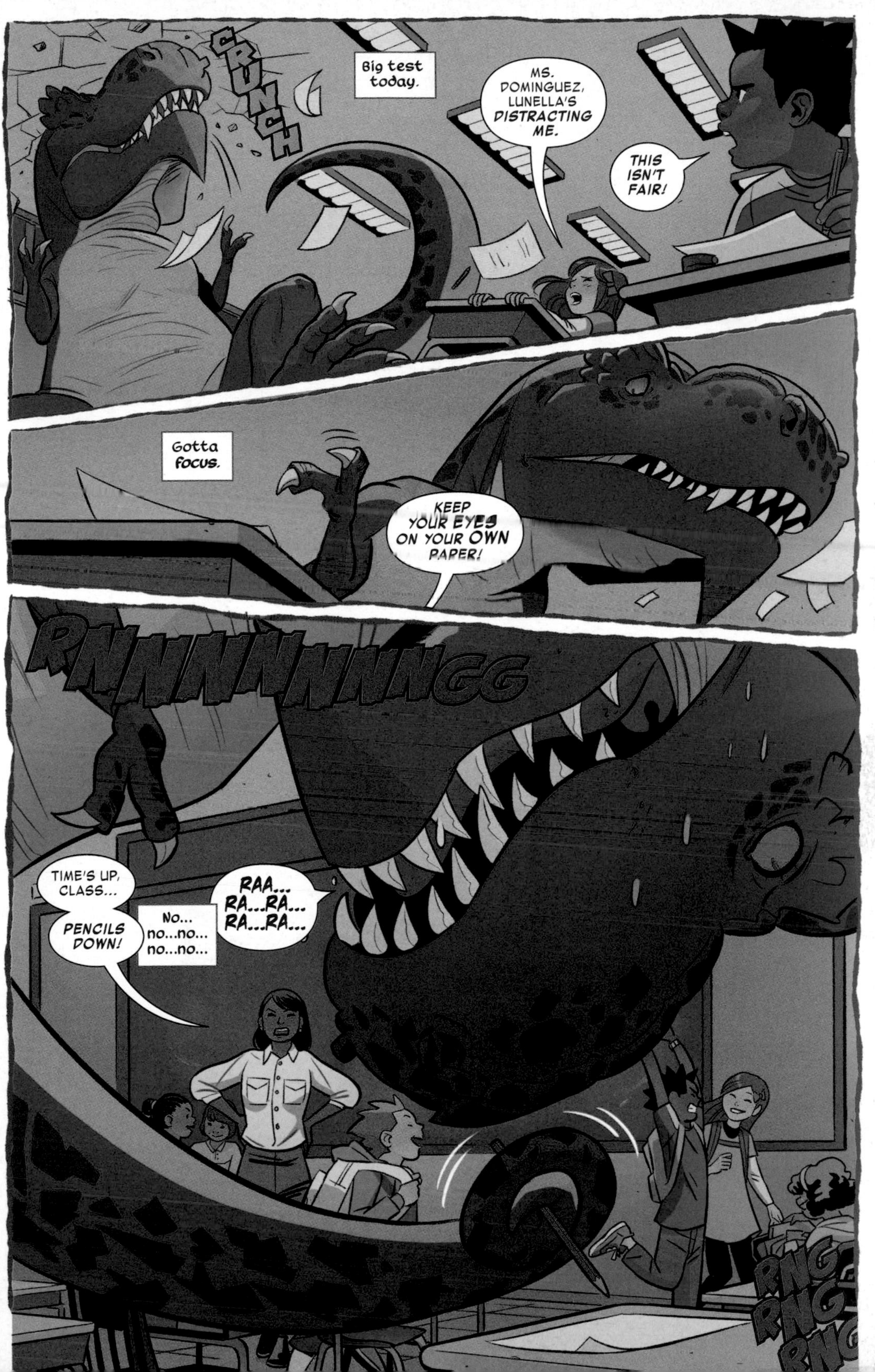
CRUNCH
Big test today.
MS. DOMINGUEZ, LUNELLA'S DISTRACTING ME.
THIS ISN'T FAIR!
Gotta focus.
KEEP YOUR EYES ON YOUR OWN PAPER!
RNNNNNNNNGG
TIME'S UP, CLASS...
PENCILS DOWN!
No... no...no... no...no...
RAA... RA...RA... RA...RA...
RNG
RNG

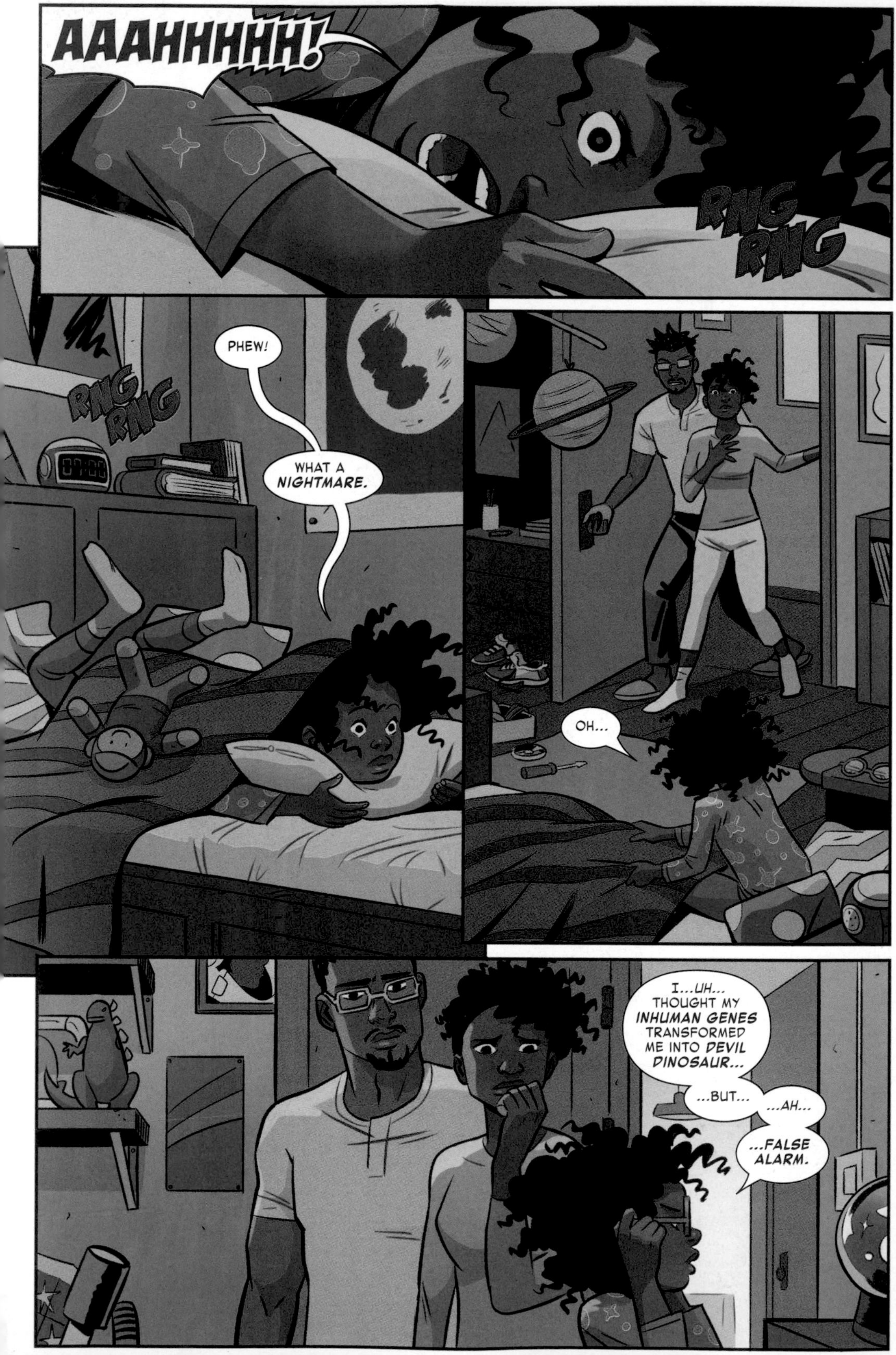
AAAHHHHH!
RNG RNG
RNG RNG
PHEW!
WHAT A NIGHTMARE.
OH...
I...UH... THOUGHT MY INHUMAN GENES TRANSFORMED ME INTO DEVIL DINOSAUR...
...BUT...
...AH...
...FALSE ALARM.

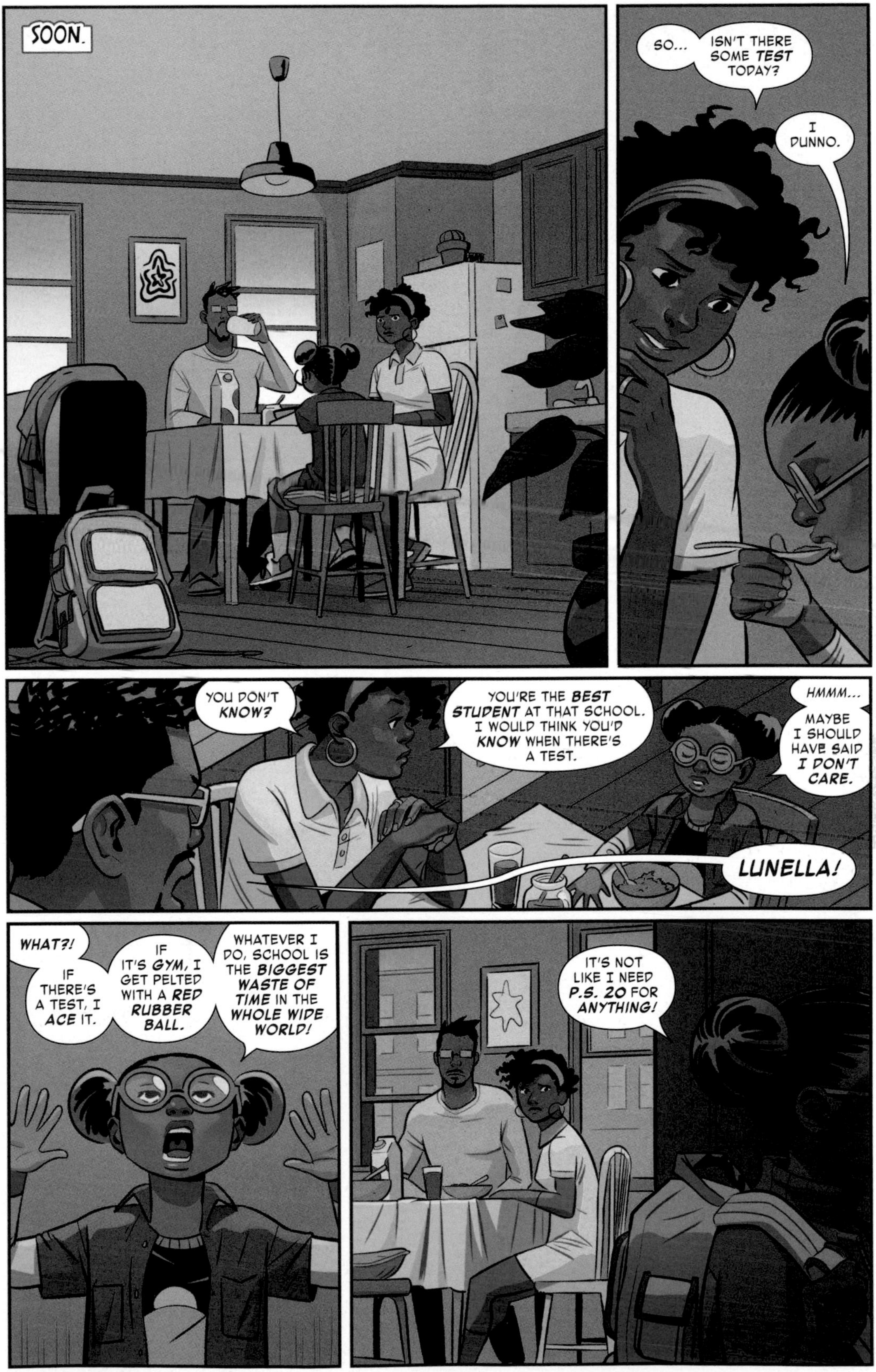
SOON.
SO...
ISN'T THERE SOME TEST TODAY?
I DUNNO.
YOU DON'T KNOW?
YOU'RE THE BEST STUDENT AT THAT SCHOOL. I WOULD THINK YOU'D KNOW WHEN THERE'S A TEST.
HMMM...
MAYBE I SHOULD HAVE SAID I DON'T CARE.
LUNELLA!
WHAT?!
IF THERE'S A TEST, I ACE IT.
IF IT'S GYM, I GET PELTED WITH A RED RUBBER BALL.
WHATEVER I DO, SCHOOL IS THE BIGGEST WASTE OF TIME IN THE WHOLE WIDE WORLD!
IT'S NOT LIKE I NEED P.S. 20 FOR ANYTHING!

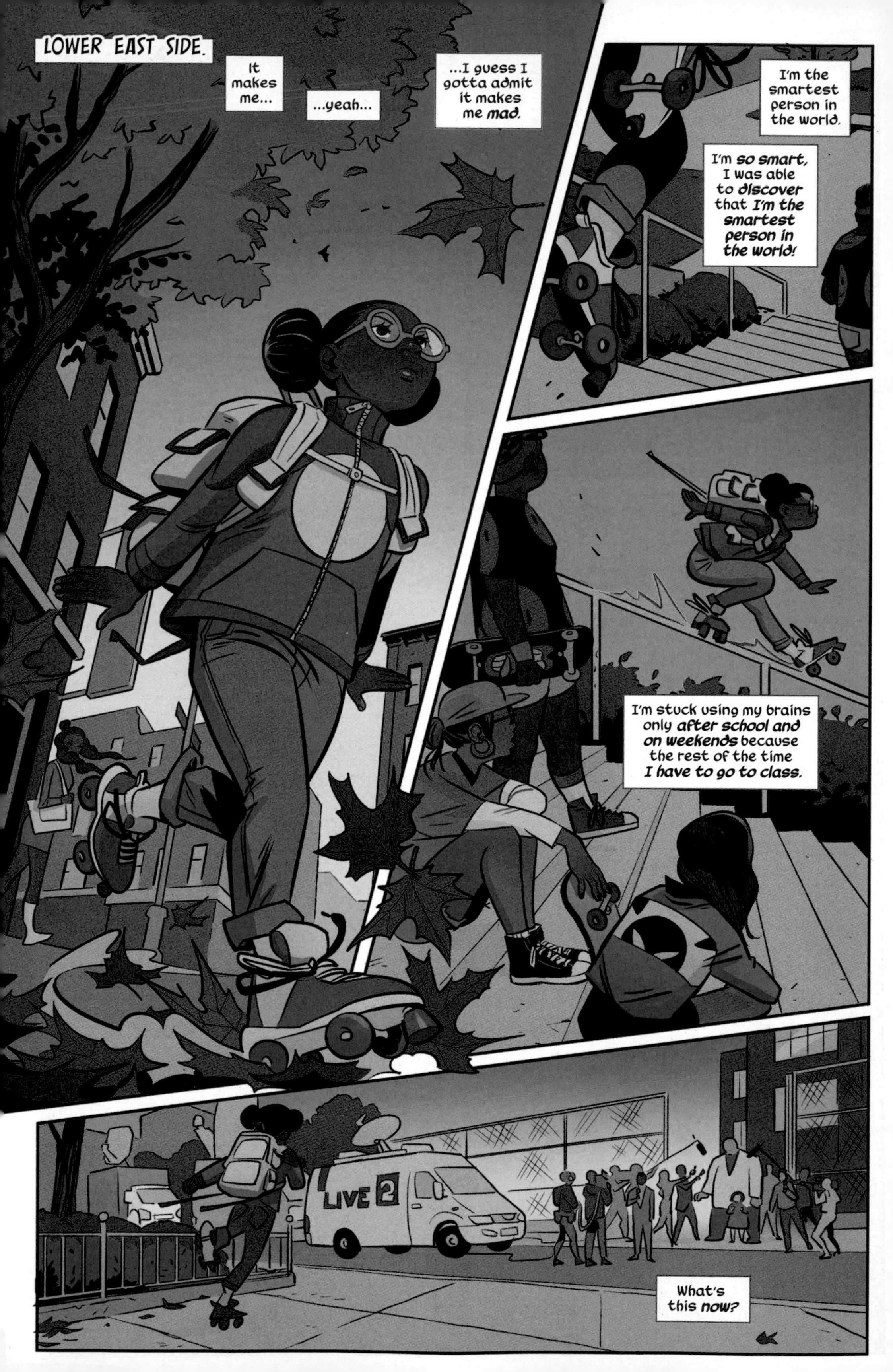
LOWER EAST SIDE.
It makes me...
...yeah...
...I guess I gotta admit it makes me mad.
I'm the smartest person in the world.
I'm so smart, I was able to discover that I'm the smartest person in the world!
I'm stuck using my brains only after school and on weekends because the rest of the time I have to go to class.
LIVE 2
What's this now?

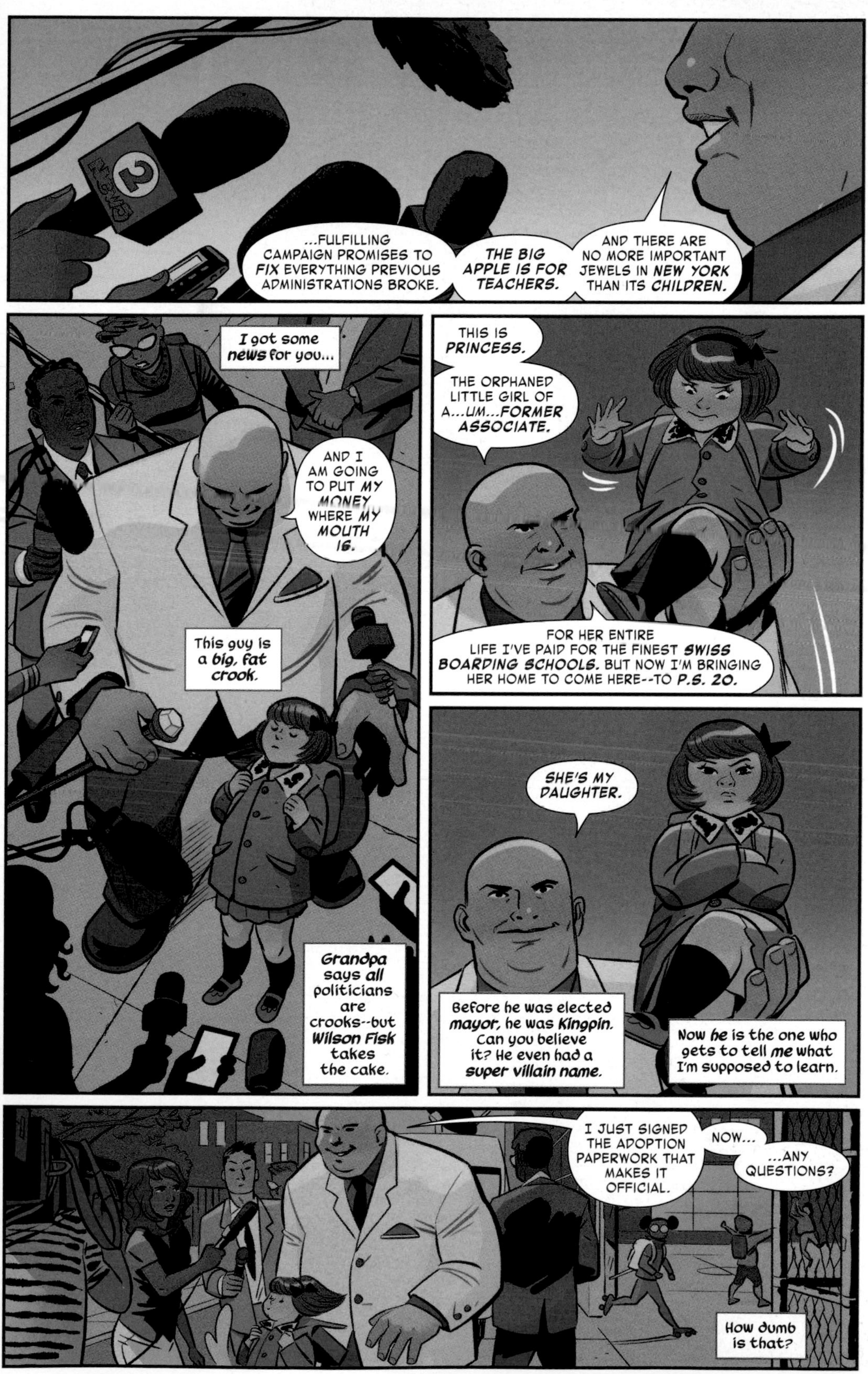
NEWS 2
...FULFILLING CAMPAIGN PROMISES TO FIX EVERYTHING PREVIOUS ADMINISTRATIONS BROKE.
THE BIG APPLE IS FOR TEACHERS.
AND THERE ARE NO MORE IMPORTANT JEWELS IN NEW YORK THAN ITS CHILDREN.
I got some news for you...
AND I AM GOING TO PUT MY MONEY WHERE MY MOUTH IS.
This guy is a big, fat crook.
Grandpa says all politicians are crooks--but Wilson Fisk takes the cake.
THIS IS PRINCESS.
THE ORPHANED LITTLE GIRL OF A...UM...FORMER ASSOCIATE.
FOR HER ENTIRE LIFE I'VE PAID FOR THE FINEST SWISS BOARDING SCHOOLS. BUT NOW I'M BRINGING HER HOME TO COME HERE--TO P.S. 20.
SHE'S MY DAUGHTER.
Before he was elected mayor, he was Kingpin. Can you believe it? He even had a super villain name.
Now he is the one who gets to tell me what I'm supposed to learn.
I JUST SIGNED THE ADOPTION PAPERWORK THAT MAKES IT OFFICIAL.
NOW...
...ANY QUESTIONS?
How dumb is that?

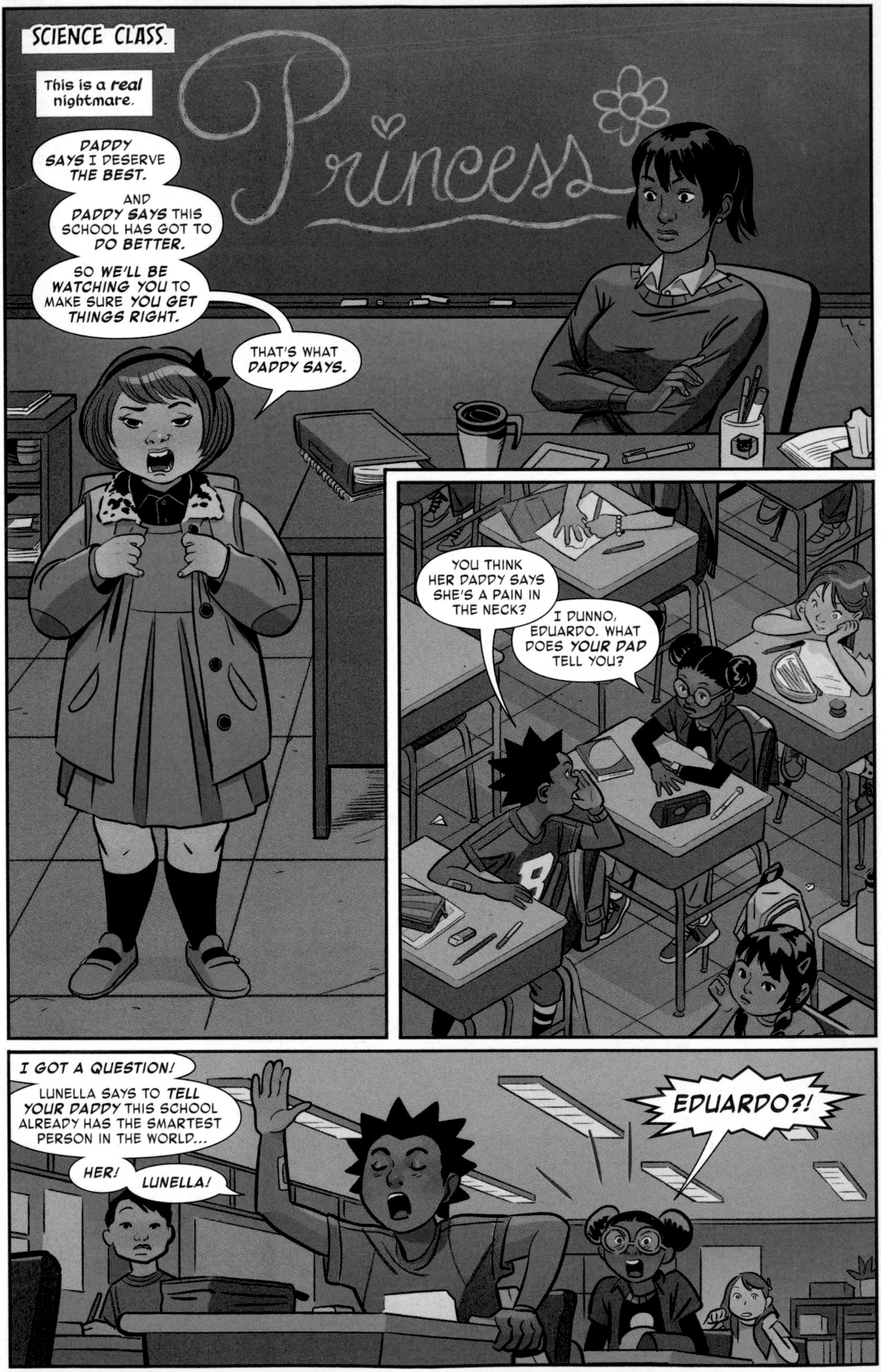
SCIENCE CLASS.
This is a real nightmare.
Princess
DADDY SAYS I DESERVE THE BEST.
AND DADDY SAYS THIS SCHOOL HAS GOT TO DO BETTER.
SO WE'LL BE WATCHING YOU TO MAKE SURE YOU GET THINGS RIGHT.
THAT'S WHAT DADDY SAYS.
YOU THINK HER DADDY SAYS SHE'S A PAIN IN THE NECK?
I DUNNO, EDUARDO. WHAT DOES YOUR DAD TELL YOU?
I GOT A QUESTION!
LUNELLA SAYS TO TELL YOUR DADDY THIS SCHOOL ALREADY HAS THE SMARTEST PERSON IN THE WORLD...
HER!
LUNELLA!
EDUARDO?!

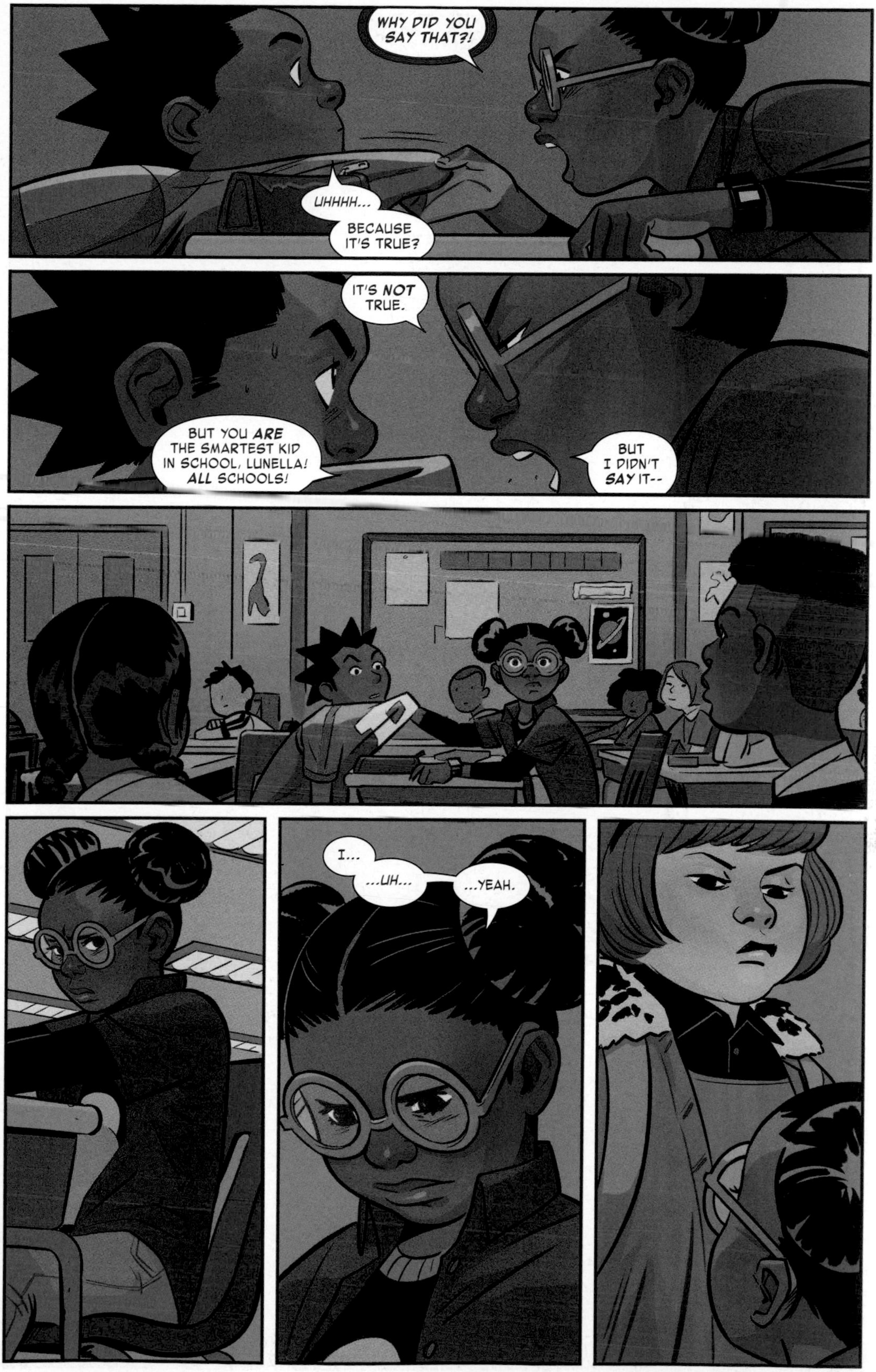
WHY DID YOU SAY THAT?!
UHHHH...
BECAUSE IT'S TRUE?
IT'S NOT TRUE.
BUT YOU ARE THE SMARTEST KID IN SCHOOL, LUNELLA! ALL SCHOOLS!
BUT I DIDN'T SAY IT--
I...
...UH...
...YEAH.

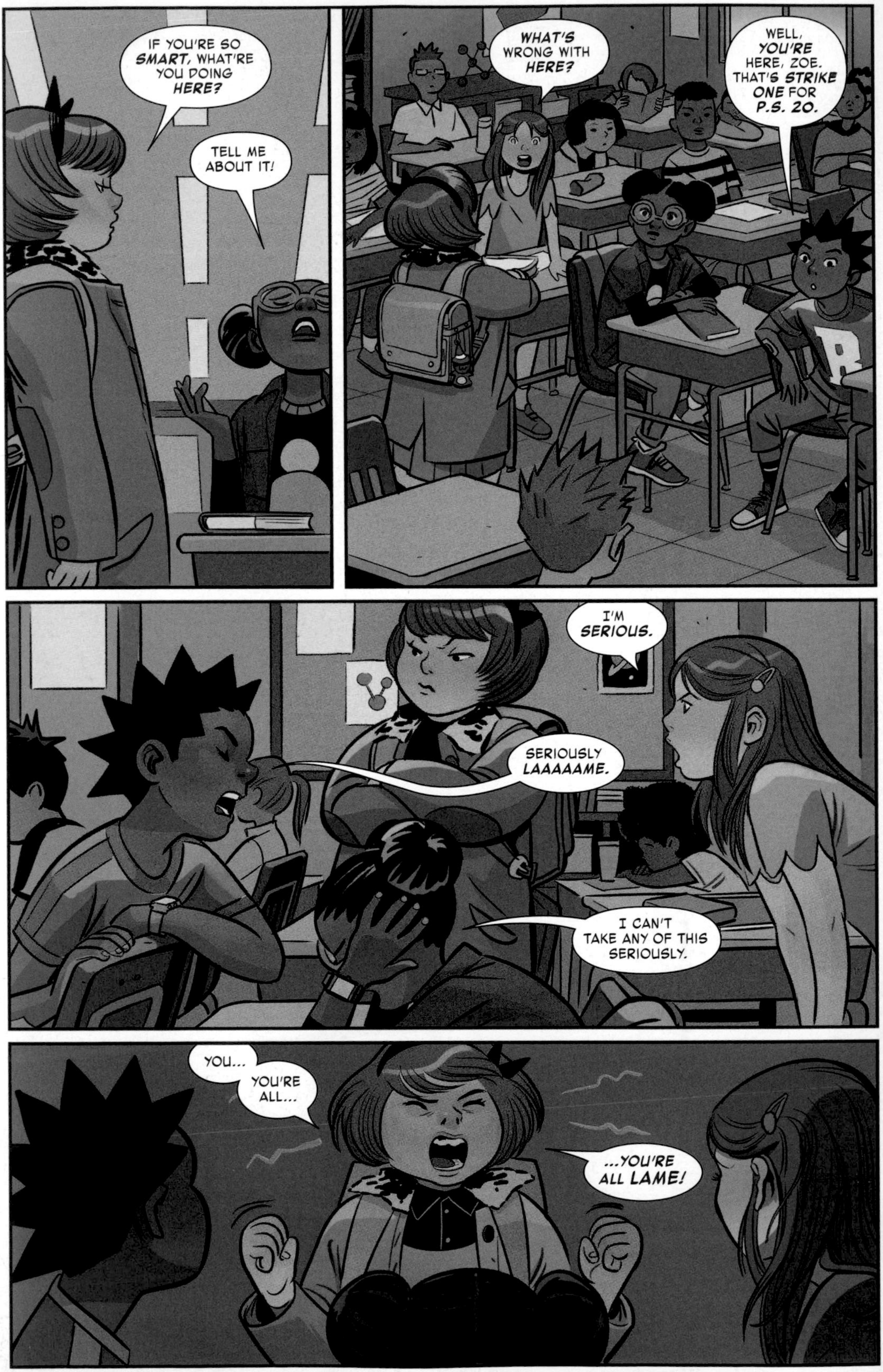
IF YOU'RE SO SMART, WHAT'RE YOU DOING HERE?
TELL ME ABOUT IT!
WHAT'S WRONG WITH HERE?
WELL, YOU'RE HERE, ZOE. THAT'S STRIKE ONE FOR P.S. 20.
I'M SERIOUS.
SERIOUSLY LAAAAAME.
I CAN'T TAKE ANY OF THIS SERIOUSLY.
YOU...
YOU'RE ALL...
...YOU'RE ALL LAME!

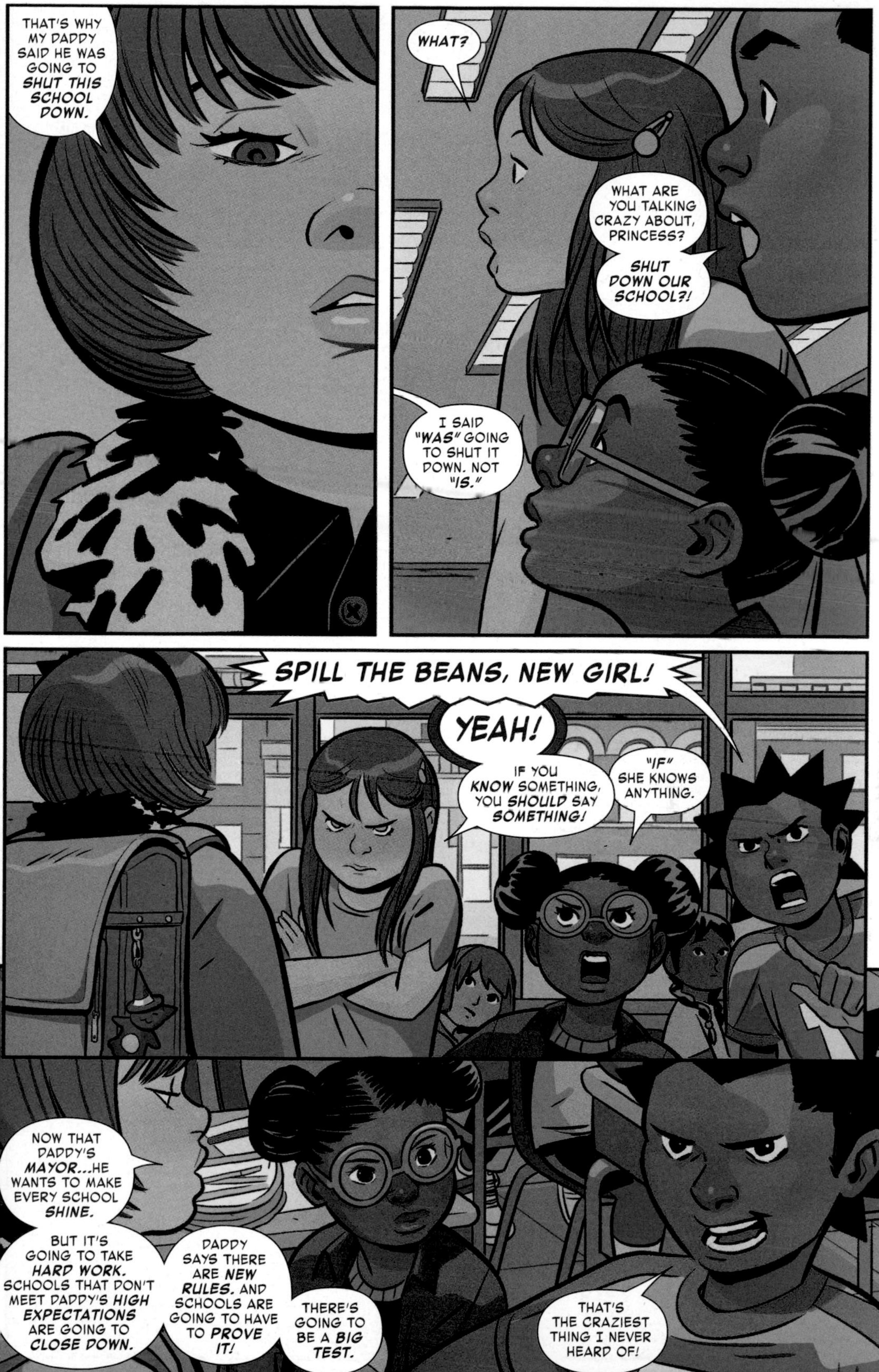
THAT'S WHY MY DADDY SAID HE WAS GOING TO SHUT THIS SCHOOL DOWN.
WHAT?
WHAT ARE YOU TALKING CRAZY ABOUT, PRINCESS?
SHUT DOWN OUR SCHOOL?!
I SAID "WAS" GOING TO SHUT IT DOWN. NOT "IS."
SPILL THE BEANS, NEW GIRL!
YEAH!
IF YOU KNOW SOMETHING, YOU SHOULD SAY SOMETHING!
"IF" SHE KNOWS ANYTHING.
NOW THAT DADDY'S MAYOR... HE WANTS TO MAKE EVERY SCHOOL SHINE.
BUT IT'S GOING TO TAKE HARD WORK. SCHOOLS THAT DON'T MEET DADDY'S HIGH EXPECTATIONS ARE GOING TO CLOSE DOWN.
DADDY SAYS THERE ARE NEW RULES. AND SCHOOLS ARE GOING TO HAVE TO PROVE IT!
THERE'S GOING TO BE A BIG TEST.
THAT'S THE CRAZIEST THING I NEVER HEARD OF!

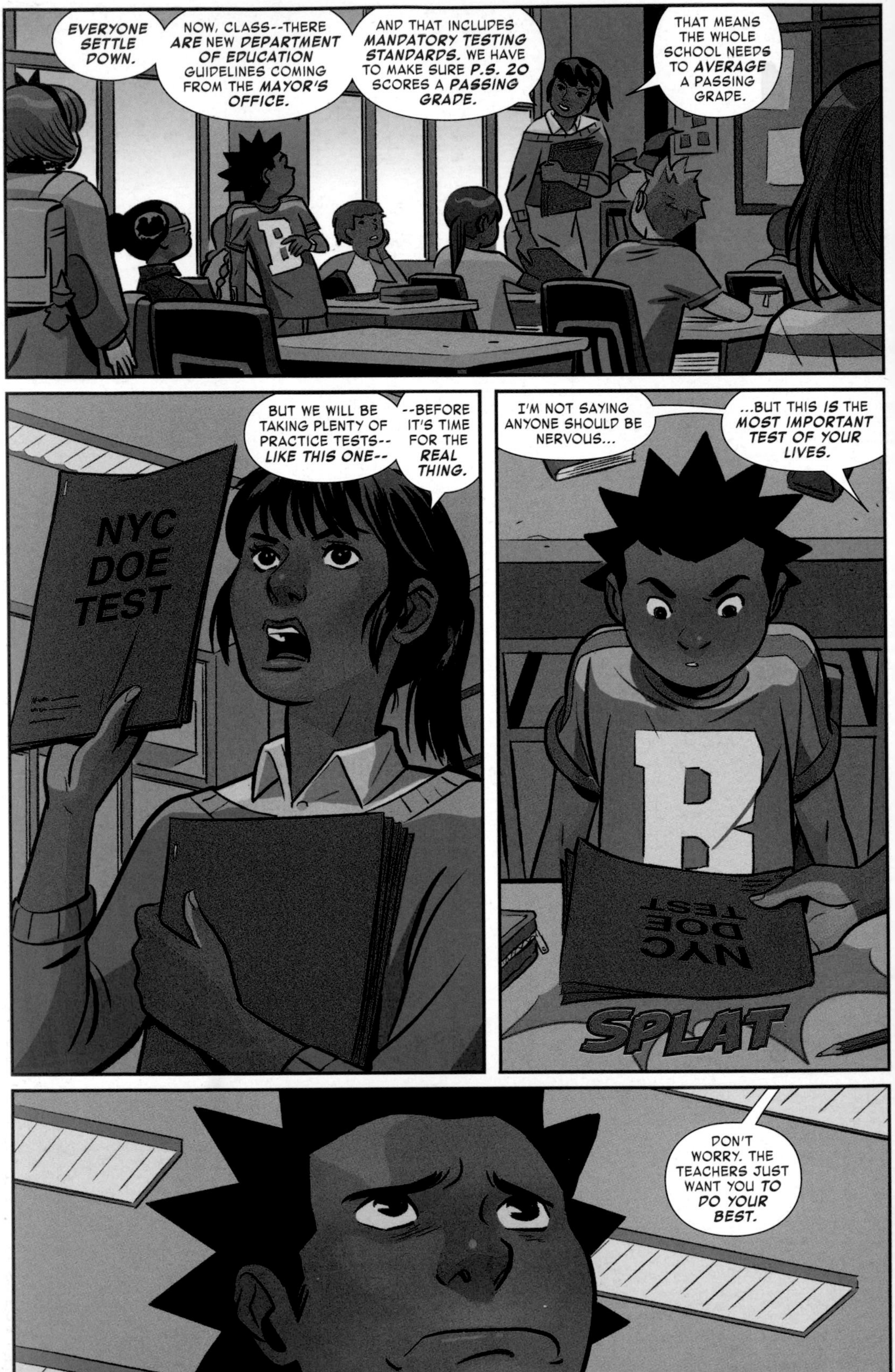
EVERYONE SETTLE DOWN.
NOW, CLASS--THERE ARE NEW DEPARTMENT OF EDUCATION GUIDELINES COMING FROM THE MAYOR'S OFFICE.
AND THAT INCLUDES MANDATORY TESTING STANDARDS. WE HAVE TO MAKE SURE P.S. 20 SCORES A PASSING GRADE.
THAT MEANS THE WHOLE SCHOOL NEEDS TO AVERAGE A PASSING GRADE.
BUT WE WILL BE TAKING PLENTY OF PRACTICE TESTS-- LIKE THIS ONE--
--BEFORE IT'S TIME FOR THE REAL THING.
NYC DOE TEST
I'M NOT SAYING ANYONE SHOULD BE NERVOUS...
...BUT THIS IS THE MOST IMPORTANT TEST OF YOUR LIVES.
NYC DOE TEST
SPLAT
DON'T WORRY. THE TEACHERS JUST WANT YOU TO DO YOUR BEST.

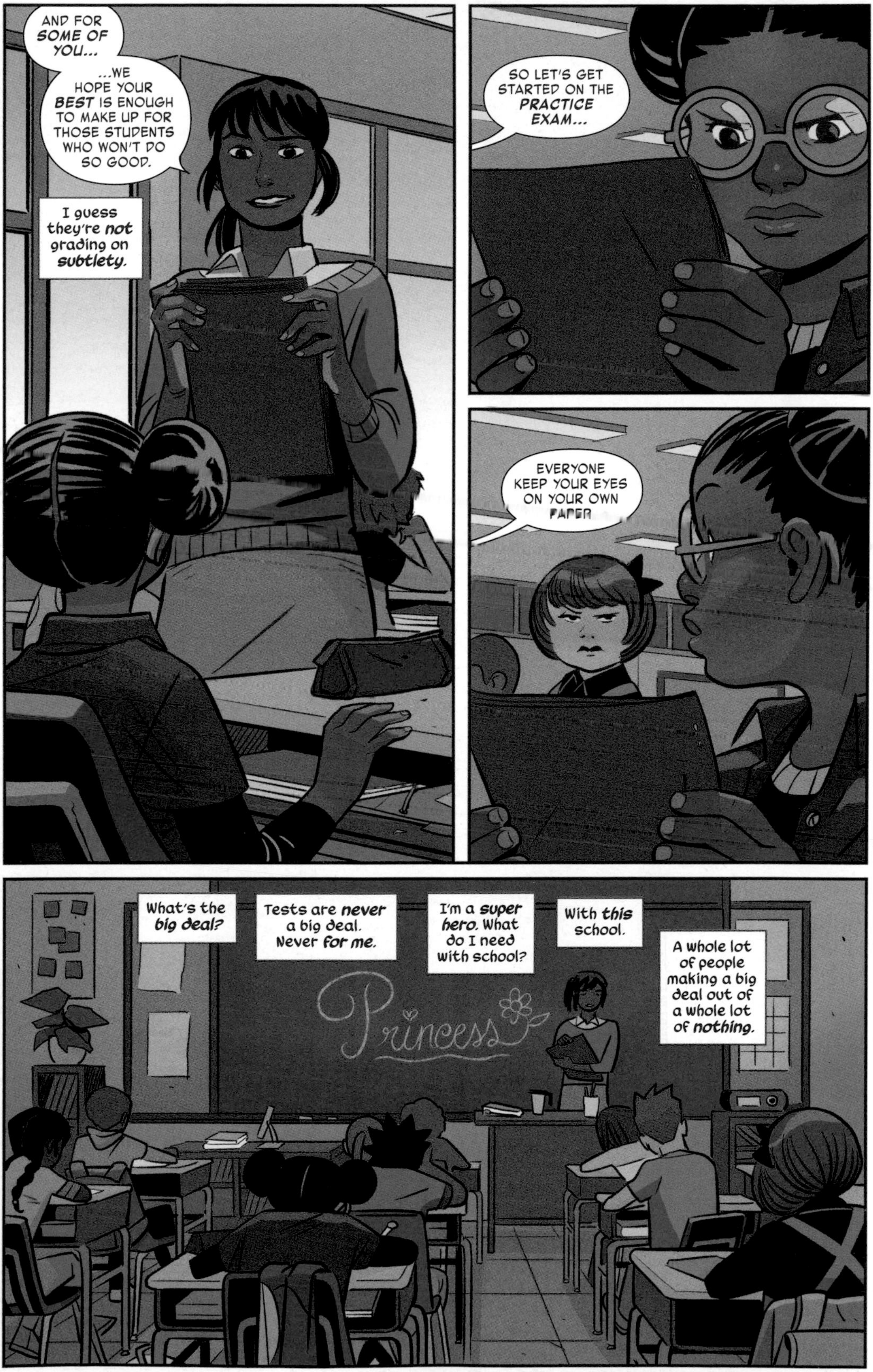
AND FOR SOME OF YOU...
...WE HOPE YOUR BEST IS ENOUGH TO MAKE UP FOR THOSE STUDENTS WHO WON'T DO SO GOOD.
I guess they're not grading on subtlety.
SO LET'S GET STARTED ON THE PRACTICE EXAM...
EVERYONE KEEP YOUR EYES ON YOUR OWN PAPER
What's the big deal?
Tests are never a big deal. Never for me.
I'm a super hero. What do I need with school?
With this school.
A whole lot of people making a big deal out of a whole lot of nothing.
Princess

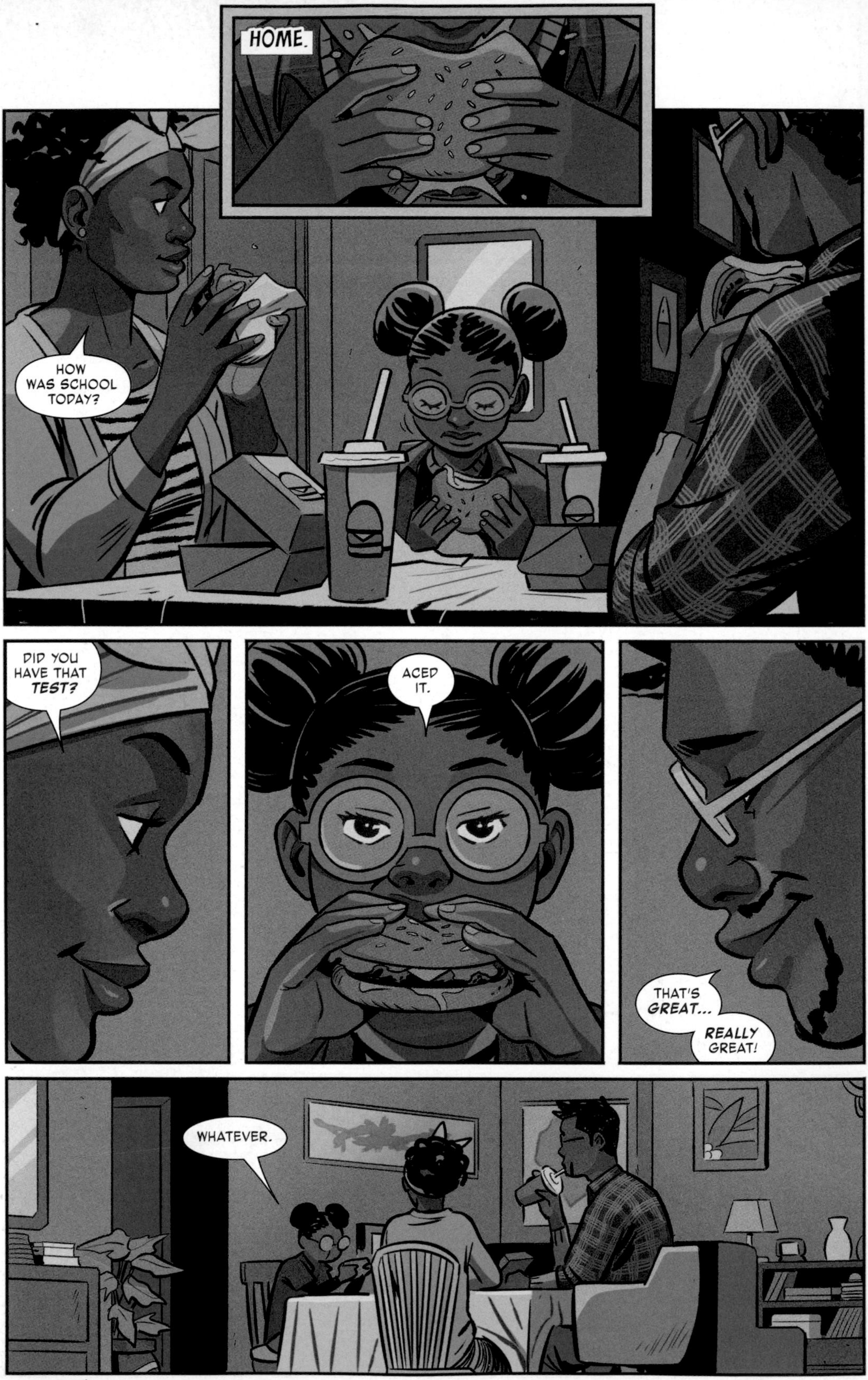
HOME.
HOW WAS SCHOOL TODAY?
DID YOU HAVE THAT TEST?
ACED IT.
THAT'S GREAT...
REALLY GREAT!
WHATEVER.

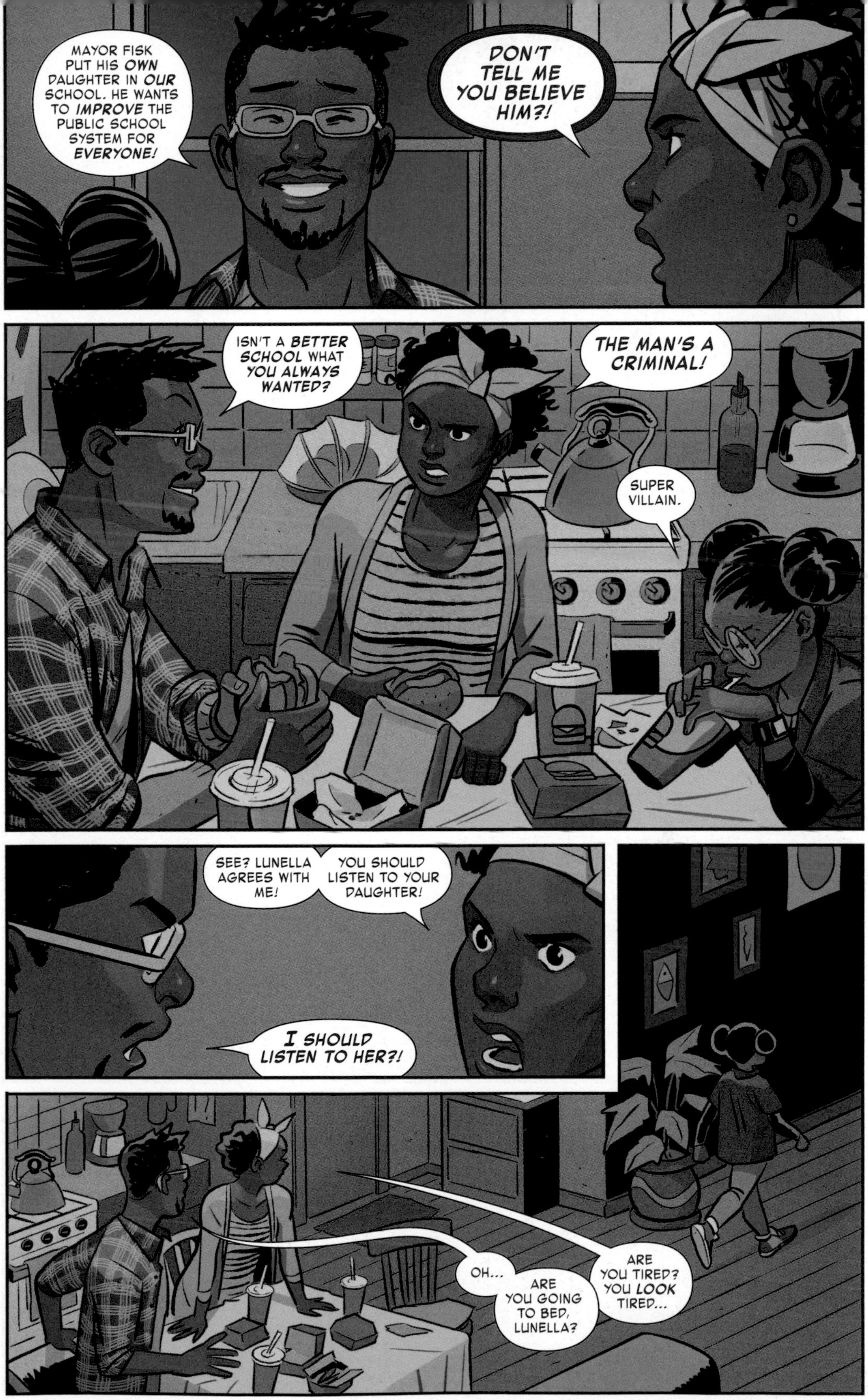
MAYOR FISK PUT HIS OWN DAUGHTER IN OUR SCHOOL. HE WANTS TO IMPROVE THE PUBLIC SCHOOL SYSTEM FOR EVERYONE!
DON'T TELL ME YOU BELIEVE HIM?!
ISN'T A BETTER SCHOOL WHAT YOU ALWAYS WANTED?
THE MAN'S A CRIMINAL!
SUPER VILLAIN.
SEE? LUNELLA AGREES WITH ME!
YOU SHOULD LISTEN TO YOUR DAUGHTER!
I SHOULD LISTEN TO HER?!
ARE YOU TIRED? YOU LOOK TIRED...
OH...
ARE YOU GOING TO BED, LUNELLA?

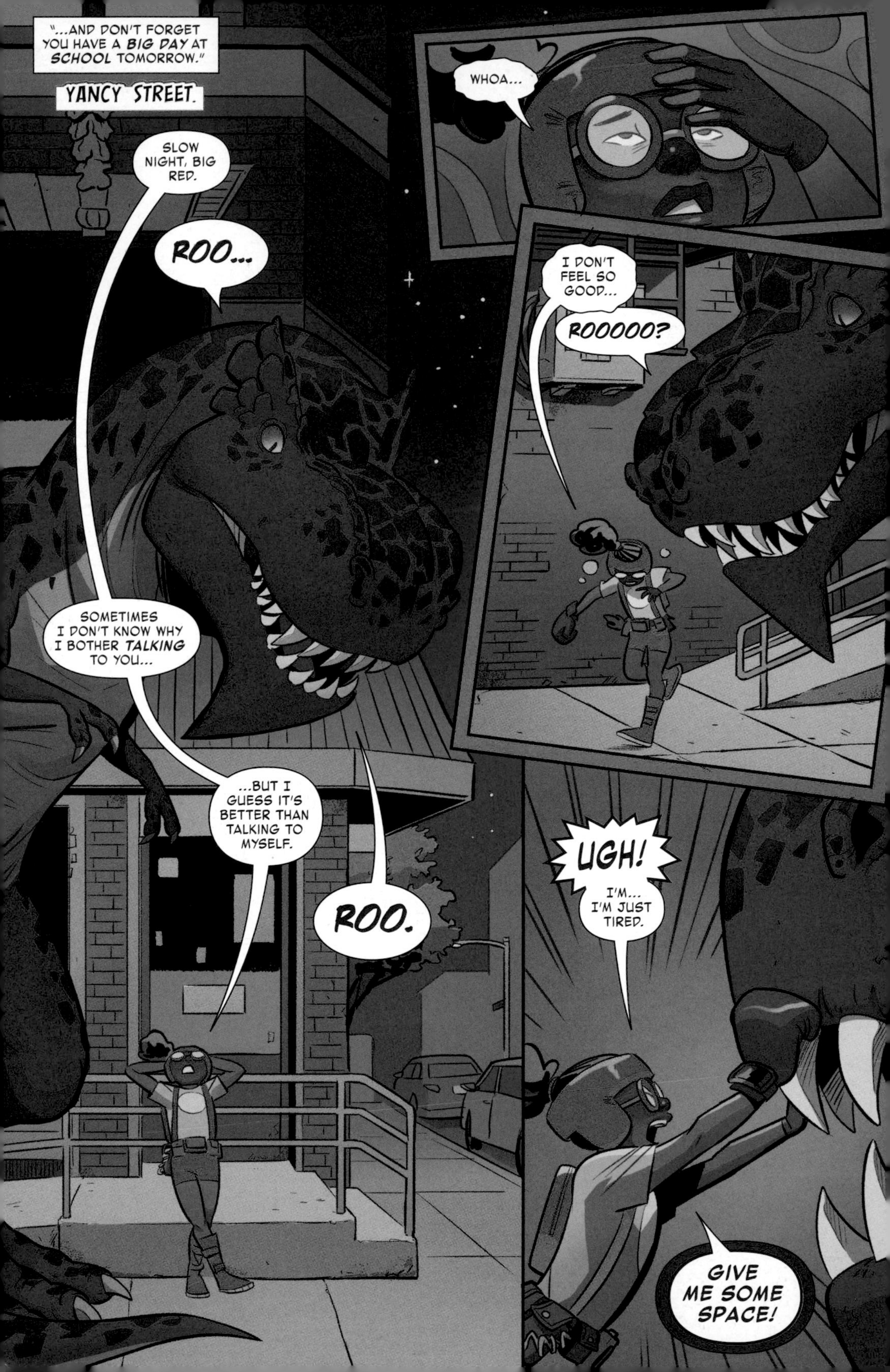
"...AND DON'T FORGET YOU HAVE A BIG DAY AT SCHOOL TOMORROW."
YANCY STREET.
SLOW NIGHT, BIG RED.
ROO...
SOMETIMES I DON'T KNOW WHY I BOTHER TALKING TO YOU...
...BUT I GUESS IT'S BETTER THAN TALKING TO MYSELF.
ROO.
WHOA...
I DON'T FEEL SO GOOD...
ROOOOO?
UGH!
I'M... I'M JUST TIRED.
GIVE ME SOME SPACE!

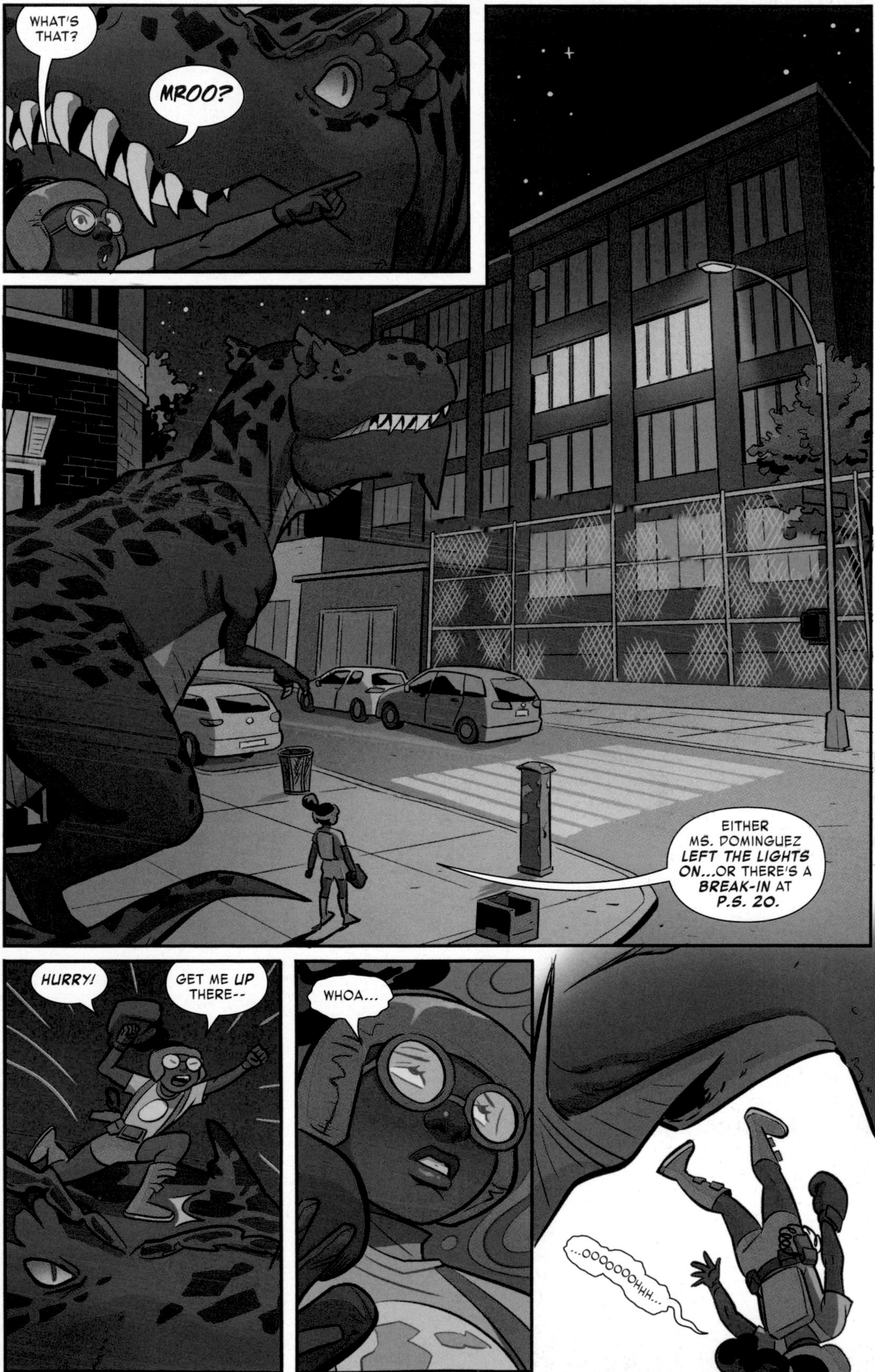

WHAT'S THAT?
MROO?
EITHER MS. DOMINGUEZ LEFT THE LIGHTS ON...OR THERE'S A BREAK-IN AT P.S. 20.
HURRY!
GET ME UP THERE--
WHOA...
...OOOOOOOOHHH...

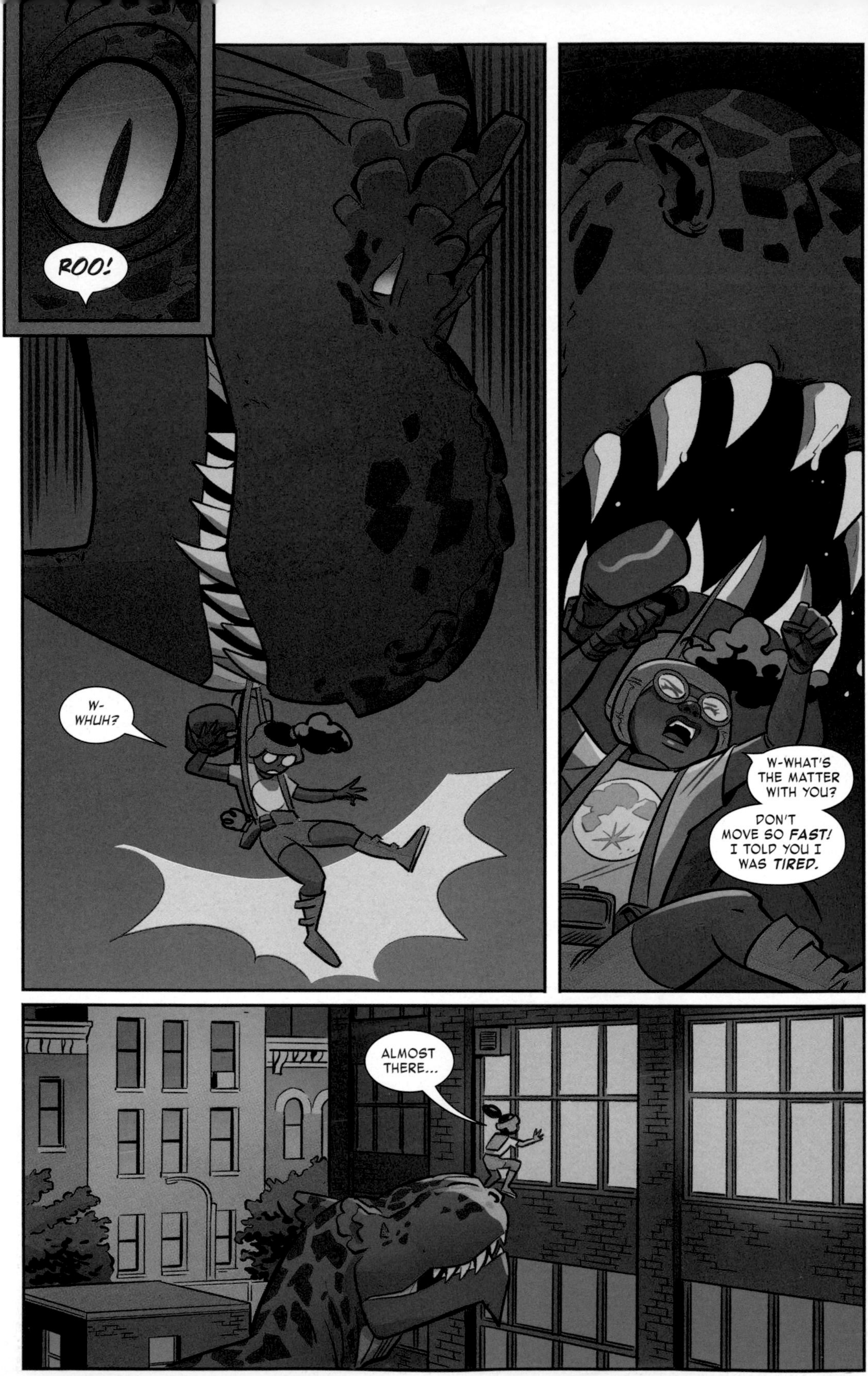
ROO!
W-WHUH?
W-WHAT'S THE MATTER WITH YOU?
DON'T MOVE SO *FAST!* I TOLD YOU I WAS *TIRED.*
ALMOST THERE...

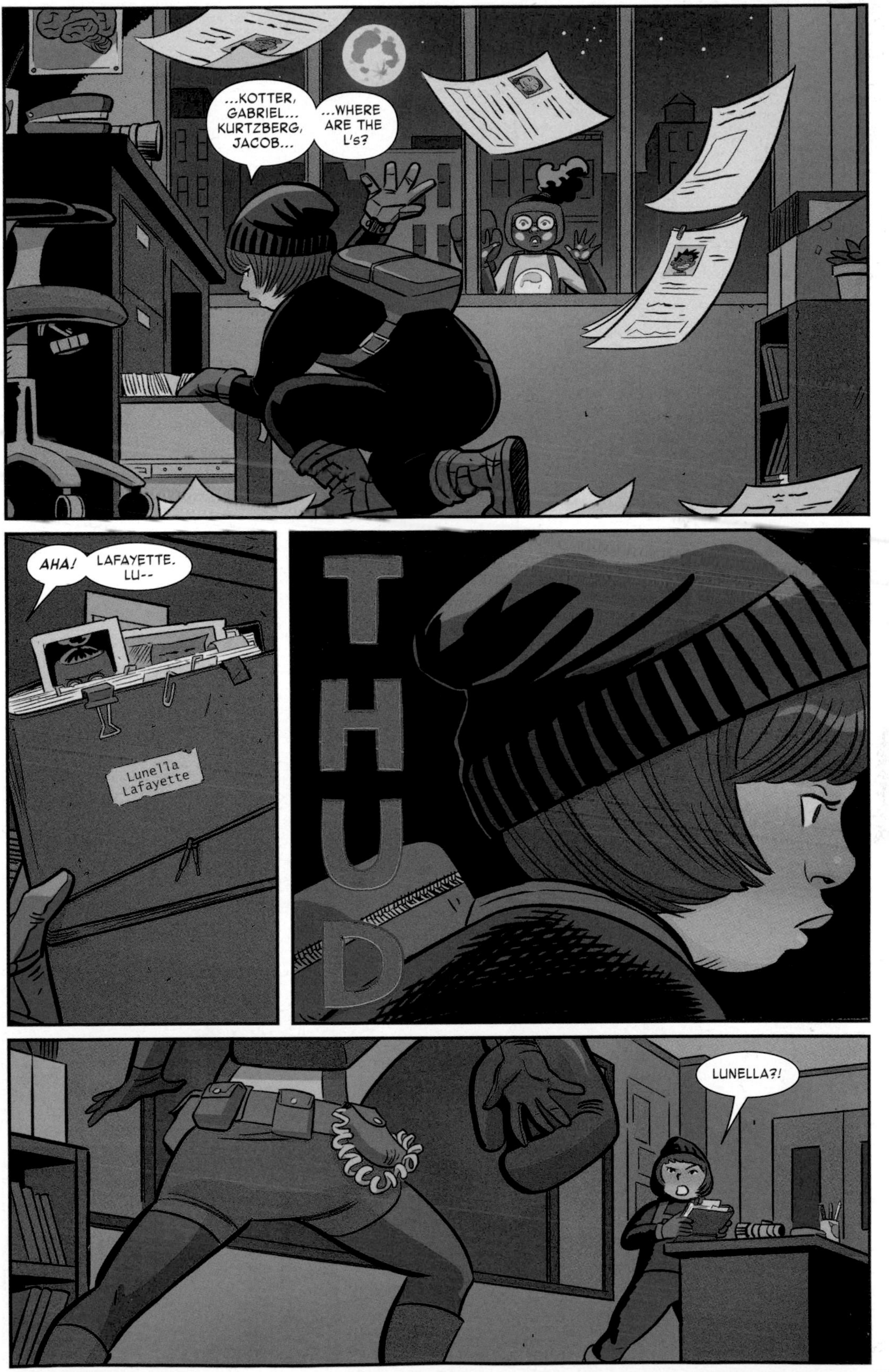
...KOTTER, GABRIEL... KURTZBERG, JACOB...
...WHERE ARE THE L's?
AHA!
LAFAYETTE. LU--
Lunella Lafayette
THUD
LUNELLA?!

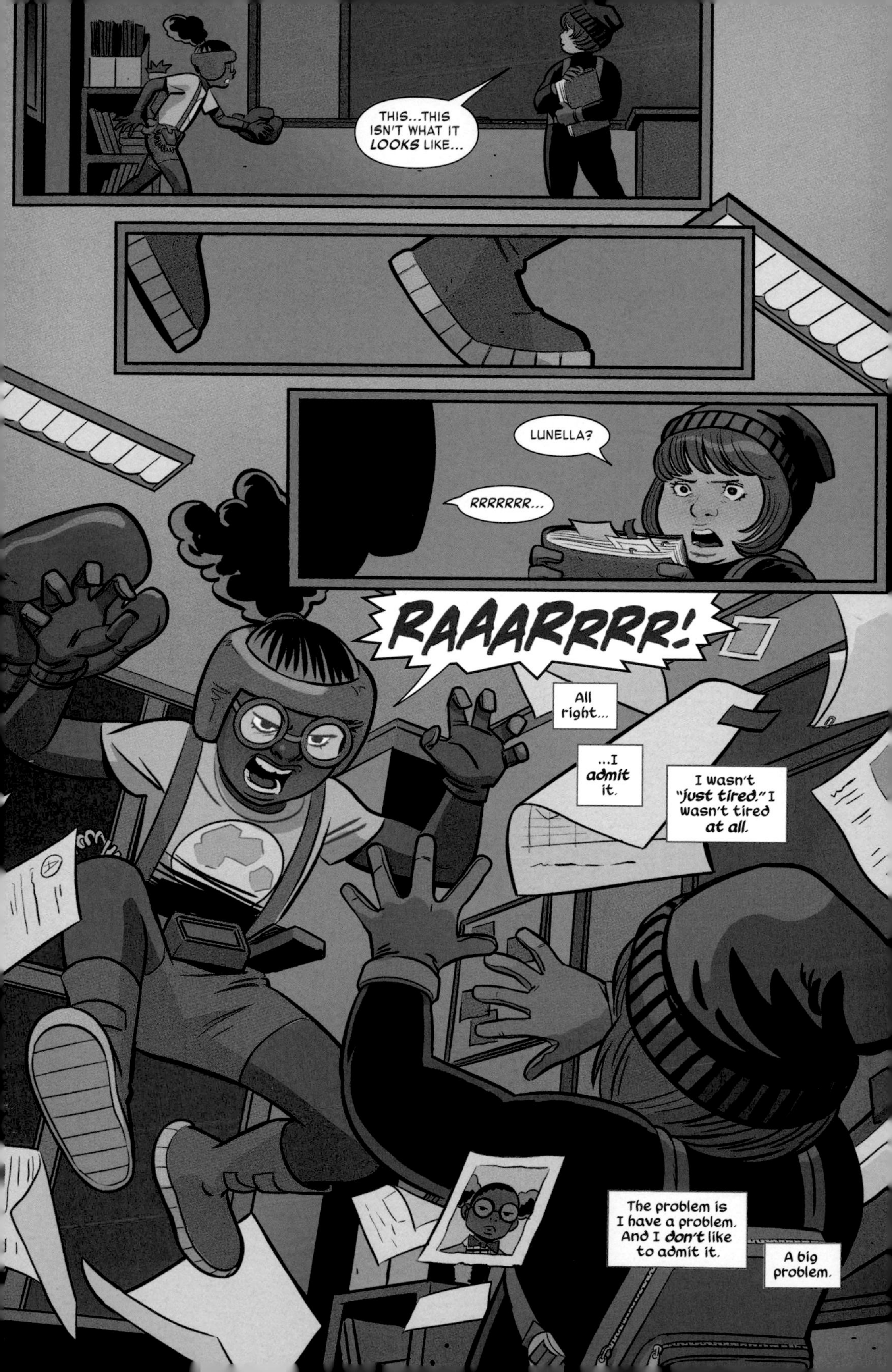
THIS...THIS ISN'T WHAT IT LOOKS LIKE...
LUNELLA?
RRRRRRR...
RAAARRRR!
All right...
...I admit it.
I wasn't "just tired." I wasn't tired at all.
The problem is I have a problem. And I don't like to admit it.
A big problem.

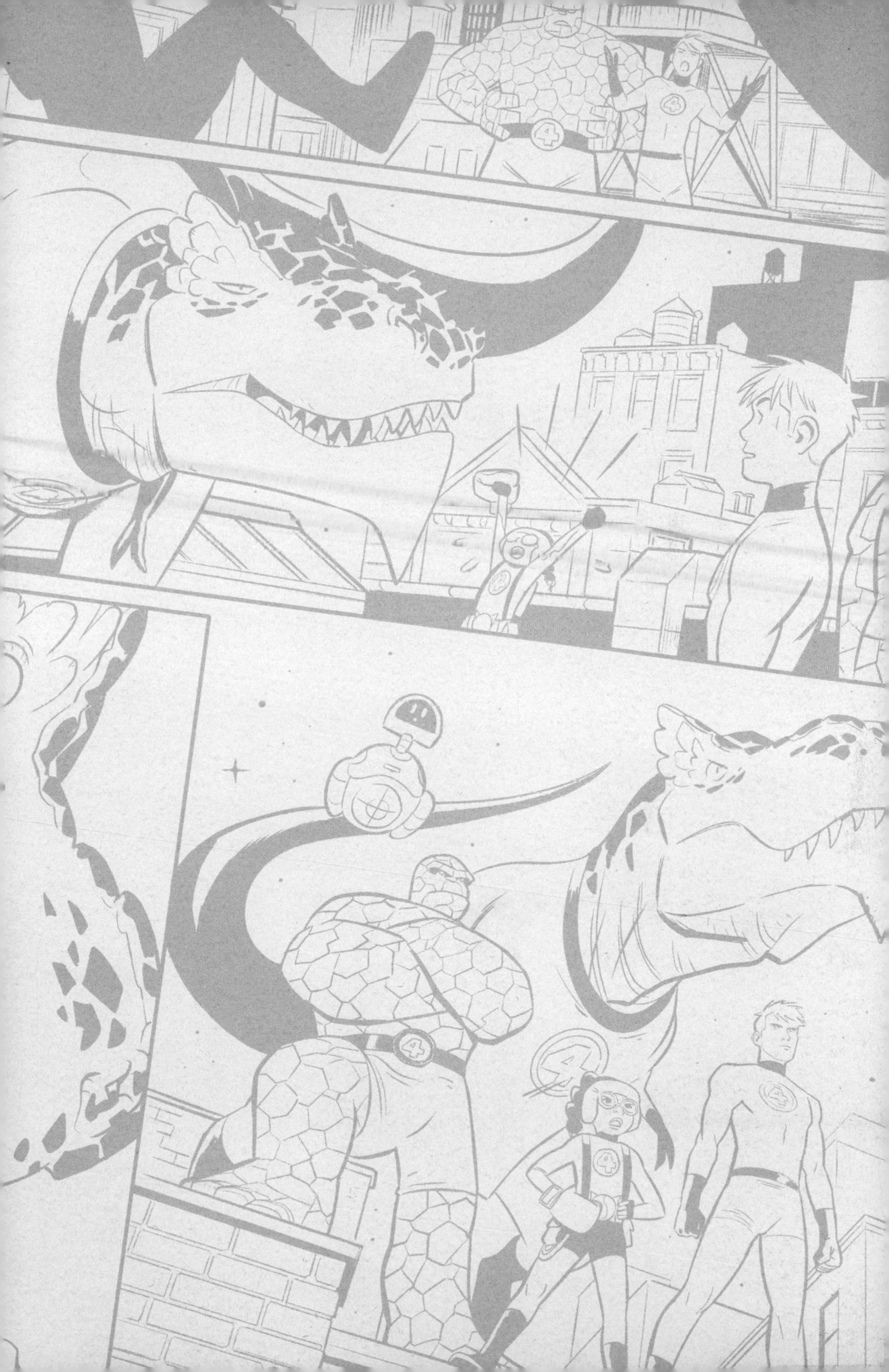

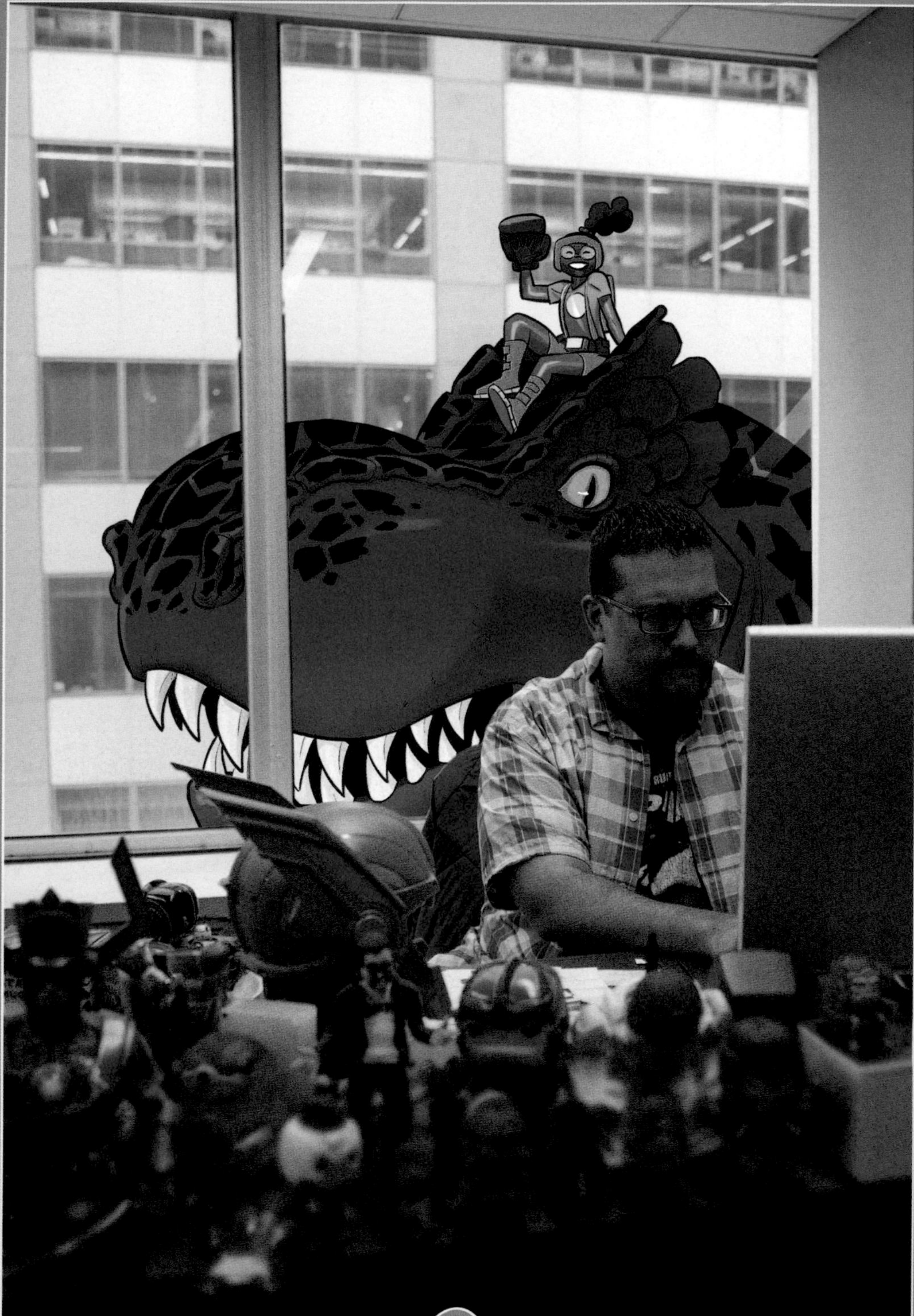

33

"DADDY'S LITTLE GIRL"

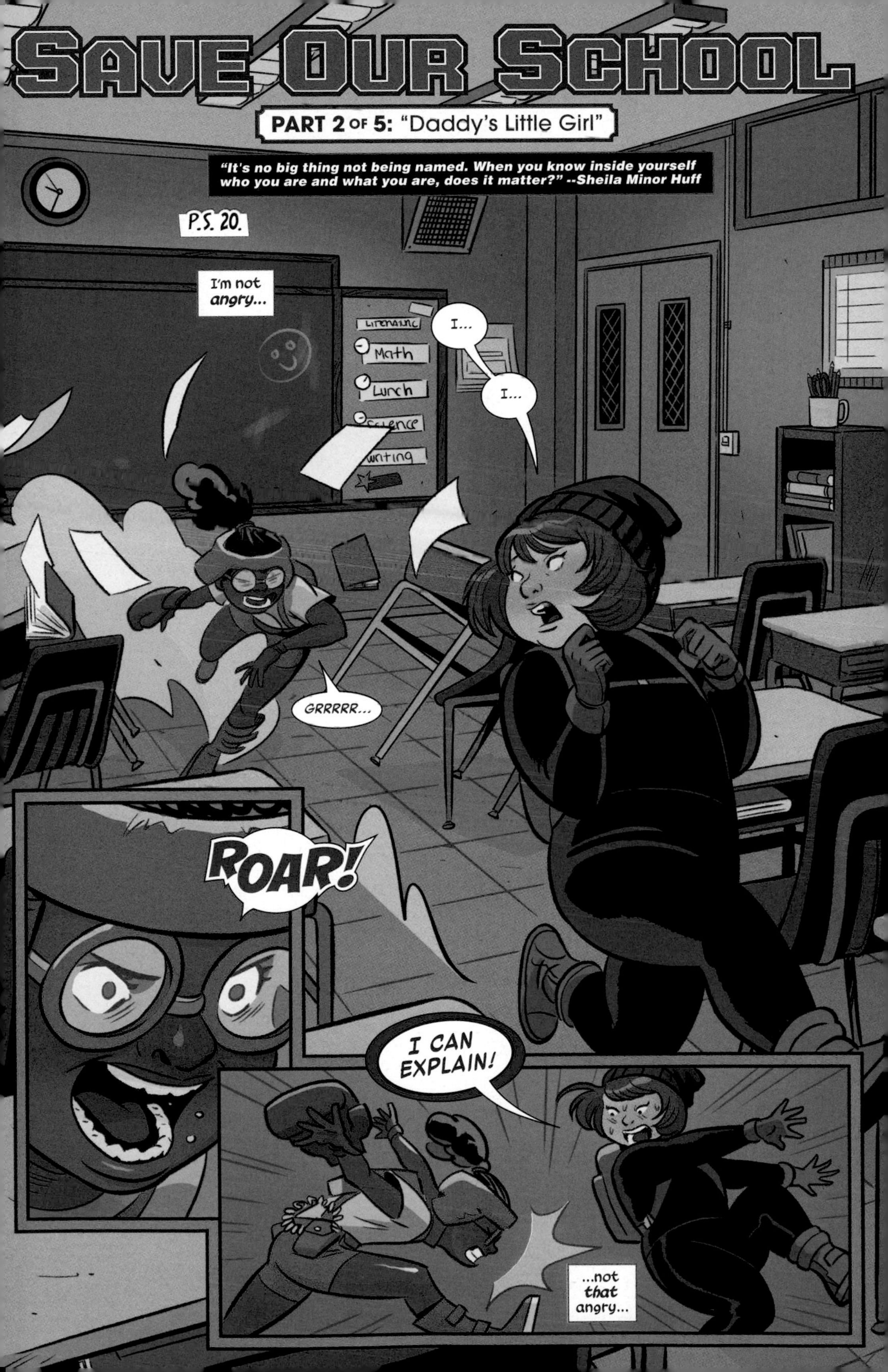
SAVE OUR SCHOOL
PART 2 OF 5: "Daddy's Little Girl"
"It's no big thing not being named. When you know inside yourself who you are and what you are, does it matter?" --Sheila Minor Huff
P.S. 20.
I'm not angry...
Math
Lunch
Science
I...
I...
GRRRRR...
ROAR!
I CAN EXPLAIN!
...not that angry...

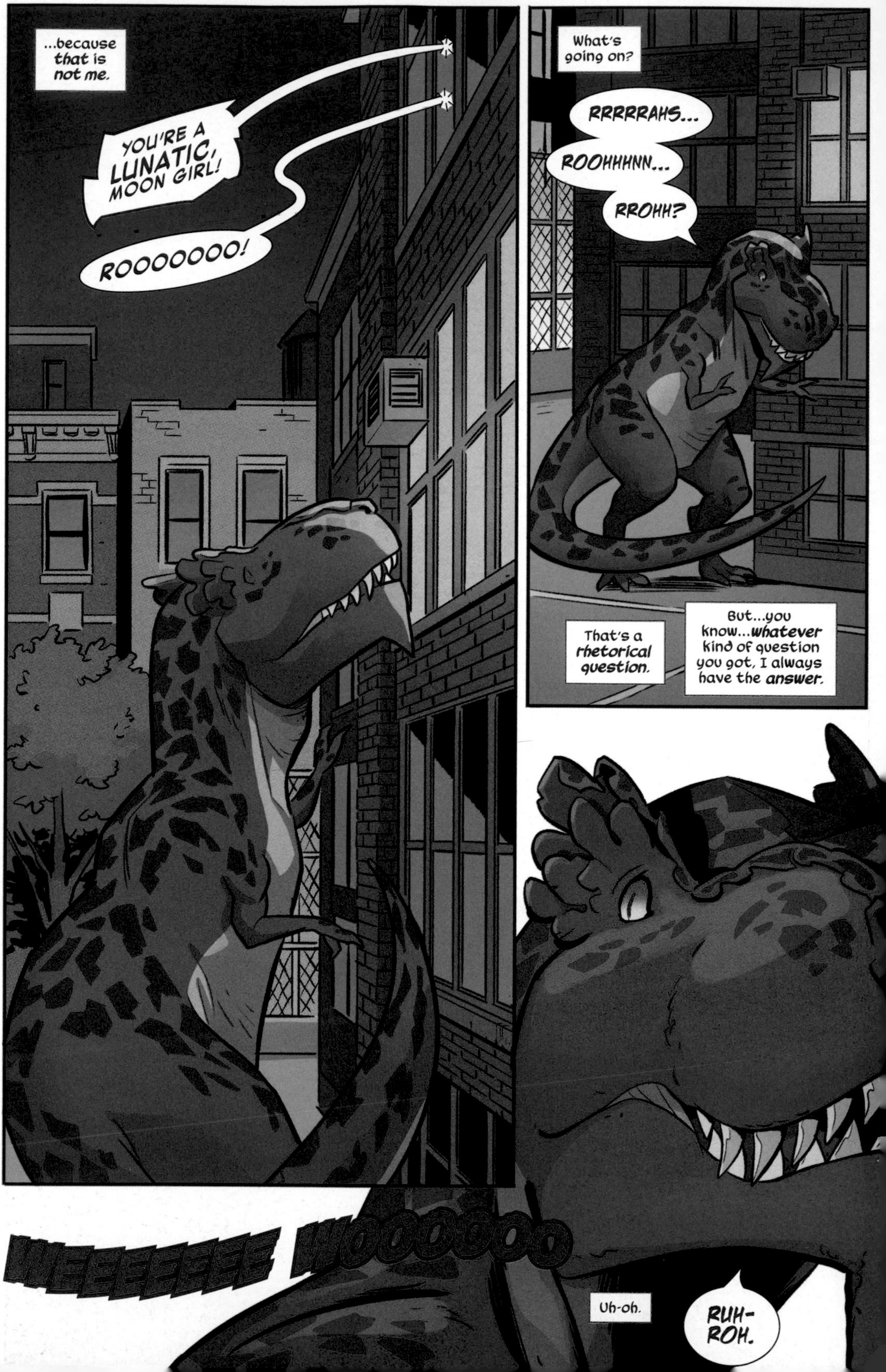
...because that is not me.
YOU'RE A LUNATIC, MOON GIRL!
ROOOOOOO!
What's going on?
RRRRRAHS...
ROOHHHNN...
RROHH?
That's a rhetorical question.
But...you know...whatever kind of question you got, I always have the answer.
WEEEEEEE WOOOOOO
Uh-oh.
RUH-ROH.

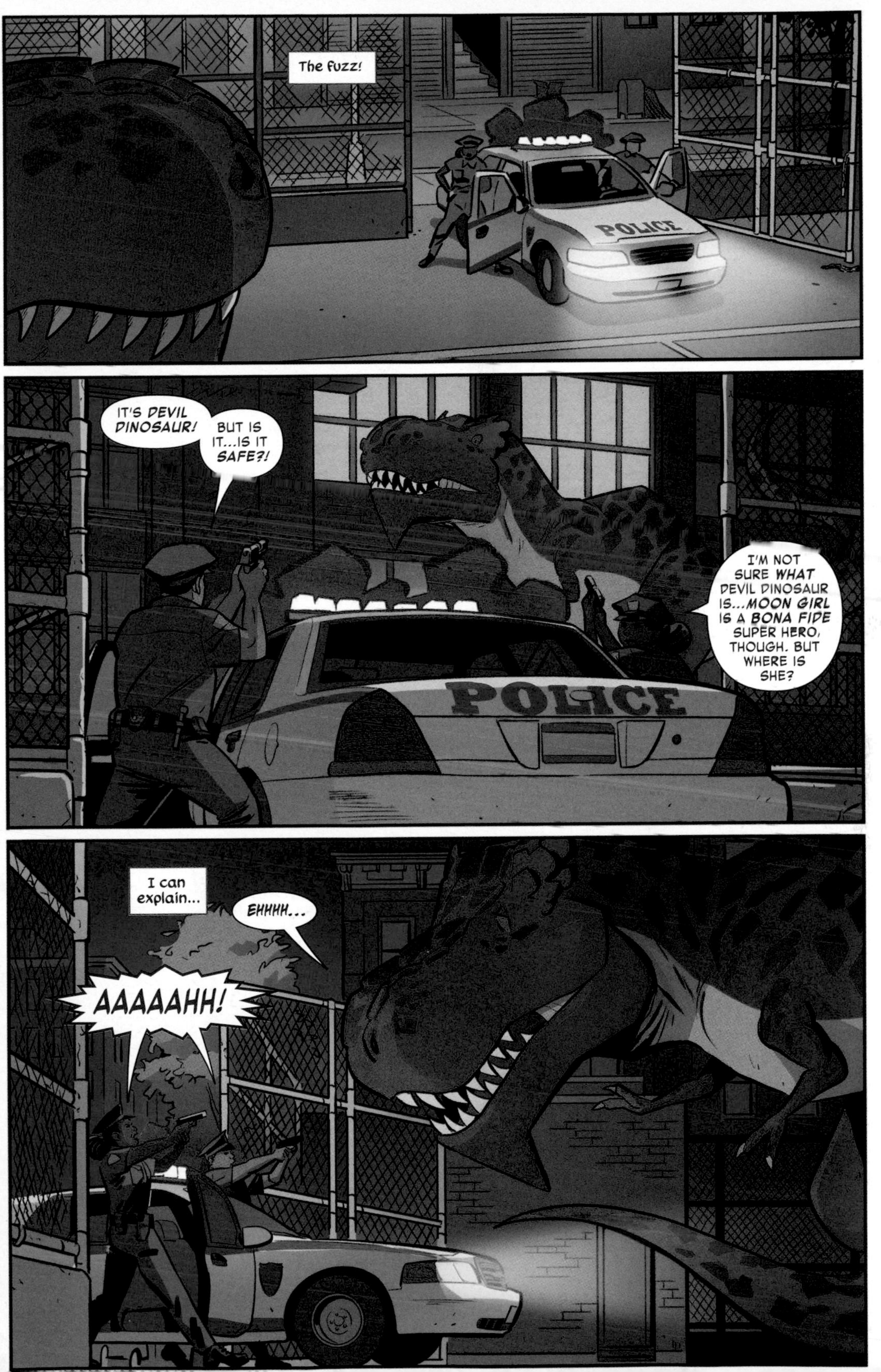
The fuzz!
POLICE
IT'S DEVIL DINOSAUR!
BUT IS IT...IS IT SAFE?!
I'M NOT SURE WHAT DEVIL DINOSAUR IS...MOON GIRL IS A BONA FIDE SUPER HERO, THOUGH. BUT WHERE IS SHE?
POLICE
I can explain...
EHHHH...
AAAAAHH!

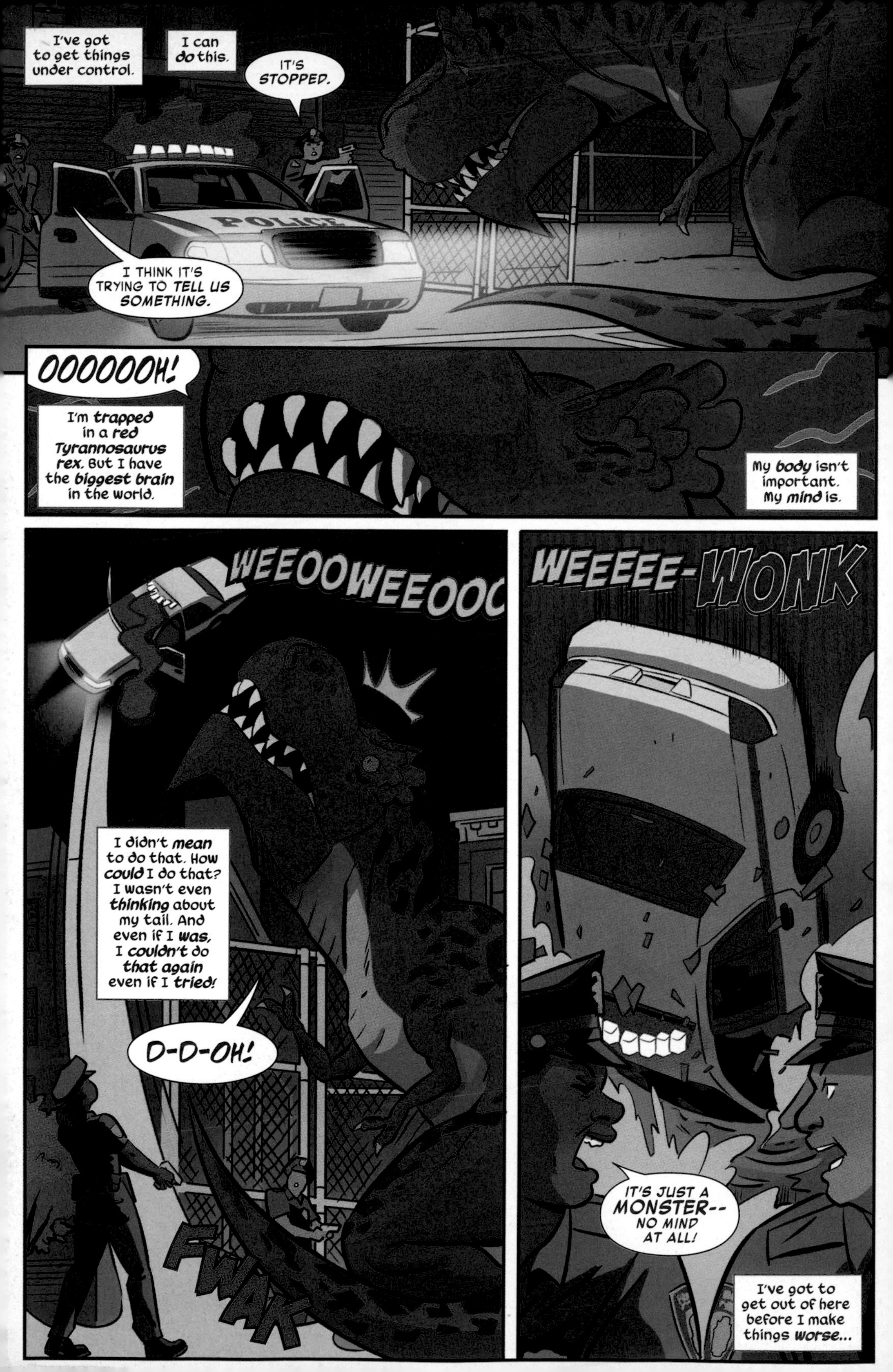
I've got to get things under control.
I can do this.
IT'S STOPPED.
I THINK IT'S TRYING TO TELL US SOMETHING.
OOOOOOH!
I'm trapped in a red Tyrannosaurus rex. But I have the biggest brain in the world.
My body isn't important. My mind is.
WEEOOWEEOOO
I didn't mean to do that. How could I do that? I wasn't even thinking about my tail. And even if I was, I couldn't do that again even if I tried!
D-D-OH!
FWAK
WEEEEE-WONK
IT'S JUST A MONSTER-- NO MIND AT ALL!
I've got to get out of here before I make things worse...

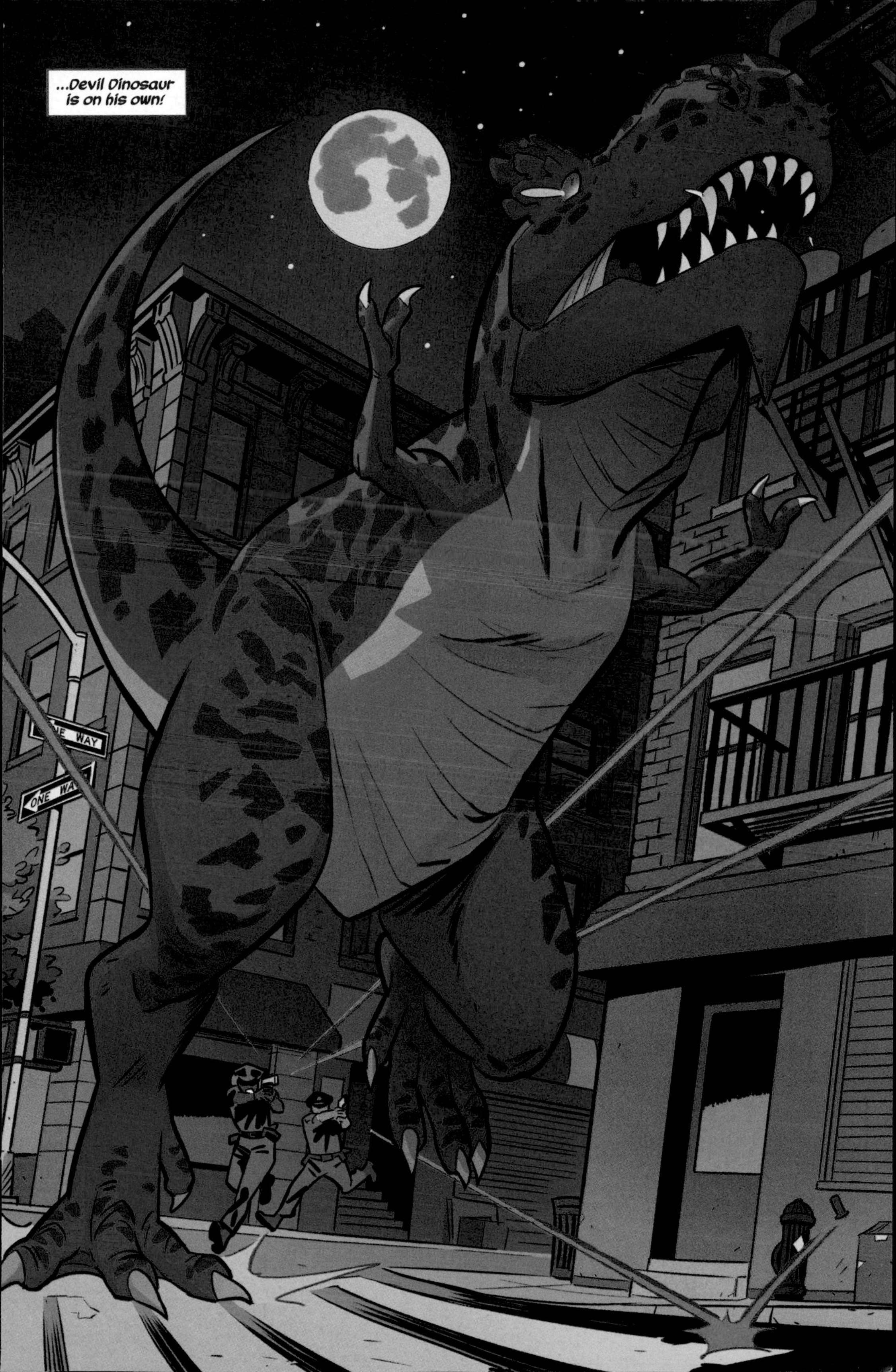
...Devil Dinosaur is on his own!
ONE WAY
ONE WAY

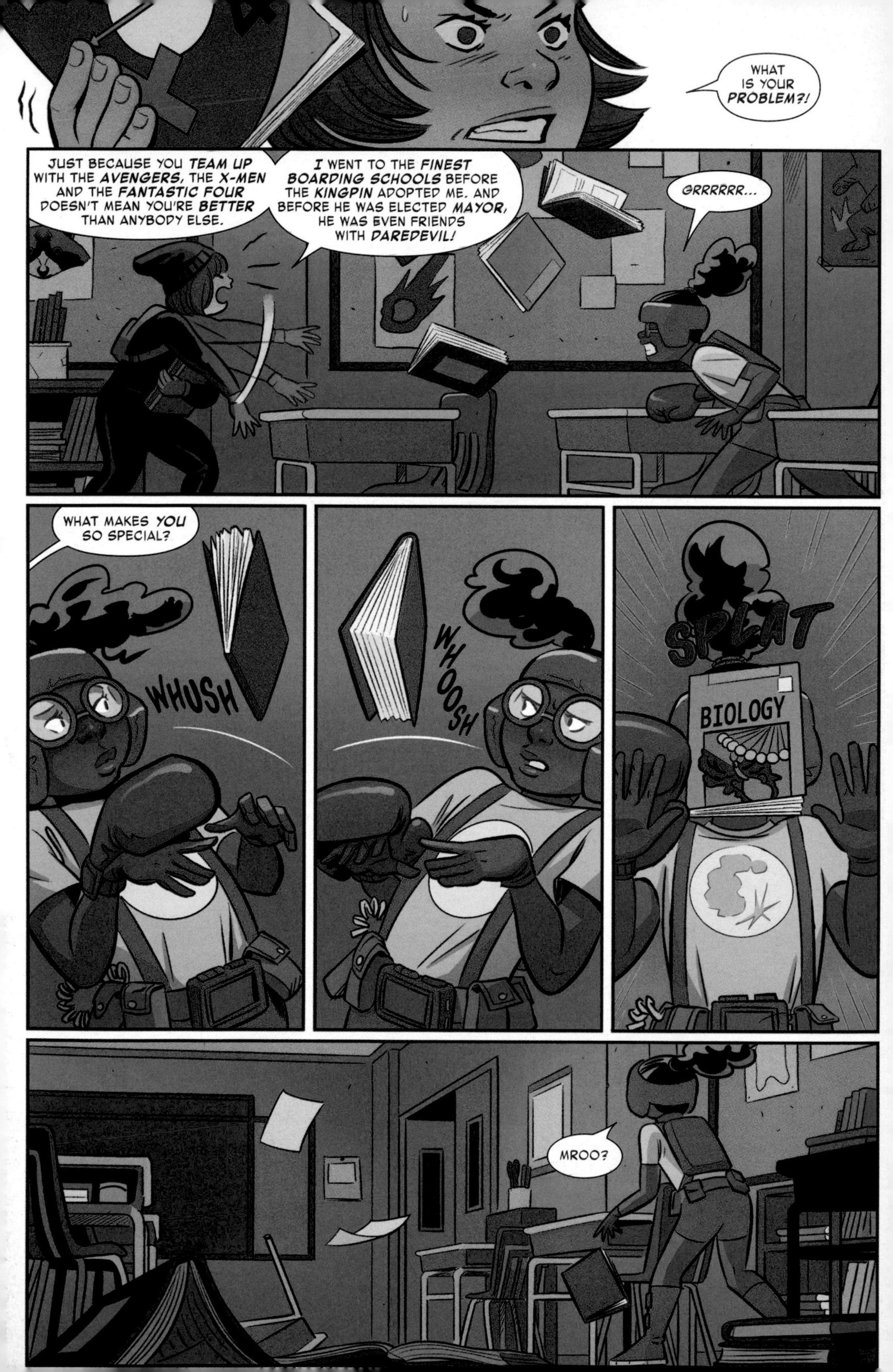
WHAT IS YOUR PROBLEM?!
JUST BECAUSE YOU TEAM UP WITH THE AVENGERS, THE X-MEN AND THE FANTASTIC FOUR DOESN'T MEAN YOU'RE BETTER THAN ANYBODY ELSE.
I WENT TO THE FINEST BOARDING SCHOOLS BEFORE THE KINGPIN ADOPTED ME. AND BEFORE HE WAS ELECTED MAYOR, HE WAS EVEN FRIENDS WITH DAREDEVIL!
GRRRRRR...
WHAT MAKES YOU SO SPECIAL?
WHUSH
WHOOOSH
SPLAT
BIOLOGY
MROO?

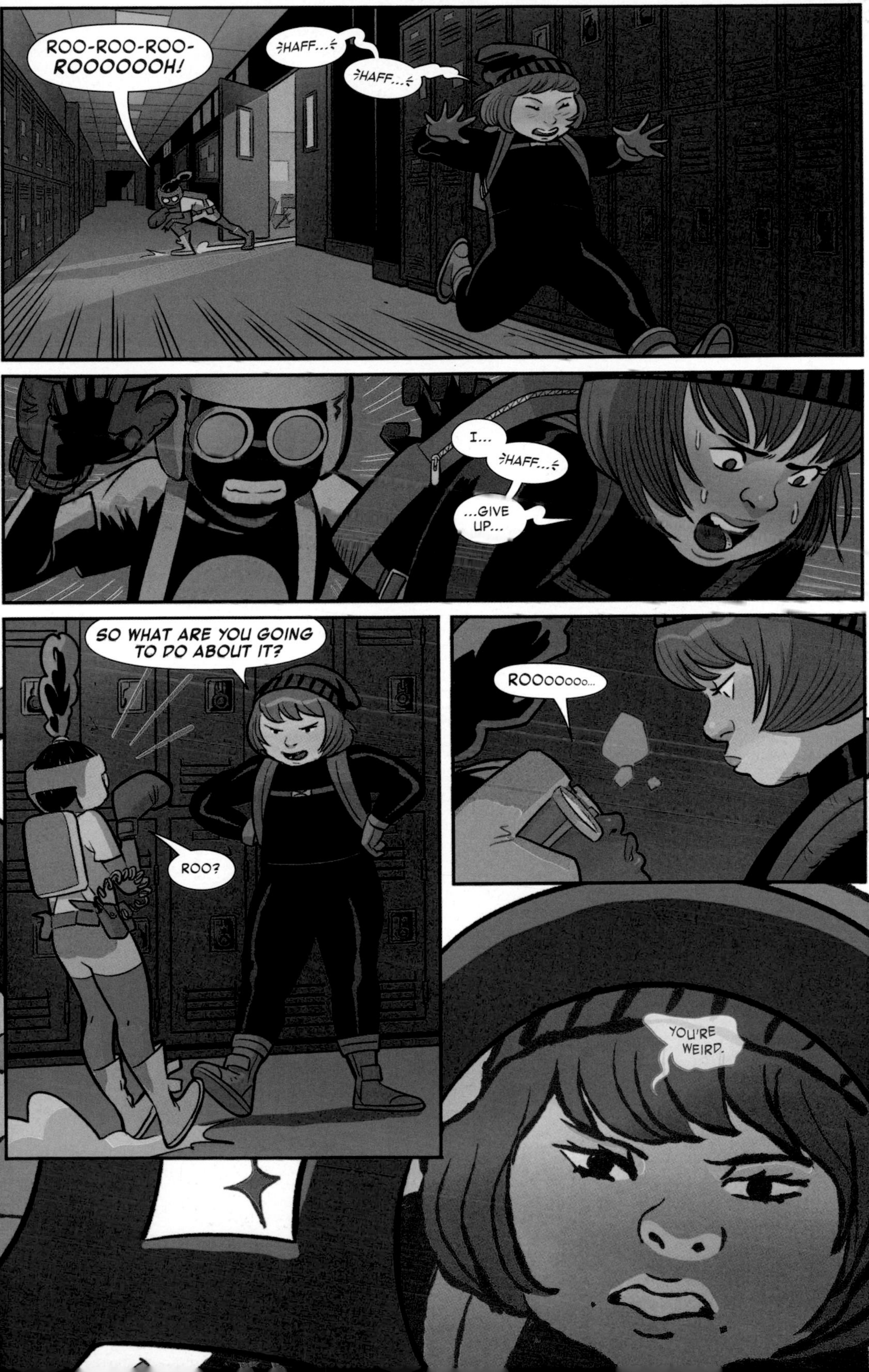
ROO-ROO-ROO-ROOOOOOH!
HAFF...
HAFF...
I...
HAFF...
...GIVE UP...
SO WHAT ARE YOU GOING TO DO ABOUT IT?
ROO?
ROOoooo...
YOU'RE WEIRD.

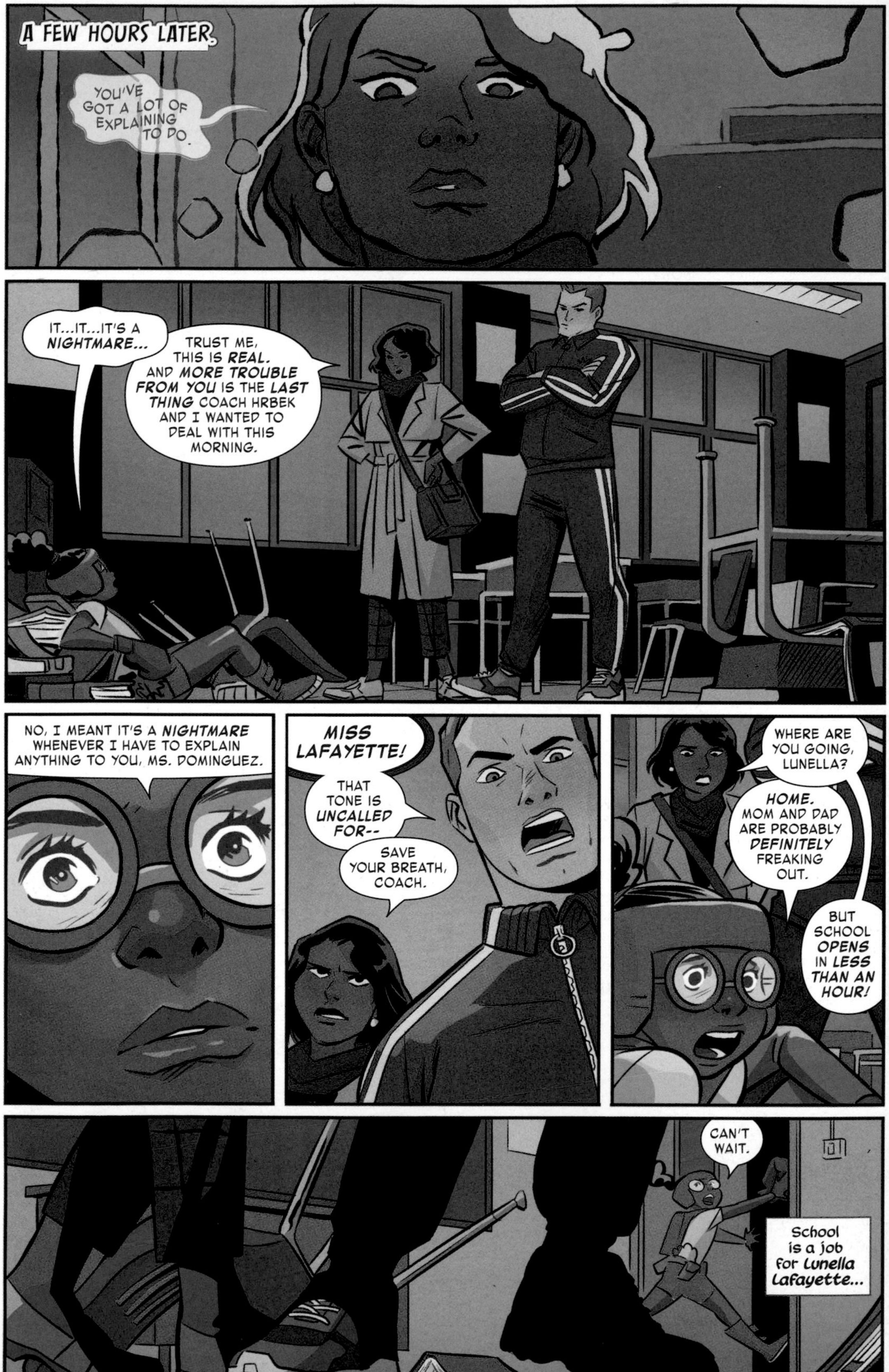
A FEW HOURS LATER.
YOU'VE GOT A LOT OF EXPLAINING TO DO.
IT...IT...IT'S A NIGHTMARE...
TRUST ME, THIS IS REAL. AND MORE TROUBLE FROM YOU IS THE LAST THING COACH HRBEK AND I WANTED TO DEAL WITH THIS MORNING.
NO, I MEANT IT'S A NIGHTMARE WHENEVER I HAVE TO EXPLAIN ANYTHING TO YOU, MS. DOMINGUEZ.
MISS LAFAYETTE!
THAT TONE IS UNCALLED FOR--
SAVE YOUR BREATH, COACH.
WHERE ARE YOU GOING, LUNELLA?
HOME. MOM AND DAD ARE PROBABLY DEFINITELY FREAKING OUT.
BUT SCHOOL OPENS IN LESS THAN AN HOUR!
CAN'T WAIT.
School is a job for Lunella Lafayette...

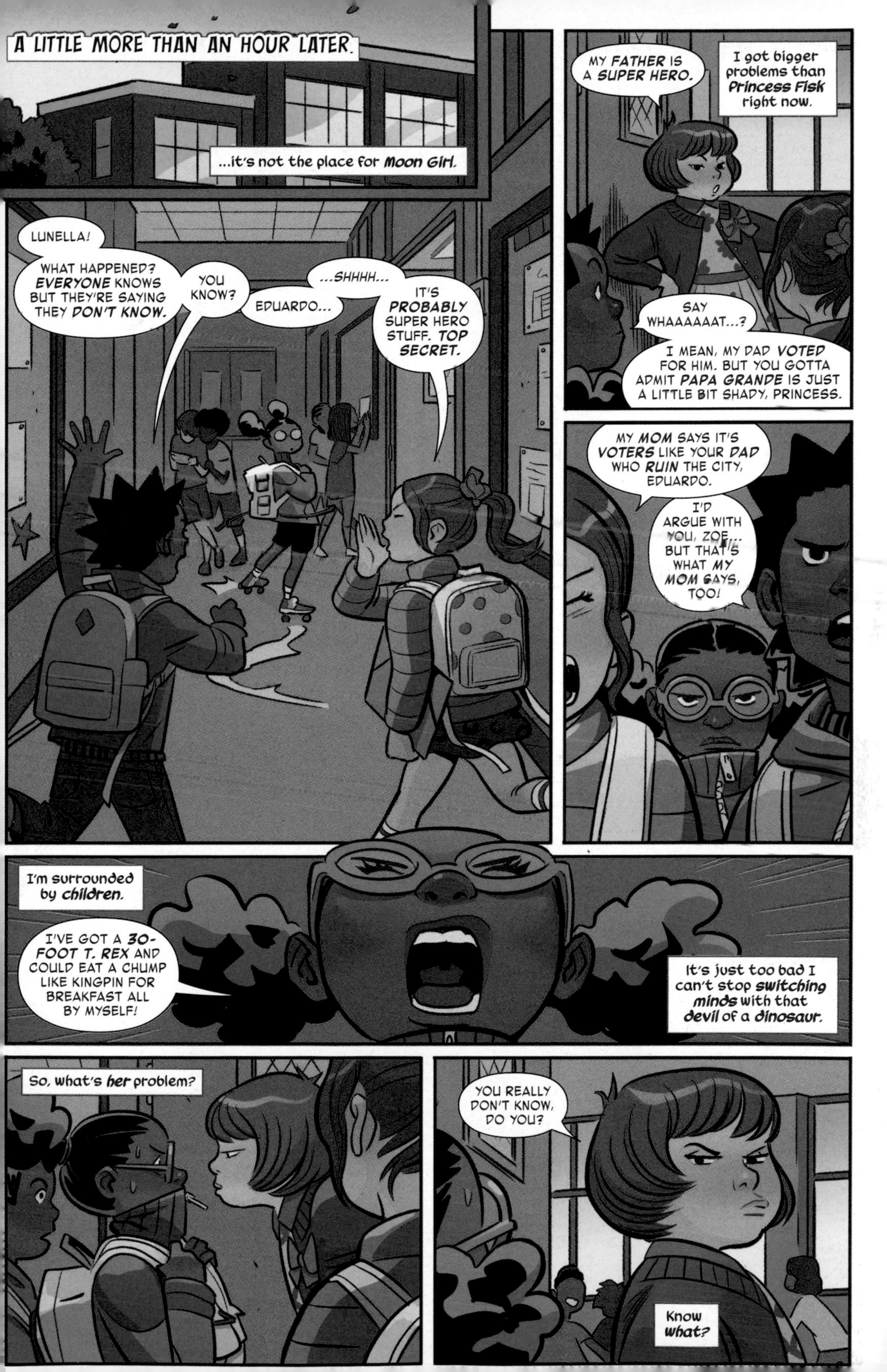

A LITTLE MORE THAN AN HOUR LATER.
...it's not the place for Moon Girl.
LUNELLA!
WHAT HAPPENED? EVERYONE KNOWS BUT THEY'RE SAYING THEY DON'T KNOW.
YOU KNOW?
EDUARDO...
...SHHHH...
IT'S PROBABLY SUPER HERO STUFF. TOP SECRET.
MY FATHER IS A SUPER HERO.
I got bigger problems than Princess Fisk right now.
SAY WHAAAAAAT...?
I MEAN, MY DAD VOTED FOR HIM. BUT YOU GOTTA ADMIT PAPA GRANDE IS JUST A LITTLE BIT SHADY, PRINCESS.
MY MOM SAYS IT'S VOTERS LIKE YOUR DAD WHO RUIN THE CITY, EDUARDO.
I'D ARGUE WITH YOU, ZOE... BUT THAT'S WHAT MY MOM SAYS, TOO!
I'm surrounded by children.
I'VE GOT A 30-FOOT T. REX AND COULD EAT A CHUMP LIKE KINGPIN FOR BREAKFAST ALL BY MYSELF!
It's just too bad I can't stop switching minds with that devil of a dinosaur.
So, what's her problem?
YOU REALLY DON'T KNOW, DO YOU?
Know what?

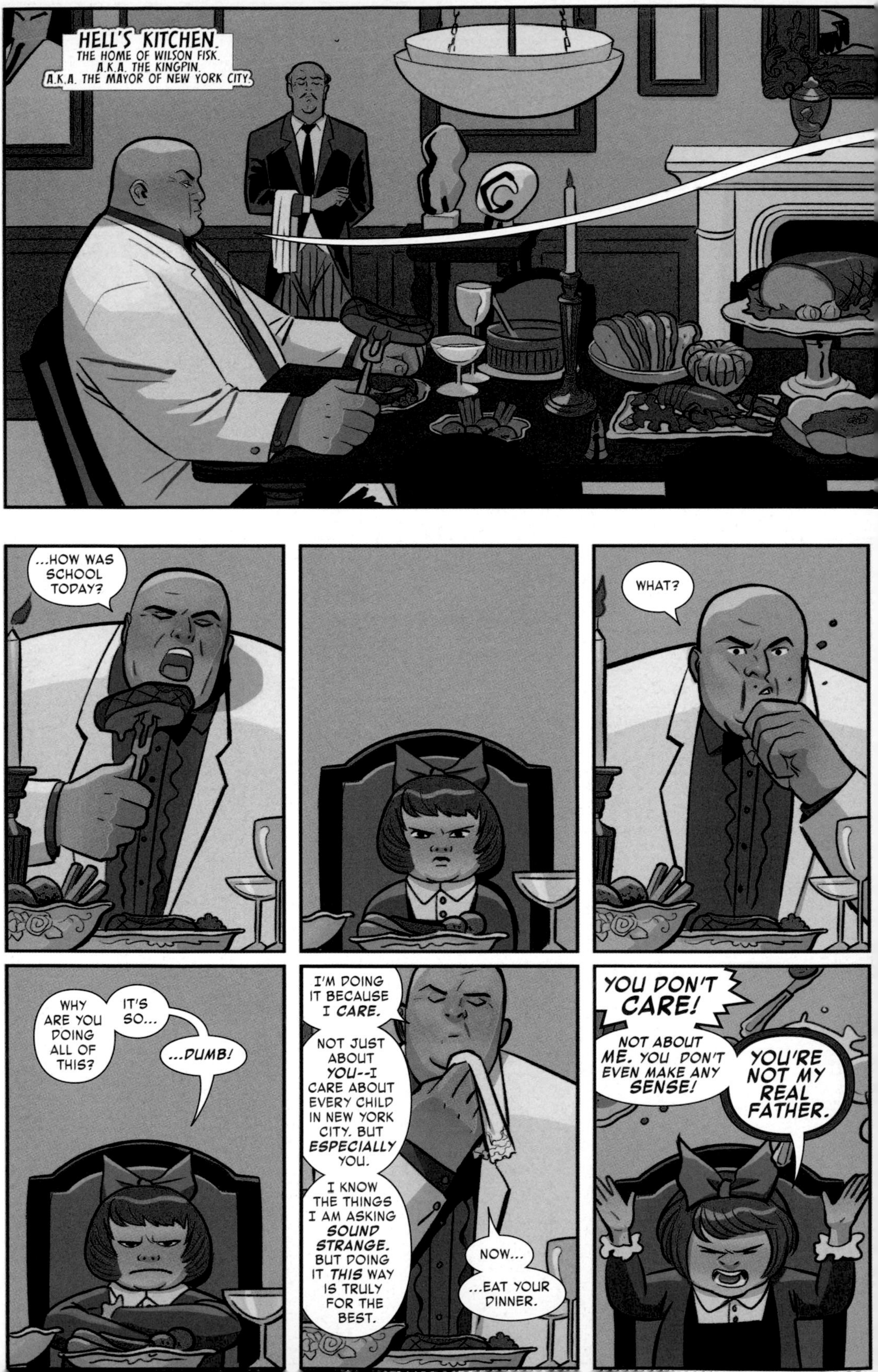
HELL'S KITCHEN.
THE HOME OF WILSON FISK.
A.K.A. THE KINGPIN.
A.K.A. THE MAYOR OF NEW YORK CITY.
...HOW WAS SCHOOL TODAY?
WHAT?
WHY ARE YOU DOING ALL OF THIS?
IT'S SO...
...DUMB!
I'M DOING IT BECAUSE I CARE.
NOT JUST ABOUT YOU--I CARE ABOUT EVERY CHILD IN NEW YORK CITY. BUT ESPECIALLY YOU.
I KNOW THE THINGS I AM ASKING SOUND STRANGE. BUT DOING IT THIS WAY IS TRULY FOR THE BEST.
NOW...
...EAT YOUR DINNER.
YOU DON'T CARE!
NOT ABOUT ME. YOU DON'T EVEN MAKE ANY SENSE!
YOU'RE NOT MY REAL FATHER.

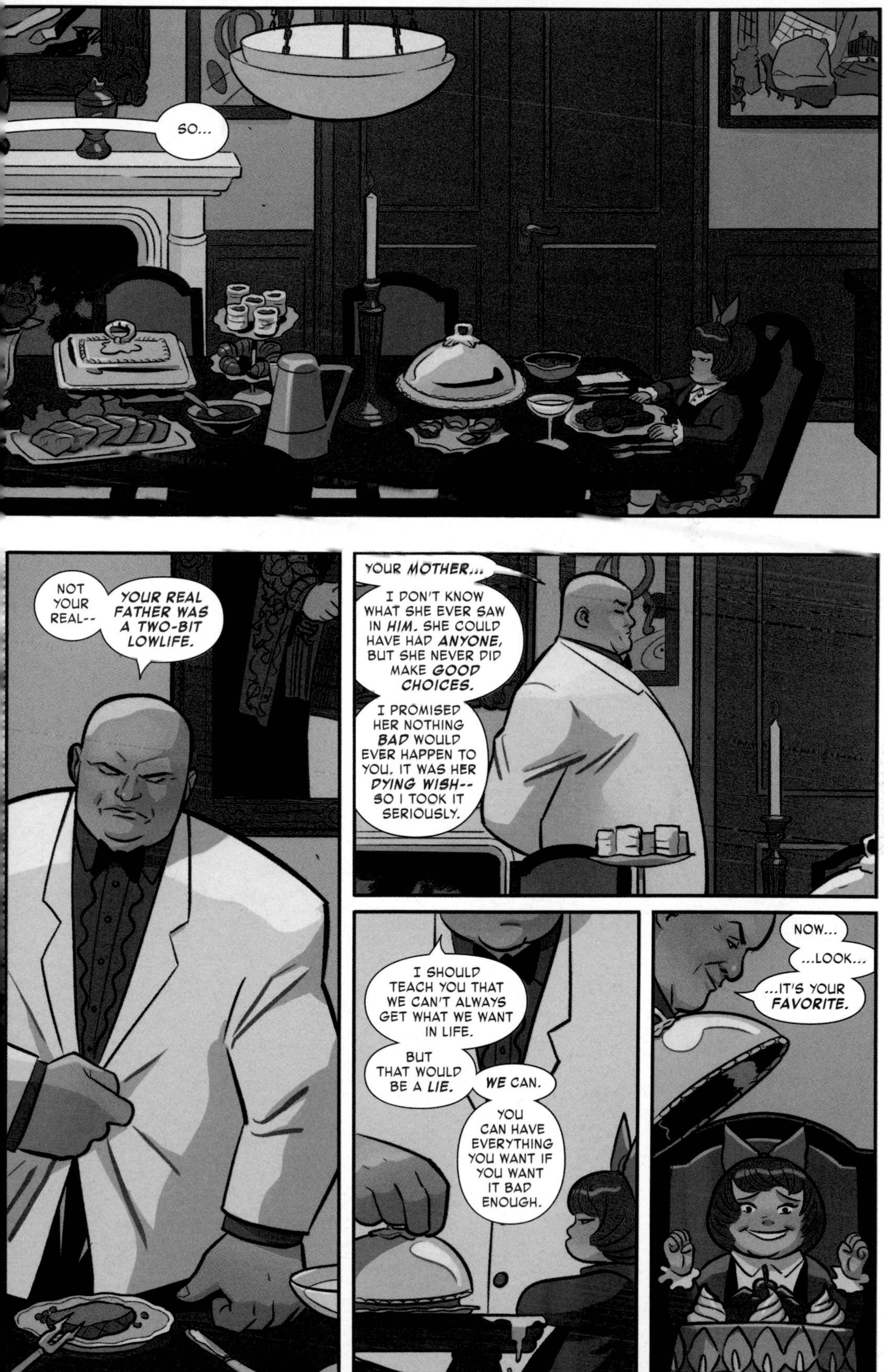
SO...
NOT YOUR REAL--
YOUR REAL FATHER WAS A TWO-BIT LOWLIFE.
YOUR MOTHER...
I DON'T KNOW WHAT SHE EVER SAW IN HIM. SHE COULD HAVE HAD ANYONE, BUT SHE NEVER DID MAKE GOOD CHOICES.
I PROMISED HER NOTHING BAD WOULD EVER HAPPEN TO YOU. IT WAS HER DYING WISH-- SO I TOOK IT SERIOUSLY.
I SHOULD TEACH YOU THAT WE CAN'T ALWAYS GET WHAT WE WANT IN LIFE.
BUT THAT WOULD BE A LIE.
WE CAN.
YOU CAN HAVE EVERYTHING YOU WANT IF YOU WANT IT BAD ENOUGH.
NOW...
...LOOK...
...IT'S YOUR FAVORITE.

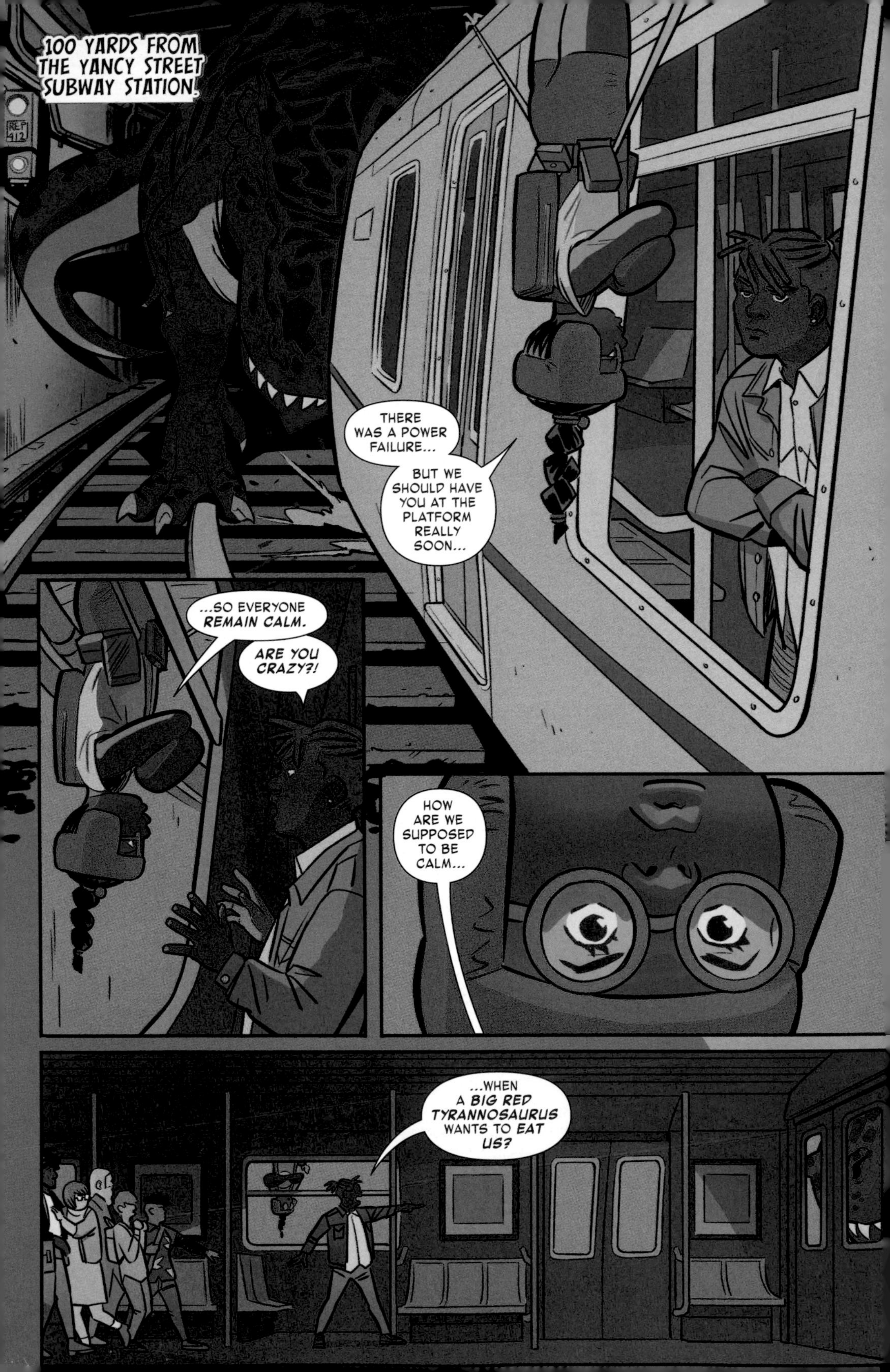
100 YARDS FROM THE YANCY STREET SUBWAY STATION.
THERE WAS A POWER FAILURE...
BUT WE SHOULD HAVE YOU AT THE PLATFORM REALLY SOON...
...SO EVERYONE REMAIN CALM.
ARE YOU CRAZY?!
HOW ARE WE SUPPOSED TO BE CALM...
...WHEN A BIG RED TYRANNOSAURUS WANTS TO EAT US?

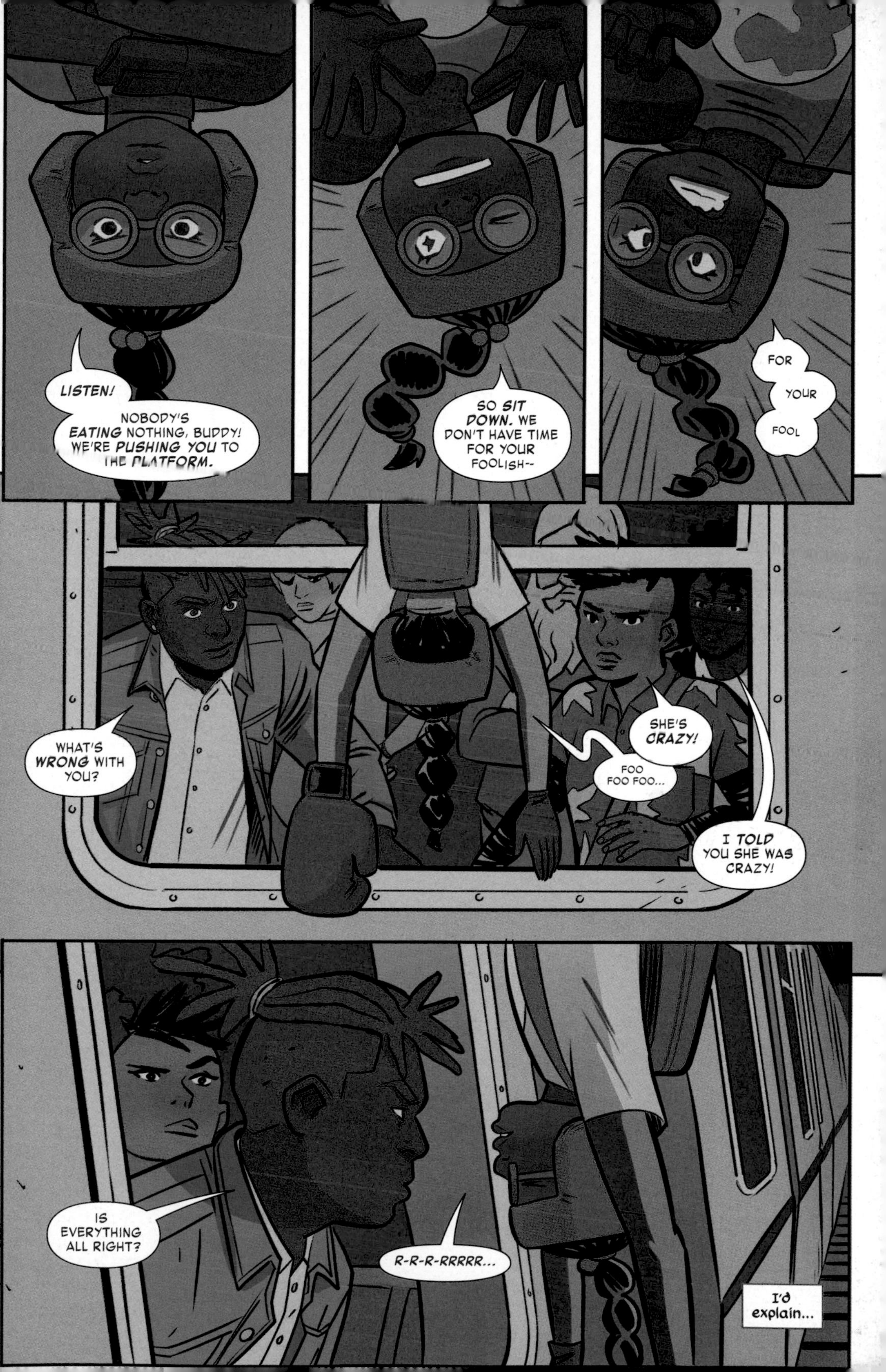
LISTEN!
NOBODY'S EATING NOTHING, BUDDY! WE'RE PUSHING YOU TO THE PLATFORM.
SO SIT DOWN. WE DON'T HAVE TIME FOR YOUR FOOLISH--
FOR
YOUR
FOOL
WHAT'S WRONG WITH YOU?
SHE'S CRAZY!
FOO FOO FOO...
I TOLD YOU SHE WAS CRAZY!
IS EVERYTHING ALL RIGHT?
R-R-R-RRRRR...
I'd explain...

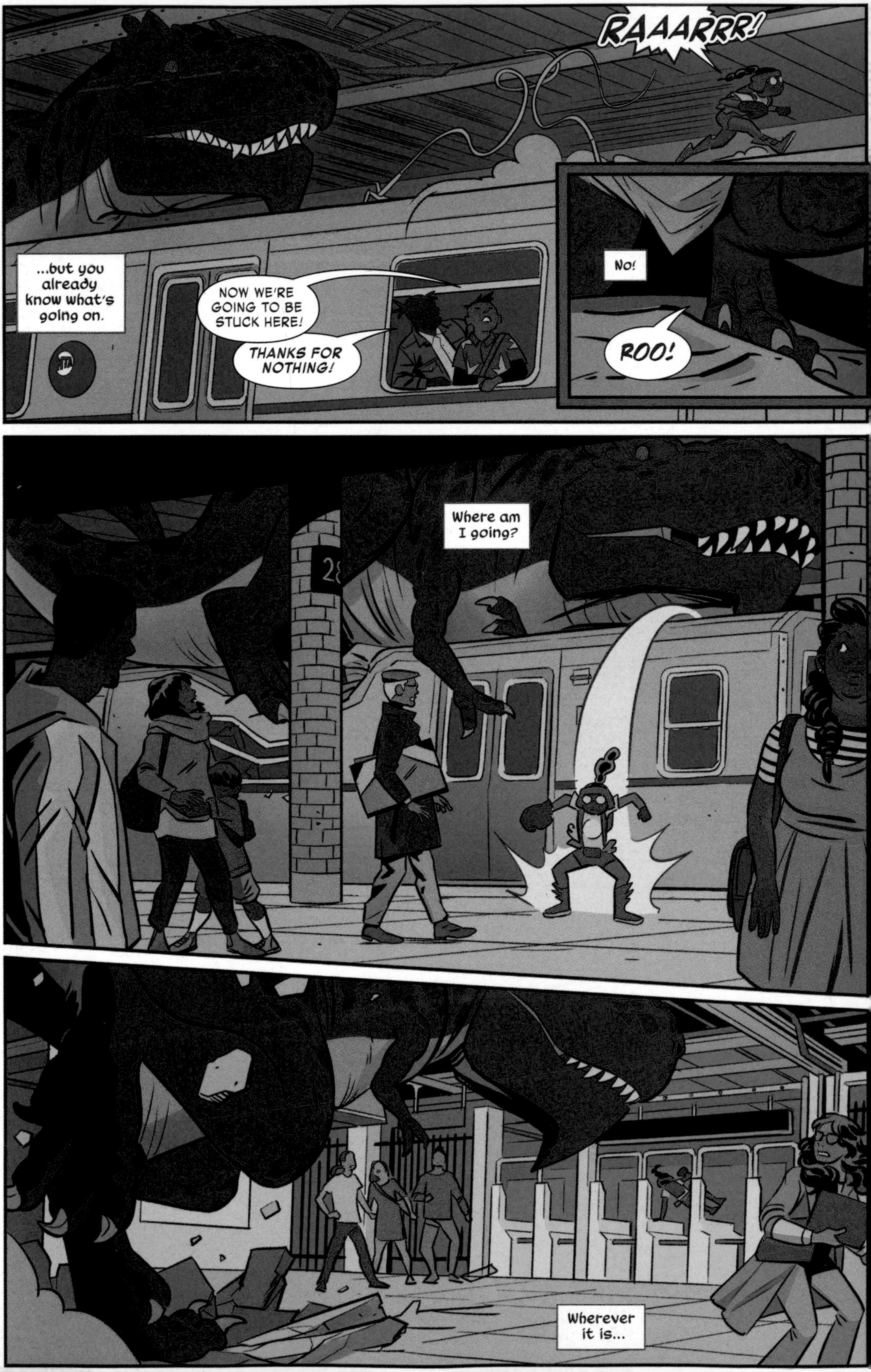
RAAARRR!
...but you already know what's going on.
NOW WE'RE GOING TO BE STUCK HERE!
THANKS FOR NOTHING!
No!
ROO!
Where am I going?
Wherever it is...

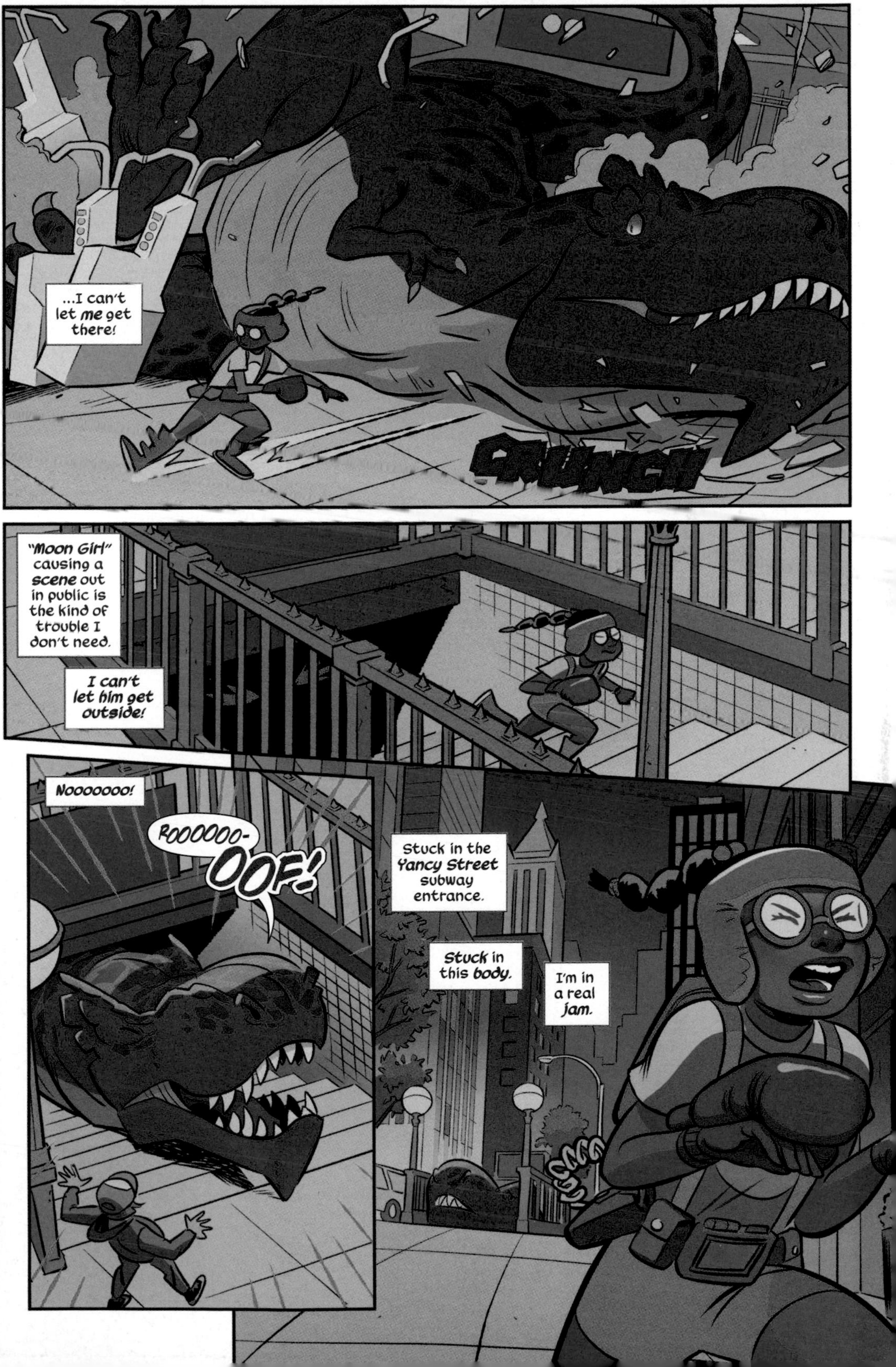

...I can't let *me* get there!
CRUNCH
"*Moon Girl*" causing a *scene* out in public is the kind of trouble I don't need.
I can't let him get outside!
Noooooooo!
ROOOOOO-OOF!
Stuck in the *Yancy Street* subway entrance.
Stuck in this *body*.
I'm in a real *jam*.

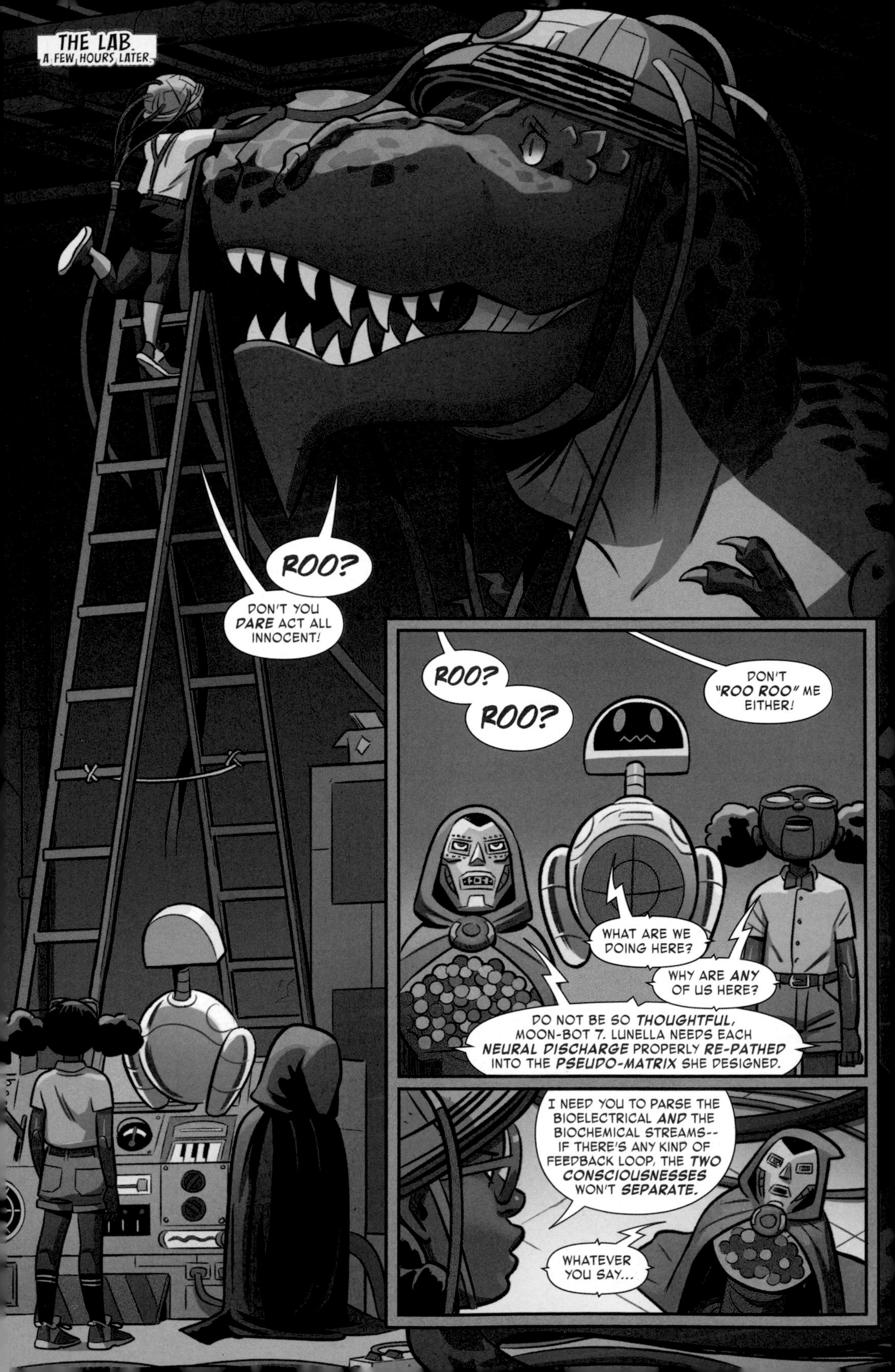
THE LAB. A FEW HOURS LATER.
ROO?
DON'T YOU DARE ACT ALL INNOCENT!
ROO?
ROO?
DON'T "ROO ROO" ME EITHER!
WHAT ARE WE DOING HERE?
WHY ARE ANY OF US HERE?
DO NOT BE SO THOUGHTFUL, MOON-BOT 7. LUNELLA NEEDS EACH NEURAL DISCHARGE PROPERLY RE-PATHED INTO THE PSEUDO-MATRIX SHE DESIGNED.
I NEED YOU TO PARSE THE BIOELECTRICAL AND THE BIOCHEMICAL STREAMS-- IF THERE'S ANY KIND OF FEEDBACK LOOP, THE TWO CONSCIOUSNESSES WON'T SEPARATE.
WHATEVER YOU SAY...

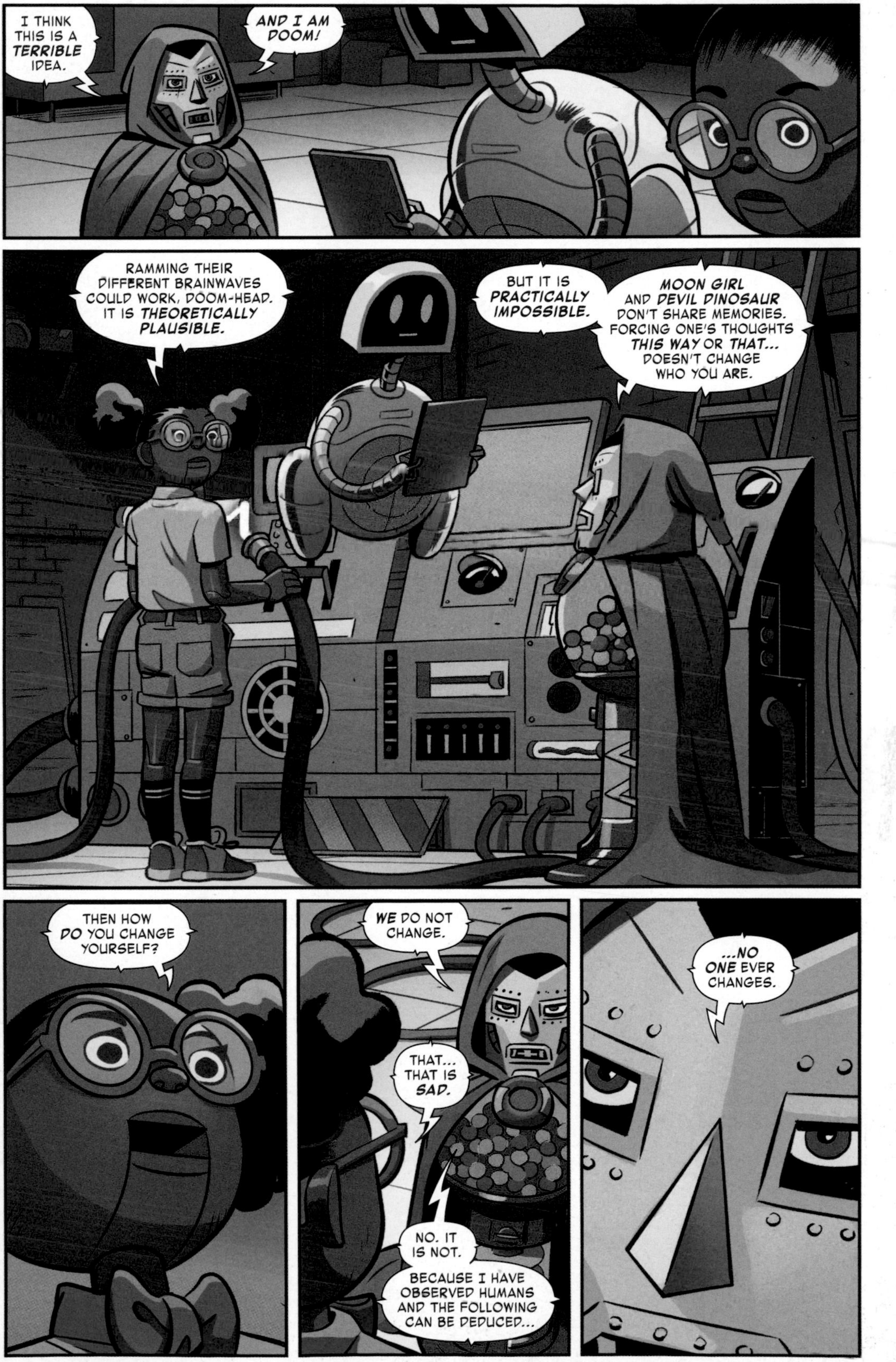
I THINK THIS IS A *TERRIBLE* IDEA.
AND I AM DOOM!
RAMMING THEIR DIFFERENT BRAINWAVES COULD WORK, DOOM-HEAD. IT IS *THEORETICALLY PLAUSIBLE.*
BUT IT IS *PRACTICALLY IMPOSSIBLE.*
MOON GIRL AND *DEVIL DINOSAUR* DON'T SHARE MEMORIES. FORCING ONE'S THOUGHTS *THIS WAY* OR *THAT...* DOESN'T CHANGE WHO YOU ARE.
THEN HOW *DO* YOU CHANGE YOURSELF?
WE DO NOT CHANGE.
THAT... THAT IS *SAD.*
NO. IT IS NOT.
BECAUSE I HAVE OBSERVED HUMANS AND THE FOLLOWING CAN BE DEDUCED...
...NO ONE EVER CHANGES.

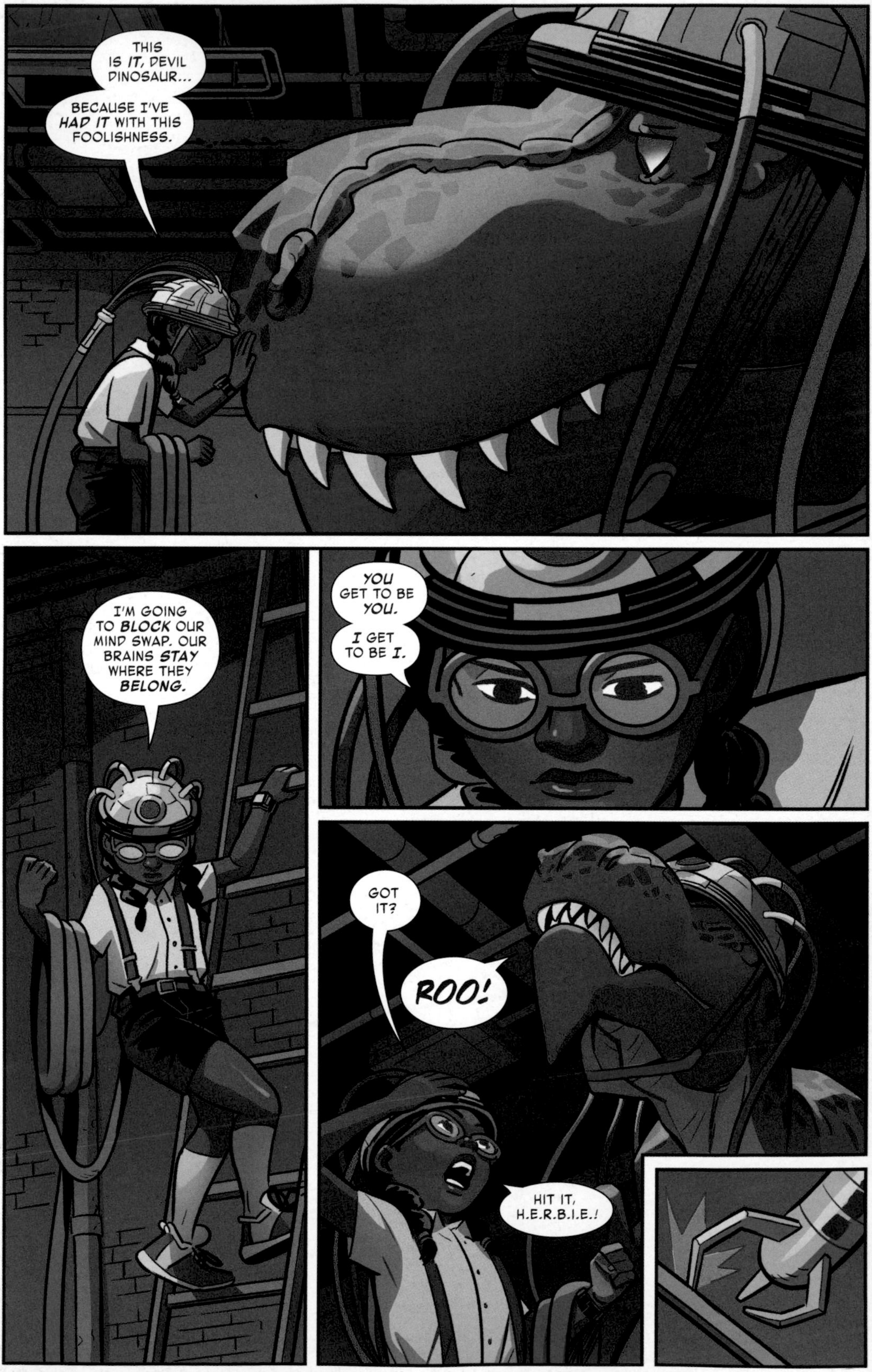
THIS IS *IT*, DEVIL DINOSAUR...
BECAUSE I'VE ***HAD IT*** WITH THIS FOOLISHNESS.
I'M GOING TO ***BLOCK*** OUR MIND SWAP. OUR BRAINS ***STAY*** WHERE THEY ***BELONG***.
YOU GET TO BE *YOU*.
I GET TO BE ***I***.
GOT IT?
ROO!
HIT IT, H.E.R.B.I.E.!

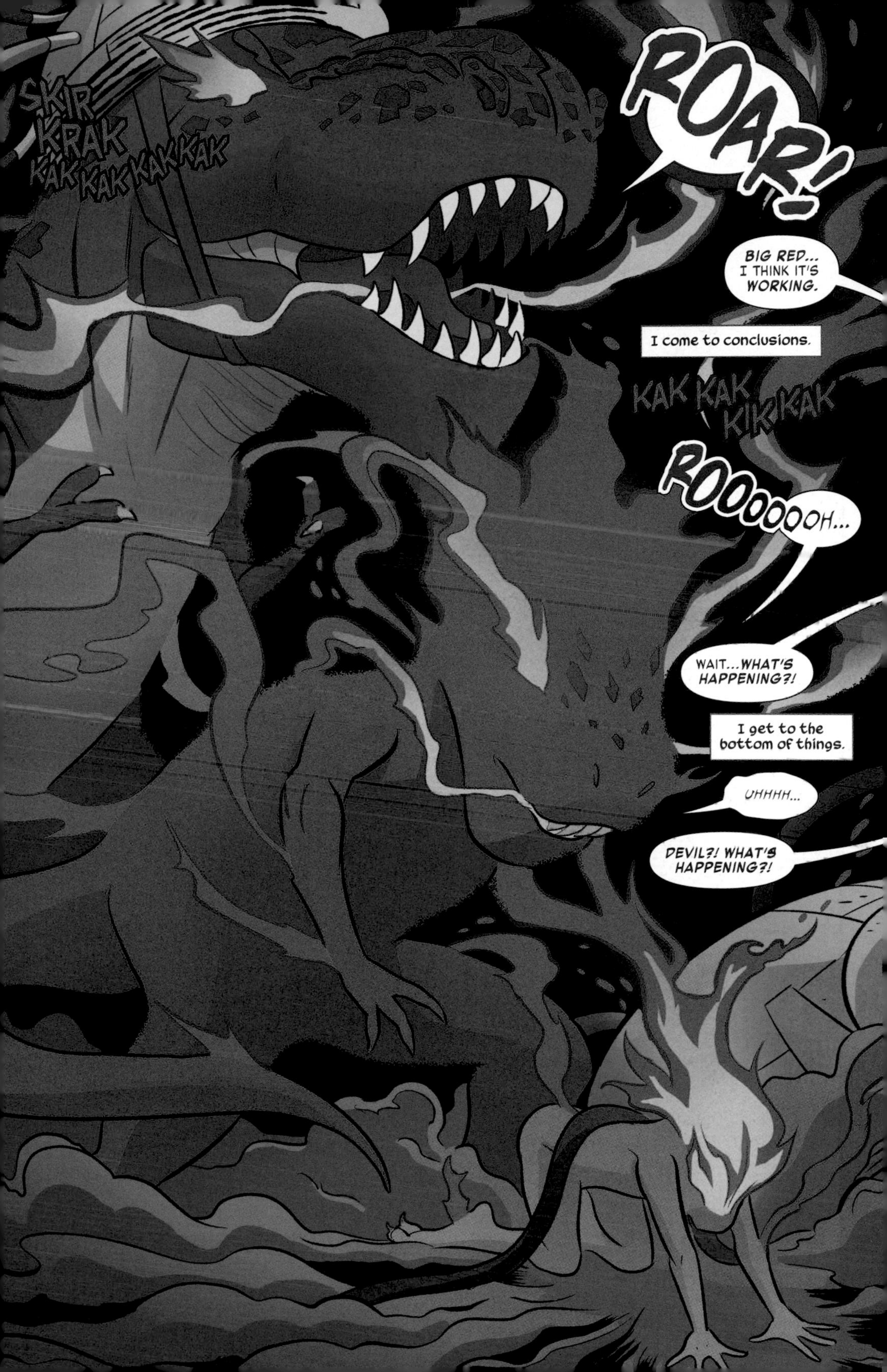
SKIR
KRAK
KAK KAK KAK KAK
ROAR!
BIG RED... I THINK IT'S WORKING.
I come to conclusions.
KAK KAK KIK KAK
ROOOOOOOH...
WAIT...WHAT'S HAPPENING?!
I get to the bottom of things.
UHHHH...
DEVIL?! WHAT'S HAPPENING?!

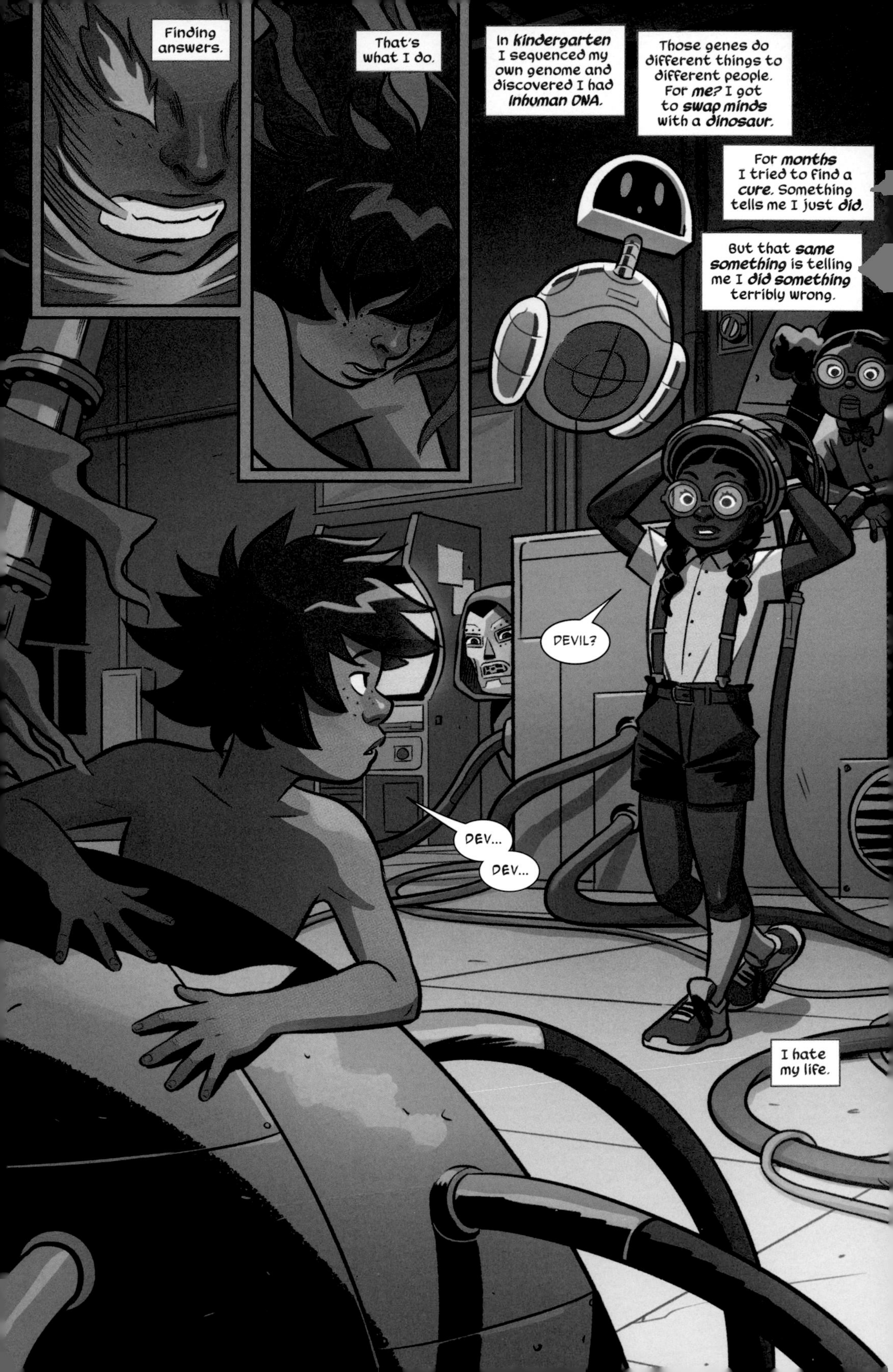
Finding answers.
That's what I do.
In kindergarten I sequenced my own genome and discovered I had Inhuman DNA.
Those genes do different things to different people. For me? I got to swap minds with a dinosaur.
For months I tried to find a cure. Something tells me I just did.
But that same something is telling me I did something terribly wrong.
DEVIL?
DEV...
DEV...
I hate my life.

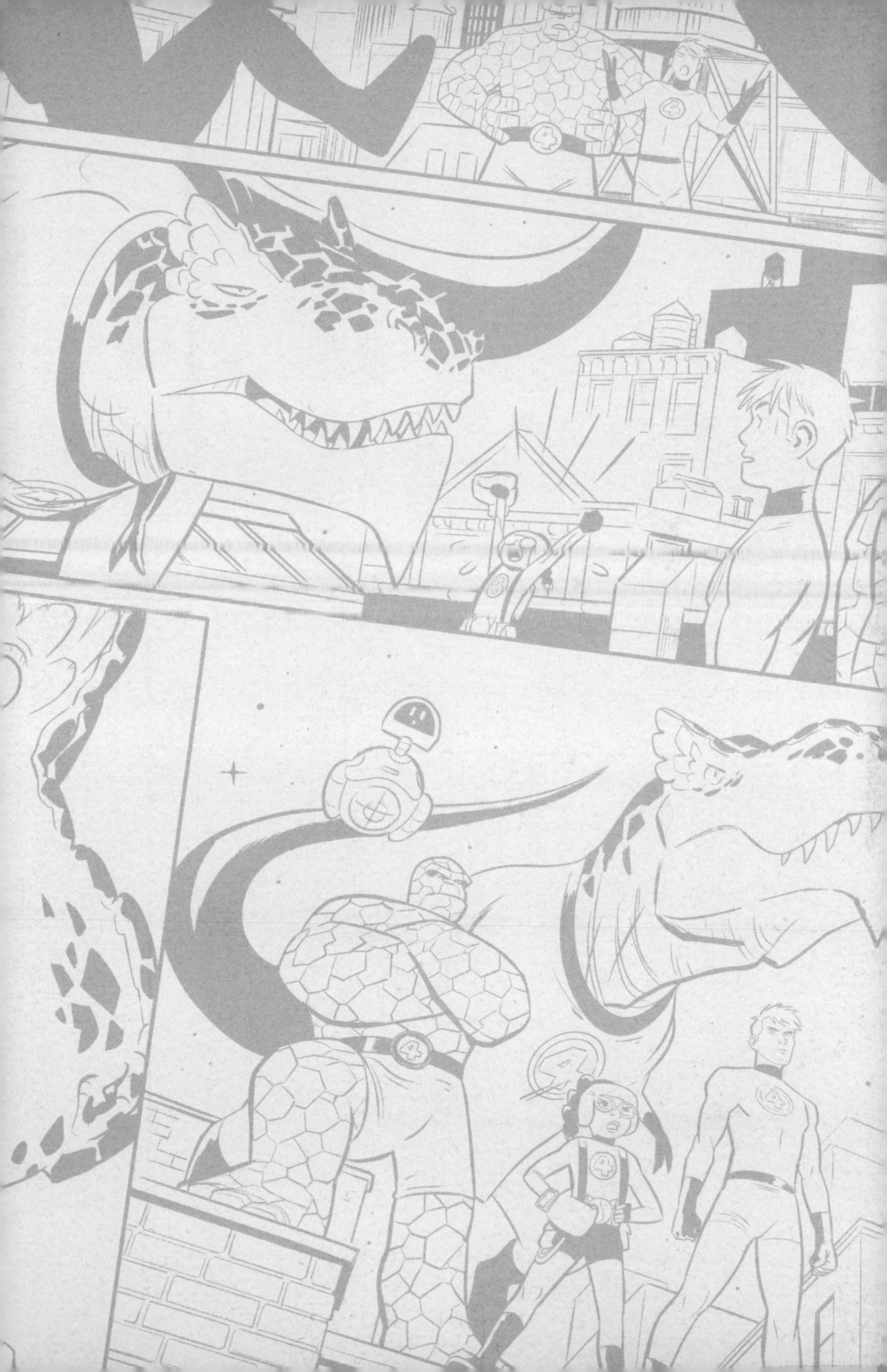

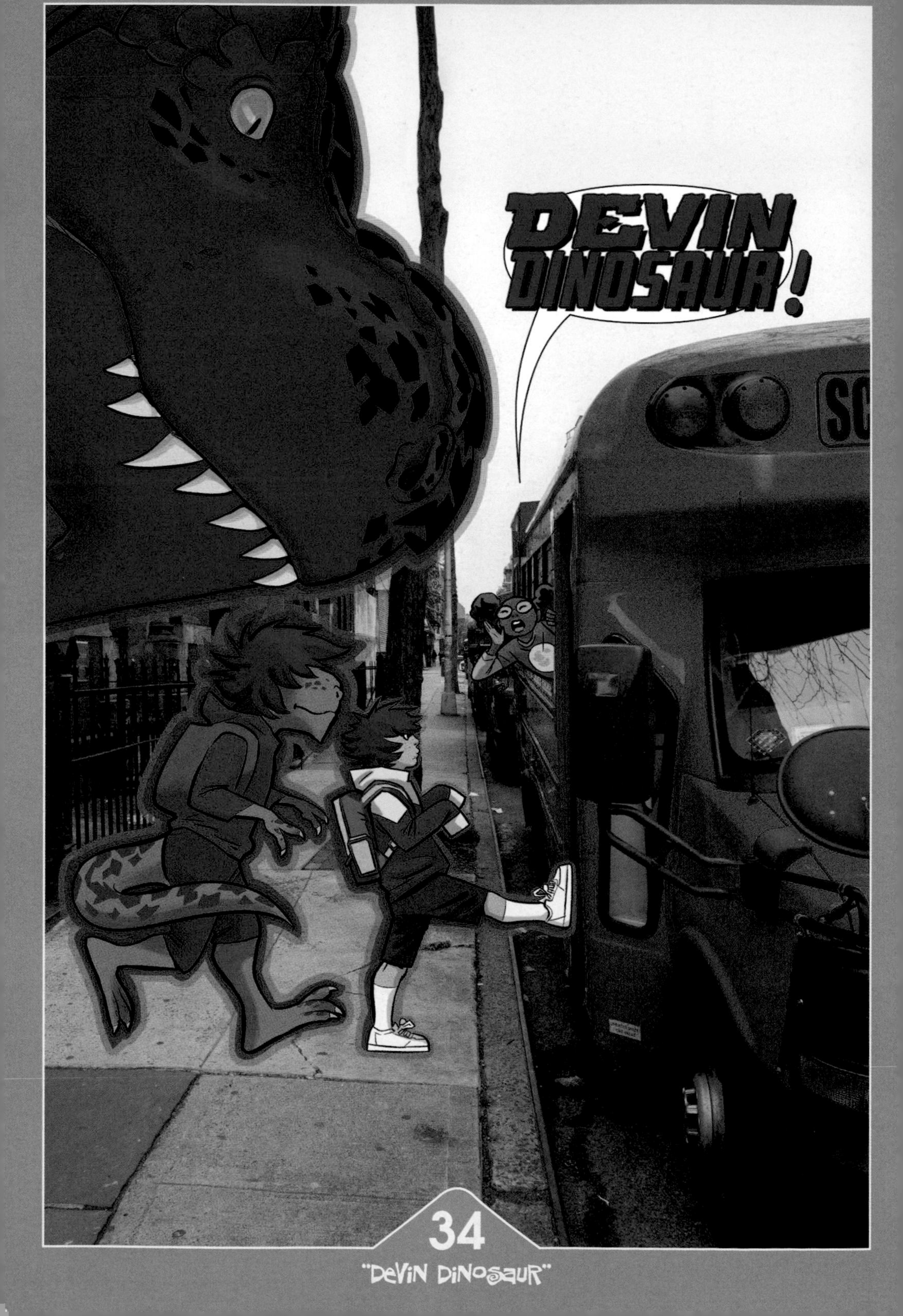
DEVIN DINOSAUR!
34
"DEVIN DINOSAUR"

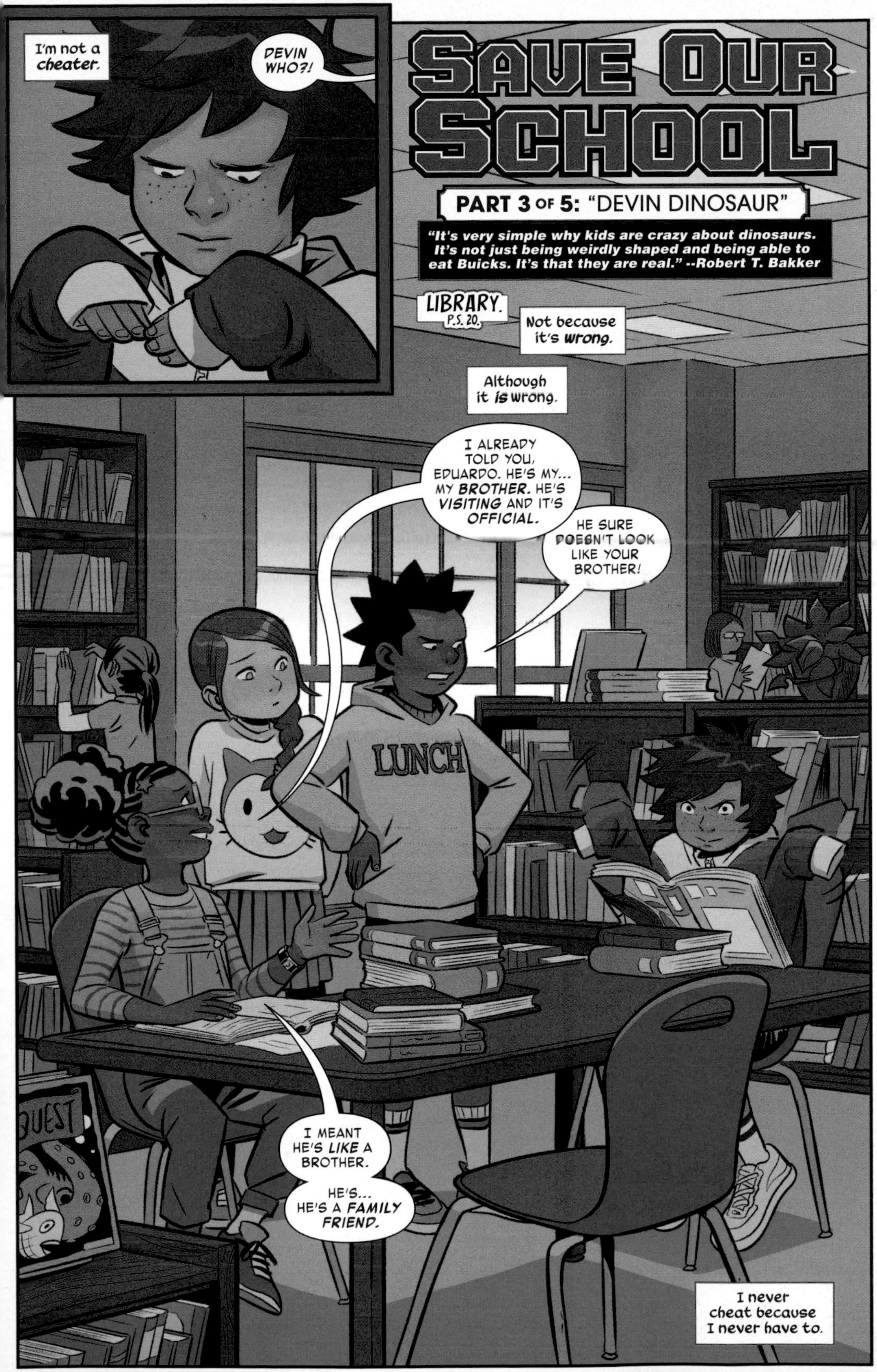

I'm not a cheater.
DEVIN WHO?!
SAVE OUR SCHOOL
PART 3 OF 5: "DEVIN DINOSAUR"
"It's very simple why kids are crazy about dinosaurs. It's not just being weirdly shaped and being able to eat Buicks. It's that they are real." --Robert T. Bakker
LIBRARY. P.S. 20.
Not because it's wrong.
Although it is wrong.
I ALREADY TOLD YOU, EDUARDO. HE'S MY... MY BROTHER. HE'S VISITING AND IT'S OFFICIAL.
HE SURE DOESN'T LOOK LIKE YOUR BROTHER!
LUNCH
I MEANT HE'S LIKE A BROTHER.
HE'S... HE'S A FAMILY FRIEND.
QUEST
I never cheat because I never have to.

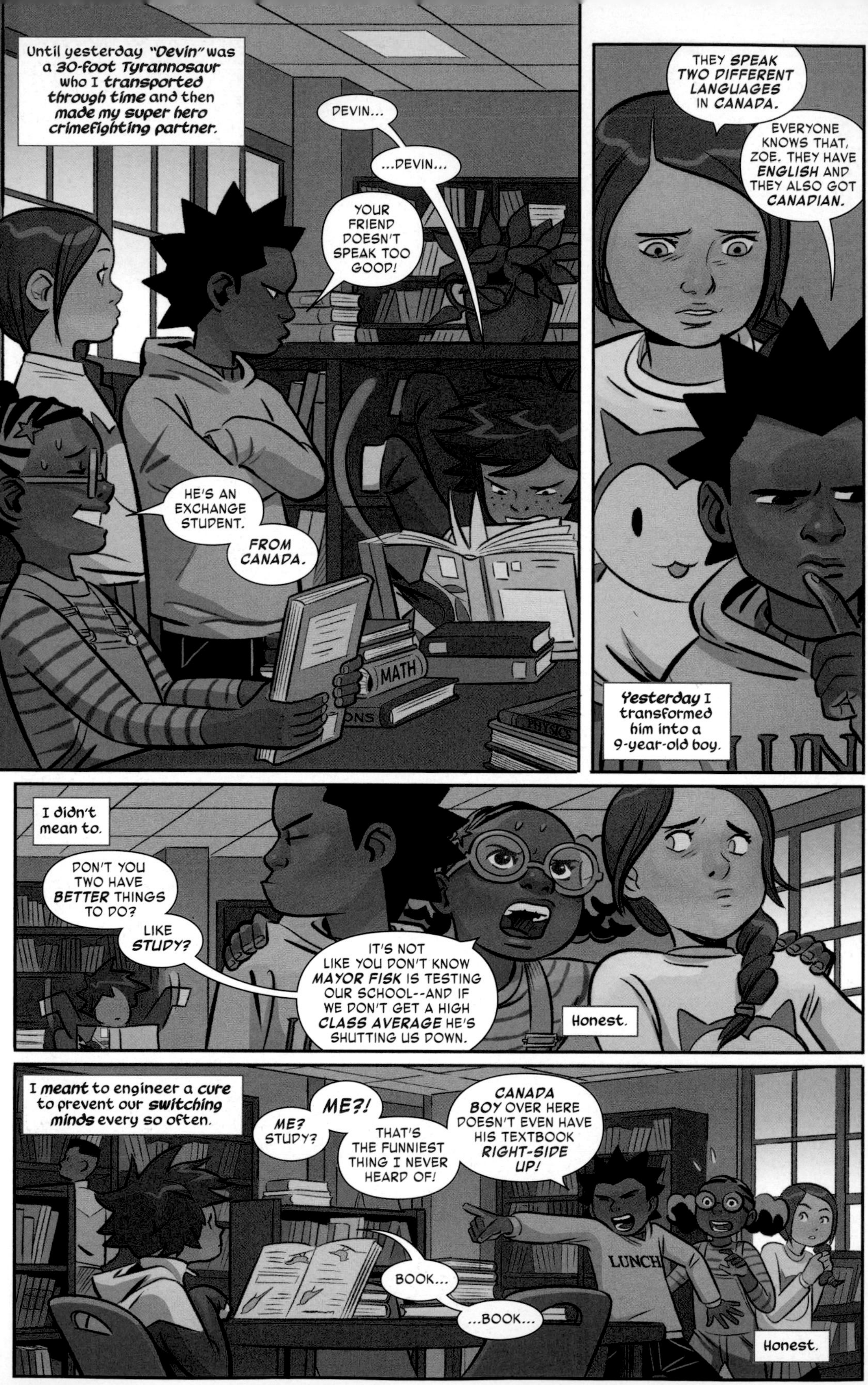
Until yesterday "Devin" was a 30-foot Tyrannosaur who I transported through time and then made my super hero crimefighting partner.
DEVIN...
...DEVIN...
YOUR FRIEND DOESN'T SPEAK TOO GOOD!
HE'S AN EXCHANGE STUDENT.
FROM CANADA.
MATH
PHYSICS
THEY SPEAK TWO DIFFERENT LANGUAGES IN CANADA.
EVERYONE KNOWS THAT, ZOE. THEY HAVE ENGLISH AND THEY ALSO GOT CANADIAN.
Yesterday I transformed him into a 9-year-old boy.
I didn't mean to.
DON'T YOU TWO HAVE BETTER THINGS TO DO?
LIKE STUDY?
IT'S NOT LIKE YOU DON'T KNOW MAYOR FISK IS TESTING OUR SCHOOL--AND IF WE DON'T GET A HIGH CLASS AVERAGE HE'S SHUTTING US DOWN.
Honest.
I meant to engineer a cure to prevent our switching minds every so often.
ME? STUDY?
ME?!
THAT'S THE FUNNIEST THING I NEVER HEARD OF!
CANADA BOY OVER HERE DOESN'T EVEN HAVE HIS TEXTBOOK RIGHT-SIDE UP!
LUNCH
BOOK...
...BOOK...
Honest.

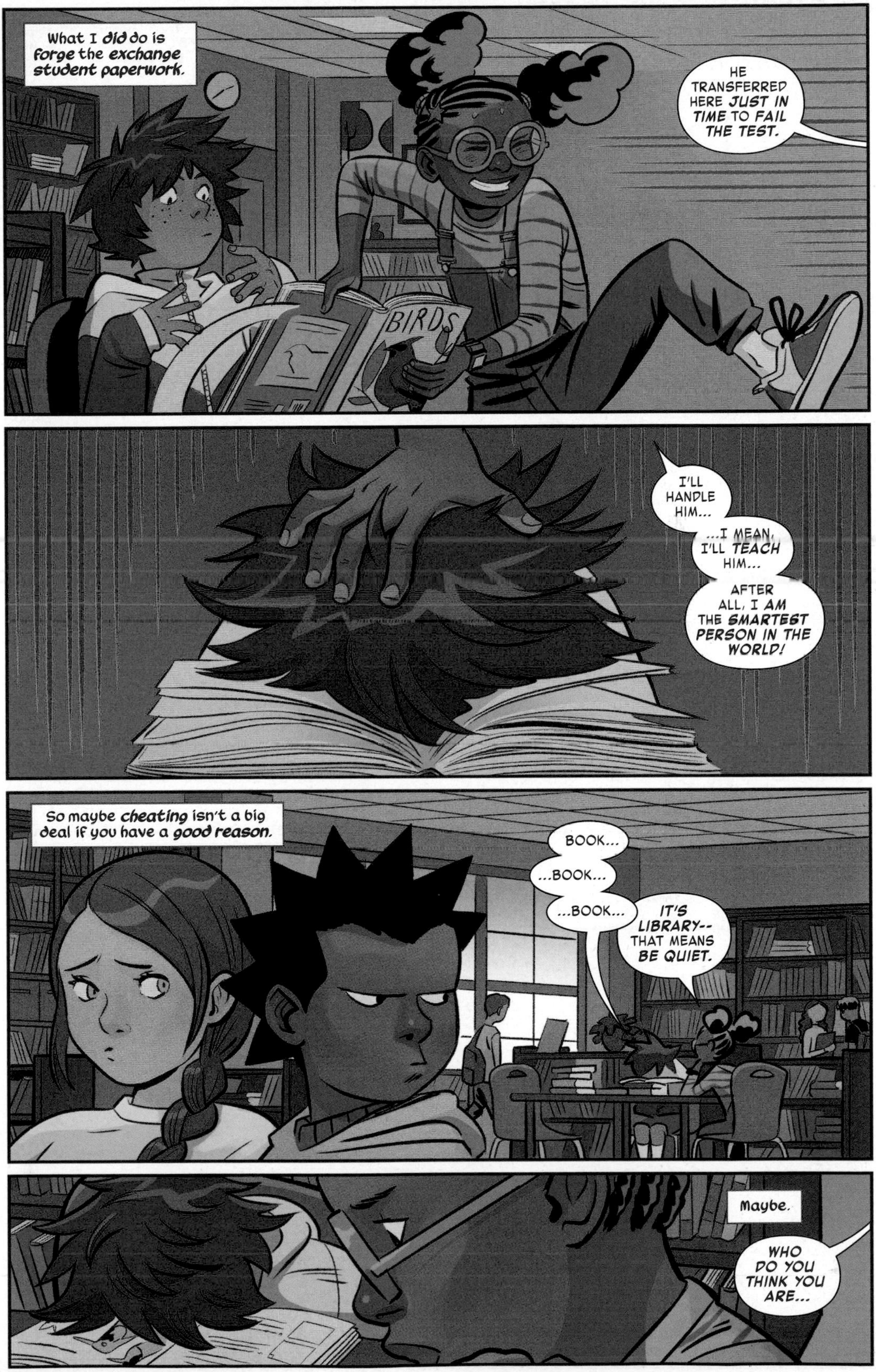

What I did do is forge the exchange student paperwork.
HE TRANSFERRED HERE JUST IN TIME TO FAIL THE TEST.
I'LL HANDLE HIM...
...I MEAN, I'LL TEACH HIM...
AFTER ALL, I AM THE SMARTEST PERSON IN THE WORLD!
So maybe cheating isn't a big deal if you have a good reason.
BOOK...
...BOOK...
...BOOK...
IT'S LIBRARY--THAT MEANS BE QUIET.
Maybe.
WHO DO YOU THINK YOU ARE...

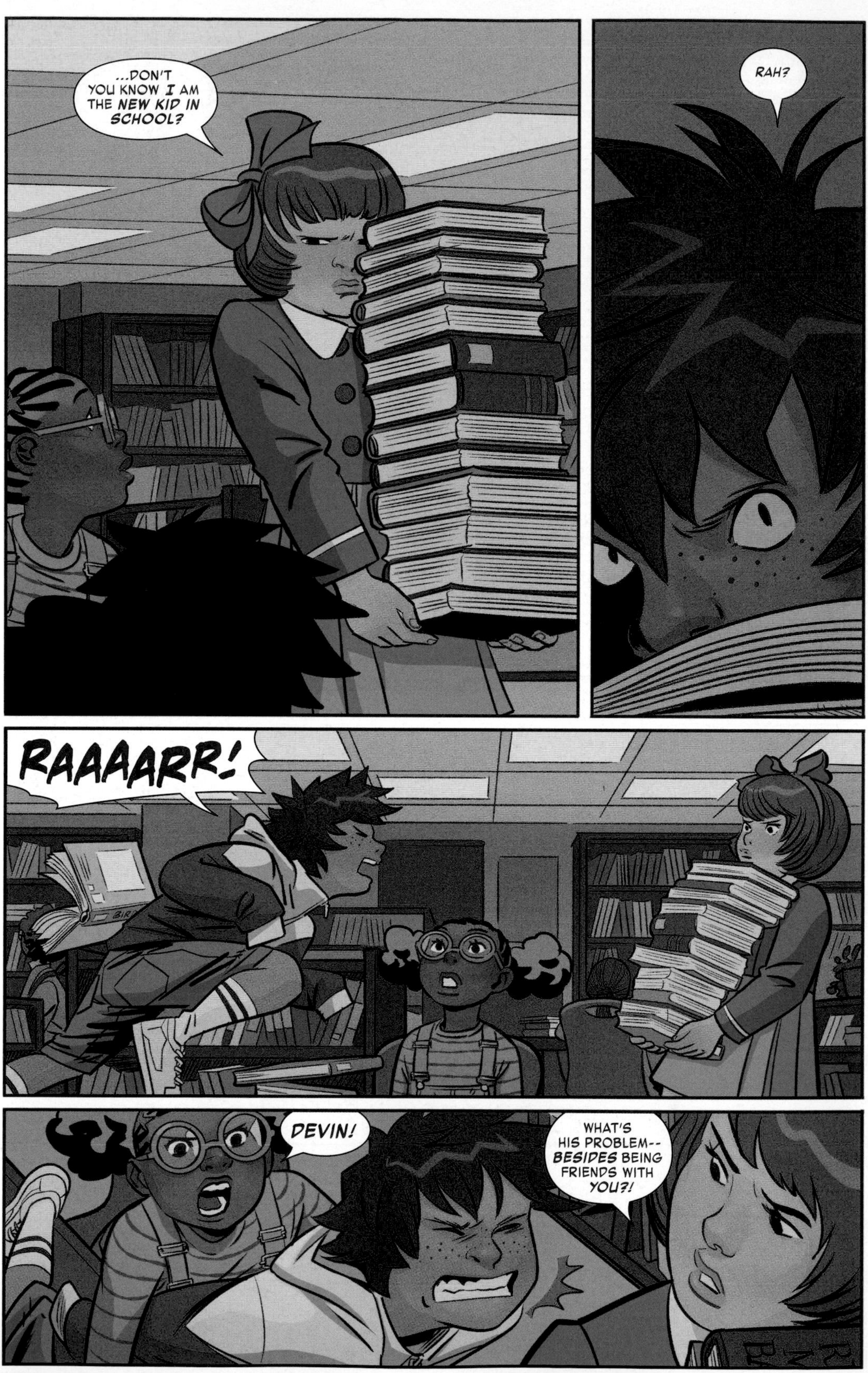
...DON'T YOU KNOW I AM THE NEW KID IN SCHOOL?
RAH?
RAAAARR!
DEVIN!
WHAT'S HIS PROBLEM-- BESIDES BEING FRIENDS WITH YOU?!

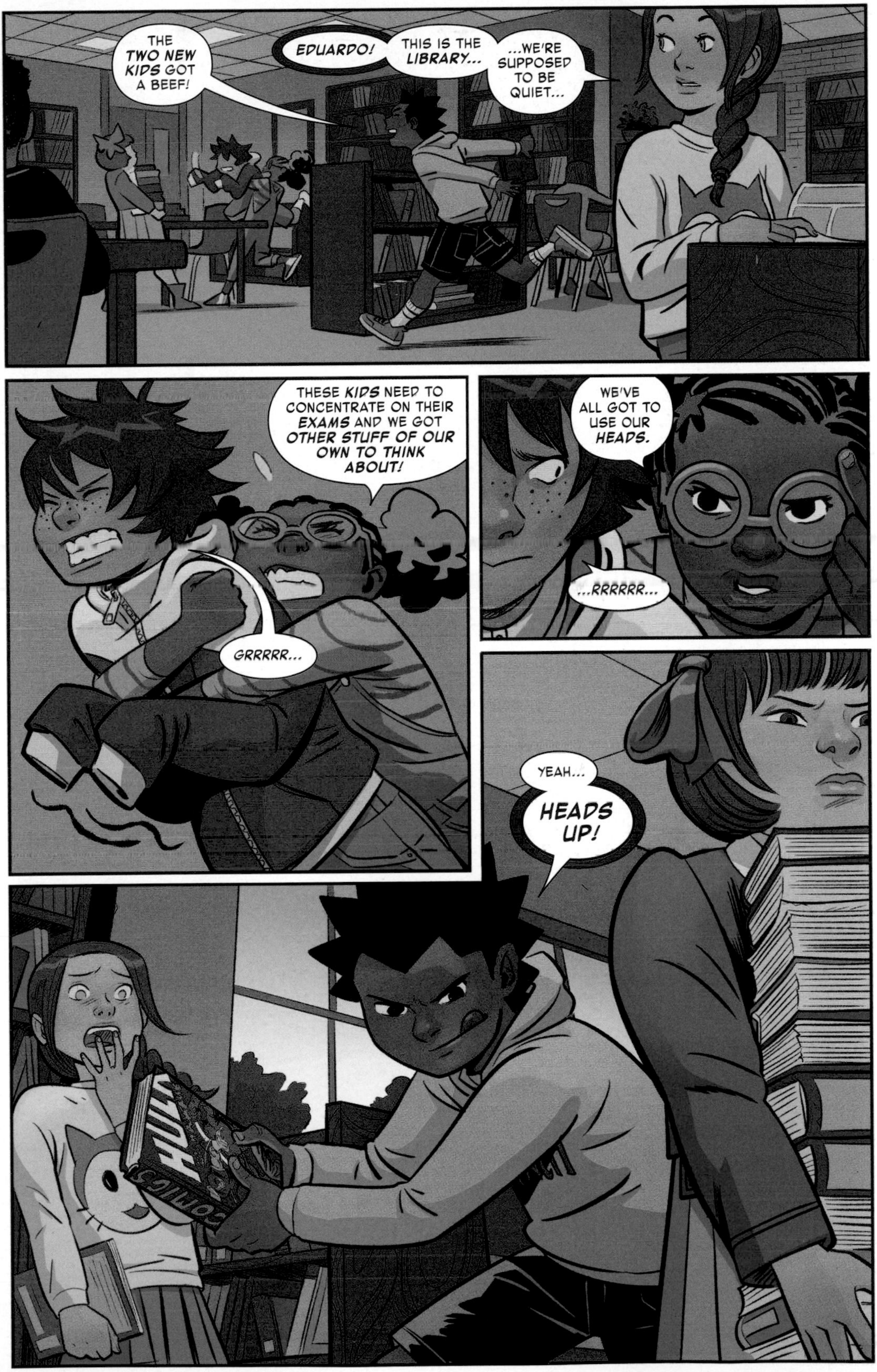

THE TWO NEW KIDS GOT A BEEF!
EDUARDO!
THIS IS THE LIBRARY...
...WE'RE SUPPOSED TO BE QUIET...
THESE KIDS NEED TO CONCENTRATE ON THEIR EXAMS AND WE GOT OTHER STUFF OF OUR OWN TO THINK ABOUT!
GRRRRR...
WE'VE ALL GOT TO USE OUR HEADS.
...RRRRRR...
YEAH...
HEADS UP!
HULK
COMICS

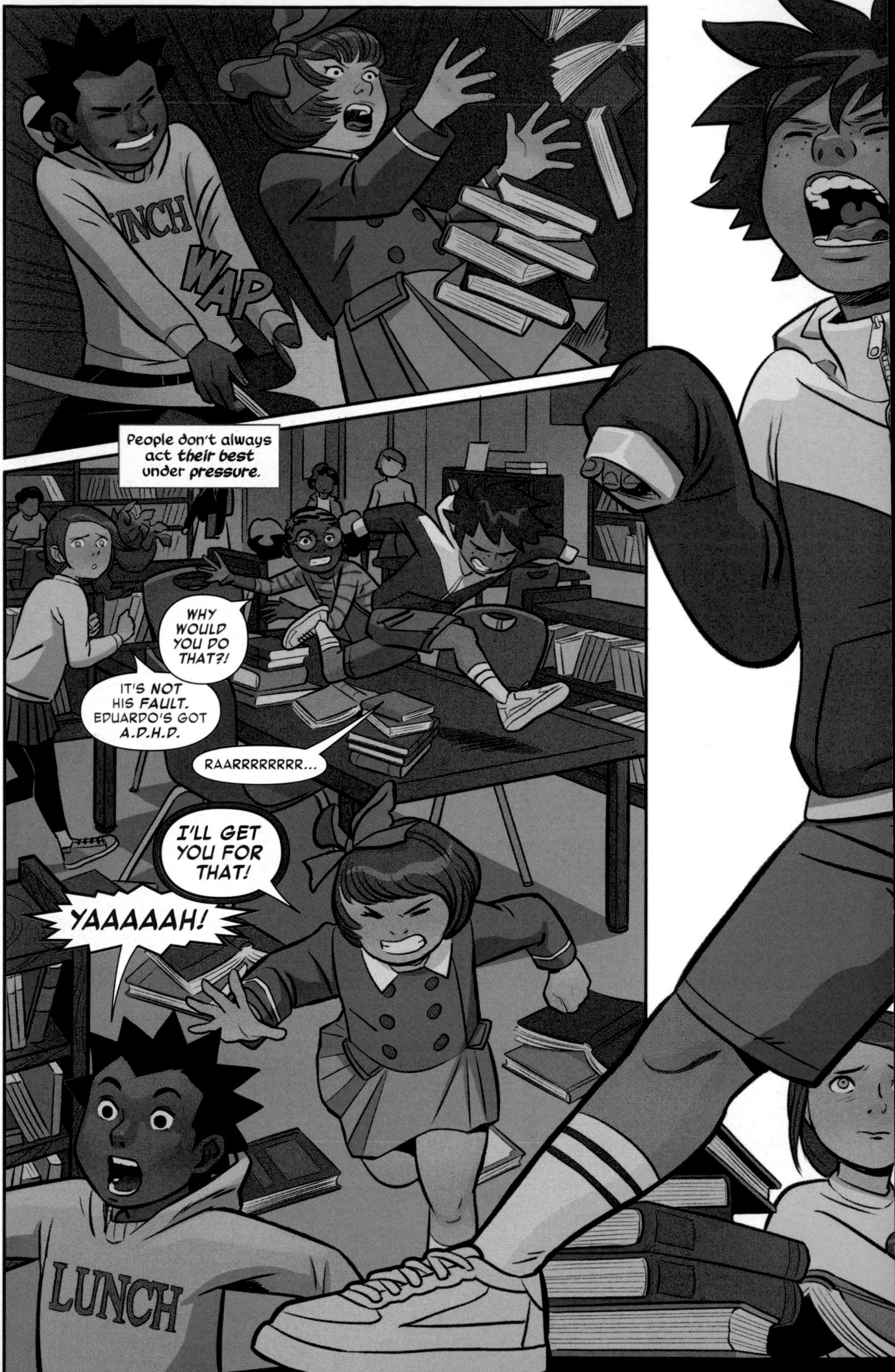
LUNCH
WAP
People don't always act their best under pressure.
WHY WOULD YOU DO THAT?!
IT'S NOT HIS FAULT. EDUARDO'S GOT A.D.H.D.
RAARRRRRRRR...
I'LL GET YOU FOR THAT!
YAAAAAH!
LUNCH

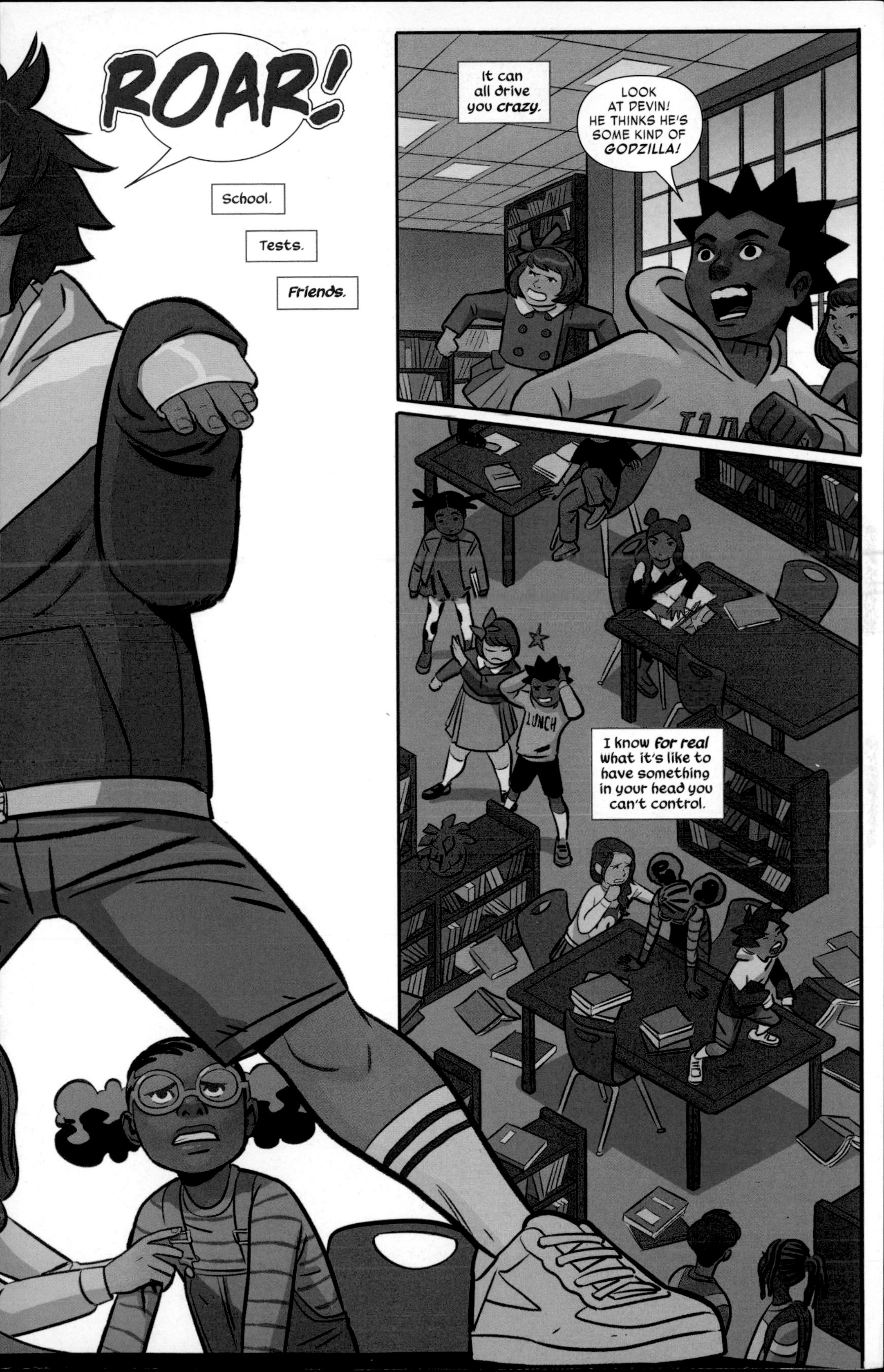
ROAR!
School.
Tests.
Friends.
It can all drive you crazy.
LOOK AT DEVIN! HE THINKS HE'S SOME KIND OF GODZILLA!
LUNCH
I know for real what it's like to have something in your head you can't control.

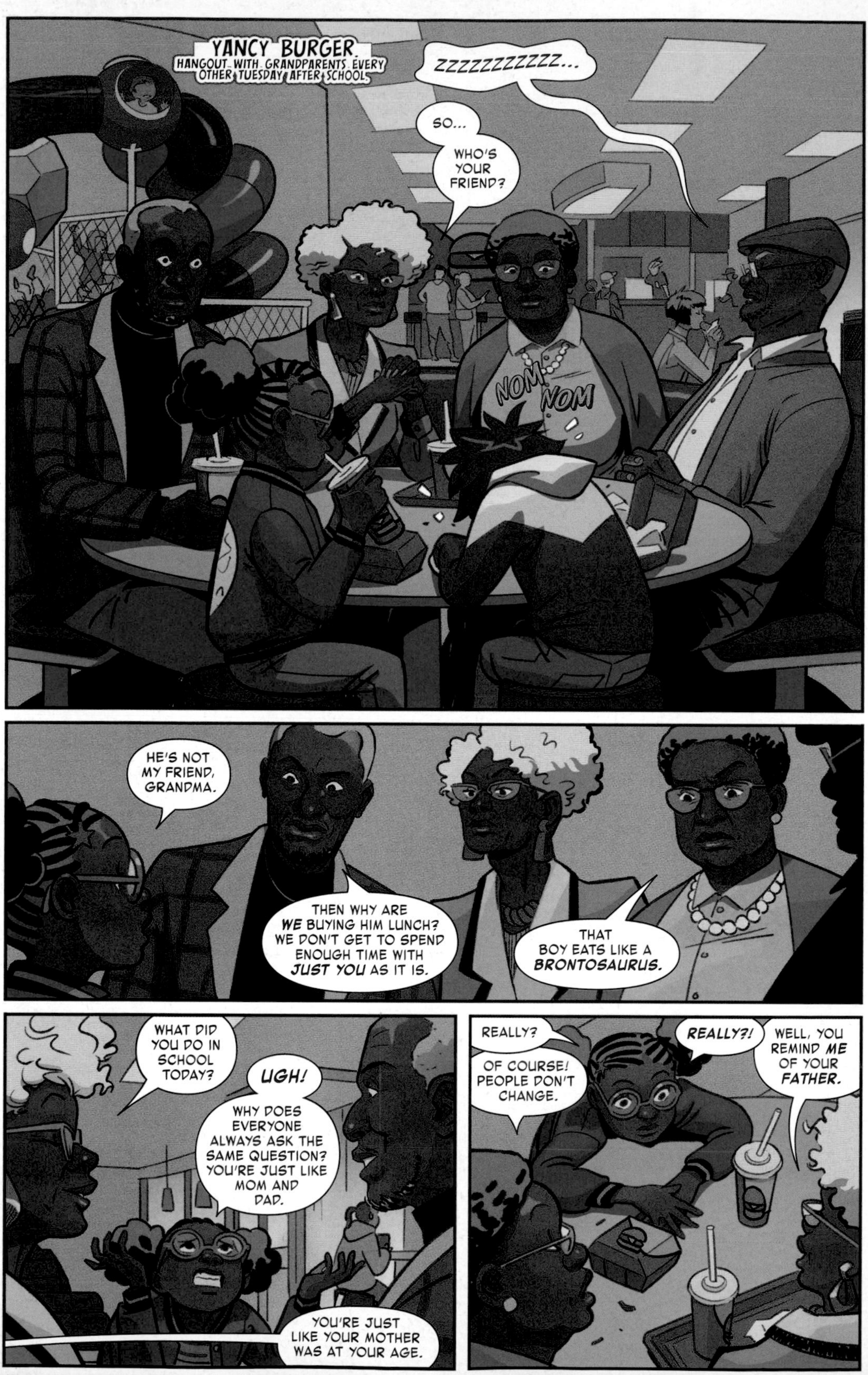
YANCY BURGER.
HANGOUT WITH GRANDPARENTS EVERY OTHER TUESDAY AFTER SCHOOL.
ZZZZZZZZZZZ...
SO...
WHO'S YOUR FRIEND?
NOM NOM
HE'S NOT MY FRIEND, GRANDMA.
THEN WHY ARE WE BUYING HIM LUNCH? WE DON'T GET TO SPEND ENOUGH TIME WITH JUST YOU AS IT IS.
THAT BOY EATS LIKE A BRONTOSAURUS.
WHAT DID YOU DO IN SCHOOL TODAY?
UGH!
WHY DOES EVERYONE ALWAYS ASK THE SAME QUESTION? YOU'RE JUST LIKE MOM AND DAD.
YOU'RE JUST LIKE YOUR MOTHER WAS AT YOUR AGE.
REALLY?
OF COURSE! PEOPLE DON'T CHANGE.
REALLY?!
WELL, YOU REMIND ME OF YOUR FATHER.

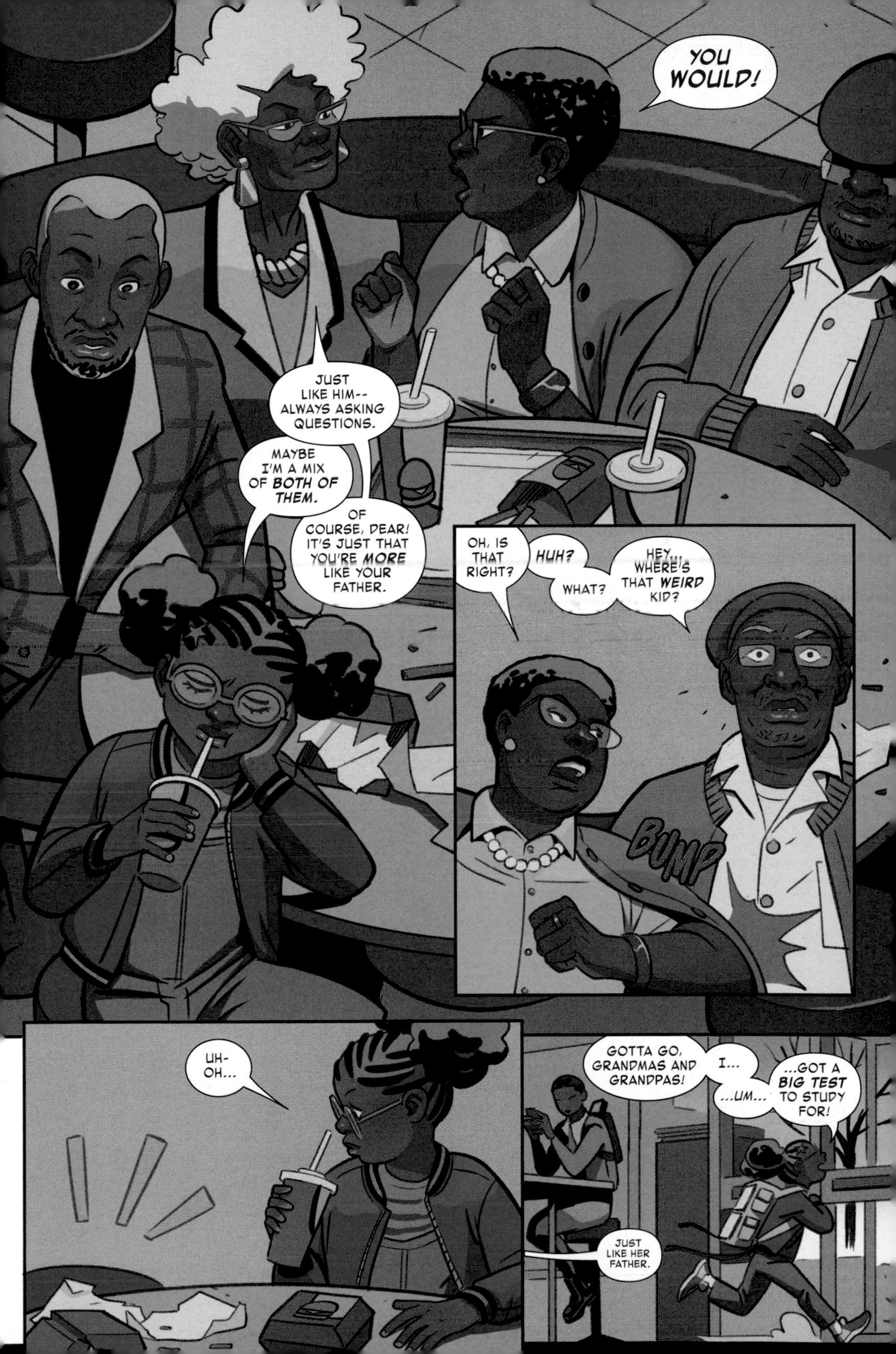
YOU WOULD!
JUST LIKE HIM-- ALWAYS ASKING QUESTIONS.
MAYBE I'M A MIX OF BOTH OF THEM.
OF COURSE, DEAR! IT'S JUST THAT YOU'RE MORE LIKE YOUR FATHER.
OH, IS THAT RIGHT?
HUH?
WHAT?
HEY... WHERE'S THAT WEIRD KID?
BUMP
UH-OH...
GOTTA GO, GRANDMAS AND GRANDPAS!
I...
...UM...
...GOT A BIG TEST TO STUDY FOR!
JUST LIKE HER FATHER.

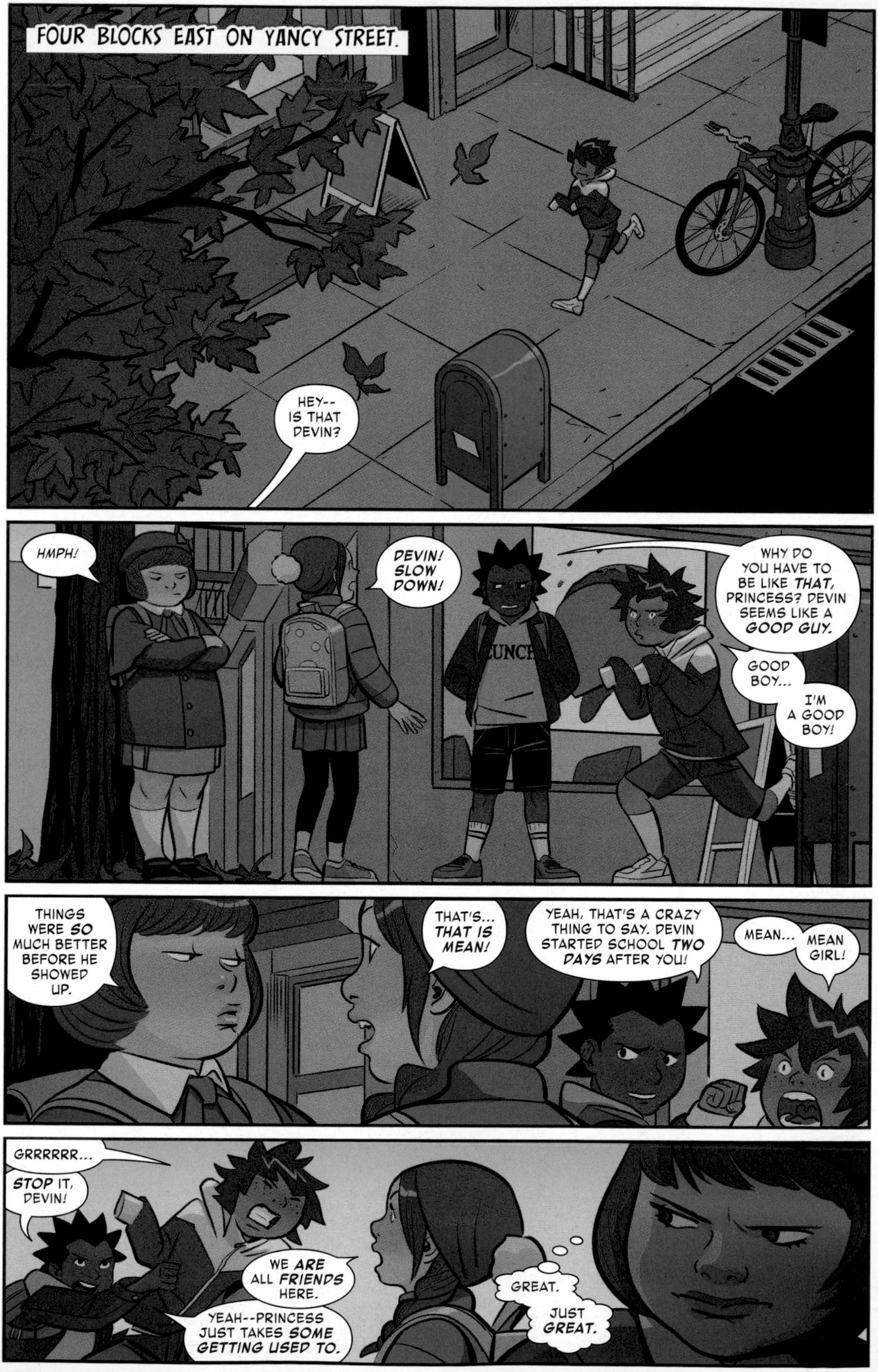
FOUR BLOCKS EAST ON YANCY STREET.
HEY-- IS THAT DEVIN?
HMPH!
DEVIN! SLOW DOWN!
WHY DO YOU HAVE TO BE LIKE THAT, PRINCESS? DEVIN SEEMS LIKE A GOOD GUY.
GOOD BOY...
I'M A GOOD BOY!
THINGS WERE SO MUCH BETTER BEFORE HE SHOWED UP.
THAT'S... THAT IS MEAN!
YEAH, THAT'S A CRAZY THING TO SAY. DEVIN STARTED SCHOOL TWO DAYS AFTER YOU!
MEAN...
MEAN GIRL!
GRRRRRR...
STOP IT, DEVIN!
WE ARE ALL FRIENDS HERE.
YEAH--PRINCESS JUST TAKES SOME GETTING USED TO.
GREAT.
JUST GREAT.

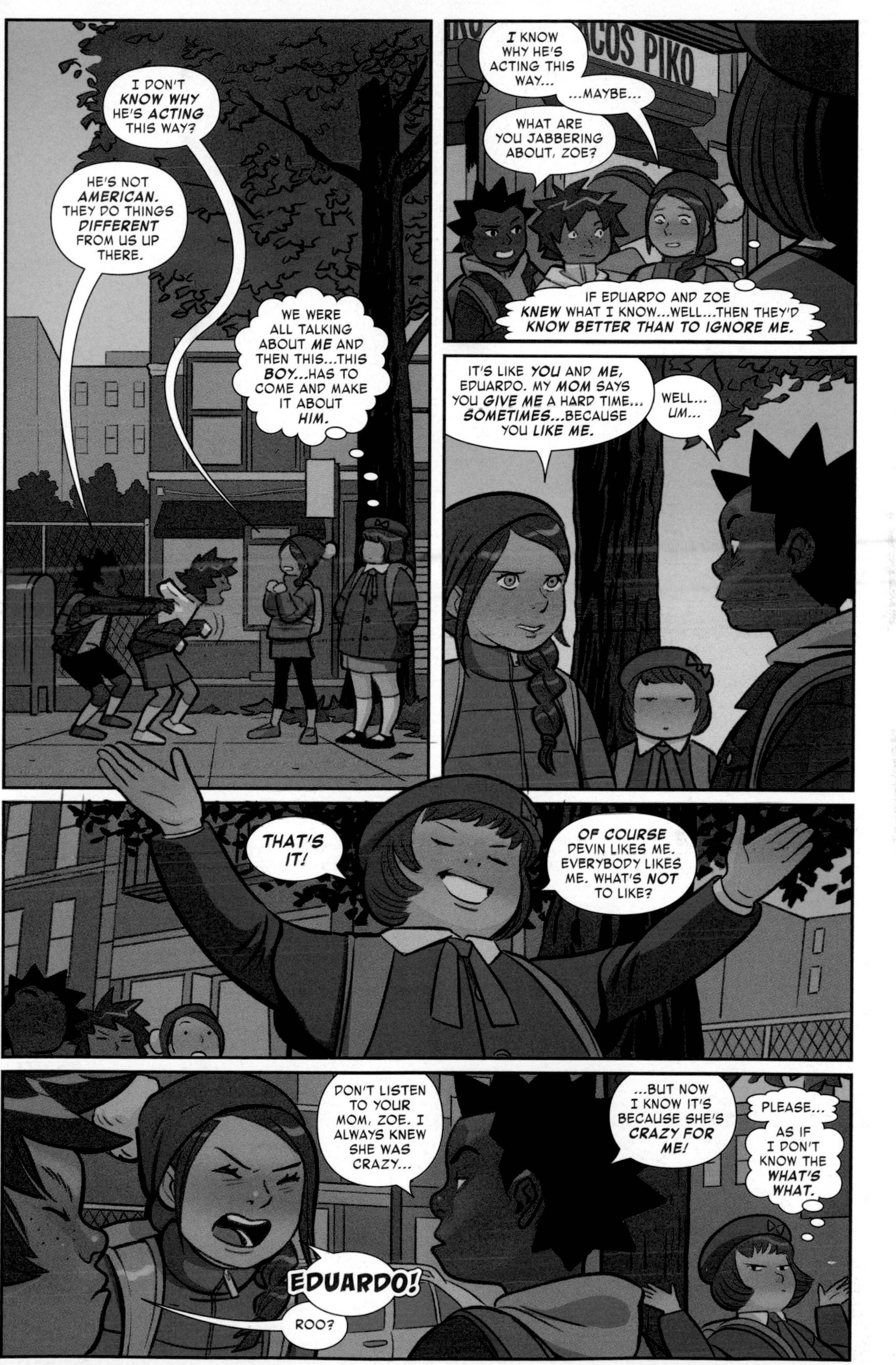
I DON'T KNOW WHY HE'S ACTING THIS WAY?
HE'S NOT AMERICAN. THEY DO THINGS DIFFERENT FROM US UP THERE.
WE WERE ALL TALKING ABOUT ME AND THEN THIS...THIS BOY...HAS TO COME AND MAKE IT ABOUT HIM.
COS PIKO
I KNOW WHY HE'S ACTING THIS WAY...
...MAYBE...
WHAT ARE YOU JABBERING ABOUT, ZOE?
IF EDUARDO AND ZOE KNEW WHAT I KNOW...WELL...THEN THEY'D KNOW BETTER THAN TO IGNORE ME.
IT'S LIKE YOU AND ME, EDUARDO. MY MOM SAYS YOU GIVE ME A HARD TIME... SOMETIMES...BECAUSE YOU LIKE ME.
WELL... UM...
THAT'S IT!
OF COURSE DEVIN LIKES ME. EVERYBODY LIKES ME. WHAT'S NOT TO LIKE?
DON'T LISTEN TO YOUR MOM, ZOE. I ALWAYS KNEW SHE WAS CRAZY...
...BUT NOW I KNOW IT'S BECAUSE SHE'S CRAZY FOR ME!
PLEASE...
AS IF I DON'T KNOW THE WHAT'S WHAT.
EDUARDO!
ROO?

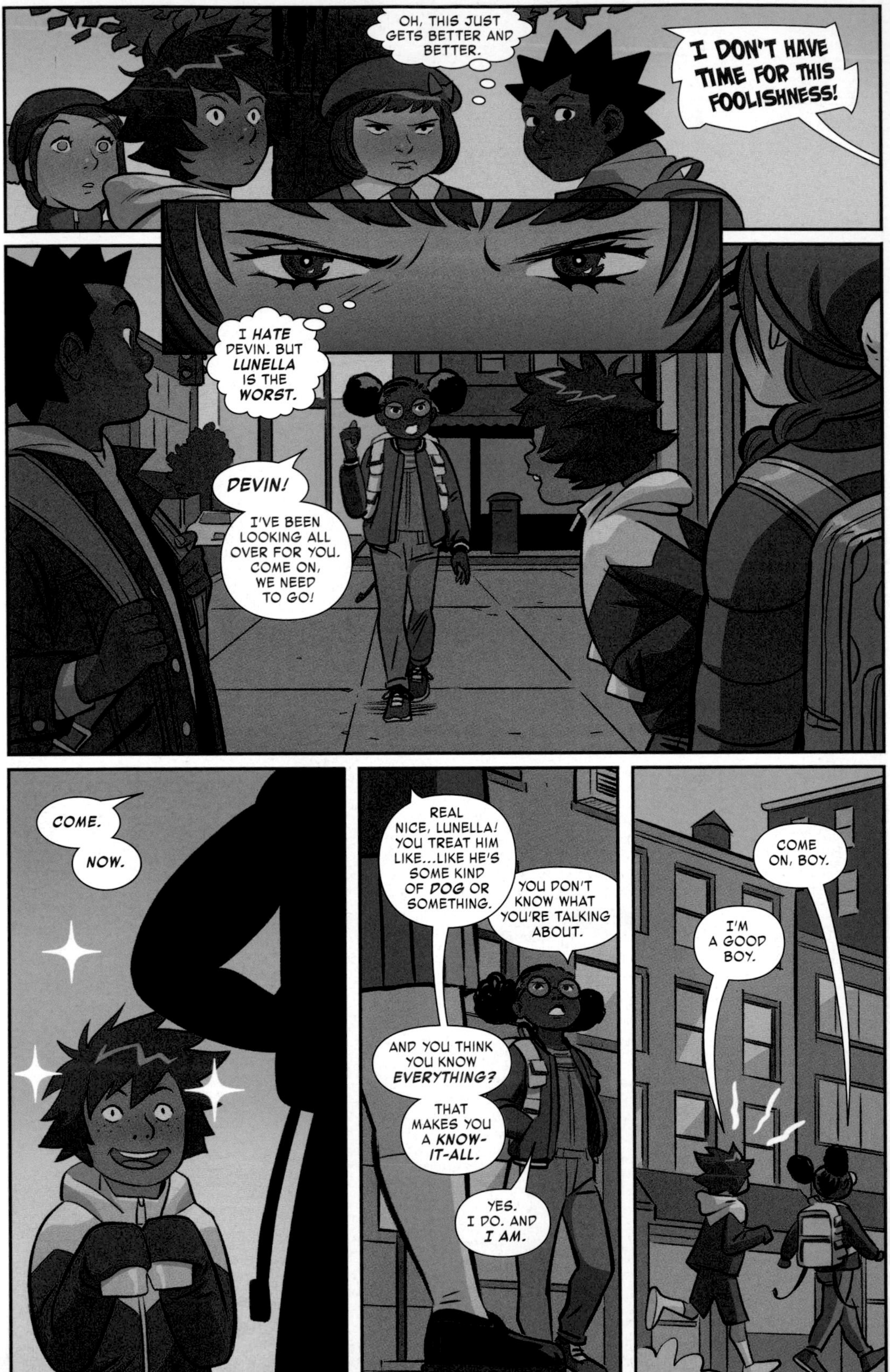
OH, THIS JUST GETS BETTER AND BETTER.
I DON'T HAVE TIME FOR THIS FOOLISHNESS!
I HATE DEVIN. BUT LUNELLA IS THE WORST.
DEVIN!
I'VE BEEN LOOKING ALL OVER FOR YOU. COME ON, WE NEED TO GO!
COME.
NOW.
REAL NICE, LUNELLA! YOU TREAT HIM LIKE...LIKE HE'S SOME KIND OF DOG OR SOMETHING.
YOU DON'T KNOW WHAT YOU'RE TALKING ABOUT.
AND YOU THINK YOU KNOW EVERYTHING?
THAT MAKES YOU A KNOW-IT-ALL.
YES. I DO. AND I AM.
COME ON, BOY.
I'M A GOOD BOY.

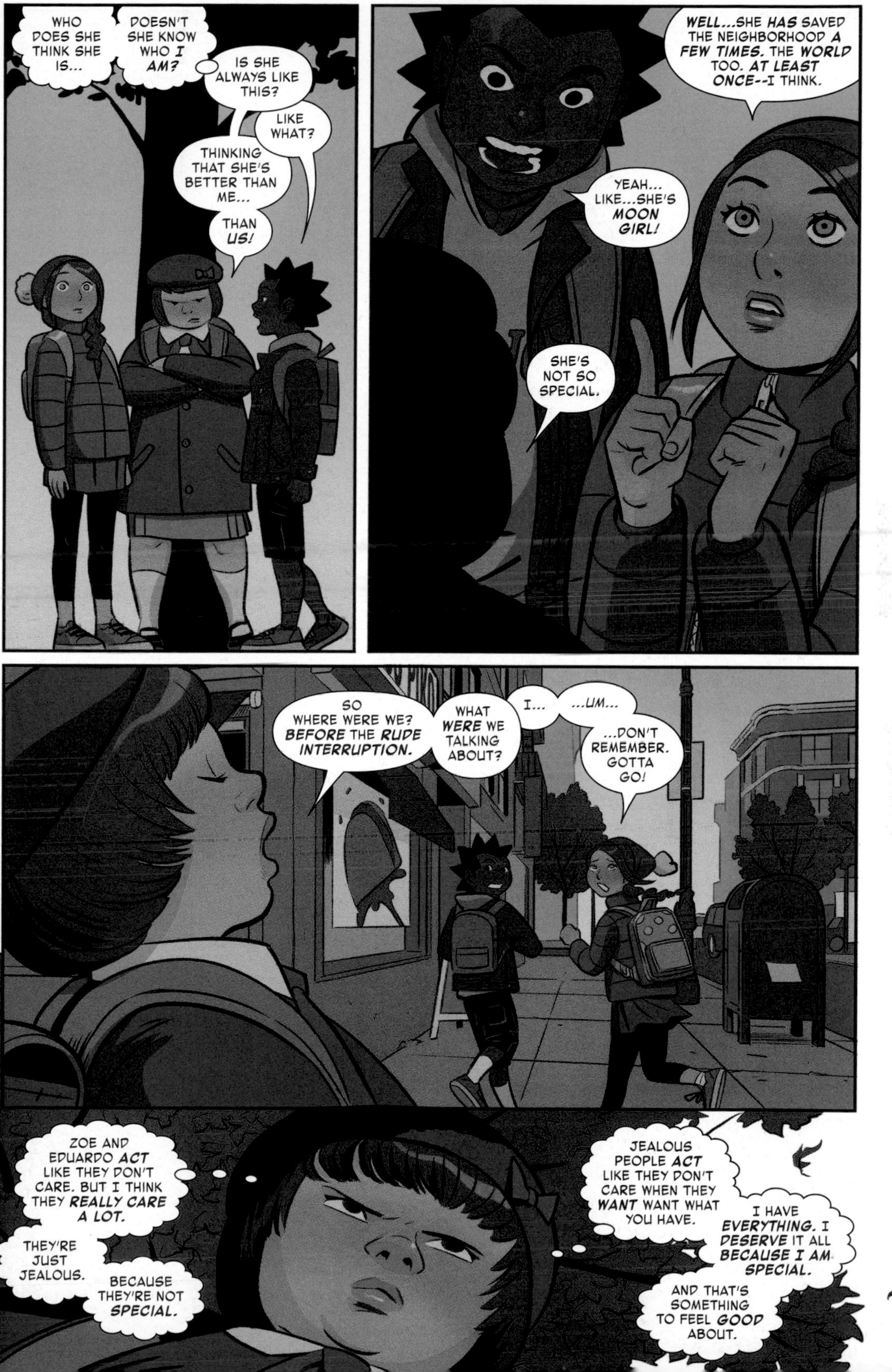
WHO DOES SHE THINK SHE IS...
DOESN'T SHE KNOW WHO I AM?
IS SHE ALWAYS LIKE THIS?
LIKE WHAT?
THINKING THAT SHE'S BETTER THAN ME...
THAN US!
WELL...SHE HAS SAVED THE NEIGHBORHOOD A FEW TIMES. THE WORLD TOO. AT LEAST ONCE--I THINK.
YEAH... LIKE...SHE'S MOON GIRL!
SHE'S NOT SO SPECIAL.
SO WHERE WERE WE? BEFORE THE RUDE INTERRUPTION.
WHAT WERE WE TALKING ABOUT?
I...
...UM...
...DON'T REMEMBER. GOTTA GO!
ZOE AND EDUARDO ACT LIKE THEY DON'T CARE. BUT I THINK THEY REALLY CARE A LOT.
THEY'RE JUST JEALOUS.
BECAUSE THEY'RE NOT SPECIAL.
JEALOUS PEOPLE ACT LIKE THEY DON'T CARE WHEN THEY WANT WANT WHAT YOU HAVE.
I HAVE EVERYTHING. I DESERVE IT ALL BECAUSE I AM SPECIAL.
AND THAT'S SOMETHING TO FEEL GOOD ABOUT.

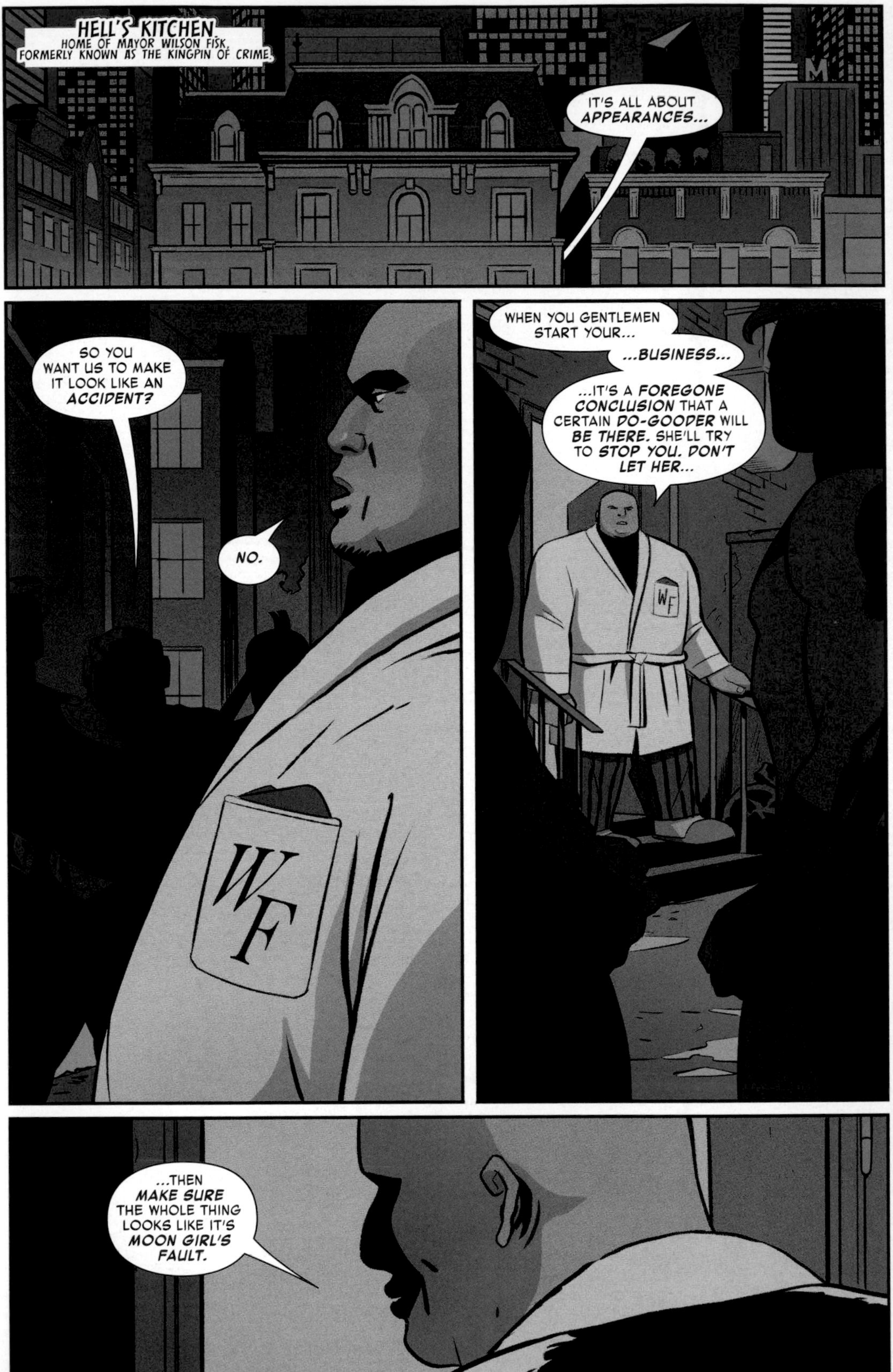
HELL'S KITCHEN
HOME OF MAYOR WILSON FISK, FORMERLY KNOWN AS THE KINGPIN OF CRIME.
IT'S ALL ABOUT APPEARANCES...
SO YOU WANT US TO MAKE IT LOOK LIKE AN ACCIDENT?
NO.
WF
WHEN YOU GENTLEMEN START YOUR...
...BUSINESS...
...IT'S A FOREGONE CONCLUSION THAT A CERTAIN DO-GOODER WILL BE THERE. SHE'LL TRY TO STOP YOU. DON'T LET HER...
WF
...THEN MAKE SURE THE WHOLE THING LOOKS LIKE IT'S MOON GIRL'S FAULT.

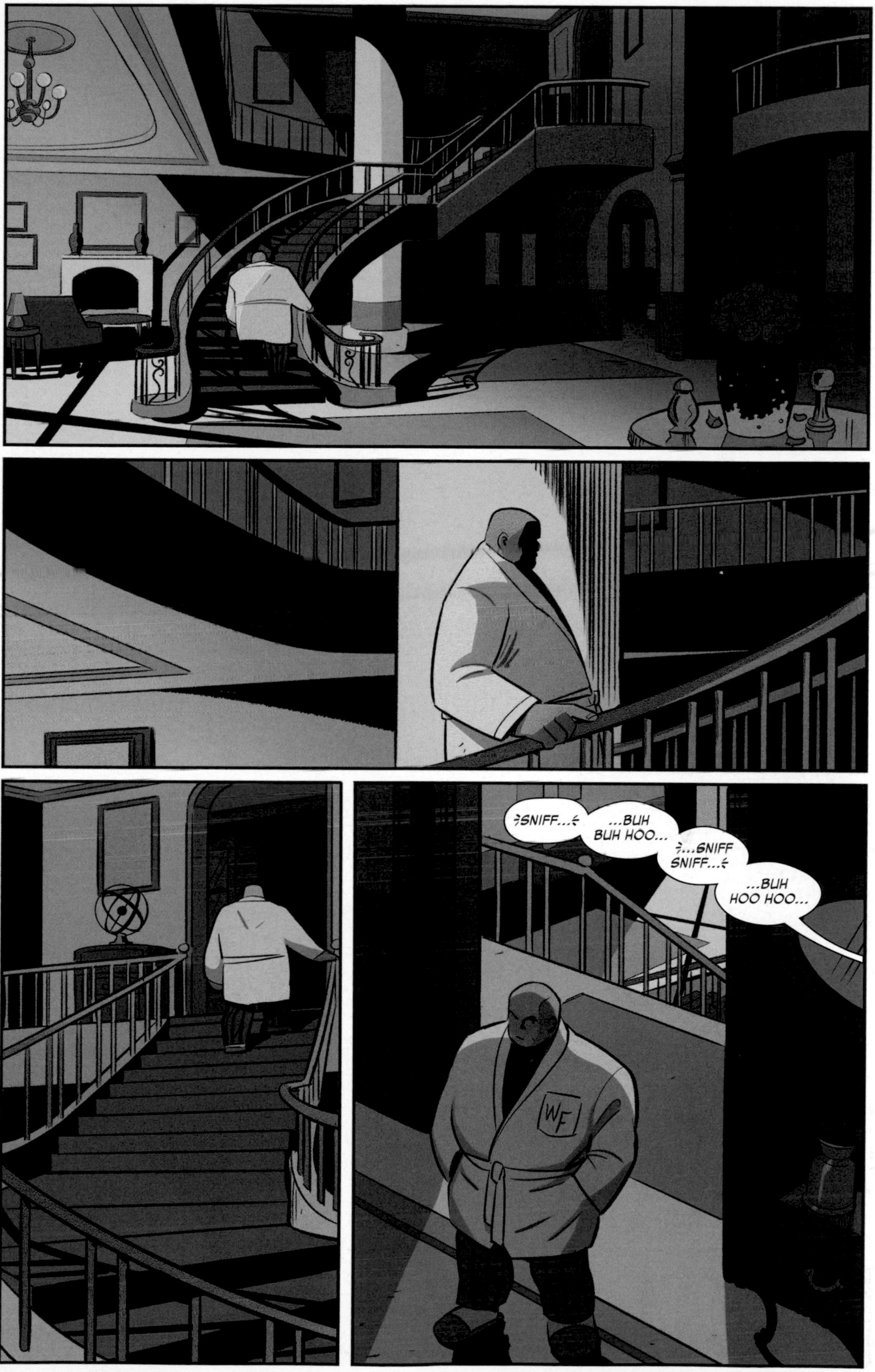

SNIFF...
...BUH BUH HOO...
...SNIFF SNIFF...
...BUH HOO HOO...

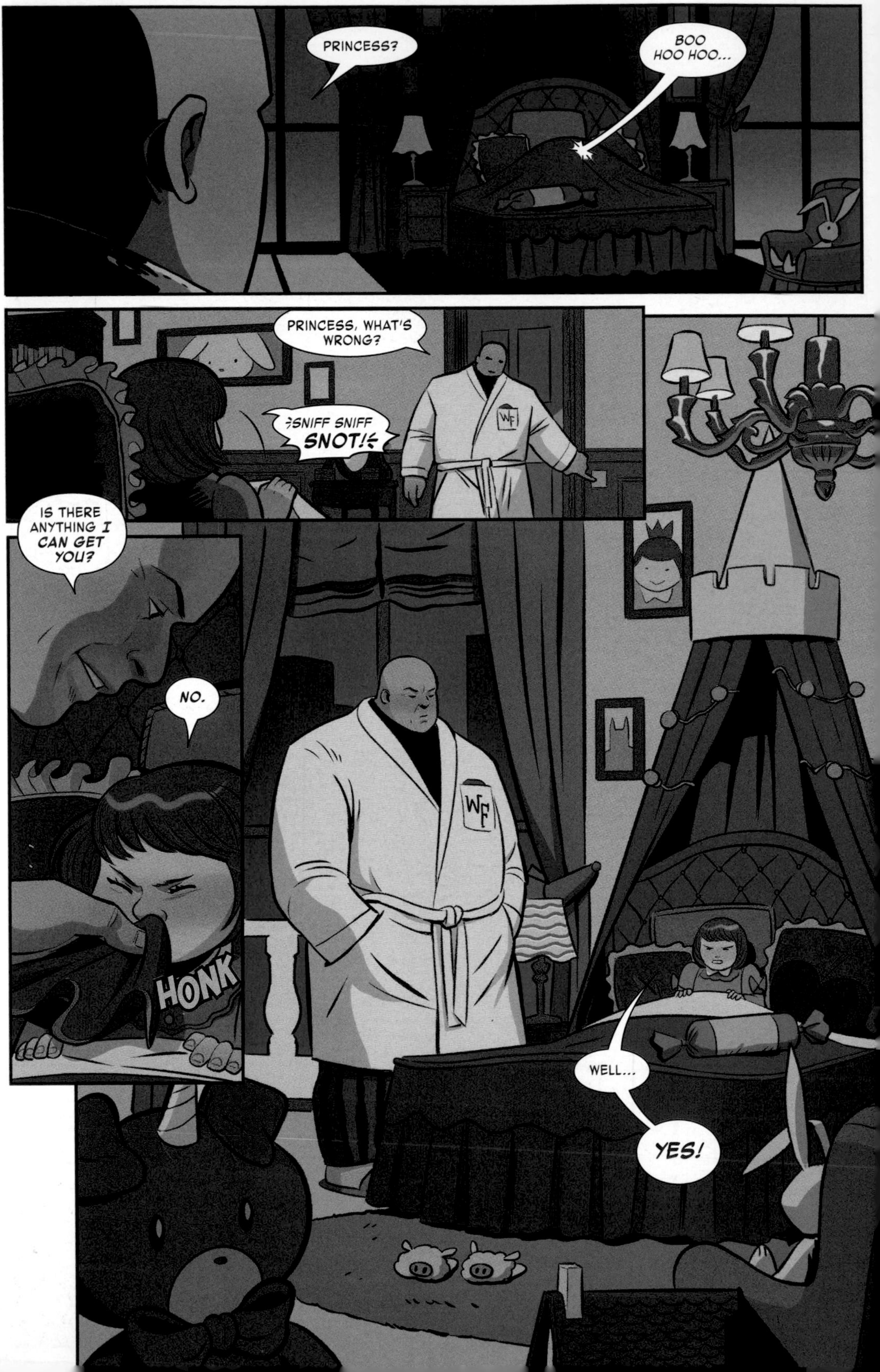
PRINCESS?
BOO HOO HOO...
PRINCESS, WHAT'S WRONG?
SNIFF SNIFF SNOT!
IS THERE ANYTHING I CAN GET YOU?
NO.
HONK
WELL...
YES!

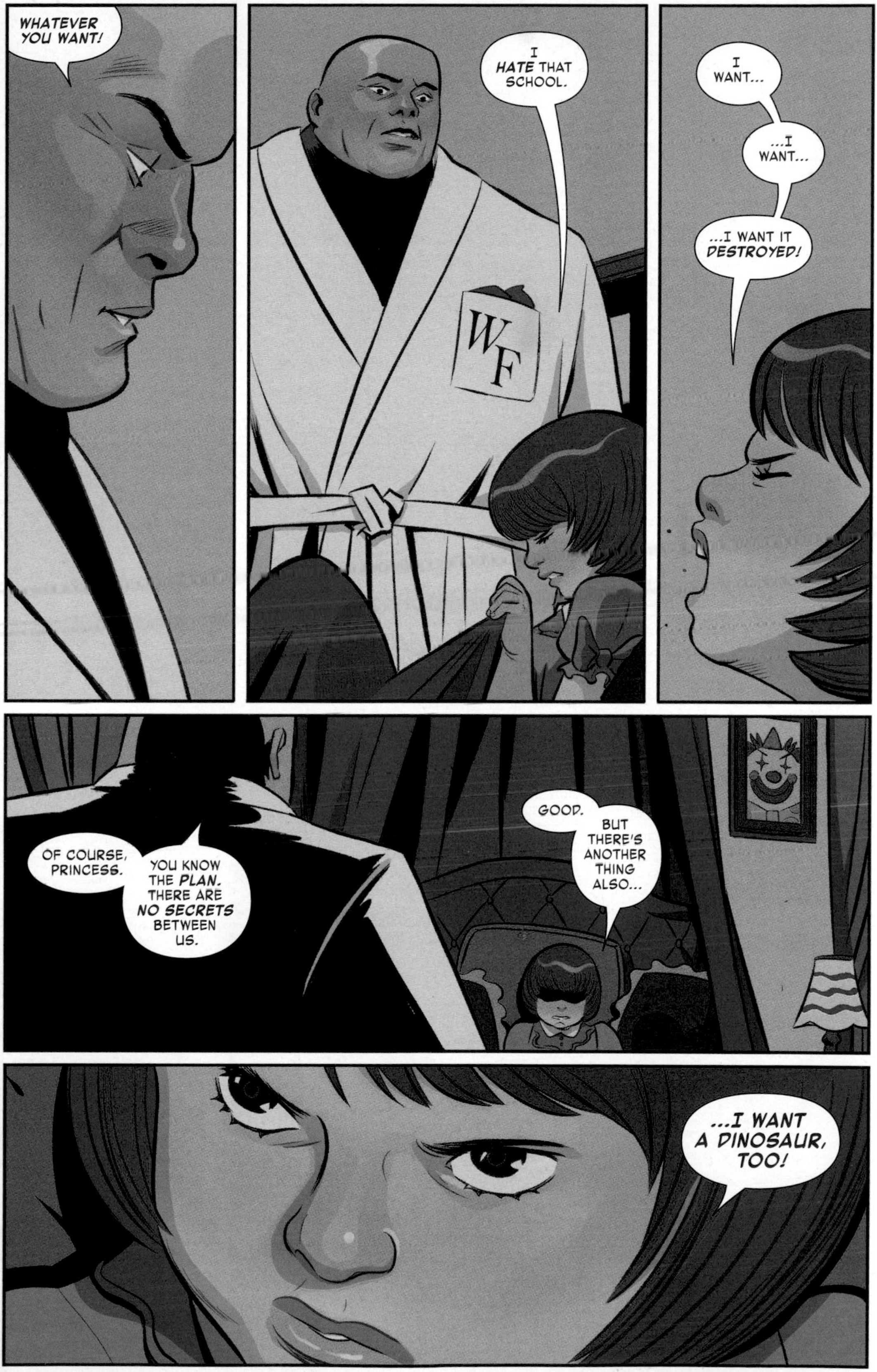
WHATEVER YOU WANT!
I HATE THAT SCHOOL.
I WANT...
...I WANT...
...I WANT IT DESTROYED!
WF
OF COURSE, PRINCESS.
YOU KNOW THE PLAN. THERE ARE NO SECRETS BETWEEN US.
GOOD.
BUT THERE'S ANOTHER THING ALSO...
...I WANT A DINOSAUR, TOO!

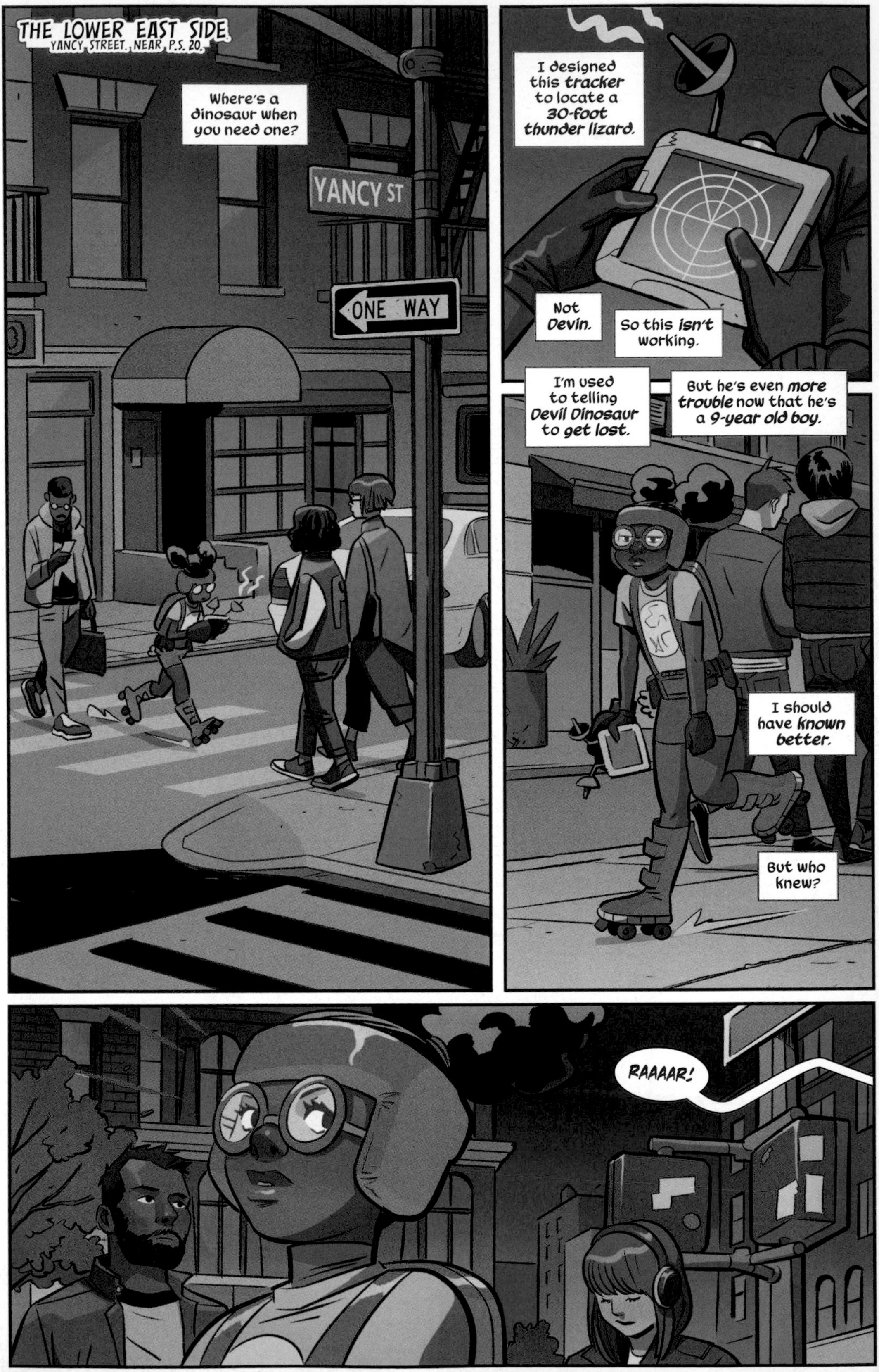
THE LOWER EAST SIDE
YANCY STREET, NEAR P.S. 20.
Where's a dinosaur when you need one?
YANCY ST
ONE WAY
I designed this tracker to locate a 30-foot thunder lizard.
Not Devin.
So this isn't working.
I'm used to telling Devil Dinosaur to get lost.
But he's even more trouble now that he's a 9-year old boy.
I should have known better.
But who knew?
RAAAAR!

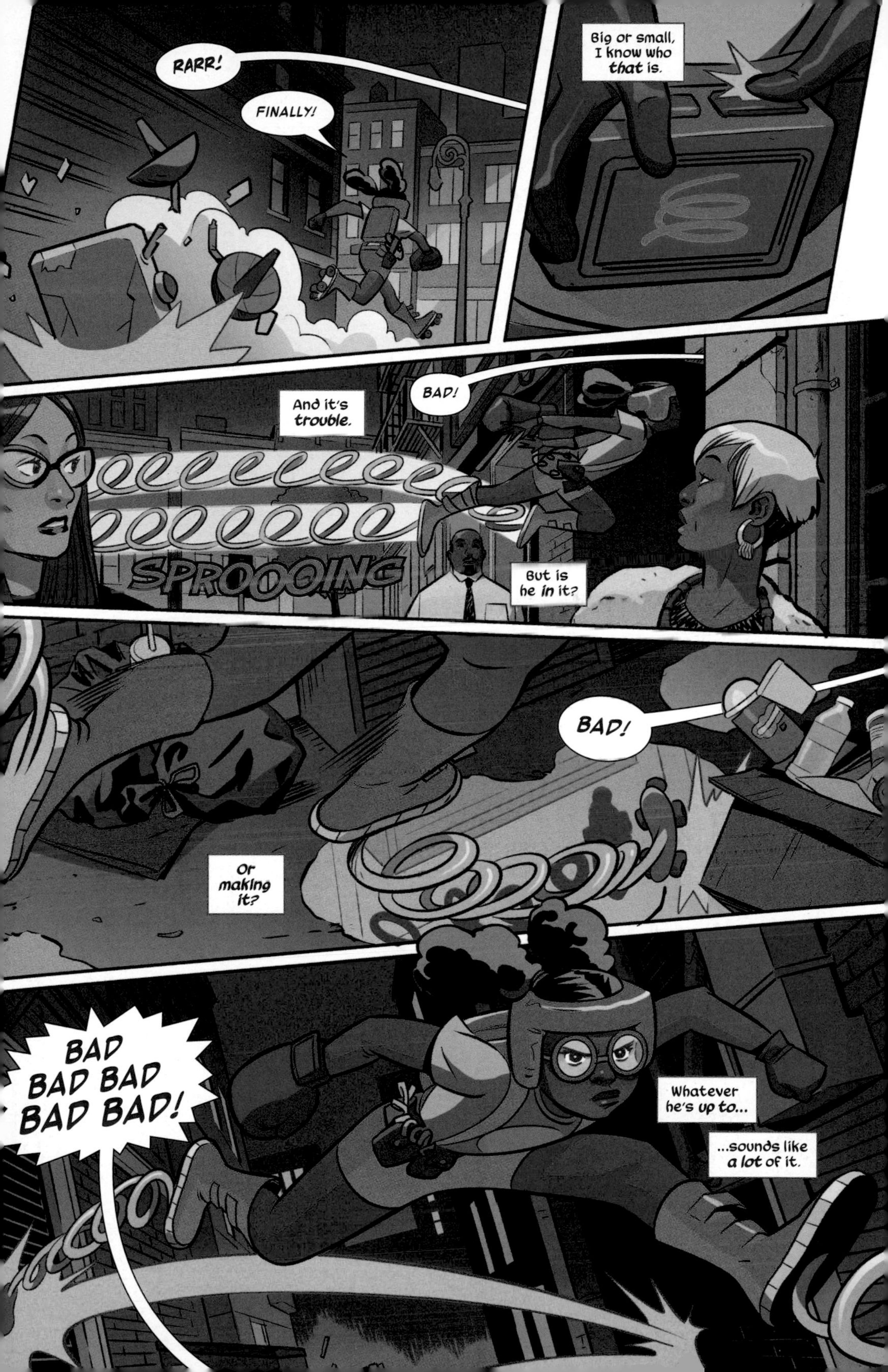
RARR!
FINALLY!
Big or small, I know who *that* is.
And it's *trouble*.
BAD!
SPROOOING
But is he *in* it?
BAD!
Or *making* it?
BAD BAD BAD BAD BAD!
Whatever he's *up to*...
...sounds like *a lot* of it.

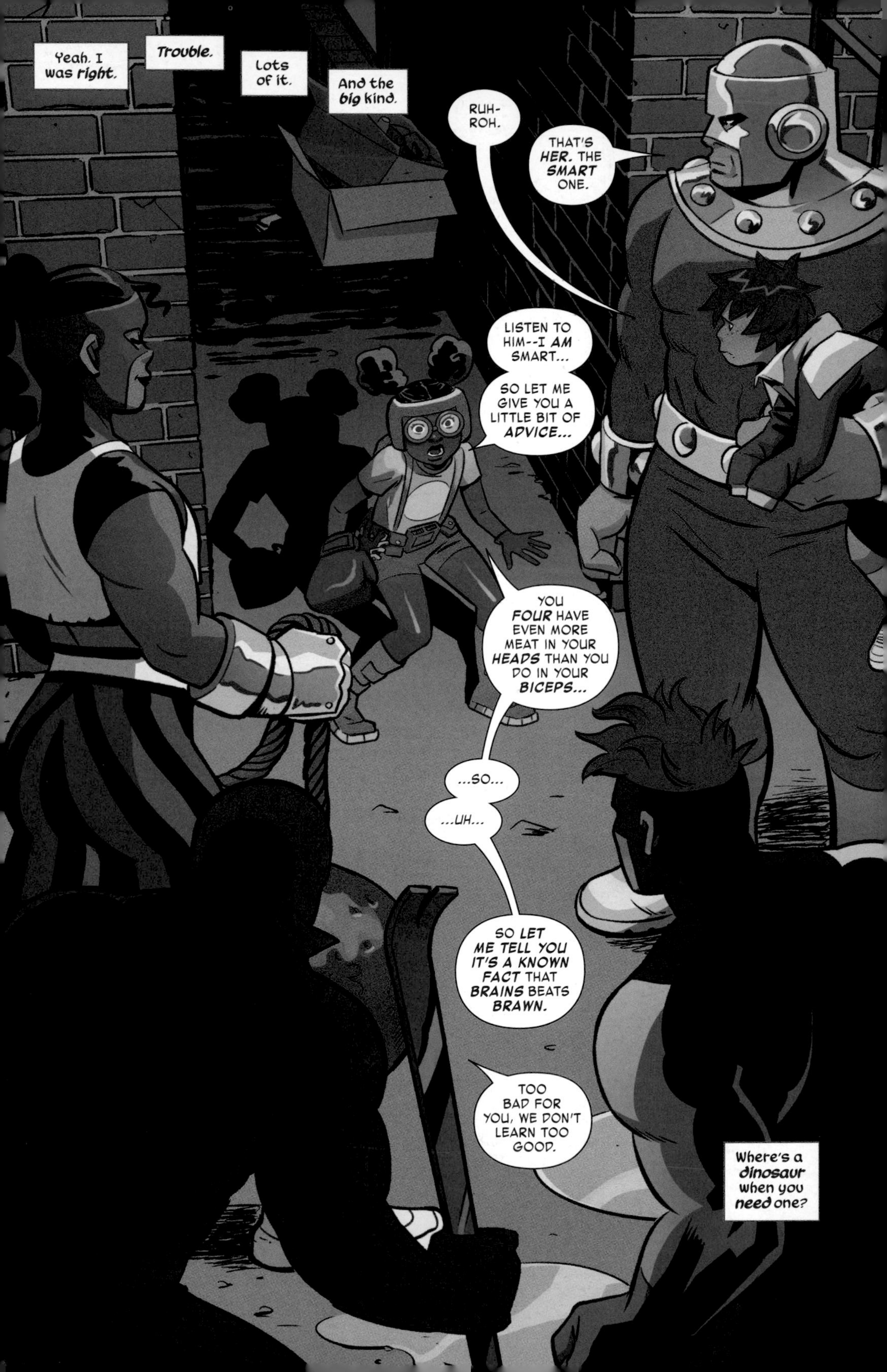
Yeah. I was right.
Trouble.
Lots of it.
And the big kind.
RUH-ROH.
THAT'S HER. THE SMART ONE.
LISTEN TO HIM--I AM SMART...
SO LET ME GIVE YOU A LITTLE BIT OF ADVICE...
YOU FOUR HAVE EVEN MORE MEAT IN YOUR HEADS THAN YOU DO IN YOUR BICEPS...
...SO...
...UH...
SO LET ME TELL YOU IT'S A KNOWN FACT THAT BRAINS BEATS BRAWN.
TOO BAD FOR YOU, WE DON'T LEARN TOO GOOD.
Where's a dinosaur when you need one?

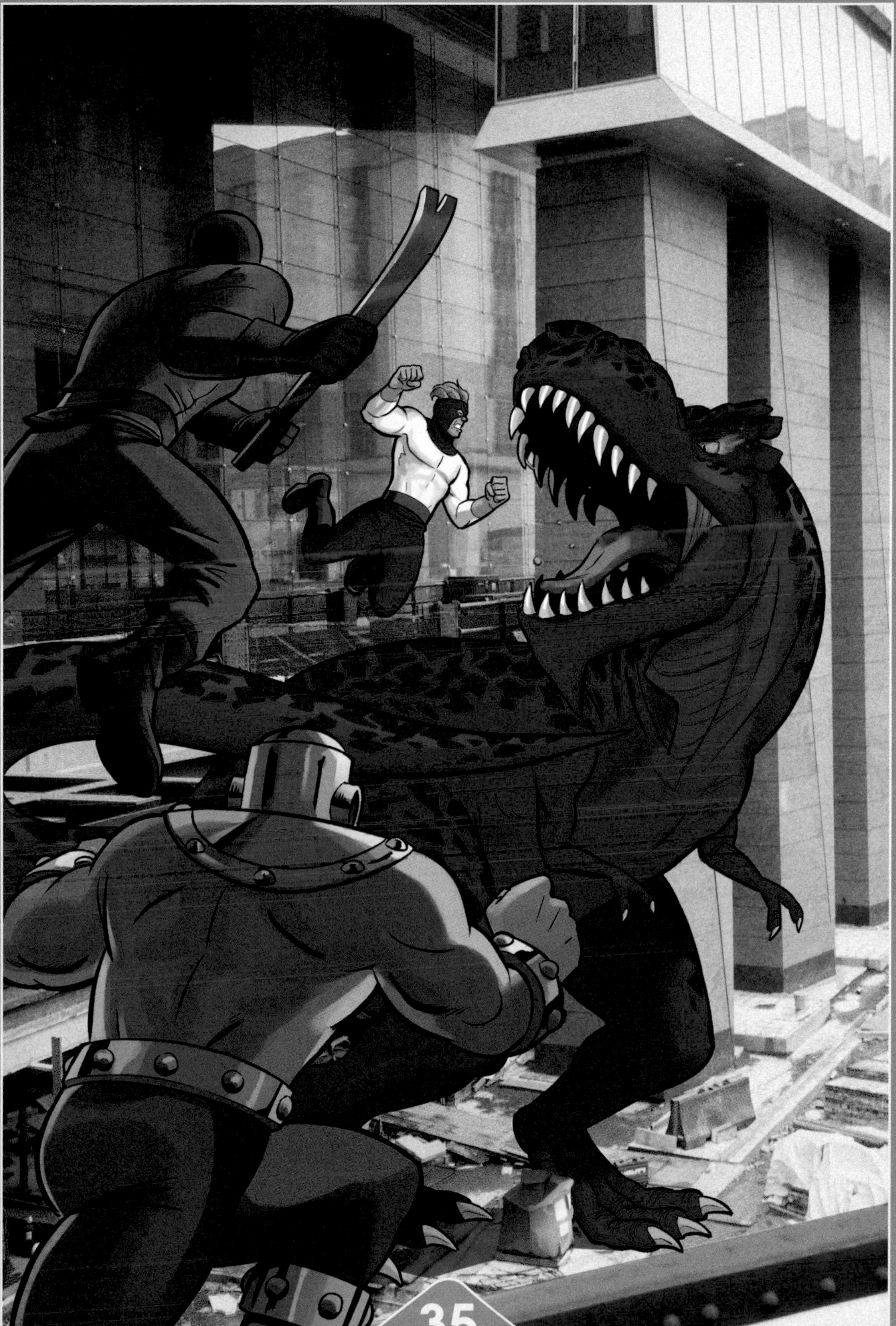

35

"What's The Big Idea?"

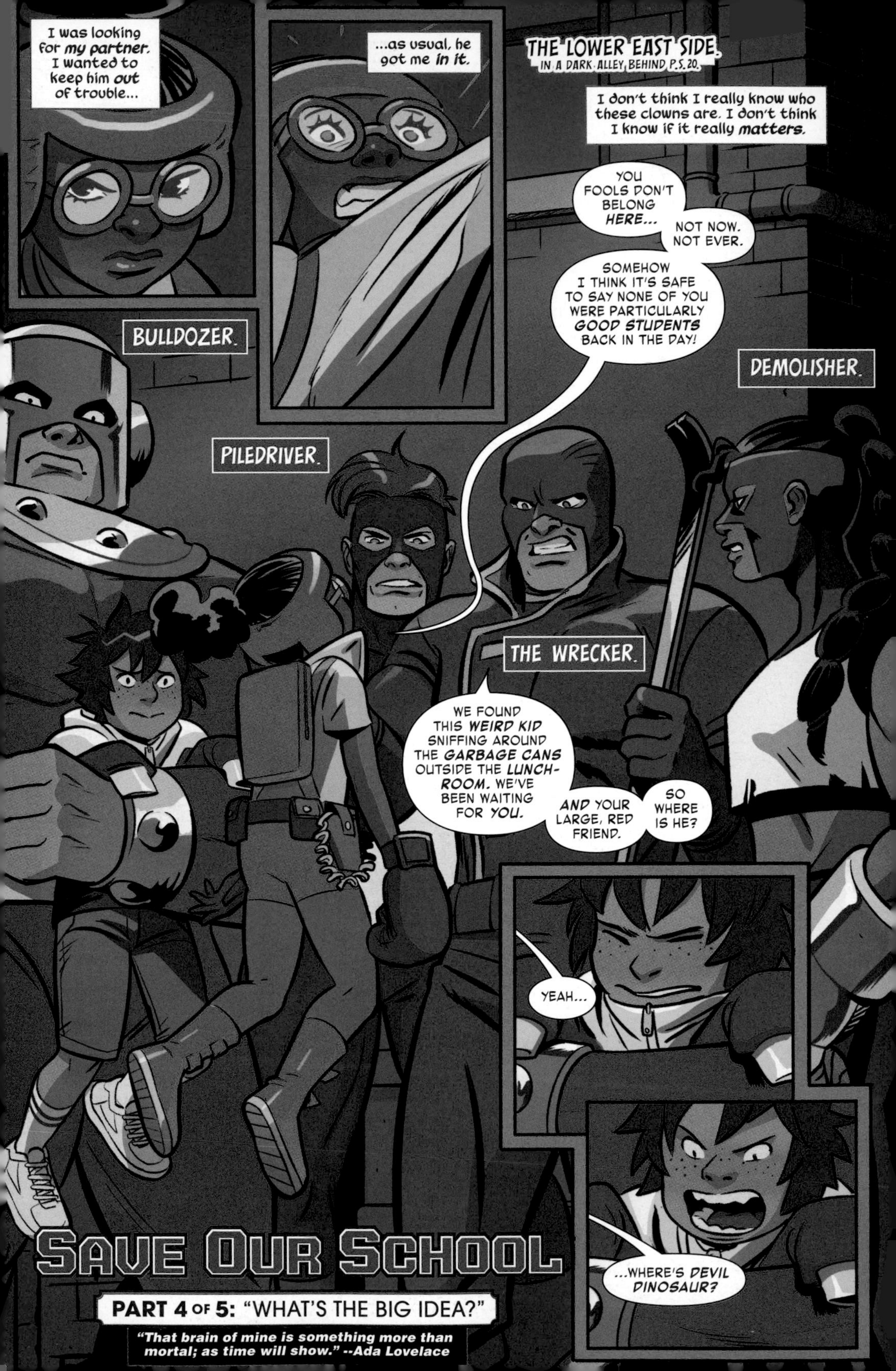
I was looking for my partner. I wanted to keep him out of trouble...
...as usual, he got me in it.
THE LOWER EAST SIDE.
IN A DARK ALLEY, BEHIND P.S. 20.
I don't think I really know who these clowns are. I don't think I know if it really matters.
YOU FOOLS DON'T BELONG HERE...
NOT NOW. NOT EVER.
SOMEHOW I THINK IT'S SAFE TO SAY NONE OF YOU WERE PARTICULARLY GOOD STUDENTS BACK IN THE DAY!
BULLDOZER.
DEMOLISHER.
PILEDRIVER.
THE WRECKER.
WE FOUND THIS WEIRD KID SNIFFING AROUND THE GARBAGE CANS OUTSIDE THE LUNCH-ROOM. WE'VE BEEN WAITING FOR YOU.
AND YOUR LARGE, RED FRIEND.
SO WHERE IS HE?
YEAH...
...WHERE'S DEVIL DINOSAUR?
SAVE OUR SCHOOL
PART 4 OF 5: "WHAT'S THE BIG IDEA?"
"That brain of mine is something more than mortal; as time will show." --Ada Lovelace

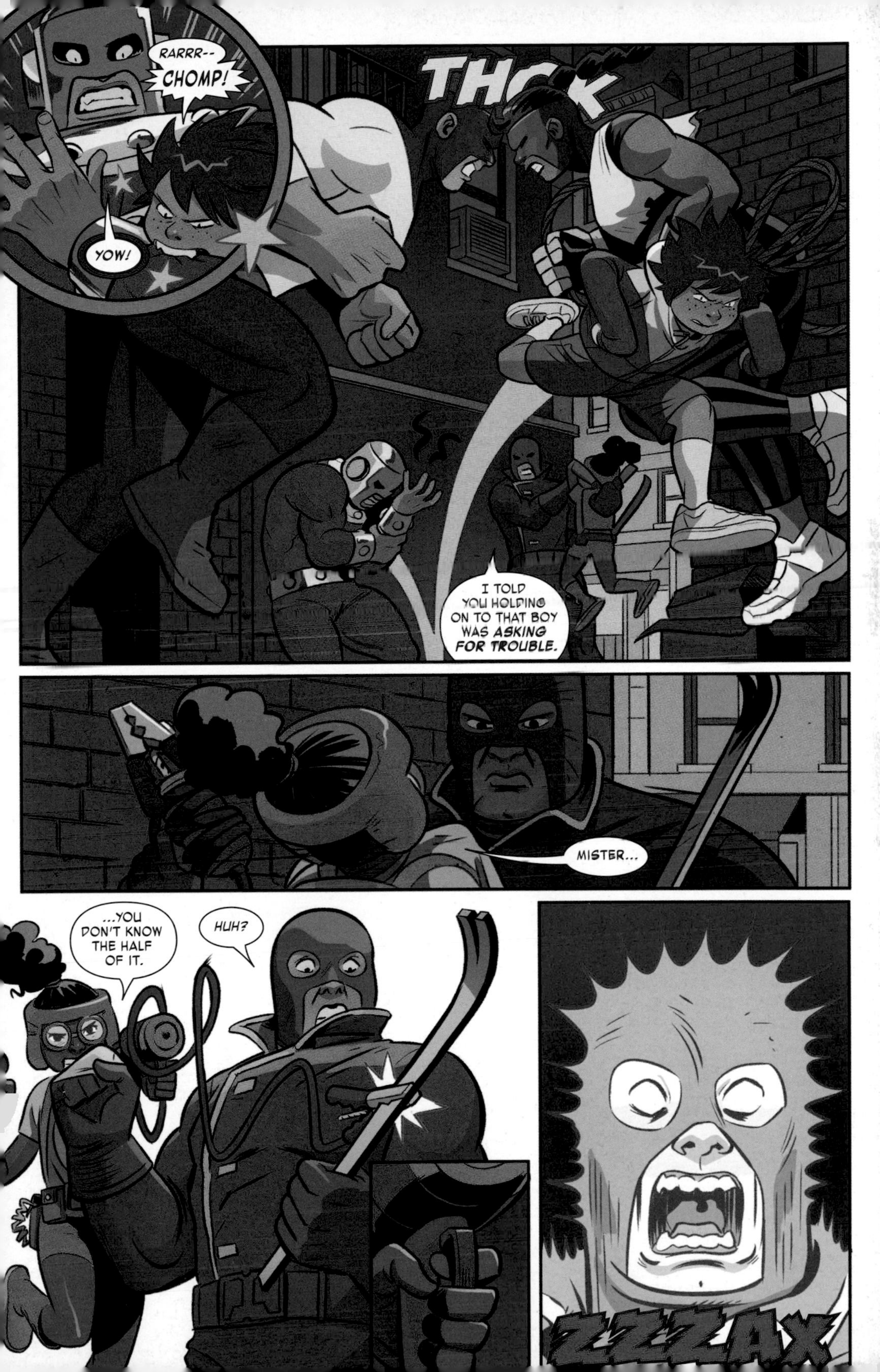
THOK
RARRR--
CHOMP!
YOW!
I TOLD YOU HOLDING ON TO THAT BOY WAS ASKING FOR TROUBLE.
MISTER...
...YOU DON'T KNOW THE HALF OF IT.
HUH?
ZZZAX

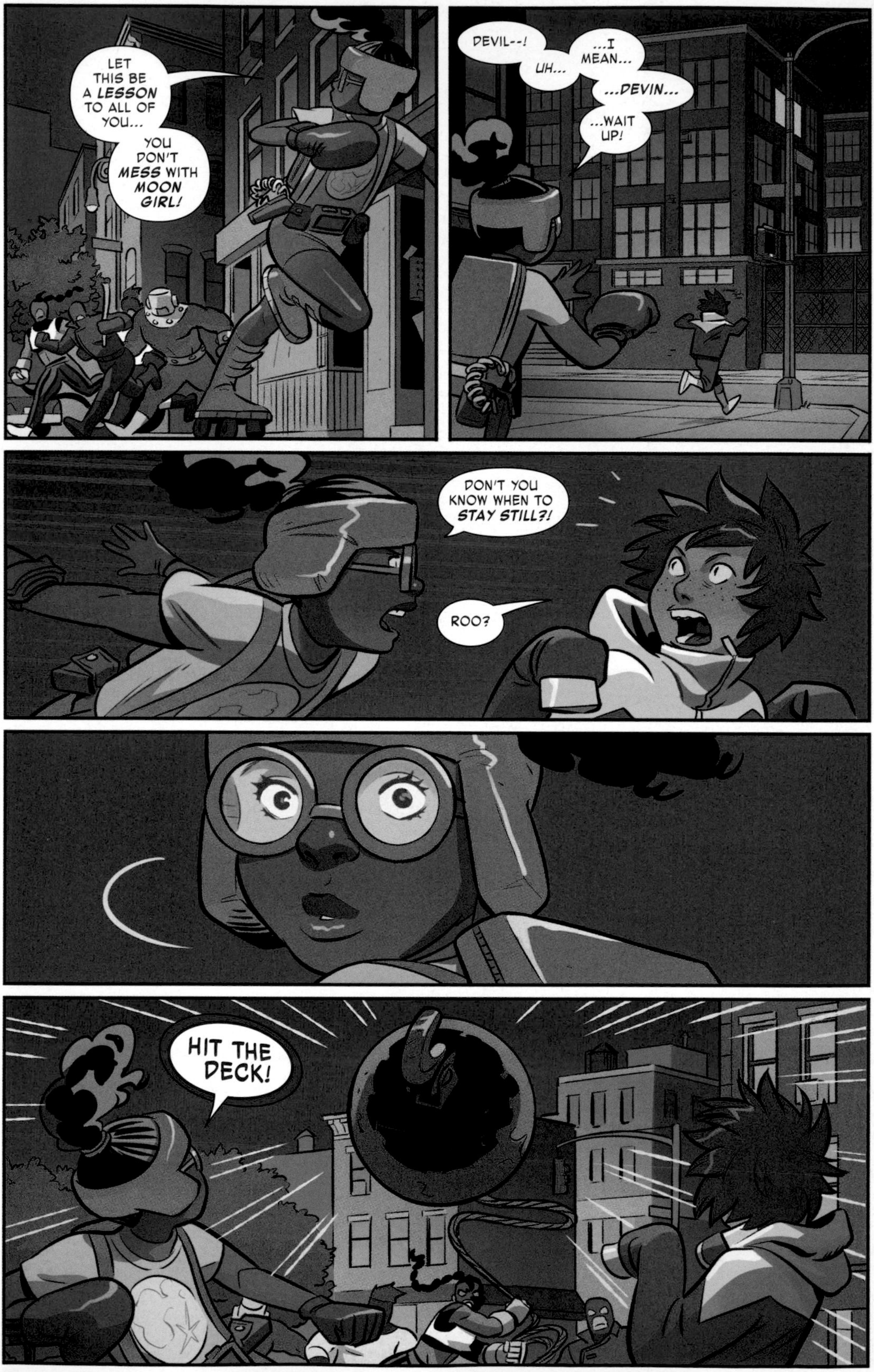

LET THIS BE A *LESSON* TO ALL OF YOU...
YOU DON'T *MESS* WITH *MOON GIRL!*
DEVIL--!
UH...
...I MEAN...
...DEVIN...
...WAIT UP!
DON'T YOU KNOW WHEN TO *STAY STILL?!*
ROO?
HIT THE DECK!

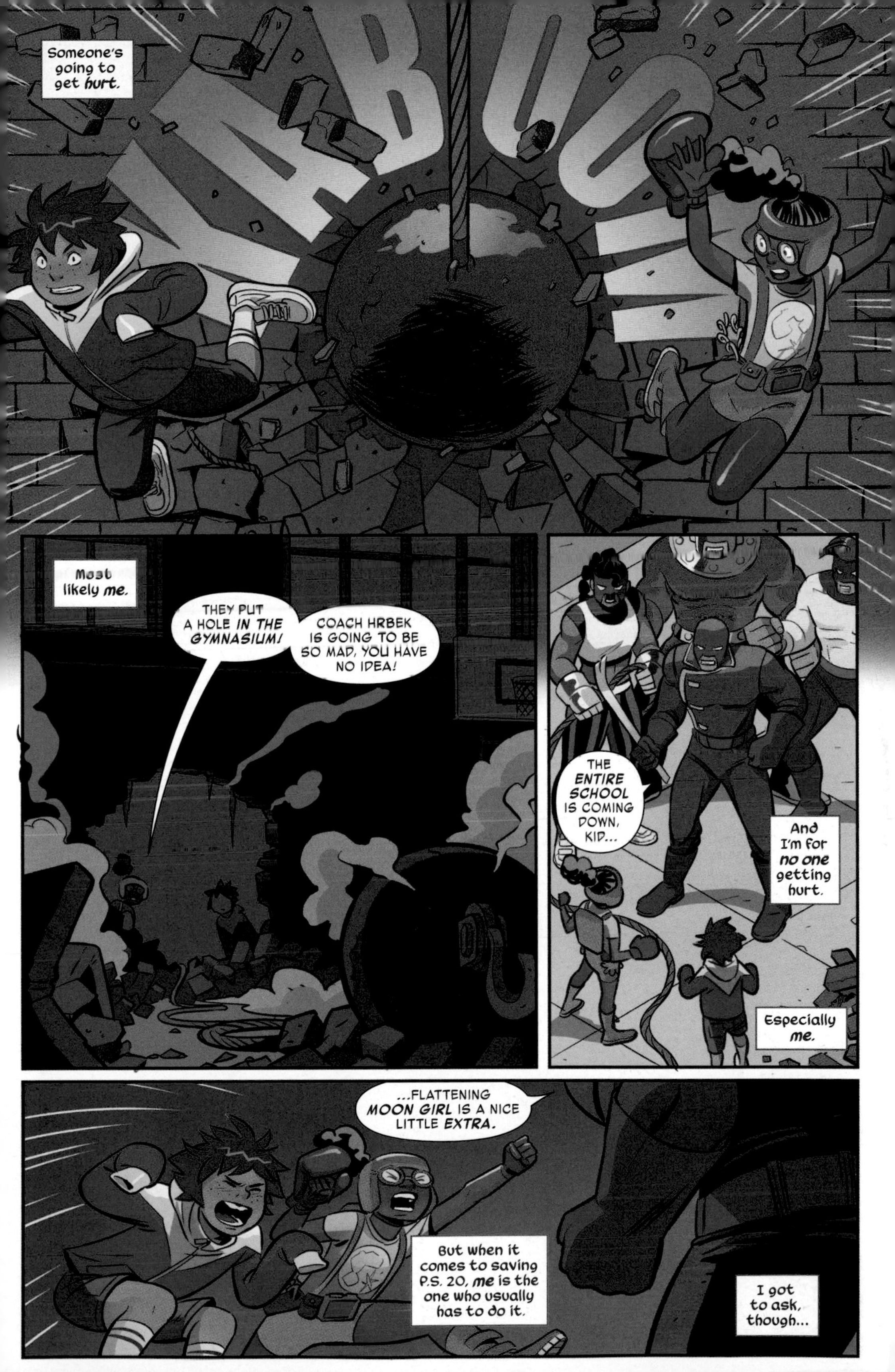
Someone's going to get *hurt*.
Most likely *me*.
THEY PUT A HOLE *IN THE GYMNASIUM!*
COACH HRBEK IS GOING TO BE SO MAD, YOU HAVE NO IDEA!
THE *ENTIRE SCHOOL* IS COMING DOWN, KID...
And I'm for *no one* getting hurt.
Especially *me*.
...FLATTENING *MOON GIRL* IS A NICE LITTLE *EXTRA*.
But when it comes to saving P.S. 20, *me* is the one who usually has to do it.
I got to ask, though...

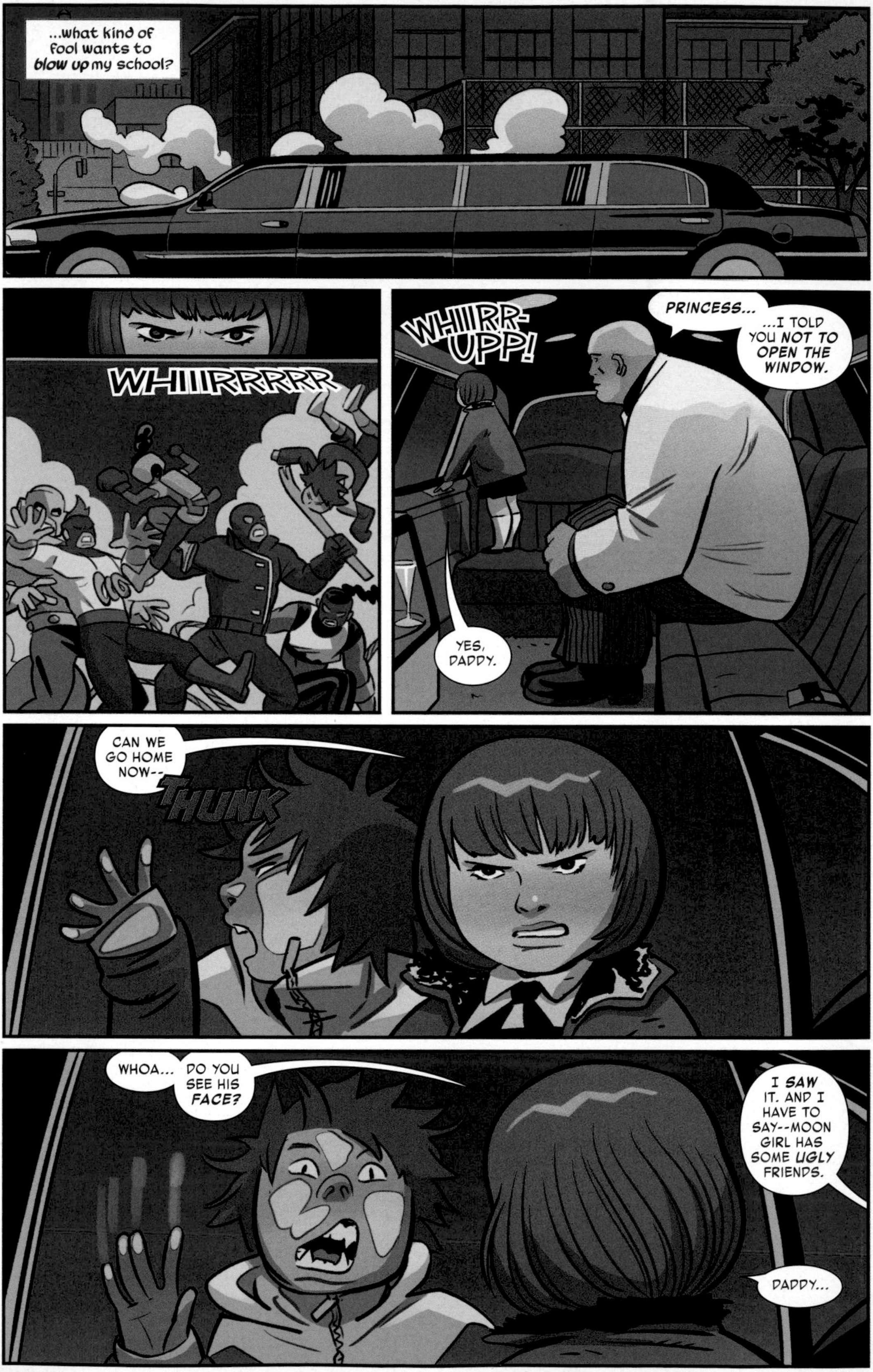
...what kind of fool wants to *blow up* my school?
WHIIIRRRRR
WHIIRR-UPP!
PRINCESS...
...I TOLD YOU **NOT TO OPEN THE WINDOW.**
YES, DADDY.
CAN WE GO HOME NOW--
THUNK
WHOA... DO YOU SEE HIS *FACE?*
I *SAW* IT. AND I HAVE TO SAY--MOON GIRL HAS SOME *UGLY* FRIENDS.
DADDY...

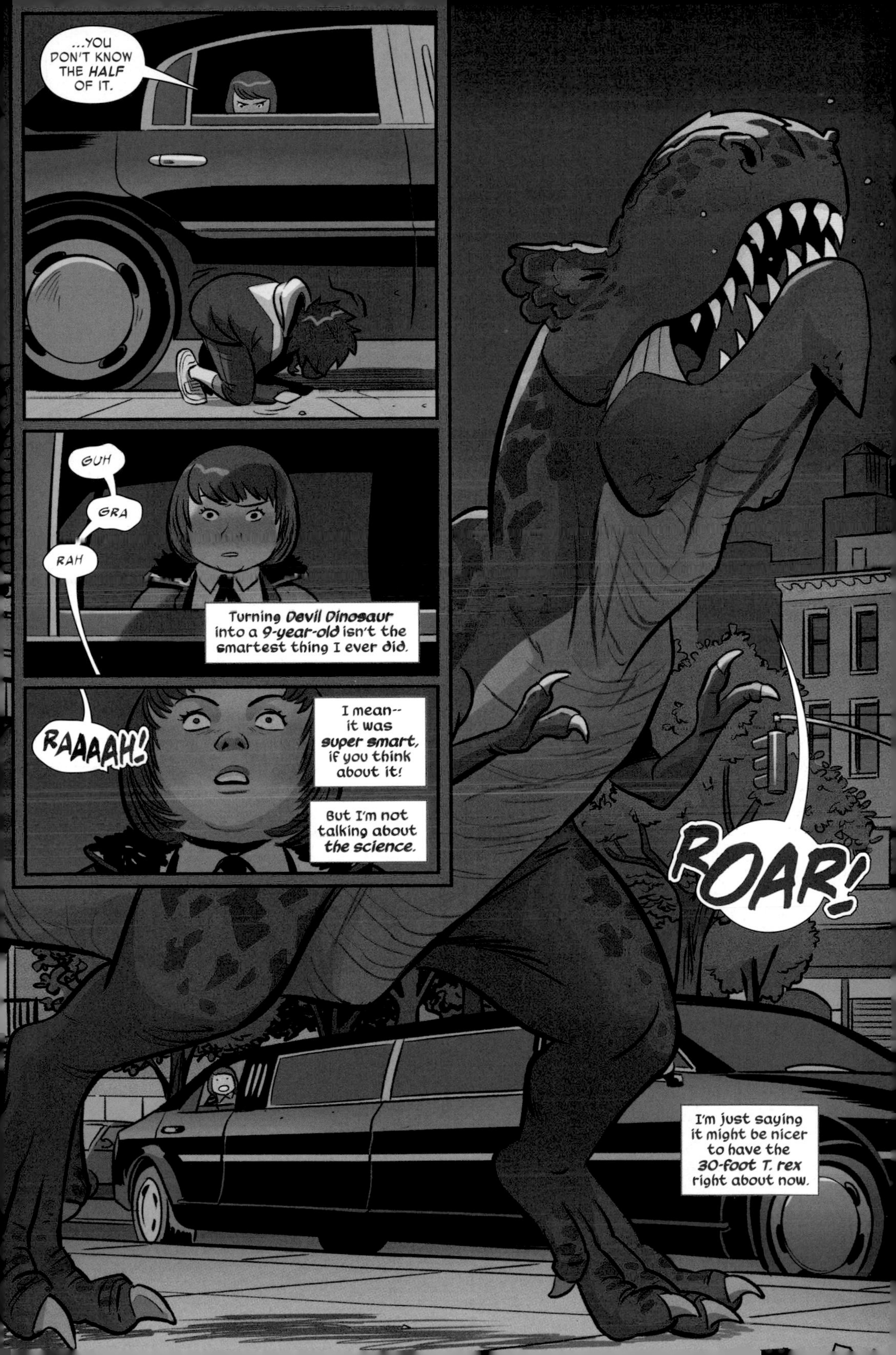
...YOU DON'T KNOW THE HALF OF IT.
GUH
GRA
RAH
Turning Devil Dinosaur into a 9-year-old isn't the smartest thing I ever did.
RAAAAH!
I mean-- it was super smart, if you think about it!
But I'm not talking about the science.
ROAR!
I'm just saying it might be nicer to have the 30-foot T. rex right about now.

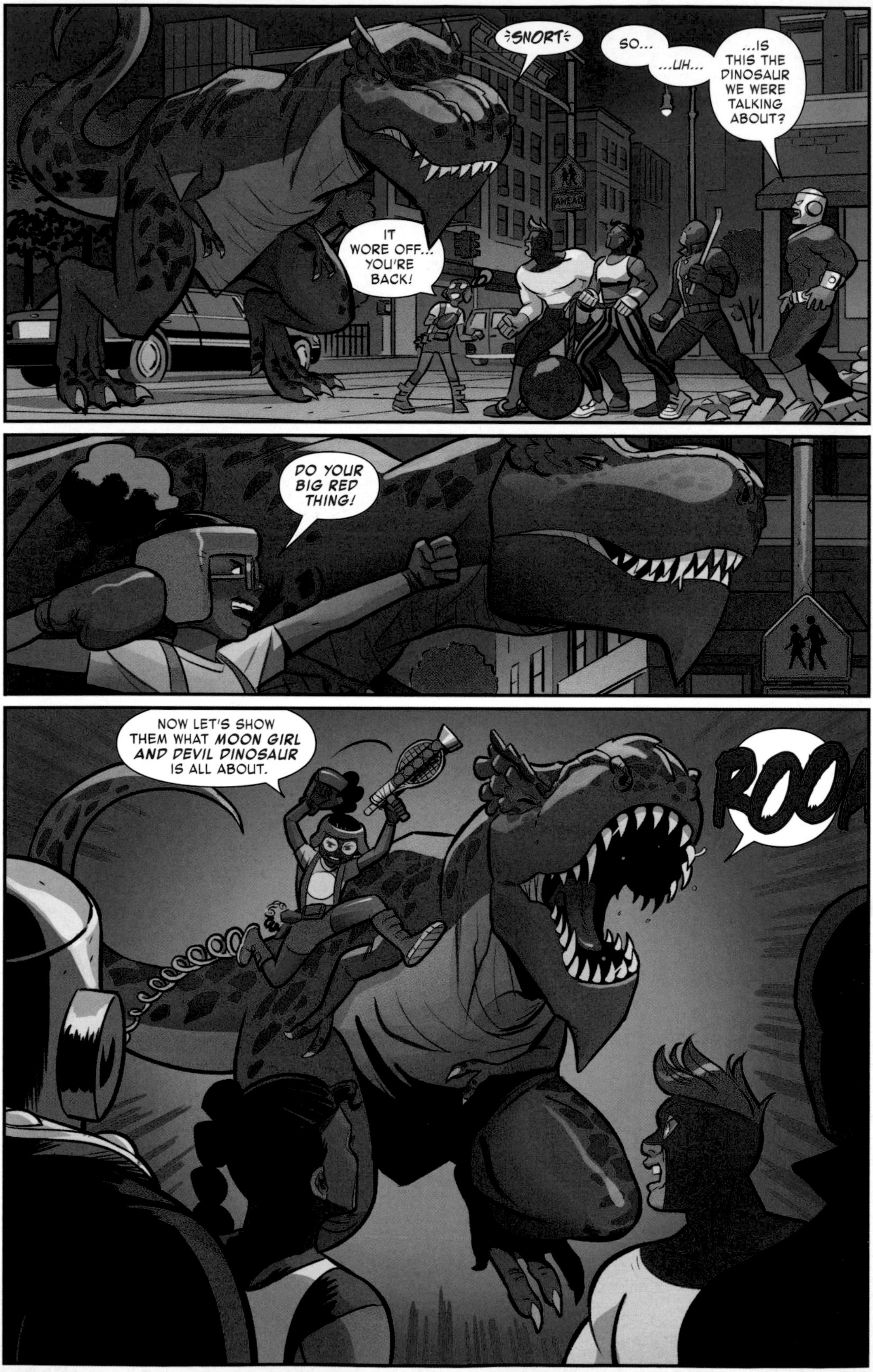

SNORT
SO...
...UH...
...IS THIS THE DINOSAUR WE WERE TALKING ABOUT?
IT WORE OFF... YOU'RE BACK!
DO YOUR BIG RED THING!
NOW LET'S SHOW THEM WHAT MOON GIRL AND DEVIL DINOSAUR IS ALL ABOUT.
ROOA

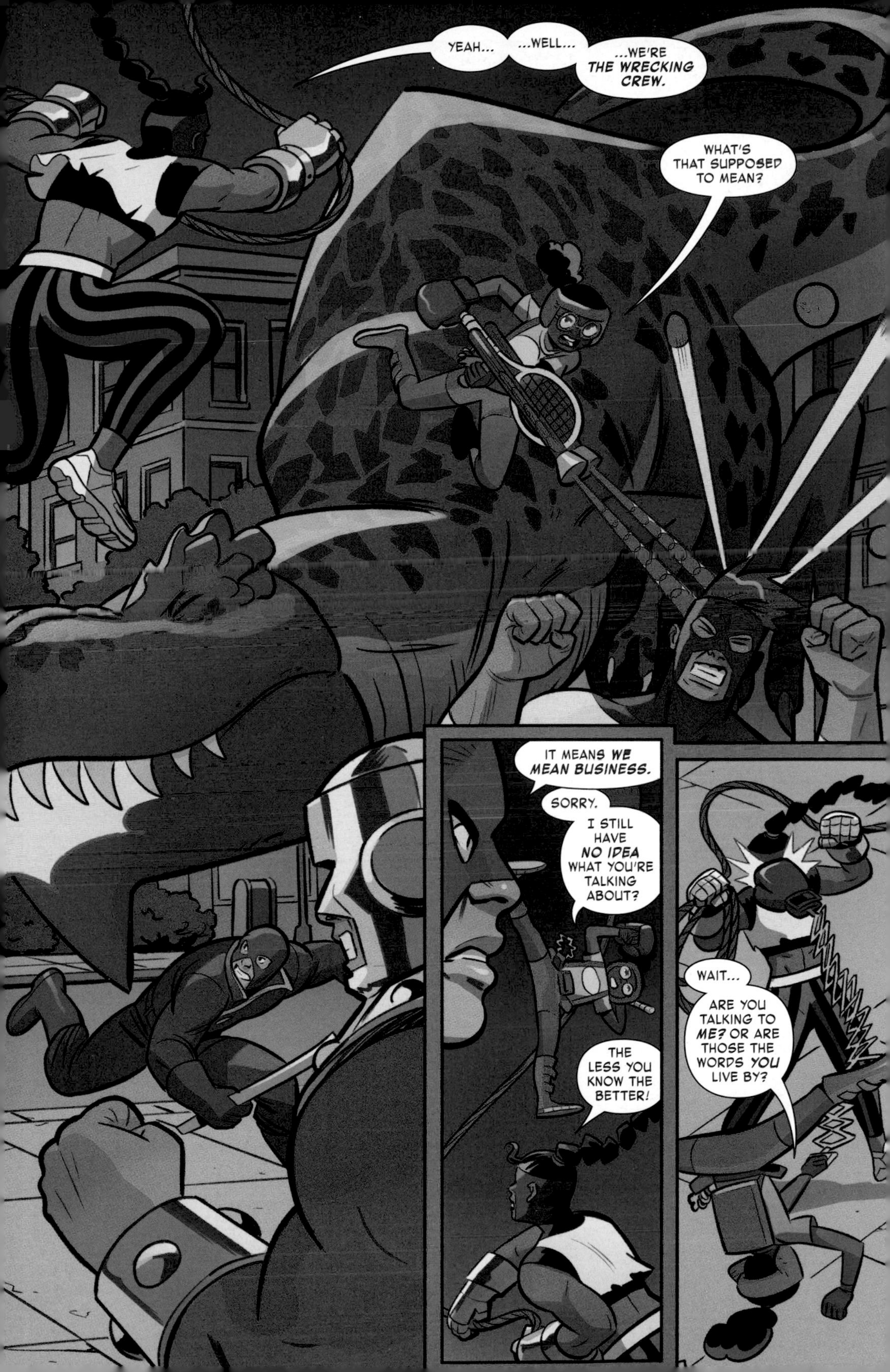
YEAH...
...WELL...
...WE'RE *THE WRECKING CREW.*
WHAT'S THAT SUPPOSED TO MEAN?
IT MEANS *WE MEAN BUSINESS.*
SORRY.
I STILL HAVE *NO IDEA* WHAT YOU'RE TALKING ABOUT?
THE LESS YOU KNOW THE BETTER!
WAIT...
ARE YOU TALKING TO *ME?* OR ARE THOSE THE WORDS *YOU* LIVE BY?

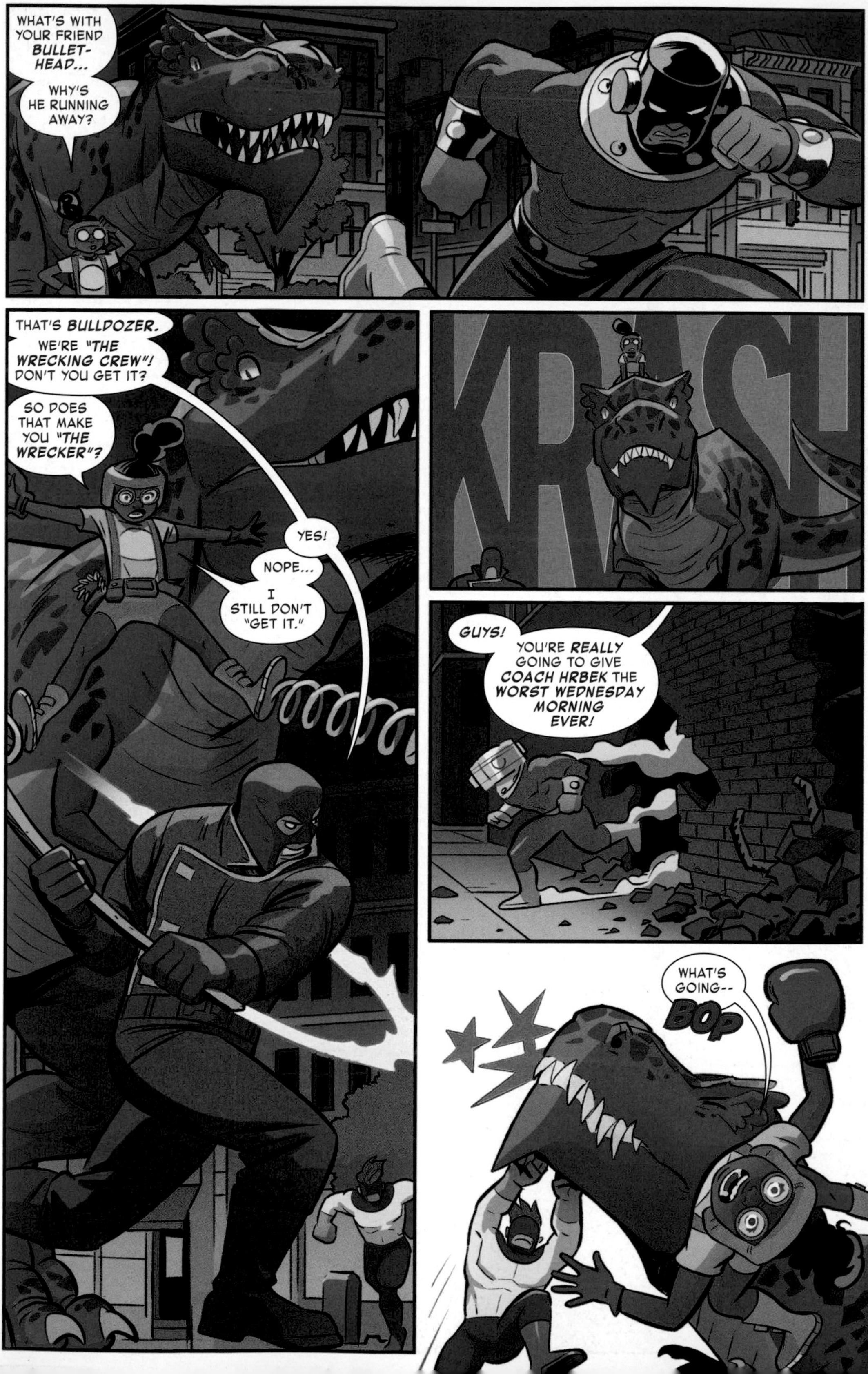
WHAT'S WITH YOUR FRIEND BULLET-HEAD...
WHY'S HE RUNNING AWAY?
THAT'S BULLDOZER.
WE'RE "THE WRECKING CREW"! DON'T YOU GET IT?
SO DOES THAT MAKE YOU "THE WRECKER"?
YES!
NOPE...
I STILL DON'T "GET IT."
KRASH
GUYS!
YOU'RE REALLY GOING TO GIVE COACH HRBEK THE WORST WEDNESDAY MORNING EVER!
WHAT'S GOING--
BOP

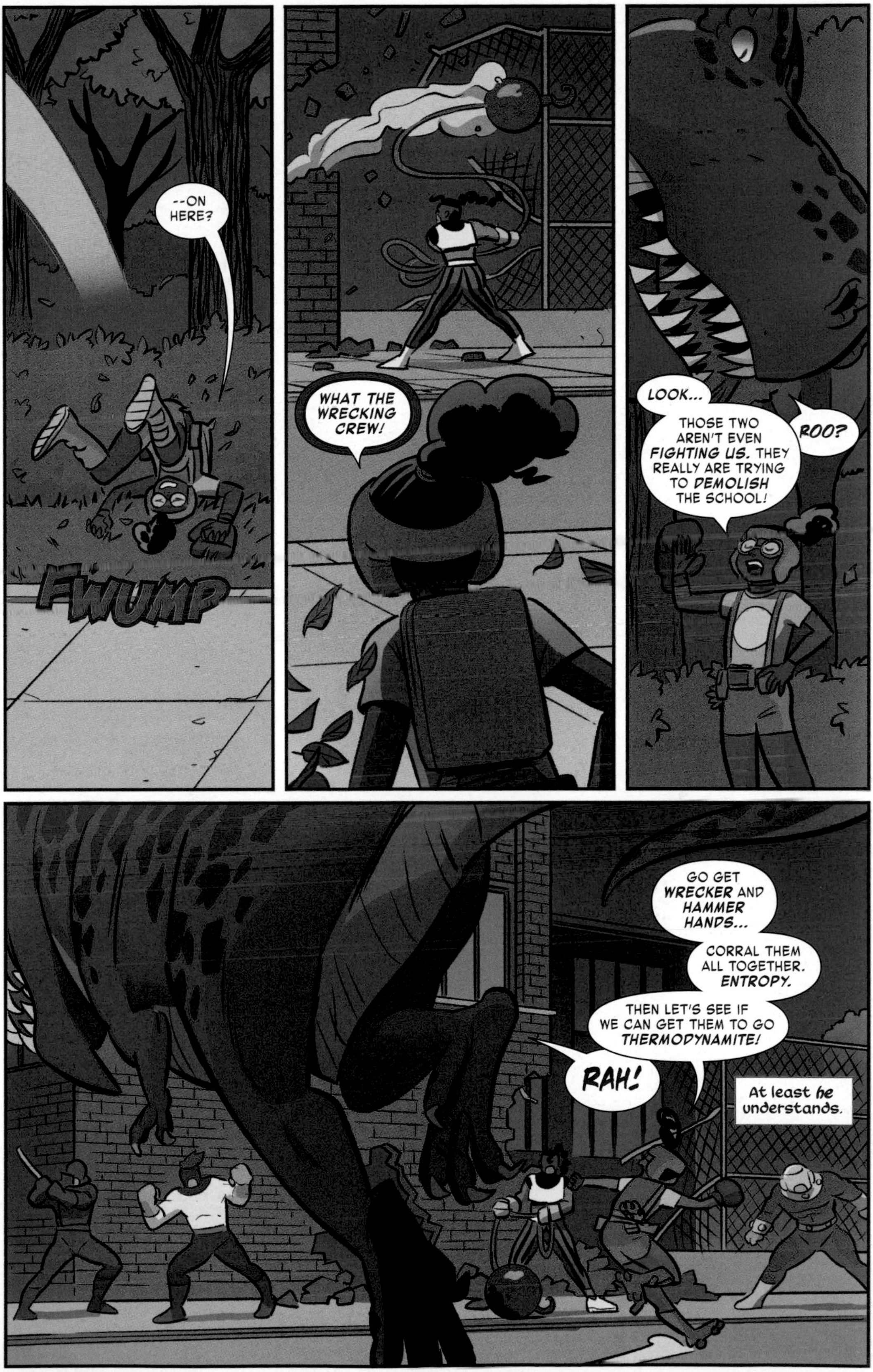
--ON HERE?
FWUMP
WHAT THE WRECKING CREW!
LOOK...
THOSE TWO AREN'T EVEN FIGHTING US. THEY REALLY ARE TRYING TO DEMOLISH THE SCHOOL!
ROO?
GO GET WRECKER AND HAMMER HANDS...
CORRAL THEM ALL TOGETHER. ENTROPY.
THEN LET'S SEE IF WE CAN GET THEM TO GO THERMODYNAMITE!
RAH!
At least he understands.

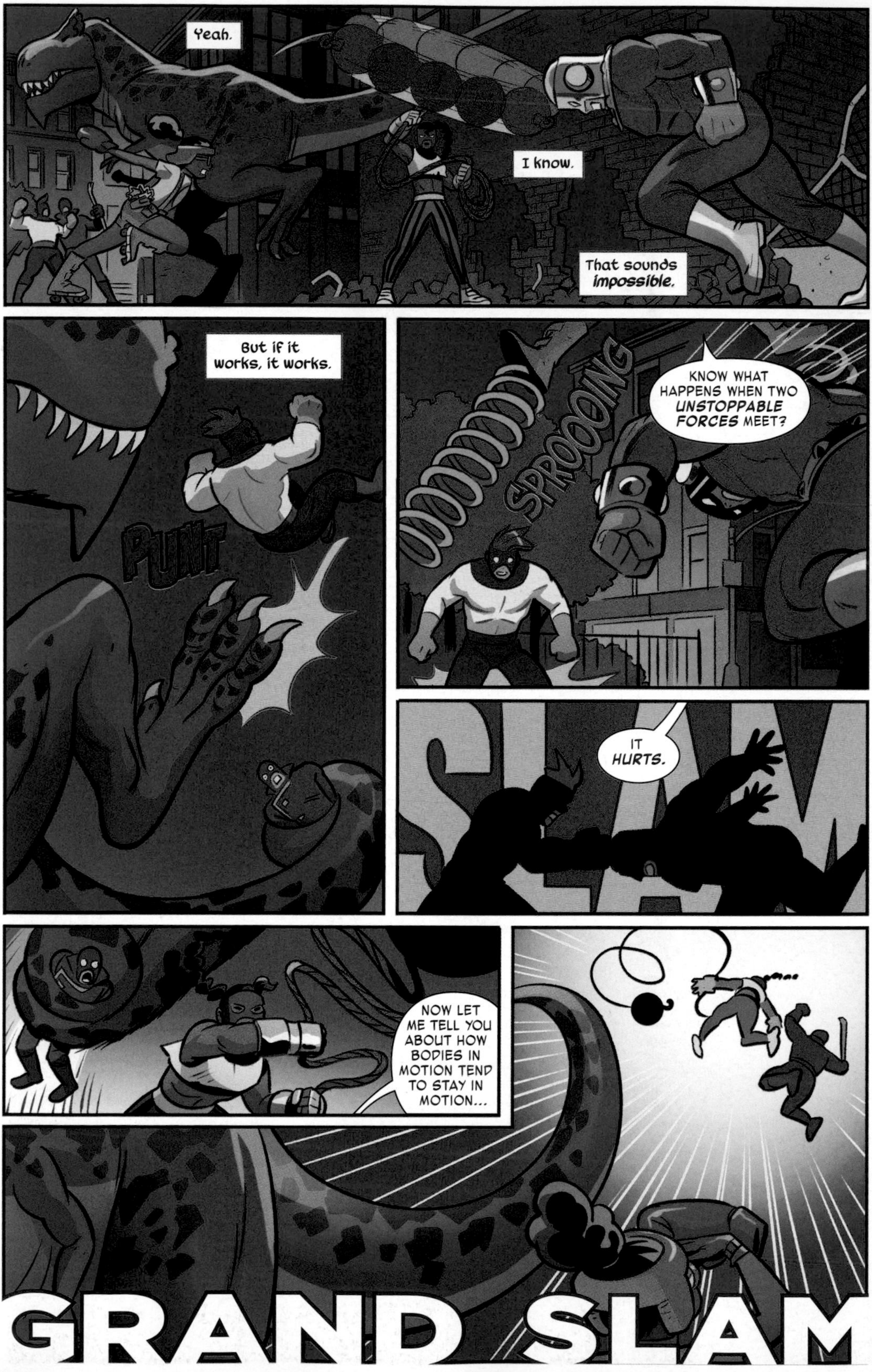
Yeah.
I know.
That sounds impossible.
But if it works, it works.
PUNT
SPROOOING
KNOW WHAT HAPPENS WHEN TWO UNSTOPPABLE FORCES MEET?
IT HURTS.
SLAM
NOW LET ME TELL YOU ABOUT HOW BODIES IN MOTION TEND TO STAY IN MOTION...
GRAND SLAM

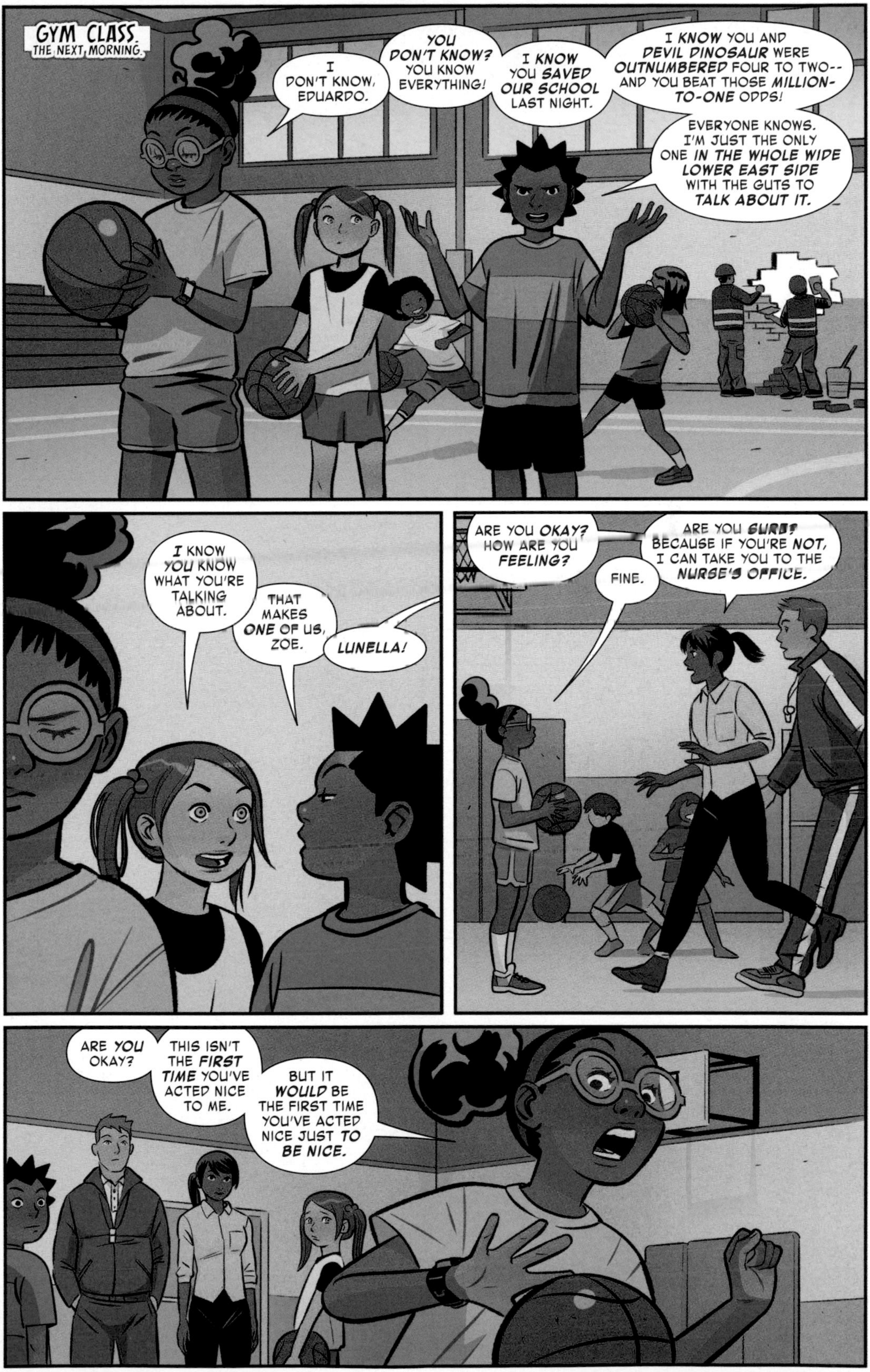
GYM CLASS. THE NEXT MORNING.
I DON'T KNOW, EDUARDO.
YOU DON'T KNOW? YOU KNOW EVERYTHING!
I KNOW YOU SAVED OUR SCHOOL LAST NIGHT.
I KNOW YOU AND DEVIL DINOSAUR WERE OUTNUMBERED FOUR TO TWO-- AND YOU BEAT THOSE MILLION-TO-ONE ODDS!
EVERYONE KNOWS. I'M JUST THE ONLY ONE IN THE WHOLE WIDE LOWER EAST SIDE WITH THE GUTS TO TALK ABOUT IT.
I KNOW YOU KNOW WHAT YOU'RE TALKING ABOUT.
THAT MAKES ONE OF US, ZOE.
LUNELLA!
ARE YOU OKAY? HOW ARE YOU FEELING?
FINE.
ARE YOU SURE? BECAUSE IF YOU'RE NOT, I CAN TAKE YOU TO THE NURSE'S OFFICE.
ARE YOU OKAY?
THIS ISN'T THE FIRST TIME YOU'VE ACTED NICE TO ME.
BUT IT WOULD BE THE FIRST TIME YOU'VE ACTED NICE JUST TO BE NICE.

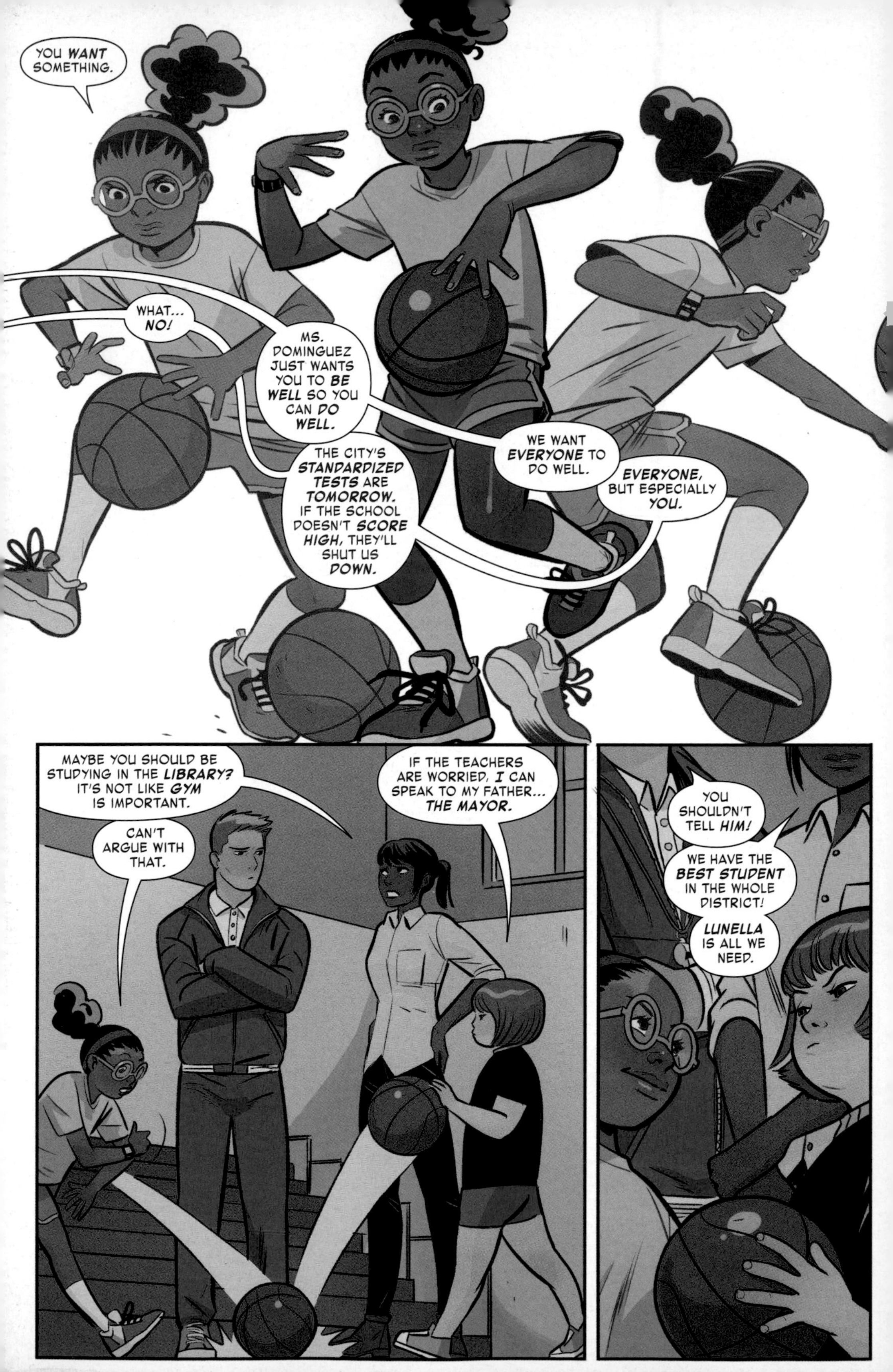

YOU WANT SOMETHING.
WHAT... NO!
MS. DOMINGUEZ JUST WANTS YOU TO BE WELL SO YOU CAN DO WELL.
THE CITY'S STANDARDIZED TESTS ARE TOMORROW. IF THE SCHOOL DOESN'T SCORE HIGH, THEY'LL SHUT US DOWN.
WE WANT EVERYONE TO DO WELL.
EVERYONE, BUT ESPECIALLY YOU.
MAYBE YOU SHOULD BE STUDYING IN THE LIBRARY? IT'S NOT LIKE GYM IS IMPORTANT.
CAN'T ARGUE WITH THAT.
IF THE TEACHERS ARE WORRIED, I CAN SPEAK TO MY FATHER... THE MAYOR.
YOU SHOULDN'T TELL HIM!
WE HAVE THE BEST STUDENT IN THE WHOLE DISTRICT!
LUNELLA IS ALL WE NEED.

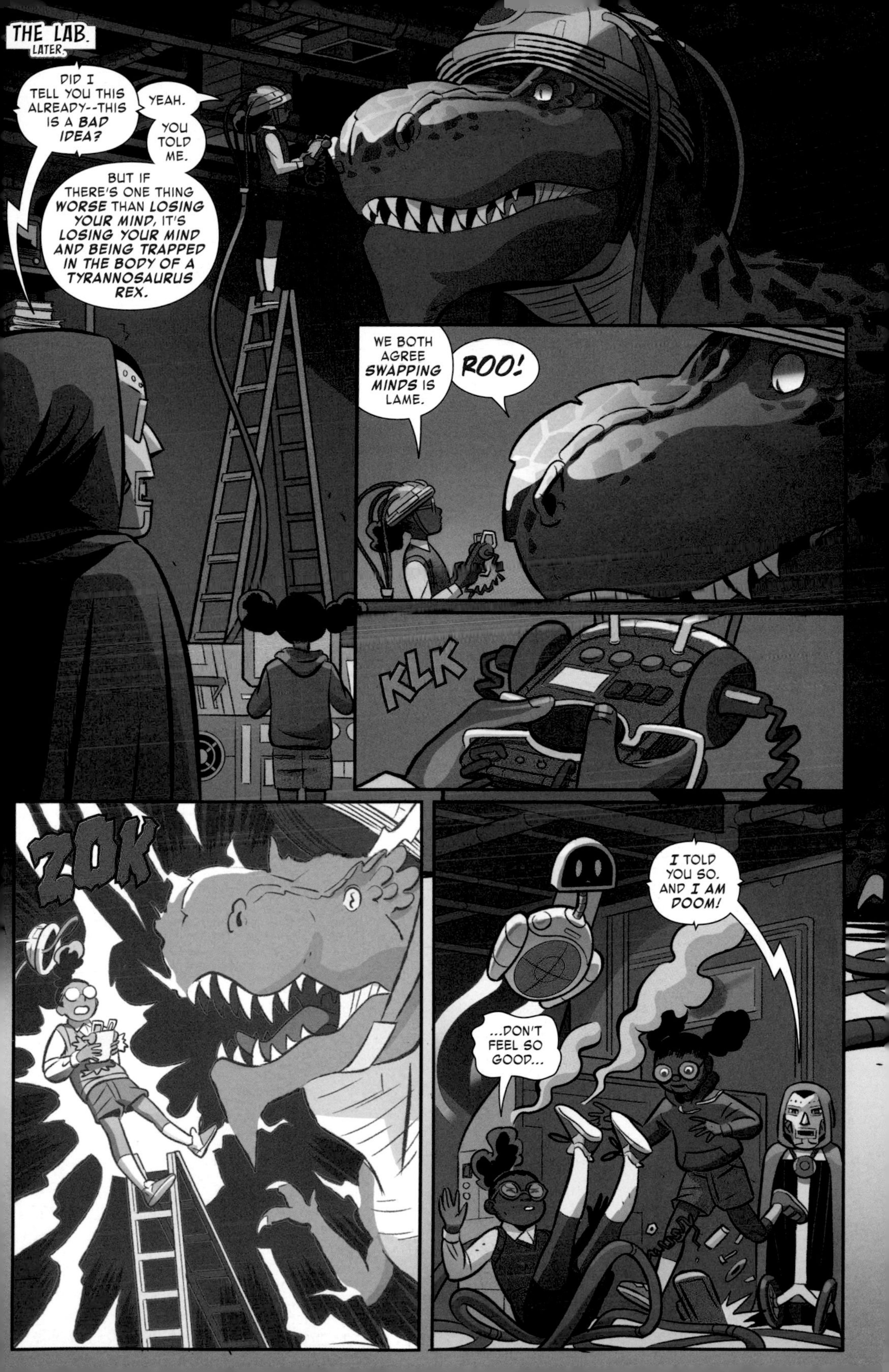
THE LAB. LATER.
DID I TELL YOU THIS ALREADY--THIS IS A BAD IDEA?
YEAH.
YOU TOLD ME.
BUT IF THERE'S ONE THING WORSE THAN LOSING YOUR MIND, IT'S LOSING YOUR MIND AND BEING TRAPPED IN THE BODY OF A TYRANNOSAURUS REX.
WE BOTH AGREE SWAPPING MINDS IS LAME.
ROO!
KLK
ZOK
I TOLD YOU SO. AND I AM DOOM!
...DON'T FEEL SO GOOD...

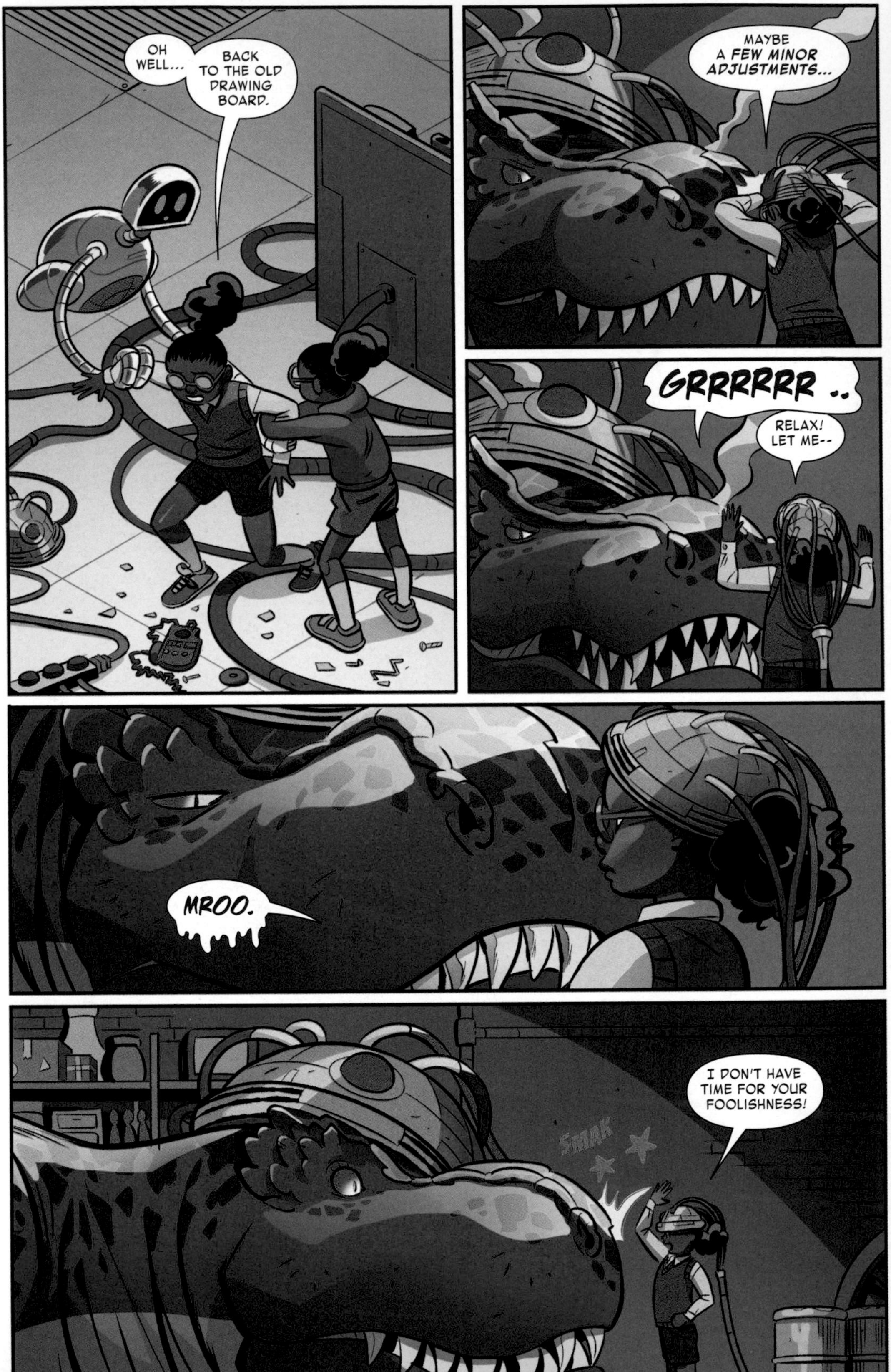
OH WELL...
BACK TO THE OLD DRAWING BOARD.
MAYBE A FEW MINOR ADJUSTMENTS...
GRRRRRR ..
RELAX! LET ME--
MROO.
SMAK
I DON'T HAVE TIME FOR YOUR FOOLISHNESS!

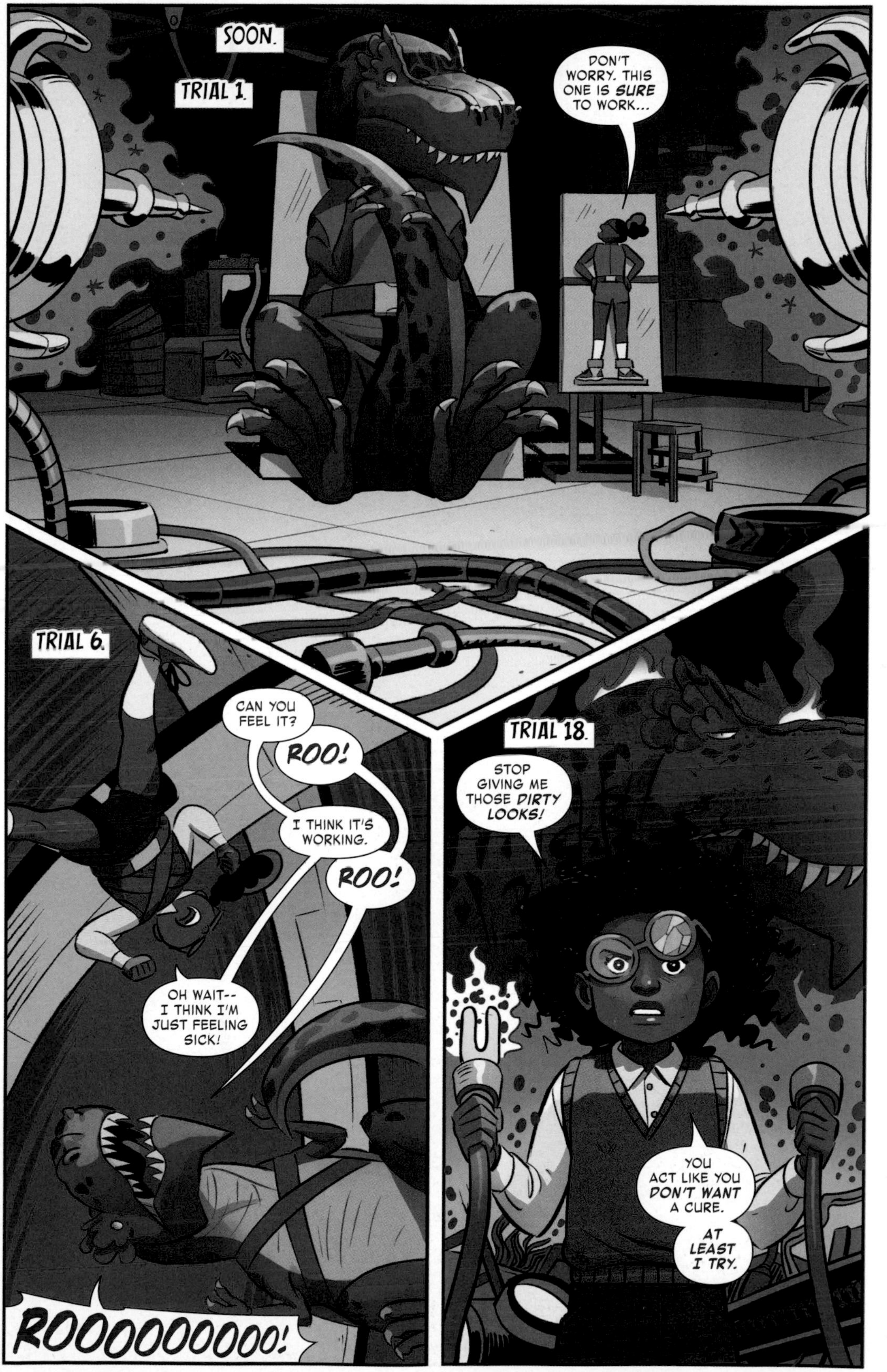
SOON.
TRIAL 1.
DON'T WORRY. THIS ONE IS SURE TO WORK...
TRIAL 6.
CAN YOU FEEL IT?
ROO!
I THINK IT'S WORKING.
ROO!
OH WAIT-- I THINK I'M JUST FEELING SICK!
ROOOOOOOOO!
TRIAL 18.
STOP GIVING ME THOSE DIRTY LOOKS!
YOU ACT LIKE YOU DON'T WANT A CURE.
AT LEAST I TRY.

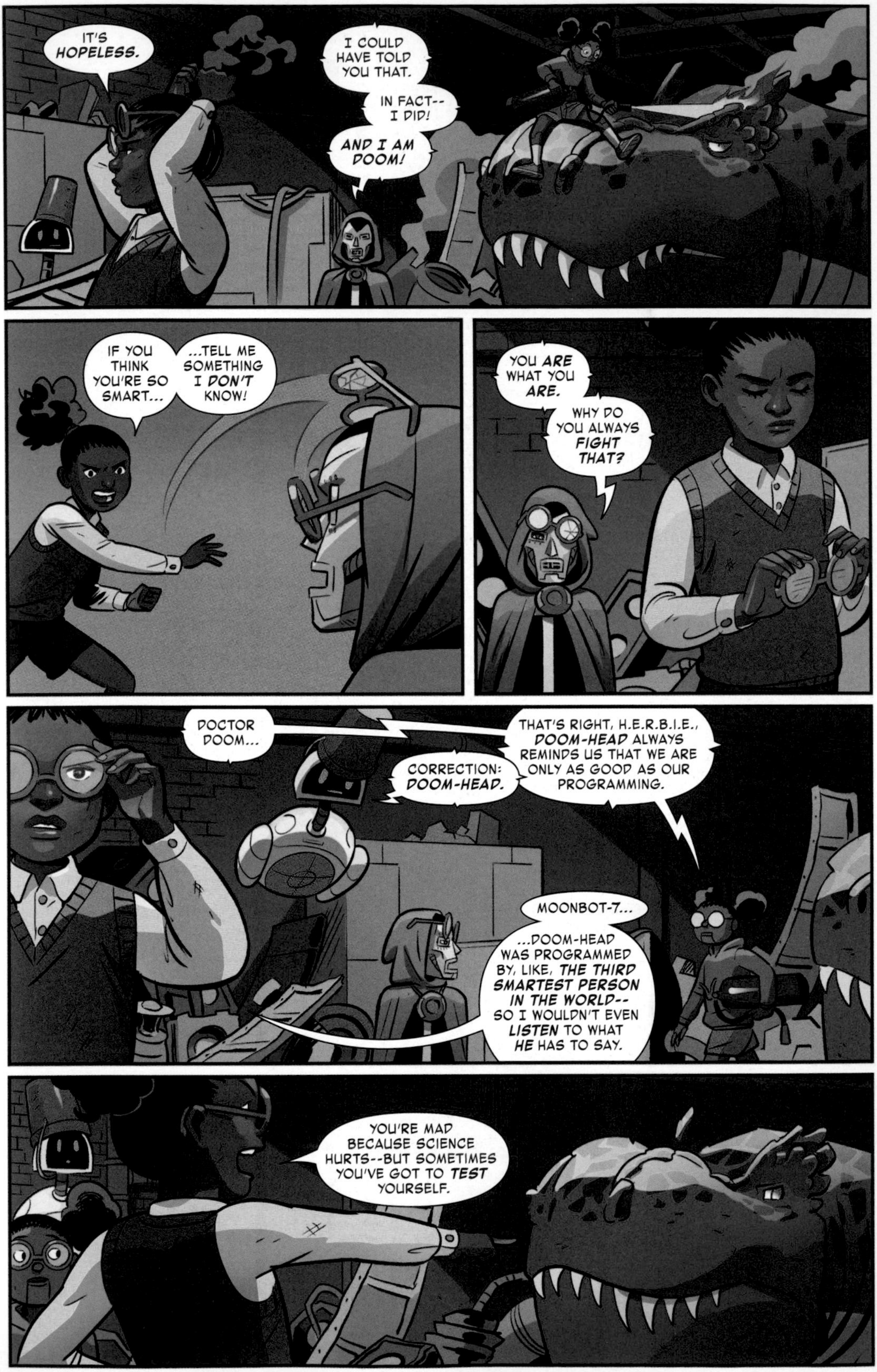
IT'S HOPELESS.
I COULD HAVE TOLD YOU THAT.
IN FACT-- I DID!
AND I AM DOOM!
IF YOU THINK YOU'RE SO SMART...
...TELL ME SOMETHING I DON'T KNOW!
YOU ARE WHAT YOU ARE.
WHY DO YOU ALWAYS FIGHT THAT?
DOCTOR DOOM...
CORRECTION: DOOM-HEAD.
THAT'S RIGHT, H.E.R.B.I.E., DOOM-HEAD ALWAYS REMINDS US THAT WE ARE ONLY AS GOOD AS OUR PROGRAMMING.
MOONBOT-7...
...DOOM-HEAD WAS PROGRAMMED BY, LIKE, THE THIRD SMARTEST PERSON IN THE WORLD-- SO I WOULDN'T EVEN LISTEN TO WHAT HE HAS TO SAY.
YOU'RE MAD BECAUSE SCIENCE HURTS--BUT SOMETIMES YOU'VE GOT TO TEST YOURSELF.

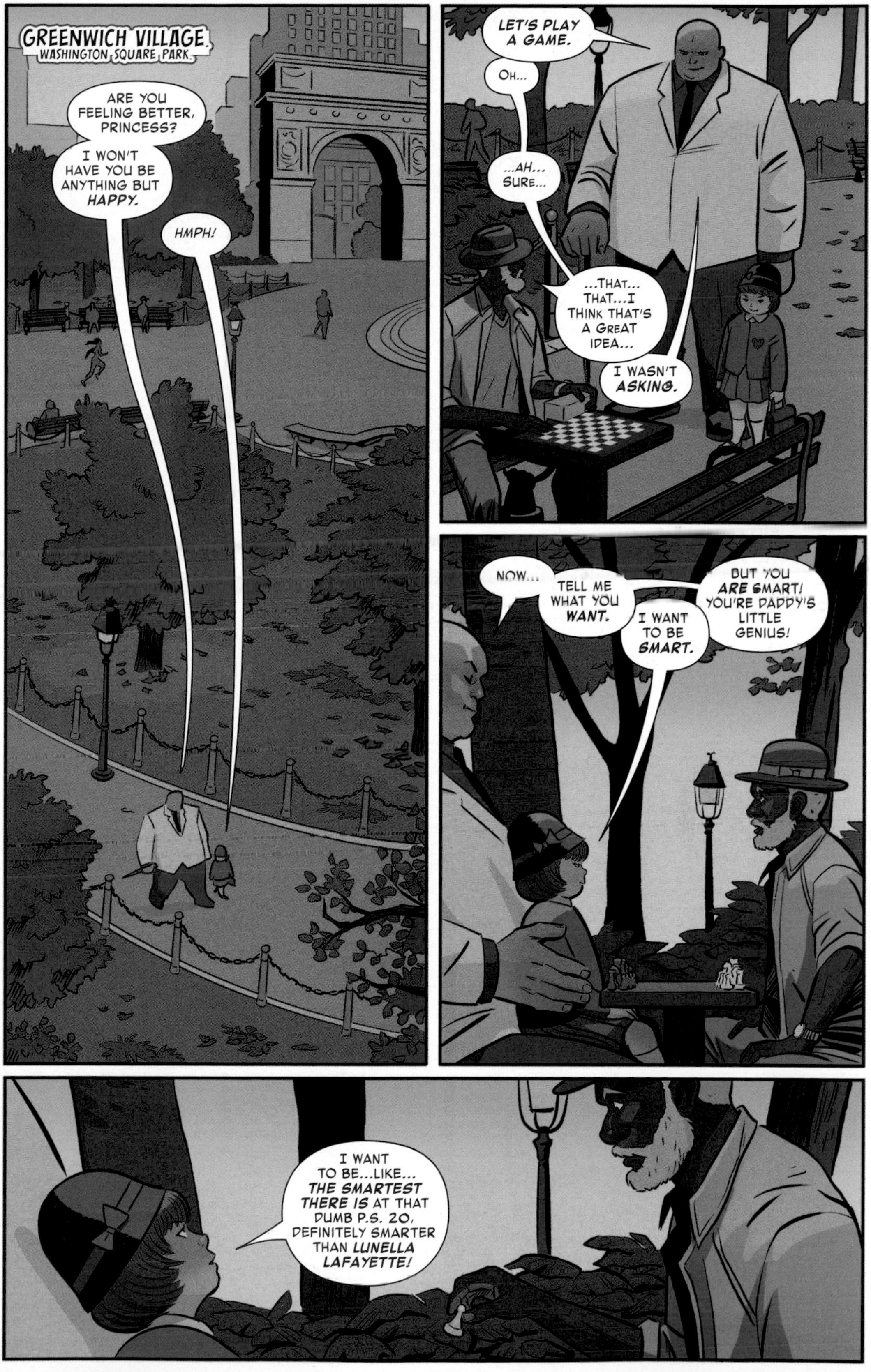
GREENWICH VILLAGE.
WASHINGTON SQUARE PARK.
ARE YOU FEELING BETTER, PRINCESS?
I WON'T HAVE YOU BE ANYTHING BUT HAPPY.
HMPH!
LET'S PLAY A GAME.
OH...
...AH... SURE...
...THAT... THAT...I THINK THAT'S A GREAT IDEA...
I WASN'T ASKING.
NOW...
TELL ME WHAT YOU WANT.
I WANT TO BE SMART.
BUT YOU ARE SMART! YOU'RE DADDY'S LITTLE GENIUS!
I WANT TO BE...LIKE... THE SMARTEST THERE IS AT THAT DUMB P.S. 20, DEFINITELY SMARTER THAN LUNELLA LAFAYETTE!

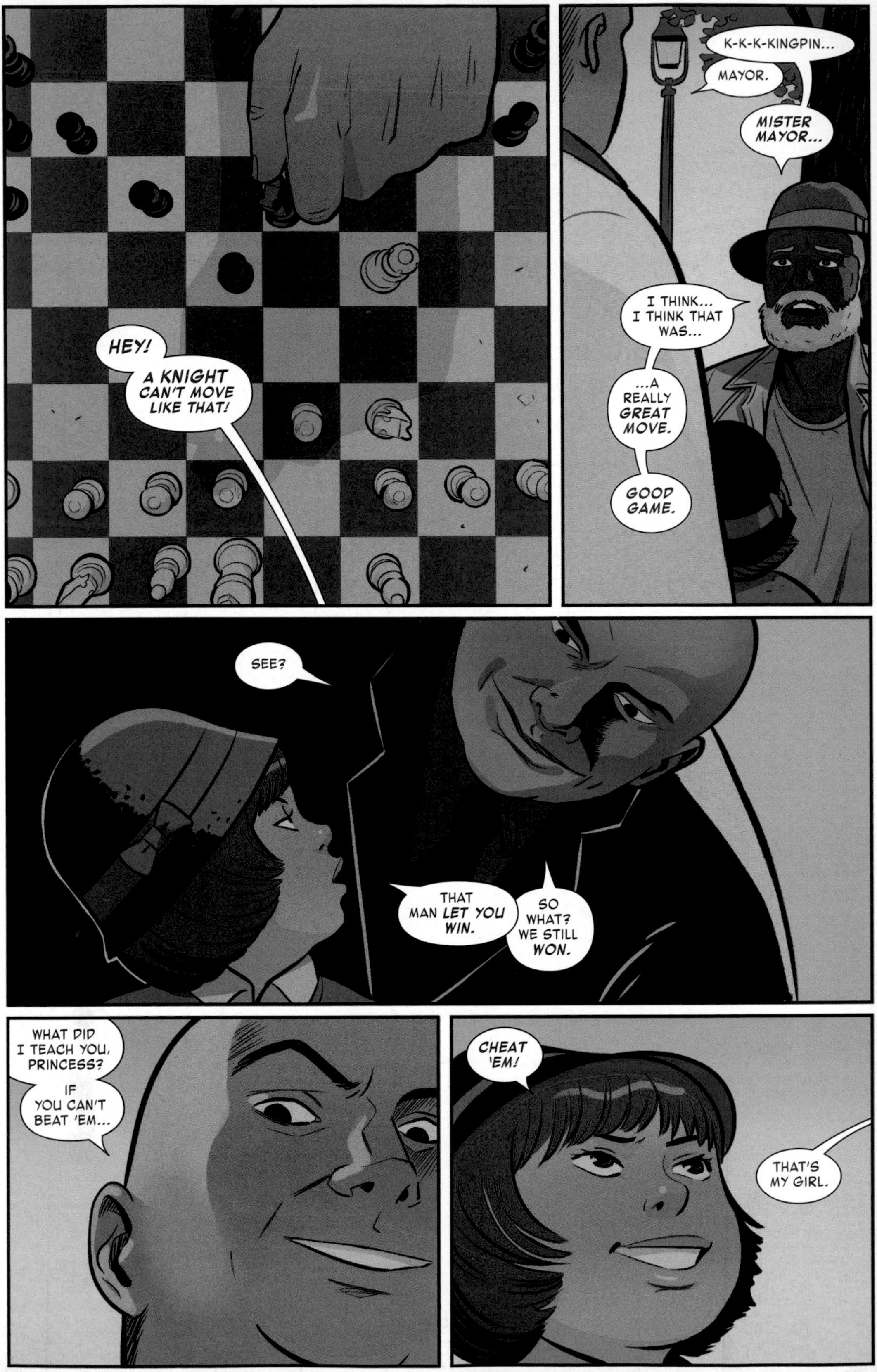
HEY!
A KNIGHT CAN'T MOVE LIKE THAT!
K-K-K-KINGPIN...
MAYOR.
MISTER MAYOR...
I THINK... I THINK THAT WAS...
...A REALLY GREAT MOVE.
GOOD GAME.
SEE?
THAT MAN LET YOU WIN.
SO WHAT? WE STILL WON.
WHAT DID I TEACH YOU, PRINCESS?
IF YOU CAN'T BEAT 'EM...
CHEAT 'EM!
THAT'S MY GIRL.

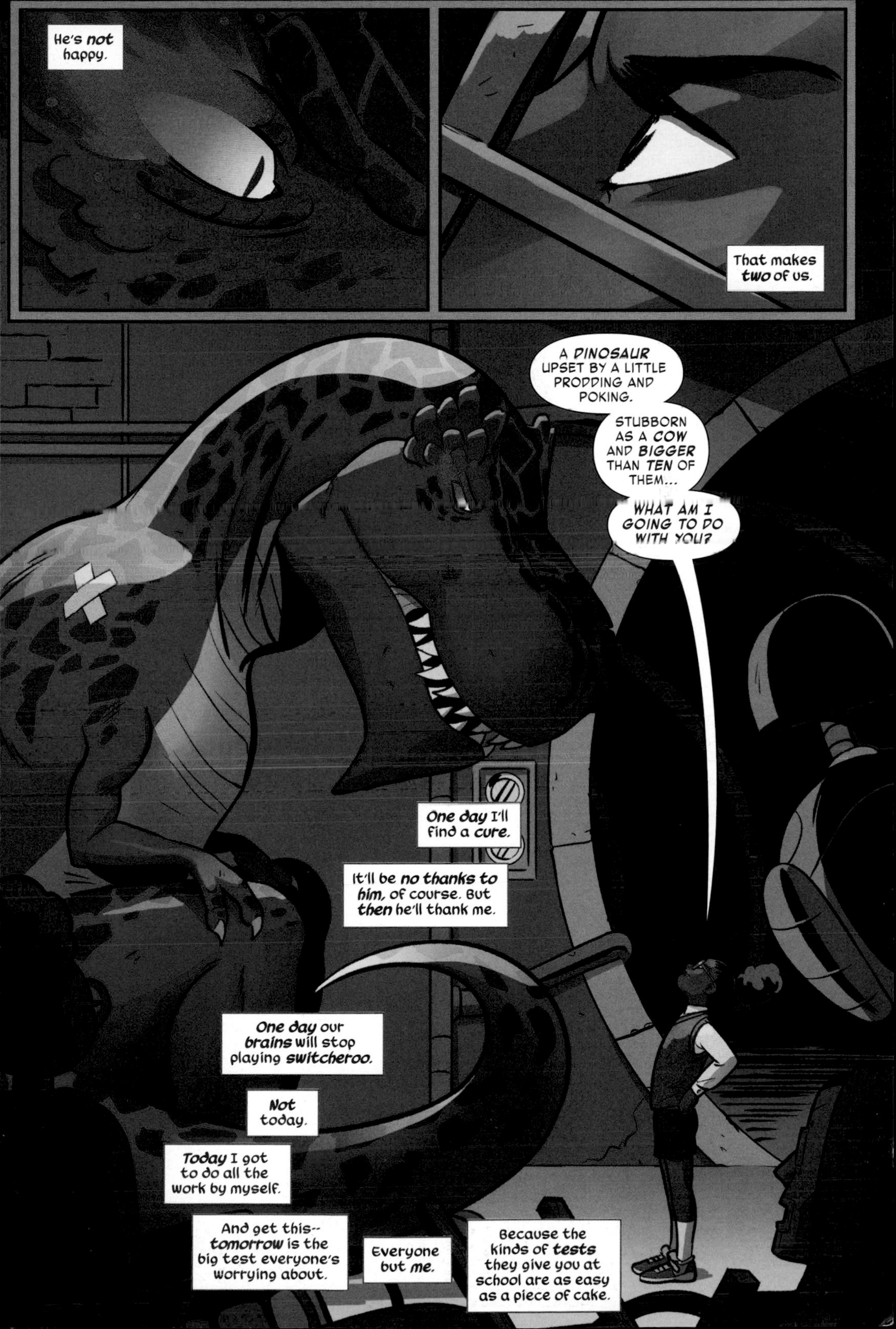
He's not happy.
That makes two of us.
A DINOSAUR UPSET BY A LITTLE PRODDING AND POKING.
STUBBORN AS A COW AND BIGGER THAN TEN OF THEM...
WHAT AM I GOING TO DO WITH YOU?
One day I'll find a cure.
It'll be no thanks to him, of course. But then he'll thank me.
One day our brains will stop playing switcheroo.
Not today.
Today I got to do all the work by myself.
And get this-- tomorrow is the big test everyone's worrying about.
Everyone but me.
Because the kinds of tests they give you at school are as easy as a piece of cake.

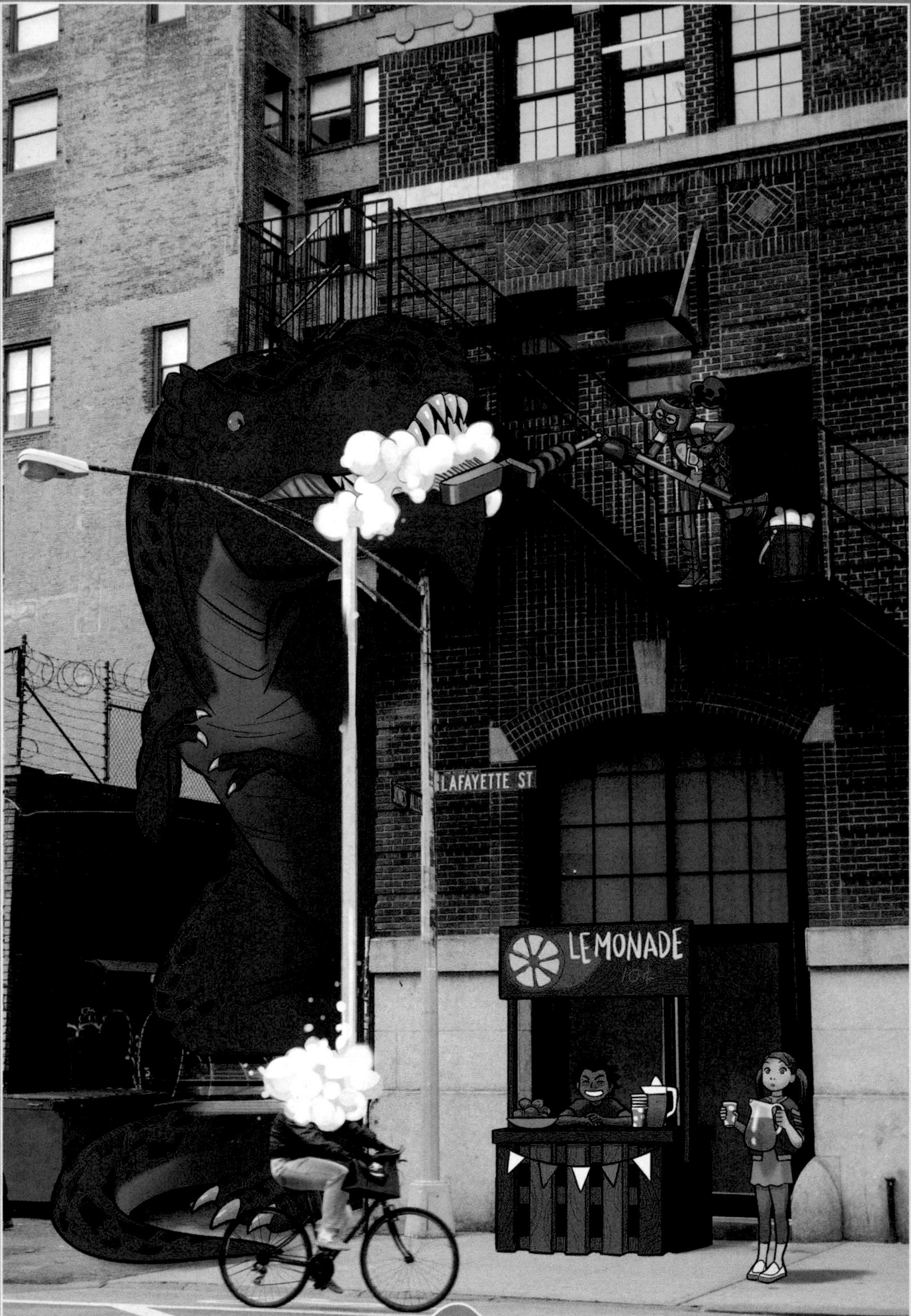
LAFAYETTE ST
LEMONADE
36

"YOU'RE NOT ASKING THE RIGHT QUESTIONS"

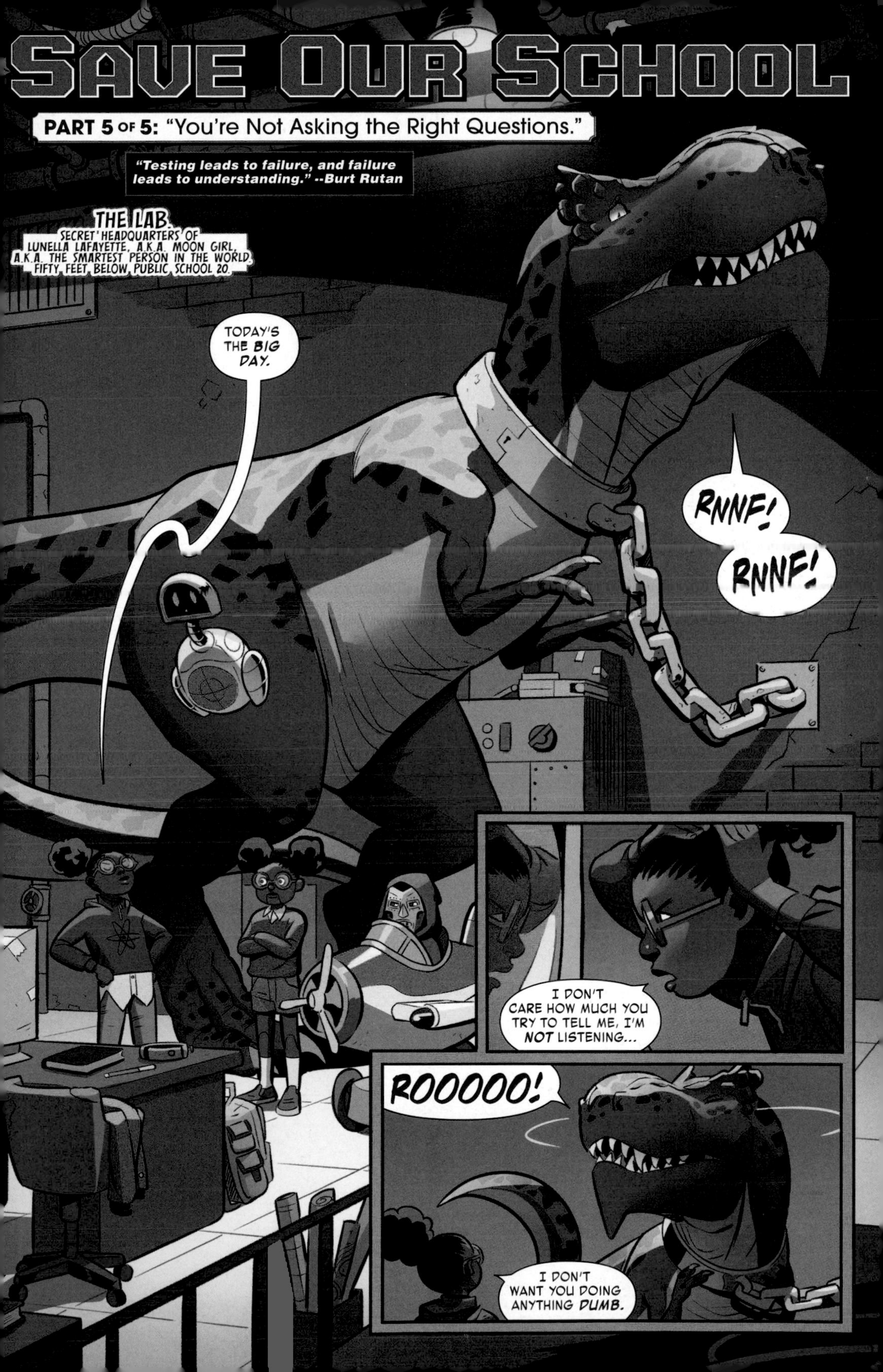
SAVE OUR SCHOOL
PART 5 OF 5: "You're Not Asking the Right Questions."
"Testing leads to failure, and failure leads to understanding." --Burt Rutan
THE LAB. SECRET HEADQUARTERS OF LUNELLA LAFAYETTE, A.K.A. MOON GIRL, A.K.A. THE SMARTEST PERSON IN THE WORLD. FIFTY FEET BELOW PUBLIC SCHOOL 20.
TODAY'S THE BIG DAY.
RNNF!
RNNF!
I DON'T CARE HOW MUCH YOU TRY TO TELL ME, I'M NOT LISTENING...
ROOOOO!
I DON'T WANT YOU DOING ANYTHING DUMB.

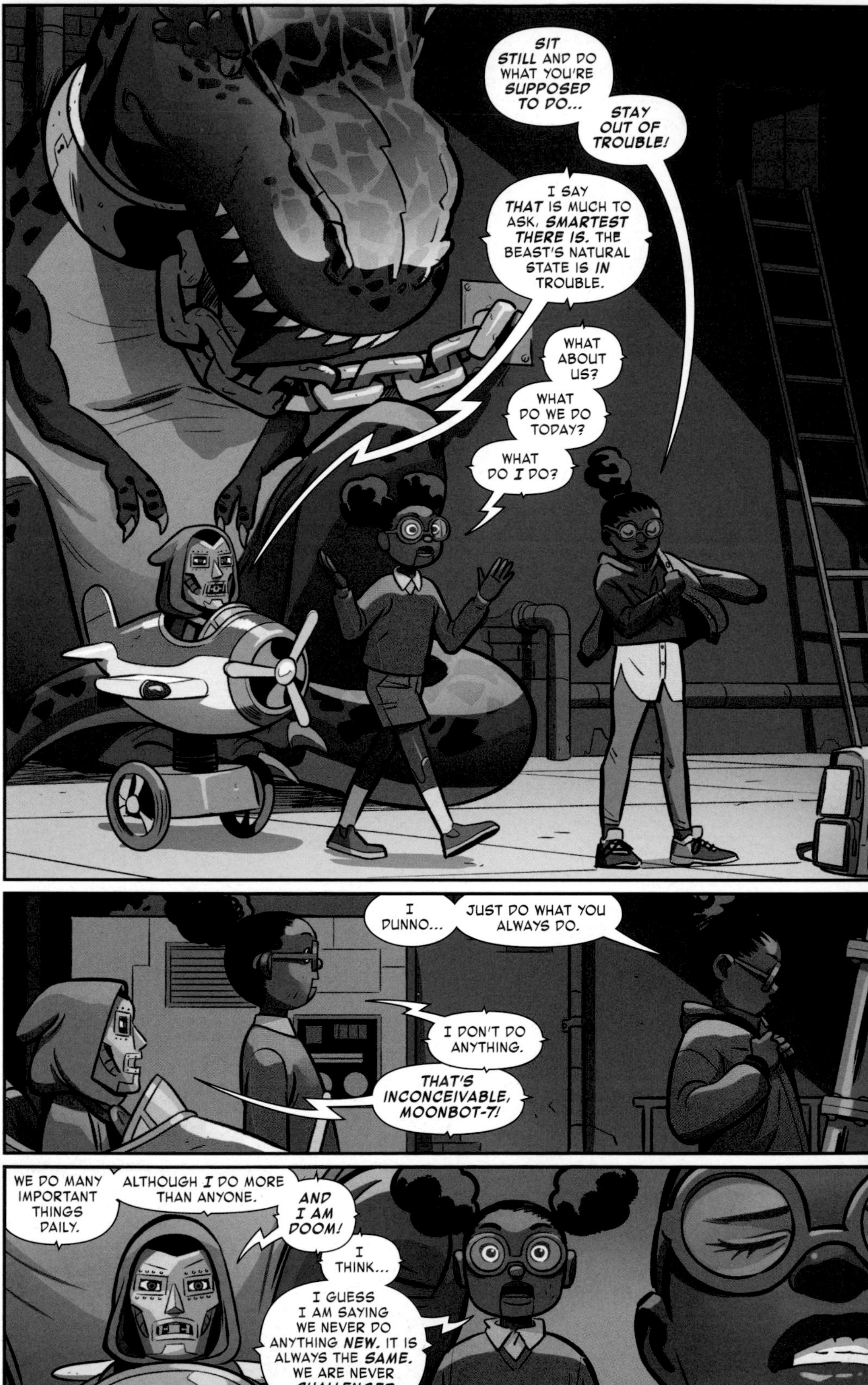

SIT STILL AND DO WHAT YOU'RE SUPPOSED TO DO...
STAY OUT OF TROUBLE!
I SAY THAT IS MUCH TO ASK, SMARTEST THERE IS. THE BEAST'S NATURAL STATE IS IN TROUBLE.
WHAT ABOUT US?
WHAT DO WE DO TODAY?
WHAT DO I DO?
I DUNNO...
JUST DO WHAT YOU ALWAYS DO.
I DON'T DO ANYTHING.
THAT'S INCONCEIVABLE, MOONBOT-7!
WE DO MANY IMPORTANT THINGS DAILY.
ALTHOUGH I DO MORE THAN ANYONE.
AND I AM DOOM!
I THINK...
I GUESS I AM SAYING WE NEVER DO ANYTHING NEW. IT IS ALWAYS THE SAME. WE ARE NEVER CHALLENGED.

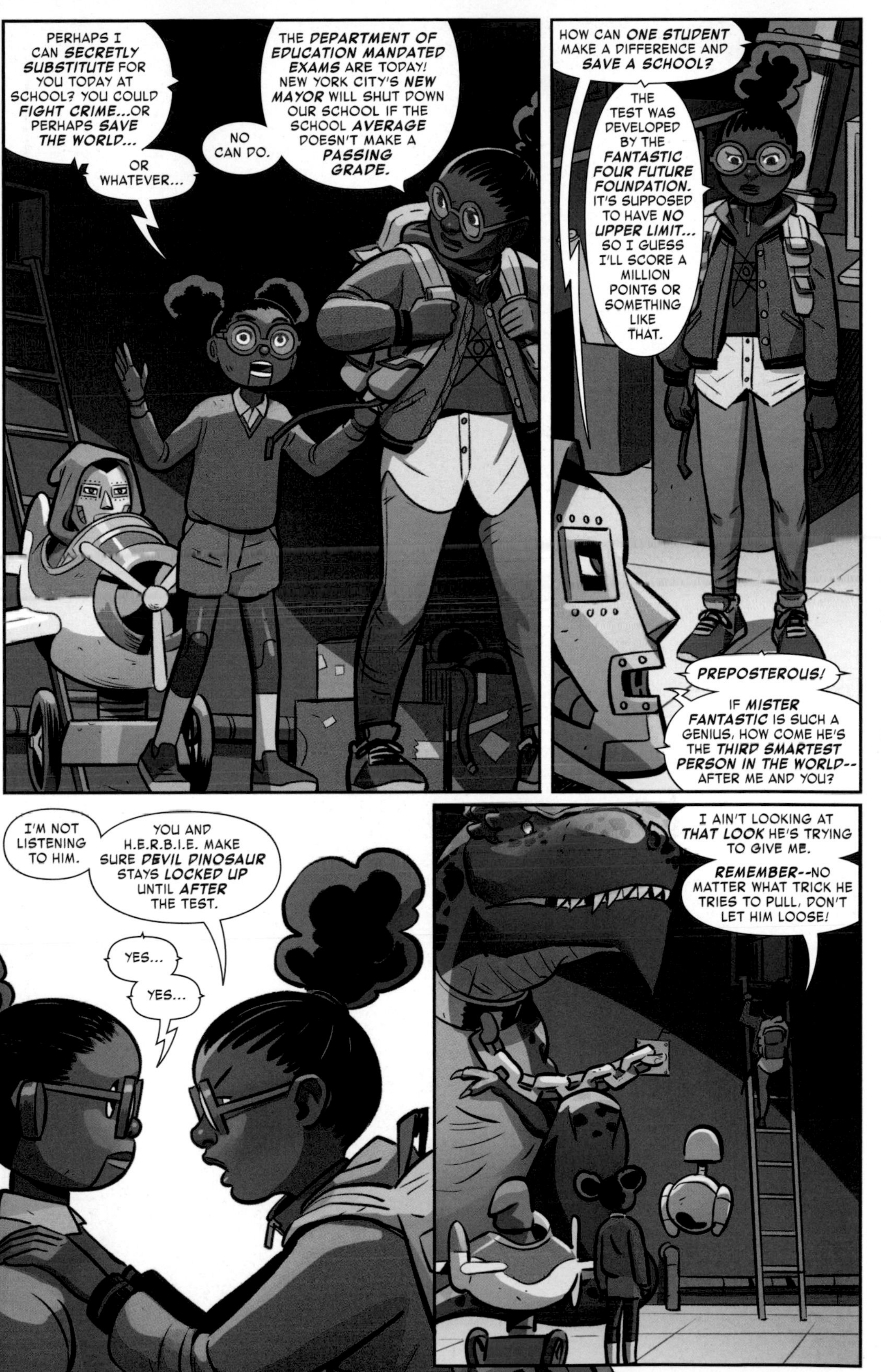
PERHAPS I CAN SECRETLY SUBSTITUTE FOR YOU TODAY AT SCHOOL? YOU COULD FIGHT CRIME...OR PERHAPS SAVE THE WORLD...
OR WHATEVER...
NO CAN DO.
THE DEPARTMENT OF EDUCATION MANDATED EXAMS ARE TODAY! NEW YORK CITY'S NEW MAYOR WILL SHUT DOWN OUR SCHOOL IF THE SCHOOL AVERAGE DOESN'T MAKE A PASSING GRADE.
HOW CAN ONE STUDENT MAKE A DIFFERENCE AND SAVE A SCHOOL?
THE TEST WAS DEVELOPED BY THE FANTASTIC FOUR FUTURE FOUNDATION. IT'S SUPPOSED TO HAVE NO UPPER LIMIT... SO I GUESS I'LL SCORE A MILLION POINTS OR SOMETHING LIKE THAT.
PREPOSTEROUS!
IF MISTER FANTASTIC IS SUCH A GENIUS, HOW COME HE'S THE THIRD SMARTEST PERSON IN THE WORLD-- AFTER ME AND YOU?
I'M NOT LISTENING TO HIM.
YOU AND H.E.R.B.I.E. MAKE SURE DEVIL DINOSAUR STAYS LOCKED UP UNTIL AFTER THE TEST.
YES...
YES...
I AIN'T LOOKING AT THAT LOOK HE'S TRYING TO GIVE ME.
REMEMBER--NO MATTER WHAT TRICK HE TRIES TO PULL, DON'T LET HIM LOOSE!

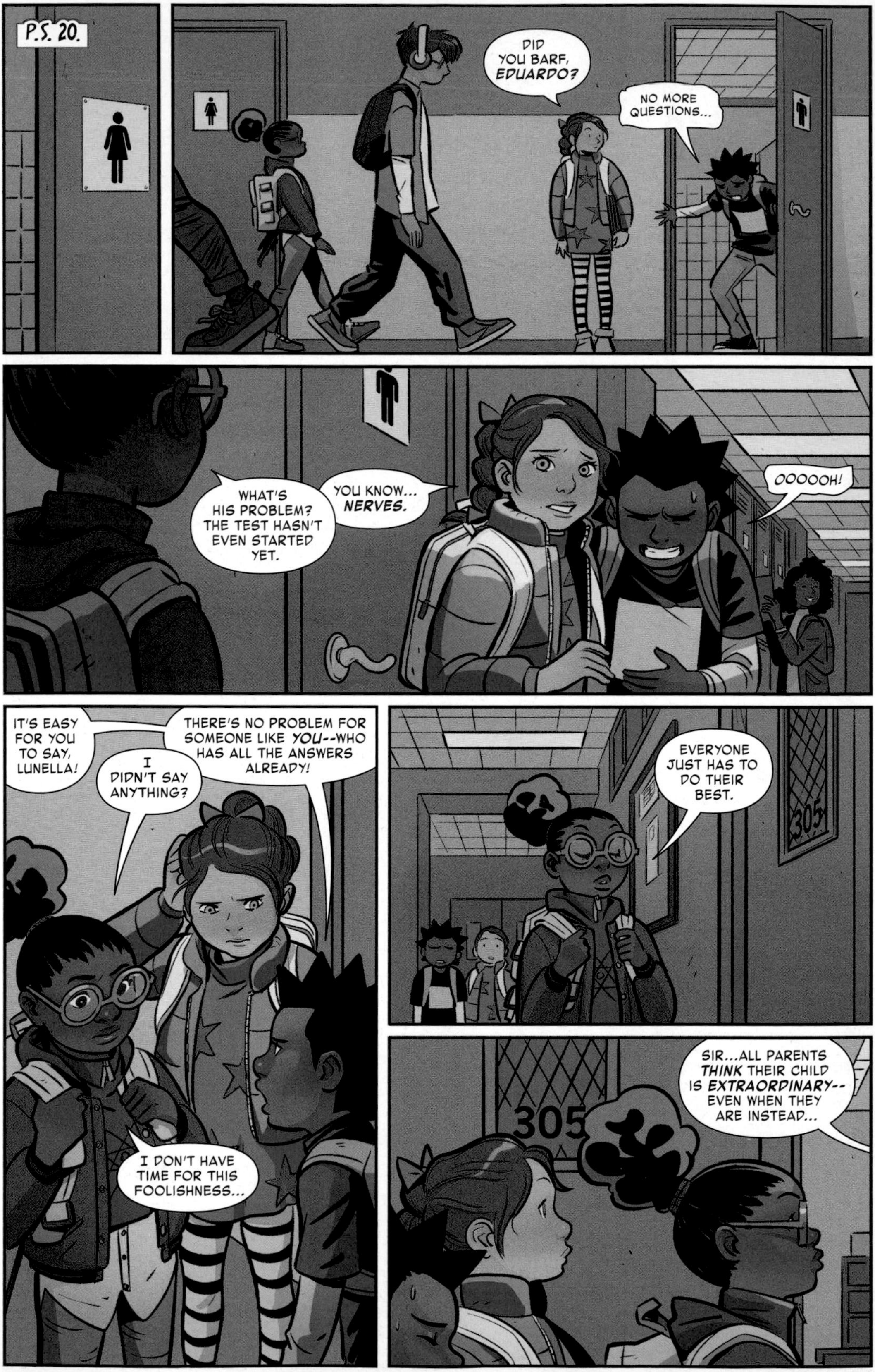
P.S. 20.
DID YOU BARF, EDUARDO?
NO MORE QUESTIONS...
WHAT'S HIS PROBLEM? THE TEST HASN'T EVEN STARTED YET.
YOU KNOW... NERVES.
OOOOOH!
IT'S EASY FOR YOU TO SAY, LUNELLA!
THERE'S NO PROBLEM FOR SOMEONE LIKE YOU--WHO HAS ALL THE ANSWERS ALREADY!
I DIDN'T SAY ANYTHING?
I DON'T HAVE TIME FOR THIS FOOLISHNESS...
EVERYONE JUST HAS TO DO THEIR BEST.
305
SIR...ALL PARENTS THINK THEIR CHILD IS EXTRAORDINARY--EVEN WHEN THEY ARE INSTEAD...
305

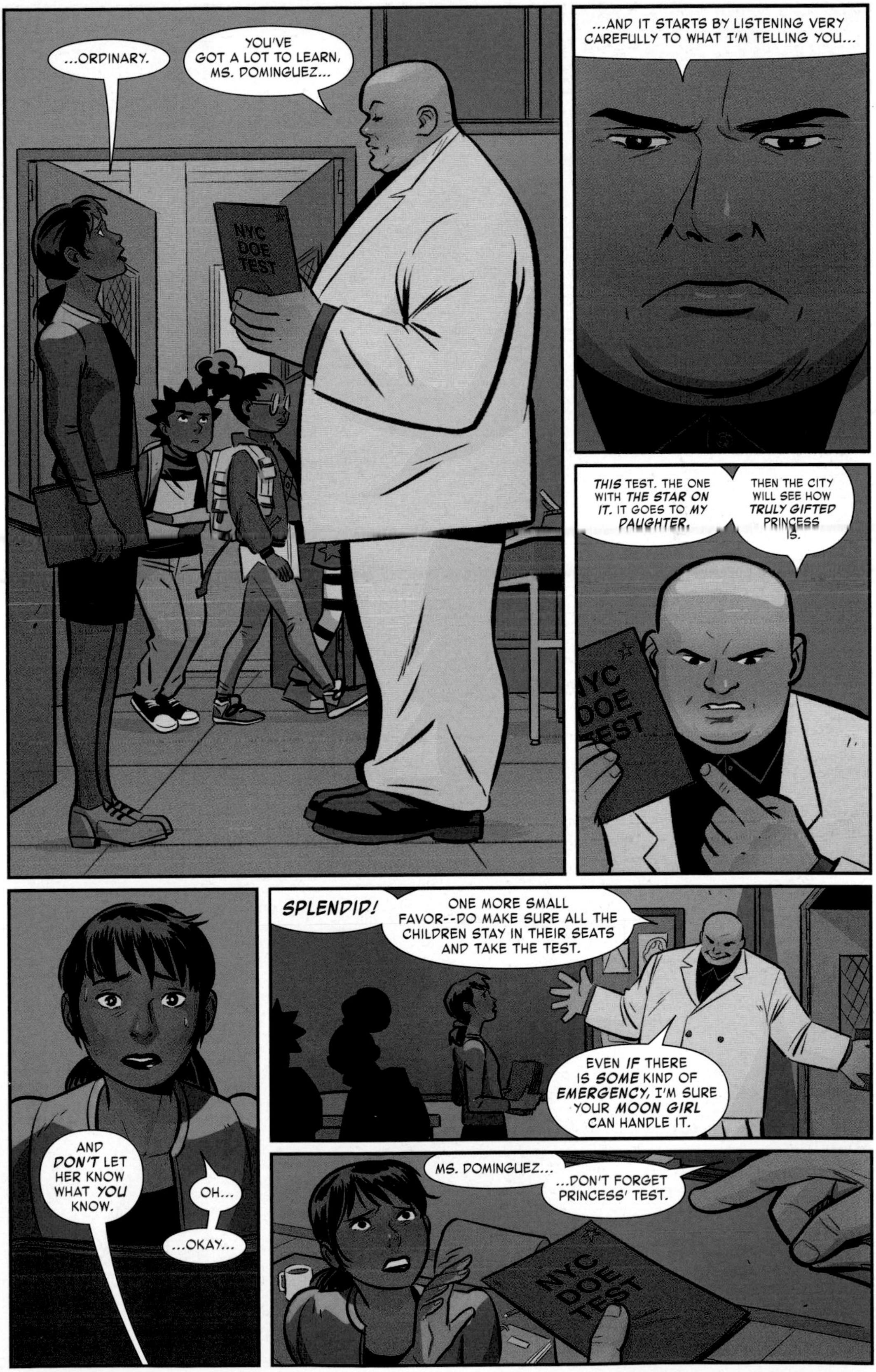
...ORDINARY.
YOU'VE GOT A LOT TO LEARN, MS. DOMINGUEZ...
NYC DOE TEST
...AND IT STARTS BY LISTENING VERY CAREFULLY TO WHAT I'M TELLING YOU...
THIS TEST. THE ONE WITH THE STAR ON IT. IT GOES TO MY DAUGHTER.
THEN THE CITY WILL SEE HOW TRULY GIFTED PRINCESS IS.
NYC DOE TEST
AND DON'T LET HER KNOW WHAT YOU KNOW.
OH...
...OKAY...
SPLENDID!
ONE MORE SMALL FAVOR--DO MAKE SURE ALL THE CHILDREN STAY IN THEIR SEATS AND TAKE THE TEST.
EVEN IF THERE IS SOME KIND OF EMERGENCY, I'M SURE YOUR MOON GIRL CAN HANDLE IT.
MS. DOMINGUEZ...
...DON'T FORGET PRINCESS' TEST.
NYC DOE TEST

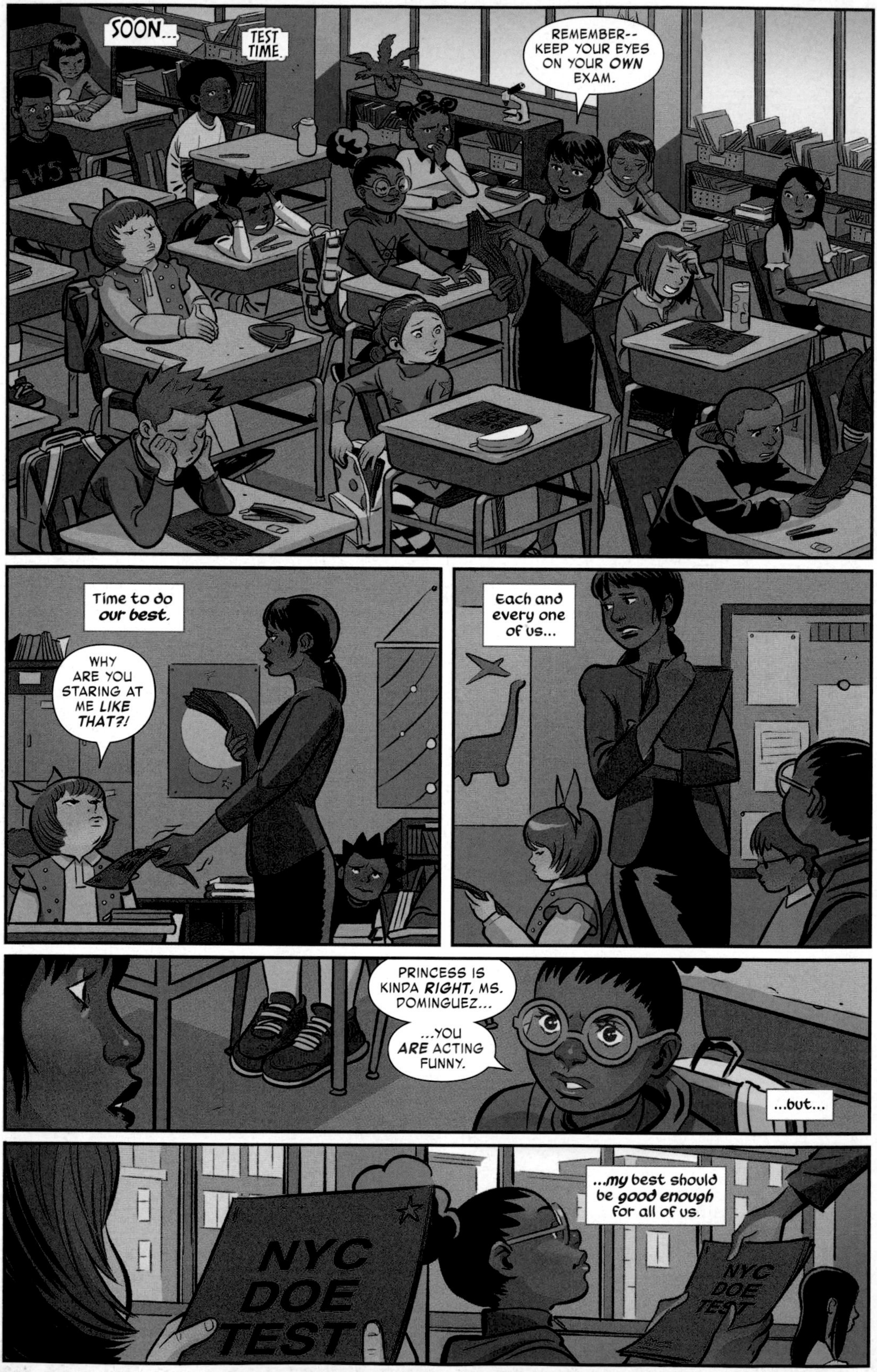
SOON...
TEST TIME.
REMEMBER-- KEEP YOUR EYES ON YOUR OWN EXAM.
Time to do our best.
WHY ARE YOU STARING AT ME LIKE THAT?!
Each and every one of us...
PRINCESS IS KINDA RIGHT, MS. DOMINGUEZ...
...YOU ARE ACTING FUNNY.
...but...
...my best should be good enough for all of us.
NYC DOE TEST
NYC DOE TEST

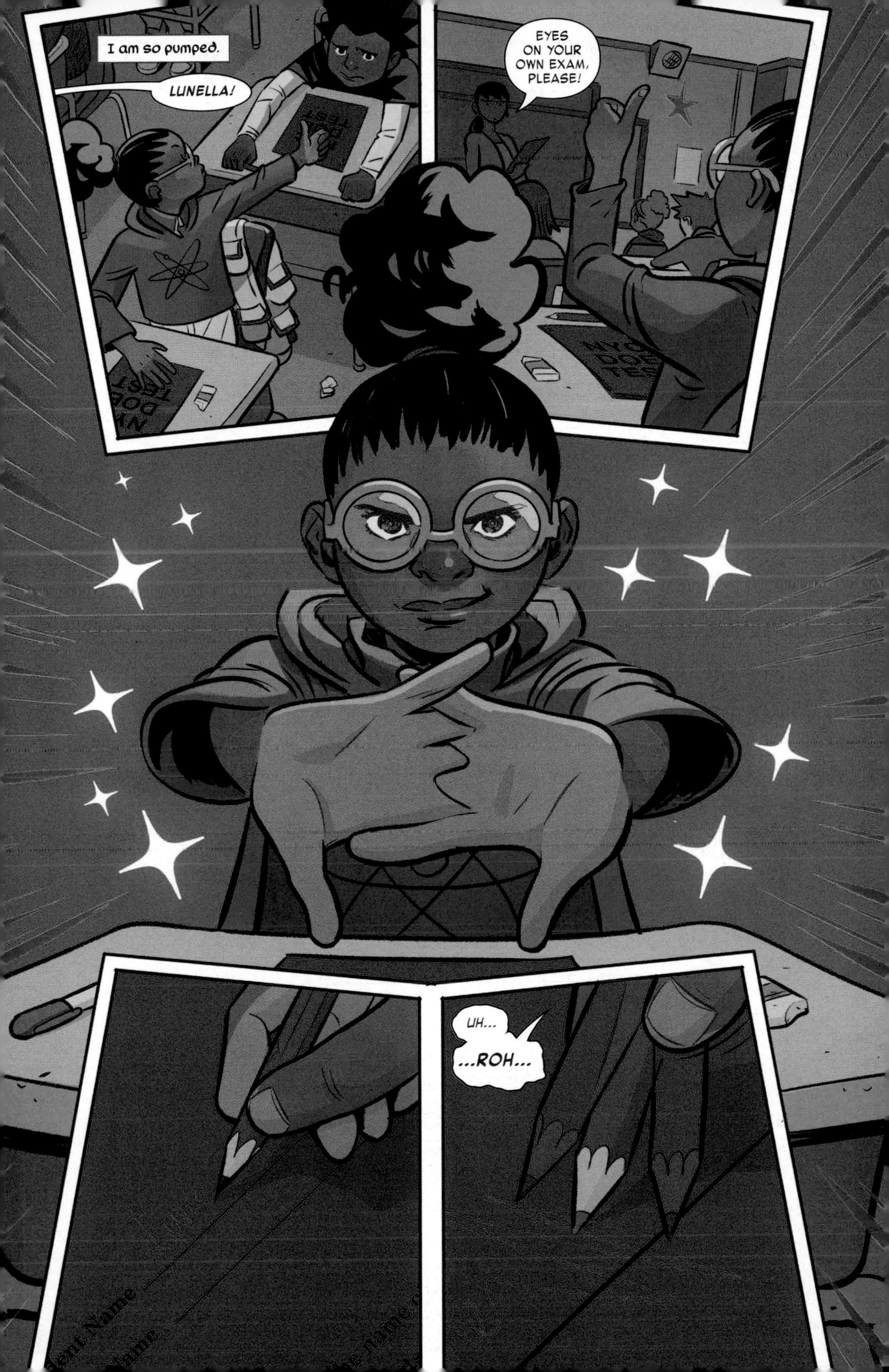
I am so pumped.
LUNELLA!
EYES ON YOUR OWN EXAM, PLEASE!
UH...
...ROH...

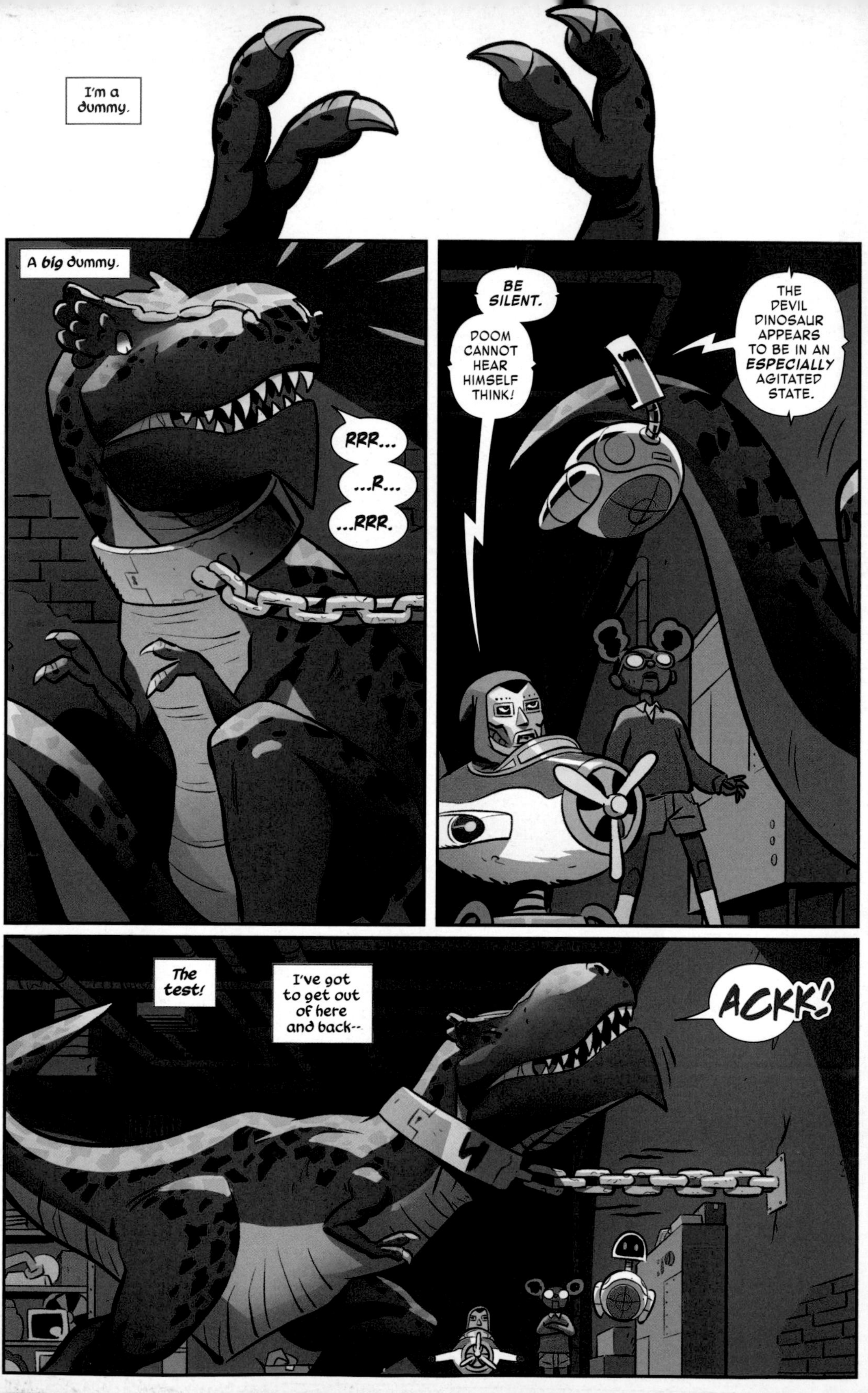
I'm a dummy.
A *big* dummy.
RRR...
...R...
...RRR.
BE SILENT.
DOOM CANNOT HEAR HIMSELF THINK!
THE DEVIL DINOSAUR APPEARS TO BE IN AN *ESPECIALLY* AGITATED STATE.
The test!
I've got to get out of here and back--
ACKK!

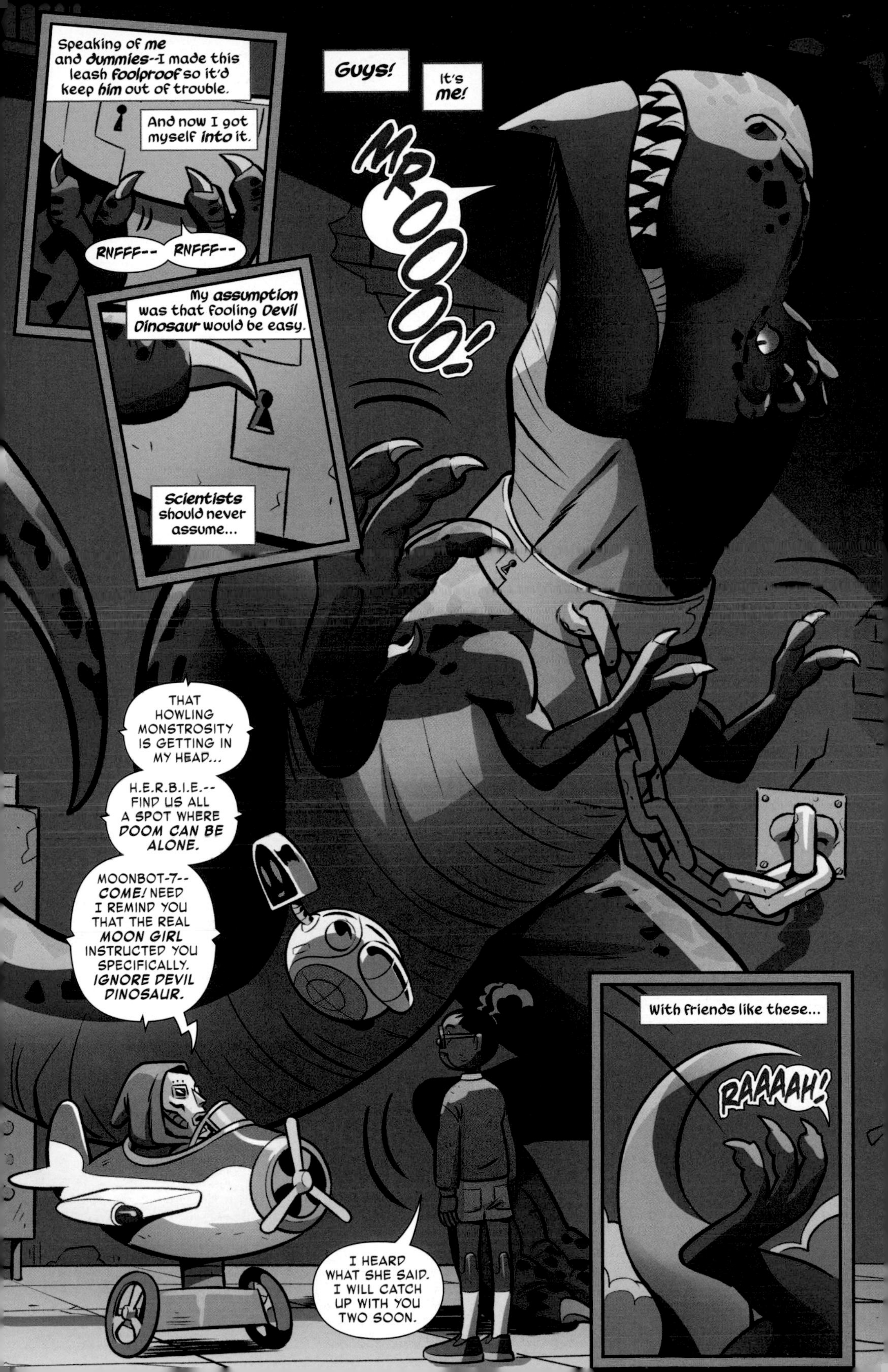

Speaking of me and dummies--I made this leash foolproof so it'd keep him out of trouble.
And now I got myself into it.
RNFFF-- RNFFF--
My assumption was that fooling Devil Dinosaur would be easy.
Scientists should never assume...
Guys!
It's me!
MROOOOO!
THAT HOWLING MONSTROSITY IS GETTING IN MY HEAD...
H.E.R.B.I.E.--FIND US ALL A SPOT WHERE DOOM CAN BE ALONE.
MOONBOT-7--COME! NEED I REMIND YOU THAT THE REAL MOON GIRL INSTRUCTED YOU SPECIFICALLY. IGNORE DEVIL DINOSAUR.
I HEARD WHAT SHE SAID. I WILL CATCH UP WITH YOU TWO SOON.
With friends like these...
RAAAAH!

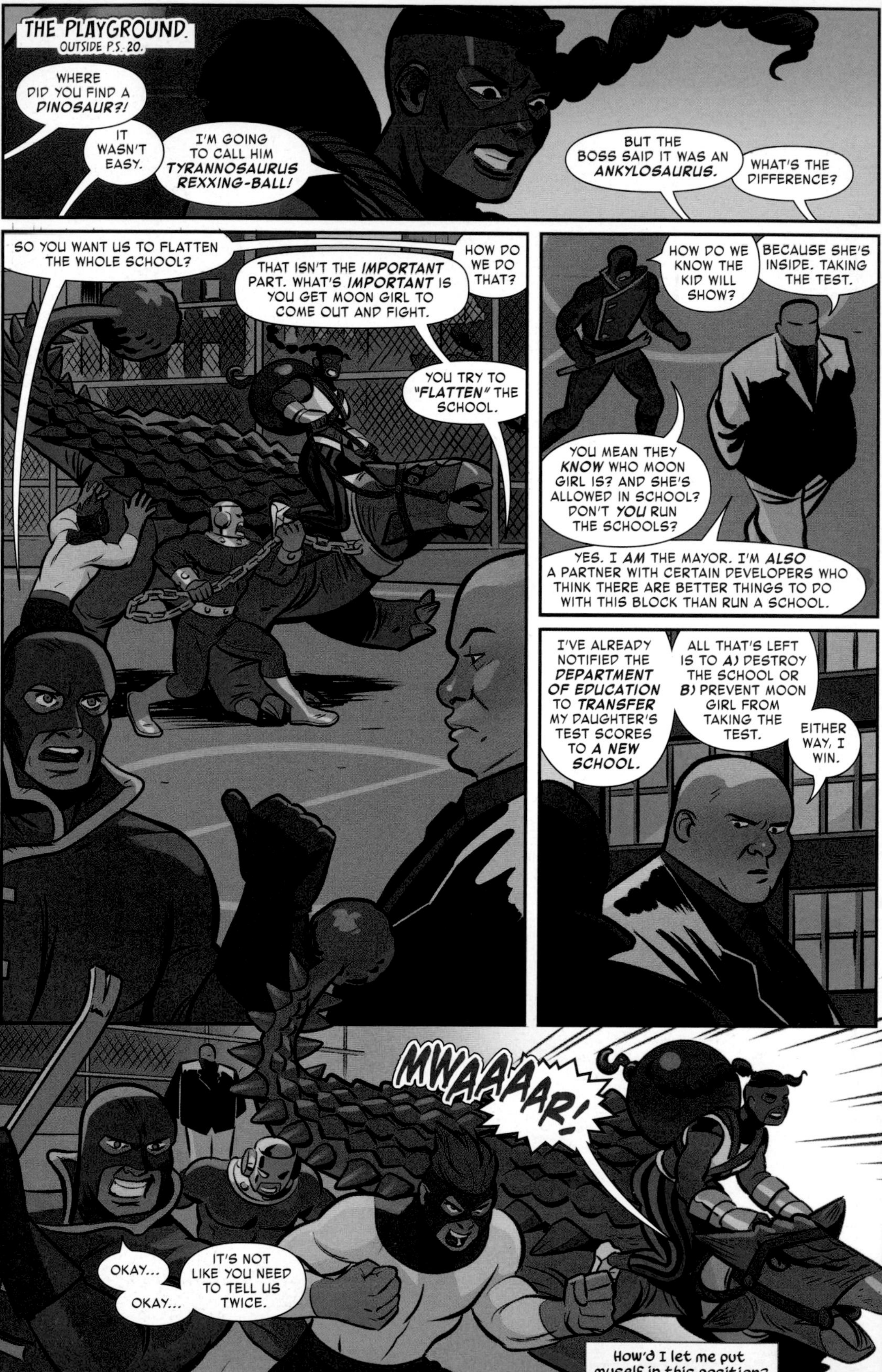
THE PLAYGROUND.
OUTSIDE P.S. 20.
WHERE DID YOU FIND A DINOSAUR?!
IT WASN'T EASY.
I'M GOING TO CALL HIM TYRANNOSAURUS REXXING-BALL!
BUT THE BOSS SAID IT WAS AN ANKYLOSAURUS.
WHAT'S THE DIFFERENCE?
SO YOU WANT US TO FLATTEN THE WHOLE SCHOOL?
HOW DO WE DO THAT?
THAT ISN'T THE IMPORTANT PART. WHAT'S IMPORTANT IS YOU GET MOON GIRL TO COME OUT AND FIGHT.
YOU TRY TO "FLATTEN" THE SCHOOL.
HOW DO WE KNOW THE KID WILL SHOW?
BECAUSE SHE'S INSIDE. TAKING THE TEST.
YOU MEAN THEY KNOW WHO MOON GIRL IS? AND SHE'S ALLOWED IN SCHOOL? DON'T YOU RUN THE SCHOOLS?
YES. I AM THE MAYOR. I'M ALSO A PARTNER WITH CERTAIN DEVELOPERS WHO THINK THERE ARE BETTER THINGS TO DO WITH THIS BLOCK THAN RUN A SCHOOL.
I'VE ALREADY NOTIFIED THE DEPARTMENT OF EDUCATION TO TRANSFER MY DAUGHTER'S TEST SCORES TO A NEW SCHOOL.
ALL THAT'S LEFT IS TO A) DESTROY THE SCHOOL OR B) PREVENT MOON GIRL FROM TAKING THE TEST.
EITHER WAY, I WIN.
MWAAAAAR!
OKAY...
OKAY...
IT'S NOT LIKE YOU NEED TO TELL US TWICE.
How'd I let me put myself in this position?

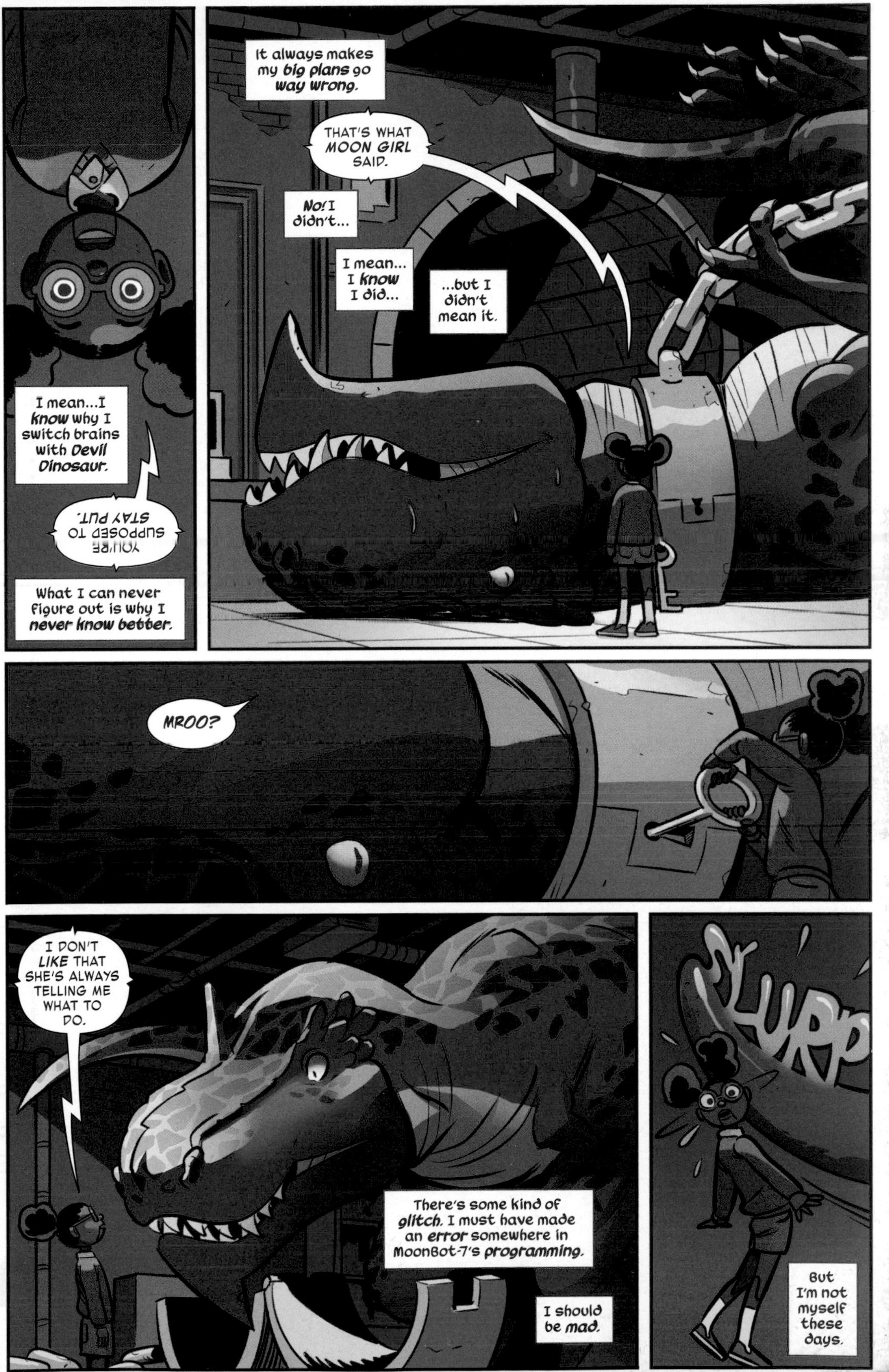

I mean...I know why I switch brains with Devil Dinosaur.
YOU'RE SUPPOSED TO STAY PUT.
What I can never figure out is why I never know better.
It always makes my big plans go way wrong.
THAT'S WHAT MOON GIRL SAID.
No! I didn't...
I mean... I know I did...
...but I didn't mean it.
MROO?
I DON'T LIKE THAT SHE'S ALWAYS TELLING ME WHAT TO DO.
There's some kind of glitch. I must have made an error somewhere in MoonBot-7's programming.
I should be mad.
SLURP
But I'm not myself these days.

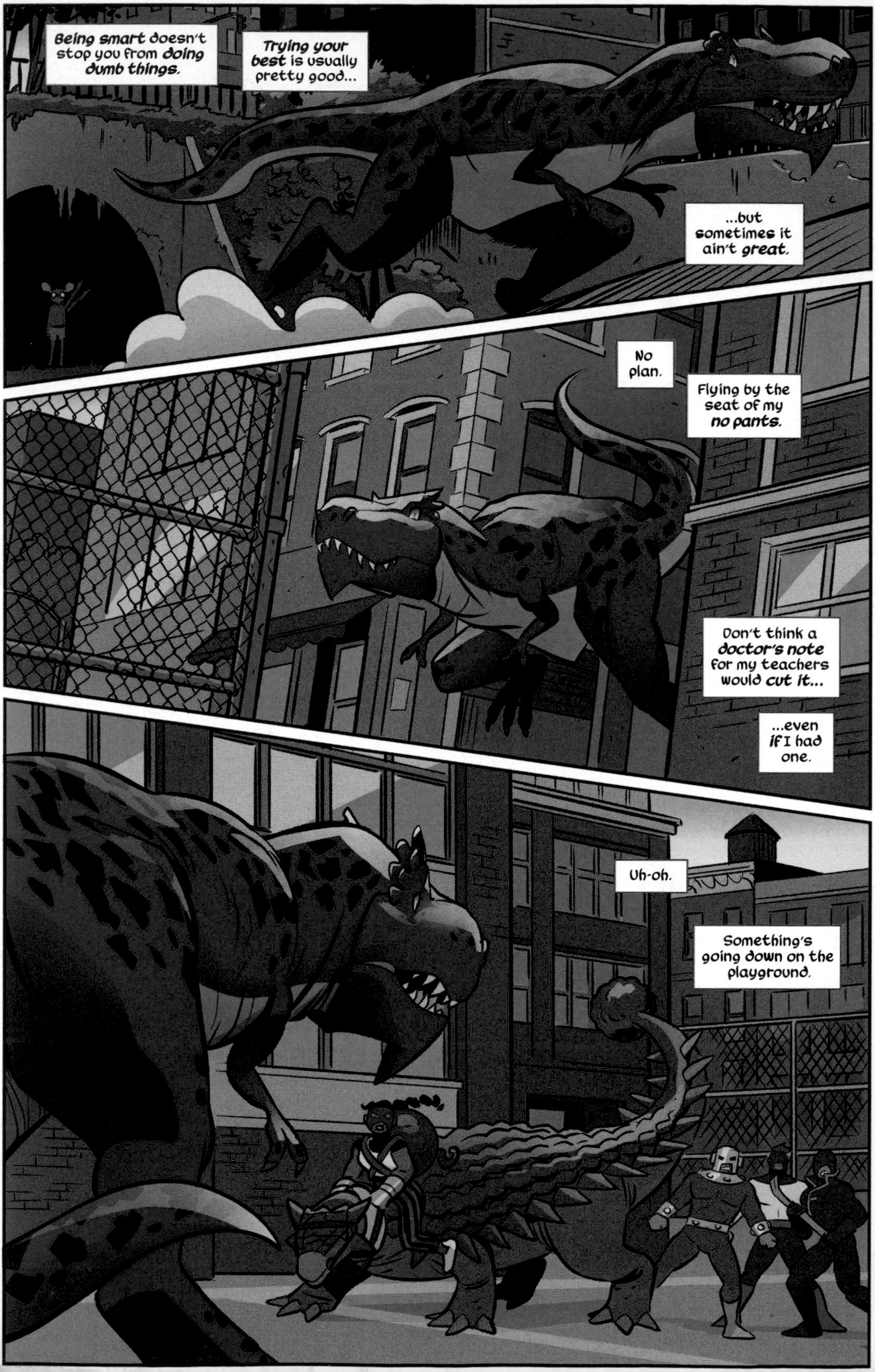
Being smart doesn't stop you from doing dumb things.
Trying your best is usually pretty good...
...but sometimes it ain't great.
No plan.
Flying by the seat of my no pants.
Don't think a doctor's note for my teachers would cut it...
...even if I had one.
Uh-oh.
Something's going down on the playground.

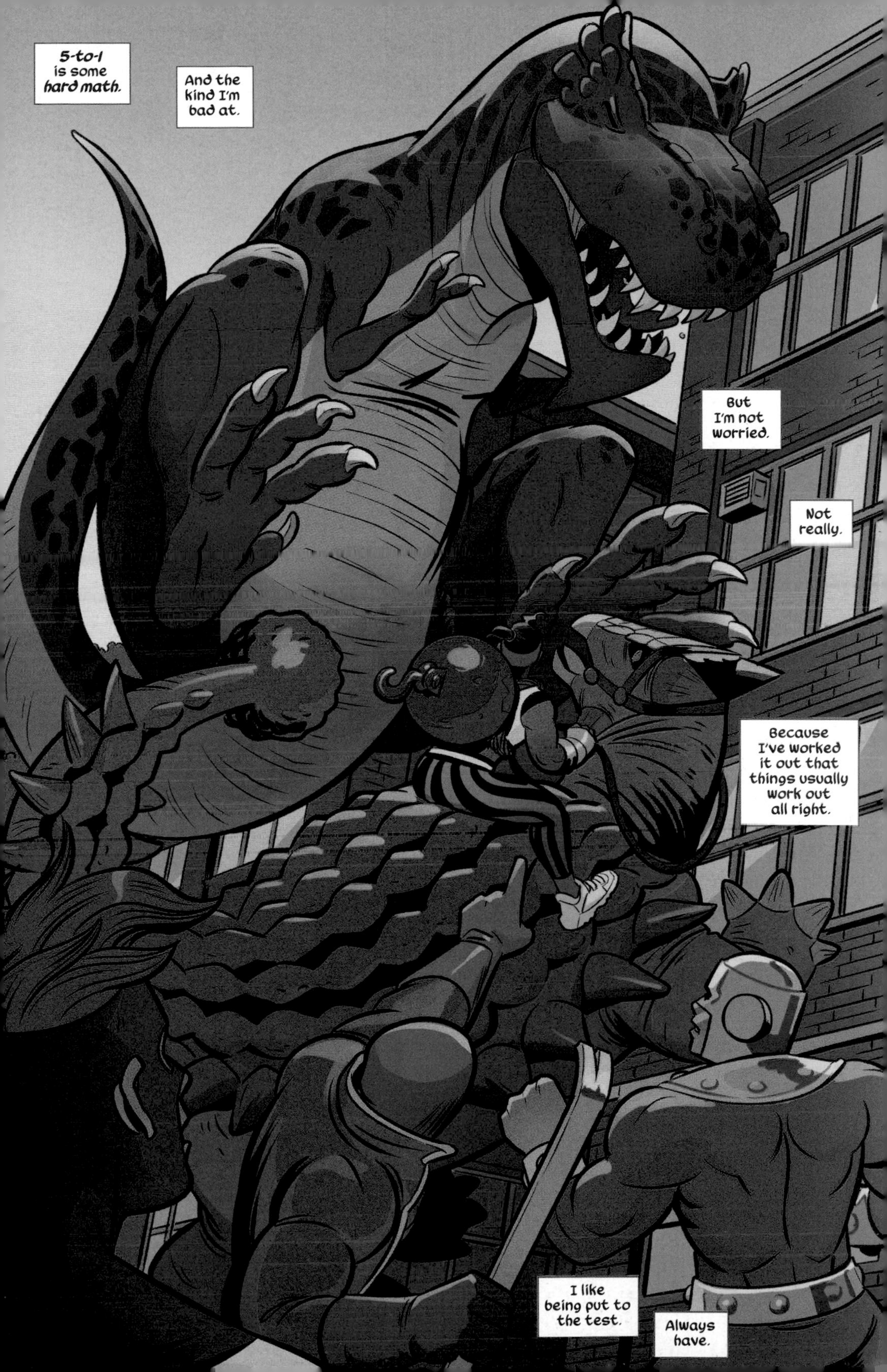
5-to-1 is some *hard math.*
And the kind I'm bad at.
But I'm not worried.
Not really.
Because I've worked it out that things usually work out all right.
I like being put to the test.
Always have.

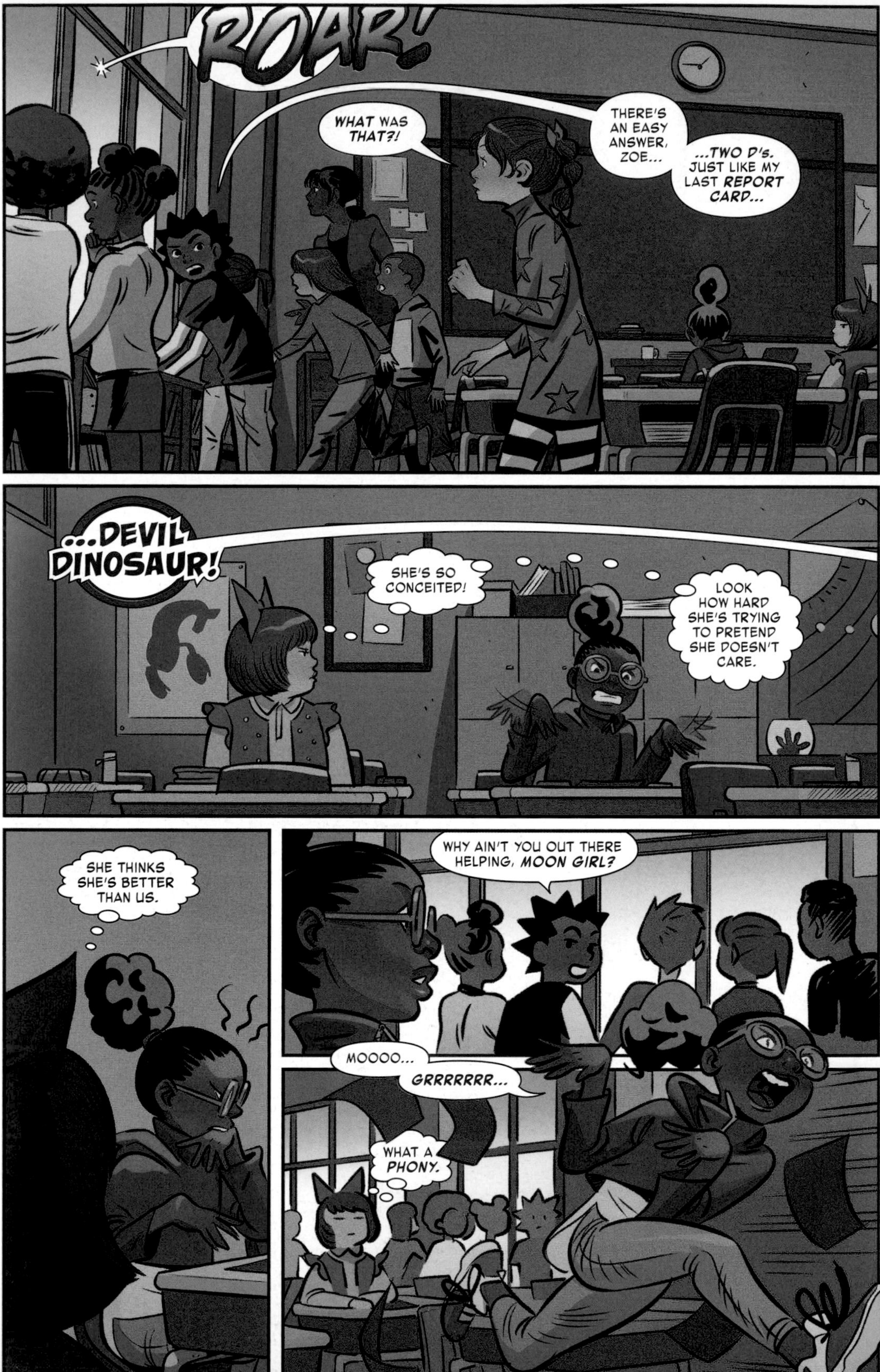
ROAR!
WHAT WAS THAT?!
THERE'S AN EASY ANSWER, ZOE...
...TWO D's. JUST LIKE MY LAST REPORT CARD...
...DEVIL DINOSAUR!
SHE'S SO CONCEITED!
LOOK HOW HARD SHE'S TRYING TO PRETEND SHE DOESN'T CARE.
SHE THINKS SHE'S BETTER THAN US.
WHY AIN'T YOU OUT THERE HELPING, MOON GIRL?
MOOOO...
GRRRRRRR...
WHAT A PHONY.

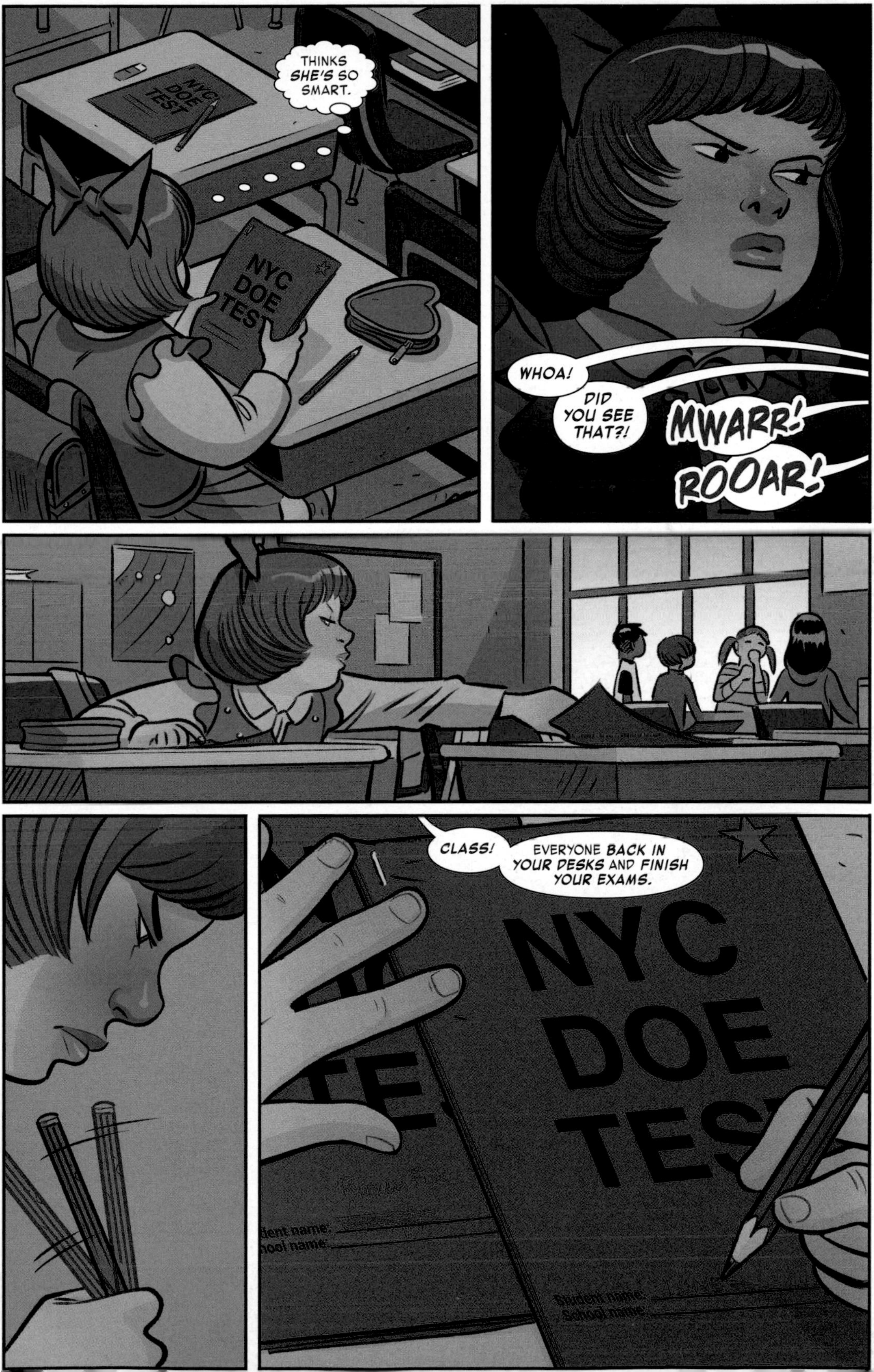
THINKS SHE'S SO SMART.
NYC DOE TEST
NYC DOE TEST
WHOA!
DID YOU SEE THAT?!
MWARR!
ROOAR!
CLASS!
EVERYONE BACK IN YOUR DESKS AND FINISH YOUR EXAMS.
NYC DOE TEST
Student name:
School name:

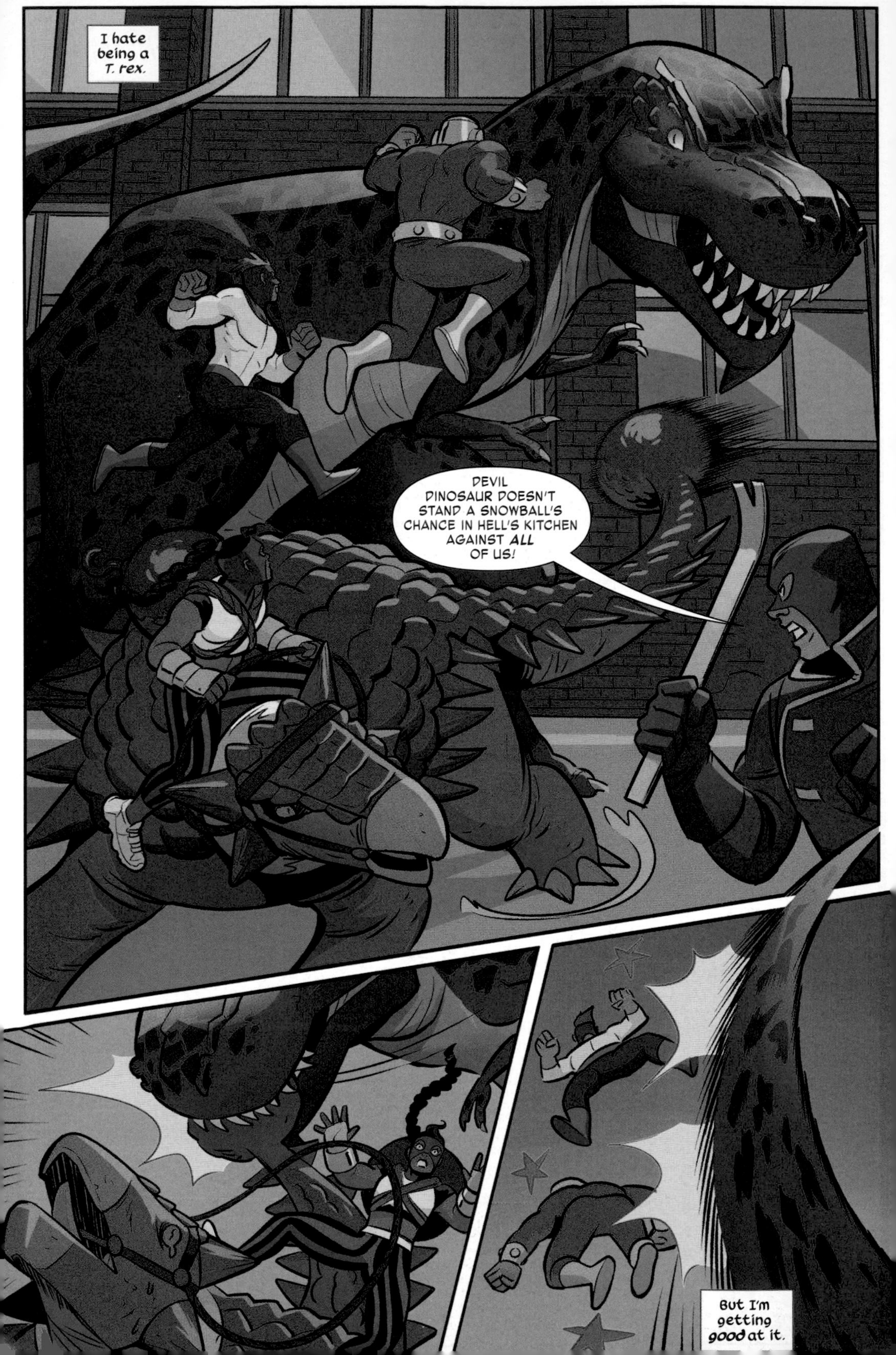
I hate being a *T. rex.*
DEVIL DINOSAUR DOESN'T STAND A SNOWBALL'S CHANCE IN HELL'S KITCHEN AGAINST ***ALL*** OF US!
But I'm getting ***good*** at it.

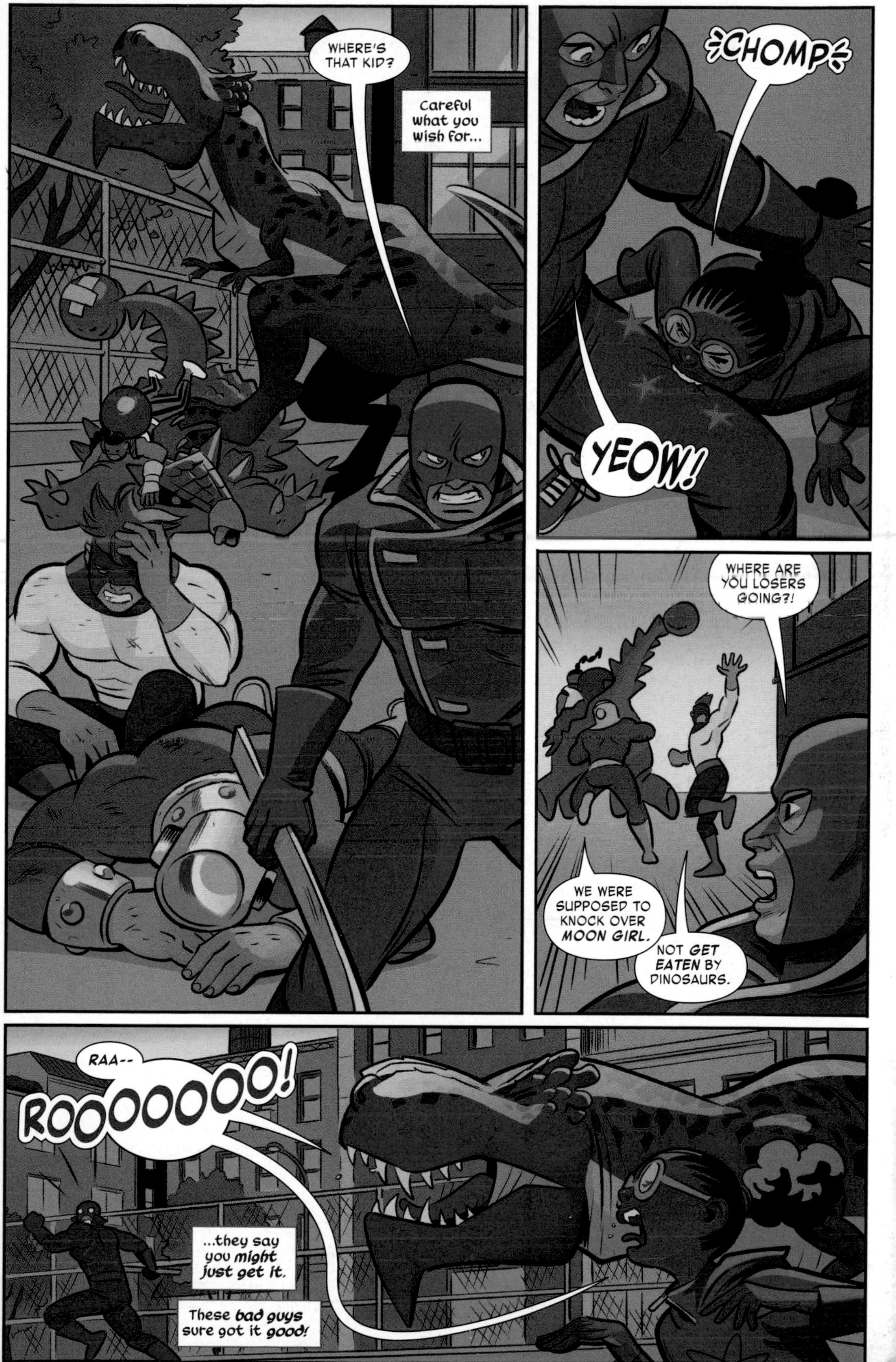

WHERE'S THAT KID?
Careful what you wish for...
CHOMP
YEOW!
WHERE ARE YOU LOSERS GOING?!
WE WERE SUPPOSED TO KNOCK OVER MOON GIRL.
NOT GET EATEN BY DINOSAURS.
RAA--
ROOOOOOO!
...they say you might just get it.
These bad guys sure got it good!

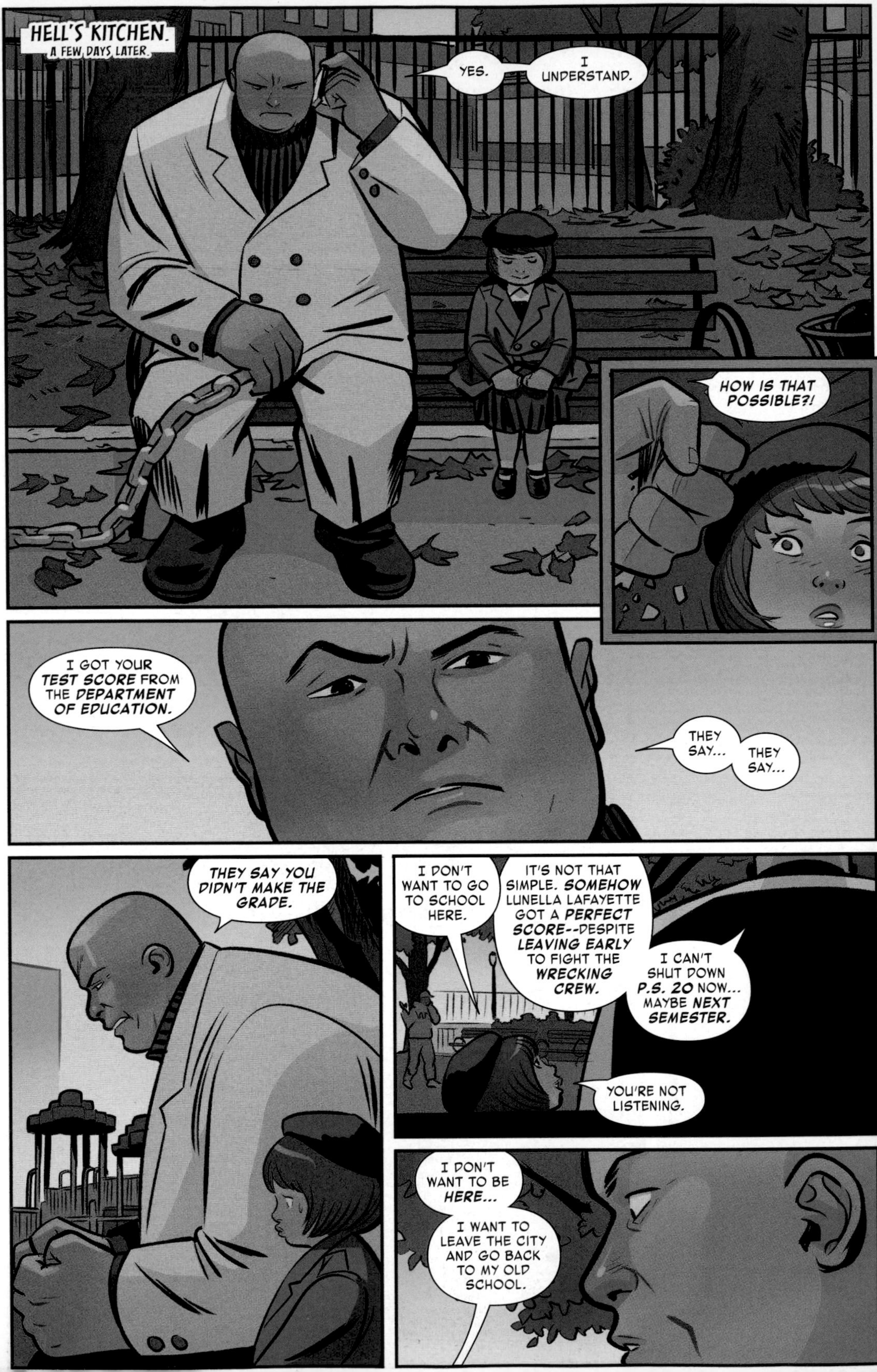

HELL'S KITCHEN.
A FEW DAYS LATER.
YES.
I UNDERSTAND.
HOW IS THAT POSSIBLE?!
I GOT YOUR TEST SCORE FROM THE DEPARTMENT OF EDUCATION.
THEY SAY...
THEY SAY...
THEY SAY YOU DIDN'T MAKE THE GRADE.
I DON'T WANT TO GO TO SCHOOL HERE.
IT'S NOT THAT SIMPLE. SOMEHOW LUNELLA LAFAYETTE GOT A PERFECT SCORE--DESPITE LEAVING EARLY TO FIGHT THE WRECKING CREW.
I CAN'T SHUT DOWN P.S. 20 NOW... MAYBE NEXT SEMESTER.
YOU'RE NOT LISTENING.
I DON'T WANT TO BE HERE...
I WANT TO LEAVE THE CITY AND GO BACK TO MY OLD SCHOOL.

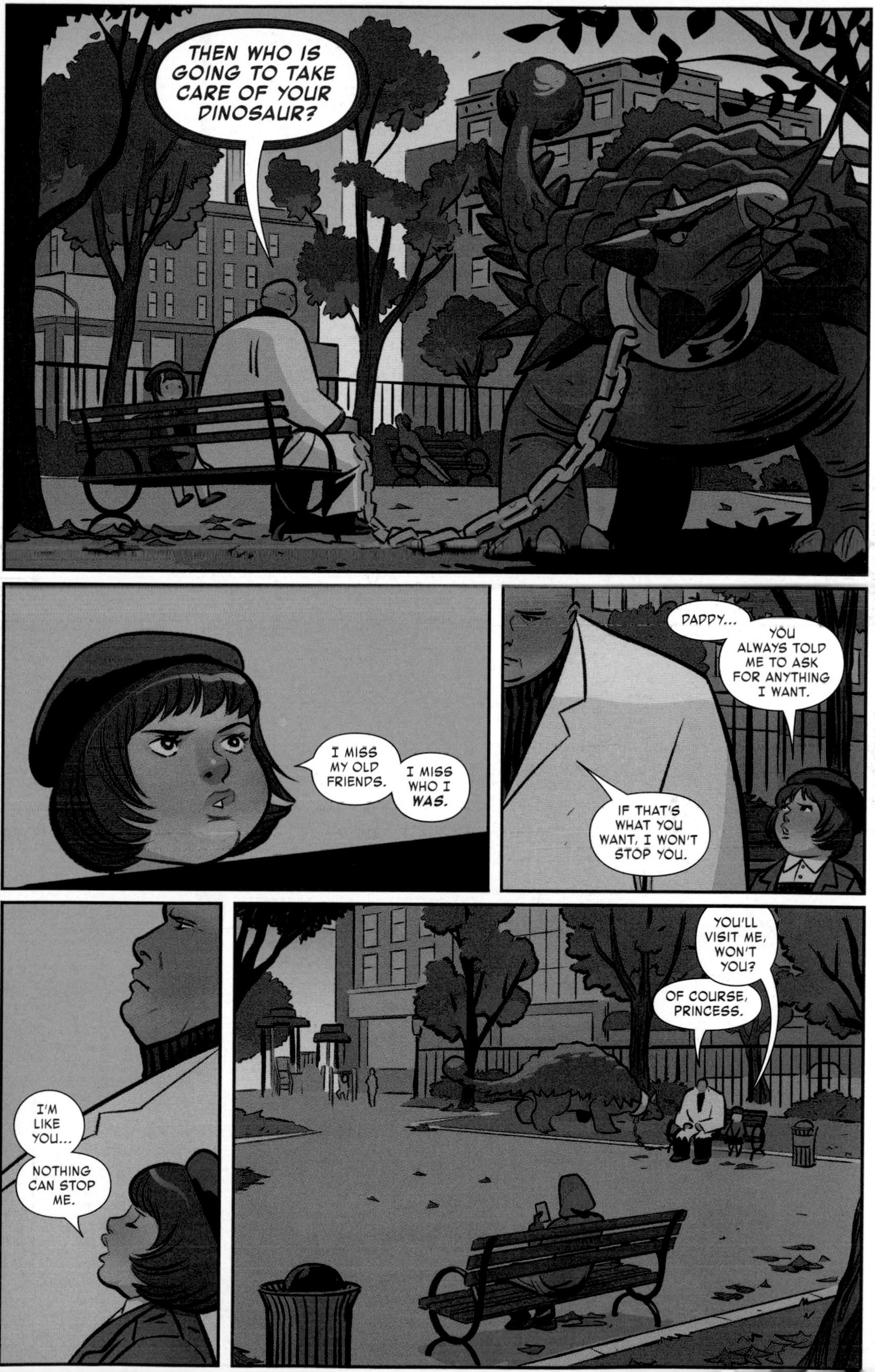
THEN WHO IS GOING TO TAKE CARE OF YOUR DINOSAUR?
I MISS MY OLD FRIENDS.
I MISS WHO I *WAS.*
DADDY...
YOU ALWAYS TOLD ME TO ASK FOR ANYTHING I WANT.
IF THAT'S WHAT YOU WANT, I WON'T STOP YOU.
I'M LIKE YOU...
NOTHING CAN STOP ME.
YOU'LL VISIT ME, WON'T YOU?
OF COURSE, PRINCESS.

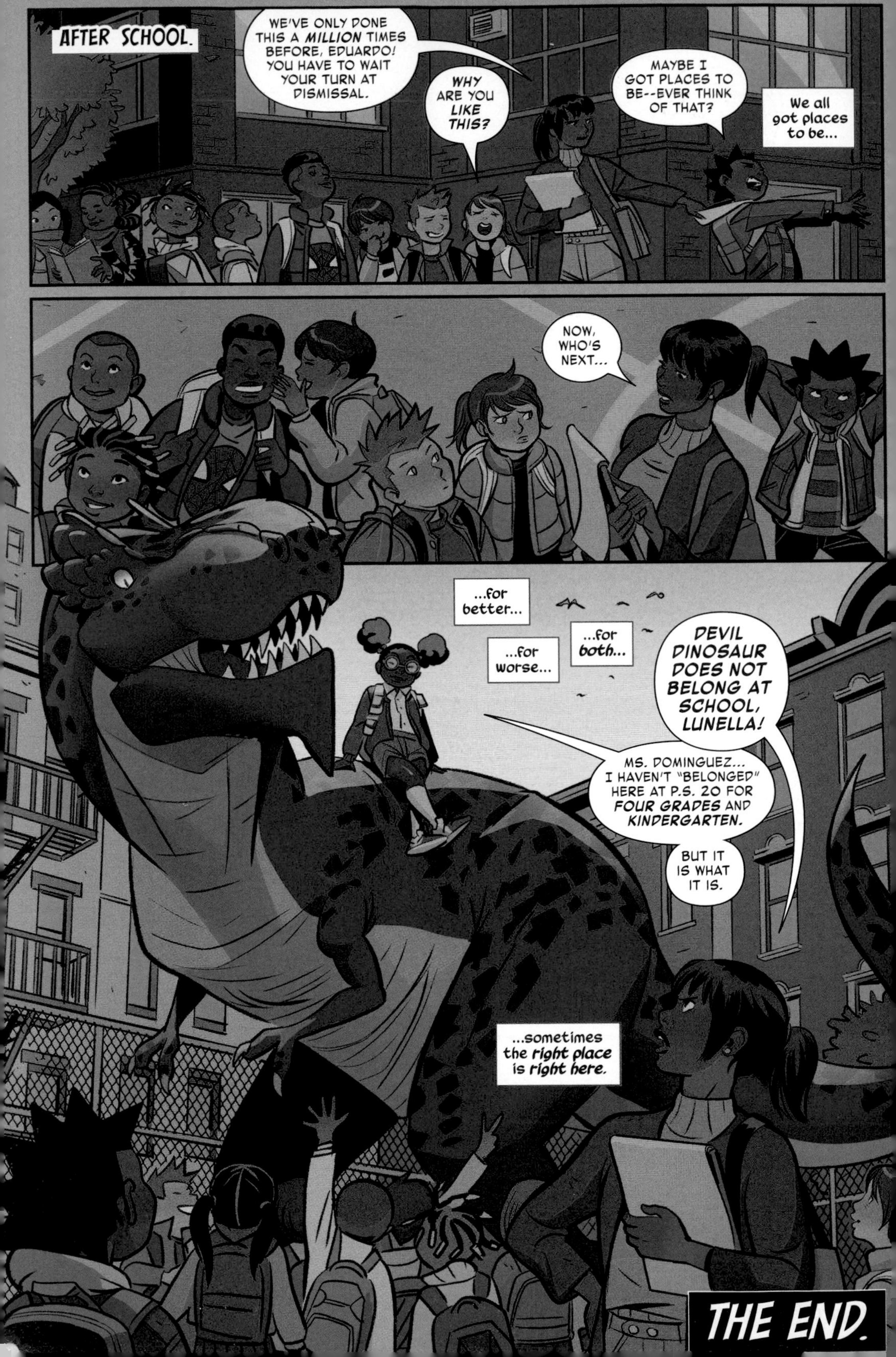
AFTER SCHOOL.
WE'VE ONLY DONE THIS A MILLION TIMES BEFORE, EDUARDO! YOU HAVE TO WAIT YOUR TURN AT DISMISSAL.
WHY ARE YOU LIKE THIS?
MAYBE I GOT PLACES TO BE--EVER THINK OF THAT?
We all got places to be...
NOW, WHO'S NEXT...
...for better...
...for worse...
...for both...
DEVIL DINOSAUR DOES NOT BELONG AT SCHOOL, LUNELLA!
MS. DOMINGUEZ... I HAVEN'T "BELONGED" HERE AT P.S. 20 FOR FOUR GRADES AND KINDERGARTEN.
BUT IT IS WHAT IT IS.
...sometimes the right place is right here.
THE END.

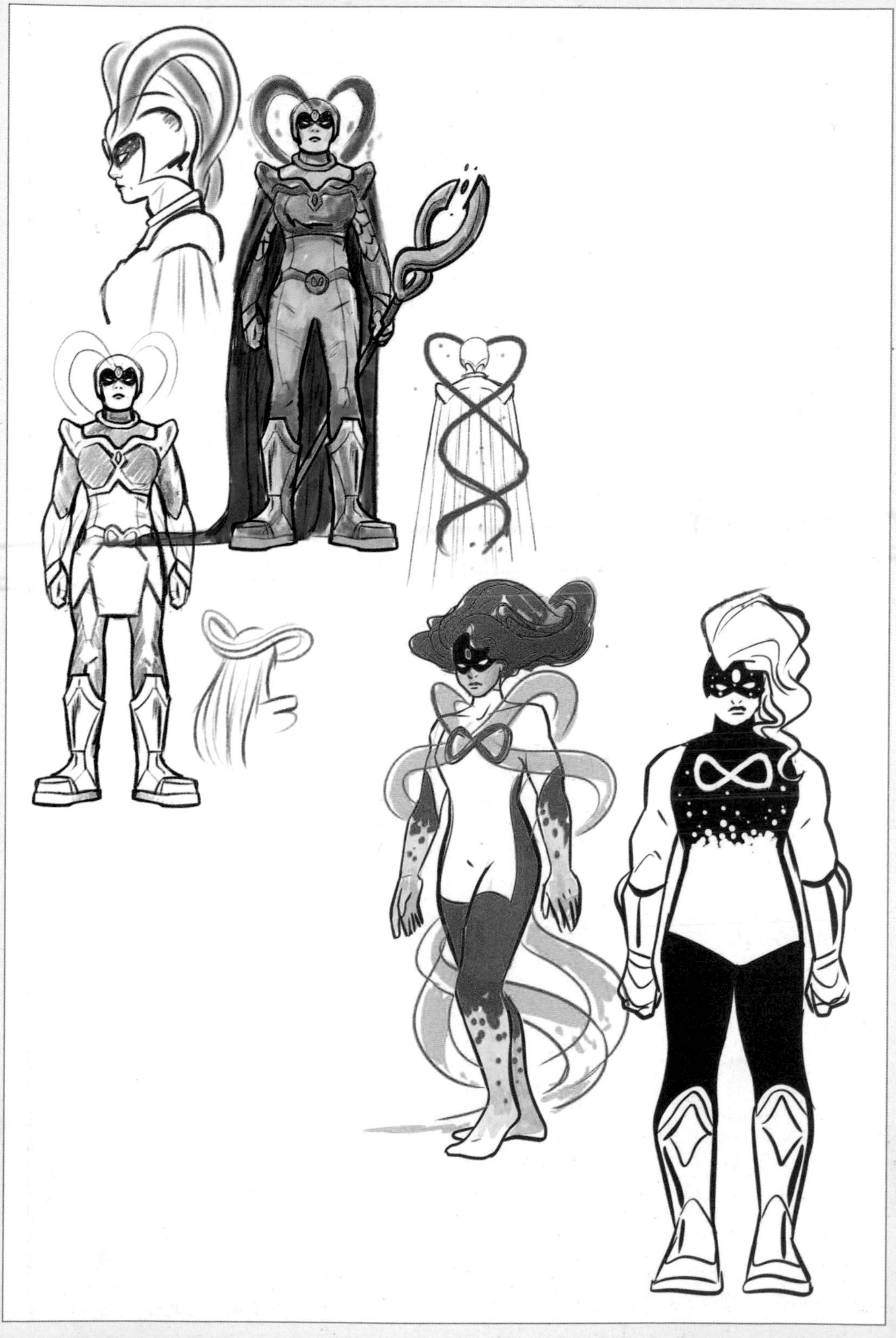

OMNIPOTENTIS SKETCHES BY NATACHA BUSTOS

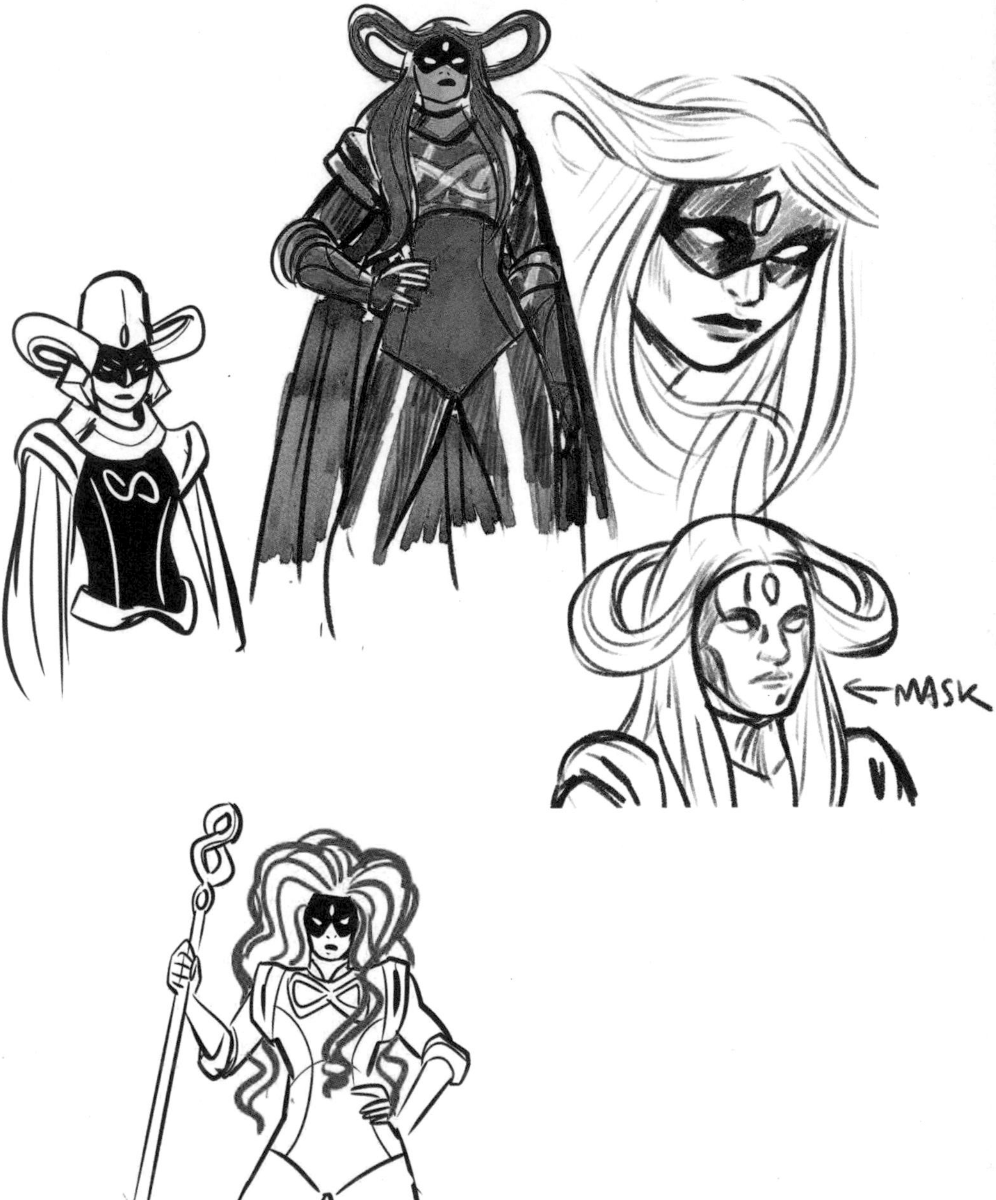

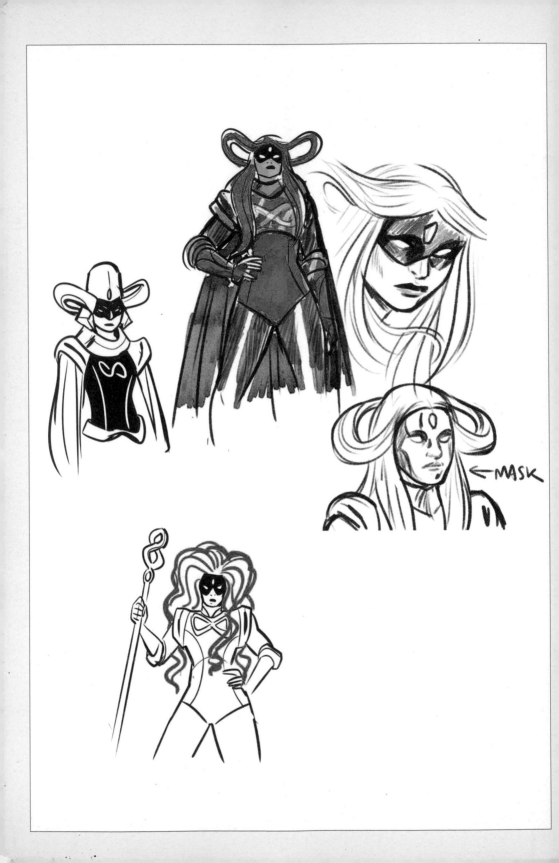

←MASK